EASTERN OCEAN

N
W E
S

Sanclar

Midpoint

GREAT HIGHWAY

Atla

HELDYN MOUNTAINS

Sylpa

Plyath

Ellisa Mitchell   2007

NATURAL ORDERMAGE

*Forthcoming

L. E. Modesitt, Jr.

NATURAL ORDERMAGE

A Tom Doherty Associates Book / New York

NATURAL ORDERMAGE

Copyright © 2007 by L. E. Modesitt, Jr.

Edited by David G. Hartwell

Maps by Ellisa Mitchell

A Tor Book
Published by Tom Doherty Associates, LLC
175 Fifth Avenue
New York, NY 10010

www.tor.com

Tor® is a registered trademark of Tom Doherty Associates, LLC.

Library of Congress Cataloging-in-Publication Data

Modesitt, L. E.
  Natural Ordermage / L. E. Modesitt, Jr. — 1st ed.
    p. cm.
  "A Tom Doherty Associates Book."
  ISBN-13: 978-0-7653-1813-8
  ISBN-10: 0-7653-1813-X
  I. Title.
  PS3563.O264N38 2007
  813'.54—dc22

                                        2007018178

First Edition: September 2007

Printed in the United States of America

0 9 8 7 6 5 4 3 2 1

For my mother,
because she introduced me to fantasy and science fiction
and because she loves the stories

OCEAN

Gulf of Austra

AUSTRA

Brysta

Valmurl

NORDLA

WESTERN OCEAN

Swartheld

Luba

Cigoerne

AFRIT

Atla

South River

MEROWEY

HAMOR

Land's End

I

Rahl . . . how are you coming on *Tales of the Founders*?" In the light of a spring afternoon, Kian glanced across the workroom toward his younger son, seated behind the battered but spotless oak copying table. The two south windows were glazed and overlarge for the workroom, but the light they provided made the work far easier.

"I've just finished the embellishments on the bottom of the last page in the fourth chapter." The black-haired apprentice scrivener smiled politely. "I'm copying those exactly as they are. That's what you wanted, wasn't it?" Rahl knew well that was what his father desired, but he'd also learned that such questions reassured the master scrivener.

"After you finish that, would you check the next batch of ink? I worry about the latest oak galls we got from Clyndal . . . and the iron-brimstone." Kian carefully set the copper-tipped iron-pointed pen down on the blotting pad, well away from the inkwell. "Folks don't take the care they used to, not at all. It was bad enough in my father's time, but these days . . ."

Rahl finished the last stroke, then cleaned his pen and set it aside. "I'll check that ink now, while the embellishment is drying."

"Don't take too long. I promised that copy to Ziertol before the turn of summer."

Rahl was well aware of that. His father mentioned it at least once a day. But the youth said nothing as he made his way out of the workroom, past the angled and padded shelf set before the small glass display window. On the shelf were sheets of parchment—samples of Kian's handwork—and a thin black-bound copy of the *Council Ordinances*. Rahl had actually copied some of that, but only a master scrivener would have been able to tell, so much like his father's was his hand, especially when he used standard hand style.

The oak door was propped ajar to let in the fresher air of spring, and Rahl had to move the heavy square gray stone blocks that served as doorstops in order to open the door wide enough to let himself out. He also had to be careful not to hit his head on the doorframe, since the door and frame had been built for Kian's sire, a man almost half a cubit shorter than Kian, and close to a full cubit shorter than Rahl.

Once he was outside, he replaced the doorstops immediately to forestall any words from his father. The late-afternoon sun had almost touched the top of the hills to the west, and the shadow of the structure that held both shop and dwelling stretched almost to the far side of the narrow paved street.

If Rahl had walked to the corner, he could have looked northward and downhill to the small harbor at Land's End. Instead, he walked around the house to the small brick shed set a good ten yards back of the rear covered porch and beside the grape arbor. A third of the shed was for ink and binding preparation, and the remainder was where his mother wove and stored her baskets before she sold them. The arbor ran from the southwest corner of the porch due west and parallel to the shed. Beyond the shed were the low square walls that held the compost heap that he periodically took from to fertilize his mother's garden. The garden itself stretched another ten yards beyond the shed to the stone wall that marked the beginning of the protected forest—such as it was—with its low pines.

Rahl slipped the catch on the shed door and stepped inside, where he checked each of the covered glazed pots that held the ink. The ink was setting up properly, as it should, although it had taken just a touch of order to stabilize the iron-brimstone. The brimstone had been a touch excessive, but Rahl had managed. He'd never told his parents of his small order-abilities. The last thing in the world he wanted was to undergo instruction in the use of order by the magisters—and risk exile and dangergeld. Besides, his abilities were modest, and he'd never even tried to use them other than for good results—even with the girls.

Even though he sensed that the ink would be fine, he dipped a thin strip of reed-paper in the first pot, another in the second, then held them away from him to dry. After a moment, he covered the pots again and left the shed. He was careful to relatch the door and to keep the ink-damp paper from touching his tunic. His mother would berate him all too thoroughly if he were careless enough to get ink anywhere but on his hands and blotting pad—and especially if he got ink on any of her reeds and grasses. If he ended up with much ink on his hands, he'd hear about it from his father.

At the separate outside door to the shop, he bent and moved the outside doorstop, then stepped inside and replaced it. He straightened and carried the two thin strips to Kian.

"Here you are, ser."

Kian set aside his pen once more. His eyes studied the strips. Then he smelled them. Finally, he pressed them against his blotting pad. "Getting there. Not quite, but they'll be ready before we finish off this batch." He looked up at Rahl. "Best get back to copying. Book won't copy itself, Rahl."

"Yes, ser." Rahl slipped back to the smaller copying desk, where he settled himself onto the square woven-reed seat of the stool—backless, unlike the one used by his father.

He opened the original of *Tales of the Founders,* and his eyes read the next few lines.

> . . . Shierra was in those days the Guard Captain of the Westwind Guards, and her twin blades were near as mighty as those of Creslin and Megaera, and her skill as an instructor in arms was unsurpassed. In less than three years, she and Captain Hyel created the Guards of Recluce, more than five squads, each squad more than a match for five squads of the best blades from any other land . . .

Rahl suppressed a snort. Five times as effective? He paused. The original Guards of Recluce had eventually become the Guards of the Council, and his brother Kacet was one of those guards at the garrison at Reflin. More than once Kacet had told him stories of how comparative handfuls of marine guards had boarded pirate vessels and destroyed entire pirate crews. From his own senses, Rahl had known Kacet had not been lying.

His eyes dropped back to the book. Still . . . five times as effective? Even against the crimson of Hamor?

II

Only a single oil lamp sat upon the oblong oak table. Spotless and shining as the glass mantel was, or had been, the light in the chamber was dim because the wick barely protruded over the edge of the brass flange of the wick tube.

Kian sat at the head of the table, his back to the kitchen area, with Khorlya to his right, and Rahl across from him.

Rahl took another spoonful of the barley-and-fowl soup. It was really thick enough to be a stew, but he'd learned years before that, no matter how thick it was, if his mother called it a soup, it was a soup. He added a small dollop of the cherry conserve to the chunk of fresh bread on the edge of the platter that held the old ochre soup bowl. He would have preferred dark bread with the soup, but molasses was getting dear again. Or so his mother had said.

So he took another small spoonful of the stew-soup, and then added another dollop of conserve to the bread. He'd learned as a small boy that small dollops were seldom noticed the way heaping spoonfuls were, particularly by his mother. After several more small spoonfuls of the soup, he added a last small portion of conserve to the bread and took a bite.

"Good bread, Mother," he said after chewing his mouthful deliberately. "It's always good. So is the soup."

"We do the best we can. Of course, we might have done better in Nylan." Khorlya glanced at her consort. "They have more coins for decorative work."

Kian ignored the sideways look. "Excellent soup. Couldn't get barley this good down south. Not near Nylan."

"No, but the fowl would be cheaper," countered Khorlya.

"Both Land's End and Nylan are better than Reflin, aren't they?" asked Rahl.

"That's like saying a snug cot and a mansion are better than a hut," replied Khorlya. "Anyway, we're probably better here . . . now."

Kian looked up, clearly surprised.

"They say that the black engineers of Nylan are working on a machine that will copy many books at one time," offered Khorlya "They won't need scriveners before long."

"Who are these people who say that?" asked Kian dryly.

"Eldonya. Her brother is a road patroller between Skil and the Black Wall of Nylan."

"How many people have repeated what he said? Skil is seven hundred kays or more from Land's End."

"Kacet says that the engineers are always working on things," Khorlya added.

"That's why they're engineers. But not everything they make is good for everyone. That's why the wall is there and why the Council is here in Land's End. I can't see the Council allowing a machine—even one bound in order—to replace the honest work of a scrivener, and that's if they can even build something that works."

Rahl concealed a smile. His father, as good and solid a scrivener as he was, was order-blind. The order in his life resulted from following the rules and careful habit. Kian couldn't have felt order or chaos if a black mage had arrived and filled the small dwelling with it or if one of the white wizards of Fairhaven had descended on white lightnings from the sky. So far, that had worked to Rahl's advantage. Still, he was careful to avoid any of the black mages. Because Kian was a scrivener, and considered a learned man, Rahl had left school earlier than many others his age—and before he'd begun to realize his small abilities with order. While he doubted he had that much order-ability, he had no desire to call attention to himself.

He had a roof over his head, good food, if plain, and plenty of time before he had to settle down.

"What do you think about *Tales of the Founders*?" asked Kian. "You're reading it as well as copying it, aren't you?"

"Yes, ser." Rahl paused slightly. He usually did in answering his father's questions, both to give himself a moment to think and to create the impression of thoughtfulness even when he didn't need the time. "I've only read what I've copied, but I don't think the writer is telling the whole story."

"That happened more than five hundred years ago," replied Kian dryly, "and you know that he left something out?"

Rahl laughed easily. "Yes, ser. All stories leave something out. Otherwise, they'd go on forever and say little in too many words. It's like copying a book. You don't tell a customer all the things you do to make the book, from the binding and gluing to the illustrations and embossing, if it has any. You just say that you copied it. Books are like that. They don't tell what people have for every meal—"

"Of course not," snorted Kian. "But that doesn't change things. You're talking about something else. Say what you mean."

Rahl wished he hadn't said so much. Still, he offered a smile. "The story says that Creslin was a master blade, and that he killed scores of Hamorians, but it also says that he was raised in the Legend in Westwind, where no men bear arms. It doesn't say how he became a master blade. You're always telling me that to be good at anything I have to study, and work, and practice. That's got to be true for a master blade, too. But there's nothing about that."

"It's a legend," replied Kian. "They leave things out."

Rahl refrained from pointing out that he had just said that, suppressing his irritation at the fact that his father had ignored what he'd said just a few moments before. His father always ignored what was inconvenient. "It's interesting, though. I'd like to know how he and Megaera ever got together. She was supposed to be all chaos, and he was all order."

"Opposites attract," suggested Khorlya. "That's something you'll need to watch out for when it's time for you to choose a consort. Great attraction beforehand sometimes means greater conflict afterward."

"He's got a consort-to-be, woman, if he'd only look. Shahyla is as good a catch as any young fellow could want. With but her one brother, she'll hold all the upper pastures and half the herds one day. Bradeon's getting grayer and frailer every eightday."

Rahl nodded politely. One way or another, Shahyla was not going to be his consort. She was pleasant enough and not bad-looking, but from what he recalled from when they had been in school together she had the curiosity of a milk cow and the brains of a stone wall.

"That's if Bradeon doesn't take a liking to some other young fellow and his family." Khorlya looked to her son. "You'll be needing to pay her a call on the end-days. I'll bake you a honey cake to take with you. You can't be calling empty-handed."

"Will you make the kind with the almonds?"

"We might be having some left," Khorlya said. "I'll see."

"You're spoiling him," replied Kian.

"It's not for him, remember, dear. It's for Bradeon and Shahyla. Poor man has no consort, and I hear tell that Shahyla's so tied up with the milk cows and the creamery, she's no time to bake properly."

"I suppose it can't hurt." Kian pursed his lips. "Be there enough for a small one for us?"

Khorlya laughed. "I could manage that, I'm sure."

Rahl finished the last of the heavy soup, and then took the last mouthful of bread, the corner with most of the conserve on it. He liked having a bit of sweetness at the end of a meal.

"Might I be excused?" he asked.

"Where are you going?" asked Khorlya.

"It's a pleasant evening. I've been inside all day. I'm going to take a walk. If Sevien's around, we'll play plaques. Otherwise, I won't be late."

"Don't be late at all," suggested Kian. "You need the sleep for a steady hand. I promised that copy by summer. Good copying can't be rushed. Means steady days, every day."

"Yes, ser."

"Let him go, Kian. I recall someone who sneaked back through the shutters more than once."

"Was different then . . ." muttered the scrivener.

His son and consort laughed.

Before Kian or Khorlya could say more, Rahl smiled and slipped off the bench and toward the door.

"Not too late!" called Kian.

"Yes, ser."

Outside the house, in the fading twilight, Rahl stopped beside the pump and the cistern. Each house had one fed by pipes from the springs supposedly found or created by the black ordermastery of Creslin hundreds of years before. He washed up carefully, brushed the dust off his brown tunic, and smoothed his hair back in place. Then he checked the truncheon at his belt. With a smile, he walked out to the street and turned southward.

At the next corner, just short of Alamat the weaver's place, he turned left and followed the street to the end, where a small wooden gate stood closed between two waist-high stone walls. Rahl unlatched the gate, entered the orchard, and closed the gate behind him. The pearapple blossoms had mostly fallen onto the sparse grass between the trees, and then faded into a white transparency, but there remained a faint scent, particularly around the trees in the higher and slightly colder southwest corner.

He walked silently down the line of trees toward the small storage barn with its closed and angled doorway that led down to the fruit cellar. To the right was an old wooden bench. Rahl took a rag from his tunic and wiped it off, then sat down.

After a time, he cupped his hands and concentrated, then did his best to imitate the soft call of a rat-owl. "Tu-whoooo . . ."

While he waited, he listened, but all he heard were the sounds of insects, and the faint whisper of leaves in the light and intermittent breeze.

Before that long, he could sense a feminine presence slipping away from the house. He stood, but said nothing as Jienela neared. She wore a sleeveless summer tunic and loose trousers, and carried something, a cloak perhaps, although the night was warm for midspring.

He took her hand. "I hoped you'd hear."

"I was afraid you wouldn't come. Father's doing his accounts tonight, and Mother's over at Aunt Denya's. They're working on the consorting quilt for Jaired."

"He's getting consorted?" Rahl couldn't imagine anyone putting up with the hot-tempered Jaired, especially since Jaired wasn't the brightest penny in the wallet.

"It's sort of a secret. With Coerlyne."

"She's . . ."

"I know, but . . . he's been seeing her for a long time, and Father and Mother finally gave in."

Rahl had the feeling that Coerlyne and Jaired might be having an addition to their soon-to-be family somewhat sooner than might ordinarily be the case. "We might as well sit down." He gestured.

"I brought an old blanket. The bench can be hard, and it's dirty."

Rahl took the blanket, folding it twice and laying it on the wood. Then he gestured for Jienela to sit down.

"You always make me feel special."

He settled beside her. "That's not hard. You are."

Carefully, oh so carefully, he brushed her with just a touch of order. Doing that, he'd discovered, not only left the girls with fairer and smoother skin, but also tended to make them more receptive to his caresses.

"Did I tell you that you're beautiful?" Rahl let his fingers caress Jienela's hand, then brushed back her long brown hair, his fingertips barely grazing her long neck.

Her eyes dropped shyly. "You're kind, Rahl, but I'm not beautiful, not like Ermana."

"Beauty is more than blond hair and blue eyes." He smiled warmly, then added, "A kind heart and a welcoming smile are more beautiful. Every time you smile, I want to smile back."

"You must tell all the girls that."

"I haven't told a single one that." He hadn't, and Jienela did have a nice smile. Besides, he tried to tell the truth about each girl. Truthful was always best, especially on Recluce. After all, they each were special in different ways, and there was no reason not to let each one know her best features. He squeezed her hand gently. "Your smile *is* special."

For a moment, neither spoke.

"What did you do today?" he asked. "It had to be more interesting than what I did. I just sat at the table and copied, and thought of you." He had thought of her, if not all that often.

"I helped Father in the morning, culling the fruit buds that were too crowded or wrong, and then worked in the house and barn with Mother."

"At least you got to move around."

"You don't just sit there and copy all day, do you?"

"Not all day." He laughed quietly. "I did go out to the shed and check on the next batches of ink, and I cut some rushes for Mother." He squeezed her hand gently once more, then leaned forward and brushed her cheek with his lips.

"We're too close to the house," she whispered. "Let's go up to the corner of the orchard. The grass is soft there, and you can still smell the pear-apple blossoms. Father won't hear us there."

"Are you sure?" he asked softly.

She leaned forward and kissed his cheek, gently. "Very sure."

He stood, giving a hand to Jienela. Then he lifted and folded the blanket over his left arm, before offering his right to her. As they walked up toward the corner of the orchard, Rahl moved easily and confidently. He had a solid *feel* for where things were in the dark . . . as well as for other matters.

III

Rahl wasn't *too* late getting home, just late enough that his parents were already half-asleep and relieved that he had returned. He'd gone to bed happily, with pleasant memories of the evening—and Jienela. It had been her idea, even if he had encouraged it subtly.

The next morning he was up as usual—just one moment before his mother was about to yell. He had to gulp down breakfast—gruel and bread—then get on with his chores. Finally, he made it to the workroom, where he settled into copying *Tales of the Founders*.

"Might be better if you got up a mite earlier," suggested Kian. "Your mother was reaching for the spare frying pan—the big iron one. And you were supposed to spar with me before we got to work. You're still not good enough with that truncheon, and there are times when a man needs to be able to defend himself."

"Yes, ser." Rahl hadn't realized about the frying pan, but he sensed his father was telling the truth about it and his sparring. Why did they always want more? It wasn't as though he were a child anymore. He was up in time, and he worked hard. He did his chores, and he didn't complain, yet whatever he did was never quite enough. He pushed back that retort and concentrated on the copying before him.

The morning was long and uninterrupted. Not a single person came by, either to have a letter written or to purchase anything. Rahl was more than ready when his mother called.

"Dinner's ready!"

He still was careful to clean and rack his pen, cap the inkwell, and close the copy of *Tales of the Founders* from which he had been copying.

Dinner was far heartier than breakfast had been or supper would be. There were chunks of mutton in brown gravy and roasted potatoes, and freshly baked bread. Of course, there were dandelion greens and winter roots, but the roots didn't taste bad in the gravy, and the greens were fresh.

Rahl only managed two mouthfuls before his mother cleared her throat.

"Rahl?"

"Yes, Mother?" He didn't like the feel behind the way she'd pronounced his name.

"Alamat's niece Quelerya said you didn't go to Sevien's last night. She saw you going through Dhostak's orchard." Khorlya looked at her son. "I'd hate to see you get tied up with Jienela. She's pretty enough, but she'll have nothing. The orchard's barely large enough to support Dhostak and his family, and she's got two older brothers. Word is that even the younger one's going to be consorted before long—and to Coerlyne. Drover's daughter, and she doesn't so much as have a single copper penny to her name. And Jienela, she'll not have much more than that, not with those two good-for-nothing louts they call her brothers. Three families'll have to live off that orchard, four if you count Dhostak and Aryla."

"She is pretty," Rahl admitted, "but I don't intend to get tied up with anyone now. I'm too young to take a consort." Why were they always nagging him about a consort?

"Intentions are all well and good, Rahl," interjected Kian, "but actions count more than intentions, and there are grass stains on the cuffs and sides of your trousers."

Rahl managed not to flush.

"There's enjoying being young," added Kian, "and there's stupidity."

"It'd be stupid to have to consort a girl with nothing," said Khorlya.

Left unsaid was the point that his father had little enough. Scriveners seldom did, especially those who did not work for the Council in Land's End.

"A girl's looks fade fast in life," continued his mother. "So you'd best find one with something other than looks. It's better to find one with a coins for a dowry, but even one who's hardworking or one who can help with your scrivening would be better than Jienela. She's sweet, but she has little enough in the way of brains and less than that in coins."

Rahl understood all Khorlya was saying. He generally agreed with her, and he had no intention of consorting Jienela. He just wished his mother would stop hammering him with her words. She didn't know when to stop.

"It only takes once to trap a young fellow," Kian added.

Not in this case, thought Rahl, especially since he'd been careful and counted the days since her time of the month. He still had some time to enjoy her favors. Rather than argue or reveal anything, he just nodded and took a swallow of the weak ale, enjoying it since they often did not have it.

Despite the hearty meal, Rahl was more than glad to leave the table and follow Kian back to the workroom and the copying table. He settled himself on his stool and opened the book from which he was copying.

"How are you coming on that, son?"

"I'm about finished with the first part. Creslin and Megaera have been consorted by the Duke of Montgren." Rahl paused. "How come Montgren had a duke, but Sarronnyn has a Tyrant, and Hamor has an emperor? Aren't they all just names for a ruler?"

"No. Rulers in different lands have different powers. The High Wizards of Fairhaven are the most powerful chaos-mages in the world, and they rule through those powers. The Duke of Montgren was not all that powerful. That is why there is no duke now, and Fairhaven rules Montgren. The Tyrant is always a woman and takes her powers from the Legend—"

Thrap!

At the knock on the door, Rahl looked to his father.

"You get it."

Rahl rose from his copying table, then crossed the workroom and opened the door. He paused as he saw Sevien's red hair. "I'm copying, Sevien."

"I thought you would be. I'm on my way down to the main keep with the amphorae that the Guards ordered from Da. I just thought you might want to come by after supper. Thorkel sent a whole bushel of early redberries, and

Mother's made some pies . . ." Sevien grinned and lowered his voice. "Jienela might come."

Rahl frowned, then smiled. "I'd love to."

"Good. Till later." Sevien smiled and turned, then hurried back toward the street.

The younger scrivener squinted in thought as he closed the door. How had Sevien found out about Jienela? Had she told Sevien's sister? That wasn't good, not at all.

"Who was that?" asked Kian.

"Sevien. He asked me over after supper. His mother is making some redberry pies." Rahl walked back to his table. For a moment, he glanced out the window, looking out into the bright spring afternoon toward the gray stone wall beyond the corner of the garden.

"Suppose it'd be all right," mused Kian, adding with a smile, "leastwise, if you don't go by way of Dhostak's orchard."

Rahl managed not to flush. "I don't plan to." He didn't have to, not if Jienela would be there anyway. Still, he'd have to ease away from her carefully. In time, but not yet.

"Best you plan not ever to go by way of that orchard."

"You and Mother have made that very clear, ser."

"I would hope so."

Saying anything more would merely have prolonged an unpleasant topic, and one that got less and less pleasant for all the repetition. Rahl smiled politely and went back to copying *Tales of the Founders*. He finished another page before there was another *thrap* on the workroom door.

Rahl immediately got up to answer it.

A trim figure in a black tunic and trousers stood outside in the sunlight. His brown hair was cut short, and he was beardless. He also bore the aura of order.

"Magister Puvort," Rahl managed, opening the door and stepping back. "Please come in, ser."

"Thank you, young Rahl. It's refreshing to hear such courtesy." Puvort studied Rahl a moment, and the faintest hint of a frown appeared and vanished before the magister turned to Kian, who had risen from his own copying table.

The scrivener bowed his head, then asked, "How might I help you, Magister?"

"I've been hearing things, Kian," began the magister. "You wouldn't have a copy of *The Basis of Order*, now, would you?"

Kian laughed. "Knowing how the Council feels about that, Magister Puvort, I'd not be foolish enough even to copy one belonging to another, let alone have one."

"I thought not, but these days, we need to ask."

"Are the engineering devils making trouble again?"

"When haven't they? A bad bargain it was the Council made with the cursed smith, but he was the only one who could turn the white demons away." Puvort shook his head sadly. "More and more of the outland traders port in Nylan, and now . . ."

Both scriveners waited.

"Now . . . they're asking the Council to let them handle the exiling for all of Recluce . . . as if we did not know who embodies chaos and who does not."

"What will the Council do?" asked Kian.

Puvort shrugged. "It has not been decided." Then he smiled. "I'd best be going. Thank you, scrivener, and you, Rahl." With a nod, the black magister turned.

Rahl found that he was still holding the door. After Puvort was out of sight, he closed it. He didn't think it had been his imagination that the magister's eyes had lingered on him before Puvort had left.

"How can the Council agree to that?" Rahl finally asked.

"How can they not?" replied Kian. "The black devils build and crew the ships that protect all Recluce. They have weapons that we cannot match. These days more than half the trade goes through Nylan. The Council must accede to them more and more."

"You've never spoken of that."

"It's not wise to do so. Being critical of the Council can put you on a ship to Hamor or Candar, or Brysta if you're lucky—unless you can get to Nylan first."

"Just for talking about them?"

"If you're not talking favorable words about the Council these days."

Rahl turned and looked out the south windows. He already knew that no one was around. That was something he'd always been able to sense, but his father had never believed him. So it was just easier to look.

"There's no one here." He closed the door and walked back to the copying table, where he sat down and looked at his father. "What is *The Basis of Order*?"

"It's the book of the Black Engineers in Nylan. They're forbidden outside the Black City."

"Why did Magister Puvort think you had one?"

"He probably didn't," Kian said. "But the magisters can tell when someone tells the truth or lies. If he asks, and I say I don't, and I'm telling the truth, then he's done."

Rahl frowned. "But . . . if you had had one, and you hid it away from the house, and said you didn't have it, you'd be telling the truth, too."

"I wouldn't be telling all the truth, and many magisters can sense that also."

"But why don't they like the engineers? They're part of Recluce, and they protect all of us, you said."

"They build machines, great creations out of metal and black iron, and when they build those machines, that creates more chaos and more of the white demons. Fairhaven gets stronger every year. Now, the white mages effectively rule most of Candar east of the Westhorns." Kian shook his head. "There's no point in saying more. Just don't talk down the Council or praise the engineers."

Rahl nodded. What his father had said didn't make total sense. Without the ships of the engineers of Nylan, the mages of Fairhaven would have conquered Recluce years and years ago, yet the Council was complaining that using the ships strengthened the white demons? It sounded to him like the Council was more afraid of losing power to the engineers than of the dangers of the white mages.

Still . . . there wasn't much a scrivener could do about that. Other things were another matter.

He smiled, thinking of redberry pies and what well might follow.

IV

Rahl could hardly wait to finish dinner, but he forced himself not to appear hurried as he washed and dried the platters and replaced them in the narrow cabinet against the kitchen wall.

"You won't be late, now." His mother's words were not a question.

"Not too late," he replied with a grin. "But I wouldn't want to leave too much redberry pie behind."

"Don't make a hog out of yourself, son. Folks'll excuse a picky eater and one with a healthy appetite, but hogs aren't welcome anywhere."

Rahl forced another grin. "I think you've told me that before."

"Doesn't make it any less true."

He smiled pleasantly, wishing that she wouldn't keep dishing up the same old sayings, time after time, as if he had no brains or memory.

When he finally finished helping his mother, he washed up in the stone-walled area just outside the kitchen, then set off. He was careful not to take the shortcut and instead to turn at Alamat's, where he could be seen by Quelerya—even in the growing twilight—as being on his way to Sevien's. What a wretched old biddy Quelerya was, watching everyone, then telling if she saw anything she thought might cause someone trouble.

The dwelling attached to the pottery works was at least three times the size of the dwelling in which Rahl had grown up, although Rahl had felt fortunate enough to have his own room, small as it was at four cubits by six, with his pallet bed against the outer wall. Many children slept in the common room or with their parents.

Rahl stepped onto the low stone stoop before the front door. The stoop was almost wide enough to be a small porch under the wide eaves. He knocked.

Sevien opened the door. "Rahl! Come in. You're the first one here."

The front door opened into a common room with a long dining table at one end, nearest the kitchen. Chairs stood at each end of the table, with long benches at each side. Two brass lanterns—each in a wall sconce on opposite sides of the room—provided a steady low light. Facing the hearth, where a brick heating stove stood, unneeded on the comfortable spring evening, were two upholstered and low-backed benches. There were even high-backed chairs flanking the benches, rather than stools, and a sideboard for platters and bowls and tankards—and several real glass goblets.

Even from the front door, Rahl could smell the aroma of baking and spices. His mouth watered, but he swallowed and smiled.

Sevien closed the door behind Rahl. "Mother, Rahl's here."

The gray-haired Nuelya turned from where she stood beside the kitchen sink. "Rahl . . . I set aside one pie for you to take home to your mother. She was so kind to bring all that fresh asparagus by the other day—and even some early brinn. It helps with burns, and handling a kiln, they do happen."

She shot a brief glance to Sevien, who glanced away from his mother. "Now . . . you won't forget it, will you?"

"No . . . ma'am. I certainly won't." He wouldn't, either, because he'd get at least two pieces out of it at home, and they didn't get redberry pie—or any pastries—that often.

"It's the one in the corner here, covered with the cloth." Nuelya turned to check something on the stove, then added to her daughter, who had stepped inside the rear door, carrying a large crockery pitcher, "Did you run the spigot a bit first?"

"Just a little." Delthea glanced at Rahl, offering an all-too-knowing smile.

Rahl smiled back blandly. "Good evening, Delthea."

"The same to you, Rahl."

"If you'd get the small plates, Delthea?" Nuelya gestured toward a tall triangular cabinet in the corner closest to the dining table.

"Yes, Mother."

"What did you do today, besides cart amphorae down to the keep?" Rahl turned to Sevien, trying to change the unspoken subject quickly.

"Mixed and blended clay. Then I shoveled the coal that Muldark delivered into the bin, except for the last bushel. I had to break that into the right-sized chunks before I loaded it into the kiln." Sevien shook his head. "Waltar used to do it. I think he slaved to get his own works in Alaren just so someone else had to handle the coal. Clendal just went to sea, and that leaves no one but me. Anyway, someone's got to do it. Mother and Da need to light it off tomorrow so that they can start firing the day after tomorrow for the next shipment for the Guards."

"That far ahead?"

"We have to preheat the kiln. Otherwise, the temperature's uneven."

All that sounded like even more work than copying books—and a lot dirtier, reflected Rahl.

"Cold water doesn't take off the coal easy. It takes forever to get clean," said Sevien.

"That's because you're not careful," suggested Delthea from the kitchen area.

"And you don't take long enough," added Nuelya.

Rahl refrained from grinning, not because Sevien was embarrassed but because sometimes all mothers sounded the same. "She and my mother could have been sisters," he murmured, barely under his breath.

"We're third cousins, young Rahl, and we've got ears like the rock-owls."

That Rahl could believe.

Sevien did grin. "Did anything interesting happen at your place?"

"Magister Puvort came by today. He was asking about some book," Rahl offered.

"He was here, too. He talked to Mother." Sevien looked toward the kitchen, where Nuelya was now setting out the small plain earthenware plates that Delthea had taken from the cabinet.

Rahl had never seen so much ceramic ware. Most people had plain platters and bowls and not much else, but he supposed that potters could make things for themselves. "He didn't seem too happy. He said something to Da about the engineers and how things weren't that good now."

"The magisters never think things are good," countered Sevien.

"Sevien," cautioned Nuelya.

"Magister Puvort was looking for a book called *The Basis of Order*. I'd never heard of it," Rahl went on. "He said that he thought someone around here might have a copy of it. I'm an apprentice scrivener, getting close to being a journeyman, but I'd never even heard of it until this afternoon."

"Sounds like they don't want folks knowing about it."

"He didn't sound very happy about the engineers in Nylan." Rahl hoped Nuelya would say something.

"The Council hasn't been happy since the engineers built Nylan," said the potter. "They're always claiming that the black wall doesn't really stop anyone. Walls don't, whether they're black walls or orchard walls."

"Especially orchard walls," added Delthea.

Rahl barely managed to avoid wincing.

Sevien grinned more broadly, then murmured, "See what I got to listen to? All the time?"

Tap, tap!

Sevien turned and hurried across the common room to open the door. A tall young man and a slightly shorter young woman stood there. Both were redheads. With Sevien's red hair, and Delthea's, Rahl definitely felt outnumbered.

"Rahl . . . this is Faseyn and his sister Fahla. They're pretty new here."

Rahl had heard that the factor who had taken over Hostalyn's chandlery had a son and a daughter. He'd seen them both from a distance but never met either. He stepped forward, smiling. "I'm glad to meet you both."

While Rahl was slightly taller than most men in Land's End, Faseyn was close to a half head taller than Rahl. Up close he was gangly, and he looked to be younger than his sister. Rahl guessed that Fahla was about his own age.

She smiled warmly. "Father's kept us so busy in stocking and reorganizing the chandlery that we haven't met anyone who hasn't come in to buy things."

"Scriveners don't buy all that much," Rahl replied. "Usually my mother's the one—"

"She must be Khorlya. She's nice," replied Fahla. "She's quick, too."

"I suspect you're very quick yourself," Rahl replied.

"So are you, and quicker with the girls you like, I'd wager." Fahla smiled mischievously.

Rahl shrugged helplessly before asking, "Where did you live before?"

"Father and Uncle Karath had the factorage near Mattra. Really, they mostly supplied the ironworks north of there. When Hostalyn said he was getting too old to keep going, Father bought him out. Of course, it wasn't quite like that, seeing as Hostalyn is his great-uncle, but Land's End is so much more interesting."

Rahl didn't think Land's End was all that interesting, but he could see that it was likely to be far more engaging than a town off the coast and on the High Road near the ironworks—and far from both Nylan and Land's End.

"Fahla really runs the chandlery," added Faseyn. "Father does the buying and trading, and that takes all his time."

Rahl had the impression that their father was without a consort, but he wasn't sure how to ask that and decided against it.

"Who else would?" replied Fahla. "You're more interested in the accounts, but someone has to sell things and tell everyone what we have and why they should buy it."

"You like doing that?" asked Rahl.

"Much more than being a consort and doing all the cooking and chores, not that I don't have to fit some chores and cooking in. Some of the older men aren't sure I should be running the chandlery, but they don't say much." She laughed. "You can tell, though, the way they get all stiff and ask where my father is. I just tell them it's their good fortune to deal with me since Father's far less compromising."

Rahl had the definite feeling that it might be easier to dicker with her father. He also found her interesting, but her directness was more than a little unnerving. When she looked at him, her eyes seemed to focus intently on him, as if she were cataloging all his abilities and thoughts and racking them somewhere in her brain.

Abruptly, Fahla turned and lifted two small pouches. "Nuelya . . . it took a while to dig it out, but here's that cobalt powder you wanted, and the scarletine, too." She slipped away and headed toward the kitchen.

Before Rahl could follow, he heard a timid knock on the door, and he sensed that the person knocking had to be Jienela.

Sevien looked to Rahl. "Why don't you answer it?"

"It would be nice," murmured Delthea, just loud enough for Rahl to hear.

He slipped around the three to the door and opened it.

Jienela smiled up at him. "Sevien said you'd be here. I hoped so."

He half bowed and gestured her to enter.

"This is nice," said Jienela as she stepped into the common room. "I've never been inside. Jaired and Jeason always come for the cider jugs."

"They may not have been in here, either. Sevien only invites his friends." Rahl guided her toward the others. He watched Faseyn's watery blue eyes fix on Jienela from the moment she turned and moved toward the group.

"Jienela," Rahl said, "this is Fahla and her brother Faseyn. Their father took over the chandlery, and they help run it."

Jienela nodded shyly.

"Jienela's family has the big orchard to the north and east of here."

"It's the only one," protested Jienela, "and it's not that big."

"The pearapples are the best, though," said Sevien with a laugh, "and the cider."

"You grew up here, didn't you?" Fahla asked Jienela.

"Father's family's been here since the first. He says that the soil was so bad then that the first trees didn't fruit for years."

"Sand on top and hard clay below," added Sevien. "That's why there have always been potters around Land's End."

"Are you going to be one, too?" asked Fahla.

Rahl frowned inside at the question. Why would she ask that? If Sevien hadn't had the inclination and talent, he would have been apprenticed out years before. Besides, most children followed either the craft or lands of their parents or their consorts' parents—if they had the talent. That was the custom, certainly.

"Haven't your parents always been factors?" asked Sevien.

"Mother was the mate on a trader. Father took up factoring after her ship was burned by pirates."

For Sevien's sake, Rahl almost wanted to shrink into the mortared gaps in the gray stone walls. How were they supposed to know that?

"Are you all ready for some pie?" Nuelya's voice rose over the conversation.

"We've been drooling all along," Rahl called back cheerfully.

"Then come over and get a piece."

Nuelya had slices cut and set on small crockery plates, with the reddish juice oozing out from the golden brown crust. "Take a plate and one of the small beakers, and settle at the long table over there. We have a bit of watered ale for you young people. Not enough to upset your folks but enough to go with the redberry pie."

Rahl maneuvered things so that he was seated beside Jienela and across from Fahla. Mostly he listened as the others chattered.

". . . Quelerya's always looking to for something she can tell . . . like a mouser . . ."

"Not so bad as Widow Wylla. She peeks through her shutters so that no one knows she's looking . . ."

As he listened, Rahl took his time eating the redberry and spaced out his sips of the ale.

After he took the plates back to the pails in the kitchen and washed both his plate and Jienela's, he eased back to where she stood at one side of the other four.

"Good cheese is hard to find, the kind that will keep," Fahla was saying. "So are good knife blades, especially here on Recluce, Father's always saying . . ."

Rahl touched Jienela's forearm. "This way . . . toward the lamp."

"But . . ."

"I just want to see if something is as I thought."

After a moment, Jienela took several steps forward.

Rahl glanced from her eyes to the lamp and back again. He smiled. "I thought so."

She offered a puzzled frown.

"The yellow-gold flecks in your eyes are the same color as the yellow in the lamp flame. Maybe that's why your eyes always look so alive." He reached out and squeezed her hand, gently, and only for a moment.

V

By late morning on threeday, Rahl had finished copying another two of the stories within *Tales of the Founders* and was beginning on the next. He also had bruises on his right shoulder and his left thigh from the early-morning sparring session with his father.

The workroom door opened, and Kian stepped inside, closing the door behind him. He carried an ancient leather folder. "What do you think of the book now?"

"It's interesting." So far the stories were more like terrible or boring, but Rahl didn't want to say what he really thought. Creslin had been an idiot to flee Westwind to avoid a pleasant life in Sarronnyn. Instead, he'd had to try to build a land on what had been a huge desert isle. He'd almost died a half score of times, and he'd been blind for much of his life and died younger than he should have. While Rahl was glad Creslin had succeeded, for his own selfish reasons, he didn't have to approve of what Creslin had done. He knew his father would hardly appreciate his comments. "Where have you been? I didn't see you leave, but you were gone when I got back from checking the ink."

"I was over at Alamat's. He wanted me to write a letter to his son in Valmurl."

"Valmurl? That's in Austra. How . . ." Rahl didn't ask why Kian had gone to the weaver rather than having Alamat come to the scrivener. These days, scriveners couldn't be too choosy.

"By ship. It will cost two silvers, and Zorbyl will have to pick it up at the portmaster's at the harbor there."

How did a weaver's son end up in Valmurl? Rahl wondered. "Two silvers for just a letter?"

"How else can he keep in touch?" asked Kian. "Lieran insulted Magister Rustyn. Rustyn told him to behave. Lieran told Rustyn that he was a useless flea on the back of the mangy dog that was the Council. They put him on the next ship out. He was lucky it was bound to Austra, and not Candar or Hamor."

"Oh." Lieran didn't sound terribly dangerous. Stupid, but hardly dangerous to the Council. "When did this happen?"

"Nine years ago. Alamat finally got the first letter from Lieran something like three years ago. It took a while for the boy to get settled, but he's a weaver in Valmurl now." Kian shook his head. "When Lieran talked to Rustyn, he'd had too much hard cider and not enough sense to go home and sleep it off. Quelerya was on her way from Feyn. They were to be consorted, but Lieran was gone before she arrived."

"And she just stayed?"

"Why not? Alamat's not as young as he used to be, and Lieran was their only boy. Quelerya's a good weaver. Your mother says she never wanted children anyway. If she were younger, she'd be a good catch for you."

Ax-faced Quelerya? Whose tongue was as sharp as her nose and eyes? Rahl repressed a shudder.

"I'd like you to take the letter down to the portmaster right now. Alamat's already paid for it, and Hyelsen is expecting it from either you or me. There's a Suthyan trader coming in, according to the ensign she's flying, and they usually run straight from here to Brysta, then Valmurl."

Rahl cleaned his pen and set it aside, then rose from his stool. He was more than happy to run the letter down to the port. Much as he didn't mind copying, he did get stiff sitting on the stool all the time, and he now had a way to stop by the chandlery and see Fahla without his parents being the wiser.

"No detours through the orchard on the way back, either," added Kian.

"No, ser. I won't be headed to the orchard." He still wished they wouldn't keep harping on the orchard and Jienela. At least they didn't know about Fahla, or they'd be telling him not to stop at the chandlery as well.

Kian handed Rahl the parchment envelope with the blue wax of a scrivener that held the imprint of Alamat's simple seal. The outside bore the inscription: Lieran, Weaver, Portmaster, Valmurl, Austra.

"Don't be long. You've got copying to do."

"Yes, ser." Rahl inclined his head, then slipped out through the door. He closed it quietly. The air was warm and still, the sky hazy, and the afternoon would be warmer than usual for midspring, almost like summer, Rahl suspected.

Envelope in hand, he turned northward and headed down the gray-stone-paved street that led from the orchard and crafthouses on the slopes south of the town down toward the center of Land's End. His sandals scuffed the stone, and the fine sand filtered around his toes. He would have liked to have boots, but decent boots were too expensive for a scrivener.

Within half a kay, the dwellings and shops were closer together, and even the gardens beside the dwellings were narrower. Before long, the street intersected the avenue that led to the harbor. After dodging behind a wagon heaped with coal, Rahl crossed to the east side and headed north. If he had turned the other way, he soon would have reached that point where the avenue became the High Road that stretched the length of Recluce, all the way from Land's End to Nylan in the south.

He walked through the crafters' quarter, passing first a tinsmith's, and then a cabinetmaker's, and beyond that the shuttered windows and closed doors of a shop that Rahl thought had been an apothecary, but it had been closed for years.

Behind the crafters' shops, on the low rises to the east, overlooking the avenue, were a handful of grander two-storied dwellings, surrounded by walls with iron gates, behind which were vast gardens and fountains. They belonged to shipowners and factors. At least, that was what Khorlya had told her son.

As Rahl walked northward on the wide avenue that was the northern end of the High Road, the closer he got to the harbor piers, the more wagons and carts appeared. Still, there were probably less than a score in the two or three hundred cubits before the avenue reached the base of the piers. Voices rose over the creak of wagons and the clopping of hoofs on the stone pavement.

". . . careful with that team!"

". . . got a consignment of fruitwood logs from Naclos . . . tell you, those are rare . . . Druids don't cut many . . ."

". . . need to be here when they port. Suthyans travel fast and keep cargoes dry, but they'd just as soon sell to whoever offers a single silver more than you . . . contracts not worth the paper they're written on . . ."

". . . frigging idiots . . . don't leave shit hanging out the tailgate . . ."

Rahl stayed on the eastern sidewalk and kept moving. At the foot of the pier was a pair of Council Guards from the keep assigned to port duty. He scanned the faces quickly, but neither was a familiar face from the handful of Council Guards he'd met through Kacet before his brother had been transferred to the keep at Reflin.

Just beyond the guards was the black-stone building that held the portmaster and the customs collectors. Rahl slipped through the portmaster's door, then stopped short of the guard stationed inside. The guard took in the truncheon at Rahl's belt and dismissed it.

That irritated Rahl, but he merely straightened, and announced firmly, "A letter for dispatch."

Portmaster Hyelsen sat on a high-backed stool. The window to the right of where he sat allowed him to look down the main black-stone pier. Three vessels were tied up there. One was a three-masted square rigger, and one was a brig. The other was a smaller schooner. Before Rahl could determine more, the portmaster turned. His eyes fixed on the scrivener.

"Young Rahl . . . I expect that will be the letter the weaver paid to have dispatched to Valmurl."

"Yes, ser." Rahl stepped up past the guard and extended the letter.

"Just in time. The Suthyan trader—the square rigger—she'll be leaving late this afternoon, on the evening winds, for Brysta. Valmurl after that." Hyelsen produced a pen from somewhere and wrote a few words on a small square of paper, then handed it to Rahl. "Here's the receipt for you."

"Thank you, ser." Rahl slipped the square into his belt wallet, inclined his head, then turned and hurried out. Something about the portmaster troubled him, but he couldn't have said what, not exactly, except that when Hyelsen looked at Rahl, he seemed to be sensing more than Rahl's words or appearance.

As he cleared the pier, Rahl took a deep breath. He was still careful to watch for wagons and carts, and for what the horses might have dropped on the pavement.

Across the paved serviceway that fronted the main pier and the two flanking it and back, past the memorial park to the east, Rahl caught sight of the time-faded black stones of the Founders' Inn.

Had Creslin really so enchanted all the Westwind Guards and the Montgren troopers with his songs that they worked together from that moment on? Rahl snorted. There had to be a limit to what song—even something like ordersong—could do.

He looked farther south and up the wide stone road that ran through the center of Land's End to where it climbed the rise south of the town to the Black Holding, where the Council still met. Rahl shook his head. No matter what the magisters said and *Tales of the Founders* recounted, Creslin and Megaera couldn't have been that great. No one could have been.

He crossed the avenue, dashing behind an empty wagon until he was on the sidewalk on the west side. Ahead he noticed fresh boards across the front of a shop. He didn't remember what it had been, but he could make out some of the painted lettering on the sign set into the bricks and partly covered by one of the boards.

"Fine tailoring," he murmured.

That could have been why he hadn't recalled it. He kept walking, past the coppersmith's and then the cooperage.

Rahl smiled as he saw the chandlery ahead on his right.

He stepped up onto the narrow porch and smoothed his hair and tunic. He tried to ease through the chandlery door quietly because he sensed someone was already inside talking to Fahla. It didn't do any good. A bell attached to the door rang. Still, he moved to one side, where he looked at the leather goods—a pack with wide straps, clearly used, and an old bridle, and a wide belt with loops—almost an armsman's or a guard's belt.

Next to the pack was a small book, one without a title on the spine. He opened it and looked at the title page, but could not read anything, except what he thought was a name: Kaorda. The book was old, and it had been written in either Hamorian or old Cyadoran, because Rahl would have been able to read High or Low Temple.

He set the slim volume down and looked sideways toward the counter behind which Fahla stood. Even from the rear, Rahl recognized Porgryn. The fuller had a voice that would have been whining without the gravelly tone.

"What's the best cheese you've got for travel? Doesn't turn green quick, you know what I mean."

"The white hard cheese," replied Fahla. "It won't even turn in midsummer so long as you don't leave it in the sun. How much would you like?"

"Don't want it now. Might need it later. Nephew's bringing a wagon of earth up from down south. It's a long trip. Need to provision him on the way back."

"The white cheese would be best. What would you like for now?"

"Ezelya said to check on needles . . ."

"We set some aside for her . . ."

Rahl waited until Porgryn turned to leave before moving away from the leather goods, stepping aside as the fuller neared. "Good day, ser."

"Good day, fellow."

While Porgryn's words were pleasant, Rahl sensed that the wiry fuller had no idea who Rahl was. That bothered him, although he couldn't say why. There was no special reason Porgryn should have known Rahl, even though Kian had made copies of several things for the fuller, and Rahl had been in the workroom.

"What can I get for you, Rahl?" asked Fahla pleasantly. Her mahogany hair was tied back with a dark blue band, leaving her forehead looking wider than when she had worn it down at Sevien's.

"Nothing today. I had to come down to the harbor, and while I was here, I thought I'd stop."

"I can let you have some special cheese that Faseyn found in Extina. Half a quarter wedge for two coppers. Your mother would like it." The hint of a smile played around the corners of her lips. They were good lips, not too thin and not too protruding.

Rahl laughed. "If you were consorted, you'd still try to sell to your consort."

"Of course." She did smile, and that softened the intensity of her eyes— for a moment. "What are you doing down here?"

"Delivering a letter to the portmaster to go by ship to Austra."

Fahla nodded. "Do you get paid a portion of the fee paid to the portmaster?"

"I don't know. Father takes care of those details. We don't do that often. Most folks can't afford to send letters that far."

"It's expensive. They have a system of couriers to do that in Hamor, Father said, and it only costs three coppers to send a letter anywhere there."

Three coppers wasn't cheap, not to Rahl, but it was nothing compared to the two silvers Alamat had paid.

"There's something like that in Candar, too, at least where the white wizards are in charge."

"We really don't need it here," Rahl replied. "We've got the High Road, and you can almost always find someone to carry a letter on it."

The bell on the chandlery door rang, and Fahla looked up. "It's Chorkeil, Rahl. Do you need anything?"

"No, not today." He could sense that she was already thinking what she'd say to the new arrival. "I'll see you later." He offered a smile, inclined his head, and turned.

"Chorkeil . . . We have the spikes you wanted," Fahla began.

Rahl nodded politely to the man although he couldn't say he knew him. Chorkeil ignored Rahl, not even giving him a glance.

The way back felt longer, although Rahl certainly didn't dawdle.

He'd barely stepped into the workroom when his father looked up.

"That took you long enough," Kian said mildly.

"I'm sorry, ser. There were three ships in the harbor, and it was crowded. The portmaster said the letter would go on the Suthyan trader today." Rahl paused. "Oh, here's the receipt." He stepped forward , took the paper square from his wallet, and handed it to his father.

"At least, you remembered the receipt. Best get some water before you settle back into work."

"Yes, ser."

Kian was already absorbed back in working some sort of embellishments on parchment, perhaps a copy of one of the declarations, when Rahl returned from the outside pump and settled back onto his stool and more copying of *Tales of the Founders*.

VI

Eightday dawned bright and sunny, and Rahl had a spring in his step, although it was still early morning, if well past dawn, when he made his way from the tiny chamber out to the common room for breakfast. He enjoyed the end-day because, unless his father had an urgent commission, after chores, the day was largely Rahl's.

Lukewarm gruel, bread, and some peach conserve awaited him at the table, along with a small mug of redberry. Khorlya was finishing a basket, and Rahl could smell something baking. He settled before his modest breakfast, then looked to the other end of the table. "Baskets on an end-day? And baking?"

"Have you forgotten? You're going to see Shahyla today. I was up early. The honey cake is almost ready."

Rahl hadn't exactly forgotten—more like put the thought at the back of his mind. "Oh . . . that's right."

"You could show a bit more enthusiasm, Rahl."

"I'm still a little sleepy." That was true enough, but not the reason.

"She's a pretty girl, and she could use a young man like you. You're handy and polite."

Rahl knew that, but he just took a large spoonful of gruel to avoid saying anything. Why did they keep pushing on the consort business? Couldn't they just let him be?

"After you finish breakfast and your chores, wash up and put on your good tunic. You'll need to start soon to get there just after midday. It's at least four kays, and you don't want to hurry and arrive all sweating."

"You told them I was coming?" That was even worse.

"I said you might when I saw Shahyla at the market on fourday. What would be the point of my baking and your walking that far if the girl didn't happen to be there?"

"Did you say when I'd be there?"

"Just that it would probably be past midday. Now, finish eating and get on with things." Khorlya set the basket aside and moved to the old tiled stove. "I did make another honey cake for us. You can have yours when you get back."

"They aren't one-god worshippers, are they?"

"I doubt anyone in Land's End is, and they're not single-twinners, either," offered Kian from the doorway.

"Single-twinners?" Rahl hadn't heard of that belief, but for him the idea of order and chaos was enough, without believing that the world was controlled by some invisible deity using strange rules.

"There aren't any here. The magisters don't allow them. Now . . . enough dilly-dallying. Finish up and get on to your chores."

Rahl finished eating, then washed his bowl, and racked it before turning to deal with chamber pots and his other chores, as well as checking the newest batch of ink.

Later, he did take his time washing up and dressing. He'd just donned his better tunic when he heard his mother.

"Rahl? Are you about ready?"

"I'll be right there."

Khorlya was standing by the front door, holding the basket she'd been working on earlier. "Here you go."

Rahl took the basket, his eyes checking it. Right above the base was the linked chain, woven out of the rushes soaked in thinned ink so that they took up the blackness. The chain swirled up and into the handle and then down the other side. It took a special talent to weave and braid a design so intricate that it looked as though a black chain was actually imbedded in the basket itself. The basket was one that would have sold for a half silver. That wasn't good, not at all, not when his mother was sending him off with one of her best.

Kian moved toward them from where he'd been sitting at the table, but the scrivener did not speak.

"The honey cake needs to be kept moist," Khorlya added. "So tell her what it is immediately."

"Yes, Mother."

"You're going to court a girl, not to exile." Exasperation colored Khorlya's words.

He was being told to court a girl he didn't want to consort who lived on lands four kays from anywhere, and it wasn't exile?

"Now . . . you take the High Road south, until you get to the base of the long rise that leads to the Black Holding. There's a lane that heads east, with two stone pillars there, and a set of horns on the right pillar. You take the lane almost a kay until you get to the fork . . ."

Rahl listened carefully. The last thing he wanted was to get lost—and then have to admit it and ask someone for directions.

"I hope you have a pleasant day, and if you run into trouble, try to talk before you use that truncheon." Kian opened the door, a clear sign that Rahl was to be on his way.

"And make sure her day is pleasant, too," added Khorlya.

"I'll do what I can."

"Do better than that," suggested Kian.

"Yes, ser." Rahl inclined his head, then stepped out into the sunlight.

Once he began to walk southward, he felt better. The breeze was just brisk enough to be cooling. At the corner, he saw Quelerya and Alamat sitting on the weaver's porch. He grinned and waved with the hand that wasn't carrying the basket. "Good day!"

"Good day, Rahl," Alamat called.

Quelerya said nothing, but Rahl could sense curiosity from the old biddy. He kept walking. As he passed the short lane to Sevien's dwelling, he glanced down it, but he didn't see anyone there. He walked almost half a kay before his sandals were on the smooth stone-paved surface of the High Road.

He looked southward. He had at least another two kays before he reached the lane. His eyes strayed to the low black-stone buildings at the distant crest of the rise. Were his parents doing the same thing to him that Creslin's mother had done to him? He shook his head but kept walking.

Behind him, he heard hoofs, and then a voice called out, " 'Ware on the left!"

He eased to the right side and glanced up as a rider in the black of a Council Guard went by. The woman didn't even really look at him as she hurried past. She could have offered a greeting, but some of the Guards thought they were so important. He snorted. They were all errand runners for the Council. From what he'd heard and seen, the black engineers in Nylan were the ones who did the real fighting and protected Recluce, not that he was about to say that to either his parents or Kacet.

And why were they suddenly so intent on his courting Shahyla? While Rahl had seen and talked to Shahyla more than a few times growing up, he'd never walked all the way to her father's holding. Why was he doing it? Why were his parents so insistent? Was there something to what his mother had said about machines being used to make books?

But wasn't there something he could do besides learn to become a herder? Or a Guard? He'd much rather be a factor, even, and working with Fahla, he suspected, wouldn't always be easy. But it wouldn't be boring. He grinned at that thought.

He looked up and watched as a cart approached. A gray-haired woman walked beside a mare, holding the mare's leads loosely. The cart held potatoes. They had to be from the previous fall and probably had been stored all winter in a root cellar.

"Good day," Rahl said politely as he neared her. "Potatoes for the Guard keep?"

"Indeed, young ser. How did you know?"

"It's end-day, and the markets aren't open. It would have to be one of the inns or the keep. That's a lot of potatoes for an inn." Rahl grinned.

The woman smiled back as she passed.

Rahl continued on his way, occasionally passing, and being passed by riders and wagons. None of the teamsters going his way offered him a ride, and he found that irked him, especially when he thought about the man who had an empty wagon.

Before long, he reached the point on the High Road where it began to climb and found the first set of pillars easily enough although he was blotting his forehead by then. Before setting off down the lane, he took off his tunic and tied it around his waist. The light undertunic felt far more comfortable, but when he reached the fork, he wasn't all that much cooler, but he wasn't sweating as much as he had been.

The right fork wound between two hills. Just beyond the hills were the gate and stone walls that marked the edge of Bradeon's holding. Rahl stopped and blotted his forehead. He found a spot on the wall shaded by an old pine and sat down to cool off.

After a time, he redonned the tunic and climbed over the wall rather than fiddle with the elaborate latches on the gate. The lane beyond the gate was even narrower and rutted as it rose gently perhaps ten cubits over a quarter kay.

Rahl studied the lands on both sides of the lane. Those to the north were lush meadows or pastures. He wasn't sure what the difference was. Those to the south looked to have been more heavily grazed and not so fertile. There were trees scattered here and there, and beyond the walls to the south, perhaps a kay farther on, rose the scrubbier juniper and pine protected forests, although in places, he could see the greener and thicker growth of leaved trees.

Just below the top of the low rise was a cluster of buildings—several shedlike barns, smaller sheds, and a long gray stone house perhaps twice the size of the one in which Rahl had grown up. As he neared the dwelling, he could see that at least one of the small sheds held chickens. A hissing told him that there were also geese.

Shahyla stood under the eaves that shaded the front porch, clearly waiting for him. She was a tall girl, taller than Sevien, with wavy brown hair cut just at neck level. She had a pleasantly curved figure, Rahl noted, and clear skin. Her nose was crooked, and her left eye twitched. She wore dark brown trousers above scuffed boots and a clean but faded pale blue shirt. When he stepped up onto the porch, she smiled. The boards of the porch creaked.

"You walked all the way out here?"

Rahl grinned. "How else would I get here?" He extended the basket. "This is for you and your family—both the basket and the honey cake in it."

"Rahl . . . the basket is lovely."

"Mother made it for you."

"Oh . . . I'm forgetting manners." She gestured toward the battered bench set against the outside front wall of the dwelling, between the door and the small square window, open to capture the breeze. "You must be hot and tired. It is a long walk. Please sit down. I'll get you some ale. That's all right, isn't it?"

"Ale would be wonderful."

"I'll also put the honey cake in the cooler. That should keep it moist."

Rahl settled onto the bench, careful not to bang the truncheon on the wood. He did watch Shahyla as she turned and entered the house, appreciating her grace and her shapeliness. Her figure was better than Jienela's. For that matter, it was better than Fahla's as well.

He blotted his forehead. He might as well enjoy the afternoon, especially since he was in no hurry to start the long walk back into Land's End.

Shahyla returned with two large mugs, more like tankards in size. One was half-full, the other almost overflowing. She handed him the full one. "One nice thing about company is that Father doesn't complain if I have a little ale."

"Thank you." Rahl took a swallow. "It's good."

"It should be. Father makes his own." She settled onto the bench beside him.

"You have quite a spread here."

"It's the last of the old large holdings near Land's End." Shahyla sipped her ale. "It keeps all three of us busy."

Rahl's eyes took in the two shed-barns he could see and the chicken shack. "Do you grow everything you eat here?"

"No. We grow a lot, but it's better to make the cheese and sell it and some of the steers every year than to spend too much time on growing things. We have a house garden, and that helps."

"You must do a lot here, the cooking and helping with the animals."

"Ma was a better cook, but Father and Semmelt don't complain."

"I'm sure you cook well, and you probably do everything else well also."

Shahyla dropped her eyes, looking down into the tankard mug. After a moment, she lifted them. "You know I don't read much. I've always had to work, since Ma was so sick. I do know my letters."

"People make too much over reading," Rahl said. "Doing is what matters, and you do a lot, more than any woman I know."

"You're a scrivener . . ."

"I'm sure you could read what I write, but it wouldn't help with the cows or the cheese." Rahl took another long swallow of the ale. It was stronger than what he got at home, but he had to admit that it was good. He reached out and touched the back of her hand just momentarily, caressing it with order. "It's quiet out here."

Shahyla gave a short, giggling laugh. "It isn't in the morning. The roosters are crowing, and the cows want to be milked, and Father and Semmelt are shouting about what needs to be done."

"Until you get everything in order?"

She looked down again.

"You're the one who keeps everything going, I'd wager."

"You're nice, Rahl," Shahyla said. "Do you like cows and bulls? Or horses?"

"I never thought about it. I haven't ever ridden a horse or driven a team, and we don't have a dog. They'd chew on the binding hides, Father says."

"They might. We don't have them because Father says they chase the cows, and it's not good for the milk." Shahyla smiled and gave the slightest giggle. "I think that's because he doesn't like them. The geese tell us if anyone's coming, and the cats take care of the rats and other rodents."

Abruptly, she looked at Rahl. "You didn't have dinner today, did you?"

"I'm fine."

"Your stomach was growling. Leastwise, you should have some good cheese and bread." Shahyla rose. "Come on inside."

Rahl wasn't about to object too strenuously. He was hungry, and his stomach had been muttering its discomfort.

Shahyla set him in the chair at one end of an ancient table that could easily have seated more than half a score, and then brought out a huge wedge of cheese and half a loaf of bread that was still warm. "We had plenty left after dinner." Absently, she pressed the side of her thumb against her left eye to stop the twitching.

"I don't deserve this . . ." Rahl grinned at her after several bites of bread and cheese. "But I can't tell you how much I appreciate it."

She seated herself on the end of the dining bench to his right, putting her tankard mug before her. "I made the bread."

"It's very good. What else do you do when you're not cooking?"

"Oh . . . I milk the cows and churn the butter, and take care of the chickens and collect the eggs. The garden's mine, too, and I do most of the skinning when we slaughter. Semmelt's too rough, and that's hard on the hide. Could make a silver's difference in what we get. I do what needs to be done."

"What do they do? Besides feed and chase the cattle?"

"Everything." Another giggle-laugh followed her words. "Yesterday, Semmelt and Father worked all day gelding and marking the male calves. They use a special curved knife. It's real sharp." Shahyla slipped off the bench and walked to the sideboard. "Here . . . see."

Rahl looked at the knife. It almost seemed to be covered in a shifting reddish white film. Just looking at the knife made him uneasy. It wasn't the gelding that bothered him; it was the gelding knife. He forced himself to nod. "It looks like it was made for just that."

"It's been in the family for a long time, Father said." She replaced the knife in the drawer and returned to the bench. "Your stomach's not growling."

"No . . . and it thanks you. So do I." Rahl touched her wrist gently—and briefly.

"What sort of books do you copy?"

"All kinds," he replied. "I've been working on *Tales of the Founders*."

"Can you tell me about it?"

"I may not remember everything, but I'll try." Rahl took another swallow of ale, then cleared his throat. "Creslin was the son of the Marshal of Westwind . . ."

He told Shahyla the first two tales he'd copied and was about to start the third when the door opened.

"Ah . . . it'd be young Rahl, sure as I'm standing here."

Rahl turned at the rough voice to see Bradeon coming through the doorway, barefoot. "Later, when you have time, Shahyla, if you'd be washing off my boots," Bradeon went on. "Semmelt's still over at the spring. Another of those clay pipes feeding the field troughs cracked. Made an awful mess. Some of the cows ripped up the grass there. Take all summer to grow back." The herder shook his head.

Belatedly, Rahl eased to his feet.

Bradeon glanced out the small window toward the west, then back to his daughter. The sun was well past midafternoon. "I'd be thinking . . ."

"I know, Father." Shahyla rose, then turned to Rahl. "Thank you for coming." She looked to Bradeon. "He brought us a honey cake."

The herder inclined his head. "Much obliged. Semmelt'll be even more obliged." Bradeon settled into the chair at the other end of the table, turning it sidewise so that he could rest his feet on the bench.

"I'd best get to what needs to be done," Shahyla said. "I'm so glad you came." She smiled broadly, revealing perfect, even teeth. "We're not that far from town, but we don't get that many folks coming out." Her left eye twitched several times.

Rahl tried not to look at that, but just smiled. "It was a pleasure. I'm the one who's glad to have come. I really liked the ale and the cheese."

He followed Shahyla out onto the porch.

She stopped. "You'll have to come more."

"I'd like that." He squeezed her hand gently, then released it before smiling at her one last time and heading down the steps toward the lane.

A hundred cubits down the lane, he turned. She was still on the porch. He waved. She waved back.

As he walked back along the lane, then along the High Road, Rahl considered the day. Shahyla was nice, if no-nonsense, and better-looking and smarter than he'd recalled. She was also interested in him. On the other hand, the gelding knife had bothered him. No, it had more than bothered him. It had disturbed him, so evil had it felt.

Still . . . there was no harm in visiting Shahyla. Jienela might not like it, but he hadn't exactly promised her anything, and he could always tell her that his parents had insisted. That certainly was true.

His feet were more than a little sore when he finally stepped into his own house to find his parents eating dinner at the table.

"How did it go?" asked Khorlya.

"She's sweet, and she's a good person."

"Is that all you can say?" asked Kian.

Rahl forced a smile, glad that his father could not sense his thoughts. "I'll have to see her more often, ser. She's not the kind to say yes after a visit or two." He turned to Khorlya. "She really liked the basket. She could tell it was one of your best."

"That's good. Tell us what happened."

Rahl laughed genially and settled himself at the table.

"I got there, and Shahyla brought me some ale Bradeon had made. It's very good. We talked for a while, and then she insisted on getting me some of their cheese and bread. Then Bradeon came in, and he'd been replacing pipes that fed water troughs, and Semmelt was still doing that. I had to go then, because she had to get to her afternoon chores. She works hard." He looked toward the kitchen worktable.

"Yes, Rahl," Khorlya said. "There's honey cake left for you."

Rahl smiled. It hadn't been a bad day at all. Not at all.

VII

For the next two eightdays Rahl did little besides copy from *Tales of the Founders* and then *Natural Arithmetics and Other Calculation Methods*. Unbelievable as most of the tales were, they had been at least interesting. He could not say that for *Natural Arithmetics*.

He hadn't even had to explain anything to Jienela about his end-day visits to Shahyla. The last eightday or so, Jienela had been in Extina. She'd been sent there to help her mother's younger sister Joslyn. Jienela's aunt had nearly died in childbirth, even with a black healer present.

Rahl could not say that he truly missed Jienela except for the pleasures she had afforded him, but he'd also not been able to stop by the chandlery more than a time or two, and never long enough to talk with Fahla for more than a moment, if that. Still, he had had another pleasant afternoon with Shahyla.

The last three mornings had dawned gray and drizzling, unusually so for late spring and early summer in northern Recluce, and fourday was far colder than twoday and threeday. Rahl was trying not to shiver as he worked on copying a page that held formulae and exercise problems.

"For darkness' sake, Rahl," snapped Kien, "go put on a heavier tunic or a jacket. You can't keep a steady hand if you're shivering. You young folks have no sense at all. I saw your friend Sevien coming out of the chandlery the other morning in a sleeveless tunic. His arms were near–dark blue, and yet he had the audacity to tell me he wasn't cold. His teeth were chattering so much I barely understood a word he had to say."

Rahl decided against trying to point out that anyone who wore a heavy winter tunic in spring, or summer, or darkness forbid, an actual jacket, would have to suffer silent ridicule in the eyes of his friends for at least an eightday, if not longer. He did set aside his pen and rise to follow his father's order. He could always hide the tunic if his father sent him on an errand away from the shop.

When he returned to the workroom, Kian nodded. "Much more sensible. You'll get more work done without errors, too."

Rahl hated it when his parents talked about sensibility. He knew what was sensible, even when they didn't, but he said nothing and went back to work.

He finished another page and started on the next.

"Frig!" Kian murmured.

"What is it?"

"There must have been something wrong with the pen point. It just snapped. That shouldn't have happened. Hardly put any pressure on it at all." Kian shook his head.

Rahl winced silently, wondering if that had been the pen he'd dropped in cleaning up the night before.

"Why don't you run down to the chandlery and pick up the nibs. They should be there by now. I'd already ordered some from Kehlyrt. He's the new factor."

"Factor?"

"Well . . . he's taken over the chandlery, but he's adding things, goods we haven't seen in years. Good prices, too. It's getting more like a factorage than a chandlery."

"Yes, ser."

"And don't strip off the tunic as soon as you leave the workroom."

"No, ser."

"I mean it, Rahl."

"Yes, ser." Rahl did manage to keep his voice pleasant as he cleaned his pen and set it in the holder. "Do I need silvers to pay for them?"

"Hardly," snorted Kian. "I had to pay in advance. That goes for anything he orders from Nylan. It's still cheaper and quicker than getting them from Lydiar or Hamor." He frowned. "I still wonder how that broke." He shook his head. "That nib was getting worn anyway . . . why I'd ordered another pair."

Rahl stood and headed toward the door.

"Don't take too long."

"No, ser."

Once outside the workroom, Rahl thought about pulling off the heavy winter tunic, but it was cold, and he could sense his father watching. With a resigned shrug, he headed down the street toward the factorage.

The cold and bitter wind blew steadily out of the northwest, driven by clouds that were almost black. Whitecaps dominated the part of the ocean Rahl could see beyond the harbor breakwater. The piers were empty of ships—a good sign that a storm was headed toward Land's End. Rahl picked up his pace.

A light stinging rain, with droplets like ice, began to lash at him by the time he neared the harbor, and he was glad to climb the steps and enter the dim confines of the chandlery. He could sense that there was no one else besides him and Fahla there.

She stood behind the counter, a concerned expression on her face as he approached. "It's raw outside, isn't it?"

"It's started to rain. The drops feel like sleet. The harbor's empty, and the clouds to the northwest are really dark."

"The last coaster raised sail almost at dawn. The Austrans left well before dawn. They have a better sense of weather." After a pause, she asked, "Do you have any business today, Rahl, or are you just here to warm yourself going one way or another or to bend my ear?"

"Business. Father thought that the pen nibs he ordered might be here by now. He's already paid for them."

"They came late yesterday, I think. The supply wagon from Nylan usually arrives on threeday." Fahla opened the small ledger to her right and flipped through several pages. "Yes, they did, and your father did pay for them."

Rahl wanted to say that he didn't like being questioned on what he'd said. He didn't. Instead, he smiled. "Thank you. I'd like to take them."

"Just a moment, Rahl. They're in the racks in the back." Fahla slipped through the open door to the storeroom.

Rahl smiled at the combination of efficiency and grace she embodied.

In moments she returned with a small pouch. "Here they are."

"Thank you. How has your day been?"

"It's always slow when it's cold and rainy. Faseyn likes it because he can finish the account entries and work on his mathematical puzzles. Did you know he's studying natural mathematics with Magistra Reya?"

Rahl didn't even know who the magistra was. "No, I didn't. He must be very good for her to tutor him personally."

Fahla nodded. "Did you ever think about studying with the magisters? You're bright enough."

"So are you," he pointed out.

"I'm more interested in practical things. I don't like studying." She laughed, ruefully. "I'd get bored doing that. I'd wager that you read every book you copy."

"You have to."

"That's not what I meant. You read them all to see what they mean, and you probably even argue with the ones you think are wrong."

"You can't argue with a book," Rahl said reasonably.

"You know what I mean—"

"Fahla!" A man's voice called from the storeroom.

"That's Father. He must need help with something." Fahla started to turn, then stopped. "Rahl . . ."

"Yes?"

"I'm glad you have enough sense to wear something warm."

He couldn't help flushing slightly, thinking that he almost hadn't.

"Good day, Rahl."

"Good day, Fahla."

As she turned, Rahl shook his head. The whole world seemed to be against his spending any time at all with Fahla. If it weren't a customer, then it was Kehlyrt wanting something from her, and he'd forgotten to ask her if the chandlery was going to become a factorage, although that question would have just been to satisfy his own curiosity.

As Rahl stepped out of the chandlery, he saw a figure in black at the foot of the two steps leading up onto the narrow porch. Rahl would have preferred not to meet Magister Puvort, but trying to avoid the magister would have been all too obvious. He did step aside to allow the magister direct access to the door. "Good day, magister."

Instead of heading inside, Puvort stepped onto the porch, under the eaves, and out of the still-light rain, and looked directly at Rahl. "What brings you to the chandlery? Might it be the young lady?" Puvort's smile was meant to be cheerful, but it bothered Rahl.

"I like seeing her, ser." Rahl didn't dare lie, not when the magister could have told he was telling an outright falsehood, but he could tell the truth in a less damaging way. He held up the pouch. "But I was here to pick up the pen nibs my father ordered. He had work to do, and he sent me."

"You're very careful in what you say, aren't you?"

"I try to be, ser."

"That wasn't what I meant, Rahl." The magister's eyes seemed to look right through the young scrivener. "You never tell an untruth, but sometimes you don't tell the whole truth. That's what the mages in Hamor do, you know?"

"Ser?" Rahl didn't like the reference to Hamor.

"You might think about applying to the Council for mage training, Rahl. It's clear that you have at least a little ability with ordermagery. You know instinctively that you shouldn't lie, and you're right. Lying reduces order-skills."

Rahl didn't know quite what to say. "I . . . I never thought about that."

"You should. Right now, your skills aren't developed enough to be that dangerous, but you're still young. If you become more powerful, you'll either have to have training or leave Recluce. You might have to, anyway, but training now would make your life easier. Much easier."

"Ser . . . I don't . . . my father . . ."

"That kind of training is not like school where your father has to pay. The Council would pay for it." Puvort paused. "Of course, you wouldn't be earning anything, either, but you should still consider it." His eyes dropped to Rahl's truncheon, and he nodded slightly.

"Yes, ser."

"Do think about it, Rahl." With another enigmatic smile, the magister stepped away from Rahl and into the chandlery.

Rahl stepped off the porch and headed southward, the wind at his back, tearing at his tunic. He had the feeling that, despite the magister's offer, Puvort hadn't really wanted him to consider it. Or the magister thought he wouldn't take it.

Should he tell his father about what Puvort had said?

That didn't seem like a good idea at all, but he couldn't have said why, and that bothered him as much as what the magister had told him.

The wind picked up, driving the rain, which had become sleet, into his back.

Rahl walked even faster, almost at a trot. He just wanted to get home and out of the cold. Then, he'd think things over.

VIII

Rahl was still working his way through the tedious mathematics text on fiveday afternoon when Kian came hurrying in with a small sheet of paper and a stack of larger and heavier paper posterboards.

"We've got a commission from the Council, but it has to be finished before sunset today. Put aside the textbook. You'll have to help."

"What is it?" Rahl asked, not that it mattered to him, except that anything would have been less tedious than the page before him. Despite what Fahla had wagered, he hadn't really read much of the mathematics text, except for the obvious matters like how to calculate areas and volumes, and simple formulae.

More important from his point of view was that a good commission from the Council meant his father would be in a better mood when Rahl said he was going to Sevien's house after supper.

"Here. You can read the words while I work the spacing and letter size for the posterboards." Kian handed the thinner, smaller sheet to his son, adding, "They must have gone to every scrivener in Recluce to get these done."

Whatever the paper said, then, it had to be important. Rahl read it, although he had to struggle in places because the writing was both hurried and cramped. When he finished, his eyes went back to the opening lines.

> The Council of Recluce has determined that the frequency and severity of piracy has increased significantly and that such piracy has been largely undertaken by Jeranyi vessels. With the failure of the ruler of Jerans to abate such reprehensible acts . . .
>
> . . . all in Recluce are hereby notified that any and all trade and commerce with any vessel bearing a Jeranyi flag or crewed by Jeranyi or owned by Jeranyi is hereby forbidden. Purchase of goods from Jerans is also prohibited, and any merchant or factor holding such goods must dispose of them within an eightday of the date of this notice—or turn them over to the Council for partial compensation. Any trader or merchant from Jerans is to leave Recluce within an eightday of the date of this notice. All who fail to do so may have all goods and coins confiscated, at the determination of a justicer appointed by the Council . . .

After a moment, he looked toward Kian. "What good will this do? Why don't they just go out and destroy the pirates?"

"The oceans are vast, and Recluce has but few ships compared to the size of those oceans . . ." began Kian.

"—and the ships that can catch and destroy the pirates belong to the engineers in Nylan, and they don't want to spend their time chasing pirates?"

Kian shook his head. "It's not that simple. They've caught and sunk a score of pirate vessels, or so I've heard, but some of the pirates fly different flags in every port they enter and change the names on their ships. The important part is the expulsion of the traders. Factors, merchants, and traders account for far more coins than do the pirates, especially those who work with the pirates and sell their plunder."

"The Council wants the traders to put pressure on the Duke of Jerans to stop the piracy," Rahl suggested.

"He's an autarch, I think. Or maybe a consul who theoretically pledges allegiance to Sarronnyn. But they have that in mind. What will happen is that our factors and traders will trade more with those they know and trust and less with those they don't. They won't like it, but the magisters will come back and ask them, and if they lie, they'll be exiled as well."

"What if they're honestly mistaken?"

"Then they'll be warned and watched more closely."

Rahl wondered what that would do to Fahla and her family.

"Now . . . I'll make the first one, and you can use that as a model," Kian began.

Rahl watched and waited, then began on a third copy while Kian started a second one.

Neither spoke much as the afternoon waned.

When Rahl finished his last copy, the sun was low in the sky, low but still not close to twilight. Kian waited for the posterboards to dry because the heavier stock absorbed more ink.

"Ten fair copies in an afternoon, with the Council embellishments! A good day's work. A good day's work," repeated Kian, before turning to Rahl. "You can start cleaning up. But check the new batch of ink first."

"Yes, ser." Rahl stretched and then headed for the door.

Kian's request to check the ink was as close to a compliment as Rahl was likely to get, because it meant Kian had no complaints about Rahl's latest work. But then, reflected Rahl, his hand was as good as his father's. Also, because he could feel what was happening, his inks usually turned out better than his father's, not that he was going to say that. He just wished at times his father would recognize it.

Outside in the mild air that had followed the storm earlier in the eight-day, Rahl couldn't help but think about what Magister Puvort had said. The more he thought about it, the more it felt like a trap. Yet, at some point, Puvort might mention it to Rahl's parents. He would need to tell them, but at the right time.

Rahl used his order-sense to help the melding and mixing of the oak galls, the bit of added iron-brimstone, and the tree gum. When he'd been younger, he'd wondered why his parents didn't see when some things didn't go together. They'd just looked at him blankly, and, after a very short time, he had stopped asking.

He closed the shed door carefully and went back to the pump and washstones to clean up. By the time he had finished and walked back into the house, his father and mother were seated at the table. Supper was simple—bread, cheese, and a leftover soup/stew that had been reheated more times than it should have been.

Still, it was after sunset before he left the house. In the dimness he passed the orchard. Someone was there, waiting. Jienela?

"Rahl . . ." The whisper came from the trees beyond the orchard wall.

He walked to the wall and leaned against it, as if waiting. Even if Quelerya saw him, what could she say to his mother? That he was leaning against the wall? "What is it?"

"I . . . I needed to talk to you, but you never came."

"I didn't know you were back." He'd suspected that she might be . . . but he hadn't actually known, and he really hadn't wanted to go looking for Jienela, not with his parents' disapproval and constant comments. Besides, Fahla made Jienela look . . . well, dull. Sweet and pretty, but dull. Even Shahyla had more spark than Jienela.

"I've been back since twoday." There was a pause. "I've missed you."

He could sense her sadness . . . and longing. "I've missed you." What else could he say? "Jienela . . . my father's gotten really strict."

"He's always been strict. That's why you've had to sneak out to see me. That's what you told me. Can't you come back later, when it's darker?"

"I can't. He and Mother found out about us. Quelerya's been watching, and she told Mother."

"You knew they wouldn't like it, but . . ."

He could sense a swallowed sob.

"Father's forbidden me to see you. If he gets really angry, he could throw me out."

"He . . . he wouldn't do that . . ."

"Why do you think Kacet is in the Council Guards? He started out as an apprentice scrivener, too, but he crossed Father too often, and Father told him that he wouldn't put up with it any longer." That much was true, but Kacet had been the one to make the decision. He'd left on his own. Still . . .

In the silence broken only by the whisper of the breeze through the leaves of the apple and pearapple trees, Rahl could sense dismay and sadness . . . and something else. What that other feeling was, he couldn't determine.

"For a while, at least, I don't dare try to sneak in to see you," he finally said. "I'll have to see how things go."

"Please try . . . you have to try, Rahl. You *have* to . . ." Then the sobs became louder.

"I'll see . . ."

"Please . . ."

Rahl looked around. There was someone on the porch at Alamat's. "I need to go. Someone at Alamat's is looking this way."

He straightened up and began to walk toward the weaver's. He waved to Alamat as he passed the porch, but the elderly weaver did not look up. Rahl didn't see anyone else for the rest of the walk to Sevien's.

Sevien opened the door even before Rahl reached it. "Come on in."

Rahl stepped inside. Except for Sevien and himself, no one was there. "Where is everyone?"

"Oh . . . Mother and Delthea are over at Selstak's. They're all working on a consorting quilt for Coerlyne. She deserves it, even if Jaired doesn't. Father went down to the tavern to play plaques with some of his friends." After a moment, Sevien went on. "You know Jienela's back?"

"I just found out." Rahl offered a sour smile, one that mirrored his own mixed feelings. "My parents are pushing me to ask for Shahyla's hand."

"They want you to become a . . . herder?"

"They haven't said that. Not in so many words, but Mother keeps talking about the machines the engineers are building that will make books by the score and how no one will need scriveners anymore."

"The Council won't let them, will they?"

"They can stop the machines from being used outside of Nylan, but how would they stop the books? Are they going to inspect every book coming out of Nylan—or on every ship porting in Land's End? And if people get books that cost less, why would they pay Father or me more for the same book?"

"You sound like Faseyn," replied Sevien. "He's always talking about how what things cost affects the world."

"What do you think of him?" Rahl asked.

"He's all right. He likes doing the accounts at the chandlery. Columns and columns of numbers, and he *likes* keeping track of them. Fahla showed me."

Rahl forced a polite smile. "When I've been there, she's the only one in the shop."

"Most times, she is. That's what she told me."

Rahl liked Sevien, but he was also interested in Fahla, and he needed to avoid mentioning Shahyla to Fahla. All that meant he'd have to be careful. Very careful.

There was a knock on the door, and Sevien bounded to open it. "Fahla!"

Rahl watched closely, but the redhead merely smiled and nodded politely to Sevien as she stepped inside.

"Faseyn said he didn't feel like coming tonight when I couldn't promise redberry pie." Fahla laughed, then turned to Rahl. "Were the pen nibs satisfactory?"

Rahl laughed in return. "Father didn't complain, and if there's anything in the slightest wrong, he will." Because she was so indifferent to anything except trade, at least with him, he asked, "Have you heard about the Council order?"

"No. Why would I? How do you know?" A faint curiosity lay behind her words.

"While you two are talking about the Council," Sevien said, "I'll get some redberry juice. There's enough for the three of us, anyway."

"It's about trade," Rahl explained, "and the Jeranyi pirates. Because, I'd guess, of all the piracy, the Council is forbidding all trade with Jerans and Jeranyi merchants, and all of them have to leave Recluce within the eightday, and all merchants and factors have to sell anything from Jerans within the eightday or turn it over to the Council . . ."

As he finished explaining, Rahl could sense a growing tension in Fahla.

"How do you know this?" Her voice was almost playful but with a tightness behind it. "Is it true or just what you heard somewhere?"

"I had to make four copies of the notice this afternoon. After that many copies, you do remember what something said. The effective date is tomorrow."

Fahla's lips tightened. Then she stepped back, and called, "Sevien, I have to go."

"You just came," the young potter protested.

"I . . . forgot . . . something." Fahla hurried toward the door, then opened it. "Good night, Sevien, Rahl." With a wave, she was gone.

Sevien strode over to Rahl. "*What* did you say to her? She was happy until you two talked."

"I just told her about the newest Council edict. We worked all afternoon copying it. It was about trade, and how the Council is forbidding trade with Jerans because of the pirates." Rahl glanced toward the door, still slightly ajar. "She was worried. I wonder if her father's been trading with the Jeranyi, or even with the pirates."

"Father says he has good prices, better than the other factors." Sevien looked at Rahl. "Did you have to tell her?"

"I thought she'd want to know. Besides, all she ever talks to me about is goods and trade, and things like that."

"That's all she ever says to me, either," Sevien retorted. "But what I say doesn't make her run off."

"I'm sorry, Sevien." He was, but he was also worried about Fahla. She was always so sure of herself, and when she'd hurried off, she hadn't been that way at all, not inside. "I think I'd better go."

"You . . ."

"I'll see you later." Rahl offered a smile, then hurried out, closing the door behind him.

Once outside, he started home.

As he passed the wall to the orchard, he couldn't help but worry about Jienela. She'd been upset as well, but he hadn't promised her anything, and she'd been the one who'd encouraged him. Besides, she'd wanted him to do what he had.

Fahla's abrupt change in attitude and feelings weighed on him more. She'd arrived cheerful, then almost run out the door. How could trading with Jeranyi upset her that much? Or were she and her family involved in more than that?

It was probably stupid—and possibly dangerous—but he decided to walk down to the chandlery. After all, it wasn't *that* late.

He walked confidently through the darkness, knowing that he could find his way better than most people because he had a clear feeling for where things were.

Even before he reached the chandlery, he could sense people around it, but the shutters were closed, and no lamps showed. Rahl had the feeling that whatever was happening was at the loading docks in back. He retraced his steps to the narrow alleyway beside the alchemist's and eased his way into the deeper gloom near the wall. His left hand rested on the butt of the truncheon for a moment before he grasped it and slipped it out of the leather loops.

Why was he doing this?

He had no idea, except that he was worried about Fahla. She'd acted like she was in trouble, and she never had done that before.

Ahead of him he could sense two wagons backed up to the chandlery's loading dock. He slowed and hugged the stone wall as he moved silently toward the wagons.

He tried to hear the whispers.

". . . sure about this . . ."

". . . copied the notice . . . quoted it word for word . . ." That was Fahla.

". . . be here in the morning . . ."

". . . can get to the east cove and wait . . ."

Rahl smelled vinegar. At least, he thought it was vinegar, or maybe pickles.

". . . sure that's wetted down good. Wouldn't want an explosion now . . ."

". . . vinegar and water . . . done solid . . ."

Although Rahl was trying to catch the words, his darkness senses registered someone moving toward him from out of the shadows on the south side of the loading dock.

The man felt as though he carried a red-tinged shadow as he moved toward Rahl, except it wasn't a shadow exactly. Rahl lifted the truncheon.

The man said nothing, but lunged and thrust at Rahl with a long blade.

Rahl near-instinctively slid/parried the thrust, then stepped inside the blade and kneed the man in the groin while slamming the truncheon across his temple.

Rahl swallowed hard, because a sense of redness—and death—washed over him, even before the man toppled onto the dusty stones. How could one blow from a truncheon have killed a man?

"You hear something? Where's Hondahl?"

Rahl backed away from the dead man and slipped back down the alleyway as quickly and quietly as he could. He couldn't believe that the man was dead, and he still worried about Fahla, but he was much more concerned about his own safety.

He stayed close to the wall and kept moving, as well as trying to check to see if any other guards might be nearby, but he didn't hear, see, or sense any.

Only after he was well away from the chandlery and headed back home did he consider the implications of what he had seen and heard—and done. Somehow, Fahla and her family were tied up with the Jeranyi traders and possibly the pirates. That was probably how they kept their prices low. They also feared more than losing goods if they were loading wagons in the darkness, without a single lamp lit, and had guards ready to kill people.

He was still holding the truncheon in his left hand when he reached his dwelling, and he'd been looking over his shoulder the entire way back.

"Rahl?" called Khorlya a moment after he closed the door.

"Yes. I'm back."

"Good. Sleep well."

Sleep well? After everything that had happened?

"Good night," he finally said as he moved through the darkness to his own small chamber and narrow bed. He closed the door, close as it made the room feel.

After undressing, he lay on his pallet, looking up into the darkness and thinking. Should he have gone to the magisters? But how could he after having killed a man? He knew that was cause for exile, if not worse, even if he had been attacked. But he'd been attacked because he was where he shouldn't have been after he'd probably revealed something he shouldn't have to someone who was guilty.

But . . . he hadn't known that. He hadn't even realized that Fahla was guilty until after he'd seen her face at Sevien's. And then what could he have done?

He shook his head.

IX

Rahl had finally managed some sleep on fiveday night, after persuading himself that he really hadn't done wrong. He'd only been trying to defend himself against someone who'd wanted to kill him. But he had wondered about the reddish white shadow around the bravo, something that he'd felt, but not seen. Even after getting some sleep, he'd felt tired when Kian had wakened him on sixday.

Then his father had insisted on sparring before breakfast.

Rahl had taken another bruise or two. He had to admit that his father was good with the truncheon, and he probably owed his life to his father's training, but he wasn't about to tell him—not for a long time, if ever.

While Kian washed up, Rahl oiled the scarred area of the truncheon where he'd slipped the attacker's blade, then studied the wood. The scar wasn't that noticeable, unless he looked very closely. Then he washed up, finished dressing, had breakfast, and headed to the workroom.

There he laid out the mathematics text. He was almost finished, with just a few pages left to copy. As he settled in, Kian appeared with a broad smile.

"You're almost finished, aren't you?"

"Yes, ser."

"Good. I'll be able to start binding it on oneday, and you can take over the copying of the *Philosophies of Candar.*"

Rahl thought that might be even worse than *Natural Arithmetics.*

"I need to finish the frontispiece, though, and I'd like you to hurry down to Clyndal's to pick up a book from him. I'm not sure if it's properly a book, but his nephew's been apprenticing with him, and Clyndal's grown fond of the fellow, and he wants to give him a copy of his formulae so that he can set up his own alchemy shop in Lydkler. There isn't one there, and it's probably one of the few towns of any size in Recluce that doesn't have one."

Rahl stood. "I can do that." It would also give him a chance to see what had happened around the chandlery.

He did slip the truncheon back into his belt loops before he left the workroom, turning it so that the scarred side was against his trousers, not that anyone was likely to notice or comment on a scrape on a truncheon.

The sky was a hazy greenish blue, and the stillness of the air made the morning seem warmer than it probably was as he headed down the street toward the center of Land's End. The avenue seemed more deserted than normal, and usually it was more crowded on sixday.

As Rahl neared Clyndal's shop, just south of the chandlery, he could see two Council Guards standing post on the porch of the chandlery. The shutters remained closed, and the front door was chained shut. Rahl couldn't help but wonder what had happened to Fahla and Faseyn, although he wasn't about to ask the Guards.

He opened the door to the alchemy shop and stepped inside. The air smelled of all sorts of odors that shifted as he stepped toward the counter set directly facing the door, less than four cubits back. Clyndal turned from the workbench and moved to the counter. His face was lined, and his gray hair thin. His water green eyes smiled with his mouth. "Young Rahl, I thought your father might send you. What I have here is in a leather folder, but if he could copy it, and then bind both, I'd be much obliged. I'd pay for the extra binding, you understand. He said a plain binding would be a gold."

"I can't offer a price, ser," Rahl said with a smile. "Not when he's already talked with you."

"Smart son." Clyndal handed the stained thick leather folder to Rahl. "Be most careful."

"That I will, ser." Rahl paused, then asked, "I see that the chandlery is locked and guarded . . ."

"Aye. The magisters came with the Council Guards late last night. The magisters left, but the Guards have remained. I've heard not a word as to why, but . . ."

Rahl waited.

". . . I've been wondering about their prices. Hostalyn was a tight man, but he never wanted to charge two coppers when one or one and a split would do. This Kehlyrt, he charged even less, and I'd be wondering where he got his goods, especially after the Council notice."

"About the Jeranyi and the pirates?"

"Exactly my thought, young Rahl. Exactly my thought."

"What did they do with the factor and his family?"

"Heard that he was a widower, but what happened to him and the girl and boy . . . you'd have to be asking the magisters. The place was like as to now when the sun rose this morning."

"I suppose we'll find out in time," observed Rahl, offering a pleasant expression he didn't feel. He lifted the heavy folder. "We'll get this back to you, with both books bound, as soon as we can."

"That'd be good. You don't know as your father wants any more of the good iron-brimstone, would you?"

"I'd judge he will in another eightday."

"I'll make sure to have some."

The door opened behind Rahl. He turned to see Hyelsen entering.

"Clyndal! Has that shipment of cuprite arrived yet?"

"No, ser. I'm expecting the wagon any day."

"We need that to soak the planks and timbers for the next one. Without that, the oak's just food for the shipworms."

"I know that, ser, but it comes from Worrak, and I can't make 'em sail any faster."

"Good day, portmaster." Rahl nodded politely.

"Good day, Rahl." Hyelsen turned back to the alchemist. "It's not good to be waiting. We ordered in plenty of time . . ."

As Rahl stepped out of the alchemy shop, he looked toward the harbor. The chandlery remained closed, with the same pair of Council Guards posted on the porch, but farther on, Rahl saw a Guard wagon outside the coppersmith's.

As he watched, two burly Guards marched out a slender figure and set him on the rear bench seat, then shackled him there. The coppersmith followed, just standing there, watching, his shoulders slumped. Even from where he stood close to two hundred cubits away, Rahl sensed the anger walled away—anger and sad acceptance. He could also hear the prisoner's protests.

"I didn't do anything . . . I didn't! It's all wrong! I didn't do anything."

"Tell it to the magisters, fellow!"

"I didn't . . ."

The Guard driving the wagon flicked the leads, and the wagon moved toward Rahl. He just stood and watched as the three Guards rode past. As the wagon came by Rahl, he recognized the prisoner—Balmor.

". . . I didn't do anything wrong . . . I was just helping Da with the forge . . ."

At those words, Rahl looked more closely at Balmor. For the first time, he could sense the reddish white around the young man—the same kind of shadow that he had sensed around the man who had tried to kill him the night before. It had to be the aura of chaos. He'd read and heard about it, but he hadn't thought about its being on Recluce. Was that why the Council had closed the chandlery? Because Kehlyrt had been using chaos?

Rahl frowned. He was certain he would have sensed something on Fahla. He'd watched her closely enough.

After a moment longer, he turned and began to walk back up the avenue toward the southern section of Land's End and home, carefully carrying the heavy leather folder. He couldn't help but wonder what was happening. He didn't recall anything like the chandlery being shut down or people being dragged off by Council Guards. Or had he just not seen what had happened?

He still worried about Fahla . . . and even about why Jienela had been so upset. He'd been careful not to promise anything to Jienela, very careful, but it was clear by her actions that she thought he had, and that could be a problem.

He walked quickly, and it was still close to midmorning when he stepped back into the workroom.

"Did you get it?" asked Kian. "You took a while."

"It's all loose, but he wants them bound, too." Rahl held up the folder. "The magisters shut down the chandlery. It's chained shut, and they have guards posted. I was leaving Clyndal's, and Council Guards from the keep were dragging Balmor away. He kept saying that he didn't do anything wrong."

"Balmor? Balmor . . ."

"He's Fherl's oldest. I remember him from lessons when we were younger."

"Dragging him away?" Kian frowned.

"Well . . . really, they shackled him to a seat on one of their wagons and drove off with him. He kept saying that he didn't do anything except help his da with the forge." Rahl suspected that had somehow involved chaos, but saying that directly might reveal too much about his own abilities.

"Must have been using chaos." Kian shook his head. "The magisters don't like that at all. Did Clyndal know anything about the chandlery?"

"I asked, but he just said that the magisters and Council Guards came in the night. He didn't know why, but he thought they might be involved with the Jeranyi." Rahl carried the leather folder across the room and handed it to his father.

"Thank you. Some folks never learn. You just don't cross the magisters." Kian set the folder on the narrow table that held work yet to be copied. At the moment, the folder lay there alone. "You need to finish up with the arithmetics book."

Rahl settled himself back before his copying table and opened the mathematics text to the next-to-last page.

He finished that page before dinner, and then the last page in early afternoon. After he stretched and checked the ink, he came back to find Kian setting another book on the copy-stand.

"The *Philosophies of Candar*. You can start with the text . . . here."

"Yes, ser."

While he copied, Rahl still couldn't help but worry about Fahla. The magisters wouldn't have executed her, would they?

As the afternoon was coming to a close, and the sun hung just over the low mountains to the west of Land's End, there was a knock on the workroom door.

"Rahl . . ."

"I'll get it." Rahl got up and headed on to the door.

Magister Puvort stood there.

"Magister," Rahl inclined his head, "how might we help you?"

"Is your father here?"

"Yes, ser."

"Good. I need to talk to both of you."

Rahl stepped back, and Puvort moved into the workroom, a stolid presence of order, embodying a blackness even deeper than the black of his tunic and trousers, or the polished black boots he wore.

Kian started to rise.

"You can keep your seat, Kian. I won't be long." The magister offered a smile, an expression of courtesy, carrying little warmth. "You may have heard that the Council has been forced to act against those who would bring chaos into Recluce. We have acted, and we will continue to act, as we must." He looked to Kian. "Although you have no abilities in handling order, scrivener, you have always acted in accord with order, and for that the Council is pleased." His eyes went to Rahl. "For those who may have ability with order, there is always a choice—order or chaos. That is not as simple as it sounds, because failing to make a choice is also a decision, and that apparent lack of decision often leads to chaos."

The magister offered another smile and moved toward Kian. "Your work on the notices was excellent." He extended a small pouch. "Here is your payment, and it includes an additional token for timeliness and craftsmanship."

"Thank you, magister. We do appreciate it."

"As does the Council." Puvort glanced at Rahl. "And Rahl, I trust you'll come to me with your decision on oneday. I'll be . . . traveling . . . until late on eightday." With a slight inclination of his head, Puvort turned and departed.

Not until the magister was well out of earshot did Kian speak. "What did he mean by saying you had to decide, Rahl?"

"Well . . . ser . . . on fourday, when you sent me for the pen nibs . . ." Rahl explained what Puvort had said about his small order abilities and the possibility of training by the magisters and magistras.

"And you don't want to do it? Rahl . . . are your brains all in your trousers? Do you see the garments the ordermasters wear, and how respected they are? No scrivener is ever that well-off and respected."

"I could end up in Nylan or exiled," Rahl pointed out. "Puvort said that was always possible."

"So you could," admitted Kian. "And if you have those abilities, and they are not properly trained, do you think you'd end up anywhere else?"

For a moment, Rahl just stood there, thinking. He didn't like to admit it, and in fact, he hated the idea, but his father had a point. He took a deep breath. "Best I go and see Magister Puvort first thing on oneday."

"Why not now?"

Rahl gestured at the window, which showed a sun already touching the rugged horizon. "They close the Black Holding just before sunset, and Magister Puvort said he wouldn't be there until oneday and to see him then."

"Sometimes . . ."

Rahl knew what Kian would have said, that at times Rahl put off doing things when he shouldn't. Still, there was little enough he could do at the moment.

"I'll go see Shahyla on end-day and Magister Puvort early on oneday." He thought the mention of Shahyla might divert his father's attention from himself.

"Do you like her?"

"She's pleasant, and pretty enough, and she's brighter than I recalled," Rahl said.

His father laughed.

Rahl forced himself to laugh as well, little as he felt like it.

X

Sevenday dawned hazy and warm, but at least Kian hadn't insisted Rahl join him in a sparring session, and there had even been a piece of leftover green-apple-cracker pie for breakfast. Midday dinner had been even better, with breaded cutlets and brown gravy with roasted potatoes.

That had taken Rahl's mind off all the things that were nagging at him. He still worried about Fahla, and Jienela, and especially about having to go to the magisters for instruction in using order. To be a scrivener, he didn't need instruction, but after he'd seen Balmor carted off, he couldn't afford not to take the magisters' instruction and teaching. But that didn't make him any happier about it, especially not after what he'd seen and heard during the past eightday.

With all those thoughts on his mind, the afternoon dragged, and he had trouble concentrating on *Philosophies of Candar*. Each stroke of the pen took special effort.

"Rahl . . . Rahl . . . are you listening?"

Rahl jerked himself to attention. "Yes, ser?"

"I said I'm going down to see if Clyndal has gotten in any iron-brimstone. Or if he knows who might have backing clips." Kian shook his head. "You get a good factor, and he's never satisfied. They're either sloppy and could care less, like old Hostalyn, or they're doing what they shouldn't, like that Kehlyrt fellow. I don't know how long I'll be. You did a good job on *Tales of the Founders* and on the *Natural Arithmetics*, but you'll need to be even neater on this one."

After his father had left, Rahl looked out the windows at the corner closest to the garden, where a traitor bird had landed on the low stone wall, calling out to anyone who would listen that a cat—or something—lurked in the parsley and brinn patches. His mother had harvested some more of the early brinn and had taken some sprigs to Elantria, the old healer who lived in a neat but modest cottage beyond Sevien's dwelling.

Finally, Rahl forced himself back to the copying at hand. The philosophy book was easier . . . and harder than the mathematics book had been. It was easier because he could read it as he copied, but harder because the words seemed to twist back and around on themselves. He read the paragraph again.

. . . there is no school of thought or of mental debate developed within or upon Candar that cannot cite or claim in its defense at least one obscure principle from the fragments remaining from the Code of Cyador . . . yet presented within this tome will be a unified and concrete cosmological system of thought, developed in complete synchrony with its own categoreal notions and implications, which can stand any test raised by the philosophy of organism, since all relatedness has its foundation in the relatedness of actualities, relatedness being established as that which is dominated by quality and subordinate only to quality as defined in Cyadoran sense of sensibility . . .

He'd read that part at least three times, and while he thought he understood the meaning of almost every single word, he still did not have the faintest idea what all the words together meant.

Thwump!

Rahl looked up with a start.

A stocky young man with truncheon in hand stood just inside the workroom. It was Jaired—Jienela's brother. The grower stepped toward Rahl, who hastily cleaned his pen and set it aside.

"Jaired . . . what can I do for you?" The question sounded inane, even to Rahl, but he had to say something.

"You'll take her for your consort," announced Jaired. While he was not so tall as Rahl, Jaired was older and stockier, and he did have his truncheon in hand.

Rahl's was still in his small sleeping chamber. He'd never thought he'd need it while he was copying.

"Take who for what?" Rahl attempted to show surprise. "What are you talking about?"

"You know well enough what I'm saying."

"You're wrong," Rahl persisted. "I have no idea what you're talking about or where you got this idea." He rose from behind the copying table and closed the *Philosophies of Candar.*

"Jienela," snapped Jaired. "She's going to be your consort, one way or another."

Rahl smiled easily. "I'm sorry. Why would I do that? I'm but an apprentice scrivener."

"Because you're the one who got her with child."

How could that be? Jienela? Rahl hadn't sensed that she was . . . anywhere near that time, but Jaired bore an air of complete conviction.

"Are you so sure of that?" Rahl didn't want to say he hadn't slept with her.

"Who else could it be? You're the only one she's been looking at or walking with," retorted Jaired.

"That's what you've seen. Maybe we haven't done anything more than that. Walking with a girl doesn't get her with child."

Jaired flushed. Then his face hardened. "You'll not be slandering my sister. She'd not be doing what she shouldn't."

Rahl refrained from pointing out that Jienela couldn't be carrying a child without having done something Jaired felt she shouldn't have been doing. "And I suppose that was true of you and Coerlyne?"

"You leave her out of this!"

Rahl was between the copying table and the back stone wall of the workroom, and still without any weapon. "You've come in here and accused me of something without even letting me say a word. Don't you think I should be able to say something?"

"I'm not for talking. It's what you do to make things right that counts."

"Let's talk about what you want me to do."

"You ask Da for her hand. There's nothing else to talk about."

"Then what?" asked Rahl. "After that, I mean."

"You become consorts. That's what."

"And will your da pay Jienela a stipend?"

"A what?" A momentary look of confusion crossed the young grower's face.

"Coins. Apprentice scriveners don't make that much. My father barely brings in enough coins for himself and my mother."

"You shoulda thought a' that. That's your problem, Rahl."

"If . . . if I did what you say, it is," admitted Rahl. "But . . . if you insist on our becoming consorted, it becomes Jienela's problem as well. Do you really want your sister not to have enough to eat? Or not enough warm clothes come winter?"

"You shoulda thought a' that," repeated Jaired.

Rahl was getting tired of that phrase, but he was in no position to object strenuously. Not yet.

"If . . . as I said, I did what you think, I should have. But if I didn't, why would I?"

"You did it. I know you did."

"Oh . . . and I suppose Jienela told you?" Rahl's voice was gently scornful.

"Jienela's protecting you, but you'd not be deserving that." Jaired raised the truncheon.

"But she is."

Jaired stopped.

"If . . . if I did it, then you don't want to injure me because how would I support your sister? If I didn't do it, you shouldn't injure me because I didn't do anything wrong."

"You twist words worse than a magister," growled Jaired.

"I'm only pointing out that trying to beat me with that truncheon won't do anyone any good. Neither will coming in here and yelling at me and telling me I have to do something that I never promised to do and that my parents are against." Rahl moved away from the copying table and toward the narrow heavy frame Kian used to stretch leather for binding. There was a long knife in a battered sheath fastened to one side of the frame, the side shielded from the young grower.

Rahl had never liked using the knife; it bothered him almost as much as the gelding knife Shahyla had showed him. But Jaired didn't have to know that.

Jaired frowned. "You think you're so smart."

"Everyone's smart at different things," Rahl said, taking another step toward the frame. He extended a hand as if to straighten the frame, then let his hand drop to the knife hilt, grasping it and sliding it out.

Jaired looked at the long knife and at Rahl.

Rahl smiled.

"You'd better think about what you're doing," the grower said. "Just because your da's a scrivener, you can't get away with hurting my sister. You'll see."

"I certainly didn't force your sister to do anything," Rahl said. "I don't like being blamed and threatened for what she wanted to do. I never promised anything." He took a step forward, holding the knife low. The afternoon light coming through the windows glinted on the polished dark iron.

Rahl could sense the other's fear. In a strange way, that amused him, how Jaired had been so sure of himself when he'd thought he'd had the only weapon and the upper hand. Was confidence all about who believed himself to have more power?

"You can't do that to her," Jaired said.

"I'm not doing anything to anyone," Rahl said. "I'm just saying that you can't force what you want on me." He took another step forward.

"This isn't over," blustered Jaired.

"I tell you what," Rahl said quietly. "You just get out of here, and you think about things over the end-day, and so will I."

"You better think hard, scrivener. You'd better." Jaired backed up to the half-open door, then turned and left, hurriedly, but not quite at a run.

As soon as he was certain Jaired was well away from the house and workroom, Rahl replaced the binding knife with a shudder of relief. Then he quickly hurried to his sleeping chamber. There he reclaimed his truncheon before returning to the workroom. He laid it on the side of the copy table.

Should he tell his father and mother? He might as well—or at least suggest part of the problem. They'd find out before long and not necessarily in the way least unfavorable to Rahl. But . . . when . . . that was the question . . . and how much?

He didn't know how much time had passed, but it wasn't long before the workroom door opened and Khorlya peered in. "I was coming up the road, and I saw someone leaving . . ."

"That was Jienela's brother Jaired."

"What would he have been wanting?"

"To know if I intended to ask for Jienela's hand. I don't know where he got that idea."

"It might have been that you spent more than a little time in the orchard with her."

"I never said anything about consorting her, and I said so. He wasn't happy when I told him that. He threatened me with a truncheon."

"He's concerned about his sister."

"That doesn't give him the right to barge in here and demand I consort with her."

"Rahl . . . I told you that you shouldn't see her."

"I stopped seeing her—eightdays ago. Jaired didn't like that, either."

"He always has been a hothead, but—"

"From what I've heard, he's always been hot elsewhere."

"Rahl!"

"Yes, Mother."

"Did you sleep with her?"

"She's a year older than I am," Rahl pointed out.

"You're not answering the question."

"I did . . . once." That was partly true. He had slept with her once, then several times more. "She surprised me." That was totally true, not that he'd been displeased.

"Rahl . . ." His mother shook her head. "This could make things very difficult."

"You know that when you told me not to see her anymore, I didn't. And I didn't promise anything."

"Sometimes, actions are promises," Khorlya said tiredly. "What you do is more important than what you've said."

Rahl could feel himself getting both angry and irritated. "She was the one who started things, and now Jaired and you are both blaming me. I wouldn't have done anything if she hadn't been the way she was . . . and I didn't let it last very long."

"Rahl . . . what's done is done. Who was more to blame isn't the question."

Rahl disagreed with that—violently—but there wasn't any point in saying so. The idea that he might have to consort Jienela because she'd been the one who wanted to sleep with him was wrong. He'd even tried to make sure that she didn't end up with child. And now, his mother, his own mother, was telling him that he might have to consort a girl she'd not wanted him to consort.

"Your father should be here in a moment. I thought I saw him heading up from the harbor. He's not going to be pleased."

That was an understatement, Rahl knew, and he certainly didn't want to talk to his father about Jaired and Jienela, but there was no help for that.

Within a few moments, Kian stepped into the workroom. His eyes went from Khorlya to Rahl and back to his consort. "What's the matter?"

Khorlya shook her head. "Jienela's brother was here. He wants Rahl to consort Jienela because he slept with her."

Kian looked at Rahl.

Rahl could feel the combination of anger and sadness. There wasn't much to say. "She took me by surprise. It was her idea, and after that I broke it off as quick as I could."

"That doesn't help much." Kian's words were hard and condemnatory.

"Ser . . . I didn't know much about women . . ."

"You were told. You were warned." Kian's voice increased in volume. "All you had to do was keep your trousers on and call on Bradeon's daughter. But no, first you play in the orchard and then you start visiting the chandlery. You don't think I didn't hear about that, too."

"I never even kissed Fahla," Rahl retorted, "and I did what you wanted."

"It was a little late for that," Kian said sourly. "You may have made your future far harder than it ever had to be. You might even have to consort a girl who has nothing and never will."

"Why?" asked Rahl. "She was the one who encouraged me."

"You let her. It takes two, as you should have discovered," replied Kian sadly.

"But she—"

"It doesn't matter. Don't you understand? If someone tells you to hit someone with your truncheon and steal his wallet, does that make it all right?"

"No . . . but I didn't hurt anyone, and I didn't steal. If anything, she's trying to steal what I might do."

"Most people won't see it that way, not in Recluce. All you had to do was to say no."

All he had to do? When she'd been taking his clothes off and kissing him?

"Your mother and I will talk it over, and then we'll see what can be done. We might be able to get one of the magisters to look into it. There are precedents . . . but I wouldn't count on that."

"What about tomorrow?" asked Rahl. "I was supposed to call on Shahyla."

"Yes, you were, but this . . ." Kian frowned. "Have you told anyone else?"

"No, ser. Jaired was just here."

The scrivener nodded. "We still might have a chance . . ." He looked at Khorlya.

She said nothing.

"If you can keep your trousers on and promise Shahyla *nothing*," replied Kian, "then a simple visit can't make matters any worse than you have. Or has she *encouraged* you as well?"

Rahl flushed. "No. Nothing like that." He could feel that his mother didn't agree with his father about visiting Shahyla, but she said nothing.

"You can finish the page you were copying before supper. Your mother and I have some talking to do. And you aren't going out tonight, not anywhere."

Rahl had already figured that out, and right now he didn't need to do anything else to get them even more upset.

XI

On eightday morning, Rahl was careful to say nothing that was not deferential and polite, and he was scrupulous about doing his chores and straightening and cleaning the workroom. Only when he was certain that he had done everything required did he wash up and prepare for the long walk to Bradeon's holding to see Shahyla.

As Rahl was preparing to leave, his mother appeared with a plain basket, containing two bundles—one of brinn and one of sage.

"Herders can always use brinn and sage, and Bradeon's a practical man." Khorlya looked at Rahl. "Your father and I don't agree about this, but it may be that you won't have to consort Jienela. I don't see how we can avoid that, but . . . he thinks he may be able to work something out. Don't promise anything to Shahyla today, and don't say anything about Jienela. And for darkness' sake, don't make matters worse. Keep all your clothes on."

Rahl laughed, ruefully. "That won't be a problem. Either her father or her brother is always near."

"Smart girl. Smarter than you deserve," observed Khorlya. "You might be fortunate, at that, but don't count on it yet."

Rahl bit back what he might have said. "I could use that fortune."

"Yes, you could, son, but you may be one of those who has to learn things for himself." After a moment, she added, "Go on. You might as well enjoy the day, as you can."

Rahl nodded. "I'll be back before sunset."

"That would be good."

As he stepped out through the front door, he could sense her concern and sadness.

All because of Jienela's brother? And because Jienela had wanted Rahl? Somehow, it didn't seem fair. It wasn't as though he'd done anything to hurt anyone, or that he'd done anything that she hadn't wanted. And then, his mother saying that he had to learn things for himself, as if he had no brains at all, as if he never listened. He'd listened, and he knew all about women and their times of the month. He'd done his best, and because things hadn't gone as they were supposed to, everyone was blaming him.

Still, because he didn't want to risk seeing Jaired—or Jienela—he took the path through the edge of the protected forest that came out farther to the south, well past Alamat's. That meant he had to walk several hundred cubits farther, then cut back. All in all, it added a good half kay to his walk, but the last thing he wanted was to see either Jienela or one of her brothers.

Although the day was pleasant, with only a scattering of puffy white clouds in the green-blue sky and a light breeze at his back, Rahl only encountered a few wagons and riders on the High Road, and no one else on foot. That was not surprising, because the road was not that heavily traveled on end-days.

It was slightly past midday by the sun when he started up the lane to Bradeon's holding. Before long, he could see Shahyla standing on the porch, waiting for him, but this time, she left the porch and strode down the path to meet him. As she passed the geese, they stopped their hissing. She was graceful enough, he noted, but in a muscular fashion. She was clearly a herder.

"I hoped you'd come today." Shahyla smiled warmly.

Rahl handed her the basket. "It's more practical—brinn and sage."

"That's wonderful! I've never had the knack of growing brinn, and there's never enough sage for the sausage. Father will be very pleased." She laughed ruefully. "I think Semmelt would have preferred another honey cake or the apple bread you brought last time. He ate most of them."

They turned and walked back up to the house and onto the shaded porch.

"Would you like some ale?"

"Yes, please."

Rahl settled himself on the bench while Shahyla took the basket inside. Within moments, she returned carrying two of the tankard mugs. She handed one to Rahl, then settled onto the bench beside him.

"I'm glad you came. It's so nice to have something special to look forward to at the end of the eightday."

"So am I." Rahl was halfway surprised to realize that he meant the words. "How are you doing?"

She offered a half-smile and a shrug. "There's always more to be done than we can do. It took longer than he'd thought for Father to replace the broken pipes to the troughs. We lost a calf to a flux, and we had to pay a healer to check the others. She found one other with it, and we put it in a separate pen. Semmelt isn't sure whether it will live."

"I'm sorry."

She smiled. "Usually, it's best when nothing happens."

Rahl considered that for a moment, then nodded. He hadn't thought of things that way, but most happenings that were interesting weren't all that good. His experiences of the past eightday were good examples.

"Has anything interesting happened in Land's End?" she asked. "We're always so busy here that sometimes it's days before we find out things."

"Well . . . the Council issued a declaration forbidding trade with Jerans and Jeranyi merchants and goods. That's because of the pirates. They closed down the chandlery—"

"Old Hostalyn's place? They closed it?"

"Kehlyrt—he's a trader from the south—bought it from Hostalyn."

"Oh . . . was that why the redheaded woman was there? I thought she was maybe a niece or something and that he'd been ill." Shahyla absently pressed the side of her thumb against her left eye to still the twitching.

"No, he's a widower, and his son and daughter help him . . . or they did. No one seems to know why the Council shut it down and posted guards. Oh, and then the Council Guards carted off Balmor because he did something. I was coming out of the alchemist's when that happened, and he kept saying he hadn't done anything." Rahl took another swallow of the full-bodied ale. He did like it better than the watered ale he sometimes got at home.

Shahyla frowned. "I didn't know Balmor that well, but he never seemed like he'd do something wrong. All that sounds like the Council is worried about something."

"And . . ." he'd wondered about saying anything, but decided to anyway, "I'm probably going to have to take some training with the magisters."

"That's wonderful! Will you be a mage, then?"

Rahl shook his head. "Magister Puvort says that I have a little talent with order and that, unless I learn about it, I could get myself in difficulty."

"Puvort?" Shahyla's face clouded. "Semmelt says he's trouble, that he's always looking for the worst in folks."

Rahl was glad that someone else felt that way, but he only nodded. "I've wondered about that, but he finally came to the house on sixday. I'm supposed to see him tomorrow."

"Be careful."

"I'll be as careful as I can."

Abruptly, she stood. "You're hungry. Don't your parents feed you?"

"Before I leave, but it's a long walk."

"If you're like Semmelt, you need to eat all the time. Let me get you some bread and cheese."

"I can come in . . ."

"You've had a long walk. I'll be right back."

Rahl didn't protest but sat back in the bench and waited for Shahyla to return. Even if all they did was talk, he was enjoying the afternoon.

XII

Because he was thinking all too much about what oneday might bring, Rahl didn't sleep very well. It wasn't because his parents had lectured him, either. When he'd finally walked into the house late on eightday afternoon, his parents had been at the table. Once they'd confirmed that he'd done nothing untoward in dealing with Shahyla, the conversation had quickly turned to innocuous subjects. That had concerned him more than if they had lectured him, but he wasn't about to bring up anything that would only bring more criticism. He'd had enough of that already, especially when so much of what they found fault with hadn't been his doing.

Pleasant as his afternoon with Shahyla had been, once he was lying in the darkness of his own small sleeping chamber, the pleasure of the afternoon was not enough to stave off his worries—from the veiled warnings from Puvort, Rahl's own concerns about Fahla, the more direct threats from Jaired, and the possibility that he might actually be forced to consort Jienela just because he'd gone along with her desire to sleep with him.

He woke early, without prompting from either parent, ate, and finished his chores.

Before he was finally ready to set out for the Black Holding, his father called him aside.

"The less you say to Magister Puvort," cautioned Kian, "the better. Just tell him that you've thought over his words and that you've realized the wisdom of his suggestion."

"Yes, ser."

"After you return," Kian said, "then we'll visit Jienela's parents."

"Her parents?"

"Her brother has demanded you consort her, has he not? That's not properly his position. Her parents may not wish a consorting with a penniless scrivener. Or we may be able to make other arrangements. Much of that will depend on what Magister Puvort determines. You might ask him, as well, if his training has any restrictions. If he asks why, you could certainly tell him that your parents wanted to know."

Rahl wasn't sure he wanted to meet Jienela's parents, but with the way his father was talking, it was clear he had little choice. "I don't know how long I'll be."

"I've not seen any of the magisters chewing the wind long."

Neither had Rahl. "I'll be back when I can."

Kian gave Rahl a firm thump on the back. "Off with you."

Rahl had thought to take the woods path, but if he did, he'd have to explain more to his father than he wished. So, with his truncheon in his belt, he started off. The sky was hazy, and clouds were building to the northwest, but they were still well out over the ocean. Any rain that might come would not arrive until afternoon.

There was no one on the lane—not until he was almost past the orchard wall. Then two figures sauntered out from the gate—Jaired and his older brother Jeason, who was far taller and broader than Jaired.

"We thought you might be sneaking off somewhere." Jaired's voice held a sneer.

"I'm supposed to meet with one of the magisters."

"A likely story," replied Jeason.

"So . . . when are you coming to ask for her hand?"

"My father and I will come to talk to your parents after I return from seeing Magister Puvort." There was no point in not admitting that, not the way Kian had been talking.

"What about right now?" Jaired's inquiry was anything but a question.

"Because I'm going to see Magister Puvort," Rahl said calmly. He could sense the rage in Jaired. Was that because Jaired didn't want Rahl to escape being consorted? Because he'd been forced into agreeing to consort Coerlyne?

"You're not going anywhere, little scrivener," Jaired said, "except to see our da. Right now."

"I'm afraid that's not possible." Rahl started to turn away from the two.

A flash of something—power or order—flashed toward Jaired, and all the grower's restraints dropped away. He charged Rahl.

Rahl's hand dropped to the grip of his truncheon, and he had it out well before Jaired was upon him.

Jaired attacked like a maddened bull—straight at Rahl.

The younger man dodged, gave a kick to the side of Jaired's knee that unbalanced him. Then, in the moment while Jaired was struggling to catch his balance, Rahl slammed his truncheon across the other's lower forearm.

"Ohhhh!" Jaired's yell was loud, half scream. His truncheon lay on the road stones, and he had to use his left hand and arm to grasp and support his right forearm. It was clearly crooked.

"Friggin' little scrivener!" Jeason charged wildly at Rahl, his truncheon held far too high.

As his father had taught him, Rahl dropped, then half pivoted and used his shoulder to drop Jeason onto the stone surface of the road. Before the older grower could shake his head to clear it, Rahl slammed his truncheon against Jeason's wrist. Bones cracked, and Jeason's truncheon dropped from his hand.

"We'll get you, we will. You're a white demon . . . the magisters will take care of you," muttered Jeason through nearly clenched teeth.

"I don't believe anyone will be getting anyone," added another voice, "and the magisters will indeed take care of matters." Seemingly from nowhere, Magister Puvort had appeared.

Rahl swallowed hard. He'd sensed the order bolt, and that meant he'd been set up. But why would Puvort do that? Why would a magister use order to encourage Jaired to attack Rahl?

"You . . ." Rahl thought about asking that question, then closed his mouth. How could he prove it, except by showing he had more order-ability? That might mean he'd broken some other rule. Puvort had already implied that more than minor order-ability required training. No matter what Rahl did, he was in trouble.

Puvort nodded, but only said, "I told you that you needed training." He turned to the injured growers. "You both need to see the healer. I suggest you start off to her place right now."

"Yes . . . magister," replied Jeason.

Jaired said nothing. He just held his arm gingerly and followed his brother in the direction of the healer's cottage.

"We'll wait for your parents," Puvort said. "They heard the yells, and they'll be here in a moment."

"But . . ."

"Silence. Drop the truncheon."

Rahl did. He couldn't see any point in protesting. Who knew what Puvort could do to him? He wouldn't have put it past the magister to be provoking him. He just didn't understand what Puvort had against him.

"Rahl!" called Khorlya, coming to an abrupt stop a good dozen cubits from her son as she saw the magister standing there. "What happened?"

Kian was only moments behind. He halted, and his face settled into impassive stolidity when he beheld Puvort, but Rahl could sense both fear and concern behind the facade.

"Your son used order and his truncheon against the two growers," Puvort said mildly.

"But they attacked me, and there were two of them," Rahl protested, now that his parents were there.

Magister Puvort smiled sadly. "You could have killed them." He paused. "You did know that someone killed one of the smuggler's guards, didn't you? He was killed with a truncheon."

"Smuggler's guard?" asked Rahl. "Who . . . ?"

"Oh, the factor who bought Hostalyn's place was really a smuggler. He was fronting for the Jeranyi. He found out what was going to happen a day earlier than we'd thought he would." Puvort looked at Rahl again. "But it didn't matter."

"What happened to them?" asked Kian.

"Oh . . . the smuggler and the guards were executed. They even had barrels of cammabark. What need does an honest chandler or factor have for explosives? At least, they were wetted down with water and vinegar. The two young people were indentured to an Austran merchant. They'll be leaving on the next ship that comes in bound that way. His agent here has a standing order for those exiles who've been involved in wrongdoing and are talented or good-looking."

Rahl stiffened. He wanted to use his truncheon on the magister, not that he could with it lying on the road. Puvort looked so smug. What were Fahla and Faseyn supposed to do? Turn their father over to the magisters? For not doing that, they were enslaved?

"But Rahl . . . he might be a father, and he was going to be consorted," offered Khorlya.

"I'm afraid that doesn't matter," said Puvort.

"What do you mean?" asked Khorlya. "Of course it matters."

Kian winced at his consort's tone.

"Not now. Rahl used order improperly, and he injured two men. If he hadn't been attacked, he'd be on trial. He could even have been executed. The Council will make the final decision. But he'll either be exiled or be on the next Guard wagon to Nylan. He might fit there. If not, he'll be exiled from Nylan as well. He certainly doesn't belong here. He's been given advice a number of times, and he doesn't seem inclined to listen."

"But . . . Jienela . . . the child?"

"As you said earlier, Khorlya, it takes two. Rahl was telling the truth. Jienela did encourage him, and she, as well as he, should have known better."

Rahl had been angry before, but he was close to seething. Puvort had known about it all, and he'd been toying with Rahl, like a cat with a mouse, just waiting to set things up so Rahl would be forced to do something that could get himself killed or exiled. Even Jienela was a tool, or so it seemed.

Puvort smiled.

Rahl thought it was a greasy smile, the kind that traveling peddlers used, but he said nothing.

"What are you going to do with Rahl?"

"What is necessary. He'll be taken before the Council immediately. Then, after the Council decides, he'll either be released or held at the keep until he's put on a ship or sent to Nylan. That's for everyone's protection." Puvort looked at Rahl. "As matters stand, I can't imagine that you won't be sent to Nylan at the very least."

"But they attacked me. I was only defending myself," Rahl protested.

"You used order in your defense, and you injured two men. The use of order is not necessarily forbidden, nor is self-defense, but after Jeason was on the road stones, you broke his wrist. That was unnecessary and showed your lack of control."

"I was supposed to let him get up and attack me again?"

"Silence. You can tell it to the Council."

"Can we . . . see what happens before the Council?" asked Khorlya.

"Council hearings involving order misuse are always closed. I'm sure you can understand why," replied Puvort smoothly.

Although Rahl could sense the truth of the magister's words, he had the feeling that Puvort was pleased.

"But . . . he's our son," protested Khorlya.

"If the Council finds against exile or removal to Nylan, you'll see him this afternoon."

"If not?" asked Kian.

"You might do well to say good-byes now. Once someone has been found guilty of improper order usage, he cannot be allowed to roam free."

Khorlya rushed forward and threw her arms around Rahl. He could feel her shivering with silent sobs. Finally, she straightened. "If . . . if things . . . don't . . . please take care . . . We love you. We always have." Then she hung on to him.

Rahl heard the sound of a wagon approaching from behind him.

"If you have anything to say, scrivener . . ." offered Puvort.

Khorlya released Rahl.

Kian stepped forward and grasped Rahl's forearms. "Whatever happens, son . . . we care." He paused, gathering himself together. "Try to think things out first."

For a moment they stood there.

Rahl didn't know what to say. Finally, he nodded. "I'll do my best. Take care of Mother, and . . ." He just shook his head. He'd always been able to find words, but at the moment none came to mind.

Puvort cleared his throat.

Kian stepped back.

The magister's face was impassive, but Rahl still felt that Puvort harbored a hidden inner satisfaction.

The wagon stopped short of Puvort. It was the same type of small black wagon with two seats that had carried Balmor away. A single Council Guard drove.

"Do we need to chain you?" Puvort's voice was not quite ironic.

"No." Stunned as he felt, yet furious beneath the shock, Rahl knew that resistance at the moment would be useless. Even if he could escape the magister and the Council Guard, where could he go? Between the magisters and people who didn't wish to anger them, he'd be tracked down within days, if not sooner, and probably face worse than whatever was about to occur.

"You can be very sensible, Rahl. It's too bad you weren't that sensible earlier."

"He's barely more than a boy," protested Khorlya.

"He's enough of a man to do a man's work and get a woman with child," countered Puvort. "That means he's enough of a man to understand the laws of Recluce. A man doesn't misuse order without paying for it."

Khorlya looked at the magister directly. "It seems like you're more interested in punishing folks than helping 'em. Rahl was on his way to see you to ask for that training."

"He should have done so earlier. It's easy to claim you were about to do something."

"You *know* he was."

Kian moved beside his consort, and murmured, "It won't do any good."

Rahl could hear the words, low as they were. He had no doubt that the magister could as well.

"Enough, woman." Puvort gestured to Rahl. "The rear seat."

Rahl took his time in carefully climbing up and into the wagon.

Puvort climbed up and settled himself beside the Council Guard. He didn't bother to look back, but as the guard flicked the leads to the pair of horses and the wagon began to move, Rahl could sense that the magister was using order to watch him.

Rahl looked back and waved to his parents, trying to convey a hopefulness he didn't feel. His father now held Rahl's truncheon. Rahl would have liked to have used it on Puvort's skull. It was all too clear that the magister had set matters up to get him off Recluce, or at least to Nylan. For one thing, Puvort had to have summoned the wagon even before Jaired and Jeason had attacked him—long before. Second, there had been that sense of power emanating from somewhere, after which Jaired had attacked and Puvort had appeared. Third, now that he had thought about it, Puvort had been watching him for a while, and far more closely than Rahl had realized.

What Rahl didn't understand was what he'd done to upset the magister, but from what Puvort had said to his mother, the magister wasn't about to reveal that.

At the end of the street, the wagon turned east, and before long they were on the High Road, heading up the long, gradual slope toward the Black Holding. Rahl wondered if that was where they were heading, but he wasn't about to ask Puvort anything. Not a thing.

Neither the Guard nor Puvort spoke until the wagon halted in a black-walled courtyard on the south side of the Black Holding. A pair of Council Guards stepped forward as Puvort swung off the wagon.

"You'll go with them to the waiting room," Puvort stated.

"Yes, ser." Rahl vaulted out of the wagon, almost slipping as his sandals skidded on a patch of fine sand on the dark gray paving stones of the courtyard.

"This way," said one of the guards, not unkindly.

Rahl could feel Puvort's eyes on his back as he was escorted through an open gate and along a covered walkway to a small structure with a black-slate roof. The guard opened the door.

Inside was a small chamber with two benches, one against the wall facing the door, the other to the left.

The shorter guard pointed to the wall bench.

Rahl sat down on it. One of the guards sat on the side bench, while the other stood by the door. Each guard bore a short sword and a truncheon.

Time passed slowly. Exactly how long Rahl didn't know, but the guards changed places several times, and from the light coming through the single small window, it was close to midday when another guard appeared. "They're ready."

The three escorted Rahl back outside and along the walkway to the Black Holding itself. Although the courtyard and the small building where he had waited looked old, they were almost newly built in comparison to the original structures of the Black Holding itself, which radiated age.

"In through the door," stated the shorter guard. "Then just wait for them to summon you."

Rahl opened the door and stepped into an oblong chamber. The two guards followed.

The room was comparatively low-ceilinged and not that large, no more than eight cubits wide and twelve in length. At the far end was a long black table, set sideways, behind which sat three magisters in black. One was a gray-haired man, another a woman who might have been his mother's age, save that her face was unlined and her hair nearly white-blonde, and the third was Magister Puvort. Rahl hadn't realized that Puvort was on the Council.

"This is a disciplinary session, handled by the justicing subcouncil. Bring forth the accused."

"Step forward and stand before the magisters," murmured the Council Guard closest to Rahl.

After a momentary hesitation, Rahl stepped forward, then inclined his head.

"You are Rahl, son of the scrivener Kian and the basketmaker Khorlya?" asked the woman.

"Yes, magistra."

"You are accused of misusing order. What do you say to that?"

"Magistra . . ." Rahl paused for a moment. What could he say? "I did not even know that I had any abilities with order until Magister Puvort suggested that I might. He told me that I should consider coming here to take training from the magisters. That was less than an eightday ago. At first, that seemed impossible. I did not believe I had such abilities. Then, last sixday, he came to our house and suggested it again. In fact, he said he hoped to see me today. I talked this over with my parents, and we all agreed that I should do what the magister said, but since he said that he would be traveling until today, I waited until this morning. It did not seem that would be too long since Magister Puvort had first mentioned it. Once my chores were done, I set out . . ."

As simply as he could, Rahl related what had happened. He did not mention the feeling of order from the hidden magister Puvort, but otherwise, he told everything. ". . . and then Magister Puvort appeared. He said that I had misused order, but I was only defending myself against two men who are both older than I am, and I didn't use order. I just used my truncheon. I wouldn't even know how to use order."

"Yet you broke the wrist of a man who was on the ground," observed Puvort.

"He wasn't going to stay there, ser," replied Rahl, "and they both threatened me."

"That is supposition, not fact," said Puvort mildly.

"Be that as it may," added the gray-haired magister, "you misused order in your seduction of young Jienela, and you attempted to avoid consorting with her. You tried to avoid—"

"Ser! She's older than I am, and Magister Puvort even said that she was as much at fault as—"

"Silence!"

Rahl decided against saying more. It was clear that Puvort had already persuaded the magisters that everything was Rahl's doing and fault.

". . . and you only decided to seek order training after it was clear that you would risk punishment or exile if you did not."

The woman in the center looked to Puvort, then to the gray-haired magister. Then she looked back at Rahl. "The Council has decided that you are not suited to remain on that part of Recluce under the control of the Council. You may not be suited to remain in Nylan, either, but that decision will be made by the engineers. You are hereby sentenced to removal to Nylan, and you will remain in the custody of the Council until you arrive in Nylan." She nodded brusquely. "That is all. Remove the prisoner."

"But . . ." Rahl closed his mouth. Nothing he could say would change matters.

"Very wise, young Rahl," said Puvort quietly. "Very wise."

XIII

Rahl sat on the edge of the pallet bed. His cell was on the lower level of the keep in Land's End. All that the cell held were the pallet, the pallet frame, a chamber bucket, and a water bucket. He'd been in the cell for close to two days, and all he'd seen were the guards when they brought him his single daily meal—a bowl of gruel. The bucket of water had to last the entire day.

The more he thought about what had happened, the angrier he felt. The Council, or the sub-Council, hadn't even heard a word he'd said. They'd all decided to send him to Nylan before he'd ever walked into the hearing chamber. Puvort had probably planned it all for eightdays, if not longer, just the way he'd planned to kill Khelyrt and send Fahla and Faseyn off into slavery. He'd told Rahl's parents that Jienela was equally to blame, and then told the Council that it was all Rahl's fault. They hadn't even given him a chance to explain anything, or the fact that Rahl would have consorted Jienela if his parents had insisted.

What did Puvort have against him? He'd always been polite to the magister, and he'd never been discourteous, uneasy as the magister had sometimes made him feel. And why had the other magisters gone along?

After a time in the dimness, he looked up. He thought he'd heard footsteps and sensed someone, but so far as he could tell, he was the only one in any of the six cells.

A guard walked by, glanced around, then stopped. He was a different guard from the other three he'd seen in the past day or so.

"You're Rahl?"

"Yes." Rahl's response was careful.

"You got a brother named Kacet?"

"He's my older brother. He's at Reflin."

"Thought so." The guard shook his head. "You'll be headed to Nylan tonight, right after dark."

"After dark?"

"They don't want folks to see when exiles leave for Nylan."

"Are there many exiles?"

The guard laughed. "Not many go to Nylan. Maybe one every other eightday. Most get shipped straight to Austra or Candar."

"Why is that? Do you know?"

"Simple. Folks who are chaos-touched get sent from Recluce right off. Folks who use order wrong get sent to Nylan to see if they fit there. Most don't, they say. Some go to Lydiar, or Nordla, but most of them get sent to Hamor." The guard shook his head. "No one in his right mind wants to go there."

"Why not?" Rahl had never heard anything about that, just that exile was bad.

"If you got chaos or order-abilities there—doesn't matter which— you're sort of a high-level slave to the emperor or one of his people. If you're not chosen for that, you end up in the ironworks at Luba or the quarries."

"But I didn't do anything . . . not really."

The guard laughed. "Doesn't matter. Once the Council decides, that's it. 'Sides, who ever wants to admit they didn't do quite right?"

"Everyone does something that's not quite right now and again."

"Don't we all?" The guard laughed again. "But the Council decides, not you or me, young Rahl. Those that rule, they decide."

"But . . . they're supposed to do justice."

The guard just shook his head. "Best I be going."

Rahl just watched as the man turned and left, his steps echoing in the empty corridor.

After having seen the injustice of the Council, Rahl had been thinking exile wouldn't be that bad. But the best he could hope for in Hamor was to become a high-level slave? He didn't even want to consider being a laborer in the ironworks or quarries.

That meant he had to swallow any pride he had and do whatever he could to stay in Nylan. He just had to, and at least that wouldn't be nearly so bad as Hamor.

XIV

The closed Council wagon that carried Rahl from Land's End did not leave the keep until well after sunset. The Guard drivers stopped periodically, and Rahl had a chance at water and to relieve himself, but no food was offered until they arrived at the keep in Reflin in late midafternoon and Rahl was placed in another cell there. Again, he found he was the only one confined.

Well after sunset, right after a Council Guard had checked on him, Rahl heard another set of steps. Even in the dim light of the single lamp on the stone wall outside his cell, he recognized the face of the Council Guard.

"Kacet!" Rahl jumped off the low pallet bed and hurried to the iron-barred door.

"Shsshhh!" Rahl's brother raised his hand. "I'm not supposed to be here. I can't stay long, but Drosett passed the word that you'd be coming." Kacet glanced toward the archway to his left. "What did you do?"

"I don't know." Rahl shrugged tiredly. "I mean . . . they said I was mis-using order, but I never did. I wouldn't know how. Magister Puvort claimed I have order-abilities, but he was waiting when Jeason and Jaired attacked me. I used my truncheon to break Jaired's arm and Jeason's wrist, but I never used order."

"Ah, Rahl . . . they just attacked you?"

"Well . . ." Rahl paused. "I got a little too close to their sister. They wanted me to ask for her hand—right then and there. I was supposed to see Magister Puvort first that morning . . ." He raced through what had happened, including his problem with Jienela and the fight with her brothers and how Puvort had appeared and what had followed. ". . . and I didn't want to consort Jienela, but I would have, but no one listened to me. Puvort had me set up."

Kacet shook his head slowly. "Puvort's a nasty one. He sounds so good, but most of those who get exiled are because of him."

"Why do they let him do that?"

Kacet was the one to shrug. "How are you doing? No one's beaten you or anything?"

"No. The Guards have been all right. Not much food, but I haven't been that hungry."

"That's good. Sometimes they aren't, except that's usually with exiles waiting for a ship. Sometimes, they get a little too friendly with the women."

Rahl hoped that hadn't happened to Fahla, but she was pretty, and she'd been exiled as a slave. That was something else he owed Puvort.

"I know about the food. I brought you some hard cheese and some bread." Kacet eased a worn cloth pouch through the bars. "I'd have brought ale, but that would have been more than Captain Vorsa would allow."

"The captain let you . . ."

"The captain's a good woman. She doesn't care for the Council that much, but she never says anything. Told me not to take too long, though." Kacet paused. "How are Mother and Father? How did they . . . take it?"

"Mother was upset. She tried to point out to Puvort that I hadn't done anything wrong. He told her to shut up. Father had to quiet her. He was upset, but he didn't say much. Puvort wouldn't allow them to come to the Council meeting where they sentenced me to be sent to Nylan."

"Bastard," muttered Kacet.

"Don't cross him, Kacet," Rahl said. "He'd exile you as quick as me."

"I can't say as I understand, Rahl. You're just a scrivener, barely more than an apprentice. So you got a girl with child. That happens enough. You didn't refuse to consort her, did you?"

"We never got to that," Rahl said. "Mother, Father, and I were going to talk to her parents later that day. After I went to see Magister Puvort."

"Real bastard."

A low whistle echoed from the end of the corridor.

"I've got to go," Kacet said. "Sustel's a traitor bird for the Council. Hide the food till he's gone. Be real careful in Nylan."

"I'll try."

Kacet vanished from the cell door, and Rahl hurried back and sat on the edge of the pallet bed.

Nylan

XV

From what Rahl could calculate, the Council Guard wagon came to a slow stop late on oneday—more than an eightday after the Council had sentenced him to exile in Nylan. He heard voices.

"Hallo, Council Guards. What do you have for us today? Another exile? What was the charge?"

"Misuse of order. Here are the papers."

A long silence followed before anyone spoke again.

"You know where to take him. We'll expect you back here shortly."

From that Rahl decided that he and the wagon had finally arrived at the black-stone wall that separated Nylan from the rest of Recluce. With a slight lurch, the wagon moved forward.

Through the barred window in the back of the closed wagon, Rahl could only see the upper section of the wall, but he could sense that the wagon was headed down a gentle grade. Shortly, it came to another halt. After several moments, the rear door opened.

"You can get out now," said the one of the Guards.

Rahl eased his way out and onto the stone pavement. He was stiff and sore from the long trip. He looked around. The wagon had halted on a flat paved expanse. The sun hung above the ocean to the west. Before him was a city of low buildings built on a hillside that sloped down to a harbor. Every structure seemed to have been constructed of black stone, with slate roof shingles of dark gray or black. Higher on the slope, near where Rahl stood, the houses were far enough apart that grass and trees were plentiful, giving Nylan the air of a park. To his right was a long black-stone building.

A muscular woman wearing black trousers and a short-sleeved black shirt walked toward the Council Guards. Her hair was red and short, barely longer than Rahl's. Rahl could sense the Guards' unease.

"Another one your Council doesn't like?" she asked.

"Here are the papers, magistra."

The woman radiated power, enough that she made Puvort seem puny in comparison, for all that she was a good head shorter than Rahl. She took the papers without looking at them and walked past the two Guards toward Rahl, stopping several cubits short of him. "What did you do?"

"I was charged with misuse of order, magistra."

"I'm sure the papers say that. I'd like to know what you did."

"Two men attacked me. I broke one man's forearm with a truncheon and his brother's wrist. Magister Puvort said that I misused order because I had order-abilities and had not asked the Council for training. That was even though I was on my way to make that request."

She nodded, then read the papers. She turned to the Council Guards. "You can go. One way or another, he's our responsibility now."

Rahl didn't like the words "one way or another." He said nothing.

The two men quickly climbed onto the wagon seat.

The magistra said nothing until the wagon was headed back up the stone-paved High Road toward the gate in the black-stone wall.

"I'm Magistra Kadara. You're Rahl?"

"Yes, magistra."

"What haven't you told me?"

Rahl didn't quite know how to answer that. "About what, magistra?"

"A cautious one. Ah, well, let's get you get washed up and set up with a room in the transient quarters, and then we'll get you something to eat, and you can tell me what you really don't want to say."

As pleasant as Kadara appeared, Rahl felt that she was far more dangerous than Puvort.

"Follow me, if you will."

Rahl didn't see much choice.

They took a stone-paved walk that skirted the uphill side of the building to the west of where the wagon had stopped. A long oblong flower garden extended a good fifty cubits farther uphill. Ahead was a two-story stone structure with evenly spaced windows. The path led to a doorway on the downhill side. Kadara paused on the wide stone stoop.

"This building holds the transient quarters, and you'll eventually meet— or at least see—everyone here. Right now, most of them are still at work." Kadara opened the door and led him down the hallway to the third door. She opened it. Rahl noted that there was an inside bolt but no lock. The room was small, but still twice the size his own sleeping chamber at home had been. The bed was narrow and set against the far wall, but it was a real bed. Folded on the end were a blanket and a towel. There was a wall lamp, and a set of pegs on the wall for garments, and a writing table and a stool. The floor was polished gray stone. The large window was glassed, with inside shutters.

"All the rooms are the same. In the morning, we'll find some clothing and boots that will fit you. Those of you on probation all wear light gray. The jakes and the wash showers are in the enclosed area just outside at the north end of the building. I'll meet you where the wagon dropped you after you take care of things. Don't be long." With that, she turned and left Rahl standing in the room.

Rahl hurried, but the lower edge of the sun was touching the surface of the ocean by the time he finished washing up. He hurried to meet Magistra Kadara.

As if she had sensed him, Kadara stepped out of the building. "We'll walk down to the mess area. It's a little early, but they should have something for you to eat. How long were you in that wagon?"

"If I counted right, seven days. Most nights I was in a keep cell."

"Someone must like you, or you've been very careful."

Her words puzzled Rahl, because he didn't sense any sarcasm behind them. He'd been accused of something he hadn't done, exiled from his home, and packed off to Nylan, and she was saying that someone must have liked him?

"That amazes you?" Kadara asked.

"Yes, magistra."

"That's not completely surprising." She gestured to the squarish structure ahead. "This is the eating hall, otherwise known as the mess. You get three meals a day here. They're served at first morning bell, noon bell, and evening bell. That's when the bells in the tower there ring." She nodded toward a slightly taller square structure that stood on a low rise to the west of the eating hall. "If you want to eat at other times, the canteen in the corner of the mess is open from dawn to the lamps-out bell. But you don't pay for the meals in the mess, and you do pay for anything you eat in the canteen. Is that clear?"

"Yes, magistra." It was also clear that he'd be eating in the mess because he didn't have a copper to his name.

The mess was large and simple—with a half score of long tables, flanked by benches on each side. Each table looked to seat between ten and twelve people. At the east side of the hall was a set of serving counters, and several men and women were in the process of setting out large earthenware crocks and covered platters.

"Just pick up a platter at the end there and fill it with whatever you'd like," Kadara said. "You can have as much as you can eat, but if you're not sure, just take a little and come back for seconds. Your eyes might be bigger than your stomach after an eightday on low rations. We'd prefer you didn't waste food. When you're done, you take your platter and mug to the cleaning area and rinse them and set them in the racks."

Rahl followed her advice and took only moderate portions of the mutton in brown sauce and the lace potatoes. He took a slightly larger portion of the baked pearapples, and a small mug of ale. Then he carried his food—and the utensils he'd found at the end of the serving tables—to the table where Kadara stood.

"You're not eating, magistra?"

"I'll eat later. I haven't been starved for an eightday."

Rahl settled onto the bench. He looked at Kadara.

"Go ahead."

He didn't need any more encouragement.

"While you eat, I'll fill you in on a few matters I'm sure that the magisters in the north have failed to mention," Kadara began. "First, if anything, Nylan is more concerned about order and the Balance than is the rest of Recluce. Because we deal with black iron and machines, we have to be. We don't tolerate any free chaos at all, and we don't allow any chaos-wizards anywhere except on passing ships in the harbor. Second, everyone here works. Third, if you commit any offense or wrongdoing, and that includes failing to work, you'll face immediate exile. Are those points clear?"

Rahl swallowed a mouthful of the baked pearapples, then nodded. "Yes, magistra."

"Now . . ." Kadara laughed gently. "I doubt that you've told me the entire story, Rahl. No one ever does. Let's start at the beginning, though. What skills do you have?"

"My father is a scrivener. I was his apprentice and assistant."

"So you can write High and Low Temple?"

"Yes, magistra. High Temple is a little harder."

"Do you know Nordlan or Hamorian?"

Rahl frowned. "Do Nordlans speak differently from what they write? I've copied their books, and the word order's different, but not that bad."

"Some would say so." She seemed absently pleased by his response. "What about Hamorian?"

"No, magistra. I've copied their books once or twice, but I just had to copy the words letter for letter . . ."

"Have you read most of what you have copied? In Temple, that is?"

"Yes, magistra."

"Do you understand what you have read?"

"Mostly. I had trouble with the higher mathematics book and the *Philosophies of Candar.*"

Kadara laughed again. "Most would."

The questions seemed to go on and on. Rahl could tell that it had taken a while because the mess area had filled up with people eating, then mostly emptied out. While several people had looked in his direction, none had approached him or the mage, as if they knew what was happening and not to interfere.

Finally, when the light outside had faded into late twilight, Kadara looked straight at Rahl. "You're going to have a hard time here in Nylan. I can tell you that. I can't promise that you'll stay here, and if you do, you won't be a scrivener, but we do have a need for translators and printers. Usually, people with some order-skills who work with words can pick up other languages quickly. We'll start you with Hamorian, and then, if you have a talent for it, with the finer points of High Nordlan. That is, if you're willing to work."

"I've always worked, magistra." Rahl was willing to work at whatever it took not to be exiled to Hamor.

"For at least the next three or four eightdays, you'll be expected to study order and languages in the mornings, and work in the print shop and wherever Magister Sebenet needs help in the afternoons."

"The print shop?"

"Oh . . . we have a printing press. It makes multiple copies of books. The typesetting is harder than writing, but once it's set, we can print as many copies as we need."

Rahl could only wonder at how his mother had known, or from whom she had heard what she had said about scriveners no longer being needed. "Is this . . . machine . . . new?"

"No. Not really. It's something else that the Council of Recluce would prefer we hadn't developed." Kadara smiled. "Now . . . one last thing. You've danced around it, but never really explained why those two men attacked you."

Rahl swallowed. "They claimed that I had gotten their sister with child, and they wanted me to go with them at that very moment to ask her father for her hand. My parents and I had planned to go later that morning, after I had seen Magister Puvort . . ." Rahl repeated all the events of that morning.

"Did you get her with child?"

"I didn't see how I could have, but I did sleep with her. Not many times, and it was her idea, and she is several years older."

"Would you have taken her as consort?"

"If I had had to," he admitted.

"Did you want to?"

"No."

"At least, you're mostly honest."

Mostly? Rahl thought he'd been more honest than anyone else in his position would have been.

"I'm going to repeat a few simple rules, Rahl. First, and it may seem obvious, but some people don't understand, you are not to go through the wall gate. We could care less, but the Council cares a great deal, and there is an outpost of Council Guards less than half a kay to the north. If they capture you and discover you're an exile, your life is forfeit on the spot. Second, you will obey any magister. You can question how to do something, but not whether to do it. Third, you are to realize that only if you fit within Nylan can you remain here permanently."

"If you decide I do not fit, what will happen?"

"You will be exiled, although you will be given training and information about where you will be exiled. We're far less cruel with those we exile."

Rahl had his doubts. Exile was exile.

"Do you have any other questions?"

"Do you meet every exile?"

"Darkness, no. I'm the duty mage. Whoever has the duty takes care of exiles. Yesterday, it was Tamryn, and tomorrow it will be Leyla. It's not that much of a problem. We don't get that many exiles."

Rahl couldn't help but frown.

"It's simple. If someone is chaos-tinged they get exiled immediately from here or from the north because we don't take someone with chaos in their blood. Likewise, we don't take anyone who has killed someone or anyone who has committed a premeditated offense. That doesn't leave that many." Kadara looked squarely at Rahl. "You're very lucky not to have been exiled directly. You have promise, but you have this tendency to want things to go your way, regardless of what it costs others. That's very close to chaos."

He hadn't meant to kill the smuggler, and didn't everyone want things to go their way? What was wrong with that? She wasn't suggesting that Rahl couldn't have things go his way if there happened to be any costs to anyone else, was she? It certainly sounded that way. Rahl was getting the feeling that Kadara didn't care that much for him, and she was sounding a lot like Magister Puvort. Still . . . the last thing he wanted was to be shipped off to Hamor.

"I have a lot to learn." That was certainly safe to say, and honest as well.

"That you do." Kadara sighed. "I just hope you can." Then she stood. "You can wander around and meet people after you take care of your dishes." She gestured at the handful of people around the hall. "Or you can walk the grounds. I'd suggest you stay close to the buildings you know until you're more familiar with Nylan. You're expected to be in your room—or at least in the transient quarters—shortly after the lamps-out bell. That will be the next bell you'll hear. It won't be for a while yet. In the morning, wait here after you eat, and Leyla will find you and get you some proper clothes and boots."

With a brief smile and a nod, the magistra turned and walked from the hall.

Rahl just stood stock-still for a moment, then carried his platter and mug to the corner and dipped them in the rinsing buckets and racked them.

He turned and took several steps, then stopped, wondering exactly what he should do next.

A muscular young man, perhaps a year or two older than Rahl, walked over. "You're new, aren't you? I'm Khalyt."

Rahl could sense the other's charm, a charm fueled by order. He forced a smile. "I'm Rahl. Are you from Nylan?"

Khalyt shook his head. "I'm from Feyn. That's where Brede came from."

Rahl had no idea who Brede was.

"Brede was the one who saved Dorrin and made Nylan possible. Kadara's named after his consort." Khalyt shrugged. "Not many people know that."

"What do you do here?"

"Work and study, the same as anyone else, the same as you'll do. I'm studying to be an engine designer. They say that the engines on the black ships can't be improved, but anything can be made better. Have they told you what you'll be doing?"

"Studying languages."

Khalyt shook his head. "Better you than me." He turned as a petite young woman approached. "This is Meryssa. Meryssa, this is Rahl."

Meryssa's short black hair glistened almost with a light of its own. Her black eyes fixed on Rahl. She smiled politely. "Welcome to Nylan, home of the dedicated, dispossessed, and distressed."

"Which are you?" replied Rahl.

"All three. Most of us are. Recluce doesn't want us, and the rest of the world would only enslave us. So we become very dedicated to avoid further dispossession and distress. If we can. You'll see."

Rahl was afraid he might. "Work hard and well or see the world?"

"That's the way it is. The magisters don't put it quite that way," replied Meryssa.

"You're giving him a bad impression." Khalyt looked to Rahl and offered a smile, one short of falsity and not quite ingratiating, but barely. "She's so direct it can be unsettling."

"That's true." Meryssa continued to study Rahl. "I work at it."

He thought he sensed something—sadness, perhaps—behind her bright black eyes. "What are you studying?"

"Nothing. Not anymore. I'm going to be an assistant purser on one of the trading ships. I'll find out which one in the next eightday or so."

"Is that good?" Rahl honestly didn't know.

"Good? No. It's better than the alternatives." She smiled to Rahl, then nodded to Khalyt and slipped away.

"I'd better be going," Khalyt said. "I'll see you here and around."

As Khalyt left, Rahl realized that he stood alone in the hall. After a moment, he shrugged and began to retrace his way out of the hall and back to his quarters. On the way, he saw others, usually in pairs, seated on benches or on the low stone walls, but no one else made any move to approach him, and he certainly didn't feel like approaching them.

He was tired, and he could use a good night's sleep—if all the thoughts and feelings swirling through his mind would let him sleep.

XVI

Rahl had been tired enough, but sleep eluded him for a long time as he lay in the solid bed in his new quarters, looking up into the darkness. It wasn't the bed; it was more comfortable than his own had been. The easy charm of Khalyt had disturbed him more than the hidden sadness of Meryssa, but both had bothered him. The chilling matter-of-fact statements by Magistra

Kadara hadn't helped much either, nor had her skeptical and almost dismissive manner. Nor had the number of people bustling through the eating hall. How many exiles were there, and where had they come from?

Eventually, he did sleep . . . and woke with the dawn bell.

He only washed up, rather than showering, since he had showered the night before, and he wasn't ready for another cold shower. He did shave, not that his beard was that long, with the small razor that had been wrapped in cloth and under the towel on his bed, along with the square of soap.

He was more than a little surprised to find several women swathed only in towels making their way back from the washstones. While one was more than a little shapely, another looked to be more the age of his mother. None of them gave him even a single glance, and from that he decided that manners meant not looking.

Back in his room, he finished dressing, then made his way to the eating hall. As he stepped forward to serve himself, he realized that most of those in the hall were dressed in gray, and that his brown and tan garments made him stand out.

He filled his platter and found an empty corner of a table. Someone sat down. He looked up to see a girl seated across from him. Then he realized she was older than that. She just looked girlish because she was thin and had a narrow face and long brown hair braided and coiled into a bun at the back of her head.

"Hello."

"Hello," Rahl replied cautiously.

"I'm Anitra. I just got here last eightday. I'm from Huldryn. You've probably never heard of it. It's a hamlet west of Enstronn."

"I haven't heard of Enstronn," Rahl admitted. "I'm Rahl."

"You must be from the north."

"Land's End." He took a sip of ale.

"Is the Black Holding really on a hill that overlooks the harbor? Have you ever been there? Is there anything about it that makes you think of Megaera?"

"I've been there. Once. That was when the Council decided to send me here. I never saw anything that might have been made by the founders . . . except the stonework. It was good."

"I'm sorry. I just wondered. I didn't mean to bother you." She put her hands on the edges of her platter, as if to slide it away or move down the bench away from him.

"Don't go. I'm sorry. You just surprised me." Rahl tried to study her, to feel what she was like. He could sense nothing.

She laughed, ruefully. "You look like all the mages when they meet me. They can't sense anything about me. That's why I'm here. It makes them uncomfortable. Are you a beginning mage?"

"I was a scrivener. I don't know what I'll be. They said I might learn languages."

"Oh . . . that would be so good. I'd love to learn how people in Hamor and Nordla and Austra speak."

"The Nordlans and the Austrans speak pretty much the same as we do. At least, the letters in their books look the same." Rahl took a large mouthful of the heavy bread, slathered with thin mixed fruit conserve, and then a bite of the breakfast sausage. He followed it with a swallow of ale, thinking, as he did, that it was far inferior to what Shahyla had given him. He almost wished that he'd just courted her and left Jienela alone—except he still recalled the gelding knife and how that had bothered him . . . both the knife and the casual way in which Shahyla had handled it.

"I'm studying to be a machinist."

"A machinist?" Rahl had no idea what that even was.

"Machinists work with the engineers to cut and grind metal for machines, especially for the black ships. I've got good hands for that, Ludwyn says."

"How do you cut metal? With a chisel?"

"I suppose you could, but we use wheels with sharp edges . . . and grindstones to smooth the edges. Special grindstones. The engines power 'em all." Anitra stood up.

Rahl realized that she'd been eating as fast as she'd talked.

"I'll see you later, Rahl."

"Oh . . . yes."

"Better finish that up quick. Won't be long afore you got to be somewhere." With a wave she was gone.

Rahl didn't exactly gulp down the remainder of his food, but he did hurry.

Even so, there was a magistra approaching him as he rinsed his dishes.

"You must be Rahl. I'm Leyla." She had an open cheerful face and attitude.

"Yes, magistra." Rahl inclined his head. Behind her facade, he could feel even more of the blackness that he associated with magisters than he had with Kadara, and far more than with Magister Puvort.

"You've eaten. So we'll get you some proper garments and some boots that fit, and then we'll come back to the academy building, and I'll give you the basics on the Balance and handling order. After that, you'll be in the lower-level order tutoring and the introductory Hamorian language and customs class. Later on, we'll get you into weapons training."

Weapons training? Rahl didn't verbalize the question.

"Sooner or later, everyone with order-skills of your potential will have to fight or defend themselves. We teach you how to do it properly."

Even in Nylan?

Leyla did not answer that unspoken question. "This way. The wardrobing shop is west of here, past the bell tower."

The wardrobing shop was partly set into the hillside. It looked more like one of the livestock sheds on Bradeon's holding than a shop, except that the stonework was far better, and it had several small windows, and the roofing slates were lighter and of far better quality. The oak door was slightly ajar.

Leyla stepped inside. "Elina! I've brought you another one to outfit."

Rahl entered the dimness of the shop.

There stood an angular woman of indeterminate age, raking him with her eyes. "Hmmm . . . northerner . . . broad shoulders. No hips to speak of . . . We'll see what we can do." She turned and walked down an aisle between open cabinets in which were stacked all manner of folded garments.

Before long she returned with several, all of them of a pale gray color, the same color most of those in the eating hall had worn. "Trousers, drawers, undertunic, summer tunic, belt." She gestured toward the front corner of the shop, where a curtain hung on a bar. "Try 'em on."

Rahl took the garments and walked to the corner. He pulled the curtain closed . . . or mostly closed, since it did not quite stretch from one end of the bar to the other. Even with the curtain shielding him, he felt uneasy disrobing. He shook his head and climbed out of garments that were far too soiled, and began to don the new ones.

For all their drab coloration, the quality of the grays was far better than what he'd been wearing, and they seemed to fit better.

"Let's see, young fellow," growled Elina.

Rahl bristled inside at her tone, but pulled back the curtain and stepped forward.

Both women studied him.

Leyla nodded. So did Elina.

"They'll do," added the magistra.

"Now . . . for some boots. This way," ordered the wardrobe mistress.

Rahl followed her to another series of bins, from which she extracted three pairs of brownish boots. He tried on five pairs before he and Elina were satisfied.

Then she handed him another set of grays and extra drawers. "That'll do you."

Leyla looked at him. "Just leave old ones. They'll wash them and use them for rags in the engineering halls."

"Washrags?" he blurted.

"There's no sense in wasting them, and they're pretty worn. You're expected to wear relatively clean clothes every day, and you're responsible for washing them. You get two complete sets of garments, and four sets of underdrawers. You can put the second set in your room on the way back."

Washing his own garments? Rahl didn't mind chores, but washing was for women. Again, he bottled away the irritation.

Rahl was definitely feeling unsettled by the time he had unloaded his new garments and was walking into the building Leyla called the academy. The wardrobe mistress had measured him without touching him, and he'd seen more clothes, casually stored, than he'd ever seen anywhere in his life. He had the kind of boots merchants or Council Guards only wore, and his old perfectly serviceable clothes would be washed and then turned into rags. He'd met another exile whom he couldn't sense, discovered he'd have to do wash and who knew what else, and found out about skills he'd never heard of. And it was still early in the day.

"We'll go to the duty study. This is where you'll meet the duty mage— or whoever's working with you—every morning after breakfast. If someone's not here, wait." Leyla stepped through the entry arch, narrower than the others Rahl had seen, and opened the door.

"Yes, magistra." To Rahl, the black stones of the building felt older than either the quarters building or the eating hall.

She led him into a small study with a square table and four chairs. At one side was a writing table, set under the window. "Sit down." She closed the door and seated herself at the table.

Rahl took the indicated chair, across from the magistra.

"Before we start, do you have any questions? About anything."

"The Council Guards said that there weren't that many exiles sent to Nylan," Rahl began, "but I saw a lot of people in the eating hall. The mess."

Leyla nodded. "There aren't that many from any one town in Recluce north of the wall, but there are scores of towns, and it takes anywhere from two seasons to a year, sometimes two, to train them to fit into Nylan or prepare them for exile. Unlike the Council, we just don't throw people on ships or indenture them to merchants or slavers in other lands."

Rahl still had his doubts about that, but merely nodded.

"Anything else?"

He had more than a few questions, but he really didn't know how to ask them or whether he should. "I might later, when I've seen more." He paused. "There is one. Can I write letters to my family to let them know where I am?"

"You can write all you want. The post fee is two coppers a page, roughly, for it to be carried to Land's End."

"I don't have two coppers."

"Right now, you get three coppers an eightday if your studies and your work are satisfactory. After four eightdays, if you're still in good standing, it goes to five. You don't get paid the first eightday, but after that you'll get paid at the counter in the corner of the mess on sevenday after the midday meal."

Three coppers wasn't that much, but he didn't have any real alternatives, and he was coming to like that less and less.

Leyla looked at Rahl. "What do you know about order? Tell me."

"All the world is a mixture of order and chaos. Order is the structure of the world, and chaos is the destructive energy of the world. . . ." Rahl went on to repeat what he'd learned from the magisters in Land's End.

When he finished, Leyla nodded. "That's what most magisters in the north teach. It's mostly correct, but you need to know more. I'm going to tell you the basics, then I'm going to give you a book to read while you're learning. You are to read at least five pages every day." From somewhere she produced a black-covered book and handed it to Rahl. There was no title on the spine or the outside cover.

He opened it to the title page—*The Basis of Order*. He managed not to swallow as he realized it was the book that Magister Puvort had said was banned.

"For right now, you are not to discuss this book with anyone except a magister. Later, things will change."

"Ah . . . could you tell me why?" Rahl still couldn't believe what he held, and he wasn't sure whether to be glad or worried.

"Because you don't know what you think you know, and what you think you know is not what is, and both will conflict with what you will be reading. Talking with anyone who has not read and studied the book will just confuse you more at first. Later, we'll encourage you to discuss it with others who have studied it." She cleared her throat. "Why do you think we're having you read this?"

"Because I might have some small ability with order?"

"Rahl . . . we wouldn't bother with someone who had small abilities. Nor would that magister have sent you here. He'd either have ignored you or exiled you directly from all of Recluce. You can sense something about how most people feel, can't you?"

"Sometimes," he said cautiously.

"That's how you got into trouble with the girl, wasn't it?"

Rahl could feel himself flushing. He could feel some anger. What right did she have to accuse him?

"Wasn't it?"

"Yes." He tried not to sound sullen.

"Rahl!"

The power and the force in his name snapped him upright.

"You have abilities with order. Everything you do will affect someone. Either you learn what those abilities are and how to control them, or you will end up in someplace like Cigoerne—or the ironworks at Luba. You have great potential. Great power demands great responsibility. That is what you must learn if you expect to remain in Nylan."

Magistra Leyla might well have been correct, Rahl thought, but he hated being lectured. That was one reason why he'd left lessons in Land's End as soon as he could. Not only were lectures boring, but the people who lectured assumed that they knew better than he did what was good for him. Just like Puvort, who'd thought exiling Rahl was better than helping him. Or that Fahla should have been enslaved for not betraying her father.

Rahl forced a smile.

Leyla sighed. "You don't really believe a word I've said. I just hope you read the book carefully. If I can't get through to you, maybe it will." She stood. "Right now, there's little point in saying more. Let's get you over to the Hamorian class."

She opened the door and waited for Rahl to join her in the corridor. He glanced down at the wear-polished stone floor tiles. For all the cleanliness of the building, there was also a sense of great age, from the depressions worn in the stones to the slight rounding of the corner stones.

"We use immersion language studies. You'll step into a setting where people are doing simple tasks, and all of them will be speaking Hamorian. You are not to say anything, except in Hamorian."

"But . . . I don't know any Hamorian."

"You'll learn," the magistra said. "I'll meet you in the eating hall after the midday meal to take you to meet Sebenet. Now . . . this way."

She opened the third door on the left, motioning for Rahl to enter before her. She followed, then bowed to a magister dressed in crimson. What the magistra hadn't said was that a number of the other students were children, some as young as eight or nine.

Rahl had no idea what she said, but when she gestured to Rahl, he bowed slightly.

The magister replied in the Hamorian Rahl didn't know, then motioned for him to join several children seated on cushions in the corner of the chamber. One held up a book and opened it.

As he seated himself, Rahl thought she said something like, "*Sciensa livra y miendas.*"

Between the activities and trying just to hear the words, Rahl had a headache by the time the midday bell rang, and the class was over. He *might* have learned a few words.

He was among the later ones to arrive in the mess and found a seat at one of the unoccupied tables. He didn't see Meryssa, or Anitra, or Khalyt, but a thin man, a good five years older than Rahl, perhaps more than that, eased over toward Rahl.

"You're new. I'm Darrant. Would you be from Reflin?"

"No . . . Land's End."

"Oh . . . I was just hoping . . ."

Rahl shook his head. "I don't even know anyone in Reflin."

"Thank you."

Wondering what Darrant had wanted, Rahl finished his meal and took care of the dishes. Almost as if she had been watching, Leyla appeared and escorted him out of the hall and even farther downhill and to the west, to yet another building set into the hillside. A muffled thumping issued from the structure.

"That's the new printing press. We finally worked out a circular press rather than a powered letterpress."

Once more, Rahl hadn't the faintest idea what she meant, but from the sounds and the thin line of smoke issuing from the chimney, he had the idea that whatever was making the rhythmic thumping was powered by a steam engine. Such engines were forbidden in the rest of Recluce, except on ships porting at Land's End.

Before long, Leyla was introducing Rahl to Magister Sebenet, a swarthy and stocky black-haired man perhaps the age of Rahl's father. He wore an ink-stained canvas apron over a short-sleeved black shirt and trousers. He smiled broadly at Leyla. "You found me a typesetter?"

"No, Sebenet, I found you a scrivener who can read High and Low Temple. You'll have to train him. This is Rahl."

Rahl bowed slightly.

After Leyla had left, Sebenet turned to Rahl. "A former scrivener, is it?"

"Yes, ser."

"You're about to become a typesetter, young fellow, as well as handle all the dirty jobs that go with it."

Sebenet was patient enough, taking Rahl through the shop and explaining each piece of equipment.

"... the engine's what powers the press. Coal level should be about where it is now, but you have to sense the heat, too ... Stay clear of the belts, break your arm or neck before you knew what happened ... water feed's here ...

"... paper trays are here ... use a web to feed into the press ...

"Each box has the same letters in it. You pick the letters and put them in place. Here are the spacing bars. You lay out the text like so ..."

Rahl had to concentrate. Even so, he knew there were things he would not remember.

By the time he finished his time as an apprentice typesetter and then ate supper, alone, he was exhausted. He straggled back to his room and collapsed onto his bed.

His last thought before his eyes closed was that being a scrivener looked to be less work and far easier than everything he'd tried that afternoon— and he hadn't even gotten anywhere close to the harder work of setting type and making up the pasteboards for the press cylinders.

XVII

As he rolled out of bed, Rahl froze. He'd been so tired the night before that he'd forgotten to read the pages of *The Basis of Order*. He scrambled to the writing table and picked up the book, opening it to the first page, eyes scanning the words.

> Order is life; chaos is death. This is fact, not belief. Each living creature consists of ordered parts that must function together. When chaos intrudes beyond its limits, its energies disrupt all, and too great a disruption can only lead to death.
> Order extends down to the smallest fragments of the world . . .

Rahl read to the bottom of the page, then set the book on the table and put on his new gray garments. Then he sat on the stool and pulled on his boots.

He picked up the book once more. The words on the second page seemed to leap out at him, although there was no sense of power embodied in the book itself.

> Learning without understanding can but increase the frustration of the impatient, for knowledge is like the hammer of a smith, useless in the hands of the unskilled and able to do nothing but injure the user who has not both knowledge and understanding. Learning is like unto chaos, a power useful only for destruction without the order imposed by understanding . . .

Rahl frowned. The book seemed to be suggesting that there were uses of chaos that were not all evil, and that some use of order might be evil. Was that why the magisters did not wish the book anywhere outside of Nylan?

A wry smile crossed his lips. He could certainly tell of some uses of order by the magisters of the Council that were anything but good. Perhaps he would, when the time was right. He read another page, then slipped the book inside his tunic and hurried to the mess.

All of the tables were occupied, but he found a corner of one where he could sit a bit away from two women, both older than he was, he judged, but not by more than a few years.

As he ate, he tried to read another page, but he couldn't help but over-hear some of the conversation between the two, low as their voices were.

". . . say that I'll never understand . . . going to send me to Suthya . . . position with a trader there in Armat . . ."

". . . not bad . . . least you got somewhere to go and coins coming in . . ."

". . . didn't want to go . . ."

". . . magisters decide, dearie. They sent Durolyt to Southport."

". . . he hates the Legend . . ."

". . . why they sent him, if you ask me . . ."

Rahl felt cold all over. Was that what he had to face? Promises that could only lead to exile in a place he hated?

He still hadn't finished eating, and his appetite had almost vanished, but he forced himself to swallow the last mouthfuls. He knew he'd be hungry before midday. Then he read the last half page of the five pages he'd been told he should read every day before tucking away *The Basis of Order* and heading for the rinse buckets.

Yet another magister met him outside the study where Leyla had instructed him the previous day. He was slender and wiry, more than a head shorter than Rahl, and his hair was whitish silver, yet not the color of an old man's, and his face was unlined. Rahl had recalled the stories saying that Creslin had possessed such hair, but he'd never seen anyone with it.

The magister laughed. "Yes, it's the silver hair like Creslin's, and no, I'm not a direct descendant of his, not that I know of, anyway. I'm Tamryn." He gestured toward the study. "We might as well get started."

Rahl walked in, then waited to seat himself until Tamryn did.

"Have you read any of *The Basis of Order*?" asked the magister.

"Yes, ser."

"Do you have any questions before I start asking you about what you read?"

"Ah . . ." Rahl wondered whether he should ask, but suspected it would come out one way or another. "There's a part that seems to suggest that chaos is not all evil, that if it's used somehow within order . . ." He didn't know quite what else to ask.

Tamryn nodded. "Not many exiles pick that up quickly. Have you done any studies with the magisters in the north?"

"No, ser. I was going to see them when . . . everything happened."

"Ah, yes, Leyla and Kadara both wrote up their reports on you." Tamryn nodded. "Well, in answer to your question, our . . . brethren . . . north of the wall wish to think of the world in simpler terms than is realistic." Tamryn frowned, then paused for a moment. "While few speak of it, all living creatures, and that includes me and you, contain both order and chaos. It's more complicated than what I'm about to say, but you can think of it this way. Chaos is like the coal or the wood in a stove. It provides the energy or the warmth that keeps us alive. Order is like the stove itself. Without the structure of the stove, the fire would consume all around it or burn out uselessly. Without chaos, there would be no life, just a dead body."

Rahl nodded. "Are there good uses of chaos and bad uses of order, then?"

Tamryn pursed his lips. "Yes . . . but with a condition. Those who use chaos frequently may indeed use it for purposes that are worthy. I understand that the junior mages of Fairhaven often are employed to clean their sewers with chaos-fire. Chaos-mages at times accompany patrollers in both Fairhaven and Hamor and help keep order. However"—Tamryn paused—"the continued use of chaos predisposes a mage toward destruction, rather than building, and very, very few powerful chaos-mages have ever been known whose good works outweighed their evil ones."

"Do you know of any, magister?"

"It is said that Cerryl the Great of Fairhaven was one of those. Certainly, in his rule, all was peaceful, and few fled to Recluce, and few indeed had harsh words for him, but we do not know what evil he did because he was so powerful that few to whom he might have done evil would have survived."

"About the evil use of order, magister?"

Tamryn looked at Rahl. "I trust you are not playing at some game, or that you will not long continue it, Rahl."

"It is not a game, ser. I have feelings about this, but I would say nothing until I understand more." Rahl wanted to make sure all the mages in Nylan understood how things really were in Land's End, and questions were always a better way to get older people interested.

"Very well. The evil that can be accomplished with the misuse of order is most different. It is more akin to building a very tight and well-constructed prison. Everything must be so ordered, and follow such rigid rules that nothing is allowed to change."

That sounded like Land's End. Puvort certainly hadn't wanted anything to change, even the way books were produced, not that the prohibition had been bad for Rahl's father. "I was a scrivener, ser, and I did not know that a machine existed to print books until yesterday. That was when Magister Sebenet showed me the printing press."

"We're aware of that, Rahl. Let's leave it at that for now."

Rahl could sense Tamryn's irritation, and he nodded. "Thank you, ser." He tried to remain calm himself, but he didn't like being treated like a child or having his questions brushed away when the mage had asked if he had those questions. The engineers and the mages of Nylan had the power to change the north. Why didn't they?

"Now . . . for today, Rahl, I'd like you to consider why Creslin was forced to found Recluce."

How could he talk about that? Rahl paused, then began slowly. "I know some of the legends, and I have read *Tales of the Founders*. I had to copy it, but I read it as well."

"You don't think he was forced to found Recluce, then?"

Rahl hated being put into corners the way Tamryn was doing to him, and he detested the fact that the mage could sense what Rahl was feeling, and yet didn't understand what was behind those feelings. Nor did he or the others seem to care. "There's a lot missing from the book. I don't understand why he fled from Westwind, then ended up consorting the woman he didn't want to consort."

"Did you fit in Land's End?"

"I was doing fine. I mean, I was until those two attacked me, and I never used any order at all."

"Let's see. You got a girl with child, and you broke the arms of two men . . . and you were doing fine?"

"They wouldn't have attacked if Magister Puvort hadn't used order on one of them to make him charge me." Rahl wished he hadn't said anything the moment the words were out.

Tamryn's head snapped up. "You didn't mention that before."

"I couldn't say anything before the Council. They were already charging me with misusing order. If they knew I could feel that, they would have exiled me right there."

"Why didn't you tell Kadara or Leyla?"

"It would have sounded like I was . . . well, like I was making something up."

Tamryn sighed. "Don't you think we can tell that?"

"The Council knew that I hadn't done anything really wrong, but that didn't stop them," Rahl pointed out.

"Actually, they did you a favor. If you'd have stayed in Land's End, even if you had taken instruction from the magisters, exactly how long do you think it would have been before you were in real trouble?"

"I made a mistake with Jienela," Rahl said. "I didn't mean to . . ."

Tamryn laughed. "It always happens."

"What?" Rahl was confused.

"If you use order to make a girl feel better, there's nothing wrong with that, if it's just a touch, but more than that, and there's a Balance there, too. If you use order that way, and you sleep with her, she's far more likely to end with a child."

Rahl could sense the absolute truth of what the magister said.

"That's just another reason why you need instruction and training. You have ability, but you're going to get yourself in real trouble someday if you don't stop feeling angry and sorry for yourself and start learning what order is all about."

Tamryn might be right, Rahl thought, but in his own way, he was as arrogant as Puvort and all the Council. Were all the magisters in Recluce like that?

Still . . . it wouldn't hurt to learn what he could.

XVIII

For the next several days, Rahl managed to meet with the three magisters without upsetting them or himself by carefully reading *The Basis of Order* and asking questions that interested him. He answered their questions honestly, although that took the extra effort of forcing himself to consider himself as someone else and replying factually.

The Hamorian classes were disconcerting at first, but then, as he realized that there was nothing at all hidden, he began to enjoy them, even with the children, just letting himself relax and learn what he could.

The printing was neither as taxing as dealing with the magisters nor as enjoyable as learning Hamorian. Each task, just like copying, had to be perfect. Unlike copying, if Rahl made a mistake, and if Sebenet did not catch it, pages and pages of print could be ruined. That only happened once, when Rahl did not check one of the corner fasteners on a pasteboard page-set on fiveday afternoon.

The page-set tore apart, and ink ended up everywhere, and Rahl missed supper and had to work until almost the lamps-out bell to clean up the mess. Sebenet worked with him, but the printmaster said nothing.

He didn't have to; Rahl could sense his disapproval. But then, after seeing the mess, Rahl couldn't blame Sebenet—unlike the magisters, whose questions and instruction continued to grate on Rahl whenever he thought about it. He tried not to think much about it.

Sixday went better, and when he arrived in the mess for supper, Rahl felt vaguely relieved to have survived the print shop without any more mistakes. After serving himself, he saw Meryssa sitting by herself.

"Would you mind company?"

"Oh . . . no. Please . . ." She gestured vaguely across the table.

"Do you know when you'll be leaving or what ship you'll be on?" asked Rahl, after seating himself and taking a small swallow of the ale in his mug.

"They say I'll be on the *Legacy of Westwind.* It's an older steamer that runs between Nylan and different ports in Candar, and once in a while to Hamor."

"What does a purser do?"

"I'm going to be the assistant purser. Pursers take care of obtaining supplies and provisions, for obtaining passage fees from passengers and ensuring their billeting, and for overseeing the mess, and for maintaining all the accounts for those. On some ships, the chief purser handles all the ship's accounts. There are other duties as well." Meryssa offered a faint smile.

"But . . . why . . ." Rahl shook his head.

"Why being a purser instead of an exile? According to Magistra Leyla, that's because I'm not really angry or chaos-driven, but somehow dissatisfied, and I'll always be dissatisfied until I see how people live elsewhere, but seeing it should be enough, instead of having to live there."

Was her underlying sadness because of that dissatisfaction? Rahl wondered. He took a bite of the fish fried in egg batter. He didn't recognize what he was eating, but it was mild and warm and filling.

"How are you finding Nylan?" asked Meryssa.

"I can't say I've seen much of anything except around here. I've been so busy."

"It's that way for everyone for the first few days. You'll have sevenday afternoon and eightday off. Then you can walk around and see more."

"What should I see?"

"Oh . . . you should go down to the harbor and the market squares there. It doesn't matter what day it is, there's always someone selling something. I like taking the west walk, along the cliffs to the west. You can look down at the beaches below and out at the Gulf, and it's beautiful, especially near sunset. There aren't many people there, either."

"Hello there, you two!" Khalyt's voice jolted Rahl, pleasant as the greeting was.

"Khalyt . . . I'd thought you'd be here earlier," said Meryssa.

"I was working late with Kyltyn. I've got an idea, and I think it will really work," Khalyt announced as he slid into the place at the table beside Meryssa.

"What sort of idea?" asked Rahl.

"Steam engines are reciprocating . . ."

Rahl had no idea what Khalyt meant. Once more, he had understood every single word the young engineer used—and what he said made no sense.

"The way they work, the steam from the boiler forces a piston back and forth and you have to use a crank or a drive wheel to turn that into a circular motion to drive the screw shaft . . ."

Abruptly, Khalyt stopped and took out several sheets of paper and a grease marker and began to sketch. When he had finished, he had a crude diagram.

This time Rahl understood, at least in general terms.

"Pushing those heavy shafts back and forth takes a great amount of chaos-energy. To contain that requires masses of black iron. That's heavy. So the more powerful the steam engine, the more weight the ship has to carry, and the more chaos-energy it takes to move it. I've been thinking about how we could use the steam from the boilers directly. . . ."

Once more Khalyt began to sketch, but the diagram looked more like a pole with vanes extending from it. "Now this would fit inside a housing, and if we get the stream pressure high enough and run it through the vanes here, they'll turn the shaft directly, and we won't lose as much power with all the conversion machinery. This turbine, even all made out of black iron, weighs much less . . ."

Rahl frowned.

Khalyt stopped. "You look doubtful."

"Ah . . . no. Not . . . well, I don't know anything about engines, and I don't know much about machines, except what Magister Sebenet has taught me about the printing press. Yesterday, I made a mistake. It was a little mistake. One of the fasteners that holds the pasteboard page-set on the press wasn't set just quite right, and the press only turned a few times before everything ripped apart." Rahl laughed ruefully. "I was cleaning up the mess until close to lamps-out. Now, if I understand what you're saying"—he pointed to the sketch of what Khalyt had called a turbine—"this is going to be turning very fast, far faster than the press. How are you going to make sure everything stays tight and in place and balanced?"

Khalyt looked at Rahl, then laughed. "My friend, you should be an engineer! That is the biggest problem. Every one of the turbine vanes will have to be precisely the same as every other one, but I have calculated a way to do that, using order-forging and black iron. Anything that must be strong and thin and deals with great forces must be made out of black iron. Regular iron or steel will break. That is why the inside of the turbine will be made of black iron."

"Will this make the black ships faster?" asked Meryssa.

"So much faster . . . you cannot imagine how much faster. That is necessary because the Hamorian warships are getting to be almost as fast as the black ships."

"Where are the black ships?" Rahl had heard of them all his life, but he'd never seen one. They didn't port in Land's End. That he knew.

"In the harbor. When they are in port, they are moored at the western pier. You can't get on the pier unless you're crew or an engineer. The main engineering hall is just above there. You can see it from just below the bell tower."

"And this idea will work?" asked Meryssa.

Khalyt shrugged. "The idea is the simple part." He turned to Rahl. "Making all the parts so that they fit together is what is hardest."

Meryssa laughed, and the laugh held sadness as well. "Making anything work is the hardest part. It is so easy to talk and think."

Rahl held his frown within himself. He'd always found doing things easier than thinking or learning. Copying was far easier than thinking about what he had just copied. Sometimes, like when he'd had to learn truncheon handling, discovering how to use what he'd learned was hard for a while, but just doing things was simply physical work.

"You have a funny look on your face, Rahl," Meryssa said.

"I was just thinking about what you said."

Meryssa turned, half rose from the table, and gestured. "Aleasya!"

The woman who turned and moved toward Meryssa was broad-shouldered and muscular, possibly a few years older than Rahl, with a squarish chin, green eyes, and neck-length brown hair. Her summer tunic and trousers were a darker gray. "Meryssa."

"If you wouldn't mind joining us?" Meryssa inclined her head. "Have you met Rahl?"

"I have not." Aleasya set her platter and mug on the table next to Rahl, then slipped gracefully onto the bench.

"Aleasya's an arms instructor, but she's best with blades," Meryssa said.

"I'm not nearly so good as Zastryl or Fhiera. They're true armsmasters."

"You're good enough to have done a tour as a ship's champion."

"Anyone who's trained here and made arms level can do that," demurred Aleasya. "They don't really take arms that seriously in any of the port cities, especially in Candar or Austra. In Hamor, if there's real trouble, they bring in mages. We're the only sea traders who need armsmen on every vessel."

Rahl just listened.

"She started as a trading marine," explained Meryssa.

"It's better to be a staff arms trainer here. Easier to keep in shape and condition, too."

Abruptly, Khalyt and Meryssa stood.

"We need to go," explained Meryssa.

"You need more practice," Aleasya said. "Pursers can't just handle coins and supplies, especially around Jerans."

"On oneday?" acceded Meryssa.

"In the morning, I can work you in somewhere."

"I'll be there."

Aleasya took a swallow of ale, then turned to Rahl. "She could be a good blade if she'd work out more."

Rahl didn't want to get into that. He wouldn't have known what made a good blade and what didn't. "Why do you and Khalyt eat here in the mess? You don't have to, do you?"

She laughed. "It's all about coins. The staff doesn't pay to eat here. I'm not consorted, and I'm not interested in anyone. So I save my coins and buy shares in one of the trading companies. Someday, I'll be able to sell them and have the coins to build a place of my own. I already have a piece of ground out east, just south of the wall . . ."

"Are you from Nylan?"

"Oh, yes. I wouldn't live anywhere else. My mother is one of the port pilots, and my father is an assistant harbormaster."

"But you eat here?"

"You wouldn't want to eat what either of them cooks, when they cook . . . if they cook." Aleasya shook her head. "I love them dearly, but their idea of food is cheese and black bread, with some sort of sausage or meat and whatever green or fruit is handy."

"You train people in arms. Will you be training me?"

"I'll probably see you when you start arms training, but I won't work with you."

"Why not?" asked Rahl. She seemed friendly enough and open, and that was more than some of those he had met in Nylan.

"You're listed as a probable black mage, and that means you won't get more than a basic fam with edged weapons."

A probable black mage? Was that what Tamryn and Leyla had meant by order-skills? Why hadn't they just said that? "They said I might have some ability with order."

That brought another laugh. "They never tell you. They're afraid that things won't work out, and then you'll be angry or disappointed."

"But why . . . it seems . . . cruel not to let people know . . ."

"Rahl . . . it is Rahl, isn't it? I'm not that good with names. Black mages and black engineers are the ones who run Nylan. They're the important ones. Everyone looks up to them. For all the young people who show some order-ability, only a few get to be mages. It's not just talent, and it's not just work, but it's also a way of looking at the world. Some can handle it, like Khalyt. He'll never have more than a slight bit of order-skills, but he understands engines, and he'll do something special some-day."

Rahl nodded. "This way . . . of looking at the world. What way is that?"

Another laugh followed his question. "I wouldn't know. I'm a good blade trying to get better and close to being an armsmaster, if I can. It's just what I've heard."

"What have you heard about that way of looking at the world?"

Aleasya looked sideways at Rahl, almost sharply. Then she shrugged.

"It's only what I've heard. To be an effective black mage, you have to be able to look at the world as if you did not matter."

Rahl almost snorted. He found it hard to believe that mages like Puvort or Kadara didn't put themselves first. Puvort certainly hadn't gone out of his way to steer Rahl in a less dangerous path, and Kadara had had her mind made up about Rahl from the time she'd first seen him. "Do you really think they all do that?"

Aleasya offered a broad smile. "No. But most of those I know try hard, and sometimes I'd wager that they get to that point." Her smile vanished. "If you want to stay here in Nylan, you'd better concentrate on doing your best and stop worrying about everyone else."

Rahl smiled politely. "I'll have to keep that in mind, but it's hard when they're the ones who will decide your future."

Aleasya shook her head. "You decide your future. They judge you on what actions you take to make that future possible. Look, Rahl, it's like using a blade or any weapon. How you handle the weapon decides whether you survive, not what people think about how you handle it." She stood. "I need to be going. Best of fortune, Rahl."

"Thank you." Rahl watched her go. She seemed the most honest and open, and yet she sounded like everyone else. Do your best, and everything will be fine. Be honest, and things will work out. He'd done his best, and he'd been honest. So why was he in Nylan, and why were people telling him he might not be able to stay?

XIX

On sevenday morning, Rahl still had to meet with one of the mages and attend the Hamorian class, but he did not have to go to the print shop in the afternoon. Even so, after he finished eating, as he made his way to the small study, he wondered which mage he would be seeing. He didn't have to wonder long. Kadara was sitting at the table waiting for him.

"Good morning, magistra."

She motioned for him to sit down, then waited until he was seated. "How far have you read into *The Basis of Order*?"

"A little over thirty pages, magistra."

"What have you learned?"

Rahl wasn't that certain he'd learned much of anything except some clever sayings and a number of commonsense observations. "There are a number of observations and cautions, but I have not read anything that is instructive."

"You do not feel cautions that will prevent you from getting yourself into danger are instructive?" Kadara arched her eyebrows.

"Magistra, I have no doubt that such cautions will be most useful, but . . ." Rahl stopped, trying to find a way to express what he thought without offending Kadara.

"But what?"

Rahl forced himself to ignore the edge hidden behind the seemingly mild question. "I have the feeling that the book was written by someone of far greater ability than I possess for those of equal ability. I do not think I have the ability or knowledge of order itself for these observations to be as useful as they could be or that they might be."

"You don't think such cautions and observations are that useful to you now?"

Kadara's patronizing and superior tone grated on Rahl, but he forced a smile. "It's probably my fault, magistra, but I've never been terribly good at learning things when people are telling me what not to do rather than showing me what I should do."

"Perhaps you should consider changing how you learn. It's apparent that you haven't been that successful in the way you have been learning . . . or failing to learn."

Rahl had to wonder why Kadara was deliberately trying to anger him. She couldn't be that inflexible, or that stupid. Yet . . . he couldn't really ask that.

"By saying that," Kadara went on, "you're basically excusing yourself from learning. You're saying that you can't learn because you have to be taught, and no one's teaching you. *The Basis of Order* provides the limits. It's up to you to figure out how to work within them—if you want to stay in Nylan. Life doesn't provide you with private tutors, Rahl."

That wasn't much help, thought Rahl. He knew all that, but outside of a few things like sensing how people felt and making girls feel better, he didn't really know anything about order, and he scarcely knew where to start. "I understand that, magistra, but I have no idea where to start."

That did surprise Kadara. After a moment of silence, she said, "You know what most people feel, don't you? How long have you known that?"

"I always had a little feel for it, but I've been able to sense more in the past few years."

"That's an order-ability. Don't tell me you didn't know that?"

"I knew that, but I don't know of other order-abilities or how to discover them or what they might be. There are hints in the book, but I can't sense when it might rain, and I can't feel what's under the ground. I can feel a bit when things aren't put together right, like ink, and I can sometimes sense where things are in the dark."

Kadara laughed, harshly. "You have more order-abilities than some who call themselves mages, and you've done less with them. Don't expect anyone to feel sorry for you."

Rahl wasn't asking that. "I'm not. I'm asking how I can learn to improve and expand what I know."

"Have you thought about looking at everything in the way you sense it through order? From the food you eat to the way the printing press is put together? Or looking at the rain that way? Or a building? You can't do anything until you understand how order and chaos work within it."

Rahl had to admit that made sense, but he hated admitting it.

"You have to ask questions about *how* things work before you ask *why* people do what they do," Kadara went on. "You're too wrapped up in Rahl and why everyone's against poor Rahl. You left a girl in Land's End with a child. You left your parents behind. You broke two men's arms. And you're feeling sorry for yourself."

Inside himself, Rahl bristled. He wouldn't have had to break Jeason's and Jaired's arms if Puvort hadn't made them attack, and he wouldn't have had to leave Land's End if Puvort hadn't been so intent on driving Rahl out, even to the point of lying to the Council. But he'd already told the magisters that, and no one paid any attention.

"There are reasons behind what happened. You've told us," Kadara continued. "It doesn't make any difference. The arms are broken, and the child will be born fatherless, and all that is because you didn't think far enough ahead. You waited until it was too late to go to the magisters. You decided you knew enough that you didn't need instruction. You avoided your responsibilities, and when your failure to think ahead created a problem you couldn't escape, you blamed people who only saw the results of your failures and acted on what they saw."

All that might be, Rahl fumed, but magisters were supposed to help, not stand aside and watch things go wrong, then blame and condemn.

"Now . . . the choice is yours. You can start thinking ahead and trying to explore your talents, or you can keep blaming us. I don't see much point in discussing order and chaos any further at the moment. It won't do any good until you start thinking for yourself instead of blaming everyone else for your problems." Kadara stood. "You can talk it over with Leyla on one-day." With that, she turned and left the study.

Rahl just sat there for a moment, furious, his fists clenching, his jaw tightening, thoughts careening through his mind. *Don't offer any real guidance except to look ahead and develop skills you don't know about and that no one will tell you about except what not to do. Don't get angry, and just accept everything we say. And don't bother us until you admit everything is all your fault.*

Finally, he rose and headed for the Hamorian class. It wouldn't matter if he arrived there early, and he might as well do something from which he could learn—unlike the largely useless sessions with the magisters.

When he walked into the large room, one of the younger girls ran toward him. "Rahl, *escara amia?*"

He couldn't help but smile. "*Escio amia,* Coraza."

Even after less than an eightday, he'd learned more than a few words and phrases of Hamorian, and it seemed as though each day he learned more. More important, Magister Thorl was only concerned about his learning language and customs.

Coraza's cheerfulness and enthusiasm helped Rahl to put aside Kadara's stinging and unfair comments for the time while he was learning Hamorian.

After leaving Magister Thorl's session, Rahl made his way to the mess, where he took a heaping platter of lace potatoes and baked sea bass, along with a mug of ale. He actually took a swig of ale, then refilled the mug before he left the serving area.

"Rahl!"

He looked around and saw Aleasya sitting with another woman. She was motioning for him to join them. Rahl could sense the darkness that signified a magister around the other woman, although she wore dark green, and he hesitated. How could he avoid them? The last person he wanted to meet was another magister.

"Come on!" Aleasya called cheerfully.

With an inner shrug and sigh, Rahl headed for the two. He slid onto the bench beside the weapons instructor.

"Rahl . . . I'd like you to meet someone. This is Deybri. She's one of the healers here."

Deybri was almost as broad-shouldered as Aleasya, but her hair was light brown and curly, barely neck length, and her eyes were brown with gold flecks. She was clearly older, perhaps as much as ten years older than Rahl, but beautiful in a quiet way.

"Oh . . . I'm glad to meet you," Rahl managed.

"You were worried that I was a magistra, weren't you?" asked Deybri. "Don't fret. I'm not. I don't judge, lecture, order, or teach anything but how to heal." She smiled warmly and reassuringly.

Rahl could sense the warmth she radiated, and that warmth felt real. He just returned the smile. "I'm still learning my way around Nylan. In fact, I feel like I'm still just beginning."

"It takes time, and you haven't been here long, Aleasya tells me."

"Less than an eightday."

"I was just leaving." Aleasya stood and lifted her platter and mug.

While she was doubtless finished with her meal, Rahl had no doubts that the meeting with Deybri had been at least partly planned. "I hope I'll see you later."

"I'm sure you will." Aleasya nodded and hurried toward the rinse buckets with her platter and mug.

There was a brief moment of silence before Deybri spoke.

"Aleasya says that you're a possible mage."

"That's what she told me. The magisters haven't bothered."

"They probably think you know that."

Rahl shook his head. "I don't even know what a mage can do. Not really."

"You know what you can do right now. That's what a mage can do. Some can do more, and some can do less."

"What's the difference between a mage and a healer?" asked Rahl.

"I think it's not so much ability as inclination. Mages tend to want to move and manipulate things and to understand how they work only so far as such understanding is useful. Healers want to see everything as knit together in some form of harmony. So far as I know, Dorrin was the only great mage who was also a healer and an engineer. All three take orderability, but how that ability is used is very different."

"How does a healer use order?"

Deybri smiled. "You're asking that like a mage."

"How would a healer ask?"

"That's a problem. Most healers don't ask. They feel the lack of order, or the wound chaos and try to do something about it. The hardest part for the healers who are just beginning is knowing what not to do."

Rahl almost shook his head. Again . . . they were talking about what not to do, rather than how to do it. "Ah . . . how can you start by not doing?"

"I suppose I didn't say that right. Let's say that someone comes in with a broken bone. If I had enough order strength, I could align the bones and tie them together with order. But they wouldn't heal right because that order isn't as strong as the order that the body creates when it heals. So the best thing a healer can do is align the bones, splint the arm to hold it in place while it heals, and remove any wound chaos that would stop proper healing. Most young healers want to do more, because that will reduce the pain . . . but it slows proper healing. Mostly. If there's too much pain, that also slows healing, and you have to work out the best balance for the injured person."

"Thank you." Rahl felt that he'd gotten the first really informative reply from anyone. "Why can't the magisters explain things that simply?"

"Why should they?" Deybri's tone was not quite mocking. "You're assuming that they have an interest in making order-magery widely available. Their main concern is engineering and in minimizing chaos and the misuse of order-magery. Too many ordermages is as bad as too many chaos-mages. They're the same thing, really."

Rahl had to think about that. How could too many ordermages be the same as too many chaos-mages? "The Balance?"

Deybri nodded. "Having more ordermages leads to more concentrated free order, and that requires more concentrations of chaos." She rose. "I'm sure I'll see you around." She smiled . . . warmly.

Rahl sat at the table, thinking. What Deybri was implying was that the magisters were more interested in weeding out those would-be mages who couldn't find their own way than in helping those who didn't understand.

That meant, like it or not, he had to figure things out. He also needed to get away from the training center.

He finished the last of his meal with a final swallow of ale, and then rose and made his way to the rinsing buckets. From the mess he headed outside, where a brisk but warm wind was blowing out of the south and up from the harbor. At the side of the main road, he paused and glanced back.

With a shake of his head, he turned and started downhill, toward the harbor. The dark gray paving stones of the road, as well as those that formed the sidewalks flanking the road, were so closely fitted together that almost no mortar was needed to provide a smooth surface. He glanced down toward the western piers, where the black ships were supposedly moored. He could barely make out the western piers, because there was a haze around them, yet the other piers were clear. Some sort of order shield? He'd have to see when he got closer to the harbor.

Each dwelling was orderly, not that he would have expected otherwise, but Nylan was even more so than Land's End. Not only was there no garbage or trash in the road or side lanes, but there were no loose shutters, no peeling paint, not even cracked slate roof tiles. Seeing such profound order made him even more uneasy.

Despite the breeze and the light summer tunic he wore, he was sweating after he'd walked little more than a few hundred cubits. Before long, he entered an area where shops fronted dwellings, and where he could see an occasional eating place. He saw more and more folk on the streets, most moving briskly toward whatever their destinations might be. The side streets became slightly narrower, but only slightly, and the house-shops were side by side, their walls touching, although he could sense courtyards farther back. The smell of the harbor wafted toward him, but it held only the odors of the sea itself—salt and seaweed, and a faint fishlike scent—fresh fish, rather than spoiled or rotten.

As he neared the harbor and was able to catch a glimpse of the ship masts and the water, the sidewalks became more crowded, not uncomfortably so, but with far more bodies close together than he'd ever seen in Land's End. People hurried along the sidewalks, swiftly, but pleasantly enough, avoiding each other. Those who stopped and talked stepped back almost against the stone-walled buildings.

Rahl stopped at the glass display window of a cabinetmaker, as much for the shade of the awning as to look at the furniture. In the center was a square table with inlay work that displayed a large ryall in the center, a black bloom done in lorken, outlined in golden oak. A smaller and more delicate bloom adorned each corner. While Rahl marveled at the crafting skill, for what would such a table be practically used? Playing plaques? But only the wealthiest factors and merchants could afford such crafting. Then, perhaps it was on display for the traders from the ships in the harbor.

He made his way to the waterfront and the wide stone avenue that ran along the edge of the water. The seaward side of the avenue was marked by a waist-high stone wall that dropped straight into the waters of the harbor— except where the piers extended from the avenue out into the harbor. On the shoreward side were factorages specializing in specific types of goods, chandleries, and other commercial enterprises, interspersed with taverns and an inn or two. At the foot of each stone pier was a guard stand, and each had a pair of patrollers. The patrollers faced the harbor. Moored at one of the piers was a two-masted, red-hulled steamer with paddle wheels on both sides. Behind it was a long schooner. The wagons on the pier suggested that both were loading or unloading cargo.

Rahl turned westward, in the direction of where Khalyt had said the black ships were moored. Just ahead was an open square off the avenue on the shore side past the foot of the closer pier. As he neared the square, he could see vendors and buyers, and tents whose sides billowed in the strong breeze off the water. The sounds of voices haggling and talking mixed with orders and epithets from the teamsters and stevedores on the piers. He could also smell food being cooked, roast fowl and sausages and other items he could not identify.

Toward him walked a pair of patrollers in black, with the uniforms trimmed in white. One of the patrollers glanced at Rahl, took in the grays, and nodded politely, before turning his eyes back to the peddlers.

As he stepped into the market square, with the neat lines of carts, small tents, and tables with wares upon them, Rahl sensed something ahead—a fainter reddish whiteness. He glanced around, but could not see anything obviously amiss. He passed a table displaying knives, from some of which emanated a dull reddish whiteness, but he could still feel a stronger sense of the reddish white elsewhere.

Then, just ahead of him, he saw a smallish man wearing faded blue trousers and shirt, who ambled along the line of vendors' tables, then slowed. Rahl could almost sense the man getting ready to dart toward an older woman at a small table piled with dried fruits. She was engaged with a bearded man well dressed in a maroon tunic and dark blue trousers, who was gesturing vociferously.

". . . not more than three coppers for the whole tenth!"

". . . I could not part with them for less than a half-silver . . ."

Rahl stepped forward, about to speak, when the man in blue darted toward the older woman and grabbed her cashbox.

The woman lunged for him, but got tangled with the would-be buyer.

"Thief! Thief!"

Rahl stuck out his foot, and the thief sprawled forward, then curled into a ball, still holding on to the wooden box, and straightened. Rahl pivoted and slammed his booted foot into the side of the man's knee.

As the fellow toppled, Rahl grabbed the box and stepped back, looking for the woman. The man in maroon had his arms around her. Seeing Rahl, he let go of her and turned, vaulting over another table.

Rahl handed the cashbox to the vendor. "I think everything's there." He glanced around, but the thief in blue had vanished, and so had her accomplice.

Several of the nearby vendors were offering comments.

". . . went that way . . ."

". . . patrollers'll catch them . . ."

". . . won't either . . ."

"Oh . . . thank you . . . young man." The fruit-seller drew herself up. "They were a pair. I should have known better. No one haggles that much over dried fruit, but I so seldom get to bargain."

Rahl couldn't help smiling.

"Would you like to buy some, young man?"

Rahl laughed. "I can't. I don't have a copper to my name. I don't get paid until the end of the eightday."

Clutching the cashbox, she smiled at him. "Well, take one morsel anyway. I'd offer more, but it's been a hard year."

"Just a little one," Rahl replied, taking a slender sliver of dried pearapple. "Thank you."

"My thanks to you, young man."

"I just did what I could." Rahl felt a little embarrassed.

"Would that more did," murmured someone.

After slowly eating the dried pearapple, Rahl eased away, looking at the variety of wares spread on the tables. He saw carved wooden boxes; brass lamps of various sizes and styles; lacework; hand tools, including chisels, hammers, mallets, planes, augers, and others; platters out of hammered brass; and even bright shimmersilk scarves, guarded by two large armsmen.

Rahl still sensed the reddish whiteness, now in the corner of the market square to his right. Had the two thieves hidden there? He moved away back toward the left, stopping briefly to admire a fine vest of black linen, trimmed in crimson.

Then, he turned and began to move down a line of collapsible booths that seemed to hold more artistic goods—small carved stone figures, decorative breadboards meant to be hung rather than used, pewter tankards—and several stalls with glassware. Ahead were what looked to be decorative woodworks and ivory.

Rahl could hear voices, if barely, from somewhere behind one of the vendor's tents to his left, about where he sensed the reddish white.

"Burned my leg, he did . . . he's the one."

". . . leave him alone . . ."

". . . no mage . . . put a knife in him . . ."

Rahl slipped behind an angular man in soiled blue, probably a foreign sailor, then past a heavier man in richer brown, who stood before a table bearing figures carved from bone or ivory.

From nowhere, the man in blue appeared, darting toward Rahl with a shimmering blade enshrouded in reddish white.

Rahl darted to one side and grabbed what looked to be a carved wooden truncheon from the seller's table. He jerked sideways, but the knife slashed across his upper right arm. The cloth of the tunic caught the blade for a moment, slowing the thief.

Rahl attacked, kneeing the man in the groin and slamming the makeshift truncheon across the side of his forehead. What Rahl had thought was a truncheon snapped into pieces that flew everywhere.

The thief dropped to the ground. He did not move.

Rahl just looked at the fallen figure for a moment, then at the slash in his tunic and the blood staining the cloth.

"Murder! Thief . . . !"

"He attacked the boy! I saw it."

Two patrollers appeared from nowhere, then two more. One of them produced cloth and bound Rahl's wound. Another summoned a cart, and the body of the dead thief was removed.

A magister Rahl had never seen arrived with a fifth patroller.

Then the questioning began—and Rahl never had gotten to look at the wharf that held the black ships.

XX

The questions by the patrollers and the magister lasted until well into mid-afternoon, when another junior magister appeared with a wagon and drove Rahl and the older magister back up the long, inclined road to the training center. Then Rahl had to sit alone on a bench outside the study while the older magister talked to Kadara behind the closed door.

Rahl was not looking forward to meeting with her, although he had no real idea what else he could have done—except let the thief steal the cash-box and escape, and that would have felt very wrong. He continued to sit on the bench, shifting his weight from time to time and occasionally standing to stretch his legs.

Finally, the hard-faced magister who had questioned him stepped out of the study. "You'll need to talk to Magistra Kadara." With a perfunctory nod, he turned and left the building.

Kadara was waiting in the study. Rahl closed the door and seated himself at the table opposite her.

She looked at Rahl. "The first time you go to the harbor, and what happens? You come back with patrollers." Her eyes went to his bloody sleeve and the dressing beneath the rent tunic.

"The patroller said that you tripped a thief and recovered a woman's cashbox. Is that true?"

"Yes, magistra. There were two of them, and I was about to warn her, but they acted before I could say anything."

"Two of them?" Kadara did not seem surprised, but was seeking something, Rahl felt.

"One was distracting her by haggling . . ."

Kadara nodded. "That's one way they work. Then what happened?"

"She gave me a small piece of dried fruit. I would have bought some, except I don't have any coins. Then I was walking through the rest of the market, and I heard someone say that I was the one. I didn't want to get into another fight. That didn't seem like a good idea, and I tried to slip away, but the man in blue came after me with a knife, and there was nowhere to go.

I grabbed for something to block the knife. I thought it was just a smooth piece of wood, and I parried the knife and hit him across the temple. I kneed him as well. He didn't get up. I didn't realize I'd hit him that hard. I still don't see how I could have."

"You didn't." Kadara sighed.

For the moment, Rahl realized that she actually looked as though she cared.

"He was off one of the Hydlenese ships, and he was . . . what you might call chaos-driven. You're at least a low-level order focus. When you hit him with that ivory, you destroyed all the chaos in him, and that included what he needed to live."

Rahl didn't know what to say, not really. "I didn't have that in mind, magistra. I was just trying to defend myself."

She nodded brusquely. "We know. The patrollers checked with everyone. The thief never should have been allowed off the pier, but those things happen. He might even have avoided the pier guards. No one's going to be upset about his death, and the training center will pay the vendor for the broken ivory. The larger question is what to do about you."

Rahl gave a start, then winced. His arm was sore. But why was he once more a question? He'd tried to avoid trouble. He truly had.

"Rahl . . . in some ways . . . let's just say that you present a particular problem, and a very serious one for both Nylan and for yourself. Most mages show some trace of their talent early, but you didn't. Your talent appeared strong and late, and that meant you didn't get the training you should have when you should have. You're also stubborn. Most mages are. We're going to have to rethink your training. I don't want to say more right now, not until I talk things over with the others." Kadara paused. "Have you been to the infirmary? Do you know where it is?"

"No, magistra." Rahl took a deep breath.

"It's on the hillside above the bell tower—" She broke off and looked at Rahl. "I'd better go with you, and you're going to need something to eat before we get there." She stood.

Rahl was truly confused. Was this the Kadara who had lectured him that very morning?

During the entire walk to the canteen, since the mess was not serving, Kadara kept watching Rahl, and she even sat him at a table and got him a bowl of maize chowder with chunks of ham, some dark bread, and a mug of ale.

He had to admit that he'd been slightly dizzy before he ate, and that he felt steadier after he finished the last of the chowder.

Kadara studied him. "You've got more color, but I still want Deybri to take a look at you and that wound. She's the duty healer today. Have you met her?"

Rahl nodded. "I met her at dinner."

"Good. No one needs any more surprises." Kadara gestured toward the door that led outside from the canteen.

Rahl followed her out, then northward on the walk beside the building that held both the mess and the canteen. The next walk to the left brought them past the bell tower, where they walked up a low rise to another small building.

Kadara opened the door. "Healer!"

Deybri was moving toward them when she saw Kadara and Rahl. Her eyes widened, then lingered on his wounded arm.

"Rahl ran into a chaos-driven Hydlenese at the harbor square. Rahl stopped him from stealing a vendor's cashbox, and he went after Rahl." Kadara offered a lopsided smile. "The thief is dead, but he did slash Rahl, and I thought you should look at the wound."

"Chaos-driven . . . I should." Deybri gestured to a stool before the window. "Sit down here, if you would."

Rahl was happy to sit down. Even after eating, he was still tired, as if he'd worked all day spading his mother's garden.

Deybri unbound the dressing, then took a bottle of liquid from the plain cabinet set against the wall and soaked a cloth before cleaning the top of the slash, as well as the area around it. The liquid stung, but not badly. Her fingers rested just at the edge of the wound.

Rahl could feel a warm/cool darkness touching and penetrating the gash. "Is that order?"

"You can feel that?" asked Deybri.

Kadara leaned forward slightly, looking at Rahl.

"Yes, healer. I mean, I feel something that's there, but not there, and black and warm and cool all at the same time."

Kadara and Deybri exchanged glances.

For a moment, Rahl could feel the air tightening around him—except that it wasn't.

"Did you feel something?" asked Kadara.

"Something pressing in on me."

Deybri glanced to Kadara.

"He's not aware of his shields. No wonder they sent him here."

Rahl glanced back and forth. Again, people were using words he knew, but they didn't make much sense.

Kadara looked to Rahl once more. "There's a way to use order to keep either order or chaos from touching you. That's what I meant by shields. Most mages have to learn how to create such shields. You're doing it without understanding what you're doing. In fact, you're doing a number of things with order without thinking about them. That can be very, very dangerous, and, if you don't learn to control them, you will get in a situation that will kill you. It's only a matter of time. If you don't learn control, your failures may kill people around you as well."

Rahl looked to Deybri.

She nodded.

"There wasn't much wound chaos there, almost none at all." Deybri turned to Rahl. "Did a mage dress it?"

Rahl nodded.

"That explains it."

"Or most of it," Kadara added.

The healer took a fresh dressing from the cabinet. Her hands were swift and gentle as she re-bound the wound. "You're to come here every afternoon after the midday meal until we tell you that you don't have to. Even if you're supposed to be somewhere else. Do you understand?"

"Yes, healer."

"I'll make sure the other magisters know," added Kadara. "Now, we need to get you some rest."

Rahl stood. He wasn't light-headed, but he had felt better than he did at that moment, usually much better.

As Rahl stepped out of the infirmary, Kadara leaned back inside the doorway and said in a lower voice, "I'll be back later."

Deybri did not speak in reply, and Rahl could not see or sense any gesture in response.

Then Kadara returned. "We need to get you back to your room. You need some rest and a good night's sleep after that."

Since putting one leg in front of the other was getting more and more difficult, Rahl had to agree. He walked silently beside the a magistra until they reached his chamber.

"You don't need to think about everything right now. You need to get some rest. Just lie down until supper."

After Kadara left, Rahl stretched out on the bed. What had he done? The thief had said that Rahl had burned him, when Rahl had tripped the man. Rahl certainly hadn't been aware of using order when he'd hit the man with the ivory carving, but what else could explain why the thief had died? He'd only felt that reddish whiteness that strongly once before, with the man with the sword in Land's End.

He swallowed. Had the conflict between order and chaos been what had killed that man as well? Was that part of the reason why he was so tired?

He had more questions, but he found his eyes closing, even as he tried to think of what they were.

XXI

Rahl didn't really want to get up early on eightday. His arm ached, and he felt even more exhausted than he had when he'd gone to bed the night before, but he knew he wouldn't feel better unless he ate, and, if he wanted to eat, he had to get up while the mess was still serving.

He washed up and forced himself to shave, but didn't shower, not with the dressing on his upper arm. Then he walked to the mess. There were perhaps fifteen people in the hall, and he knew none of them. Tired as he was, he found himself eating two complete helpings of cheesed eggs and sausage and almost half a loaf of bread, with two mugs of ale. He didn't feel nearly as tired after he'd eaten, but he also didn't feel all that energetic as he walked back to his quarters.

While it was too nice a day to sit inside, he didn't have that much energy. Still, he forced himself to go to the washing area and wash out his dirty garments and undergarments—except for the one ruined summer tunic—and hang them out to dry. On oneday, he'd need to see if he could get a replacement tunic. He just hoped he didn't have to pay to replace it . . . because he couldn't.

At that moment, he realized that Kadara had to have paid for his meal in the canteen the afternoon before. He hadn't even noticed that.

Her words about his being able to do things with order without thinking about it also came back to him. Was that why the Council had pushed him out of Land's End and sent him to Nylan? Kadara had clearly thought so. But why?

Rahl thought about the magisters and magistras he'd met in Nylan. Almost all of them seemed more powerful than those on the Council. Had Puvort set up Rahl to be sent to Nylan because he could have been as powerful as the northern mages? Or because they feared that he would become powerful? Kadara had said that Rahl could be a danger to himself and others, and those words had felt true.

But . . . how . . . and why?

He shook his head. He was still tired, and he needed to know more.

Finally, he decided that he might as well read *The Basis of Order.* If he tried to relate what he read to what he knew or had done, maybe that would help. After a little wandering around, he found a secluded stone bench near the garden and settled there, opening the book and letting the morning sunlight warm him.

He had read several pages when his eyes slowed in reading one passage. He went over it carefully, and then reread it.

> . . . all that is, everything that exists, is little more than the twisting of chaos within a shell of order, and the greater the complexity of those twistings, the more solid the object appears. A thumb of lead or gold may appear more solid than a flower, and may indeed overbalance the scales, yet there is no difference in the fashion in which they are constructed, only that the chaos is twisted more lightly and that the shell of order is stronger. Hard coal is heavier than wood, and, as such, when it burns it releases more chaos-fire . . .

Rahl frowned. Was that why black iron was heavier, because it contained more order and chaos than simple iron? That would also explain why Khalyt had been so excited about his ideas for building a steam turbine to propel ships, because it would use less black iron and provide greater power.

He read another page, and then another, before coming to another section that struck him as interesting.

> In substance, there is no difference between chaos and order, for neither has substance in and of itself, but as a result of how they

are structured. Likewise, that structure determines how much order and chaos can be encompassed and how it will be released, if it can be, should the structure fail or be caused to fail . . .

Be caused to fail? The book didn't mention how that might happen, just like it didn't go into details about how much was accomplished.

He read through several more pages until he came to another section.

If one studies the light from the sun, it is like chaos, and yet it is not. It has a power not unlike chaos, yet its structure is more like unto water, and it flows through the air like a breeze, yet it weighs so little that it might be as nothing . . .

Sunlight like water? With weight . . . and flowing through the air?

After several pages more, he closed his eyes, leaned back against the stone wall behind the bench, and let himself doze.

XXII

In the darkness of eightday, not long before lamps-out, Rahl walked along the path in the garden. The afternoon nap had helped, but he still felt a little tired. As he walked, he kept his eyes closed, confirming that he navigated more in deep darkness by his order-senses than by his sight. Still, he was trying to sense more than just the general position of things, but where exactly they were and how solid they might be.

Still without using his vision, he followed the stones through the patch of brinn, trying to put his boots down in the exact center of each hexagonal stone. When he had crossed the brinn, he stopped on the narrow walk that separated it from the sage on his left and the mint on his right. The sage bed was elevated a good span and a half above the mint and grew in drier and sandier soil.

He opened his eyes and checked his location. He was on the edge of the stones, but that wasn't too bad. The first time, he'd almost tripped on the raised border of the sage bed.

As he stood in the cool of the evening, he also tried to recall the difference between seeing and sensing. After a moment, he closed his eyes and began to move forward.

Then he sensed someone approaching on the main walk, but not who.

He opened his eyes.

It was an older man, dressed in the same grays as Rahl wore. He looked at Rahl, then inclined his head. "Good evening."

"Good evening."

Rahl waited until the other was out of sight before he resumed his exercises in the garden. He couldn't sat why, but he felt that he needed to learn *something* about order before long.

He'd discovered more than a few aspects of order by trying things, but what he had not discovered was *how* he did what he did. Once he considered the possibility of doing something, it was almost as though he could either do it, or he could not—even when he knew that other mages had been able to accomplish what he tried.

As the time neared for the lamps-out bell, Rahl made one last order-sensed navigation through the garden, this time between the mint and the parsley, before opening his eyes and making his way back to his quarters.

There he lit the lamp and reclaimed his towel before heading to the washstones to wash up before climbing into bed. He finished quickly and returned to his chamber.

Absently, he put out the wall lamp by tightening a miniature order shield around the wick. He could do that, but he could not erect a shield such as that around anything living—even to protect it. He'd tried to shield a tree-rat from a terrier, and that hadn't worked. He hadn't even been able to put shields around insects.

Then he laughed. He hadn't even thought of it, but he hadn't really needed to light the lamp at all.

Was that part of his problem, that he still was doing too many things by habit rather than asking if he should be, or whether he could handle them in a different fashion?

He began to disrobe, stifling a yawn. The end-days had been long.

XXIII

On oneday, Leyla met Rahl outside the small study. "We've decided to change what you're doing. You won't be working with Magister Sebenet any longer."

What had he done wrong there?

"It's not your work. In fact, Sebenet's not at all happy about it. He thinks you have the makings of a good typesetter and printer, but that's not going to help you. From here on, you'll be spending all morning in Hamorian classes. Magister Thorl says you have a great ability with languages, and your experience there and with the printing indicates that you learn better by doing than by reading."

Rahl had only been trying to tell the magisters that for an eightday, but he just nodded.

Leyla glanced at his arm. "You'll be doing arms training in the afternoon. There's plenty you can do with that while you're healing. Deybri says it's not that deep."

"Thank you."

"Don't thank me. It was Kadara's suggestion—after your difficulties over the end-days. She said you're one of those who has to learn everything the hard way. Learning arms will be very hard for you. Probably not the truncheon or the staff, but everything else."

"What about studying order?"

"That's up to you. You have your copy of *The Basis of Order*. We'll answer any questions you have." Leyla's eyes met his. "Frankly, if you don't figure out better control, you won't be able to stay in Nylan, but you're spending as much time and effort fighting us as trying to learn. We think that your only hope is to learn on your own—at least for the next few eightdays. Then we'll see."

Rahl found himself bristling inside once more. They hadn't wanted to tell him all that much, and now they were saying that it was because he was fighting them. Of course he was fighting them. He was trying to get them to tell him something useful. The only one who'd really been all that helpful hadn't been a mage at all, but a healer. Rahl wasn't certain that Kadara would have said nearly so much as she had if Deybri hadn't been there.

"Oh, Rahl," Leyla said tiredly, "please do stop it. You want us to give you easy and simple answers on how to handle a set of complex skills you haven't investigated, haven't tried to figure out, and don't seem to want to. You have natural order-talents, but they'll never be more than that until you look into yourself and see what you're doing and how, and that's not something we can do for you."

"You could tell me how things are supposed to work."

"Such as?"

Rahl found his thoughts going in all directions. He hated being put on the spot, trying to come up with a quick reply, as if it were all his fault if he didn't. "How do you put order into things?"

"Unwisely, if you look at it that way." Leyla sighed. "Let me try to explain this in very simple terms. You have both order and chaos in your body. If you use the order in your body and put it elsewhere, you're going to unbalance your body, and you'll get sick or die, because the remaining chaos will overpower the order and break down parts of your body. Now . . . there is a certain amount of free chaos and order around us all, but it's spread out thinner than the air we breathe. A strong mage can gather either and use that. If he gathers too much, it's likely to result in attracting an equal amount of chaos—or draw someone who holds that much free chaos within them. If there are reasons why that does not happen, then a focus of the opposite force will appear somewhere in the world, more likely nearer than more distant. You have the ability to draw some of that free order from around you, but you're not really aware of it, or how you do it. I suspect that's why the thief had to attack you, although he wasn't aware of it, because his chaos was drawn to your order. That's why we maintain strong defenses against chaos here in Nylan, because the black iron of our machines represents concentrated order. That's also why we discourage order-magery in Nylan, except for healing, because it makes matters worse."

"You're saying I caused the thief to attack me? I caused it?" Rahl couldn't believe that.

"Not directly. Not in the way you're saying. Let me give you an analogy. Let us say you have a coal stove, and you need to add more coal, but when you open the door to the fire chamber to shovel in the coal, there's a hidden string from your coal scoop to a pitcher of lamp oil in the rafters overhead, and the oil runs down the string all at once into the stove. What will happen?"

"You'll get a flare-up in fire, I suppose."

"Well . . . that's sort of the way you're going about things right now. You have a hidden order string that attracts chaos because you aren't aware of that tie, and every time you use your order-skills you're risking some sort of fire. Now . . . you're potentially a powerful mage, and your shields are strong enough that most of us can't sense what you're about to do until you do. Frankly, we'd rather not get burned in your fires. Do you think you'd want to if you were in my position?"

"So what am I supposed to *do*?"

"Learn Hamorian, read *The Basis of Order,* and learn more about arms and how they're used. Every time you use order-skills, try to feel how you're doing things. You might even try to figure out other ways to do things, even if they're not as easy, because that will help you understand."

Rahl understood that Leyla was trying to help him, but what she said didn't seem all that useful or practical. Besides, he'd already been trying some of that, and while it helped some, he hadn't had any great insights from what he'd tried.

"Now . . . you can join Magister Thorl. I'll meet you at the weapons center after you see the healers. It's the square building about two hundred cubits west of the infirmary."

Rahl left the study half-understanding and half-angry. Why couldn't anyone explain anything clearly? Leyla had explained why he was a problem, but she hadn't given him any solid advice or suggestions except to consider what he was doing. People had been doing that for years, and Rahl hadn't found such advice to be particularly helpful. It was just an easy way of making sure it was his fault whenever anything went wrong.

Magister Thorl did offer a smile when Rahl appeared, and both Coraza and Yanyla ran to greet him.

"*Mes amias!*" Rahl declared.

"*Ista tuo de ceriolo . . .*"

Rahl caught most of what Coraza was saying and smiled.

He felt far more cheerful when he left Thorl for dinner in the mess. He wasn't even upset when Anitra joined him at his table.

"Sokol said you killed a thief in the market on sevenday. That true?"

"He tried to knife me because I stopped him from stealing a vendor's cashbox."

"He was Hydlenese. They're all thieves. Even their traders are thieves."

Rahl nodded and kept eating, listening and occasionally making a remark or two.

After he finished and rinsed his platter and mug, he made his way to the infirmary. He had to sit and wait a while before Deybri appeared.

"Good afternoon, Rahl," said Deybri. She hadn't been the duty healer on eightday. That had been an older man—Natran. "How's the arm?"

"Sore, but not quite as stiff."

"Let's take a look." She didn't actually remove the dressing but merely let her fingers rest on his skin above and below the cloth. "Another few days, and you won't need the dressing. We'll give you some ointment to put on it. That will keep it from itching and keep the scarring from being too bad."

"Is that all?"

"For today. You're fine. I have some others who aren't." She smiled, then turned, heading toward the long wards to the rear of the building.

Rahl felt vaguely let down as he left the infirmary and followed the walk westward toward the squarish building where Leyla had said she would meet him.

She stood just outside. "How's the arm?"

"Deybri says the dressing will come off in a few days." He paused. "Can I get another summer tunic . . . or do I have to wait until I have enough coppers to pay for a replacement?"

Leyla laughed. "Just stop by the wardrobing building and tell them I said it was all right. You probably saved us more coins than the tunic cost."

"Ah . . . ?"

"If the thief had escaped, people would have lost coins. If he'd been captured, he would have had to appear before a justicer, and he would have had to be fed for a day or two. All of that costs. Even quick justice isn't free."

Rahl understood. He just hadn't thought of it in that way.

The weapons hall was a long building, and most of it was just open space between walls with areas for practicing. In some places, there were mats on the floor. In other areas, the stone was covered loosely with sand. In one section was what looked to be part of a ship's deck.

Leyla led him into one of the few separate rooms, in which there were long rows of plain wooden tables. There, the man who bowed to Leyla wore black, but trousers and a shirt that were neither tight nor loose-fitting, but somewhere in between. He also held a slight aura of order.

"Rahl, this is Magister Zastryl."

"Magister." Rahl bowed slightly.

"If you would, Rahl," said Zastryl, "I'd like you to walk up and down the tables and pick the weapon that feels the most comfortable. Not the one you think would be best, but the one that feels that way." He gestured toward the tables. "It doesn't matter whether you know how to use it . . . you'll learn."

Rahl could sense that every weapon had somehow been infused with something. To him, some even held the reddish white that had to be a form of chaos. He slowly walked along the nearest table. He could have played games with Zastryl, and picked up one of the blades or a long knife, but Leyla, standing on one side, would have caught that. He suspected that was one reason she was there. He looked up and smiled at her.

She did not return the smile.

In the end he was honest. There was no reason not to be. He brought both a truncheon and a staff to the armsmaster. "I can't decide. I might be favoring the truncheon because I've used it, but I don't think so."

Zastryl looked to Leyla.

She nodded. "There's no discernible difference."

"That's interesting," noted Zastryl, looking at Leyla.

"Until later," she said, turning and leaving the narrow chamber.

"Since you have a sore arm, and you know something about the truncheon," Zastryl began, "we'll start with the staff. Later, you'll get the basics of handling a blade, mainly defense, and a dagger." He turned and walked out of the weapons room and into the main area, expecting Rahl to follow.

Rahl did.

Zastryl stopped at one of the racks on the wall, from which he removed two dark wooden staffs. Both were heavily padded on the ends.

On one side of the large chamber, Rahl noticed two solid-looking men in olive black uniforms he hadn't seen before. Both of them were looking at him.

Zastryl followed his gaze. "Naval marines. We train them, too, and make them go through refresher courses periodically." After a moment, he raised his voice. "Khaesyn, Stendyl! You aren't sparring when you're looking." He turned back to Rahl. "If you don't concentrate, the padding won't help much. Let's start with your feet . . ."

Rahl was sweating heavily by the time Zastryl dismissed him in late afternoon. He was also exhausted although he'd never actually crossed staffs with the arms magister, just practiced moves and footwork, time after time.

Leyla was waiting for him when he finished the session.

"You were considering picking up one of the blades just to confound everyone, weren't you?" she asked.

Rahl understood that the question was almost rhetorical. "I thought about it. I decided there wasn't much point to it."

"Could you have picked up one of the razor-edged blades?"

"Yes, magistra." It would have been hard, but he could have.

She nodded. "We need to have a talk, Rahl. A very serious talk." She looked toward the mess. "It won't be that long."

Rahl waited.

"It's early to tell, but you may be one of those mages who can handle a certain amount of disorder and chaos. This is both desirable and undesirable. It is desirable from your point of view because it makes you less vulnerable to chaos-attacks. It is undesirable because you will attract even more free chaos than a practicing pure black ordermage. In your case, this could prove dangerous or fatal if you do not attempt to learn more about *how* you use order." She paused. "Believe it or not, I understand your frustration. You are looking for guidance on how to use order. There's one problem with that. Order-use cannot be taught. It remains an art that can only be *learned* by each mage on an individual basis. No two mages use order in precisely the same way. That is one reason why *The Basis of Order* provides only observations and statements about how order and chaos appear in the world and what the results of balanced or unbalanced use may be."

"But . . . magistra, in a way, that is true of everything. When I was learning to be a scrivener, my father could not take the pen and move my hand, but he could show me what the letters looked like. He could show me the best way to hold the pen."

"True," Leyla acknowledged. "Now . . . what if you could not see the letters he wrote on the page, and he could not see those you wrote? And the only way in which he could determine how well you copied was by how well someone else read what you wrote? That's not a perfect analogy, but it should give you an idea of the difference. When you attempt to manipulate order, I can tell that you are doing it. I can tell that you have done it, and I can view the results, but because the means by which you do so are within you, I cannot see or sense what techniques you use."

Rahl was silent, thinking over what she had said.

"Until you can describe and feel what you are doing with order and how you are doing it," she went on, "we cannot offer ways in which you might improve your skills."

"But I don't really know how."

"Exactly. And if you can't say how you are doing it, how do you expect us to offer advice on what techniques might be useful when we cannot see or sense how you do what you are doing?"

Rahl didn't have an answer to her question, but he still felt that the magisters were being singularly unhelpful.

"Think about it, Rahl. I'll see you on fourday."

Rahl watched as she took the walk northward. After a moment, he started toward the mess. He was hungry . . . and irritated, if not as angry as he had been.

XXIV

Surprisingly, the entire eightday and more passed smoothly for Rahl. Part of that was because he did not meet with any of the magisters or magistras. He did keep reading *The Basis of Order*, and he found it helped a little to keep in mind what Leyla had said. He tried to understand the book more as just a statement about the world and how order and chaos fit into it, rather than seeking direct answers about how to do something. He also decided to avoid the harbor for a while.

He enjoyed the additional time spent in learning Hamorian, perhaps because he was beginning to be able to talk in complete sentences, if short ones, and because he could instantly tell whether he was saying things correctly.

On sixday, close to two eightdays after his encounter with the Hydlenese thief, he stepped out of Magister Thorl's Hamorian class and headed to get something to eat. Despite the breeze and the light summer tunic, even walking from the one building to the mess left him perspiring. As he stepped into the slightly cooler mess, he blotted his forehead. Then he made his way to the serving table.

Fried fish again. As well as it was prepared, he was getting tired of the fish, and the boiled early potatoes weren't exactly a favorite, either, but with only three coppers to his name, he couldn't exactly afford to be choosy. He filled his platter and mug and stepped away from the serving tables.

"Rahl!"

At the sound of Deybri's voice, Rahl turned. The healer was sitting alone at one end of a table that had three others at the far end. She motioned for him to join her. With a smile, he carried his platter and mug over and sat down opposite her.

"I haven't seen you in a while." He saw the circles under her eyes and sensed her tiredness. "You look like you've been working hard."

"We've been busy. A Spidlarian ship had a boiler explosion."

"That doesn't sound good."

"It's not, but I'd rather not talk about it now. How is your training with the staff coming?"

"Well enough. I hadn't realized how effective it can be against someone with a blade."

At that moment, an attractive young woman, a good ten years younger than Deybri, passed the table. She made an effort not to look in Rahl's direction.

Deybri laughed. "A little obvious."

"About what?"

"Looking at you while trying not to."

Rahl couldn't help but be somewhat flattered but didn't want to say so. He just shrugged.

"Don't pretend that you don't know you're good-looking."

"I hadn't thought about that."

She smiled. "That means you know it. People who are handsome and know it never have to question whether they are."

Because her words were so good-natured and the feeling behind them so open, Rahl didn't bother to hide the wince. He even laughed. "That might be, but I still hadn't thought about it."

"You're too much of a pretty boy," Deybri added. "Especially now that you're putting on more muscle from your arms training."

"Did you mean that as an insult?" Rahl had not sensed any hostility, but more a feeling of amusement from the woman.

"No. If it weren't for the complications—and that I'm exhausted at the moment—I'd be interested in taking you into my bed, but I'm a forever person. Besides that, I don't want a child right now, and I don't have the order-skills to keep from having one, not with you, and you don't know enough yet to do it either."

"But . . ." Rahl was confounded by the warmth and honesty of her words, and the sudden confusion within Deybri. He finally said, "I barely know anything."

"That's the problem. You have great order strength, but not much discipline."

Rahl sighed. "Deybri . . . how do I get that discipline? The magisters don't tell me much except to read *The Basis of Order* and think about what I do before I do it. I don't even know how I can do what little I can do. And I've been trying to puzzle that out."

Deybri nodded. "That's a problem. I can only suggest a few things. You can probably see well at night, can't you? Well, try finding your way around with your eyes closed or with a blindfold, then think about the difference between seeing and feeling your way. You also might try sensing how everything around you is put together." She paused. "You have a little time before you have to go to arms training, don't you?"

"A little."

"Come with me to the infirmary. I think you'll be able to learn something there, too. You might be able to help me as well."

Rahl hurriedly finished his fish and potatoes, then swallowed the last of the ale. After rinsing off his platter, he walked with Deybri toward the infirmary.

"The boiler in a Spidlarian merchanter exploded, and that filled the engine spaces with steam. Some is high temperature and high pressure, and they breathed it. If they breathed more than a little, slowly they lose the ability to breathe. It's as if they breathed pure chaos. The ones who were closest have already died, but there's one who might make it, except that . . ." She shook her head.

"What?"

"You'll see. I don't want to say more yet." She walked several more paces before adding, "What you'll see won't be pleasant. Can you handle that?"

"I'll handle it."

Deybri laughed mirthlessly. "Just don't look appalled."

Rahl thought he could manage that.

Once they reached the infirmary, Deybri led Rahl past several empty beds. In looking at them, he could sense an aura of . . . something. Past the vacant beds was an area that was curtained off.

"Here." She drew back the curtain slightly and held it so that Rahl could step through.

A man lay on the bed, his upper body propped up. The sailor's eyes were closed. His forearms were swathed in dressings, and his face was swollen, a mass of blistered skin. With each labored breath, his chest shuddered with a gasping sound.

"He's unconscious. Can you sense something within his chest?"

Rahl tried just to feel. Then he nodded. Within the man's chest was a mass of whitish redness. It reminded him of both of the men who had attacked him. It wasn't quite the same, but it was similar.

"He's just on the borderline. If . . . if there were just a little less chaos there." Deybri shook her head. "I just can't do any more."

Rahl looked at her, realizing that she was somehow . . . frailer. Not in body, but in something. Then he recalled what Leyla had told him about order. Deybri didn't have any more to give as a healer.

He moved closer to the sailor until he stood almost next to the man. What could he do?

After a moment, he bent over and extended his hands, so that his fingers were almost touching the man's chest, one set on each side. Then he tried to touch the man with gentle strokes of order across and within his chest.

How long that took he didn't know, but when he began to feel lightheaded, he stopped, then stepped back.

"That's better," Deybri said softly. "Can you hear the difference?"

Rahl wasn't sure than he could. Was the sailor gasping less, breathing more easily? He looked at the man again, trying to sense the chaos. He *thought* there was less, but he really could not tell.

Deybri stepped back and lifted the curtain. "You've done all you can."

Rahl stepped back beyond the curtain, and she let it fall.

"Thank you."

"I hope it helped."

"It did. We'll just have to see how much." She paused. "You'd better tell Magister Zastryl that you were helping me heal. You won't have as much strength for a while."

"I will."

After they walked toward the front of the infirmary, away from the injured sailor, Rahl turned to the healer. "Is there a difference between wound chaos and chaos? They don't seem quite the same to me."

"They're not. To me, wound chaos is a little darker and redder."

"It's uglier."

Deybri nodded. "I think that's because it's part chaos and part sickness."

"Couldn't a white mage help healing by using the chaos to destroy the sickness?" asked Rahl.

"That would take very good control. Pure chaos destroys things. If you'd used chaos on him, you would have destroyed his lungs."

"Oh . . ." Rahl shook his head. "Of course."

"I've been told that there have been chaos healers, but they almost have to be gray mages."

Rahl had never heard of gray mages. "There are gray mages? Who can do both black and white magery?"

"It's more like some of each," replied Deybri. "Some say that Cerryl the Great had to have been a gray mage because he built too much that lasted for it to have been accomplished by a white wizard."

Rahl really didn't want to leave, but he was already late for arms practice.

"You need to go, but tell Zastryl what you were doing. He won't mind."

Rahl hoped Deybri was right. He smiled at her. "I hope I'll see you later."

She only smiled in return, enigmatically.

XXV

Rahl struggled to get up on both sevenday and eightday morning, but it was harder on eightday. Was that because he didn't have that much to do, except read *The Basis of Order* and think?

He took a shower, and the sun-heated water was almost lukewarm, probably because it was getting into late summer, when the days and nights were warmer, and on an eightday when not so many people got up early to bathe and wash up. He dressed and made his way to the mess, where he was sitting alone, slowly eating, when Kadara walked into the hall and sat down across from him.

"It was good of you to help Deybri the other day."

"She needed it. How could I say no?" He paused. "I suppose I should have asked how he is doing."

"He died last night."

Rahl winced. Should he have gone back and offered more help?

"You couldn't have done any more. He didn't die from the lungs. He was older, and his heart gave out. Healing doesn't always work, even when you do everything right. I'm not here to blame you. You did what any good mage would have done."

"You're telling me so that I don't remind Deybri about him?"

Kadara shook her head, but Rahl sensed no negative feelings. "Sometimes, you understand so much . . . and other times . . ." She rose. "I just wanted you to know."

"Thank you, magistra."

After Kadara left, Rahl pondered what she had said . . . and what she had not.

He also couldn't help but worry about his own lack of progress in understanding what he was doing with order. It seemed as though he could either do something, or not do it, and when he could do things, he couldn't figure out how he had done them. He just did them. When he couldn't do things, he didn't seem to be able to figure out how, and sometimes he didn't have the faintest idea how to accomplish tasks that the book suggested were simple.

Rahl dawdled over his breakfast, but finally finished the last mug of cider, and was about to roust himself to rinse his dishes when he saw Meryssa hurrying into the mess. She glanced around, then walked toward Rahl. "Have you seen Khalyt? I thought he might be here."

"No. I haven't seen him this morning." Rahl looked at her, then asked, "Is everything all right?"

"Yes." Her smile was rueful. "I should say that everything is going as it's supposed to. I just wanted to say good-bye to Khalyt," Meryssa said. "I'm leaving this afternoon. Well . . . I won't be leaving Nylan yet, but I have to report to the ship."

"The ship is that *Legacy* one?"

"The *Legacy of Westwind*."

Rahl offered an encouraging smile. "You'll do well."

"I might, but you're just humoring me."

"I'm wishing you well by saying that you will do well."

"I like that better, Rahl." Meryssa glanced around the mess. "You take care of yourself."

"Thank you."

Rahl waited until she had left the mess before standing and taking his dishes to the rinse buckets. Then he stepped out of the hall into the bright summer sun and hot early morning that promised a sweltering day.

He walked slowly to the infirmary, where he opened the door, stepping inside cautiously.

Within moments, Kelyssa appeared. Rahl had only met the younger healer once before.

"Rahl, isn't it?"

"Yes. I was looking for Deybri."

"She's not here. She has today off, and tomorrow. She said she was going off somewhere."

Rahl could understand that. At times, he wished he could go off somewhere. "Thank you." He offered a pleasant smile, then slipped out of the infirmary.

He didn't want to stay around the training center, but he didn't want to walk down to the harbor either, even though he had not yet seen the black ships. With the summer sun beating down, it would be unpleasantly hot. Someone had mentioned that there was a pleasant path that overlooked the cliffs to the west.

He nodded and started out.

Even by the time he reached the two stone pillars that flanked the opening in the wall at the western end of the grounds for the training center, he was blotting his forehead. Across the street were several dwellings, set among a groomed parklike setting. On the south side of the northernmost one, two children were playing ring-catch. The oldest could not have been more than six or seven.

For a moment, Rahl just stood and watched as the boy spun the ring into the air and the younger boy danced around, trying to catch it with his wand. Rahl smiled. Ring-catch had never appealed to him, but that might have been because Sevien had been the only one his age living nearby, and Sevien never could catch the ring, and his throws had been even worse.

Then Rahl turned uphill and followed the sidewalk a good half kay before both the street and the walk ended in a circular paved area with three dwellings clustered around it. Between the one to the north and the one to the west was a walk. Rahl took it. The path was smoothly paved with gray stone, although the stones had been cut only about two cubits wide, and their centers were hollowed out from years of use.

Past the two houses were open meadows, with grasses almost waist high, and an occasional acacia tree. To his right, almost a kay up the gentle grassy slope, stood the black wall, featureless from that distance but not appearing all that tall. To his left, the grassy meadows sloped gently down to the edge of the black cliffs, precipices that rose from little more than a height of ten cubits immediately northwest of the harbor reportedly to more than a hundred cubits above the narrow sandy beaches just short of the black wall.

The walkway Rahl took ran almost due west until it intersected the one that followed the cliff edge. Rahl thought the cliff path ran all the way from the harbor to the wall in the north, but he had not walked it. Before long, he reached the cliff-edge walk. On the downhill side was a stone wall, also about two cubits high, but it was of a hard flagstone, and each flag was less than a full thumb length in thickness, but close to three cubits in length, and all were mortared in place.

A light and cooling breeze blew off the Gulf, but the waves seemed almost languid, with barely a whitecap in sight. Ahead of him, he saw a couple walking in the same direction as he was. They stopped, and the woman pointed out to sea. Rahl followed her gesture. There was a large sea turtle swimming through the low swells, parallel to the sheer black cliffs.

Rahl kept walking for another half kay or so. Two couples walking southward passed him, and both the men and women offered him pleasant smiles. The couple he had been following walked all the way to the end, where the path ended at the black wall. Then they turned and walked back.

Rahl stopped and stepped onto the graveled shoulder of the walk to let them by.

"Thank you," said the man, a blocky figure who carried a touch of order about him.

"You're welcome." Rahl nodded.

After they passed, he glanced out at the Gulf again. He looked for the giant sea turtle, but he didn't see it, or anything else except the various birds that swooped and then rode the air currents high and higher, before diving at the waves. A sea eagle caught a fish with its claws and carried its prey to a ledge in the cliffs. Rahl watched for a few moments more, letting the wind blow past his face, before he continued northward.

The walk ended in a stone-paved hexagon. One side ran against the cliff wall, and another against the black wall. There were two backless black-stone benches set so that whoever sat on them could look out at the Gulf.

Instead, Rahl straddled one so that he could study the wall and the order that it embodied, although he could not say that it actually emanated order.

The black wall looked to rise a good six cubits in height above the ground, and the stones were so precisely cut that Rahl could not see any noticeable difference in size, no matter how hard he looked. There was only the thinnest line of mortar between the stones.

How had the builders set order into the stones themselves?

With the sun falling on his left side, Rahl tried to let his senses just take in the wall, to feel the order. From what he could feel, the order overlapped a lesser chaos, almost in linked fashion, as if the order were both a frame and a surface, with the power of the contained chaos supporting and strengthening the framework.

But from where had the chaos come?

The heat of the sun on his face called to mind the section of *The Basis of Order* that had stated that sunlight was both like chaos and order, or had it been chaos and water? But the book had said that sunlight held both chaos and structure. Had the builders of the wall done the same with the stones?

He turned his attention back to the wall. Could he try to see how the order was structured over and around the stones? Or was it within them? Order had definitely not been stretched over sections of the wall. Rather, each stone had an order framework, and there were links between the stones.

Rahl extended what he thought was a thin line of order, just touching the link between two stones. That link felt more like a knot, but there was something "behind" it. He tried to lift or twist the link, but that didn't seem to work. Then he tried to see how the order twisted back into itself.

CRUUMMPP!

Even before he heard the explosion, Rahl felt himself being thrown backward.

Darkness flared across him.

"Ooooo . . ." He realized that he was making the sound and shut his mouth, slowly struggling to his feet amid the grass into which he'd been flung. He felt bruised all over, but he didn't seem to have any gashes or cuts. His eyes went to the wall, and he swallowed.

The last ten cubits of the wall were little more than rubble, cracked and splintered black stones frozen in a black cascade, part of which had spilled over the paved area and part of which had overflowed the low cliff wall and fallen onto the sands of the beach below. Pieces of stone were also scattered across the pavement and around both benches.

How had all that happened? He hadn't been trying to do anything, just investigating how the wall had been order-linked. He certainly hadn't meant to unlink anything.

Now what was he supposed to do?

After staring at the destruction for a time, he turned and began to walk back toward the training center. There was no point in doing anything else. Sooner or later, the magisters would discover that he had been the one, and best he tell them well before that.

He glanced back at the wall over his shoulder, once more, then tightened his lips. He didn't even want to think about what Kadara would say. Or what his latest mistake might do to his already slender chances of avoiding exile.

He kept walking.

When he got back to the training area, he went straight to the study used by the duty mages. It was closed, and Kadara was nowhere in that part of the building. He tried the mess, then the canteen. He was headed for the infirmary, and then to the weapons-training hall when he saw the magistra on a path south of him.

"Magistra!"

Kadara turned, stopped, and waited.

Rahl hurried across the grass between paths to her.

"You might have taken the walks, Rahl. I'm not going anywhere."

"I'm sorry, Magistra Kadara . . . I was trying to follow your advice . . . and I did something wrong."

"You did something wrong?" The magistra sighed. "What?"

"I *think* I undid all the order-links in a part of the black wall. The western end where it meets the walk."

"Did it fall down?"

"Ah . . . part of it exploded."

Kadara looked at Rahl intently, then asked, "Can you ride?"

"Not really."

"You're about to learn, and it's likely to be another lesson you won't enjoy. Follow me." She turned and marched along the walk, turning onto another stone walk that ran southeast.

Rahl almost had to run to catch her.

Before long, he found himself bouncing on the back of a mount that the training center duty ostler had assured him was as "gentle as an old dog in front of a fire." That might have been, but Rahl spent more than a little effort holding on to the rim of the saddle as he followed Kadara along a riding trail through the meadow grasses, seemingly halfway between the stone walkway he had followed earlier and the black wall.

When she reached the end of the riding trail—which ended a good hundred cubits short of the end of the wall and the paved space with benches—Kadara just continued riding through the grass until she reached a point a few cubits short of the benches. There she reined up, but did not dismount. She just studied the ruined end section of the wall for a time. Rahl could sense her order-probing the stones and the ground beneath the wall.

Finally, she turned in the saddle. "Tell me, as well as you can, exactly what you did." Her voice did not sound angry, but tired, almost resigned, and that disturbed Rahl far more than anger would have.

"I was sitting on the bench there." He pointed. "I could feel both the breeze and the sunlight, and I was thinking about how *The Basis of Order* said that sunlight was chaos with a structure. The black wall had a lot of order in it, and it felt sort of like the description of sunlight. I was sitting on the bench, and I was just trying to feel how it was all put together, and . . . then everything came apart, and I was thrown into the grass. When I managed to get up and look at things, the wall was like it is now."

"You didn't try to unlink or take anything apart?"

"No, magistra. I was just trying to figure out how the links worked. You and Magistra Leyla had both told me that I needed to look more into things and try to figure them out for myself."

Kadara studied Rahl. She shook her head. "You're lucky you don't have to think about shields. Otherwise, you'd be dead. Look at all those stone fragments around the benches. Do you see that arc?"

Rahl did.

"Your shields stopped them. That's the pattern." She turned her mount. "We might as well head back. Tomorrow morning, you'll need to meet with all of the mages at the training center."

Rahl managed to get his mount turned and headed back behind Kadara, thinking that her calm and resigned words were far more frightening than had been the sentence of exile to Nylan handed down by the Council.

XXVI

On eightday night, once more, Rahl did not sleep all that well, even though he had tried to read himself to sleep with *The Basis of Order*. Usually, when he tried to read it at night, he immediately fell asleep, but the order-chaos explosion at the wall kept going through his mind. All he had been trying to do was to see how the builders had constructed the wall and how they had linked the order in the way in which the chaos structured by order had actually strengthened the stones of the wall and the wall itself.

He got up earlier than normal, showered, shaved, and put on his cleanest tunic and trousers before making his way to breakfast. He didn't feel that hungry, but decided he'd best eat well with what faced him. He took the eggs scrambled in with sausage and half a small loaf of dark bread and a mug of ale. Often he had cider in the morning, but he'd felt he needed the ale with what lay ahead of him.

Perhaps since he was earlier than usual on oneday, there weren't quite as many people in the mess, and most who were wore the training grays. Because the mess wasn't that crowded, and because he really didn't want to talk to anyone, he picked the empty end of a table, but no sooner had he seated himself than Anitra got up from where she had been sitting. She made her way immediately to his table, settling down right across from him.

"Someone blew up part of the black wall in the west. Did you hear that?"

"They did?" That was a safe enough answer for Rahl.

"Engineer Selyrt said it had to be a chaos-mage. Someone else said a Hamorian warship fired a cannon at it. What do you think?"

Rahl took a swallow of ale before answering. "I don't think it could have been either. The black ships would have known if a warship were that near, and almost any magister around would have known about a chaos-wizard who was strong enough to do that."

"Then who could have done it?"

"Probably someone with the best intentions who didn't realize what would happen." That was certainly true as well.

"Doesn't that beat all." Anitra shook her head. "Engineers weren't happy. Selyrt said it would take a lot of work to repair it."

"It's a tall wall, and damage to even a small part would take work. What do you think?"

"Don't know, but I think you know more than you're saying."

"I probably am." Rahl forced a laugh. "Isn't that true of all of us?" He took a mouthful of eggs and sausage, hoping that would discourage the apprentice machinist.

"I don't know. I say what I know . . . mean what I say."

"You're more honest than most. Most people have things they'd rather not have others know."

"You have things like that?"

"Yes."

"Want to tell me?"

Rahl smiled. "I'm like everyone else in that. I'd rather not. I've done stupid things, and it's painful to remember them, let alone repeat them." He grinned. "And then, I'd feel that everyone would know I was stupider than I am."

Anitra looked at him, then nodded. "Suppose so. Wager that's true for all you mage types." Then she stood. "I'm off. Going to meet Sheyna. We always walk down to the engineering hall together."

"Have a good day."

"We will. She makes the walk fun."

Rahl couldn't help smiling for a moment. Then he ate the last of the eggs and bread and ended with a swallow of ale.

He forced himself to take his time in cleaning up his dishes and in making his way to the training hall.

Early as he was, Kadara was already there. So was Leyla.

"You can wait in the study," Leyla said. "One of us will get you when it's time for you to come before the board in the hearing chamber."

The board?

"The training center's board of magisters," added Kadara.

As the two departed, Rahl took a seat in the study. The door was left ajar, but, unlike what had happened in Land's End, when he had come before the Council, there were no guards. In fact, Rahl realized, he hadn't seen anything like the Council Guards in Nylan. There were patrollers, but they didn't seem to be the same. Was that because they were more interested in keeping law, rather than enforcing the will of whoever ran Nylan? But then, where could anyone go in Nylan and not be found before long?

Try as he might, even with his order-senses, Rahl could hear nothing.

After a time, he shifted his weight in the chair. Then he stood—and reseated himself . . . and squirmed in the chair some more. What were they saying? How difficult could it be to decide to exile him?

Finally, Leyla reappeared at the door. She just nodded.

Rahl rose and followed her down the corridor into the hearing chamber, a room even smaller than the Council chamber in Land's End. At one end was a long black table, behind which there were four chairs. Three were occupied, and the vacant one at the left end was doubtless for Leyla.

Leyla stopped several cubits short of the table and half turned so that she could address both Rahl and the other three magisters. Rahl knew Kadara and Tamryn, but not the older gray-haired magister.

"Rahl," Leyla began, "this is the board. Magister Tamryn, Magistra Kadara, and Senior Magister Myanelyt, this is Rahl." She nodded to the single chair set behind the small table that faced the longer table. "If you would be seated, Rahl."

Rahl took the seat. Somehow, with the table before him, he felt less attacked than he had in Land's End. But he still felt attacked.

Leyla slipped into the vacant seat at the long table.

There were several moments of silence.

"Most of you know Rahl," Tamryn began, "and Magister Myanelyt has reviewed the reports on his progress and been briefed on his actions and accomplishments. The reason for this hearing is that yesterday, Rahl unlocked enough order and chaos to destroy the last fifteen cubits of the black wall. Most ordermages would have difficulty doing this even after years of training. What is disturbing about this is not Rahl's strength and ability, but his apparent inability to understand and master control of the techniques behind his actions." The silver-haired magister paused, then looked directly at Rahl. "Is it fair to say that you have this difficulty?"

It wasn't at all fair, but Rahl couldn't see any point in saying that. "Magisters and magistras, it is true that I have had some problems in using order, but those problems are not quite as Magister Tamryn has stated. When I do what I know I can do, I have had no problems. The problem is that when I am trying something new or different, I can either do it or not do it, and I don't always know what will happen. Sometimes, nothing happens, and there are things that most mages seem to be able to do that I cannot." Had he said too much? He decided to stop.

Tamryn glanced to Leyla and Kadara.

Kadara nodded. "I would grant young Rahl the correction. He can do some tasks with great proficiency and little difficulty, and for some that seem minor, such as sensing the wind or what lies immediately beneath the ground, he has no ability. His problem is that his mastery is incomplete, and his efforts to obtain it could pose great dangers."

How was he supposed to learn if he couldn't at least try? First, they'd told him to try, and now that he had, they were claiming he was a danger.

The senior magister looked directly at Rahl.

Rahl met his gaze.

Myanelyt nodded. "Everything must be balanced. Our world is one where maintaining a balance is both difficult and often unfair to individuals. Your situation is one of those cases. It is not fair to send someone into exile when he has tried to follow the instructions of the magisters. On the other hand, it is not fair to subject all those in the training center and in Nylan to the dangers you present to them. In this regard, the most disturbing aspect of your latest . . . effort," continued Myanelyt, "is the fact that you had no idea how you accomplished such destruction. You are in fact the perfect natural ordermage."

From his tone and stern demeanor, Rahl was most certain that description was anything but a compliment.

"Consequently, given our responsibilities, and particularly given the limited area of Nylan, we feel that there is little alternative to some form of exile," Myanelt went on. "This is not, as most exiles are, a permanent exile. You are at heart basically a mage of order, but you lack adequate forethought, and your control of your skills is far less than the amount of power you can wield. We are charged with maintaining order here in Nylan, and we have a responsibility to all who live here. At this time, you present a danger at any time you attempt to use order in any significant fashion. Furthermore, you do not seem able to discern what uses of order are significant and what are not. Whether or not your exile is permanent depends on you. At any time you feel and can demonstrate a knowing mastery of order, you may claim passage on any Recluce ship and return to Nylan to show that mastery to the magisters."

Myanelt turned to Kadara.

"Because you show great promise," Kadara went on, "you may remain here in Nylan until you have gained greater mastery of the Hamorian language and customs and of skills in arms, and some basic information about Hamor. Remaining here to finish this training is contingent upon one condition. You are not to attempt *any* active use of order-skills during this time. You should know the difference. If you actively use order-skills, you will immediately be placed on the next available ship to Hamor."

Rahl couldn't help but wince. He certainly didn't want that to happen.

The gray-haired senior magister cleared his throat once more. "In order that you will not be thrown to the mountain cats, so to speak, if you complete your training here satisfactorily, you will be given a position as a clerk with the Merchant Association of Nylan in the Hamorian port of Swartheld. This is not a permanent position, but it will remain available to you for a full season from the time of your arrival. That time limit will not be made known to anyone, nor will the fact that you are an ordermage."

Leyla nodded, and Rahl had the feeling that provision had been her doing, for which he was grateful—or at least as grateful as he could be under the circumstances.

"I appreciate the consideration." Rahl managed to bow his head, hard as it was. They might be gentle about throwing him out, but they were still exiling him.

"Your schedule will be much the same for the next four eightdays," Kadara went on, "save that you will practice arms all afternoon until the evening meal. After the evening meal, Magister Thorl has agreed to work with you most nights on learning more about Hamor."

Rahl nodded again.

"It would be to your interest," interjected Leyla, "only to tell those here in Nylan that you are being posted to Swartheld as a clerk to learn more about Hamor. Even the director in Swartheld is only being told that you are a temporary exile and being sent to Hamor to better understand yourself and the world. That's not unusual, and he won't complain because we're paying part of your wages there."

For a moment, Rahl frowned. Why would it be to his interest not to tell everyone how poorly he was being treated? But then, if he did say that, it might be passed on, and he couldn't afford that, not if he wanted to avoid immediate exile.

XXVII

The power of a ruler rests upon three pillars: his control of his people, his control of order, and his control of chaos. To be able to control a people, a ruler must control order and chaos. To control chaos, that ruler must control order. Thus, the ruler who maintains complete control of order within his lands holds the most important tool necessary to maintain his power . . .

Ideally, a ruler should be an ordermage of the highest abilities. In the world as it is, this is seldom the case, and thus, a ruler must control such ordermages. Strong ordermages can protect themselves against chaos, but are vulnerable to other weapons and to the greatest vulnerability of all, which is poverty and want. For if they use their order-skills to obtain power without justice and mercy, in time they will lose such abilities. Since, in our rough and uncertain world, power is seldom obtained through justice and mercy, ordermages can be persuaded to serve a just ruler, even if that ruler must use means that are neither merciful nor just to those who would oppose him in order to assure justice for all . . .

Introduction
Manual of the Mage-Guards
Cigoerne, Hamor
1551 A.F.

XXVIII

Rahl evaded the blade thrust and parried. The padded end of the staff caught Zastryl's hand, and the long hand-and-a-half blade went flying.

"Enough!" Zastryl shook his head. "You know more than enough about the staff and truncheon, and trying to teach you more is getting too hard on these old bones of mine." He rubbed his hand. "Now, you're going to get to the painful part of your arms training. You're going to learn to use a blade, or blades. The sabre, the falchiona, and a blade like that one." He nodded toward the blade on the floor. "You won't be as good, and it will be painful to use them, but you need to know something about them."

Rahl wondered if Zastryl just wanted him to suffer a little.

But then, he really couldn't complain. For the past two eightdays Zastryl had been working hard to help Rahl perfect his abilities with the staff and truncheon, just as Magister Thorl had been inundating him with words and information about Hamor, both in the mornings and evenings.

What he didn't understand was why everyone was willing to spend so much time and effort preparing him for exile and yet why no one had expended a fraction of that effort in trying to teach him what would have prevented him from making the mistakes that had led to his sentence of exile.

Zastryl walked over and picked up the blade.

"Magister Zastryl!" The loud call came from the naval marine, Khaesyn, who had often been at the training hall.

"Yes, Khaesyn?" Zastryl bent and picked up the blade.

"How come you don't let Pretty Boy spar with anyone except you, Magister Zastryl?" Khaesyn made the title sound like an expletive. "Don't you think he needs some variety?" The marine swaggered across the stone floor toward the armsmaster. The other marine followed. Both were smiling broadly.

Zastryl glanced to the muscular blond man, then shrugged. "I take it that you wish to provide that variety?"

"Well . . . me or Stendyl here."

"You want to use staff or truncheon?"

"Why not blades against his staff?"

"You need the work with the truncheon," Zastryl said dryly. "After you try the truncheon, if you still want to, you can try the blade."

"That a promise, Magister Zastryl?"

"So long as no one gets hurt first."

Khaesyn grinned. "You got to keep Pretty Boy in one piece so you can deliver him to the merchants, that it?"

"Something like that."

Rahl could sense two strong emotions from Zastryl—both amusement and distaste of the marine. Neither were reflected in the armsmaster's voice.

Zastryl tossed a truncheon to Rahl and one to Khaesyn. Rahl caught his one-handed, then extended the staff to the armsmaster.

"Only to disarming or to surrender," Zastryl declared.

"That'll save someone," muttered Stendyl.

Khaesyn just grinned. "You about ready, Pretty Boy?"

Rahl dropped into the sense of being just where he was, all senses focused on Khaesyn.

Khaesyn's first move was a feint, and Rahl eased to one side, slightly, just enough not to reveal he knew it was a feint.

Then came a slash thrust, one that Rahl evaded, sensing the possible trap.

"Don't fight by running," taunted the marine.

Rahl said nothing, instead offering a lightning jab to the marine's free forearm, and pivoting away.

The bigger man charged, clearly willing to take a hit, as he brought a cut-slash that would have snapped bones had it struck.

Rahl slipped it.

The blond's arm was overextended, and he was off-balance, with all his weight on this right foot. Rahl could have snapped his knee, but instead he pivoted and yanked Khaesyn's tunic, driving the bigger man into the padded mat face-first, then jumping back.

A laughing titter came from somewhere, then cut off abruptly.

Khaesyn jumped to his feet and circled toward Rahl. "Little dancer . . . dancing doesn't win."

The marine jabbed again, and Rahl avoided the jab and delivered a slamming blow across the side of Khaesyn's hand, so that the blond's truncheon took some of the force. Khaesyn's truncheon dropped to the mat, and he looked at Rahl, who had stood back but not lowered his truncheon.

Then Khaesyn grabbed his weapon.

"Enough!" snapped Zastryl.

"I was just getting started," bellowed Khaesyn.

"You were just getting started on the way to getting yourself permanently maimed or killed. Perhaps you didn't notice, Khaesyn, but you never touched Rahl. At one point, he considered breaking your leg, but only put you on the mat. If you keep trying to kill him, at some point you're going to get hurt very badly. You might even get killed."

Rahl noticed how the magister used a touch of order to emphasize the last few words, enough so that Khaesyn finally shook his head.

The two marines turned.

"Wouldn't last a moment on a deck . . . can't dance like that . . ."

Rahl lowered the truncheon and waited.

"He's right about that, you know," said Zastryl.

"Yes, sir, but I wouldn't have waited in that kind of fight."

"I didn't think you would." Zastryl paused, then frowned before speaking again. "I have a question for you, Rahl. It's one I don't want you to answer. In fact, I forbid you to answer me. I just want you to consider it."

"Yes, ser."

"You clearly respect me. Just as clearly, you do not respect most of the other magisters. Why is that so? I'd like you to think that over."

Rahl pondered the question.

Why had Zastryl asked the question? Was it that clear that Rahl respected Zastryl? But why did he respect the armsmaster? Because Zastryl didn't hide behind words? Or didn't patronize Rahl?

"Not now," said Zastryl with a laugh. "We need to start you with a blade. That's going to be much, much more difficult, and you'll have a much harder time using it against someone like Khaesyn."

But why would Rahl have to? He could carry a truncheon anyplace he could carry a blade.

"Because," Zastryl answered the unasked question, "you may well be someplace where the only weapon is one you can take from someone else, and that is most likely to be a blade. In weapons, as in many things in life, we don't always get the choices we want."

That was becoming increasingly clear, Rahl admitted. He didn't have to like it, though.

XXIX

After the midday meal on sevenday, Rahl took a nap, then washed up and headed down the long road to the harbor. He was looking forward to the evening because Magister Thorl had invited him to the evening meal—it was dinner in Hamor, not supper—at a harbor eatery that served Hamorian food. While Rahl had avoided the harbor for a time, even after that, he had never really properly explored the area around it, and now he did finally have a few coppers to his name, not that he intended to spend them. Some few were to go to send the letter to his parents that he had yet to write, and the rest were for what he might need in Hamor.

After walking a few hundred cubits downhill, Rahl took a wider road on the right, one that seemed less traveled for all its width.

Shortly, he arrived at a small park, square in shape. Low trimmed hedges, no higher than midthigh, formed an outer wall. Almost hidden within the hedge were tiny yellow and orange flowers. Stone walks circled through the grassy area within the hedges, and carefully trimmed evergreens, with soft and bushy long needles, were set almost at random within the space, but somewhere near each of the evergreens was a stone bench.

At the west end, where there was one of the larger grassy spaces, five children played hoop tag. After watching the game briefly, Rahl crossed the park and took the street nearest the southwest corner, which looked to run close to the western end of the harbor. Instead of the haze that usually blurred the western piers, where the black ships were moored, he thought he saw almost a light shadow. He glanced skyward, but there were no clouds that could have cast such a shadow.

The black-stone houses along the street seemed far older than those along the more traveled main route to the harbor, and several, neat and well kept as they were, looked old enough to have dated back to Nylan's early days. One bore a brass plaque, but Rahl would have felt strange crossing the street just to read what it said.

Just above the harbor, he came to a walled area where the street he had followed ended at another street perpendicular to it. The wall rose at the edge of that street's sidewalk. All Rahl could see above the wall were three long slate roofs. There was no gate in the northern section of the wall, which stretched almost half a kay to his left and right.

Rahl turned west, walking a good three hundred cubits before coming to another street that ran southward to the harbor. Small neat stone dwellings stood side by side, separated by only narrow gardens, on the west side of the street, opposite the wall. Belatedly, he realized that the wall enclosed the engineering hall and its outbuildings.

When he reached the end of the wall, he looked eastward, then nodded. A large gate stood in the middle of the southern wall. He decided against walking back to view the gate, because just ahead, past a cluster of workshops, he could see what looked to be a harbor wall and the vague outline of piers beyond.

As he passed the closed doors of the workshops, still smelling of hot oils, metal, and even sawdust, he could see that the street he followed also ended at a black-stone wall. Several hundred cubits to his right, at the intersection of the street in front of the wall with another street was a guard post. It stood in front of the open iron gate manned by two soldiers or marines in black uniforms.

Since Rahl couldn't see the piers or through the gate from where he was, he turned and began to walk westward. The closer he got to the gate, the more puzzled he was because the guards bore strange-looking weapons. Were they rifles? Why would anyone bear a rifle when loading one of the clumsy weapons was slow and when even the hint of chaos would cause gunpowder to explode?

He frowned. The large barrels were of black iron. Would that contain chaos? Still, the barrel seemed too large for a rifle. In addition to the weapon each guard bore, there were racks beside them that held similar weapons.

He refrained from shaking his head, but he couldn't help but wonder what the weapons were, if they weren't rifles. He glanced through the gate but managed to keep walking. Afternoon sunlight fell on the piers, and yet there was a shadow of some sort—an order shadow!

Rahl had to remind himself not to use any active order investigation. He definitely wasn't ready to go to Hamor. Even so, he could sense the solidity of several vessels at the piers, although he could not see them with his eyes—clearly some sort of black magery. He wished he dared explore that, but shook his head. *Not now.*

Ahead of him was another black-stone wall.

He shrugged and turned, walking steadily, but not hurriedly, back east-ward, staying on the sidewalk across the street from the guards. He could feel their eyes on him, but he did not hesitate. Before long, the wall to his right made a right angle into the harbor. He glanced at it, but since it ran well into the water, he could not see the vessels tied at the piers.

He had no doubt that they were the feared black ships, but why did they need to be hidden? Especially in Nylan? Was that because so many vessels visited Nylan and because it would be easier to study them closely when they were moored? Or was it to add to their mystique?

Rahl laughed silently. So much for seeing the black ships.

There was a wide expanse of water, a good half kay, if not more, between the walled mooring of the black ships and the next set of harbor piers. Only a small fishing boat was moored on the west side of the first pier, clearly battened down and empty. On the east side was a larger schooner, and crewmen were carrying crates of fish to a wagon on the pier.

Rahl didn't want to see any more of the piers, not for the moment. He turned to his left, away from the water, at the next lane. Immediately, he found himself walking up between the small shops that lined both sides of the way. The first offered scarves of all sorts, in more shades and colors than he could have dreamed possible.

The next held leather goods—vests, belts, scabbards, sturdy belt wal-lets, and even small decorative leather boxes, some of them gilded. Then came a shop filled with decorative brasswork.

Rahl took his time, looking, because that was all he could do with his lim-ited coins. Even so, he had far from explored more than a few square blocks around the harbor, or so it seemed, looking through shops, then going to the seawall and taking in vessels from Hamor and Candar, as well as from Nordla and Austra, and viewing more goods in more shops, before he realized it was getting close to the evening bell, when he was to meet Magister Thorl.

He didn't know exactly where he was, but he recalled the directions that the magister had given him, based on starting at the market square. He had to walk quickly, but it wasn't that far, he discovered, and he reached the bright green-and-yellow awning of the eatery that was less than two blocks from the market square before the magister did.

At least, he didn't see Thorl when he stepped inside.

A slender graying man dressed in spotless khaki trousers and shirt, with a crimson vest edged in silver thread, turned to Rahl and offered an apologetic smile. "You wish a table, ser? I fear that we cannot . . ."

"I'm supposed to meet Magister Thorl here."

"Ah . . . ha . . . he said you would be here. I apologize, ser. This way . . ." The vested man turned.

Rahl followed him to a corner table under a brass lamp suspended from the beamed ceiling by a large brass chain. The table held two people and one vacant chair. With Magister Thorl was Deybri.

"Ah . . . good evening," Rahl offered.

Thorl gestured expansively to the empty chair. "I did not mean to upset you, Rahl, but Deybri is my niece, and since you two get along, I thought it would be more enjoyable with three of us."

His niece? Thorl didn't look that much older than Deybri. "Oh, I'm not at all upset. I'm surprised, but pleasantly surprised. Very pleasantly surprised."

Deybri laughed. "You're gallant, but it's nice to know that you also meant it."

Rahl slipped into the chair.

Thorl was speaking to the man who had escorted Rahl to the table. "The leshak with the pashtakis for the first course, and then . . ."

"Your uncle," murmured Rahl to Deybri, "I didn't realize . . ."

"Talents for handling order—or chaos—do tend to run in families. You'll find that many of the magisters and magistras and healers are related," Deybri explained. "That can be a problem."

"Oh, because people don't like consorting with those who have order-talents? And those who do can only find relatives?"

She nodded.

"Your timing was excellent, Rahl," began the magister in Hamorian. "We had only been seated a few moments. I wanted you to have some understanding of Hamorian food. That was Kysant himself who brought you here. I asked him to look out for you. His place is the only true Hamorian-style eatery in Nylan. His grandfather was the cook on a Hamorian warship. He claims it was the fleet commander's vessel. I've had my doubts about that, but the cooking is authentic."

Rahl nodded, wondering how Thorl might have known that.

"Uncle Thorl spent several years in Atla," Deybri added, if in halting Hamorian.

Rahl almost laughed ruefully. When those around him could sense what he felt, before—and whether—he expressed it or not, the whole nature of conversation changed. "This takes getting worked . . . used to, I mean," he replied, also in Hamorian.

"You will do well in Hamor," Deybri continued in Hamorian. "You have no accent. I do."

"I learned from your uncle and the children."

"Actually, he does have an accent, but it will work to his advantage," said Thorl. "He speaks as I do, and that will tell people he is from Atla. That way, he will be considered Hamorian—but excused for not knowing all that he might about Swartheld."

At that moment, a server appeared, wearing the same khakis as the owner had but a pale green vest. He set three goblets on the table and a large pitcher. Then came a circular bone porcelain platter with scalloped edges, which he placed in the center of the dark oiled wood of the table. On the platter were fried folded shapes that were roughly octagonal.

Thorl poured a clear liquid from the pitcher, half-filling each goblet. "Rahl, you must taste the leshak—it's a wine from greenberries and white grapes. Drink it in moderation. It's more powerful than it tastes."

Rahl lifted the goblet, noting that the wine had the slightest of green tinges. He took a small sip. The wine was smooth and cool, with a taste that was unlike anything he'd ever had. Perhaps the closest might have been a cross of pearapple, green-apple juice, with a hint of honey, and an even tinier hint of pine.

"Although they use greenberries liberally, the taste is totally unlike the vaunted greenberry brandy of the north," Thorl added.

Rahl had heard of the brandy, but no scrivener could ever have afforded it, nor could any of his friends or acquaintances.

"The pashtakis are a favorite and common dish everywhere in Hamor. They are spiced crab and mushroom filling inside a crispy fried pastry. The ones in Hamor are sweeter, because the southern crabs are more . . ." At that point, Thorl used a word that Rahl had never heard and could not discern from context.

"More what, ser?"

"Juicy and tasty . . . succulent."

Rahl concentrated on holding the word.

"These are still good, and perhaps better," the magister went on. "They aren't as likely to be cloying if you eat too many." Thorl paused. "Cloying . . . too sickeningly sweet."

"Thank you."

Rahl sampled one of the pashtakis. The appetizer almost melted in his mouth after a single bite into it, leaving a piquant taste that was neither mushroom nor crab, yet both. "Good."

"I thought you might like them," replied Magister Thorl. "By the way, meals are far more social in Hamor than in Recluce. The midday meal is luncheon, and light, but an occasion for planning or business. The evening meal is late, well after twilight, and much more substantive—solid—if you will."

"Do men and women eat together in public?" asked Rahl. "I had heard . . ."

"Only if they are consorted, or if a woman is accompanied by a male relative. Now . . . women can eat together in public, and groups of men and women can eat together at the same place if they are at separate tables. Among families or in private, it does not matter. Only the appearances matter."

Rahl almost laughed. That sounded like Land's End.

"That may be because their customs are more directly Cyadoran, as is the language itself, which is decadent Cyadoran mingled with High Temple and fermented by time. Also, certain subjects are not discussed in public. They are not forbidden, but a sign of bad manners. One does not discuss family difficulties, nor order or chaos, or anything personal about the Emperor . . ."

Rahl listened intently.

Abruptly, Thorl broke off as the server reappeared and removed the platter that had held the pashtakis and replaced their platters with clean ones before placing two serving dishes before them. One held sheets of very thin pan bread, seemingly barely thicker than parchment, and the other long light brown cylinders.

"Biastras. Each slice of meat is braised in spiced oil just enough to brown it on each side, then rolled around sweet peppers that have been marinated—soaked in a mixture of special oils and spices for days," Thorl explained to Rahl, "and each tube is braised just enough to warm the peppers. Then the meat is dipped in an egg and corn flour mixture and fried briefly in very hot oil." After a moment, he added, "They actually make this with marinated wild horse meat in the far east of Hamor. I think it tastes better with horse meat than with beef or lamb, but you can find all three kinds of biastras."

Rahl took a small bite of the end of the cylinder. Even the small mouthful left his mouth and nose burning. Sweat popped out on his forehead.

"I think I forgot to mention that they can be very spicy." Thorl grinned.

Deybri laughed softly, then turned. "That was cruel, Uncle."

"Somewhat, but had I told Rahl how hot it was, he would not have tried it." He looked at Rahl. "Have a bite of the bread. That will cool the taste more than leshak or anything you drink. Too many sailors have ended up in the ironworks or the quarries for the Great Highway because they thought leshak would cool their throats." He laughed jovially. "It will, but the cost can be rather exorbitant. High," he explained, seeing Rahl's momentary puzzlement at the unfamiliar word.

"Another way to eat them," suggested Deybri, "is to wrap them in the thin bread and eat bread and biastras together. That's what I do."

Rahl followed Deybri's example and found that the taste was merely close to unbearably spicy rather than intolerable.

"Burping or slurping . . . or smacking one's lips," Thorl went on, "is considered very common and bad manners . . ."

As he ate carefully, Rahl continued to listen. He also only sipped the leshak.

Before long, the biastras and bread had vanished, and the server placed another platter before them.

Magister Thorl gestured. "Khouros. Two cinnamon pastry tubes—one inside the other and tied together with a thin layer of honey. The inner tube is filled with sweet creamy cheese."

Rahl enjoyed the dessert greatly, perhaps because he'd missed true sweets and perhaps because the khouros removed all the aftertastes of the spicy Hamorian dishes.

When he finished, he looked at the magister and inclined his head. "Thank you so much. This is the best meal I've had since I came to Nylan, and certainly with the best company." He turned to Deybri. "With the exception of those I've had with you, but neither the food nor the other company was so good."

Thorl laughed. "That was the best sentence you've uttered in Hamorian, and a perfect conclusion to a meal."

Deybri just shook her head.

Thorl turned to Rahl. "I'd be most appreciative if you would walk Deybri home. It's not that far."

"Uncle . . ." Deybri half protested.

"Humor me, if you would. I have certain matters to take care of with Kysant."

"Of course."

Rahl rose, scarcely before Deybri did. He inclined his head to the magister once more. "Thank you again."

"It was my pleasure."

Neither Deybri nor Rahl spoke until they were out on the street.

"Which way?" Rahl asked.

She laughed. "You don't have to speak Hamorian any longer."

"Oh . . . I'm sorry."

"Uncle said you had a gift for languages. You certainly do." Deybri gestured. "Up the main road. We'll turn east a little less than a kay along."

"Did he teach you Hamorian?"

"He tried. I spent a little time, just a few eightdays, in Atla years ago."

"I can't imagine you were exiled."

"No, but the magisters felt I needed to see what happened when only strength of some sort ordered a land. So I was sent as a healer to work with a trading company. I was ready to come back to Nylan after a few days . . . and very grateful to be allowed to."

Rahl couldn't help but shiver at the implications of her words. He remained silent for a time as they walked uphill.

"You have great promise, Rahl . . ."

"But?"

She did not respond immediately, as if thinking what exactly to say in reply. Then she pointed. "Along this lane."

"How far?"

"Three or four hundred cubits. It's not that far from Kadara's dwelling. The original Kadara, that is."

"What were you going to say?" he asked.

"You have great promise," she repeated, "but you need to think and feel beyond yourself without prompting. Especially to feel."

The dwelling before which she stopped was small, no more than fifteen cubits in width, with a door in the middle. "It was once a small barn, but I don't need much space, and it's very quaint."

"I'm sure it's lovely inside."

"I think so, but we'll forgo your finding out tonight. You're sweet at heart, and someday you'll understand the difference between thinking you know what you feel and knowing with all your being what you feel."

"Is that a promise?" Rahl replied lightly, although her words had somehow burned in a way that he could not have explained.

"No. I can't make promises for you." Deybri smiled, opening the door. "Good night, Rahl. Thank you for walking me home."

"I enjoyed it." He offered a smile, then stepped back and let her close the door.

Despite their age difference, Deybri was interested in him, but she wasn't going to let him get closer to her, or herself to him. Was it just because he was being exiled? No . . . there was something else he was missing, something beyond the words about feeling.

But why couldn't people just say what they meant?

He turned and began to walk back toward the training center and his own bed.

XXX

For almost an eightday, Zastryl had drilled Rahl with various blades, forcing him to learn the basic moves. Holding the blades had been uncomfortable, and more tiring than using a staff or truncheon, even though the ironbound staff was heavier than all but the big two-handed broadsword. But Rahl didn't have any difficulty handling the discomfort. He did wonder why Zastryl insisted he spend so much time practicing by himself. When Rahl had asked why, the answer had sobered him.

"So long as you just practice moves, it'll be slightly painful to most of you black types. Once I make you spar, it's going to hurt a lot. There's no point in hurting you while you're learning the basics. That would just slow things down, and you don't need that."

Then, on threeday, Zastryl appeared with another weapon and handed the scabbard and sheath to Rahl. "This is a falchiona. It's the most common blade in Hamor. It's a cross between a sabre and a falchione, with a few nasty touches." The armsmaster smiled. "The naval marines call it a bitch blade. It has a few peculiarities you won't find anywhere except Hamor. For most of the length of the blade, like a sabre, it only has one edge. But from the tip back for the first hand, both sides are edged. The means you can slash from either direction at the tip, but you don't sacrifice the strength of the body of the blade. It's harder to handle well. That's why we didn't start with it." He nodded. "Draw it."

Rahl suppressed a wince as he did. The shimmering Hamorian steel felt evil, far more so than the other blades he'd handled.

"You can sheathe it. I'm going to give you a practice blade like it. There aren't any edges, and you'll need to wear some padded armor while you spar with Aleasya. Even without the edges, a blow can break an arm or fingers just like that."

Rahl handed the falchiona back to Zastryl.

In turn, Zastryl extended another blade, less menacing, but just as heavy and more lifeless. "Just practice your basic moves with it, while I get Aleasya and the gear you'll need."

Rahl took a stance on the stone floor and began to practice with the substitute blade. It was better balanced than he'd thought, yet he felt somehow off-balance using it, even though he could tell that, physically, he was not.

After some time, Zastryl returned with Aleasya. He carried what looked like a padded coverall over one arm. She wore formfitting black, although Rahl thought he sensed some sort of light armor under the shirt-tunic, and held a practice blade.

"Have you met Aleasya?" asked the armsmaster.

"We've met a few times." Rahl inclined his head to her.

"Let's get you into the coverall," Zastryl said.

Rahl was feeling more than a little warm in the coverall but suspected he might well need it. As broad-shouldered and muscular as Aleasya was, and as a former ship's champion, whatever that was, Rahl knew he'd be fortunate to escape with only a few bruises.

"Aleasya will begin with some of the standard openings," Zastryl offered. "Do your best to stop them, but don't worry. Right now, she won't carry through."

"Yes, ser." Facing the weapons trainer, Rahl felt chaos, almost as if it were trying to climb up from the blade through the hilt into his hand and arm. Every time he lifted the blade, a twinge of fire streaked up his arm. He could feel the sweat beading on his forehead, but the heat was coming from the blade and his struggles with it, not from the warmth of the partly armored coverall.

Aleasya began with a quick exploratory thrust, one that Rahl managed to deflect.

From there, it got harder, as much because Rahl had to fight the chaos-pain of handling the weapon as much as he had to fight Aleasya. At a pause, he blotted his forehead.

"Are you all right?" asked Zastryl.

"So far. Just let me have a moment." Could he use his shields to block the chaos from striking back up the blade at him? If he could just concentrate on Aleasya . . .

He thought—and abruptly, the pain of the chaos vanished. He could sense it, just below his hand, but now he was free to concentrate fully on learning and using the falchiona. With each pass, he began to sense more and understand more about the blade and what lay behind the moves.

Zastryl began to offer quick comments in between the short encounters where Aleasya demonstrated various attacks and maneuvers before using them.

"Most of the time," the armsmaster called from the side, "a lead from the edge side is a feint. But not always, especially if the aim is to disable or disarm you."

"That's a setup for an arm slash . . ."

"Don't drop the blade tip!"

When Zastryl called a halt, sweat was pouring from Rahl's forehead, and he felt light-headed, almost unsteady. He'd certainly worked harder and longer with the staff before without such effort tiring him so much, but he could have been getting overheated in the heavy coverall.

He began to unfasten the padded and sweaty coverall.

"I've never seen a mage type handle a blade that well, or learn it so quickly." Aleasya glanced to Zastryl. "Have you?"

"No. He's done something." Zastryl began to walk toward the pair.

As if a giant wave had risen from a shore where he stood, Rahl could feel his shields crumpling under that unseen wave and redness rising around him. He could feel himself falling . . . forward into reddish blackness.

When he could see again, he was on his back looking up at the beamed ceiling of the arms-training building. Hovering over him was someone, but for several moments, the image was a swirl of indistinct color. Then he could make out the face of Kelyssa, the younger healer.

"Kelyssa?"

With that single word, Rahl's head felt as though it were being hit with a heavy mallet and splitting apart, and his eyes burned.

"What did . . . you can tell us later. How do you feel? Can you see me?"

"Yes. My eyes burn, but I can see you."

"And you can hear?"

"Yes."

"Can you feel your fingers and toes?"

"They hurt, but I can feel them."

"Wiggle them."

Rahl did.

"Now move your arms and legs, just a little, and gently."

Rahl could sense a reassuring aura of black order from the healer as she probed his body. Then she straightened. "I think he'll be all right, but we ought to watch him at the infirmary for a while."

"Do we need to get a cart for him?" asked Zastryl.

"Just let him rest for a while, and I'll be able to walk him over there. I think he should be fine in a day or so, but I'll have Deybri look at him to make sure." Kelyssa turned back to Rahl. "I'm going to help you sit up."

Gingerly, Rahl rolled to one side, then sat up on the hard stone. At that point, he realized that the coverall had been stripped from him. He glanced around and saw the padded armor lying in a heap several cubits away.

"They thought you'd had a heat bout," said the healer.

After a short while, Rahl finally got to his feet. Kelyssa insisted that he take her arm as they walked from the weapons-training building toward the infirmary. Each step hurt, and Rahl felt as though he'd been beaten with a staff. Yet he hadn't taken a single blow from Aleasya.

Once he was in the infirmary, Kelyssa had him sit in a padded chair and sip ale. The ale helped with the light-headedness, but not with soreness. While the throbbing in his head subsided, it did not vanish so much as retreat into a muted dull pounding.

He had just about finished the beaker of ale when Deybri appeared.

She glared at him. "That was even stupider than taking on the black wall. You could have killed yourself, you know?"

Rahl just looked at her. From shielding himself from chaos?

"I went and talked to Zastryl and Aleasya first. You have to have blocked yourself."

"I just shielded myself from the chaos in the falchiona," Rahl protested.

"Weren't you told not to use active order?"

"But shields aren't active . . ."

She shook her head. "Didn't Kadara and Leyla keep warning you about the dangers of trying things when you don't have an understanding of how it works and why? You couldn't block chaos from the blade. There wasn't any actual chaos in the blade. That's the way your mind interprets the potential chaos of using a blade and the disorder that use causes. Your shield was actually fighting yourself, as well as whoever you were sparring against."

"Aleasya," Rahl admitted.

"Why did you do it?"

"Because it hurt to use the blade and fight the chaos—or what I thought was chaos—and I wasn't learning and being very good at it."

The healer snorted. "You're an ordermage. You're not supposed to be that good. They just want you to be able to put up enough of a front with a blade so that you can buy time to use order. You're supposed to learn how to handle it *with* the pain. Didn't they tell you that?"

"Not exactly. Magister Zastryl said that it would be painful and that I might have to use them . . ." His words trailed off.

"For what?"

"To keep people off me for a short time," Rahl admitted. Still, Zastryl hadn't been anywhere near as clear as Deybri had been. He hadn't told Rahl that one of the points of the exercise was to deal with the pain. Why couldn't people be clear? He was having a hard enough time learning what he had to learn without trying to figure out what they really meant. He was more than a little tired of guessing.

Deybri shook her head. "You'll be all right. Go over to the mess and eat—as much as you can without getting sick. Then take it easy and get a good night's sleep. No sparring against anyone for two days. When you resume, don't do what you just did—even if it hurts like the demon's whiteness. You might not recover a second time."

That worried Rahl more than anything she'd said. But, even with the worry, he was also getting angry again because he wouldn't have gotten so close to killing himself if he hadn't been getting incomplete answers or nonexistent answers to his questions. The magisters and magistras acted as if everything were spelled out in *The Basis of Order*, and whenever he tried to get an answer, he was either chastised or told to find it out himself . . . and then, when he had attempted to discover something on his own, they'd declared him a danger to all Nylan.

"Rahl . . . that's life."

"What?"

"You're getting angry again because things haven't been explained to your satisfaction. Do you think that people are going to explain everything that seems evident to them just to make you comfortable? You have the ability to think. Your problem is that, because certain skills come to you easily, you just use them without thinking about them or what they might do to you or to others."

"Wait a moment," he replied. "Let me put it a different way. You and all the others here are perfectly willing to explain things endlessly to those who have few abilities and take a long time to learn things. Yet you're not willing to make a similar effort in explaining the implications of what I can do. Just because I'm able to do things, everyone seems to think that I should know what happens next."

"That attitude is exactly why you're being exiled," Deybri said calmly, almost sadly. "You have enough order-talent that most ordermages would give an arm or a leg for that ability. They've worked for years to master and understand what they do. You can do things easily and with minimal effort, and then you complain and get angry when the magisters expect you to spend some time and effort thinking before you act. And this is another time when you got into trouble doing what you were told not to do. No . . . I won't say much about it, and I will say, if asked, that you honestly didn't understand that shields were active order-magery. It's also the last time I'll help you if you use one single bit of active ordermagery." A faint, almost rueful smile appeared. "Now . . . go get something to eat."

Rahl set the not-quite-finished beaker of ale on the side table and rose from the chair. "Thank you."

As he left, he was still angry, if not at Deybri. At least she offered some explanations.

XXXI

On fiveday morning, Rahl found himself in the small study again, wondering if he was being sent off as a result of his problems with the falchiona, or if he'd made some other mistake. Tamryn sat across the table from Rahl.

"Yes, ser?" asked Rahl politely.

"I understand you had a little trouble the other day. This isn't about that. This is about your assignment in Swartheld . . ."

Exile merely an assignment? Rahl had his doubts about that.

"You'll be leaving in about an eightday," Tamryn went on. "Until then, you'll be working every afternoon at the Merchant Association building down in the harbor. You'll wear the standard clerk's attire. We'll take a moment for you to pick that up at the wardrobing building—and a pack for your clothing and gear. From now on, you'll wear the clerk's garb from breakfast until you're dismissed by Ser Varselt. He's the managing director in Nylan."

"Yes, ser."

"And Aleasya and Magister Zastryl have agreed to spend a session with you every evening after meals. They did mention something about not cheating on pain." Tamryn smiled. "There's a price for everything, Rahl, and it's either paid fairly when due or with interest and penalties later."

Tamryn made it sound like order-skills were trade goods subject to usury.

"Now head over to wardrobing. Elina's already got your garb ready for you. Wear it while you're with Magister Thorl as well. The association of Hamorian with the garb will help when you get to Swartheld."

How that might be, Rahl couldn't imagine, but he didn't doubt Tamryn on that. "Yes, ser. Is there anything else I should know?"

"Not right now." Tamryn stood.

So did Rahl, bowing politely to the silver-haired magister.

Tamryn left, and Rahl followed him out, then headed for the wardrobing shop.

After he picked up the garments, he hurried back to his chamber and changed, leaving the empty canvas pack on the bed. The clerk's garb consisted of light brown trousers, darker than the khaki worn by Kysant and his staff at the eatery, a light tunic of a darker brown, with three-quarter-length sleeves, and an even lighter undertunic.

Magister Thorl only nodded in acknowledgment when Rahl slipped into his session.

Tamryn appeared, as the magisters often did, just as Rahl had finished rinsing his dishes at the mess. "We'll take a cart down today, but you'll have to eat more quickly—if you're walking down there and if you expect to be there in a timely fashion."

"Yes, ser."

Rahl followed Tamryn to the cart that waited outside.

The magister drove, and Rahl sat on the narrow seat beside Tamryn as the cart moved downhill behind a dun mare.

"The more you can learn at the Merchant Association, the better you'll do in Swartheld," Tamryn observed. "It's very different from either Land's End or Swartheld. As I'm certain Magister Thorl has indicated, the laws are far more stringent. If you break a minor law, you might get off with a flogging. If you break a major law, you'll end up in the quarries, the ironworks, or dead. Oh . . . one of the major laws is a restriction on use of order- or chaos-skills unless you are registered with the mage-guards. As an outlander, you can have the talent. That's not forbidden. Using it is unless you're registered. Citizens of Hamor with any magely talents must register. Minor uses in one's own dwelling don't count. Almost all active uses in public do."

Rahl almost swallowed. Magister Thorl had only told him to be very careful and scrupulous in obeying the laws. "Is there anything else that I'm likely to stumble into through ignorance?"

"The Hamorian Codex is based on that of Cyador."

Rahl didn't have the faintest idea what Tamryn meant, but before he could say so, the magister went on.

"That means that once you're taken into custody by patrollers or by the mage-guards, you're assumed to be guilty, and you have to prove that you're not. That's a very good reason not to even look like you're breaking the laws."

To Rahl, that didn't sound all that different from Land's End.

"How do they look at use of order- and chaos-skills?"

"If they're used as the Emperor wishes, that's acceptable, and those who serve him directly are respected. Only outlanders or healers are allowed to serve others."

Rahl wasn't sure what else to ask, and Tamryn seemed reluctant to volunteer more on the rest of the ride down into the harbor area.

The Merchant Association building was set slightly east and north of the main shipping piers, but on an avenue that ran along the seawall. The second-story windows were narrow but tall, while those on the ground level were high and narrow. The oiled door was of dark oak, a gold so deep it was almost brown. Tamryn eased the cart to a halt, vaulted off the seat, and tied the mare to an iron post painted black. "We won't be long, lady," he said to the mare.

Then he walked toward the door, which he opened, and stepped inside. Rahl followed and closed the door behind himself. They stood in an open area bordered on all sides by oak counters as old and as oil-polished as the front door.

Two clerks sat on high-backed stools behind the counters, whose surfaces were just slightly higher than a dining table, one on the right, the other on the left. Beside each were various stacks of paper. The stool at the counter opposite the door was vacant. Farther to the rear of the open chamber was a paneled wall, and in the center was an archway, off which at intervals were several doors.

From one of those hurried a tall but round-faced man so bald on top that his remaining silver-blond hair formed a furry ring around a tanned and shining scalp. Handlebar mustaches filled the space between his upper lip and nose and flowed out almost to his ears. "Magister Tamryn . . . you caught me checking a cargo reconciliation."

Tamryn nodded politely. "We did not mean to interrupt." He inclined his head. "This is Rahl, Ser Varselt. As we explained, he was trained as a scrivener and has a good head for neatness and is capable with figures. He knows High and Low Temple, as well as having a working and speaking knowledge of Hamorian."

"He'll be most useful here for now, but Master Shyret in Swarthold will be most pleased. A scrivener with a good and working knowledge of Hamorian—we don't see many of those. No, we don't."

Rahl could sense the veiled curiosity from the two clerks.

"He'll be available every afternoon, starting now until his ship comes in," Tamryn said.

"We'll have plenty of work for him," Varselt promised, "that we will."

"Then I'll leave Rahl in your capable hands." Tamryn bowed, turned, and departed.

Varselt gestured toward the vacant stool. "For now, that will be yours, Rahl. Gorot and Wulff will instruct you on how each form is to be filled out. Now in Swartheld, some of the forms—the ones that go to the Emperor's tariff enumerators—must be filled out in Hamorian, but here the tariff declarations are done in High Temple. Not that there's really much use of words—mostly figures, but they must be precise. No smudges. No . . . no smudges at all." Varselt bobbed his head cheerfully, and his ample jowls shook as well.

Rahl made his way to the stool, undecided about whether to climb onto it or wait.

"Take a seat. Take a seat," said Varselt jovially. "Look over the forms. You'll get a smudged and crumpled one from the ship's master or supercargo, and your task is to provide three fair copies, one for the ship, one for the association, and a final one for the tariff collectors. They'll check the cargo against the copy the ship gives you, but they'll want both the one they seal and a clean copy." The managing director nodded to Gorot. "I need to get back to that reconciliation. Take him through the declaration first."

The thin-faced Gorot hopped off his stool and walked to where Rahl sat. The clerk set a partly filled-out printed form on the counter.

At that moment, Rahl could definitely see a reason for the use of Magister Sebenet's printing press, especially with three copies for every vessel.

"This is what the straight declaration of cargo looks like," Gorot began. "Two sections, one for everything off-loaded and one for everything on-loaded. There has to be one for every port the ship makes. Of course, we only have to do the ones here in Nylan, but sometimes we have to make copies for ports where there's no association representative. Purser or supercargo has to put down everything that has more than a token value. Captain has to sign it. Right now, a token value means more than a silver . . . but that doesn't mean that a trader can get away with not listing a keg of nails or spikes because a single spike is less than a copper. Token value applies to the units in which a cargo is usually traded. Cloth-yards for fabric, kegs for nails, amphorae for oils . . . you get the idea. The cargo declaration is not the same as the manifest. The captain's manifest is usually kept by the purser or supercargo, and it's a listing of all cargo carried from port to port. There's a separate manifest for each leg of a trading voyage, and at the end, we have to go through them and reconcile the declarations with the manifests. You probably won't do many reconciliations in Hamor because the home port of all Association vessels is here in Nylan. If you do, of course, everything should balance."

Wulff looked around and, seeing no one near, laughed. "Never does. Never. But Ser Varselt and the other directors don't say anything if the difference is a few golds or less. More than that, they call the captain in. Bad business, that. Captains know it, too. Sometimes, they'll sneak in with a different declaration."

"And?" asked Rahl cautiously.

"You got to look at 'em and decide. Was the original right, or is the one he holds right?"

Rahl could see that might be a problem for most clerks, even if they could tell.

"If it's a lot, you just tell 'em you can't do it, because Ser Varselt or the directors'll bring in a mage. Most captains won't try it unless they made a mistake on the original and are just trying to set it right. Thing is, they got to make the coins balance, too."

Rahl hadn't even considered this side of trading.

XXXII

Rahl followed the routine dutifully for more than an eightday, still trying to perfect Hamorian in the morning and working at the Merchant Association in the afternoon. Almost immediately, Wulff and Gorot had given him the job of making the second and third fair copies of the various forms. Even so, after just a few days, he had mastered the standard terms and usages in the most-used forms.

What was far more difficult was the arms training with Zastryl and Aleasya. Some evenings, his entire body felt as though it were on fire when he collapsed into his narrow bed, even as he improved enough so that they only struck him infrequently. He did discover that the chaos-pain was far less if he only defended himself rather than attempting any sort of attack.

He also finally got around to something else he'd been putting off, and that was writing a letter to his parents. He didn't really want to tell them his exile was permanent, and there was a chance it might not be. So he just said that he was being sent as a clerk to Swartheld, and how he did there would determine what might happen next. He added that he'd been learning Hamorian and that he'd received more training with staff and truncheon, as well as instruction in his new duties. He told them not to worry and that he would write as he could. What else could he really say?

On and off, he looked for Deybri at meals, but never saw her. Was she avoiding him?

Even Anitra no longer plopped herself at his table in the mess, and it had been eightdays since he'd seen Khalyt around.

Then, on sevenday, Kadara found him on his way to the evening meal.

"The *Legacy of Diev* ported this afternoon. That's the ship that you'll be taking to Swartheld. You'll report to Captain Liedra before midmorning tomorrow. As a clerk of the Nylan Merchant Association, you'll be expected to help the purser in minor ways, copying manifests or cargo declarations. Nothing you shouldn't be familiar with by now . . . You can take the gray trousers, but I'd leave the gray tunics. Those won't be that welcome in Swartheld."

"What if I take one—just for the voyage? Not to wear in Swartheld."

Kadara actually grinned. "Might not be a bad idea. Especially since you've not been seafaring." The grin faded. "Don't be late."

"No, magistra."

With that, Kadara was gone.

After making his way to the serving table and filling a bowl and taking some dark bread, Rahl made his way to the unoccupied corner of a table in the mess. He sat down and looked at the fish stew over noodles. He ate one bite, then another, before taking a swallow of ale. He looked to the west-facing windows and the white-golden light slanting through them. *Tomorrow?*

He'd known he'd have to leave Nylan, but he hadn't expected it to happen quite so suddenly. He was being sent to Hamor all because he didn't fit what the magisters expected of a beginning mage. Do it our way, or be on your way. That was what it amounted to, and it wasn't as though he hadn't tried. He had tried, but sometimes things just didn't follow their precious *Basis of Order.* Of what use were rules and precepts when they didn't apply? And what wisdom was there in denying that sometimes the rules weren't applicable?

The problem was that it didn't matter what he thought or what made sense. The magisters and the Council had the power to exile him, and he couldn't do anything about it that wouldn't make his own situation even worse.

He slowly finished his meal.

Then, after rinsing his dishes and washing up, in the light of early twilight, Rahl walked downhill, then eastward to Deybri's small house.

He hoped she happened to be there, although he saw no light behind the curtains in the front window. Still . . . he rapped on the ancient oak door, its surface golden brown and showing a tracery of age lines.

There was no response, and he rapped again. He could sense someone there, and he thought it was Deybri.

Finally, the door opened halfway, and Deybri stood there wearing trousers and a short-sleeved collared shirt. She was barefoot. "You would know that I was here."

"I came to say good-bye."

"When are you leaving?"

"Tomorrow, I think. I have to be on the ship in the morning. It might be oneday or twoday. I don't know how long it takes them to off-load and on-load."

"Usually a day, sometimes two, usually not more than three."

Rahl was puzzled by the combination of indifferent tone and the concern lying behind her almost flat words. After a moment, he said, "You've been interested in me, but you've kept me at a distance. It's not just because I'm younger, is it?"

"No." Deybri smiled sadly. "It's because you won't come back." She held up a hand to forestall any interruption. "If you fail to find what you need to discover, you won't be back. If you do, Nylan will be too small and confining for you, and you won't be back." She shrugged. "I'm not someone who does things by half. Or in smaller fractions. For some people, every small bite of life can be tasted by itself. For me, it can't. So I pass on some sweet morsels because the memory of their taste would turn bitter."

Rahl stood there, thinking about what she said.

"You don't look back, Rahl. That's not in your nature. I'd wager you scarcely even think about the girls you liked or loved in Land's End. I'm not blaming you. You are what you are. Each of us is. You live for the now and the future. I live from the past into the present and don't dwell on a future that I can only experience when it arrives each morning. That's also why you won't be back. The past has no hold on you." She bent forward and kissed him gently on the lips. "Perhaps this will remain with you for a time." Then she stepped back. "Good night and good-bye, Rahl."

He just watched as she closed the door, so gently that it did not even *click.*

Then he turned and headed back toward the training center . . . for his last night there, thinking about her words. "The past has no hold on you." No hold on him?

XXXIII

On oneday morning, Rahl was finishing breakfast at the mess—his last breakfast there, he reflected, when Aleasya stepped through the south door and walked over to his table. "I brought you something. It's from Zastryl and me." She extended a truncheon, along with a half scabbard for the weapon.

Rahl stood, then just looked for a moment. The truncheon was of lorken, the hard black wood that resisted even black iron and steel, with a black-iron band just below the swordlike haft. Simple as it looked, Rahl could tell that the workmanship was outstanding.

"Go ahead. Take it. It's yours."

Rahl wanted more than anything to grasp it. "How can I? It's too good for me. I couldn't . . ."

Aleasya smiled. "You have to. We had it made for you. Hamor is no place for an unarmed person."

Finally, Rahl took the weapon, turning it in his hand. "Thank you. I can't tell you . . . how much . . . this means."

Aleasya beamed.

Rahl could tell she was pleased.

Then the smile faded. "Zastryl asked me to tell you something else. He said it was important, and that you should know it. First, don't forget to take your copy of *The Basis of Order.*"

"I won't." Even though he was often doubtful of the book's usefulness, Rahl had no intention of leaving it behind.

"Second, any references to a staff in the book also apply to truncheons. The book doesn't say that, but they do. He said that it could be very important to you in times to come, but not yet, probably not for a year or so."

Rahl wondered why the armsmaster would have emphasized *The Basis of Order*, but he respected Zastryl. If Zastryl had said that, then it was important. He'd have to reread the book on the voyage to see if he could discover exactly why Zastryl had sent the message. "I'll keep that in mind."

Abruptly, Aleasya stepped forward and hugged him. "Take care." She stepped back and was gone.

Rahl stood there, holding the truncheon and sensing belatedly the concern she had expressed. Why hadn't he noticed that before? Or was it something that had only become real to her once she'd heard he was leaving?
Yet . . . much as he appreciated the warmth and the hug, he wished it had
come from Deybri . . . who had told him that the past had no hold on him.

He sat down slowly, setting the truncheon on the bench beside him. He
looked at it once again before turning back to his platter. He finished his
breakfast quickly, then belted the truncheon in place before making his way
back to his quarters, where the canvas pack holding his few belongings
waited.

After taking a last look around the chamber, he picked up the pack,
shrugged and left, closing the door behind him. Outside, the sun beat down
through a clear green-blue sky, promising another hot day. As he crossed
the grounds, none of the magisters or magistras appeared to wish him well,
and that irritated him, but he turned downhill. He wasn't about to go looking for them.

Before reaching the piers, he stopped at the Merchant Association to say
good-bye.

Varselt was actually out in the front talking to Wulff.

". . . be especially careful these days in listing the declared value on
goods coming out of Biehl and Jera . . ." He turned, and his eyes fixed on
the pack Rahl carried. "Come to say good-bye?"

"Yes, ser. I've been told to report to the *Legacy of Diev* this morning."

"That you have. That you have. Give my regards to Captain Liedra and
my thanks to the magisters for your efforts here." Varselt's jowls flexed as
his head bobbed up and down. "I'd wager you'll be doing a fine job for
Shyret in Swartheld as well. Now . . . best you be on your way and not keep
the captain waiting."

"I won't, and thank you for the training, ser." Rahl nodded. He could
tell Varselt had other matters on his mind

As he stepped outside, he could hear the few words from Gorot.

". . . poor bastard . . ."

He almost nodded, but managed a wry smile as he headed for the piers.
It might have been his imagination, but he thought that the harbor was more
crowded than usual, with several ships at each of the piers, and parts of the
avenue beside the seawall with carts, wagons, sailors, and tradespeople.

The *Legacy of Diev* was tied up at the long pier closest to the market
square. She was broad-beamed compared to the Nordlan vessel moored

inshore of the *Diev* and on the opposite side. The *Diev*'s hull was of dark oak, and she had paddle wheels mounted aft of midships on both sides. The paddle-wheel housings were dark green, as were the painted surfaces of the ship above the main deck. She had two full masts for sail plus the bowsprit.

Rahl hesitated short of the gangway, then squared his shoulders and walked up onto the main deck.

A sailor wearing a short green vest over a gray shirt and trousers that were almost white turned from where he had been watching the cargo crane and stepped forward. His broad and square face was clean-shaven and weathered. "Welcome to the *Diev*. Who are you looking for?"

"I'm Rahl. I'm supposed to report to Captain Liedra."

"News to me. I'm Gresyrd, bosun's mate. Captain didn't mention it."

"I'm being sent as a clerk to Swartheld. I think I'm supposed to help the purser, though."

"There was something about that. No problem. Captain's up on the bridge deck." Gresyrd turned. "Borlye! Watch the hoist and the quarterdeck for a bit."

"Yes, Boats," replied a lanky but muscular woman.

Gresyrd gestured to the narrow steps to his right. "Up this ladder." He clambered up, expecting Rahl to follow.

Rahl did.

Captain Liedra stood on the forward edge of the bridge deck, beside the pilothouse, watching the crane that lowered pallets in a cargo net into the forward hold.

"Captain?" asked the Boatswain's Mate. "You've got a clerk here."

The captain turned. She was a wiry yet muscular woman, who wore a short-waisted green coat with black braid on the cuffs over a plain gray shirt. Her jet-black hair was shot with streaks of brilliant white, both set off by a tanned and slightly weathered angular face. Her eyes were a piercing green. "I'm expecting him. I'll take it from here."

"Yes, ser." Gresyrd nodded, then turned and hurried back down the ladder.

Liedra studied Rahl for a moment before speaking, her eyes taking in the canvas pack. "So you're the one headed to Swartheld. Almost too much of a pretty boy. You handle arms?" Her eyes dropped to the truncheon at his belt.

"Yes, Captain. I'm better with a truncheon or a staff, but I know something about a blade. I'd rather not use one, though."

"You're one of those blacks who might be a mage, then?"

"So I've been told. I've also been told that I have a great deal to learn."

"Don't we all?" Liedra laughed, a quiet sound that bore amusement. "Might as well get started. You'll be acting as the purser's assistant on this leg. You know something about the forms and procedures?"

"Something. I've been working in the Merchants' Association for the past eightday or so, and I was trained as a scrivener." Rahl added quickly, "Ser Varselt asked me to convey his best to you, ser."

"He would." She shook her head. "A scrivener. Ought to be able to read your writing, then. That's an advantage. You know anything about ships?"

"Nothing, ser. This is the first one I've been on."

"Been aboard," Liedra corrected him. "You'll learn. The *Diev* was built to carry cargo on the Nylan–Hamor run, but we also have four passenger cabins and a steward, and most runs we're full up. There's a spare bunk in the steward's space. That'll be yours. We'll drop your gear there." She walked swiftly to the ladder on the side away from the pier, swung herself around one-handed, and was on the main deck before Rahl actually had his hand on the ladder rail.

"Lively now!"

Rahl scrambled down after her, following her through a hatch and down a narrow passageway.

"Mates' cabins here. Crew's forward in the fo'c's'le. Steward's cubby's the last." She held open a narrow door.

There was less than two cubits clearance between the bulkhead and the bottom bunk. The top bunk was a half cubit narrower than the one on the bottom. Above the foot of the upper bunk was a narrow shelf with netting running from it to the overhead.

Liedra pointed to the netted area. "That's where your gear should go. Just leave the pack on the upper bunk for now. Make sure it's stowed before we leave port."

Rahl eased past her and swung the pack onto the bunk, then followed the captain back down the passage and out into the bright summer sun that made the ship every bit as hot as the pier and far warmer than the training center had been up on the breeze-swept hillside.

A short and blocky man sat on a stool just aft of the open cargo hatch. "The last net! How many kegs of Feyn indigo?"

"Fifteen, ser."

". . . makes sixty altogether . . .

Liedra waited until the man had jotted something down on the paper fastened to an oblong of polished wood, a portable writing surface. "Purser?"

"Captain . . . we're going to be short on the dyes from what they promised . . ."

"We can sell what we have." She gestured. "Rahl, this is Galsyn. He's the purser. Galsyn, this is Rahl. He's being sent to Swartheld as a clerk there for the Merchant Association, but he's your assistant for this leg." Liedra smiled. "He can make clean copies of your forms and do whatever else you need along those lines. Teach him what you can. The more the clerks know, the easier it is for us." She offered a brisk nod, turned, and headed back across the deck to the ladder.

"Rahl, is it?"

"Yes, ser."

"If I call out things, can you write them down?"

"Yes, ser. There might be some special words I can't spell right."

"For on-loading that doesn't matter so long as it's close, and you'll learn them when we do the final manifest." Galsyn stood and pointed to the stool. "Sit."

Rahl sat.

Galsyn handed him the writing board and the marker. "Just list what I call out underneath the last entry. When you run out of space, start a new sheet." He turned and gestured. "Let's get that net moving!"

Rahl watched as the crane swung another load from the wagon on the pier toward the open cargo hold. Galsyn stepped forward slightly, his eyes traveling from the net to the hold and back to the net. "Easy now . . . those are amphorae."

Rahl waited to write down whatever the purser said. He just hoped he understood it all.

XXXIV

From the moment Rahl took over the marker and writing board on oneday, he jotted down, in the best hand he could, not only the cargo in the nets and pallets, as Galsyn called the items out, but what seemed to be even more in the way of notes. With a short break for the midday meal, they worked until sunset. Then, after supper, Galsyn went over what Rahl had written and spelled out the corrections and terms.

Twoday was more of the same, until midafternoon, when all the outbound cargo had been loaded, the last of the wagons had left the pier, and the crew was battening down the hatches.

Smoke began to rise from the twin stacks just aft of the pilothouse, and the acrid odor of burning coal drifted across the ship.

Rahl watched as Gresyrd's deck crew took in the gangway and swung that section of the wooden railing back into place.

"Single up!" came the order from the bridge.

Before long, the midships paddle wheels began to turn, with a dull, slapping *thwup, thwup.*

Rahl stood at the railing, just aft of the bowsprit, as the *Diev* backed down and away from the pier, out into the harbor. Then the paddle wheels stopped for a moment, and a dull *thump* shivered through the ship before the paddle wheels resumed turning, this time in the opposite direction, now carrying the ship forward and westward toward the channel between the outer breakwaters.

Rahl turned, first to the westernmost piers, but they were empty, and there was no order-haze across them. Did the black ships spend most of their time at sea?

He looked back at the buildings of the harbor, and the black-stone dwellings with their dark slate roofs, rising gradually up the hill, interspersed with trees and greenery.

"Rahl!" called the purser.

Rahl turned slightly to see Galsyn gesturing.

"Now that everything's on board and stowed, we need to get to work on the manifest for this leg. We can use the long table in the mess. That's the one the passengers usually eat at."

"Yes, ser." Rahl glanced back once more at the black-stone piers and the black-slate-roofed buildings on the hillside above the harbor structures. He thought he could see the training center, but he wasn't certain. He wondered if he would ever see Nylan or Recluce again, or if Deybri had been right.

He also had to ask himself if he would ever see his parents.

"Rahl!"

"Yes, ser." He walked toward Galsyn.

Swartheld

XXXV

The paddle wheels were silent, and the boilers were cold as the *Diev* flew southwest under full sail. Even at noon in late summer, the spray off the bow was chill at those times when the ship nosed through the heavier swells.

Rahl stood by the railing just aft of the bowsprit, watching a seabird circle up, then dive for a meal. In a bit, once the steward cleaned the ship's mess, he'd have to meet Galsyn there to continue working on the cargo declaration for what was to be off-loaded at Swartheld. He would have preferred to spar with Mienfryd, the ship's champion, dour as the man usually was. Rahl found that he could hold his own with the truncheon and not get too badly bruised with the practice wands so long as he concentrated on defense. But it would have been far more painful if the wands had not been wooden.

He half turned, glancing aft. Farther to the northwest was a low line of dark clouds. They looked to be larger and nearer than they had been at midmorning, but he'd already learned that estimating distances at sea wasn't all that easy.

His eyes came to rest on the silent paddle-wheel assemblies. At that moment, he recalled Khalyt's comments about engine design and about screws. If screw propulsion were faster, why didn't the trading ships use it instead of paddle wheels? Although Khalyt had never said so directly, Rahl also had the feeling that the hulls of the Recluce warships were black iron. But Rahl had never seen any trading ships in Nylan that were metal-hulled.

Was building a ship of metal too expensive? Or was there another reason?

One of the passengers, a darker-skinned man who was a Hamorian factor of some sort, made his way along the railing toward Rahl.

"Good afternoon," Rahl offered in Hamorian. "How are you faring?" He'd wanted to ask how he liked the voyage, but those words escaped him.

The merchant looked up. "You speak Hamorian?"

"I'm still learning. You are a trader?"

"Yes, a factor in cloth and in wool. The black wool of Recluce is much desired in Hamor. I came to pick out that which is most suitable."

Rahl nodded. "Wool is warm, but is not Hamor too warm for wool garments?"

The factor laughed, a sound with vast amusement. "For tapestries and rugs. Because it does not have to be dyed, it lasts far longer. I also travel to the west of Austra, where there is an orange wool. It is even harder to find, and it is not as durable, but the weaving masters wish it and pay well."

Rahl knew that the *Diev* carried raw wool that would be sold in Swartheld by the Nylan Merchant Association. So why would the Hamorian spend coins and time to buy wool himself when he could get it without traveling? Did the Association increase the price that much?

"You are Rahl. You are an assistant to the purser, I heard. I am Alamyrt." The trader inclined his head politely and smiled, showing tannish teeth.

"For the voyage," Rahl admitted. "I'm being sent as a clerk to the Nylan Merchant Association in Swartheld."

"Ah . . . they wish someone who can speak Hamorian." He laughed. "Still, language alone will not help. They should bargain more. We love to bargain." Alamyrt paused. "Do you come from a trading family?"

"No, ser. I was a scrivener."

"You write Hamorian, too?"

"As I speak it. Not as well as I would like."

The trader shook his head. "You will not remain with the merchants. You will learn too much. If you choose to leave, go see my brother. He is Calamyr of Doramyl and Sons."

"Doramyl was your father?"

Alamyrt laughed again, almost delightedly. "Alas, no. He was my great-great-grandsire. We are an old trading family."

Over Alamyrt's shoulder, Rahl caught sight of Galsyn, standing in the hatchway of the passage that led to and from the mess and galley. He held a large leather case and gestured with the other.

"Ser . . . you must excuse me. The purser needs me."

"You are excused, young Rahl. Perhaps we can talk later."

"Yes, ser." Rahl could sense a rueful amusement in the trader, almost verging on . . . something he couldn't define. Still, he inclined his head politely before turning and heading across the deck toward the purser.

"What did his mightiness the cloth factor have to say?" asked Galsyn.

"He just said that he was interested in black wool from Recluce and orange wool from Austra, and that the Merchant Association needed to bargain more."

"Ha! He'd like that. He'd bargain you out of your skin and make you think he'd done you a favor." The purser snorted. "Anyway, we've got a lot to do on the declaration, and I'd rather do it now while we've got good weather. Can't check everything in heavy weather, end up with papers every-where, and without the declarations being complete, the captain won't want to off-load in Hamor."

Rahl frowned. "But doesn't all the cargo go to the Merchant Association there first?"

"Aye, it does." Galsyn cleared his throat. "But we have to give the decla-ration to the Imperial tariff enumerators before we can off-load. Then they check the declaration against everything that hits the pier. Anything that doesn't match doesn't get off-loaded, and that means a separate declaration for the stuff we miss—and the fees for another wagon and teamsters, and those costs the captain has to eat out of her share. She doesn't like that."

Rahl could understand that.

Galsyn turned and made his way down the short passage to the crew and passenger mess, with Rahl behind him. Once in the mess, the purser extracted two stacks of papers from the leather case and set them on the long table.

"I was thinking, ser," offered Rahl before Galsyn said anything. He'd wanted to ask before, but not when anyone else was around. He hated revealing what he didn't know. "Outside of the manifests and cargo lists, I don't know much about trading, but it seemed like the Nordlan ships I saw in the harbor at Nylan were narrower, and they looked faster."

Galsyn shook his head. "Trading's not about speed, young fellow. It's about coins. A faster ship, if she's under sail, carries less. If she's under steam, or steam and sail, she burns more coal, and coal is far more costly than the wind, and the coal takes space that cargo could occupy. And fac-tors and traders, for most goods, they don't pay more for getting 'em quicker. Rather have 'em later and cheaper."

"You're saying that we shouldn't use steam at all?"

The purser laughed. "Not like that at all. There are times when there's no wind, and there are harbors where it might take days for the wind to be right to make port. A good master like Captain Liedra knows when to use the engines and when not to."

"And to escape pirates?"

"Most of 'em. The Jeranyi have fast iron-hulled vessels. They carry bar-rels of cammabark. After they loot a ship, they fill it with cammabark, then fire it. The stuff explodes and burns right down to the waterline. Doesn't leave any trace of the ship—or the crew."

Rahl winced. And Fahla's father had been involved with them? "But why do we have wooden hulls, then?"

"Better for the cargo, and we're merchanters. Warships, that's another question. I've had it explained to me, and I can't say as I understand, but it's about order and metal, and too much metal in a cargo ship tends to be bad for the cargo over time. At least, that's the way I heard it. Warships, they don't have to worry about cargo. Anyway, it's not something I can do anything about." Galsyn handed several sheets of declarations to Rahl. "Sit down across from me. I'll read off something, and I want you to check the declaration and tell me if it's listed."

"Yes, sir."

"It won't necessarily be in the order on the declaration. So you might have to go through it all to find it. Don't rush. Just make sure it's there." Galsyn adjusted the form in front of him. "Twenty kegs of scarletine . . ."

"Yes, ser. Twenty kegs."

"Fifteen kegs of madder . . ."

"Fifteen kegs, ser."

"Sixty-two kegs of Feyn indigo . . ."

Rahl looked twice. "There are only sixty listed on the declaration, ser."

"Sixty? Just sixty?"

"Yes, ser."

Galsyn fumbled through the papers, then nodded. "That's right. The frigging teamsters dropped two on the pier. Smashed 'em up good. Should have remembered that. Probably did it so that they could grab some for themselves. They'd have to return it to the trader, but they could probably make off with a silver's worth in their trousers easy."

"A silver's worth?"

"A keg of good indigo will fetch five golds, maybe more." Galsyn shook his head. "Need to finish this. Ninety-three bales of Lydklerian black wool—raw."

"Is that the same as the Hamorian wool factor's wool?"

"No. Alamyrt's wool is on a separate declaration that he'll have to make. Because he's Hamorian, it has to be separate. He pays a lower tariff, but he'll also pay on his profits from it, or something like that. Now . . . next item. Ten barrels of hard wheat flour."

"Yes, ser." Rahl wasn't having any trouble following Galsyn, but he could see that being purser wasn't the most interesting job, and he wondered how Meryssa was finding it.

XXXVI

As he sat beside Galsyn at one of the crew's tables in the mess, eating tough lamb in a stew with overcooked potatoes and stringy quilla, Rahl could sense someone looking at him. Since his back was to the passenger table, he had no idea who it might be, and he didn't want to turn around and stare.

"Cook's done better than this," muttered Galsyn. "Would have been hard for him to do worse."

"Careful there," suggested Trylla, the first mate. "I could tell him, and he might try."

"Who bought the provisions, purser?" asked the carpenter from the end of the table.

"You're always telling me that it's a poor crafter who blames his tools and materials," countered Galsyn.

"Tools, not materials. Hope you're not as loose with your figures as your words."

"Some figures even you'd like to be loose with."

A series of laughs followed Galsyn's words. Even Mienfryd laughed, if dourly.

Rahl smiled but didn't laugh. For some reason, he thought of Deybri, although she certainly wasn't the type for anyone to be loose with. She had made that point more than clear to Rahl.

He finished the last of the stew and hard biscuits, then asked Galsyn, "Is there anything else you need for me to do this afternoon?"

"Not for the moment. Later, you can help me check the ship's accounts. I could do it alone, but it's faster with two."

Rahl nodded, then waited for the mate and Galsyn to rise before following them out of the mess and onto the forward deck.

The early-afternoon air was pleasant, if brisk, and the ship was only pitching moderately in strong swells rising out of the southwest. He walked to the bow, then realized that he'd be soaked before long from the fine spray coming off the bow, and retreated to a position just forward of the starboard paddle wheels.

"Young man, you are the assistant purser, are you not?" The voice was firm—and feminine.

Rahl turned, then paused, because the question had been addressed to him in Hamorian, and the woman who had asked it was the one whom all the crew stared at, and at whom all the male officers tried to avoid staring. She was black-haired and black-eyed, with flawless skin that carried a faint hint of almond. Although concealed somewhat by trousers and a black vest, her shape was clearly one of those alluded to by Galsyn.

Abruptly, Rahl dropped his eyes just slightly and tried to remember the honorifics in Hamorian. "Yes, honored lady."

She smiled, and Rahl wondered what he had said wrong.

"If I offended you, honored lady, I beg your pardon. I am still learning Hamorian."

"You speak it as a native, young man, if as a native of Atla who lived in Merowey. No, I was amused because you clearly did not wish to offend, yet you were more than properly respectful, unlike so many of those in the north. That is so refreshing." She turned to the dark-haired handsome but muscular man with her and nodded. "You may leave us, Bartold."

The man inclined his head and stepped away, although he retreated only so far as the base of the foremast, and his eyes remained on Rahl.

"How might I be of service?" Rahl asked.

Rahl could sense the amusement, and he wondered if he'd used the wrong term for service, but he waited politely.

"You may talk with me for now. There are few on board who have the time or the inclination."

"For a while, lady. Later, I will have to work."

"Accounts of sorts?"

Rahl nodded.

"This vessel seems small for both a purser and an assistant."

While she hadn't exactly asked a question, that was the fashion in which polite Hamorian society made an inquiry, according to Magister Thorl, and Rahl replied. "It is to make me more aware. I'm being sent as a clerk to the Nylan Merchant Association in Swartheld."

"Those individuals of less-than-perfect parentage who manage that establishment could use more of the courtesy you exhibit," replied the woman.

At least, that was what Rahl thought she had said. "I will try to be polite to all."

"Politeness never hurts, Rahl, especially if you give nothing except courtesy and what was paid for."

"I will keep that in my thoughts." Rahl didn't know the expression he really wanted to use.

"And in your mind."

"Thank you."

"I have seen you sparring. For one who claims little experience, you exhibit much craft."

"My father taught me the truncheon early. Blades I learned later, and not so well."

She offered a knowing nod, then gestured out at the ocean and the seemingly endless swells, just high enough to show occasional traces of foam. "The ocean appears to have no end when one can see no land."

"This is my first voyage." *And possibly my last,* he thought to himself. "You must travel often."

"More than I would prefer, but I cannot find the . . . assistants and servants I need for my enterprises just in Hamor. Those who purchase from me often have particular needs." She shrugged. "One does what one must."

"You must have a number of indentured servants, then." That was a guess.

"More than most, but my needs are greater. You are from the north of Recluce, I would judge."

"I am. You are more perceptive than I would be."

"Although you have black hair, your skin is fair, and your eyes are blue. Likewise, you are taller and broader across the shoulders than most men. Those traits are more likely in men from the northern reaches. You will find that you are taller than most men in Hamor. That may not be to your advantage outside of your trading house."

"I am among the taller men in Recluce, but there are many who are as large or larger."

"Size is not everything, young Rahl. Neither is strength."

Rahl nodded. He'd heard that often enough. "Can you tell me about Hamor?"

"I could, but then you would not see it through your eyes." She smiled.

He could sense concern, calculation, and a hint of cruelty behind the words. He also could see Galsyn appear from the port hatchway, looking around.

The woman caught his look and half turned. "I see that the purser is looking for you. Perhaps we will talk later."

"I would appreciate that, lady." Rahl inclined his head.

She did not say more as Rahl eased around her and crossed the width of the deck toward the purser.

"Ser?"

"Oh, Rahl . . . I wasn't looking for you. Have you seen the third?"

"No, ser." He paused, then asked, "Ser, who is the Hamorian lady?"

"I'm not certain she's properly a lady." Galsyn laughed. "Her name is Valdra Elamira, but I think the Elamira isn't really a name."

It meant something like "of great wonder," Rahl thought, but he only said, "She's traveling with a consort, although he looks younger."

"He's a combination of bodyguard and lover. The captain says that she is the mistress of a number of brothels in Swartheld in Cigoerne. She is quite wealthy."

Rahl managed neither to flush nor groan.

"She's had her eye on you." Galsyn grinned. "It might be fun. A bit older, but most attractive."

"I think I'd worry about the bodyguard," Rahl demurred. He was good with his truncheon, but against a true bravo?

"Wouldn't hurt to talk to her and be polite," Galsyn pointed out.

"I was, and I will be."

"None of my business, Rahl . . . but what did you do to get posted to Swartheld?"

How could he answer that without revealing too much? After a moment, he smiled ruefully. "I made some mistakes that I shouldn't have. Things that they felt I could have avoided if I'd just thought things out. I'd rather not say what."

Galsyn laughed. "Sooner or later, that's true for all of us. Sometimes, the best we can do is survive our mistakes."

"Was that how you got here?"

"That's why I never got further than the *Diev.* It's not a bad life as a purser. I get to see places I'd never see otherwise. I've got enough coins for what I need. I've got a decent cabin and a full belly, and I work for a good captain. One thing about Merchant Association ships . . . not a bad captain in the lot. Some are better than others, but the worst are better than the best from some places."

"Like Jerans?" guessed Rahl.

"Or Biehl . . . or Hydlen." Galsyn surveyed the deck. "Don't see Carthold. I'll get back to you later."

"Yes, ser."

After Galsyn turned and headed aft, Rahl glanced around the forward deck, but apparently Valdra had returned to her cabin or climbed the ladder to the bridge deck and moved aft far enough that he could not see her. Even before Galsyn had told him about her, Rahl had been a bit on edge.

He decided to find a quiet spot and force himself to study *The Basis of Order.* He *might* learn something new, although he doubted it.

XXXVII

After more than two eightdays, Rahl was more than a little tired of life at sea. The Hamorian lady Valdra had quietly avoided Rahl, as if she had measured him and found him wanting, and that nagged at him. He wasn't that interested in her, but he didn't like being enticed and dismissed. Especially by a brothel mistress, or whatever the proper term might be.

The days had gotten so long that Rahl even looked forward to copying and filling out forms for Galsyn. When he was not doing that, sleeping, or practicing with Mienfryd, if he couldn't find someone to talk to, he forced himself to read through *The Basis of Order* page by page. Mostly, it was slow going, and boring, because he could either do what was mentioned, or, no matter how hard he tried, he couldn't. Mostly, he couldn't. At least of the skills he understood.

He'd also tried to find the passages that Aleasya had said Zastryl had wanted him to read. He only found three, and one had some nonsense about not truly mastering the staff order until casting it aside. Another said that a staff could be infused with order, and the third said that a staff was only a pale reflection of its wielder. Rahl had to wonder what Zastryl had had in mind, but at least the wording of those passages had been clear.

There were more than a few passages whose ideas he didn't understand at all. One remained in his mind.

When snow falls, the flakes do not fall in a precise pattern, each flake only so far from another. Nor are the flakes of one snowfall like unto another, yet once it is fallen, one snowflake clings to another in a pattern that coats all, and one can mold snow into forms. If one melts that snow, it becomes water and only has the structure of what confines it. In the winter, one can freeze that water and sculpt it into any shape. One can also boil water and turn it into a chaotic mist. Thus, water can be ordered or not. So is water of order or of chaos?

The obvious point was that in some circumstances water was chaotic and in others ordered. But what determined those circumstances? Just how hot or cold it was? Somehow, Rahl couldn't believe that just heating something made it chaotic. Black iron was the most ordered of all metals, and it was created by great heat.

As he stood in the shaded area just aft of the starboard paddle-wheel assembly in the early afternoon, he tried to dismiss the paragraph, but he knew it was always somewhere in the back of his mind. Finally, he turned and made his way up the ladder to the bridge. Sometimes, the captain would talk to him.

At the top of the ladder in a space of sunlight falling between the full sails, he wiped the sweat from his forehead with a square of cloth. Within the last four days, the air had gotten far warmer, the sun more intense, and even the spray from the bow had lost its chill. The heavy long-sleeved gray tunic had become uncomfortably warm, and Rahl usually wore the lighter clerk's summer tunic.

The captain stood on the covered but open bridge, to the left of the helm. Rahl stopped at the edge of the bridge, waiting for either an invitation or a dismissal.

"You picked a good time to come up, Rahl." Liedra pointed ahead, just off the port bow. "If you look hard there, you can see Hamor."

Rahl followed her gesture, staring out over the gentle swells that barely seemed to move the light blue waters. A thin line of white was visible just above the blue. Farther east, but north of the white, was a line of smoke.

"The white line's the cliffs to the west of Swartheld," the captain explained. "Before long, we'll be swinging to a more easterly heading to avoid Heartbreak Reef. Don't ever want to come into Swartheld in a storm or the dark. There's a lighthouse there, but ship breakers will use fires to copy it, get unwary captains to drive onto the reef."

"There's smoke over there, ser."

"I'd guess it's a Hamorian warship. Might be one of their new iron-hulled cruisers. Nasty beasts with iron cannon. All that iron means a mage has to get really close to touch off the powder, and they don't let anyone they don't know get close. Cannon make more sense on a ship. It's harder to use order- or chaos-forces at sea."

Rahl nodded, although he hadn't noticed much difference with what he could do with order.

He stood by Liedra for a time as the smoke drew nearer, and a dark-hulled vessel without rigging appeared, moving north of the *Diev*. He squinted. "There's an iron box just aft of the bow, and two in the rear."

"Gun turret. They can point in any direction and fire. The Hamorians like guns, and lots of warships."

"Are they all iron-hulled?"

"Just the warships."

"Where do they get all the iron?" Rahl knew that there was an iron-works in the mountains north of Feyn in Recluce, but no one had ever told him about the Hamorian iron warships.

"Don't know where they mine the iron, but the Hamorians have a whole city that smelts and forges iron. Some claim that they produce more iron and steel there in Luba than in the rest of the world combined. Don't know as I believe it, but all that iron has to come from somewhere, and it's not from Candar or Recluce. They've got small mines and works in Lydiar, but that's barely enough for the east of Candar, not that Fairhaven likes to see much iron produced."

Cold iron was hard on chaos-mages. That, Rahl did know.

After a time, the captain spoke again. "Look hard just off the starboard bow, on the peninsula, inshore of the reef."

Rahl looked. In the distance was a stone tower with a shimmering dome.

"The northwest light tower. At night, a beam of light that swings from east to west." After a moment, the captain added, "You'd better find Galsyn before long. See what he needs from you. You won't be leaving until we're off-loaded. You can take the last wagon to the Association. Oh . . ." Liedra coughed gently. "I'd suggest you be very polite to folks in Swartheld. Ever since the days of the Founders, the Hamorians haven't taken that kindly to those of us from Recluce."

"That . . . that was hundreds of years ago."

"A little more than five hundred," Liedra said. "They didn't like the fact that Creslin destroyed one of their fleets and forced them to trade with Recluce."

"Five hundred years ago, and they're still mad?"

"I wouldn't call it mad, but the Hamorians hang on to grudges like no one else. They can cheat you and think nothing of it, but you cheat them, and you're likely never to be welcome in Swartheld again. They don't forget anything," the captain replied. "Now . . . on your way."

"Yes, ser." At the top of the ladder down to the main deck, Rahl looked toward the stone lighthouse and the white cliffs beneath it. Five hundred years. He still had a hard time believing that. How could they hold a grudge that long? That was truly holding to the past, and not in the best way.

XXXVIII

The *Diev* entered the harbor at Swartheld with canvas furled and under steam power in late afternoon. The port dwarfed Nylan, with ships anchored in deeper waters offshore, others tied at the long and wide piers so closely that there looked to be almost no vacant spaces.

As Liedra guided the *Diev* after the pilot boat and toward the third pier south from the northeasternmost wharf, Rahl stood by the railing, taking in everything that he could. On the western side of the bay, barely visible across the stretch of open water beyond the offshore moorings, was another set of piers, holding black-hulled warships of various sizes, with iron hulls and white superstructures and white gun turrets. Rahl tried to count them, but lost track after ten.

He turned his attention to the *Diev* and the pier.

"Full astern!" came from the bridge above.

"Full astern, ser!"

Rahl listened as the captain walked the ship into the pier, neatly between two bollards.

"Lines out!" ordered the boatswain's mate.

The handlers on the pier secured the twin lines to the bollards fore and aft.

"Double up!"

"Gangway!"

Rahl stepped back as the deck crew hurried in his direction, setting himself aft of the quarterdeck and against the bulkhead outboard of the ladder to the bridge deck.

As he waited for Galsyn to summon him to work, Rahl turned and studied the pier where the *Diev* was tied. It was not only more than six hundred cubits long, but a good hundred cubits wide, and there were wagons and carts everywhere. Already, several wagons were headed toward the *Diev*, and two vendors with handcarts were rolling them toward the gangway.

"Silks, silks . . . the finest silks from Atla . . ."

". . . the finest wools from Recluce and Brysta . . ."

"Spices . . . brinn from Candar, brinn and astra . . ."

"Tools . . . iron tools, Hamor's finest from the works at Luba . . ."

Rahl glanced toward the foot of the pier, where two vessels larger than the *Diev*—not the smallest of ships from what Rahl could tell—were tied up. So many street and cart vendors pushed around the wagons that he wondered if the teamsters driving the wagons would have to push through the crowds to force them away from the ships. While Nylan had peddlers and vendors, the numbers and variety were nothing compared to those on just the one pier where the *Diev* was tied.

"Clear the forward hatch," ordered Gresyrd. "Power takeoff for the crane."

Before that long, the first wagon bearing lettering on the side that proclaimed "Nylan Merchant Association"—rolled to a halt forward of the gangway, directly opposite the forward hatch.

At that moment, Galsyn appeared on deck, carrying a large leather folder and the portable writing board. He walked over to Rahl and handed him the writing board. "Stand by. It will be a little while."

The captain made her way down the ladder, then glanced at the purser. "Everything ready?"

"Yes, Captain. Declarations and current manifest."

Liedra nodded and walked to the section of railing that had been swung back for the gangway. Mienfryd joined the captain there, wearing his black blade.

"The manifest?" asked Rahl quietly.

"Sometimes, the tariff enumerators ask what else you have on board. They're not supposed to, but . . ." Galsyn shrugged. "That's another reason why Mienfryd stands by the captain. It's a symbol, but it helps. Most of the time."

Rahl didn't ask about what happened when it didn't work.

"Here come the enumerators," murmured Galsyn. "Just stand here." He stepped forward so that he was just slightly back of Captain Liedra's shoulder on the opposite side from the ship's champion.

Rahl watched. The two officials who walked up the gangway wore short-sleeved khaki shirts and long, matching trousers over black boots. Their belts were black, but the insignia on their collars and shirts were crimson.

"Captain Liedra."

"Inspector Salyx," returned the captain.

"You have your declaration ready." The inspector spoke in Temple rather than Hamorian.

Galsyn handed the tariff declaration to the unnamed inspector who had not spoken. The inspector studied it, then handed it to Salyx.

"The tariff looks to be ninety golds, subject to verification, Captain."

Even though he had seen the tariff calculation, and checked it for Galsyn, Rahl still found himself amazed at the amount. Ninety golds—and that was just an assessment of roughly one part in a hundred, although for some goods the tariff was one in a thousand, and for some, it ran as high as five parts in a hundred. Rahl doubted that his father had netted ninety golds in the last ten years, and the *Diev* probably made more than ten trips a year, if not more.

The captain handed an envelope to the inspector. "A letter of credit against the ship's account, held in the Exchange through the Nylan Merchant Association."

"A pleasure, Captain Liedra." The inspector signed the bottom of the declaration, then handed it to his silent assistant.

The assistant produced a circular device that fitted over a portion of the signature on both sides of the paper. He squeezed the handles, then removed the device. Rahl could see an embossed pattern across the signature as the assistant gave the declaration back to Salyx, who in turn handed it to Liedra, who passed it to Galsyn.

Then the inspectors nodded, turned, and walked down the gangway.

"See to the passengers, purser."

"Yes, ser."

Rahl wondered if he was supposed to help off-load passenger baggage, but Galsyn just handed him the leather folder he had been carrying, and the declaration, and said, "Wait here. It won't be long."

Rahl waited.

The first passenger to leave was a bearded dark-skinned man whom Rahl did not recall even having seen on the voyage, but he might have been ill or violently seasick, because his eyes were reddish, and he looked pale behind the color of his skin. A faint miasma of chaos clung to him.

Valdra Elamira did not look at Rahl as she left the *Diev.* Neither did her bodyguard.

The wool factor Alamyrt actually stopped for a moment. "I wish you well in Swartheld, and perhaps our paths will cross."

"Good fortune to you, honored ser."

"I'm certain it will be." Alamyrt laughed, then turned and walked down the gangway, carrying a large satchel-like case.

Once the last passenger had left, Galsyn turned back to Rahl. "We need to get on with tracking the unloading, Rahl."

"Yes, ser."

The off-loading continued until slightly after twilight, when the piers cleared of wagons and vendors. From what Rahl could tell, the vendors tried to sell until it was almost dark, with their warbling and piercing cries, which had become even more insistent, then hurried away. At that point, the gangway was swung up and the railing closed.

Rahl looked to Galsyn. "We're not leaving, are we?"

"No. It's just the captain's way of reducing temptation. No one gets shore leave until we're off-loaded," Galsyn said. "Not anywhere in Hamor. She says she doesn't like being shorthanded. More likely she doesn't want to lose good sailors." With a smile, Galsyn left Rahl by the railing.

The younger man stood there, looking out on the pier, feeling the warm air filled with scents he could not identify moving past him, and hearing the sounds of a strange port rising and falling around him in a rhythm he could sense, but not describe.

XXXIX

More wagons arrived on the pier opposite the *Diev* not long after dawn on threeday, and Rahl sat on a stool by the railing and wrote down the cargo items as they were off-loaded and as Galsyn checked each item and called it out.

"Fifteen bales of raw wool, ship's consignment . . ."

"Thirteen kegs of scarletine, shipper's consignment . . ."

"Two barrels of quilla flour, ship's consignment . . ."

Rahl's fingers were almost numb by midafternoon, when the last goods had been transferred to one of the wagons on the pier. He was also sweating from the heat, even though he and Galsyn had been shaded from the direct sun by a square of old canvas stretched between a frame of ancient poles.

"Better grab your gear, Rahl," called Galsyn. "Teamster won't wait."

Rahl dashed for the cubby where he'd slept for the past eightdays, scooped up his pack, and headed back out to the deck.

The captain and Galsyn were waiting for him on the quarterdeck, just short of the gangway.

Liedra extended a small cloth pouch. "Here's your pay. It's not that much, but it should help."

"Thank you, Captain. I appreciate it." Rahl was well aware that she didn't have to pay him anything. He quickly tucked the pouch into his belt wallet. "I really do."

"Everything you learned could help us all, and give my best to Shyret." She paused. "One other thing."

"Yes, Captain?"

"I just wanted to give you a few words from a woman who's been around." Liedra smiled ruefully. "Whatever you're doing when you're out of the Merchant Association, be careful. Be especially wary around the girls. Any woman seen in public with any of her body uncovered is a slave or servant. If she's paying attention to you—or any other young fellow—she's probably working to ensnare either your coins or your body. You have to watch closely, because the free women with golds often wear fabric and scarves so sheer that their shoulders look bare, but you won't see more than that. If you do . . . watch out."

"The body-snatchers get you," added Galsyn, "and you'll end up working in the great ironworks at Luba, or lugging stone on one of those great highways the Emperor's building and rebuilding . . ."

Rahl had heard often enough while at the training center about the ironworks at Luba, but he didn't recall anything about the great highways.

"Watch everything," added the captain. "Best of fortune."

"Thank you." Rahl picked up his pack and walked down the gangway toward the remaining wagon from the Merchant Association. When his boots rested on the wide stone wharf, a mixture of order and chaos swirled up around him, then seemingly receded slightly.

"You the clerk?" called the teamster from the seat of the remaining wagon.

"Yes. I'm Rahl."

"Climb on up. Need to be moving. Otherwise the red and tans get nasty."

Rahl hurried to the wagon and swung his pack up, then scrambled onto the hard painted wood of the bench seat.

"I'm Guylmor," offered the driver, a dark-skinned man with a short-cut graying beard who wore a blue shirt and trousers, both so faded that they were more like a light gray shaded blue. "Teamster for the mercantos."

Mercantos? Then Rahl nodded and asked, in Hamorian, "Do you live near the Merchant Association?"

"Where else?" Guylmor laughed, not quite bitterly. "We have a bunk room. My consort, she lives out in Heldarth. I go there on end-days." He flicked the leather leads, gently. One of the dray horses snorted, but the wagon began to move, slowly. "Where are you from? Did you grow up in Atla?"

"A long ways from there, but I learned to speak from . . . someone like an uncle . . . who lived there."

"Some of the vendors will try to cheat you. They don't think Atlans are that smart."

"Are you from . . . Heldarth?"

"My family is from south of there." Guylmor shook his head.

The wagon rolled slowly down the pier, inshore toward the buildings beyond the end of the pier. Rahl's eyes flicked from point to point, but so much was going on that he scarcely knew where to look—or for what. The wagon passed a cart with an open grill, so close that Rahl almost could have reached out and grabbed one of the spiced fowl roasting on spits there.

"No better fowl anywhere . . ." The words in guttural Temple were followed by another set in far more precise Hamorian. "The best young chickens, fattened and roasted . . ."

Voices pitching wares and more came from everywhere, or so it seemed.

"Indentured servants . . . young and in the best of health . . . young men, young women . . ."

On the opposite side of the wagon from where Rahl sat was a stage on which a young man and a girl stood. They wore little but cloths around their loins, and the girl was red-haired. For a moment, he thought she might be Fahla, but the girl was shorter and more fragile. Was that what had happened to Fahla—because she wouldn't betray her father to the Council? A flash of anger swept through Rahl.

". . . in the best of health and form . . ."

The teamster jerked his head toward the slave stage. "The only ones they show here are trouble. They're crazy or damaged in some way. They look good, but the best slaves never come to the piers. A little cheaper, though, and I wouldn't mind having the redhead, if I had the coins. Good thing about slave women—they can't tell you no."

Two darker-skinned men wearing short-sleeved shirts and trousers of a light khaki fabric stood in a loose formation at the end of the pier, just at the point between the pier itself and the stone-paved causeway perpendicular to it. Each wore a khaki cap with a blue oval above the visor. They also carried polished oak truncheons and wore falchionas at their black belts.

Rahl looked at the Hamorian patrollers, or whatever keepers of the peace were called in Swartheld. Both were hard-eyed and made the Council Guards of Recluce seem friendly by comparison.

Directly behind the armsmen was a younger man, barely older than Rahl. The younger man bore only a falchiona, but above his cap visor was a bronze or gold starburst set on a red oval. A whitish chaos-mist surrounded him. He had to be one of the chaos-mages serving the Emperor. Rahl was careful not to look long at the man, but he had a feeling that the chaos-mage still had noticed him.

Once the driver had the wagon off the pier and onto the street that fronted the harbor, the crowding eased, and the wagon began to move more quickly. On the streets heading south from the harbor boulevard, there were few peddlers or carts, but more people, and despite his understanding of the far larger size of Swartheld, all the people made Rahl feel cramped and crowded.

"How much farther?" asked Rahl.

"Less than half a kay," replied Guylmor.

The shops Rahl could see and make out carried everything, but a greater proportion seemed to deal with fabrics—silks, woolens, linens, cottons—and even costly shimmersilk. The shop that displayed the shimmersilk had two large armed men in maroon by the door. In just a few blocks were as many bolts of cloth as in all of Nylan, Rahl suspected.

Even though he had done little more than ride in the wagon, Rahl could feel even more sweat beading on his forehead and neck and running down his spine. A haze hung over the city, mostly from the heat, Rahl thought, but some of it might have been from chaos—or just from so many buildings and people. He tried to take in what they passed, but there were so many factorages and shops that he soon lost track of all that he had seen.

The teamster cleared his throat, then gestured with his left hand. "There's the traders' building. We'll be unloading in the rear yard. That's where the warehouse is."

"I need to tell Ser Shyret I'm here." Rahl glanced around, trying to take in what he could. Across the street from the Merchant Association building was a shop that displayed weapons—many shimmering in the front display window—sabres, cutlasses, an especially menacing falchiona, a huge wide broadsword, and all manner of knives and dirks. "Thank you for the ride."

"Serting together and company's welcome," Guylmor replied.

Rahl waited until Guylmor slowed the wagon to bring it through the brick-pillared gates before hopping off and hurrying toward the front door of the building. Before he put his hand on the polished-brass door lever, he paused, then firmly pressed down and opened the door.

Inside, the building was cooler than the street, but only slightly. The ceilings were high, close to ten cubits, and the walls were white plaster over brick, with occasional yellow-brick pillars. Unlike the Merchant Association in Nylan, there was no counter, but a single long desk facing the door. The blond-wood surface was not quite chest high.

The clerk seated on a stool behind the desk was turned, listening to a man at the side.

". . . be getting the cargo and declarations from the *Diev* . . ."

Rahl intended to wait, but the man turned, as did the clerk.

"You must be the new clerk."

"Yes, ser." Rahl inclined his head politely. "Are you Ser Shyret?"

" 'Director' will do." Shyret was stocky, and the top of his head barely came to Rahl's nose. The managing director was also clean-shaven, with iron gray hair cut short, and he wore a loose-fitting white shirt decorated with silvered embroidery and lace. "Say something in Hamorian." The tone was polite enough, but preemptory.

"I look forward to working here and doing my best."

"That will do." Shyret nodded brusquely, inclining his head toward the thin-faced man at the high desk. "Daelyt is the senior clerk. He will assign your duties. You are to speak Hamorian at all times when anyone else is here, even if you are addressed in Temple. The one exception is any ship's master. You reply in whatever language the captains use to you."

"Yes, ser."

"Show him his duties, Daelyt. You can see me later."

The senior clerk nodded.

Shyret turned and walked through a wide archway at the rear of the main office. There was a faint chaos-haze about him, not as much as if he were a white wizard, Rahl thought, but he wasn't sure about that.

"We might as well get you started," said Daelyt. "What do you know about manifests and declarations?"

"I worked in the Nylan Association for several eightdays, and I was the assistant to the purser on the Diev for the voyage here."

"You can write Hamorian?"

"Enough for the forms."

"You're going to make my life much easier." Daelyt smiled. "There are some differences in what the magisters want in Nylan and what the Imperial tariff enumerators want here. Set down that pack, bring over another stool, and we'll go through them."

Rahl carried a stool from the side of the room and set it close enough to Daelyt's so that he could see what the older clerk was doing. He sat down, then wiped his forehead with the cloth he'd tucked inside the light tunic. "Is it always this hot?"

"You're fortunate," said Daelyt. "You came in on one of the cooler days of summer. But it's in the high season. Some days, even the locals don't go out unless they have to. So the wealthier traders send their families to their east-hill villas or their seaside places. Once we get into fall, Swartheld won't be quite so uncrowded as it is now."

Daelyt took out a set of declaration forms and laid them on the desk before Rahl. "We'll start with the differences . . ."

After going through all the variations on the forms, then making Rahl copy one set, abruptly, the older clerk looked up. "Time to get something to eat and show you where you'll sleep."

"I was wondering about food . . ."

"We get two meals a day from Eneld's. It's the cantina across the street, beside the arms shop. We have to eat in the back, but the food's not bad, and you don't have to use your own coins."

"What about my pack?"

"Oh . . . I'll show you your alcove." Daelyt turned and walked through the archway that Shyret had taken earlier, except he went through another door into a small storeroom. "Here's your space. There's a water barrel for drawing your wash water out the back door there."

In the corner on the right side of the storeroom was what amounted to a narrow chamber without a door, but with a cloth curtain, half–drawn back.

Rahl glanced around the narrow area behind the curtain, little more than a narrow pallet with shelves above the foot of the bed and a pegboard affixed to the wall for hanging a few clothes. There was a bowl and pitcher on the shelves for washing, and one thin worn towel folded beside it. There was also a chamber pot against the wall.

"The chamber pot wastes and water go down the sewer out the rear door. It's the circular cover. Just lift it and dump. Don't toss wastes into the alley. The patrollers catch you, and it'll cost you a silver the first time, and the quarries the second."

That stopped Rahl for a moment. Finally, he said, "Thank you for the warning. Where do you . . ."

"My consort and I have rooms and a kitchen above the main warehouse." The older clerk's eyes dropped to Rahl's belt and the truncheon. "You can use that?"

"Yes."

"Good. You won't have much cause to use it most nights, but you can never tell. Not in Swartheld. We don't keep many golds here—just enough in case we need supplies or if someone pays us late in the day after the Exchange is closed. That makes the director very unhappy, but sometimes it happens."

"There's a strong room?" asked Rahl.

"Of sorts. It's really an ironbound closet in the back of his study. Now . . . let's eat, because we'll be working late on the *Diev*'s declarations."

Rahl followed Daelyt to the main door and out into the growing twilight. From what he could tell, there were even more people on the street than there had been earlier.

"The bar works better, but we can't use it and get out." Daelyt grinned as he turned and locked the main door with an oversized brass key. "The director doesn't like to be surprised when he's here alone, but he won't leave until he's seen the declarations, and we won't get them until everything's stored in the warehouse and checked off by Chenaryl and the enumerator."

"Chenaryl?"

"He's the warehouse supervisor."

"Thank you." As he followed Daelyt across the street and toward the cantina, Rahl wondered just how many more names and forms he'd have to learn.

XL

Rahl and Daelyt sat on stools on opposite sides of the small battered wooden table in the corner behind the kitchen of Eneld's cantina. The brownish wood of the tabletop was so battered, stained, and polished with years of grease that Rahl had no idea what kind of wood might have been used. The light brown crockery platter that held his dinner was so chipped along the rim that handling it there risked cutting fingers, and a fine tracery of lines through the glaze proclaimed its age and wear. The meal itself consisted of shreds of unnamed fowl mixed with various root vegetables and a grain half the size of rice and twice as tough, all covered with a pungent melted cheese and a greenish brown sauce that made his mother's pepper fowl seem cool and mild by comparison. The whole concoction had arrived wrapped in fried but still-soft flat bread and accompanied by a weak amber beer.

After he finished eating, Rahl wiped his forehead surreptitiously, then swallowed the last of the bitter beer, noting that Daelyt had only eaten about half of his dinner, but had drunk all of his beer. The meal had not been that large, either. No wonder the clerk was so thin.

"How did you like the kurstos?" asked Daelyt.

"Hot . . . but good."

"Just wait until you try Eneld's burhka. Your whole head will go up in flames." The clerk laughed.

Rahl could hardly wait. "How long have you been working for Shyret?"

"Five years come the turn of winter."

Rahl nodded. "Does it get any colder here in winter?"

"At night, you might need a heavy tunic or a coat. Fall and winter are when it rains. Not that much, but the only time it does."

Rahl quietly studied Daelyt. The clerk had to be more than ten years older than Rahl himself, and there was the slightest hint of a white chaos-haze around him. But then, there had been around Shyret as well, and a fainter haze of the same type had been present everywhere Rahl had been in Swartheld so far. Did living in Hamor make everyone slightly chaotic?

"You finished?"

Rahl nodded.

"We need to get back. It won't be long before we get the declarations back from Chenaryl, and we'll need to redo them in Hamorian." Daelyt rerolled and folded the half of his meal he had not eaten in the flexible flat bread, holding it carefully in his left hand as he stood. "We'll walk by the warehouse before we head back. You should see it, and you need to meet people." He turned and called, "Seorya . . . we're leaving. Thank you for the exquisite dinner."

"Only exquisite?" came the retort from the woman standing before the heavy iron stove.

"Excellent and exquisite."

Seorya snorted, a sound barely audible above the crackling of frying bread and fowl.

The two clerks slipped out the rear entrance into the alleyway. Rahl had half-expected garbage and offal in the alleys of Swartheld, but they held only dust and sand and a few small bits of rubbish. Daelyt walked quickly out of the alley and across the street, ducking behind a carriage with filmy side curtains that flowed with the hint of the warm evening breeze and the movement of the carriage itself. The footman was a guard with a falchiona at his belt.

Rahl dashed after Daelyt, catching up with him just in front of the gates to the warehouse area.

The massive dark-skinned guard standing just inside the gates looked toward Rahl.

"Tyboran, this is Rahl. He's the new clerk."

The guard studied Rahl for a moment, then nodded.

Daelyt kept walking, explaining as he did. "He doesn't speak. The mage-guards took his voice years ago for something, but he's a good guard."

Mage-guards? And they'd destroyed Tyboran's voice?

Daelyt stopped before a small door at the south end of the northernmost warehouse. "Just wait. I'll be right back." He opened the door and took the narrow steps.

Rahl glanced up. There were three narrow windows on the upper level, close together and overlooking the courtyard. He didn't see anyone, but he tried to follow the clerk with his senses. He *thought* Daelyt met a woman at the top of the steps, but that might have been because the older clerk had mentioned his consort.

While he waited, Rahl studied the area. All the wagons had been stored somewhere, and down by the south end of the courtyard formed by the Association building, the two warehouses, the stables, and a head-high stone wall, Guylmor was grooming one of the dray horses.

Daelyt returned empty-handed. "Let's see if Chenaryl has the papers ready for us."

Chenaryl was a black-haired, olive-skinned man with deep-set eyes. His shoulders were broad, above a more-than-ample midsection. He was sitting behind a small table just to the right of the open main doors to the second warehouse. He did not rise when Daelyt and Rahl approached, but his eyes lingered on Rahl.

"Rahl's the new clerk from Nylan," offered Daelyt in Hamorian.

Rahl was surprised at the awkwardness of the older clerk's language, but he inclined his head slightly and greeted the warehouse supervisor in Hamorian as well. "I'm pleased to meet you."

"You sound like an Atlan. Mostly, anyway."

"So I have been told. I learned from someone who had lived there."

"How much of the cargo is usable?" Daelyt asked quickly.

"Most of it. Some of the wool spoiled, and some other things. It's on the declarations." Chenaryl handed the sheets of paper to Daelyt. "You can have them. Better you than me."

"I'd rather handle paper than cargo," replied Daelyt.

Chenaryl nodded slightly. He looked and felt—to Rahl—less than happy, and there was a sense of chaos that suggested untruth in some of what he'd said.

Rahl glanced past the supervisor to a barrel set by itself. The barrel was labeled clearly "Feyn River pickles." He looked at Chenaryl. "I didn't know we shipped pickles. I've never seen any on a declaration or manifest."

"We don't," explained Daelyt from beside Rahl. "Some outlanders like delicacies, or what they think are delicacies. That was for a small trader who brought it in on a Jeranyi vessel. We're holding it for him. We store some things for smaller traders—for a solid fee."

That made sense to Rahl, except Daelyt was shading things, and Rahl couldn't imagine pickles as a delicacy . . . but who knew? He nodded. "I have a lot to learn."

"We all do. We need to get back to work."

Daelyt turned, and Rahl followed.

"We need to get to work on these," Daelyt told Rahl, as they left the warehouse supervisor and walked back out of the courtyard and past the silent Tyboran. "The Imperial tariff enumerators will want them tomorrow."

Daelyt unlocked the front door to the Association building and walked to the long desk. There he used a striker to light the oil lamp, then set the declarations he'd received from Chenaryl on the wood. He pulled out several sets of blank forms from a drawer and set them beside the original forms. Then he rummaged around and came up with another pen and an inkwell, as well as a blotting pad. Those he set to one side.

"You sit on the other side of the lamp. We'll need two copies, one for the Imperial tariff enumerators and one for our records here. This time, just to make sure you understand, I'll do the first copy, and you can do the second."

That made sense to Rahl.

He was halfway through copying the second page of the declaration, with more than a few unvoiced questions, when Director Shyret appeared from his study.

"You'll have those ready first thing in the morning?"

"With Rahl here, ser, we'll have them finished tonight and waiting for you in the morning."

"Good. You'll show Rahl how to lock up?"

"Yes, ser."

Shyret nodded and turned without another word.

Rahl returned to copying. When he finally finished, he looked up.

Daelyt was working on something else, but the older clerk immediately closed the leather folder. "You're done?"

"I am. Where do I put these, now that they're done?" asked Rahl.

"Oh . . . I'll take them. They go on the director's desk. Once he approves them, and the enumerators get their copy, he'll file the other one in the wall cases in his study." Daelyt rose and took the declarations Rahl held.

"Daelyt . . . I'm confused. The ship's master does a declaration, and then we do another in Hamorian. Are they filed together? Or separately? Is the difference just that we need one in Temple for the Association, and we need the other one in Hamorian for the tariff enumerators?"

"That's about it. We also have to remove spoilage, because we'll get tariffed on it," replied the clerk. "We need the declarations in Hamorian because the enumerators make a practice of not reading Temple. So we need both sets." He walked toward Shyret's study.

Rahl was more than confused. He was worried. He'd remembered clearly that there had been ninety-three bales of black wool, not the ninety on the Hamorian declaration he'd just finished. There had also been twenty kegs of scarletine, rather than nineteen, and sixty kegs of Feyn indigo, not fifty-nine. And Daelyt had been lying. Not about the Hamorians not reading Temple, but about the reason for the two sets . . . or something about it. Chenaryl and Daelyt had talked about spoilage, and Chenaryl had noted the "spoilage" on the original declaration that Rahl had written out for Galsyn, but Rahl knew he would have sensed such spoilage when the cargo had been unloaded. Not only that, but Daelyt hadn't answered his question about the separate files, either. Rahl wasn't about to ask twice. Not at the moment. "Seems like a waste."

"It probably is, but who listens to clerks?"

Rahl offered a laugh, then waited for Daelyt to return.

It was only a few moments before Rahl heard a second *click*, and Daelyt was walking toward the clerks' desk.

"I'm ready to head back to Yasnela."

"Your consort?"

"She's the one. Now . . . let me show you what to do in locking up. First, we check the back outside storeroom door. It should be locked, but you still check. It doesn't need a bar or bolt." Daelyt laughed. "It has three locks, and none of us have the keys. Only Director Shyret does."

That was another lie that Rahl tried to let pass without reacting.

"You don't have to worry about his study, either. I locked that after I put the declarations on his desk. We try to keep his study locked whenever he's not here. One of your other duties is sweeping and mopping the floors and polishing the brass and the wood. You don't have to do that tonight. It's late as it is, but it's up to you to take care of all that."

Rahl nodded. That made sense, but he hadn't exactly expected it.

"Let's finish up," Daelyt said.

Rahl followed the other clerk through all the checks, and they ended up at the front door.

"Just slip the bar through the iron brackets, and you'll be set."

"I will."

After Daelyt departed, Rahl immediately slid the iron bar into place. Then he slowly walked back to the long desk, where he snuffed the lamp and made his way to the narrow alcove that was his space.

Once he disrobed, lying on his back, with the light cover over his legs that he really didn't need, except that he had never been able to sleep without at least a hint of covers over his legs, Rahl looked up at the sand yellow bricks of the walls that enclosed his sleeping alcove, then at the aged brown planks and beams of the ceiling. He order-sensed them more than saw them, but he could feel the age and the strangeness.

He was in Hamor.

Hamor. Thousands of kays from Nylan. A place where even the teamsters wanted slaves. Where one of the cooler days of summer was hotter than he'd ever experienced anywhere. Where people were crowded everywhere, and yet Daelyt was telling him that the city was empty. Where no one thought much about mage-guards destroying voices, and where he already felt that matters were not right in the way the Association was being run. But who could he tell, and what real proof did he have? He could only claim he knew what was happening through his order-skills, and his past experiences suggested that making a claim based on them was anything but wise.

Beyond that, there was something about the clerk, not just the touch of chaos, or the fact that he had clearly given half his dinner to his consort . . . but something else that he couldn't identify.

Hamor—he was here, doing something that looked to be drudgery, both of mind and body, all because Magister Puvort hadn't wanted to explain anything. None of the magisters had, not really. He'd learned more from Deybri and Zastryl than from any of the magisters—and neither of them was even a mage.

He tried to calm the seething feelings within, but sleep was a long time in coming.

XLI

Chaos-mages have the ability to focus destruction and fire. Such abilities range from lighting a fire to incinerating portions of armies and melting quantities of lesser metals. Those abilities are based upon their mastery of such magery in unbinding the elements of the world that most would see as fixed and firm.

An ordermage can strengthen those bonds that a chaos-mage would sever, often to the point where the chaos-mage can do nothing. Likewise an ordermage can bind a white mage, if their strengths are equal.

An effective ruler must command both order and chaos, for he must be able to hold that which must be held and destroy that which would thwart him. Likewise, he must know where every mage of more than minor ability is located in Hamor, and each and every mage must serve the ruler, either directly or indirectly.

Failure to be registered as a mage is an offense against the land and its ruler, and must be punished severely, either by a term at hard labor or by execution, depending upon the circumstances. Ignorance of this requirement provides no excuse, except for those mages who are still children, and those must become immediate wards of the ruler, to be educated and trained to administer and carry out the wardings and duties necessary to assure that order and chaos are governed so that Hamor will be prosperous and peaceful within its borders and so that no other land can employ either order or chaos against Hamor and its peoples.

The life of any mage who lifts his abilities against the ruler or his duly appointed ministers and administrators or against those who bear arms in defense of Hamor and its peoples is forfeit . . .

Introduction
Manual of the Mage-Guards
Cigoerne, Hamor
1551 A.F.

XLII

Rahl's stomach was rumbling even before first light, enough to wake him from a vaguely troubled sleep. He was up and washed and dressed in his clerk's attire by shortly after dawn. Because the air outside was cooler, if not by much, he opened several windows. He also unbarred the door but discovered that only a key could unlock it, and he hadn't been given one. He wasn't really trapped, because he could have squeezed out through one of the windows, but where would he have gone?

From what he could tell, the cantina wasn't open yet, and there were far fewer people on the streets in the early, early morning than there had been late in the evening when he had gone to bed.

For lack of anything better to do, he went through the side of the long desk that was apparently his and looked at the various blank forms. Then he checked the inkwell and the ink and cleaned the pen he'd been given. That didn't take long.

After that, he went back to the storeroom and looked over what was there, but there was nothing out of the ordinary on the shelves, just copies of various forms, two large glass jugs of ink, several amphorae of lamp oil, and a small brass pitcher with a long and narrow spout designed to fill the lamps, some lamp wicking, brass polish, and rags. There was also a small jar of what looked to be a waxlike polish.

That reminded him of his duties, and he looked for a broom. He found both a broom and a mop, but he decided against trying to mop because he couldn't find any water for washing floors. As he recalled, there were barrels or possibly a pump or tap out the rear door, but it was locked.

Instead he swept the front part of the building and the rear corridor, then used a rag and the wood polish—sparingly—on the woodwork. The brasswork didn't look that bad. It could wait for a day or two.

He had just returned to the long desk when he heard and sensed Daelyt unlocking the front door.

The older clerk walked inside, then nodded. "You swept. Good."

"I polished the wood, lightly." Rahl paused, then added, "I should have asked, but I forgot about keys. I could have gotten out the window, if there had been a problem, but I didn't want to try to lift a chamber pot through it or try to get water . . ."

Daelyt grinned. "I would think not. You should have asked. We tend to think you know things unless you tell us otherwise. For the keys to the front door, we'll have to wait until the director gets here. He keeps the keys under lock. In the morning, you'll have to use the front door." Daelyt nodded. "Is there anything else?"

"You said we got two meals at Eneld's, and one is dinner . . ."

"The other is midday. We take shifts for that. Director Shyret wants a clerk here all the time." Daelyt laughed. "It's been difficult at times since Wynreed disappeared."

"Disappeared?" Rahl didn't like the sound of that at all.

"He went out on an end-day night and never came back. The patrollers and the mage-guards don't have any record of taking him into custody or . . . disciplining . . . him." Daelyt settled onto his stool.

Disciplining him? That suggested that the mage-guards could just dispose of people. Despite a morning that was already getting warmer than Rahl would have liked, he managed to repress a shiver, but his stomach rumbled . . . loudly.

Daelyt shook his head. "That won't do. You need to get a loaf of bread or some hard biscuits to get you through the morning. Run down to the corner, on the side beyond the warehouse. Gostof usually peddles some. You can get a loaf of rye for two coppers, if you press. The director won't be here for a bit, and he wouldn't mind on your first morning. It takes a while to get settled." The clerk's smile was helpful and friendly.

Rahl didn't sense any deception or chaos, not beyond the slight whiteness that apparently accompanied Daelyt all the time. "I'll hurry."

"That would be good."

Rahl moved toward the door.

Outside, the sun had lifted over the hills to the east of the harbor and shone through an already hazy greenish blue sky. There were more people on the street, but still not so many as the evening before, and most looked to be older and graying. Rahl hadn't taken three steps before he began to sweat. He hurried past the still-closed iron gates of the warehouse courtyard. Tyboran was standing inside the heavy iron grillwork. The guard looked at Rahl impassively.

Rahl smiled back and called cheerfully in Hamorian, "Good morning, Tyboran." He didn't feel all that cheerful, but that wasn't the point.

Tyboran just looked at Rahl, but Rahl had the feeling that the guard was at least slightly glad to be recognized.

An older man, weathered and bent, stood in the morning shade of the northernmost warehouse, so close to the corner that Rahl had to come to a halt quickly to avoid running into him.

"Loaves, just a day old, good loaves!"

"How much?" asked Rahl.

"For you, young ser, a mere four coppers. For the rye. Five for the dark."

"Old bread? Four coppers?" Rahl snorted. A half silver for a loaf of bread? Between his wages from the training center and what Liedra had given him, he had but three silvers. "A half copper is more like it."

"You've been in Atla too long, where bread and women are cheap, young ser."

Rahl grinned. "You've been in Swartheld too long, where even dung is sold as incense. Not more than a half copper."

"For your fine tongue I might accept three."

"Flattery is cheaper than coin. No more than one and a half."

"My bread may be a day old, but it is far fresher than most loaves, and of better quality."

"Only the dark bread, and who can afford that?"

In the end, Rahl paid two coppers for a loaf of dark bread, the first he'd had since he'd left Land's End. He could have gotten the rye for a copper and a half, and doubtless would have to settle for it in the days to come, but he had wanted the dark.

He walked back to the merchant association, only nodding to Tyboran as he passed. The guard did nod back.

"I see Gostof was there," observed Daelyt, when Rahl walked toward the long desk. "Take the bread to your cubby and eat it there. The director doesn't like crumbs or food out here."

As he hurried toward the storeroom and his cubby, Rahl wondered just how much else there was that Shyret demanded or didn't like. Once in the back, he ate half the loaf and wrapped the rest in one of his cloth squares before wiping his face and hands and returning to the desk.

"We need to check through your forms and make sure that you have everything," Daelyt said. "Start with the declarations . . ."

Rahl had not quite finished reorganizing his side of the desk when a slender man with a short black beard and dark eyes stepped through the door and made his way toward the two clerks. He wore the same type of loose-fitting embroidered shirt that Rahl had seen on Shyret the day before, but his was tan with brown embroidery. Despite the intricacy of the stitches, the garment had seen better days.

The newcomer ignored Rahl and looked at Daelyt. "What is the next vessel bound for Nylan, and when might it be expected?"

Daelyt slipped several sheets of paper from the drawer to his left and scanned them. "The *Legacy of Diev* is already in port, but her cargo space is all spoken for, and she's almost loaded out. The next would be the *Legacy of Westwind*. She should port here in Swartheld in about three days. Most of her cargo space is taken. The *Legacy of the Founders* is scheduled in about an eightday, and there's space for up to two hundred stones or the equivalent cubage."

The young trader frowned.

"There's more space on the *Legacy of Montgren,* Trader Forisyt," Daelyt suggested, "but you're looking at two to three eightdays before she ports. Does it have to be Nylan, or would you consider Land's End?"

"Nylan. There is little profit and less satisfaction in dealing with those at Land's End," replied Forisyt. "I'll take a hundred stones on the *Founders*. Brassworks and oils."

Daelyt began to write on a form that looked vaguely familiar to Rahl. "What is the approximate declared value, Trader Forisyt?"

"It is a cargo of insignificance, so small that it would be an insult to your association to declare a value."

"The minimum valuation is fifty golds," Daelyt pointed out, "and the reserve on that is five, and the cartage would be six."

"Insignificant as it is, it might be of greater worth than the minimum."

"That is often the case, for we will ship goods with little value, except to the shipper, and your goods are usually far beyond that."

"We might claim a value of ninety golds," mused the trader.

"The reserve would be nine, and the cartage ten. Without cargo assurance."

"As always, you will break me, but what can a small trader do?"

Rahl could sense that the trader wanted to haggle and bargain, but it was clear that the rates were fixed.

"As you may recall," said Daelyt, "the reserve is due when the consignment order is signed, and the cartage before any cargo can be manifested and loaded."

"Alas, has it not always been so?" Forisyt shrugged expressively. "I will be back on sixday with the reserve."

"The consignment order will be ready, honored trader."

Forisyt smiled wanly, then grinned, before turning and departing.

After the trader had left, Rahl glanced at the older clerk. "Could I look at that schedule? Or should I make a copy for myself?"

"A copy for you would be a good idea—after we deal with the consignment agreement. Have you ever done any of those?"

"I've seen them and had them explained, but I've never done one," Rahl replied.

"All right. I've got the rough form here. I'll tell you what to enter and why. Then you can make two copies. We need three, one for the trader, one for the ship, and one for us."

"Why don't they use their own ships?"

"Traders like Forisyt only have small cargoes. He doesn't own a vessel, and the Hamorian traders charge more per stone the smaller the cargo is. If they don't have a Hamorian shipper, they'll always try to get on one of our vessels, because we lose almost nothing to piracy, and less than most others to storms. That means less risk to them, or lower indemnity payments if they wish to pay for cargo assurance."

Rahl had never even heard of cargo assurance. "How does cargo assurance work?"

"We'll get to that after we do the consignment forms." Daelyt handed a form to Rahl. "It's all in Hamorian. First, you fill in the ship and master." He handed the sheets he had used earlier to Rahl. "Look for *Legacy of the Founders* . . ."

As he proceeded in following the other clerk's directions, Rahl was again bemused and amazed at the amount of paper required by trading.

He had barely begun when Director Shyret appeared from behind them, suggesting that he had entered through the rear storeroom door. Shyret was cheerful and smiling.

"Good morning to all, and it is a good morning, if a trifle warmish." The director spoke in Hamorian, clearly, but with an accent. "Have we had any business yet this morning?"

"Trader Forisyt has requested a hundred stones on the *Founders*," replied Daelyt. "The declarations for the *Diev* are on your desk, and Rahl will need a key if you don't want him using the windows to get in and out."

"Ah, yes, a key. We do have spares, since we had to change the locks after Winreed's disappearance. Terribly discommoding, that." He nodded to Daelyt. "If you'd accompany me, I'll take care of the key."

While Daelyt followed the director, Rahl sat at the long desk, thinking. He spoke Hamorian better than either the director or the head clerk, and that seemed strange, although he told himself that was just because of his order-skills, and not because of anything else.

Daelyt returned almost immediately and handed a heavy brass key to Rahl. "Here you are. Keep it safe. If you lose it, you pay for the new locks and keys."

Rahl nodded as he slipped the key to the bottom of his belt wallet, a wallet he was now wearing inside his trousers rather than in plain view.

"Let's try to finish those consignment forms before anyone else shows up. Now . . . the declared value won't be what the shipper says, and that can mean trouble if he wants cargo assurance. If he does, tell him that, in the event that cargo assurance is paid, it will be limited to the declared value on the consignment sheet or the cargo declaration or ship's manifest, whichever is the lowest figure . . ."

Rahl tried to concentrate on what Daelyt said, boring as it was already getting to be.

Once Daelyt guided Rahl though the form, he left the younger clerk to make the additional copies. When Rahl had finished the third copy of the consignment forms, he handed it to Daelyt, who had been working on another form that Rahl did not recognize. "Here you are."

"Thank you." The older clerk smiled politely.

"You were going to tell me about cargo assurance."

"Oh . . . the assurance is simple enough. Only one ship is lost out of every hundred voyages. It could be even less. So whoever wants to make sure he does not lose value pays five parts of a hundred of the cargo's value."

"But . . ." Rahl paused. "Is that because some don't want assurance?"

"The Association must also maintain a reserve in the Exchange here in Swartheld in the event that a ship is lost." Daelyt looked up as the outer door opened. "The tariff enumerators for the *Diev* declarations. Would you go tell the director they are here?"

Rahl eased off his stool and walked back to the archway and then to the open door into Shyret's study. For a brief moment, he just looked. Unlike the front of the office, with its plain white-plaster walls and yellow-brick columns, the study had paneled walls, with deep green hangings that seemed heavy for Hamor. The wide table desk was supported by five fruitwood legs carved into a pattern of twined vines and small flowers. The corners of the four head-high file cases were carved in the same fashion, and a circular green rug with a beige border filled the center of the chamber. There were no windows, and the heavy oak door had sturdy iron hinges and twin locks.

"Director," Rahl finally said, "the tariff enumerators are here."

Shyret looked up from an open ledger. "I'll be right there, Rahl."

"Yes, ser."

Rahl hurried back toward the front of the building, inclining his head to the two enumerators. They wore uniforms similar to the one patroller Rahl had seen on the pier, except the insignia on their collars and sleeves were not the sunburst, but a set of scales. "Honored enumerators, the director is coming."

"Thank you." The older enumerator chuckled, then turned to Daelyt. "So you managed to get an Atlan to work for you. I suppose that's the best you outlanders can do. At least, he doesn't mangle the language."

"The director does what he can," replied Daelyt, maintaining a polite smile, although Rahl could sense amusement.

"Greetings!" Shyret's voice was cheerful and hearty as he walked up to the two Hamorian officials and extended the single copy of the amended and final cargo declarations of the *Legacy of Dieu.*

"And to you," replied the older enumerator.

"You will find all is as it should be," offered Shyret.

"It always is, for which you should be thankful, Ser Director." With a smile, the older enumerator inclined his head slightly, then turned.

The younger followed him out. Both tariff enumerators bore the faintest tinge of chaos, but less than did either Daelyt or Shyret.

Shyret's smile vanished, and he turned and headed back to his study.

"You'd better start copying that schedule," suggested Daelyt. "You can add a few more vessels to the end, for both of us. I haven't had a chance to update it yet."

Rahl reached for several sheets of blank paper.

XLIII

Rahl looked at the cheese-covered wedge that the cook had set before him. Finally, he looked up and called to Seorya, who had returned to frying something on the iron stove that radiated so much heat that the street outside under the midday summer sun felt cooler. "What is this?"

"Pepper flahyl. Thought you Atlans liked things hot."

"I like them spicy, but not so hot that I cannot taste them," Rahl countered.

"You don't want to taste them."

Rahl suspected she might have a point. "Any flat bread?"

"Got a copper?"

"No. I haven't been paid."

She turned from the stove and tossed something at him. "Other half got overfried when Eneld was chewin' wind too much. Be better if he didn't think he was a cook."

Rahl caught the ragged chunk of fried flat bread. "Thank you."

After taking a small bite of the flahyl, Rahl followed it with a small bite of bread. Besides a sauce that tasted like liquid flame, the flahyl contained a mashed and flattened fried grain base with pieces of barely cooked slimy fish, pepper strips, and cheese that tried to stick to the roof of his mouth. He was just as glad he couldn't taste much of it, but he was hungry enough that he would eat it all.

"Daelyt coming over in a bit?"

"He should be, but that depends on the director and what work has to be done." He paused. "Have you ever seen his consort, Seorya?"

"No. She doesn't come here. Folks say that she has a bad leg, can hardly move it. She does needlework for Pasnyr, the fancy stuff on the fharongs."

It took Rahl a moment before he realized she was talking about the embroidered loose shirts worn by the more well-off men. "I'd wager it doesn't pay that well."

"Nothing pays well here, not unless you already got plenty a'golds."

Rahl nodded and kept eating, trying not to think about what the sauce and cheese concealed. He was successful enough that he managed to eat every last bite of the flahyl, but he had to take few small bites of the flat bread, and small sips of the bitter beer.

Finally, he stood. "As always, Seorya, your cooking was a delight to a famished man."

"You didn't say it was good."

Rahl laughed. "Delight is always good. I'll see you this evening."

She just snorted.

After stepping out into the alley behind the cantina, Rahl glanced around quickly, but there were only an old man and a youth on the far side, both in the shade, trying to escape the worst of the heat of early midday. The old man was eating something, shaking his head, and muttering, before spitting something onto the paving stones of the alley.

The youth, leaning against the brick wall of the arms shop, looked away.

Rahl hurried toward the street, belatedly sensing that the youth was following, and whistling. At the edge of the paved sidewalk, Rahl had to stop because a wagon, a coach, and several carriages were moving quickly down the street. He tried to keep his distance from all those on foot, but there were scores of people within fifty cubits.

Then, as he started to cross the street, he felt chaos, and turned, his hand on his truncheon. A youth bounced away from him, sliding onto the stone slab of the sidewalk. His eyes were wide, and fear radiated from him. The barefoot boy scrambled to his knees, and then to his feet, backing away from Rahl.

"Don't try your thievery on me," Rahl said quietly, the truncheon in his hand.

The boy turned and sprinted away, ducking behind a heavyset older woman.

"See . . . not all Atlans are easy marks."

". . . he's a big one, he is . . ."

". . . just a clerk for someone . . ."

Feeling another chaos-mist, Rahl half turned and slashed with the truncheon. He was not gentle, and an older youth reeled back, grasping his wrist. Like the first cutpurse, he dashed away.

In turn, Rahl hurried across the street, angling between two wagons. Inside, he was more than a little angry. Where were the patrollers and the mage-guards who were supposed to deal with thieves? He could feel his fingers tightening around the truncheon, and once he stepped up to the door of the Merchant Association, he forced himself to relax. He didn't replace the truncheon in its half sheath until he was inside.

Daelyt looked up from the consignment forms he was studying. "You don't look happy."

"Cutpurses. They didn't get anything . . ." Rahl paused and checked his belt wallet, concealed as it had been. "No . . . not this time, anyway."

"I try not to carry anything I don't have to," Daelyt said, shaking his head. "Little bastards will take the belt off your trousers. How did you even feel them?"

"I don't know. I just did. I hit one of them on the wrist."

"They'll either be looking for you or leave you alone." The other clerk paused. "Mean-looking truncheon you carry."

"I was told I'd need it."

"It's not iron, is it? The mage-guards frown on that."

"It's wood." Rahl decided against mentioning what kind of wood.

"That's probably all right."

"Where are the mage-guards? I've only seen them on the piers."

"They're everywhere. You don't always see them, but they see you."

"They didn't see the cutpurses," Rahl pointed out.

"With what you did, they probably didn't need to show up."

There wasn't much point in saying more, except that Rahl could sense order and chaos, and he hadn't sensed either. But he could see that there was a certain value in having people think the mage-guards could be everywhere.

"Could you make another copy of this consignment order?" asked Daelyt. "It's from Rystinyr for three hundred stones on the *Montgren*."

"I can do that."

"While you're writing it up, I'll hurry over to Eneld's. The director just left, and he won't be back for a bit. You know what to do on consignments, and you have the schedule for the ships. I won't be long. Do you have any questions?" Daelyt slipped off his stool.

Thinking about the state of his wallet, Rahl glanced to Daelyt. "Ah . . . when do we get paid?"

"Good question. At the end of the day every other sixday. The last payday was last sixday. So we get paid an eightday from tomorrow."

Rahl nodded. His coins *might* last that long, but he'd probably be reduced to the cheapest loaves that Gostof hawked.

XLIV

Sixday came and went, and so did sevenday, although Rahl and Daelyt had to work till almost dinner on sevenday, because the *Legacy of Westwind* ported, and the ship's master didn't have any intention of waiting until one-day to off-load and receive his cargo declarations. From Rahl's point of view, that had been a mixed blessing because it had meant that Shyret—or the Association—had paid for both his midday meal and the evening meal, which didn't happen on sevendays. On the other hand, he didn't get paid extra for the half day's work.

When he woke on eightday morning, later than usual, he realized, again, that the day was his and that he could do as he wished. Except for one thing—he hadn't been paid and wouldn't be for another six days, and all he had left was a little more than one silver, and that would have to go for the bread that comprised his morning meals.

After eating half of the loaf he'd bought the day before on the way back from his midday meal, when he'd realized that Gostof probably wouldn't be hawking bread on end-day, he washed up and got dressed. At least, he could walk around, and look and study Swartheld. In fact, he told himself, the more he learned the better off he would be, because in less than a sea-son, he'd be on his own. He hadn't learned anything more about how to control his order-skills, but then, he'd had little enough time, and he hadn't read much more in *The Basis of Order* either. He thought for a moment, then tucked the small black-covered book inside his summer tunic. He might find a quiet place to read.

He'd thought about writing his parents, but there was no point in it. It would be seasons before he had enough coins to pay for sending a letter to them, and anything he wrote now would have changed.

With a shrug, he slipped the truncheon into its belt straps, left his cubby, and walked to the front entrance, where he removed the bar, and unlocked the door. After stepping outside the Merchant Association build-ing, he relocked the front door, then turned, glancing around. Heavy shut-ters covered the windows of the arms shop and Eneld's cantina across the street. Farther westward, the coppersmith's was closed, as was the lace-maker's.

Where should he go?

In the end, he turned eastward. Daelyt had mentioned that it was cooler to the east, with nicer dwellings. Even as early as it was, the day was hot and muggy, and a faint silvery haze covered the green-blue sky, wash-ing it out. Unlike the previous mornings, he passed but a few handfuls of people as he walked two long blocks eastward, and the streets were largely deserted, without a single hawker or peddler. He glanced to his left, in the direction of the harbor, where there were a few wagons, but not that many more people.

Abruptly, he laughed, if softly. Had he been in Nylan or Land's End and seen the number of people he had passed, he would have thought it moder-ately busy. In Swartheld, he had already come to accept Daelyt's definition of what was crowded.

He was sweating when he reached an avenue that angled off to the northeast, but it was broad enough that the riders, wagons, and carriages headed away from the harbor took the south side, and those headed in to the harbor, the north, while the two lanes were divided by a narrow park-like strip. On each side of the parklike divider was a line of trees that resem-bled giant acacias, except the leaves were broader, and in the middle was a stone-paved sidewalk, shaded by the overhanging trees.

Rahl gratefully crossed the street and took the shaded sidewalk.

Less than two hundred cubits farther along, he saw an empty stone bench to the right, and he decided to sit down there and cool off. After wip-ing his forehead, he watched the part of avenue before him, the half for the wagons heading to the harbor. Only two empty wagons passed, and then the avenue was untraveled for a time before a covered carriage passed, hold-ing two couples. They were having an animated conversation, but Rahl couldn't make out the words as they rode by him.

Finally, he stood and resumed his walk, taking his time and appreciat-ing the shade provided by the leafy canopy of the overhanging limbs.

He passed another bench where two older men sat, side by side, not talking. Neither looked up, nor did they move. Coming down the sidewalk toward him was a large-framed young woman, pushing a small wheeled carriage with a seat. In the small seat was a child, bound loosely in place by a cloth band. Rahl had never seen such a child carriage, but then, why would he have? To make it would cost coins, perhaps a gold or more, and what purpose would it have in Recluce? Then again, perhaps the wealthier merchants and factors in Nylan or Land's End had such for their children.

Rahl nodded politely to the woman, but she was lost in her own thoughts and did not even see his gesture.

The small shops that had lined the avenue near the harbor had given way to small dwellings. All were in relatively good repair, with flat yellow tiles and stucco walls washed with white. They were so crowded together that the dwellings all shared the walls that surrounded their small rear courtyards, and the houses seemed to have common sidewalls. A man could climb up a corner wall and look into the courtyards of three of his neighbors. Even the poorest areas of Land's End were not so cramped.

Rahl kept walking.

After another half kay or so along the avenue and the walk, he came to a boulevard branching off to his left that looked as though it might lead seaward, but it was not divided or tree-lined. Rahl decided to keep following the tree-lined median parkway, although it was beginning to rise gently. Still, the avenue was certainly cooler, and besides, he wanted to see where it went. It wasn't as though he had anything else better to do.

He walked another half kay or so, coming to the top of a low rise, where he could see that the avenue ended only a few hundred cubits ahead at a street perpendicular to the avenue. Where the avenue ended, of course, so did the shaded center parkway and sidewalk.

Rahl stopped just short of the end of the avenue and looked at the cross street. On the street ahead were larger dwellings, all of at least two stories, and all set behind stone walls and gates. The roofs were all of a pale yellow tile, curved and joined, unlike the roofing on the meaner dwellings closer to the harbor, and the walls were of plaster or stucco, painted pastel shades. From the trees he could see rising behind those walls, there were gardens and courtyards surrounding the dwellings on all sides.

He studied the hillside behind the first line of dwellings, realizing that those farther east were higher—and far larger. Before him were more magnificent dwellings than existed in all of Recluce, he suspected.

Someone coughed, off to his right.

Rahl turned to see a patroller—a mage-guard, he mentally corrected himself—in khaki and black, with crimson insignia, sauntering in his direction. The mage-guard's hand was near the hilt of his falchiona, but he seemed relaxed as he stopped short of Rahl. "What are you doing here?"

"I'm taking a walk, ser. I'm new in Swartheld, and I had the day off."

"Where do you work?"

"I'm a clerk at the Merchant Association."

The patroller nodded. "Do you know where you are, young fellow?"

"The other clerks said it was cooler on the hills to the east."

This time the patroller laughed. "You *are* from Atla, no doubt about that. This is where factors and merchants live. At least, you didn't walk up here in rags."

"I was just looking for a cool and shady place. I wanted to see more of Swartheld." Rahl smiled pleasantly. All that he said was true enough.

"There's a park where you could go. It's a little west of here." The patroller pointed back down the tree-lined avenue Rahl had walked up. "About five streets down, there's a boulevard that heads north. To your right, toward the ocean. If you follow it, you'll see the park. It's a nice place. You'll fit in there."

"Thank you." Rahl turned obediently and headed back down the avenue, following the directions, back to the boulevard he had passed earlier. This time, he turned north, walking on the sidewalk that was separated from the fronts of the dwellings by a dirt strip no more than three cubits wide. There were some houses with grass on each side of the walk between the sidewalk and the front door, but even there the grass was as much browned-out tan as green. Most houses had no grass at all in front, just dusty, hard-packed dirt. For all that, Rahl saw no trash, and no sagging shutters or run-down dwellings.

After several hundred cubits, he came to what he thought might be a temple or something of the sort. While the structure was only of one story, it was tall enough for two. What made it unusual, though, was the twin spires at the end away from the street. The southern spire was narrow and rose to a point that glittered in the sun, but the northern spire *curled* and then straightened before ending in a strange convolution of metal strips or bars that faintly resembled the female form.

As he passed, he heard singing within, but could not make out the words. It had to be a temple of some sort of worshippers. He shook his head and kept walking northward, wiping the sweat from his forehead, as the sun felt more intense with every step.

Then, the dwellings on the left ended, and Rahl stood at the southeastern edge of an expanse of open ground bordered on the east, south, and north by lines of dusty-leaved acacias that offered minimal shade. To the west was a low bluff, perhaps twenty or thirty cubits above the roofs and walls of the warehouses and factorages that bordered the eastern side of the harbor. Beyond the trees to the north was a jumble of dark gray and black rock, with but occasional weeds and scrawny trees poking up from the inhospitable land.

The park actually contained areas of worn grass, as well as three groves of loosely spaced acacias with a few tables set in the groves. The pillars supporting the battered plank tabletops were of the ubiquitous yellow brick. Away from the trees were several narrow stone walks or gameways, where teams of men, two at each end, tried to skid triangular stones closest to a small stone circle of a lighter color.

The men were wearing simple short-sleeved shirts with soft collars, or no collars at all, and a number wore a kind of trouser Rahl hadn't seen at all, that ended midway between the knee and ankle. Above ankle-length flowing pants, all the women wore flowing blouses that ran from wrist to neck. Only their sandaled feet and hands were uncovered, although the light fabric of their head scarves concealed nothing. Rahl looked more closely at a woman walking by, holding the hand of her small daughter. The fabric of her garments was light, and not tightly woven. In fact, in the bright sunlight, at times, he could see the outline of her figure.

So what was the purpose of garments that covered everything, yet that occasionally revealed so much?

Rahl eased himself into a relatively shady spot beneath the nearest tree and continued to survey what was happening. Whole families had to have arrived early to claim the shaded tables in the groves, and in several places, he could see older white-haired men playing what looked to be a form of plaques.

Two men detached themselves from a group that looked to include several families under the nearest acacia grove and ambled toward him.

Rahl waited, taking their measure as they neared. Neither was as tall as he was, and while the two bore belt knives, they had no other weapons. One had drooping black mustaches, and the other had a few days' growth of beard. Both wore old and thin faded shirts, not tunics or undertunics.

"You're not from around here," said the shorter and broader figure, fingering one pointed end of his mustache.

"No. I live down near the harbor."

"You sound like you're from Atla."

"I've only been in Swartheld for a short time."

The taller man looked at the truncheon, then at Rahl. "You look too pretty to be a guard, and most bravos wear blades."

"I work for a trading association," countered Rahl. "They don't like holes in possible shippers."

The shorter man laughed. "You ever use a falchiona?"

"Enough."

"Why are you here?"

"At the park?" Rahl shrugged. "What else would I do? I haven't gotten paid that much yet."

"How about women?"

Rahl laughed. "I left the one I wanted behind, and I haven't met any here. Even if I did, why would they be interested in someone without that many coins?" As he finished speaking, he realized that what had started out as an evasion and rationalization was actually true—except that the image that had come to mind was that of Deybri.

Deybri? The healer who had told him that the past had no hold on him?

"You get any coins at all, and you'll find someone interested," replied the shorter man. "There's always someone in Swartheld."

Rahl laughed. "We'll just have to see."

Abruptly, the two exchanged glances.

"Well, best of fortune, fellow," said the shorter man.

"Thank you." Rahl nodded, but kept his attention on both as they stepped back carefully, and turned away. He used his order-skills to try to pick up the low murmurs as they walked across the sparse grass and dusty ground back toward the family group under the shade of the nearest grove.

"Nice enough . . ."

"Tough ones are . . . don't keep that pretty a face unless . . ." The shorter man shook his head.

"Mage-guards'll get him . . . 'less he's registered."

"Didn't see it."

As the two moved out of earshot, Rahl frowned. What had they been looking for? Some indication that he was registered as a mage? But he wasn't, and he'd been careful not to use any active order-magery anywhere, especially in public.

Finally, he walked northward for almost a hundred cubits until he found a tree where it was even more shaded and comfortable enough to sit down and read. He doubted he'd learn much, but he might as well try, and his feet could use a little rest.

XLV

On oneday, Rahl was almost happy to get up early and sweep and polish some of the brasswork before eating and washing up. That might have been because eightday had not proved particularly pleasant or productive for Rahl, except in leaving his feet sore and his face and neck sunburned, and costing him several coppers for a fowl stick from a vendor near another parklike area farther to the south of the harbor area.

People he'd passed on his long walk had seemed friendly enough, but like the two men in the first park, most had said a few words, then left or excused themselves. Could they sense the difference . . . or was it merely the Atlan accent?

He'd stopped in several shaded places and read portions of *The Basis of Order*, but the book remained as useless to him as ever. Of what worldly use was a phrase like "for chaos can be said to be the wellspring of order and order the wellspring of chaos"? Or the section that said that a mage shouldn't assume that what lay beneath was the same as what lay above or that it might be different? Anything was either the same or different. Why did the writer even have to write something that obvious down? Reading it not only left him irritated, but often just plain angry at the unnecessary obtuseness of the words.

Daelyt stepped into the front area of the office and glanced around. "You did the brasswork. It looks good."

"Thank you. How was your end-day?" Rahl suppressed his exasperation about *The Basis of Order*.

"Good. Yasnela and I visited some friends. Shealyr has an old mare and a cart, and he was kind enough to let me borrow them. We had a good time, but I'll pay for it later today."

Rahl let his order-senses take in Daelyt, but the clerk didn't seem that tired or even different. Perhaps there was a shade more of the white chaos-mist around him, but Rahl wasn't even sure about that.

"Usually on oneday, nothing happens early, because everyone's cleaning up and figuring out things, and then it gets rushed in the afternoon.

I stopped by to see Chenaryl, but he's still not through with the corrected cargo declaration," said Daelyt, adding after a moment, "On the cargo off-loaded from the *Westwind*." The clerk began taking blank forms from his drawers and stacking them.

"Does the Association send those from Nylan—the forms, I mean?"

"Mostly. Even with the shipping, it's cheaper. Undelsor could print them, but anything we want has to come after everyone else because we represent outlanders." Daelyt snorted. "Shyret tried to offer more, once, and he was told that was bribery, and he could be flogged for it. Locals can offer more to get their work done first, but we can't."

Rahl followed Daelyt's example and seated himself on his stool.

"What did you do yesterday?" asked the older clerk.

"I just walked around, tried to get a better feel for Swartheld. I think it will take time." He paused, then went on, carefully. "I was at the park, the one up behind the harbor to the east—"

"That's a long walk."

"What else was I going to do? Anyway, I was sitting under a tree, and a bravo came up, and two men went over and talked to him, and he left. But they watched him. They were looking for something."

"Oh . . . freelance bravos have to be registered with the mage-guards, just like the mages, and they have to wear a wristband."

"I understand about mages, but bravos?"

"They can only kill in self-defense or under contract."

"You can hire someone to kill someone?"

Daelyt shook his head. "You or I couldn't. The minimum contract is a gold, but most bravos won't work for less than twice that, and the ones that will don't last long."

Rahl just sat there, silent, for a moment. "What . . . what if they fail?"

"They have to succeed or return the fee plus a tenth more."

"What if they get killed by the person they're supposed to kill?"

"It doesn't happen often, but, if it does, that person gets the fee, and the name of the person who made the hire."

"Couldn't the person who was attacked just go kill the person who paid the bravo?"

Daelyt laughed sardonically. "No. That'd be murder. Like anything else in Swartheld, you have to pay a professional to do the job. Why do you think Shyret needs us? It's a fine for a trader or a shipper to do his own declarations. They have to be done by one of the shipping associations or by the bonded agents of an individual shipowner. That's for the handful that have their own fleets, like Kashanat, Doramyl, or Skionyl."

Doramyl? Rahl had heard the name before, but could not recall where. At that moment, the front door opened, and a man stepped into the Association building. He wore a fharong colored blue and soft yellow, and embroidered in green. To Rahl's eyes, his hands looked greenish.

"Is Director Shyret here?"

"I believe so, Dyemaster," replied Daelyt, "but let me check." The clerk hurried back toward Shyret's study.

Within moments, Shyret appeared. Rahl hadn't even realized that the director had arrived earlier through the storeroom door.

The director bustled toward the dyemaster. "Ebsolam! I have your indigo and scarletine. I sent a message."

Daelyt slipped along behind Shyret, then eased back into his stool.

"So you did, but . . . you're asking a gold more a keg than you quoted."

Shyret offered an apologetic expression. "Cartage rates are up, and the rains in Feyn fell mainly on the higher ground, and the kermetite swarms were thinner this winter. We did the best we could." A shrug followed. "I'd not hold you to the commitment, since we can't meet the quote."

"Can't? Or won't?" asked the dyemaster.

"It's the same thing. If I sell at less than cost, I won't be here long."

Ebsolam's flinty eyes fixed on Shyret.

"You can hope the Esalians might send a shipment. Their scarletine generally costs less," suggested Shyret.

"It's not as good."

"Do you want it or not?"

"I'll take it, you scoundrel. Sometimes, you give Jeranyi pirates a good name."

"As soon as we have your draft, Guylmor will deliver the kegs."

"My son will be by with the draft before midday." Ebsolam turned and left.

Rahl could sense the anger held within the dyemaster.

Only once the door had closed did Shyret turn, shaking his head. "They charge all the market will bear, and when we have to raise prices to cover our costs, you would think that the very ocean was at his door." He looked directly at Rahl. "I was about to come out anyway. I need you to take something to the enumerators' office. It's next to the harbormaster's."

"I'd be happy to, ser," Rahl said, "but I'll need directions."

"Guylmor will drive. It's not a good idea to walk that far. Not with a draft on the Exchange, and that's what you'll be taking. Just run out and tell Guylmor that he's to drive you there. Then you can come back here while he's harnessing and wait until he pulls up out in front."

"Yes, ser." Rahl slipped off the stool and headed for the rear storeroom door. Once outside, he had to go to the south end of the courtyard to find Guylmor, who was grooming one of the dray horses outside the stables there. He was sweating by the time he reached the teamster. The day was looking to be even hotter than end-day had been.

"Guylmor, the director wants you to drive me to the enumerators' place next to the harbormaster's."

The teamster looked up. "You got too much sun. Look like a steamed langostino."

"I'm not used to it."

"Be a few moments, and I'll bring it out front."

"Thank you."

"What we're here for." The teamster resumed grooming the big chestnut.

Rahl turned and walked back up the long courtyard. Shyret had gone back to his study by the time Rahl returned to the Association office and climbed back onto his stool. What was he supposed to do now?

Daelyt was painstakingly cleaning his pen and then the rim of his inkwell. After that, he looked up. "The director will be back in a few moments, he said."

"You were telling me about people being punished for doing things they weren't supposed to do. Does that mean we get in trouble if we mortar a loose brick or repair a shutter, things like that?"

Daelyt laughed. "You're taking me too seriously. It's stuff for other people. We can do anything the director tells us here at the Association, because the Association owns everything, and we work for it, and the director's in charge. He couldn't have us fix Eneld's shutters, because we're not carpenters and we're not working for Eneld or related to him. Eneld can try to fix his own shutters. He shouldn't because he makes a mess of anything but cooking and serving, but he could . . ."

"Rahl . . ."

Rahl turned to see Shyret walking toward him, carrying a large brown envelope.

"This is what you're to take to the enumerators. You say that you're new and you're delivering this to the tariff clerk from Director Shyret at the Nylan Merchant Association."

"Yes, ser."

"You have Guylmor drive you there. Have him wait, and then have him drive you back here. Make sure that you get a receipt with the enumerators' pressed seal."

"Yes, ser."

Shyret finally handed the envelope to Rahl, then turned and headed back to his study.

Rahl watched through the narrow front windows until Guylmor drove up. He wasn't holding the leads to a wagon, but to a light trap, pulled by a single horse.

"I'll be back as soon as I can," Rahl said, standing and picking the envelope off the desktop.

"Don't dawdle, but don't rush."

"I won't." Rahl made his way out to the trap and climbed up onto the seat beside the teamster.

"Rahl . . . you said we were going to the enumerators'. That right?"

"That's what the director told me. I have to deliver this envelope."

"Oh . . . Daelyt used to do that. Guess you get to be messenger now." Guylmor flicked the leads lightly, and the horse pulled the trap away from the Association building and out into the welter of carts, carriages, and wagons, heading eastward, then north on the harbor boulevard. The going was barely faster than a walk, and if Rahl's feet had not been sore, he could have walked the distance faster than he was riding.

"There's the harbormaster's up on the right, past the mage-guard post."

Rahl stiffened inside. He really didn't want to get that close to one of the mage-guards.

Ahead of them, the mage-guard sat in a chair on a raised pedestal a good four cubits high, shaded by a crimson umbrella. A pair of patrollers, also in crimson and khaki, stood in front of the pedestal, occasionally stepping forward and stopping a wagon or carriage headed toward the piers. Those stops were what slowed their progress, Rahl could see.

The patroller waved through a wagon loaded with coal, and the carriage following it, but as Guylmor eased the trap forward, the patroller gestured for Guylmor to stop.

The teamster did.

"You . . ." The mage-guard pointed to Rahl. "Over here."

Rahl climbed down and moved from the trap, still holding the envelope, to the south side of the pedestal from which the mage-guard looked down. He was far enough away that Guylmor could not hear, not easily. The mage-guard was a woman, Rahl realized, her face weathered and hard, but the white flames of chaos flickered around her as she studied him.

"Who are you?"

"I'm Rahl, ser. I'm a clerk at the Nylan Merchant Association," Rahl replied in Hamorian.

"What happened to the other clerk?"

"Daelyt? He's still there."

She nodded knowingly, but her shields blocked whatever she was feeling.

"Why are you here?"

"The director told me to bring this envelope to the tariffing clerk at the enumerators'."

"What's in it?"

"Some papers and a draft on the Exchange for them. That's what he said. It's sealed, and I haven't opened it."

"Are you registered in Atla? Or here?"

"Ah, ser . . . I'm from Nylan. I don't understand."

"You have order-energies. That makes you a possible mage. Mages must be registered."

Rahl didn't know quite what to say that would not make matters worse.

"Where do you live? Or sleep?"

"At the Merchant Association, ser. That's where I work."

"You were born and grew up in Recluce, then?"

"Yes, ser."

"How did you get an Atlan accent?"

"The man who taught me Hamorian had it. He said I'd picked it up, and that people would notice it."

"That they would," she said dryly. "Were you aware you are a mage?"

"Ser . . . I'm not really a mage, not in Nylan," Rahl said. "I have a few skills. I don't want to get in trouble with you and the other mage-guards, but I don't want to claim I'm something I'm not, either."

The mage-guard shook her head. "Here in Hamor, if you have any order- or chaos-skills, you're considered a mage. Since you work for an outland merchanting association, and were born elsewhere, and live on their premises, you are not technically in violation of the Codex." The mage-guard paused. "I would still suggest that you register as an outland mage. If you do, so long as you do not do active magery, and you wear your bracelet, we will not trouble you."

"Yes, ser. I'm new here. Where do I register?"

She smiled faintly. "I wish others were as cooperative." She half turned and pointed. "The first building to the right is the harbormaster's. Behind that is the enumerators' building. That's where you find the tariffing clerk. If you follow the lane, there's a building with crimson tiles set around the windows and the doors. If you get to the end and the bluff, that's too far. Go in the main door, and tell whoever is at the counter what happened. They'll take it from there."

"Yes, ser. Thank you, ser. Can I deliver the envelope first?"

She nodded. "On your way."

Rahl walked back to the trap and climbed up.

"What did she want?"

"To tell me what I needed to do after we deliver this."

The trap moved forward, past the patroller, and then right into a narrower way that headed due east past the small brownstone building that had to be the harbormaster's. Less than fifty cubits from the eastern end of the brownstone was a larger structure with a domed roof, constructed of a reddish sandstone.

Guylmor slowed and then halted the trap short of the main entrance. "Can't block the entry. If I have to move, I'll be farther down."

Rahl nodded and vaulted down. His feet hurt when his boots hit the stone pavement, reminding him, again, how far he'd walked on end-day. He walked another thirty cubits or so, up the three wide stone steps, and in through the sandstone archway. There, he looked around, catching sight of a guard with both falchiona and a long truncheon, one weapon on each side of his belt.

"I'm looking for the tariffing clerk."

"The arch to the left."

"Thank you."

The guard did not reply.

Rahl continued to the arch, turning there and stepping into a chamber with a waist-high oak counter set back five cubits from the arch and running from wall to wall. The wooden counter was so old that it was brown rather than even golden.

Two men stood behind the counter.

"The tariffing clerk?" asked Rahl.

"Either one of us," replied the younger man, although he was clearly close to Rahl's father's age, while the other was graying and stern-faced.

Rahl went to the man who had spoken, tendering the envelope. "This is from the Nylan Merchant Association."

"The last moment, as usual." The clerk shook his head as he opened the envelope and scanned the sheet of paper and the draft that accompanied it. After several moments, he turned to a black ledger and began to write— entering the name of the Association and the amount of the draft, Rahl thought.

Then, he took a square of parchment, roughly a span by a span, and filled in several lines, then signed it. After waiting for the ink to dry, he took a circular press-seal and fitted it over the signature part of the parchment and pressed the handles. The receipt went into an envelope that he handed to Rahl. "Your receipt."

"Thank you."

The tariffing clerk only nodded, although Rahl sensed a certain disdain.

Rahl hurried back outside to where the teamster waited and climbed back up into the seat. "We need to go somewhere else, Guylmor. Because I'm an outlander, I need to register with the mage-guards. It's in the building up there against the bluff." Rahl pointed.

"Daelyt always came right back, Rahl."

"He probably did, but he's been here a while, and they know him. Anyway, the mage-guard said that I'd have to go through that every time I saw one of them unless I registered. I don't think the director would like that."

"Suppose not. Never had this happen before."

"It's been a while since anyone came here directly from Nylan or Recluce."

"They get those travelers in black, sometimes, with black staffs. Most of 'em end up in the quarries, I hear, without any memory, either." Guylmor lifted the leads, and the mare started forward.

Rahl was not looking forward to registering, whatever that meant, but he had the feeling that not registering would be worse. That might have been because of what had happened with Magister Puvort.

At that thought, Rahl had to push back anger he had managed to forget. Here he was, having to deal with Hamorian mage-guards just because Puvort hadn't wanted to go to any trouble to explain things—and in fact because the dishonest bastard had framed Rahl. Magistra Kadara hadn't been that much better, either. She'd been skeptical of him before she'd even seen him more than a few moments.

Being angry would only make matters worse. Rahl took a deep slow breath.

"You all right?"

"I'm fine." Rahl sat quietly beside the teamster as the trap moved toward the registry building. He concentrated on calming himself.

When the teamster stopped the trap, he looked at Rahl. "I'll be turning the trap around if you come out and don't find me."

Rahl doubted he would be anywhere near that quick. "Thank you. I hope I won't be long." He climbed down and crossed the paved space between the street and the entry.

There were no mage-guards outside, and two corridors branched from the entry. Rahl stepped into the one to the right, but he could tell two things. There were no mages around, not nearby, and all the doors were closed. He went back and stepped through the other archway into a foyer with a desk. A mage-guard sat behind it.

Chaos swirled around Rahl, and he barely managed to avoid losing his balance.

The older mage-guard looked up from the table desk. "Yes?" Then he smiled, coolly. "You're here to register?"

"Yes, ser." Rahl was getting more than a little tired of saying "ser" to so many people, but he offered a polite smile. "I'm new here in Swartheld, and I work at the Nylan Merchant Association . . ." Rahl explained everything he had told the mage-guard who had stopped him on the pier avenue and what she had said. ". . . and she told me it would be best if I registered."

An ordermage had somehow appeared, although Rahl had not seen him, and he nodded. "He's clean. Almost every word true." He grinned. "He's a little fuzzy about his abilities."

"Tell me more about your order-skills," asked the chaos mage-guard.

"I can't really, ser. I mean, I can sometimes tell how people are feeling, and I see better in the dark, but I can't sense weather or what's under the ground. I can sort of see and feel when people are sick, but when I tried to help a healer, it didn't help much. I didn't hurt the man, but I couldn't heal him." Rahl shrugged helplessly.

"That's about got it," said the ordermage-guard. "He could develop more skills here, or stay the same, or even lose skills. He doesn't look to be a danger, and . . . if he's a registered outlander . . ."

There were more questions, but not many, although Rahl had the feeling that matters would have been much worse had he not been a clerk at the Association.

In the end, the chaos mage-guard measured Rahl's left wrist before departing for a time. He returned with a copperlike bracelet. On it were Rahl's name, the letters NMA, and inscription OUT-437. The mage-guard took out a ledger and, at the bottom of a half column of names, wrote out Rahl's name, place of work, and what was inscribed on the bracelet.

Rahl sensed that not many entries had been made recently, and that concerned him.

"Sign here—you can sign your name since you're a clerk, right?"

"I can sign." Rahl did.

"You don't have to wear the bracelet," the chaos mage-guard said, "not as an outlander, but you do have to have it with you if you leave Swartheld for any other part of Hamor. It will be easier for you if you have it with you whenever you leave your dwelling or work." He extended the bracelet.

Rahl nodded as he took it and slipped it on his left wrist. "Is that all? Do I have to do anything else?"

"As an outlander, you are forbidden to use active order- or chaos-skills outside your dwelling or place of work, except in self-defense. Any claim of self-defense will be tried by the justicers of mages. If you choose to leave your employer and do not work for another outlander, you must reregister and be tested and instructed like any mage born in Hamor. That costs a gold, but if you don't have the funds, just say so, and the funds will come out of whatever you get paid in the future. Don't let the lack of coin stop you. Failure to reregister could get you a flogging or worse."

That was another bit of information that chilled Rahl. "Thank you." He nodded again, then stopped. "Are there any special days . . . ?"

"No. Someone's here all the time. You might have to wait a while on end-days, though. We're usually shorthanded."

Obviously, the mage-guards worked harder than the magisters did.

"That's all, Rahl."

"Oh . . . I'm sorry. I was just thinking." Rahl turned and left.

". . . that one won't last . . ."

". . . might . . ."

Guylmor was glancing from side to side as Rahl neared the trap. Rahl kept his left arm out of sight.

"There you are. I was getting worried, Rahl."

"They had questions and some papers to sign. Let's get back." Rahl climbed back up into the seat he had been in and out of more times than he'd wanted.

"Good by me."

As Guylmor drove back along the lane, and waited for the patroller to stop other wagons so that they could get back on the harbor boulevard, Rahl sat, thinking. He couldn't stay more than a season with the Association, and once he left, he'd either have to find a way out of Swartheld or effectively put himself in the hands of the mage-guards. The more he thought about it, the angrier he got. He wasn't just in exile, but perilously close to being in worse danger than he'd ever faced.

If he could have at that moment, he would have put a falchiona into Puvort without the slightest remorse. The magistras in Nylan weren't much better, either. Anyone they sent to Hamor was almost certainly doomed to slavery or worse. And they talked about their kindness in "preparing" people for exile!

Rahl's lips tightened. What could he do? He didn't really have that much time . . . or coins.

"Rahl . . . we're here."

"Oh . . . I'm sorry. I was thinking." Rahl didn't need to be angry at Guylmor. The teamster certainly wasn't at fault.

Rahl gathered himself together and eased off the seat. His feet were still warning him not to jump down. Before he stepped into the Merchant Association building, he slipped the shimmering copper bracelet off his wrist and into his belt wallet. At the moment, the last thing he wanted was for anyone to think he was a mage, especially Daelyt or Shyret, since they were not supposed to know—if what the board members in Nylan had said happened to be true. He had to wonder at that, but he wasn't about to bring it up.

Shyret was pacing up and down the space behind the wide desk. At Rahl's entry, he turned. "Rahl, what took so long? I need Guylmor to take the wagon and the dyes to Ebsolam."

"Something must have happened in the harbor. The mage-guards were stopping everyone. They wanted to know who I was, why I was there, and who I worked for."

"Did they take the envelope?"

"No, ser. They let me deliver it to the enumerators'. Here is the receipt they gave me." Rahl extended the envelope with the sealed square of parchment.

Shyret as much as grabbed the envelope as accepted it and immediately opened it. Rahl could feel the relief from the director as soon as Shyret saw the receipt.

"Sometimes that happens. It's most disconcerting," said the director.

Rahl could tell he was lying—and that he'd been worried about that draft getting to the enumerators', worried more than just a little.

Shyret forced a smile. "Thank you."

"I'm sorry it took so long. Maybe they just stopped me because I was new. The mage-guard wanted to know where Daelyt was. It seemed better when I explained, but that took time."

The director smiled wanly. "I need to make sure Chenaryl's loaded the wagon for Ebsolam." He turned.

Rahl took a slow deep breath, then moved toward his stool. "Do you know what that draft was for?" He kept his voice low.

"No. Not exactly," replied Daelyt. "I imagine it's one of the seasonal tariff payments to the enumerators. Everyone who handles declarations and manifests is assessed tariffs four times a year. The amount is based on how much cargo passes through our warehouses. I work up the figures and give them to the director. He writes the draft and sends it. I've been taking it . . . until you got here."

"He seemed worried," Rahl ventured.

"Things have been a little slow . . . he probably waited until the last moment to write the draft—or he could have forgotten it was due. Anyway," Daelyt said with a shrug, "it's done, and I've got the declarations for the *Legacy of Westwind*. We might as well get on with it before the enumerators show up."

Rahl climbed into his stool.

At that moment, he realized where he'd heard the name Doramyl before—from Alamyrt on the *Diev*. But why had Alamyrt been traveling on a Recluce vessel when he or his family owned their own fleet? Or had the trader just been pretending to be Alamyrt? Yet he'd owned bales of wool in his own name, and black wool didn't come cheap.

"Rahl? We need to get started."

"Oh . . . I'm sorry." Rahl jerked alert. He must have dozed off. "I don't know what happened."

"Too much sun yesterday. Your skin is still red. It's hotter here than in Recluce."

"That could be." Rahl cleaned his pen and dipped it in the inkwell. "I'm ready."

"Cargo declaration of sevenday, eleventh eightday of summer . . ."

Rahl began to write.

XLVI

Thankfully, the next several days were uneventful for Rahl, and he did not have to go anywhere there might be a mage-guard. Even with the registry bracelet, he didn't want anything to do with them. He kept the bracelet in his belt wallet, although at first it clinked loudly and gave the impression he had more coins than he did. He solved that problem by wrapping it in an old square of cloth he took from the rags in the storeroom.

The *Legacy of the Founders* ported ahead of schedule on fourday, but Chenaryl did not finish the "corrected" cargo declarations until mid-afternoon on sixday. Daelyt had delegated the drafting of the clean Hamor-ian copies of the cargo declaration to Rahl and checked each page of the first copy of the declaration as Rahl finished it.

Rahl was completing the last page of the third copy when Daelyt looked up from the cargo consignment form he had been writing up.

"The declaration shows that two kegs of madder were spoiled. What happens to all the spoiled goods?" asked Rahl.

"Chenaryl will sell them for what he can get on the sevenday auctions at the Exchange Plaza," replied Daelyt. "Just like all the other spoilage. The coins go back into the accounts here, except Chenaryl gets one part in fifty for his trouble."

"I can see that it's better for everyone to get some coins," Rahl said, "but how does it work out for the traders? Or the growers or whoever made the goods?"

"Oh, they don't have to worry," explained Daelyt. "The Association buys the goods outright, except for cargoes carried under consignment. Then we resell them to factors and merchants here—or anyone else who pays the price. The spoilage and the costs of carrying goods are why they cost more here than they would in Nylan or wherever they come from."

Rahl thought about that for a moment. "So the price that the director charges others here in Swartheld has to be high enough to cover the losses and the spoilage . . . and what it costs to keep the Association going? That's why he wouldn't back down to Ebsolam the other day. Or Escoryl."

"Exactly."

"So, if spoilage gets too high, prices have to go up, or the Association loses coins."

"Both, sometimes," replied Daelyt, "and for some things he can't raise prices. The director doesn't like it when that happens."

Rahl could see why.

"Are you finished with that last copy?" asked Daelyt.

"Yes." Rahl handed it to the older clerk, thinking over what Daelyt had said . . . and what he had not, and how uneasy the other had been. "What else do you need?"

"You can make the copy of this when I'm finished. While you're doing that, I need to find out something from the director."

"I'll work on copying the new schedule until you're done," Rahl said, "now that we have dates for the *Guards* and *Black Holding*."

"That's a good idea."

Rahl actually finished a complete copy of the Association ship arrivals scheduled for the next three eightdays before Daelyt wiped his pen and set it aside.

"Here you are." Daelyt did not look at Rahl as he handed him the cargo consignment form.

"I'll get to work on it."

"Good." Daelyt's voice was a trace flat as he eased off his stool.

Rahl only waited until Daelyt was beyond the archway before following the older clerk. He just sensed that he needed to know what he had said that had upset Daelyt. He stopped just before the arch and tried to use his order-skills to pick up what Daelyt was saying.

"Ser . . . worry about Rahl . . . sounds dumb with that Atlan accent. He's not . . . lot of attention to the spoilage . . ." Daelyt's voice was low, and hard for Rahl to pick up.

"Is that so? Just watch him."

". . . see if he says more?"

"We have time, and he does good work, doesn't he?"

"... much better ... Wynreed ..."

"No reason not to use him while we can. If it looks bad, well ... he can disappear."

"... not like ... Wynreed ..."

"It doesn't matter. Who would he tell? We're within the laws here, and no one in Nylan will really care. No one wants to come here so long as we return profits on the golds they've invested."

Rahl turned and slipped back to his stool so that he was writing out the copy of the consignment form when Daelyt returned. He did not look up, but kept working, trying to keep himself composed, and concentrating on not putting too much pressure on the pen. He had a tendency to do that when he was upset.

Somehow, Rahl managed to get through the end of the day. He was glad that he and Daelyt had to eat their evening meal at differing times. It would have been hard not to reveal his worry—and his anger.

Once Shyret and Daelyt had left the Association, Rahl stepped out and locked the front door behind him. He made his way eastward, trying to ignore the faintly acrid odors of too many people in too small an area cooking too much unfamiliar food. He kept walking along the avenue with the tree-lined median until he found an empty bench under the trees. There he sat in the hot evening, occasionally wiping his forehead, watching a few riders and carriages go past, trying to think, to sort things out.

While he couldn't prove it, he was certain that most of the "spoiled" goods were not. He knew scarletine was even more expensive than indigo, and it had been valued on the manifest at something like fifty golds a keg. If Chenaryl reported a sale at ten golds, but really had sold it at fifty, and the wool at a similar difference, Shyret was making as much as forty to eighty golds off so-called spoilage on every ship. Chenaryl was making more than a few golds on the reported salvage sales. But what about Daelyt?

Yasnela had to be the key. Daelyt had as much as said that she could not walk—or not far—and that the two had rooms above the warehouse. Was the lodging and some healer support what Daelyt got? With what clerks made, Daelyt would be hard-pressed to support and quarter a consort without some accommodation by Shyret. Was that because Daelyt helped Shyret in his manipulations? It had to be, or he wouldn't have talked to Shyret that way.

Rahl looked blankly at the tree across the stone sidewalk from him. What could he do? He couldn't prove the goods hadn't been spoiled. Everything that had been declared spoiled had already been sold except for the items on the *Founders*. Shyret was the only representative of Nylan in Swartheld, and he was the one stealing from the Association, and Rahl had sensed clearly the truth of the statement about what was being done was within the laws of Hamor.

In a way, he supposed it was. The growers got paid. The ships or their captains and crews got paid. But the Association was getting cheated. The question was . . . who was the Association? What was it? How did it work? Did it matter? It had to matter to someone.

Rahl found his fists clenching and his jaw tightening. He was in Hamor, working for a thieving director, yet where could he go and what could he do? If he left the Association, unless he immediately turned himself over to the mage-guards for testing, he'd be breaking the law, and after his experiences with mages, he wasn't ready to go running to them, especially since, under Hamorian law, apparently, what Shyret was doing wasn't illegal. And Rahl would either need a gold he didn't have or have to be indentured . . . or something . . . if . . . when he left the Association.

What about seeing the factors at . . . what had it been . . . Doramyl and Sons?

He shook his head. He'd still have to register with the mage-guards.

Everything was so wrong, and so unfair! All because that arrogant sow's ass Puvort hadn't wanted to be honest or fair, and the magisters in Nylan were so worried that he might damage something. None of them gave a demon's fart about Rahl or what might happen to him.

He stood up and began to walk. He had to do *something*.

XLVII

On sevenday morning, before anyone else showed up, Rahl polished the brasswork on all the lamps—except those in Shyret's locked study—as well as on the doors and cabinet pulls. Then he swept the tile floor and mopped the entry area. He had just finished getting cleaned up and settling into place at the wide desk when Daelyt walked through the front door.

"So . . . feel guilty about getting paid, and you decided to do more of the brasswork?" Daelyt laughed.

Rahl had gotten a silver the evening before, but that was only for one eightday's pay, rather than two. While it was more than twice what he'd received at the training center, everything he had to spend coins on was far more costly in Swartheld than it had been in Nylan. "I appreciate the pay. Having coins is much better than not, but"—Rahl offered a grin before going on—"I only feel a little guilty." He really wanted to tell the older clerk that he didn't feel guilty at all, but that wouldn't have been wise.

"A little guilt is good." Daelyt set out his pen and inkwell, then lifted a folder. "The director asked for a copy of this, and we've been so busy, I never got to it. With the *Montgren* more than an eightday out, now's a good time for you to work on it."

"Ah . . . what is it?"

"Oh . . . it's the final inventory of what was in the warehouses on the last day of spring. The director has to send the Association's chief managing director an inventory at the end of each season. It includes both what was left at the end of the season, with an estimated value, as well as what was sold during the season and for what, as well as losses through spoilage and pilfering. There's also an addendum that lists what we hold in storage for others and what we receive for the storage fees. I've let it drag, but it will have to be done and sent to Nylan on the *Legacy of Montgren*. The chief managing director gets upset if the reports get more than a season behind." Daelyt extended the folder. "Director Shyret will need two copies, but just do one first, and I'll check it as you do."

Rahl took the heavy folder. "There are a lot of pages here."

Daelyt grinned. "There are. It will give you a better idea of all that we handle here."

After setting the folder in front of him, slightly to his left, Rahl began to turn the first few pages, filled with changes scrawled in the margins and smudges everywhere. With such entries going on for what looked to be almost twenty pages, he could definitely see why Daelyt would like someone else to do the fair copying.

He extracted the blank ledger sheets from his side of the desk and began to copy, taking his time, because he needed to check the figures as well as copy them neatly. Even so, it was certainly no worse than *Natural Arithmetics* and not nearly so impenetrable as *Philosophies of Candar*.

Daelyt looked over his efforts several times, then straightened as a trader came in the front entry. "Might I be of assistance, noble trader?"

"When's your next vessel bound for Nylan?"

"That would be the *Legacy of Montgren,* and it will be porting sometime after an eightday from oneday."

"I'm looking for cubage for amphorae—needlewasp honey."

"How many stones' worth?"

"Less than a hundred."

"That will not be a problem."

The trader nodded, turned, and left.

Rahl looked at Daelyt quizzically.

"You've never heard of needlewasp honey?" asked the older clerk.

"I didn't know it came from Hamor. Don't the vintners use it to sweeten and stabilize bitter wines?"

"More trades use it than you'd think. Apothecaries, vintners, brewers, even dyers." Daelyt snorted. "Working for a wasp-keeper . . . almost as bad as the quarries or the ironworks. Worse if you're the kind that swells up when you get stung."

"Where do they keep the wasps?"

"Most of the wasp-keepers are in the low marshy valleys south of Cigoerne. That's where the blue lilies grow."

"Daelyt!" called Shyret from the archway leading to his study.

The older clerk slipped off his stool and hurried away.

Rahl kept working on the seasonal inventory through the rest of the morning and into the early afternoon, before Daelyt sent him over to Eneld's for his midday repast. Then Daelyt went.

Late in the afternoon, when Daelyt had completed the draft cargo consignment form for the honey factor, Rahl cleared his throat.

"Yes?"

"Daelyt . . . I have a question, and it's going to sound stupid."

"The only stupid questions are the ones you don't ask." The older clerk gave a sardonic laugh.

"What is the Association? I've heard of it all the time I was in Nylan, and I've filled out forms for a season, but . . . all I know is that ships from Nylan carry cargoes for the Association, and it has directors and clerks." Rahl offered an embarrassed shrug.

"You have the general idea, and that's more than most people do," replied the older clerk. "Some of the ships are owned by the Association, and some are owned by wealthy factors. But that doesn't matter to us. The ships have to make golds on their own, and that's something they worry about in Nylan. The members of the Merchant Association put up golds for shares in the Association. The golds they put up paid for the buildings and the warehouses in the ports like Swartheld or Lydiar or Renklaar or Summerdock. Each director operates his office and warehouses as he sees fit. He also has to obey the laws of the land. And the end of each year, he either makes golds or loses them. Directors who lose golds don't stay directors. Each director gets a share of the profits he makes after he pays for the cargoes and sells them. The rest goes back to Nylan and gets split up among those with shares, according to how many shares they have. Oh, and directors have fixed terms in a port, and then they get moved to other ports, unless they decide to retire on a stipend. That's determined by how many years they've worked for the Association and what they've made over those years."

"How long has Director Shyret been here?"

"Five years. It'll be six next fall. That's when his term expires. Then he'll go somewhere else."

"Who was here before him?"

"Varselt. He's in Nylan now."

Rahl forbore to say that he knew that. "Do directors have shares?"

Daelyt laughed. "Anyone who has the golds to buy them can have shares. Every director, Director Shyret once told me, has to own at least two shares. Most have more than that, I'd wager, but who knows?"

"You make it sound so clear," Rahl replied. "Thank you. Our wages come from what the director makes here?"

"That's correct. So do Chenaryl's and those of the teamsters and guards."

Rahl just nodded and went back to work on the inventory form.

Daelyt had made it very clear. Shyret was cheating the shareholders and the other directors. And if he used his ill-gotten gains to purchase more shares, he could profit even more from the efforts of honest directors. Rahl wondered whether the other directors were honest—or more honest than Shyret—because the other ports were ones closer to Nylan where traders and factors were less unwelcome.

Yet . . . what could he do? He had yet to see an account or a cargo declaration—or even the inventory—that would support what he sensed to be true. And he really had no idea as to whether what Shyret was doing was condemned or tacitly accepted. A year ago he would have been sure, but after all he'd been through . . .

As he thought about it, he also realized that the inventory addendum contained no mention of storing pickles. That nagged at him, but he couldn't say why. Then, there were more than a few things that bothered him, and most were things that he had to worry about because of Puvort's dishonesty and pettiness . . . and because of the arrogance of the board of magisters in Nylan.

XLVIII

Eightday midmorning found Rahl wandering around the warehouse courtyard in a mist that was not quite rain but more like the steam that rose from a boiling kettle, if not quite so warm. He'd discovered that his key also fit the lock to the warehouse gates. That made sense, but he hadn't thought about it. He glanced up at the upper level of the first warehouse, barely visible through the mist. The shutters were closed, and his order-senses suggested that Daelyt and Yasnela were not there. From what he could tell with his senses, there were more than two rooms—three and a small study or sewing room for Yasnela—and except for the small room they were comparatively spacious, especially for a clerk. Yet, in a way, Rahl suspected, it was almost a prison for Daelyt. How could the other clerk ever say anything or leave Shyret?

Rahl glanced toward the stables, catching sight of a broad-shouldered figure—was it Chenaryl? Was something wrong? Rahl walked toward the south end of the courtyard. As he neared the stables, he realized that the warehouse supervisor was actually cleaning out one of the water troughs.

At the sound of Rahl's boots on the stone, Chenaryl straightened and brushed a lock of oily black hair back off his forehead. He wore only an old undertunic above equally faded and patched trousers, and his boots were old and scuffed, clearly a different pair from the ones of polished brown leather he wore during the eightday.

"Chenaryl . . . I didn't expect to see you here today."

"Didn't expect to see you, either. Thought you'd be tired of this place, Rahl."

Rahl shrugged. "I don't know anyone, and I never see anyone anywhere close to my age. I don't have many coins. I suppose things will get better in time."

Chenaryl nodded, then wiped his forehead with the back of his hand. "Years back, it was the same with Daelyt. It takes a while when you're in a new place."

"Does his consort have trouble walking . . . or something? He was talking about needing a cart for her?"

"Sweet woman . . . she had some real trouble . . . a couple years back. Part of her left leg was crushed . . . Daelyt helped her, and they fell in love. She can't walk far."

"He cares for her a lot," suggested Rahl. "I can tell that."

"More than most for their consorts," agreed Chenaryl. "More 'n most."

Rahl nodded. That was true enough from what he'd seen. "What are you doing here?"

"Someone has to feed the horses and check on things. Both drivers have the end-day off today. So it's my turn." Chenaryl's eyes dropped to the truncheon at Rahl's belt. "You almost look like a bravo. Walk like one, too."

"My father said I had to learn to defend myself. I was bruised most of the time growing up."

"Won't hurt you to know that here, but stay away from the west side south of the naval piers. Gangs there, and good as you might be, one against a half score isn't a good wager."

"Thank you. Is there anything you think I should see—that I can walk to?"

"If you've got a few coins, you might try Hakkyl's. Better than Eneld. It's some five blocks west and three south, opposite corner from the Triumph fountain and the square." Chenaryl frowned, and his forehead crinkled. "Not really much else to see close by. When you've got more coins, you could take a coach down to Pharoa. There's a nice inn there, only costs a half silver a night for a room to yourself . . ."

Rahl listened for a time, until Chenaryl shook his head. "Zaena'll have my head if I don't finish this and get back."

"I wouldn't want that."

"I wouldn't either."

"Thank you." Rahl nodded politely and turned away.

Just like Shyret and Daelyt, the warehouse supervisor carried a faint chaos-mist.

Rahl walked back to the gates and let himself out, but he was careful to

lock them behind him. Then he turned and began to walk. Despite the mist
that was so fine that it almost drifted around him like fog, Rahl had to get
away from the Association buildings, feeling that he could not have spent
another moment there, especially after talking to Chenaryl.

He might as well locate Hakkyl's, if only to know where the place was,
but even if it happened to be open so early on eightday, he wouldn't be eating there until far later in the day. His coins were far too few for more than
one modest meal.

Following Chenaryl's directions, Rahl turned westward, walking easily,
but not hurriedly. A young couple walked toward him, the man wearing
a white fharong embroidered in red and black, the woman in a filmy blue
blouse and scarf over white flowing pants. As soon as they saw him, they
immediately crossed the street.

Rahl frowned. He didn't look that menacing, did he? A clerk with
a truncheon?

He crossed the side street behind the warehouses, so narrow that it
was almost an alley, and so filled with the foglike mist that he could only
see a handful of cubits beyond the edge of the two-story building that
held the cotton factorage. Once on the other side of the alley or cross
street, he moved away from the shuttered windows. For the next several
blocks, he passed shuttered windows and doors with iron gratework—
and almost no one on the sidewalks, except two bent old women, and a
younger bearded man who tottered along, singing nonsense syllables to
himself. At least, what the fellow sang didn't sound like any language
Rahl knew.

Between the dampness of the air and his rapid pace, Rahl could feel
sweat beading up everywhere especially under his garments. He couldn't
do much about that, but he did wipe his forehead with his sleeve.

He turned the corner at the fifth cross street and passed a shuttered
cooperage, then a cordage shop. He began to feel something or someone
lurking in the alleyway ahead to his left. Even as he debated crossing the
street or turning back, two figures jumped out of the mist and fog-filled serviceway. Rahl pulled the truncheon out, hoping he didn't have to use it, but
he didn't want to turn his back on the pair.

"Pretty Boy . . . you know how to use that toy?" The taller man, still
shorter than Rahl, laughed mockingly through a roughly trimmed square-
cut beard. He waved a long knife.

The other man grinned broadly, showing sparse and blackened teeth and holding a long walking stick topped with tarnished brass. Both men reeked of chaos, not of the active energy of a mage, but the type that Rahl felt was more decaying and corrupt, almost like wound chaos. He eased away from the alley, moving toward the edge of the street. He could sense another presence in the next alleyway ahead. He needed to keep the three as separate as possible.

"You're going to hand over your coins, Pretty Boy, one way or another."

"I think not."

"Oh . . . an Atlan pretty boy . . . no brains at all."

Having no brains would have been handing over anything. Rahl could sense that they had no intention of leaving him alive.

The first man came in, with his knife held low and to the side.

Rahl stepped back, trying to look tentative.

"Oh, Pretty Boy's trying to give us the slip."

Rahl could sense the tension even before the first man darted in low and fast. Quick as the attacker was, Rahl was quicker. The truncheon smashed across the attacker's wrist, before Rahl reversed it into the man's jaw, although the second blow was almost glancing.

Eeeiii! With a scream, the man reeled back, then went to his knees, moaning and clutching his broken wrist.

Rahl pivoted, barely in time to deflect the walking stick that was more like a short staff, but instead of moving away, he swung inside, and half rammed, half slammed the truncheon into the spot just below the center of the man's ribs.

The second assailant crumpled, his stick flying. Rahl could sense that he was dead. Dead, because he held so much chaos?

Whhssst!

A bolt of chaos flew past Rahl and slammed into the still-moaning first attacker.

Rahl blinked. There was nothing left except a scattering of ashes and a few metal items, including a handful of coins, and the faint sound of fleeing footsteps echoed from the alleyway farther to the south.

Whhsstt! With the impact of the second chaos-bolt, the body of the dead man vanished as well, except for similar leavings.

"Very nice, friend," came a voice from behind Rahl.

He wanted to freeze, but instead he forced a smile and turned, still holding the truncheon.

A mage-guard stood there. Chaos played around her. She was another hard-faced woman, but not the one who had advised him to register. "You used a bit of order there. I do hope you're registered."

"I'm registered. The bracelet's in my wallet."

"Why don't you put away the truncheon and get it out . . . slowly."

"Yes, ser." Rahl slipped the truncheon back into its half scabbard, then fumbled his belt wallet out and extracted the bracelet. He started to extend it.

"Just toss it to me. If it's real, it won't break."

Rahl complied, lofting it gently.

The woman caught it easily without taking her eyes or senses off Rahl. Then she looked at the bracelet, and then at Rahl, alternating between the two.

For just a moment, Rahl could sense puzzlement. He also had the feeling that she had a headache and wasn't in the best of moods. That bothered him, but there wasn't much that he could do about it.

"You're an outlander?" The mage-guard's words were half statement, half question.

"Yes, ser. I work for the Nylan Merchant Association. I'm a clerk there."

She tossed the bracelet back to him.

This time, he slipped it on his wrist.

"It's a good thing I saw them attack you. Even registered, you could have had someone question your actions. Where were you going?"

"I was trying to find Hakkyl's."

"It's up on the corner on the avenue ahead, but you should have kept on the boulevard until you reached the next street. Much as we try, the footpads like the alleys here, and they seem to know when we're watching. You must have distracted them somehow."

Rahl suspected she knew how . . . unfortunately. He inclined his head. "I'm indebted to you."

She laughed softly. "You are indeed, but don't let it bother you."

"Did I do something wrong?"

"Not this time. You were attacked. Self-defense is allowed . . . if you're registered." She pointed to the coins still lying on the stone of the sidewalk. "By rights, those are yours. I'd appreciate it if you'd dispose of the other items, though. There's a waste barrel at the edge of the next alley. That was where the other was hiding, but he's long gone."

"Yes, ser."

She laughed, not unkindly. "If you keep walking in this area, I could follow you and clean up half the petty bravos in Swartheld. But that might be hard on you. This time, follow this street to the avenue ahead. If you stay on that, no one will bother you. Next time, use the main streets."

"Thank you."

"Thank you. You've just made the streets a bit safer." She nodded, turned, and seemed to vanish.

Except this time, Rahl could sense the *twisting* of chaos-forces around her that made it so that his eyes kept trying to look away from her. After collecting the coins, almost a silver's worth, and putting them in his wallet, and then taking the belt buckles and metal fastenings, he began to walk southward. He quickly deposited the metal in the waste bucket at the entrance to the next alleyway and hurried toward the avenue ahead.

Once he reached it, he glanced across to his right. Hakkyl's was still shuttered, but the yellow-brick walls were clean, and the brasswork on the door shimmered even through the mist.

He crossed the avenue to look at the Triumph fountain, just three columns in the middle of a marble basin, with three streams of water spurting up and crossing before falling into the basin. At the western side was a smaller water jet that flowed into a watering trough, set so that pitchers could be filled above the trough and horses could drink. He did not sense anyone nearby.

Finally, he turned eastward. He had not gone more than a hundred cubits before he began to feel small and faint rain droplets on the back of his neck. He kept walking, but hurried a bit more.

The avenue he was following joined the boulevard on which the Merchant Association was located. In fact, where the two joined was where the parkway he often walked began. Once he crossed to the parkway, he looked for and found one of the stone benches that was shielded by the trees. He wiped off the damp surface as best he could with the cloth that had been wrapped around the bracelet and sat down with a sigh.

If the mage-guards were really there to protect people, why had the mage-guard waited to see what he did? Rahl was glad he had only struck each man effectively once. His lips tightened. He could just imagine the mage-guard acting like Puvort, telling him he'd gone beyond self-defense.

After a time, Rahl looked at the stone walk beyond the tips of boots that showed scuffs, despite his efforts to keep them clean and polished.

Plop . . . plop . . . A reddish droplet hit the light gray stone, then another.

The rain was so fine, and the air had been so dusty for so long that the leaves of the acacias—and every other tree—seemed to be bleeding as the moisture formed a thin layer over the reddish dust and slowly washed it off, so that the droplets that fell on the stone walks and pavement were reddish splotches.

The rain was falling like drops of blood, slowly dropping, inexorably.

Rahl felt the same way, as though he were being bled of hope and possibilities, hemmed in on all sides. Recluce and Nylan had thrown him out, and everywhere he went in Swartheld, he had the feeling someone was watching, waiting for him to make a mistake. Daelyt was watching; Shyret was watching; the mage-guards were watching. And what could he do?

It was possible, he supposed, for him to try to get some ship's captain to take him as the lowest form of seaman to get somewhere else, but . . . he had no skills at all useful to them, and he'd seen enough of life at sea to know that a ship would be another prison, and there wasn't much chance that life would be any better in another land—and that was if the magisters didn't go after him for going against their exile. And if he did that . . . he'd have no chance at all of returning to Nylan.

Did he anyway? Probably not, but he didn't like the idea of closing that door. Not quite yet.

XLIX

Late in midafternoon, closer to early evening, really, Rahl returned to Hakkyl's, this time following the mage-guard's advice about which avenues to take. As he walked up the brick steps to the brass-bound door, the muscular and dark-skinned guard outside studied Rahl.

His eyes took in the truncheon. "That ironbound lorken?"

Rahl nodded.

"You registered?"

Rahl lifted his left arm to reveal the copper bracelet.

As the guard opened the door, he offered a polite smile. Behind it, Rahl felt, was a sense of amusement. "Enjoy your meal, ser."

"I hope to, thank you."

Although the guard said nothing, his confusion at Rahl's Hamorian was obvious enough that Rahl could detect it almost without using his order-senses.

Inside the door was a dimly lit foyer with walls plastered in off-white. The floor was tile, but tile of dark and shining gray rather than the deep red floor tiling Rahl had seen in many buildings. A short man in a pleated green fharong without embroidery stepped up, his eyes lingering on the truncheon, then on the copper registry bracelet. "You wish to have a meal? We are not a tavern."

"I do."

"There is nothing less than half a silver."

"That will be acceptable." Rahl would not have agreed to that, but he'd been mistaken about the coins he had collected from the two who had attacked him. When he had actually counted them when he'd been sitting on the bench, there had been three silvers and four coppers in all.

"We do have a small table for one. This way." The man turned and led Rahl through an archway whose edges were faced with green marble and into a dining chamber close to ten cubits wide and twenty long. Only a handful of tables were occupied, but all the men were wearing fharongs. At one table were three men about Daelyt's age; at another, a gray-haired man and a younger woman; at a third, two women who were close enough in appearance to be sisters. Rahl couldn't be certain exactly who was seated at the corner table, where the lamp had been wicked out.

As he followed the greeter, he tried to pick up the whispers.

". . . young bravo . . ."

". . . truncheon . . . outland mage . . ."

". . . too handsome to be a trader and too young . . ."

"Young or not . . ."

"Ailya . . ."

Rahl smiled at the last, but didn't turn his head.

"Here you are, ser." The greeter gestured to a table for two set against the right wall, between two other tables, both vacant at the moment.

"Thank you." Rahl took the chair on the far side because that allowed him the best view of the other diners.

A serving girl moved toward Rahl, but the greeter met her well away from the table, murmuring quietly.

Rahl had to strain both his ears and order-senses to pick up what he did.

"Outlander . . . talks like an Atlan, maybe lived in Merowey as well . . . talk to him . . . find out what you can."

That scarcely surprised Rahl, and he surveyed the table as he waited for the server to reach him. The cloth was a pale blue, and the utensils were of an ornate silvery bronze. He wondered if the metal were cupridium or just a Hamorian attempt at replicating the ancient material.

"I haven't seen you before." The servingwoman was fully dressed from wrist and ankle to neck, but the dark blue fabric was thin enough that at times, as she moved, it clung closely to her well-shaped body. She didn't look much older than Rahl, but there was a hardness about her. Whether she was indentured or a slave, Rahl couldn't tell, only that he doubted he could trust her.

"I haven't been here before. What might be good for a meal?"

"Our burhka is the best in Swartheld, but if you like fish, the curried whitefish with quinoa is also good. The spiced langostinos with mint-cumin butter are tasty. We also have marinated goat skewers with cheesed lacers."

Rahl was getting tired of food he couldn't taste for all the spices. "Tell me more about the skewers."

"An excellent choice, ser. The meat is from choice young goats and has been marinated for days in a mixture of olive oil and spices. It is grilled with sweet peppers and onions. It is six coppers."

"What do you have to drink to go with it?"

"The dry red wine from the Nebatan Hills. That is three coppers a goblet."

Almost a silver for a single meal? Rahl refrained from shaking his head. He hadn't had much experience in expensive dining. It could have been that the meal he'd been treated to in Nylan by Magister Thorl had been that expensive, if not more so, but he hadn't had to pay for it, and that did make a difference. "I'll try the skewers and that wine."

"Very good." The server nodded and slipped away.

Rahl looked around the dining area. The three men had clearly lost interest in him, as had the older man with the younger woman. The apparent sisters were both sipping their wine, as if they had looked away moments before. With some concentration, he could make out the couple at the darkened corner table—a man and a woman, and the woman continued to wear a filmy scarf. They were absorbed in each other and talking in low and intense voices.

"Here is your wine, ser."

Rahl glanced up at the girl. "Thank you."

"You sound like you're from Atla . . . but you're not, are you?" The serving girl smiled warmly, and not entirely falsely.

"No. I was born a long way from there and here. What about you?"

"I'm from Sendyn, but there's not much there." Her hand brushed Rahl's wrist as she reached across and straightened the three-pronged narrow fork. "Swartheld is more interesting. Don't you think so?"

"I work a lot," Rahl confessed. "I don't know much except about the harbor and the trading areas."

"You a mage for one of the traders?"

How could he answer that? After a moment, he laughed. "If you have any talent at all with order or chaos, you have to register as a mage. That doesn't mean you really are one. I work for the Nylan Merchant Association."

"Oh . . . do you know Chenaryl? He eats here sometimes."

"He was the one who said I should come here."

Her hand brushed his shoulder as she stepped back. "It shouldn't be too long before your skewers are ready. I'll make sure they're just right."

Rahl nodded, then took a sip of the wine. It wasn't sweet, and it wasn't bitter, and it went down easily.

The serving girl hadn't seemed terribly concerned or upset about the mention of the Association, and Rahl had been led to believe that people in other lands were wary of anything connected with Recluce. Was her lack of unease due to her familiarity with Chenaryl? That suggested that the warehouse supervisor frequented Hakkyl's more than just "sometimes." It also suggested that Chenaryl could afford a silver a meal without trouble, and that concerned Rahl, because it supported his feeling that golds were being diverted.

Again, he surveyed the other diners, but all seemed to have forgotten or dismissed him, even the pair of sisters.

Before long, the server returned with a large platter on which were four lines of meat, each interspersed with chunks of green and orange peppers and purple onions. On one end was a lattice of thin fried potato strips covered with a drizzling of three cheeses of differing colors.

"You'll like this," she announced.

Rahl smiled politely and turned to the food. He was hungry.

He had to admit that the cubes of marinated goat were excellent, as were the cheesed lacers, with the combination of mild and pungent, and heavy and light cheeses on the thin and crisp-fried potatoes. The wine tasted better with the food. He'd barely finished the last mouthful when the girl returned.

"Would you like some sweets?"

"No, thank you." He'd already spent more than he should have.

"How did you like it?"

"Very good. Goat fixed like that is definitely better than mutton or lamb."

"Dalsym can fix the skewers with chicken, but they're better with goat. You don't have many goats in Recluce, do you?"

"Very few, except in a few mountain places where no one lives. They're hard on the grass, and they'll eat saplings and shoots, and that hurts the land."

"You know a lot about that. Were you a herder once?"

Rahl shook his head. "I knew some."

"Were you one of those exiles?"

"No. People who are exiled directly don't get positions with the Merchant Association." That was shading matters, but it was far safer.

"Will you run it someday, do you think?"

"I don't know that I want to spend my life that way," Rahl replied, "but that's something that I'll just have to see about. What about you?"

"I've got another three years. Then, I'll see about working full wage." She smiled at Rahl. "Unless someone wants to consort, but he'd have to be handsome and wealthy. As handsome as you."

Rahl managed to keep a pleasant smile on his face. "As pretty as you are, you might not have to work at all."

She laughed softly, and for a moment, the hardness left her face. "You're kind. I'm Thanyra." She smiled again. "You can ask for me whenever you come. It's nice to serve someone who isn't old enough to be my uncle."

"That's good to know." Rahl returned the smile.

In the end, he left a silver and a copper. He hoped that Thanyra got to keep the extra two coppers. She'd worked hard enough for them.

The greeter nodded almost indifferently as Rahl left.

The guard outside—the same one as when he'd entered—offered a cheerful, "Good evening, ser."

"The same to you."

Outside, the misty fog had lifted, and the early evening was almost uncomfortably warm and damp. The infrequent sound of hoofs on stone echoed out over a low insect chorus. Rahl had no more than walked away from Hakkyl's and crossed the street, following the avenue, than he sensed the two men waiting around the corner of the building ahead to his right, lurking in the alleyway. He pivoted, deciding to head back the other way suggested by the mage-guard earlier, when another man walked down the side street from the south toward him.

Rahl could sense chaos-forces building, and his hand went to the truncheon as he tried to strengthen his order shields.

Whhst!

The white chaos-flame flared around him, but his shields held. The chaos-bolt didn't seem as strong as those of the mage-guards he had met, but he didn't want to see if the man could do worse. Rahl pulled out the truncheon and sprinted toward the chaos-wielder.

Another chaos-flare enveloped him, harmlessly.

The small squat man turned to run.

WHHSSTT! Ashes and flame swirled and then began to settle.

Rahl stopped in his tracks and began to search for another white wizard.

The mage-guard he had met earlier appeared, standing next to the wall of the building, smiling. "I thought you might come back for an early dinner. Hakkyl makes a little extra this way, but we've never been able to prove it."

Rahl replaced the truncheon and shrugged helplessly. "I didn't know what else to do. There were two of them waiting in the alley ahead off the avenue, and I was trying to stay out of trouble."

She frowned. "They're gone now. Long gone." Then she shook her head. "You'll never avoid trouble here. Not unless you become a mage-guard. You carry enough order to draw anyone who's got order- or chaos-senses, and you're handsome as well." She laughed softly, but not derisively. "If you were a mage-guard, and if I were younger, I'd enjoy working with you, I think."

"Can outlanders become mage-guards?"

"It doesn't matter so long as you can speak both Temple and Hamorian."

"Oh . . ."

"You might think about it." She inclined her head toward the ashes and metal on the stone. "It's late enough that the sweepers will get most of it, but you might need the coins, and you deserve them."

"Are you sure . . . you . . ."

"You defended yourself. Your shields wouldn't stand against a real chaos-master, but you won't run into one of those except in the services of the Emperor. Have a pleasant evening, Rahl." She turned and walked in the direction of Hakkyl's.

Rahl watched her for a moment. She'd made the effort to recall his name from when she'd studied his registry bracelet. That didn't bode well. Finally, he picked up the coins from detritus left from the attacker destroyed by the mage-guard. This time, he found two silvers and six coppers. After slipping them into his wallet, he was far better off than when he'd awakened that morning. He was also far more concerned about his future in Hamor, but he didn't like the idea of being a mage-guard, not and being what amounted to a high-level servant.

Finally, he started back toward the Association.

He made his way down the avenue carefully, using both his eyes and senses, but there were only a handful of carriages, and a few couples. The would-be assailants had vanished, and the avenue was well lit by the streetlights that resembled inverted cones set on iron posts.

As he continued, the sound of his boots on the pavement mixing with the other sounds of a quiet and damp evening in the city, he found his mind trying to sort out all sorts of matters—from trying to make sure that no one was following him or lying in wait to the fact that he'd scarcely been attracted to Thanyra, comely as she was, and that he'd found himself comparing her to Deybri.

He shook his head. It was hardly likely he'd see Deybri again.

When he neared the Association, he began to check the area around him, but he neither saw nor sensed anyone. Nor did he sense the masked chaotic eye-twisting that marked the sight shielding used by the mage-guards.

When he stepped inside the Association building, he quickly locked the door behind him, then slipped the bar in place.

It had been quite a day.

L

On oneday, in midafternoon, Rahl was at the long desk by himself while Daelyt was eating his late midday meal. A smooth-skinned man in a deep brown fharong, embroidered in brilliant gold thread, marched into the Association office.

"Understand Shyret has black wool." The statement was in accented Temple, not in Hamorian.

Rahl lifted the sheaf of papers that held the current inventory, and the approximate asking price of each commodity, scanning it quickly and replying in Temple. "There are bales of black wool available."

"How much is he asking?" The man switched to Hamorian, but with a regional accent Rahl had not heard before.

"You would have to ask him," Rahl replied in Hamorian.

"You Atlans can't even think for yourself, can you?"

Rahl saw Daelyt had entered and now stood well back of the trader, if the man were indeed that, but the older clerk did not move, just listened and watched.

"The director is the one who sets the prices." Rahl noted that Daelyt was pointing toward the rear of the office. "I would be most happy to tell him you are here and are interested in purchasing some."

"No. I won't trouble him now." The man turned immediately and walked past Daelyt without so much as looking at the older clerk or back at Rahl.

"That was Klerchyn," explained Daelyt, moving toward the wide desk. "Whenever there is someone new here, he tries to see if he can get them to quote him a price lower than what the director offers. If it's higher, he accuses you of trying to cheat him. If it's lower, he insists on having you write it up, and he'll pay for it on the spot. That way, the director's bound."

"Are there many like him?"

"There are a few, but he's the worst."

"He must do well, with all the gold-threaded embroidery."

"At everyone else's expense." Daelyt slipped onto his stool and pulled out his leather folder from one of the drawers on his right.

"Is the more elaborate needlework a sign of wealth?" asked Rahl. "Or the gold thread."

"Sometimes, but that was coated brass."

"You recognized that. Is that because of your consort? Seorya said that Yasnela does outstanding needlework," ventured Rahl.

"She did?" Daelyt actually looked—and felt, to Rahl—surprised.

"She said Yasnela did work for one of the best."

"Pasnyr's good . . . I don't know if he's that good."

"Maybe what she does makes his the best."

Daelyt laughed. "Maybe you ought to try selling things at the markets with words like that."

"I think not. When I've been walking around, I've noticed something. Does everyone wear a fharong for special times?"

Daelyt offered a rueful smile. "They're too costly for everyday wear for most of us. I only have one, and that's because Yasnela could do the needlework." He looked up as two traders walked into the office.

Rahl recognized the older man—Alamryt.

The older trader stood back as the younger man walked up to Daelyt. "I need a quote for a consignment of two hundred stones of finished metal implements to Nylan on the next available ship."

"The *Legacy of Montgren* will be porting in about an eightday, Hassynat. It might be as early as sevenday, or as late as the following sixday," replied Daelyt. "The *Black Holding* is scheduled for about two eightdays from now. What are the nature and value of the implements?"

"They are high-quality steel shears, picks, and combs. Your Association would hold them in Nylan for the buyer. The value would be at your minimum."

Alamryt looked at Rahl, smiling faintly but not speaking.

"The consignment reserve would be five golds," replied Daelyt, "and the cartage would be eleven. Storage for the first eightday in Nylan comes with the cartage. After that, it would be a half gold an eightday."

"That would be acceptable. I will be back late this afternoon with the deposit."

Daelyt inclined his head. "The consignment form will be ready for you."

Hassynat nodded briskly. "Good day." Then he turned and departed.

Alamryt followed the younger trader without looking at either of the clerks.

"That will help," observed Daelyt. "We don't have that many consignments on the *Montgren*. That's always a problem at the end of summer. Things pick up in fall."

"Why didn't the older trader get involved? Is there something about that I should know?" asked Rahl.

"Oh, he never does. Hassynat is the one who makes the consignments. He's the one who has to find space for the cargoes that their ships can't carry—either because they're overcommitted or because it's not worth their while to send a ship to a particular port at that time."

Rahl laughed. "You're acting as if I know who *they* are."

Daelyt frowned for a moment. "The way Alamyrt was looking at you, I thought you did."

"I saw him on board the *Diev,* and he said he was a wool trader. I didn't realize he was part of something larger, not when he was traveling on one of our ships."

"Doramyl and Sons is one of the largest." Daelyt laughed. "They've got almost a score of vessels. Alamyrt is one of the family. He doesn't always come, and he never talks when he does. I think he just wants to know what we're charging."

"Oh . . ." Rahl paused, then added, "He must want to get a feeling for it, too. He'd get the quotes from Hassynat."

"It doesn't matter to us, so long as they pay." Daelyt paused. "You heard it all. Why don't you write it up, and I'll check it?"

"I can do that. Is the shipper Hassynat of Doramyl and Sons, or just Doramyl and Sons?"

"Hassynat of Doramyl."

Rahl took a consignment form from his second drawer and set it directly before him. As he settled in to fill out the form, Daelyt slipped from his stool and headed back toward the archway, doubtless to tell Shyret that Alamyrt had recognized Rahl.

Rahl wanted to shake his head. No matter what he did, it seemed like something came up to create problems. Even when he went for a walk or out to find a meal.

He picked up the pen, and another thought struck him, something so obvious that he hadn't really noticed it at first. For all that Daelyt had said about Klerchyn trying to trick him into offering a lower price for the wool, Rahl had not sensed more than the faintest trace of chaos-mist around the trader—far, far less than what surrounded Shyret, Daelyt, and Chenaryl. Nor had Alamyrt or Hassynat shown any more chaos than Klerchyn.

Rahl forced himself to concentrate on the details of the consignment form.

LI

A people cannot survive in chaos, nor can a land. For this reason, the first duty of any who would rule is to maintain order. Too much order, and a land becomes a prison where nothing is accomplished, save keeping order. Before long in such a land, there will be neither food nor clothing, and order itself will vanish as each person struggles to find nourishment and shelter for himself and those he holds dear. Too little order, and no one respects anyone else, neither his neighbor nor his ruler, and that land, too, will fall into ruin and anarchy.

The lessons of history have illustrated all too clearly that, despite what people say about the need to do good and to respect the persons and property of others, most beings will only do good and respect others either when it costs them nothing or when they fear a greater power will cause them suffering should they not respect others. Using power to instill order and respect, without turning a land into a prison, that is the task of a ruler.

Power is not respected or feared when it is never exercised. Yet, if it is exercised excessively and in an arbitrary fashion, people will become unhappy and unproductive, and that will cause the order of a land to decline. People also become unhappy when power is always used harshly and disproportionately to an offense against order. Likewise, they become confused when the laws governing the use of power are complex and difficult to explain or understand.

Thus, the laws of a land must be both fair and simple. Sometimes, this is not possible, and if it is not, a ruler should err on the side of simplicity, because, no matter how hard administrators, mage-guards, and rulers attempt to assure fairness, absolute fairness is by nature impossible, and attempts to create it always lead to a wider and more complex set of rules and laws, which seem unfair because of their very complexity. In the end, attempting to create absolute fairness will create a greater impression of unfairness than maintaining a firmer and simpler set of rules.

The last precept about laws is this: Create no law that is not absolutely necessary to maintain simple order. Beyond the minimum for maintaining order, laws are like fleas or leeches. The more of them that exist, the more they vex a land and bleed it into chaos and anarchy . . .

> *Manual of the Mage-Guards*
> Cigoërne, Hamor
> 1551 A.F.

LII

The mist that had cloaked Swartheld on eightday had given way by oneday morning to high clouds that in Recluce would have promised rain. Rahl had doubts that they would and went to work sweeping and mopping the floors. The brasswork could wait a few days, but he did oil and polish the woodwork and furniture. When he finished, he washed up and dressed. He replaced the registry bracelet in his belt wallet, wrapped in cloth once more, rather than wearing it. Then he went and bought some bread from Gostof that he ate in his own cubby, before returning to the front and waiting for Daelyt to arrive.

The older clerk came in whistling, but Rahl thought the melody was a bit off.

"Good morning, Rahl."

"Good morning. How was your end-day?"

"Quiet. We slept late and went and saw friends. What about yours?"

"I explored a little and had a meal at Hakkyl's." Rahl laughed. "I won't be doing that again anytime soon."

"I can see why. I took Yasnela there once for her birthday. She told me she wouldn't stand for my spending that many coins on food ever again."

Rahl chuckled politely, even though he knew the older clerk was lying. "I suppose once will have to be enough. At least, the Association pays for our meals at Eneld's."

"In a way," replied Daelyt. "We probably get paid less, but Shyret can get the meals for us cheaper than we can."

Rahl hadn't thought of it quite that way.

The day went quickly, with traders coming in and seeking consignment space on the *Montgren*—and even on the *Black Holding*, which wasn't scheduled back until an eightday or more after the *Montgren*, or the *Diev*, which would arrive in Swartheld even later. Others came in looking to purchase various goods in the warehouse, or to see if they were available.

"We're in the last eightday of summer, getting on toward fall," Daelyt pointed out in one lull. "It gets busier then."

"And winter?"

"That's busy, too. Late summer is the slowest."

As the sun dropped lower in the west, and the shadows lengthened outside the Association, a slender man wearing a pale blue fharong hurried into the Association. "I've got a remittance for the director."

"I can take it," offered Daelyt.

"No. It has to go to him personally. The trader wouldn't be happy otherwise."

Daelyt nodded at Rahl, and the younger clerk jumped off his stool and hurried back through the archway.

Shyret looked up from the ledger open before him. "What is it, Rahl?"

"Ser . . . there's a man here with a remittance. He won't give it to anyone but you. Daelyt sent me to tell you."

The director rose, shaking his head, then ran his fingers through his short iron gray hair. "Because none of them trust their own clerks, they don't trust mine."

Rahl stepped aside and followed the director.

As Shyret approached the wide desk, Rahl could sense two kinds of chaos from the remittance man—that of a hidden blade and that of evil or corruption. His hand went to his truncheon.

The man stepped toward Shyret extending a large envelope. "Ser director, this is the remittance from Waolsyn."

Rahl's truncheon was out, and he was moving even faster than the attacker. The black wood slammed across the man's wrist, and the dagger in the hand not holding the envelope dropped to the floor.

The man whirled, dropping the envelope, and sprinted toward the front door. Rahl couldn't move around Shyret fast enough to stop him.

The director glanced around, then shuddered ever so slightly. His hand touched his midsection, his fingers lingering there for a moment as his eyes dropped to the weapon on the floor. He looked up and moistened his lips. "Have either of you seen him before?"

"No, ser." Daelyt's and Rahl's words were almost simultaneous.

"He's not one of Waolsyn's men that I've ever seen."

Daelyt bent down and picked up the envelope, then straightened and handed it to Shyret. "It's light, but there's something in it."

Shyret did not take the envelope, instead looking at Rahl. "How did you know he had a blade?"

"I didn't, ser, not until I saw that he had something in his other hand. It just felt wrong."

"It was indeed." Shyret's laugh was hollow. His eyes dropped to the dagger on the floor. "Since you were the one who stopped him, Rahl, the blade is yours."

"Thank you, ser. Ah . . . is it all right to sell it?"

"Whatever you wish." Shyret opened the heavy envelope. He looked anything but happy, and he manifested a tenseness as he extracted a short sheet of heavy paper, which he read quickly and thrust inside his beige fharong. He handed the empty envelope to Daelyt. "Burn it."

Then he turned and strode back toward his study.

Rahl looked at Daelyt. "Why would anyone do something like that?"

"This is Swartheld. You can pay for anything here."

"Even here, there has to be a reason," Rahl pointed out. "Is he undercutting other traders? Or did he do something to anger someone?"

Daelyt shrugged. "He doesn't say much about things like that."

The older clerk was lying. That Rahl could tell.

"Still smells like something got burned," mused Daelyt.

Although Daelyt was changing the subject, Rahl realized that there was the faint stench of burned hair hanging in the air.

"Watch things," Daelyt added. "I need to burn this." He held up the envelope, then glanced at the weapon still lying on the floor. "That's yours, remember."

"Oh . . ." Rahl shook his head. "There's something on it. I'll get a rag from the storeroom." Before Daelyt could protest, he dashed to the back and returned almost immediately.

As soon as he did, Daelyt headed toward the rear door.

Rahl could sense that the substance on the edge of the blade held something like chaos. Poison? He was careful to wrap the entire dagger in rags and slip it into his lower drawer. Later, after he was alone, he'd clean it, and study it.

LIII

On twoday, Rahl ate his midday meal quickly and hurried out from Eneld's to Chalyn's—the weapons shop just to the east of the cantina. As he stepped inside, he noted that the shutters were iron-backed.

A muscular balding man moved from the counter toward him. "You must be the new clerk at the Association."

"You're Chalyn?"

"The very same." The proprietor made a sweeping gesture that was clearly a mockery of a formal bow. "And you?"

"I'm Rahl. I heard your name, but I've never met you. Daelyt said that you often bought weapons as well as sold them."

"It depends. They have to be usable, and salable. Especially salable. I'm not a collector the way Eklar is."

Rahl brought out the cloth-covered dagger, unwrapped it, and set it on the counter. The dark blade was a span and a half long, dark oiled iron, with narrow gutters on each side of the blade. The hilt looked to be bone, cut in a cross-edged pattern to make it easier to grip. "What about this one?"

Chalyn moved behind the counter.

Rahl stepped to one side to avoid blocking the light from the high side window.

The proprietor lowered his head slightly and studied the dagger, then lifted it and balanced it on the side of his hand, before turning it in the light. Finally, he laid it gently on the oiled wood countertop.

"It's not a new blade. Not a real old one, either. It's a copy of a Cyadoran dagger. Assassin's weapon. Sharp edges and points, and strong enough to cut a silk vest in a direct thrust. Tang is almost as wide as the blade, but a touch thinner. It could be used as parry blade for use with a rapier or a falchiona, but this one hasn't been. Might be threescore years old, might not. Good condition."

"Who would carry this?"

"Is it not yours?"

"Only because I knocked it out of the hand of a ruffian who was assaulting the director."

Chalyn's eyes flicked to Rahl's belt. Then he nodded. "Ironbound lorken. Recluce weapon, but not the kind that gets the mage-guards upset."

Rahl waited.

"Footpad wouldn't carry this. Not that good for anything but killing . . . or showing off. It's not that decorated. No inlays on the hilt and not a hint of scrollwork or engraving on the blade or guard. Either a bravo who wants to be an assassin or an assassin apprentice, that would be my judgment. Might be a tough who was given the weapon."

"What would you offer for it?"

Chalyn laughed. "Blades are always worth something, but there'd only be a few who'd be interested in this. Sometimes, Vadoryn comes by looking for decent blades for apprentices. He'd be the only one I'd be able to count on. Say . . . a silver and a half."

"You could get three and a half from him," replied Rahl.

"And you're just the clerk?"

"The newest one," replied Rahl with a smile. "But I listen and watch."

"I still have the carrying costs, and the tariffs on inventory, and Vadoryn won't pay near what it's worth, and there might not be anyone else for seasons," countered Chalyn. "A silver and eight."

"You don't have another like it in the case or the display window," Rahl pointed out. "If Vadoryn came by tomorrow and you didn't have it, it might be eightdays, or seasons, before he returned."

"I still have to pay tariffs to the mage-guards and the patrollers, and the local enumerators. A silver and nine."

"Two and two," suggested Rahl.

"Two silvers and one. That's the best I can do."

Rahl sensed that was close to what Chalyn could—or would—pay. "Done at two silvers and one."

Chalyn left the blade on the counter, but two silvers and a copper appeared next to it, almost instantly.

"Thank you." Rahl swept up the coins.

"Young fellow . . ."

"Yes, ser?"

"I'd be watching your back. Even apprentice assassins don't like having to go back to their masters without their blades. You'll probably be having an eightday or so while he recovers from the whipping, but after that . . ."

That was something else Rahl hadn't considered. He nodded, then slipped the coins quickly into his belt wallet. "I'm always learning something new about Swartheld. Thank you."

Chalyn laughed. "If you stay alive longer, you might find me some even better blades."

By the time Rahl left Chalyn's, the clouds had lowered, and the first drops of rain had begun to fall. He hurried across the street, ducking behind a heavy-laden lumber wagon pulled by four drays, and scurried into the Association.

"It's wet out there," Rahl said as he took his place behind the wide desk. "I thought it didn't rain much here."

"It doesn't, most of the year," replied Daelyt. "We often get more rain in the last eightday or so of summer and the first two eightdays of fall than in the whole rest of the year." The older clerk rose. "I'm headed to Eneld's. I won't be long. You can handle consignments, except if they want to pay right now. Then you'll need to check with the director. Selling goods, you'll have to fetch him."

Rahl nodded and watched as Daelyt hurried out into the light rain.

After that, Rahl sat alone for a time. Belatedly, he realized the full impact of Chalyn's warning and last words. Better blades suggested more accomplished assassins. As he considered that, he could feel a slow-burning anger rekindle—or perhaps he just recognized it. Because he stopped a killing, he was going to be more of a target? He was likely to be in even greater danger . . . and it had all started with that sow's ass Puvort! Just because Puvort hadn't liked Rahl, he'd made Rahl's self-defense into a crime. The bastard had twisted the truth and misrepresented what had happened and exiled Rahl to Nylan, and there the magisters hadn't been much help, either. Everyone wanted to blame, but no one really had wanted to help or explain. And now, Rahl was stuck in Swartheld, and he not only had to worry about the mage-guards, and what he would do in less than a season, but he also had to worry about assassins, and that didn't take into account cutpurses, and the schemes of Shyret and Chenaryl.

The more he thought about it, the angrier he got. No matter what he tried to do, the future was looking grimmer and grimmer, and no one cared.

Puvort certainly hadn't cared, and Kadara hadn't been much better. The only one who'd tried to explain anything had been Deybri, and she was a healer, not a magister.

He was still seething when Daelyt returned.

"Is everything all right, Rahl? You look . . . disturbed."

"Just thinking." Rahl forced a laugh. "Sometimes, it's hard to get used to a new place."

"That's true. My first year here was hard." Daelyt paused at the desk. "I'll be back in a moment. I need more ink."

Before Daelyt returned, two traders walked in, looking for wool and various dyestuffs. From that moment on, both clerks were busy until late in the afternoon.

When the last of a continuous string of traders had left, Daelyt smiled crookedly. "Didn't I tell you that it would get busier?"

"You did."

The door opened again, and Rahl turned his head.

A swarthy young man in a clerk's summer tunic walked to the desk. "Daelyt!"

"Hylart, what are you doing here? You walk all the way from the north piers?"

"Hardly. There's a wagon outside with Sumyl and a driver. I've got what Waolsyn owes your director. With twenty golds in the pouch, no one was going to let me walk."

Daelyt inclined his head, and Rahl hurried back to Shyret's study.

"Director, Hylart is here with twenty golds from Waolsyn."

"Now? After the Exchange is closed?"

"Yes, ser."

With a sigh that seemed forced to Rahl, rather than resigned, Shyret rose from behind the fruitwood desk. "Tell him I'll be right there."

"Yes, ser." Rahl turned and headed back to his own desk. As he neared the other two clerks, he slowed slightly, taking in what they were saying.

". . . anyone else who might have known that Waolsyn was going to pay the Association?" asked Daelyt.

"If Waolsyn knows it, so does all Swartheld," replied Hylart. "He never says what he receives, but he's always complaining about all the factors he owes."

Both stopped talking as they saw Rahl.

"He'll be right here."

"Oh . . . Hylart, this is Rahl. He's new with us, the past two eightdays."
Rahl inclined his head. "I'm pleased to meet you."

"From Atla?"

"Just my speech," Rahl said, offering a smile.

"He's from Nylan," Daelyt added, "but he learned Hamorian in Atla."
As he took his seat at the desk Rahl decided against correcting Daelyt.

"You think the rain will continue?" asked Daelyt.

"For a few days. The first rains of fall always last a few days. Makes the mage-guards edgy, though. Have to be careful around them when it rains."

"That's what they say."

"That's the way it is," insisted Hylart.

Shyret approached, clearly his throat loudly, before speaking. "You have something for me, Hylart?"

"Yes, ser. The last remittance on the last purchases." The clerk handed a cloth pouch to the director. "Ser Waolsyn would like a receipt, ser." Hylart drew an envelope from his tunic. "If you would not mind signing . . . ?"

"If you would not mind my counting the golds first," countered Shyret, opening the cloth pouch and easing the coins onto the desktop before Daelyt. ". . . eight, nine, ten . . . thirteen, seventeen . . . nineteen, twenty . . . all here." He swept the golds back into the pouch, then took the pen that Daelyt handed him and signed the receipt already spread on the desk. "There you are."

"Thank you, ser director." Hylart bowed, then turned, and departed.

Shyret picked up the pouch. "We'd better have Rahl eat first tonight, before you go, Daelyt."

"Yes, ser."

Without explaining more, the director turned and headed back to his study.

Rahl looked to the older clerk.

"The director hates getting large remittances after the Exchange closes," Daelyt said. "He doesn't want to risk taking them home. So he locks them away in his study. That's why he wants you to eat first tonight and not go out after that. I doubt anything will happen, but he'd feel better knowing that someone will be here until he can take the golds to the Exchange when it opens in the morning. Tyboran and Yussyl can go with him."

Despite his genial tone, Daelyt was clearly uneasy.

"Just tell me when you want me to go," replied Rahl. What else could he say?

LIV

Rahl woke abruptly. He'd been dreaming of flame and fire, and sweat was pouring off his forehead. What night was it? Twoday? Was it only twoday? He sat up and swung his legs off the pallet and let his feet drop onto the floor tiles, reassuringly cool.

Chaos! Somewhere nearby . . .

He grabbed his truncheon and slipped out of his cubby, moving surely through the darkness of the night that seemed little more than early twilight to him. Barefoot, and in drawers and an undertunic, he didn't feel exactly ready for an intruder, but taking the time to dress seemed unwise.

He quickly checked the rear storeroom door, but it was still firmly closed, with all its multiple locks fastened tight.

As he moved toward the front of the building, the feeling of chaos grew stronger. It was clear something was happening there. Rahl eased closer to the door, sensing some form of chaos. He blinked and looked again, but his order-senses, rather than his eyes, discerned a tendril of chaos threading its way through the thinnest of gaps between the door and frame. It wasn't chaos alone, but chaos intermixed with something else, something darker. Was it order?

How could it be?

The tendril tugged, then pushed at one end of the bar, slowly shoving it out of its metal brackets. Abruptly one end of the bar clunked to the floor, then the other, and the door swung open, as if it had already been unlocked, pushing the bar aside. Rahl flattened himself against the wall beside the door, his truncheon ready.

A figure in dark garb stepped inside, falchiona extended.

The man started to turn as he caught sight of Rahl, but Rahl was faster, and his truncheon cracked the man's wrist, hard enough that Rahl could feel bones snap.

"Oooo . . . !" The bravo reeled back, out of sight, the falchiona clattering on the floor tiles.

Whhstt! A bolt of whiteness flew toward Rahl, but only the edge of it splattered on his shields.

Another bravo charged into the building, and Rahl barely managed to parry the hurried cut from the sabre—not a falchiona, he noted almost absently.

The bravo was nowhere near as good as Aleasya, let alone Zastryl, and within moments, Rahl had slammed the truncheon across the man's wrist, and the sabre was on the floor. The bravo backed away hurriedly, then turned and ran. Rahl wasn't about to chase him, not with chaos-fire coming from outside.

"We will have to handle you differently, dear boy," came the languid words from the chaos-wizard who stepped inside the front door.

The words chilled Rahl, but he forced himself toward the white-shadowed figure.

More chaos flared around his shields, but he kept moving.

At the last moment, the wizard lifted a falchiona, but one not of iron. It seemed to be made of something else, a whitish bronze, perhaps even true cupridium. Belatedly, Rahl realized that the wizard wore the khakis of a mage-guard, although his visored cap was nowhere to be seen.

Despite the greater length of the blade, Rahl managed a parry, and then to evade the blade enough so that the truncheon touched the wizard's forearm. He could sense the agony as the wizard tried to swing the blade back toward him.

Rahl stepped inside the blade, ramming the truncheon into the wizard's throat, knowing the lorken and iron had to touch bare skin to have any great effect. The wizard shuddered and brought the falchiona up, but not quickly enough. That hesitation allowed Rahl to slam the weapons aside, then smash the truncheon back across the wizard's temple with a solid *crunch.*

Light flared from where the black iron touched skin, and the wizard gave a last shudder, and then began to collapse in upon himself.

Rahl stood there breathing heavily, still almost aghast at the disintegration of the wizard. He glanced around, trying to determine if anyone else happened to be nearby. He could not see, hear, or sense anyone else. After a moment, he looked down. All that remained was a rough pile of ashes and dust and small objects coated with both. The air seemed filled with glittering reddish white motes of chaos that seemed to disperse as soon as he had become aware of them.

He eased toward the door, truncheon ready, but the sidewalk and boulevard outside were almost silent, except for the distant bells from the harbor, the faint patter of a light rain, and a muted unharmonic discord from the evening insects.

Quickly, he rebarred the door.

How exactly would he explain what had happened?

Rahl snorted. He was more than a little tired of explaining anything. This time, he wasn't about to explain. He returned to his cubby and pulled on his trousers and boots.

Then he belted his truncheon and picked up a broom and dustpan and walked back to the building entry.

He thought there should have been three blades around, but there were only two, both the bronzelike falchiona and the regular falchiona. He set them against the wall and began to sort and sweep.

Among the ashes, dust, and scraps of cloth that were all that remained of the chaos-wizard were coins—a gold, four silvers, and seven coppers. Rahl carefully wiped each off with a rag before placing it in his wallet. He had over four golds—more than he'd ever been able to call his own—and nowhere truly safe to put them, let alone any way to explain how he had gotten them. Still, he could now send a letter to Recluce, but he'd have to do it without Shyret or Daelyt learning about it, or there would be questions he didn't want to answer.

Something nagged at him, and he looked among the debris for something, what he didn't even know at first. Then, he swallowed. The mage who had appeared had been wearing a mage-guard uniform. Did that mean he was a renegade of some sort, trying to gain extra coins doing something he shouldn't be doing? Or were the mage-guards trying to cause trouble for Shyret?

Once more, Rahl had more questions than answers. But questions or not, he needed to remove all evidence of what had happened.

After unlocking the door and checking outside, he took the contents of the dustpan and walked through the light rain several hundred cubits, scattering the contents in the gutter, which had a modest flow. Then he returned to the Association and took the two falchionas and carried them back westward to the gates to the warehouse courtyard, where he set them just inside the grillwork, where they would be easily visible from inside the courtyard, but not immediately obvious from outside. He certainly could have sold the blades to Chalyn for even more coins, but everyone would know that he had, and that was the last sort of notice he needed, especially since the bronzelike falchiona would have raised far too many questions.

After that he locked up, and replaced the bar, and then went back to his pallet bed. But he left his trousers on and his boots beside his bed. Had the renegade mage-guard and his accomplices come because they had known about the golds Waolsyn had sent to Shyret? That didn't seem exactly right, but what else could it have been? Or was it an attempted burglary—another part of someone trying to get to Shyret, one way or another?

Were Shyret's methods making enemies in Swartheld as well?

Again, there were far more questions than Rahl had any way to answer or even speculate accurately on the possible answers. One thing he did know. It was unlikely that he would sleep well for the remainder of the night.

LV

Rahl took the precaution of getting up early on threeday and mopping the entry area with some of the water left in the storeroom. He also polished the brasswork, including the inside and outside door levers and kick plates, and the woodwork in the area around the door, as well as that around the clerks' desk. The clouds that had brought the rain the night before had lifted, but not vanished, and a gray dawn had given way to a gray morning by the time Rahl had gotten his day-old loaf of dark bread from Gostof and returned to the Association building. He thought it might rain later, but he'd learned in Nylan that he was far from accurate in predicting the weather.

He was at the desk, cleaning his pen, when Daelyt arrived, with a frown on his face.

"Is everything all right?" asked Rahl.

"Have you been out through the courtyard?"

"No. I brought in a bucket of water last night so I wouldn't have to this morning. I usually do because it takes so long to unlock the gates and relock them." Rahl paused, then asked, "Why?"

"Something . . ." Daelyt shook his head. "Chenaryl found some weapons by the gate. I wondered if you'd seen them."

"I wasn't out there this morning . . . well, except I walked by the gates when I went to get some bread, but they were still locked."

"Daelyt!" Shyret's voice was harsh, as well as a trace higher than usual.

Without a word, the older clerk turned and headed back to the archway where the director stood.

Even with order-senses, Rahl could not make out what they discussed, except that Shyret was gesturing and clearly unhappy. Then both walked toward Rahl.

"Did you hear anything . . . unusual last night?" asked Shyret.

"I woke up once," Rahl admitted. "I was hot all over and sweating, and I thought I heard something in the street outside, but then it all went away."

Shyret looked to the older clerk, who frowned.

"Ah . . . ser, could you tell me what's the matter? Did I do something wrong? Is this about the weapons? What kind of weapons?"

"There were two blades left on the pavement inside the courtyard," the director explained. "One was an ancient Cyadoran blade. It had to belong to a mage. The other was a falchiona."

"Why would anyone leave blades like that?" asked Rahl. "They're valuable. At the least you could sell them. I got several silvers for that dagger."

"You couldn't sell the wizard's blade without Chalyn telling the mage-guards," Daelyt pointed out.

"But even if whoever left it knew that, why would they leave the falchiona?" Rahl did his best to look puzzled.

Daelyt shrugged.

Shyret looked at Rahl, then at the older clerk.

"Is anything missing from the warehouse?" Rahl asked, trying to instill concern in his words.

"I'm going to have Chenaryl look, but it doesn't look like anyone opened the gates or climbed them." Shyret turned and headed for the rear door and the warehouse courtyard.

"Mage-blades at the gates . . . that's not good at all," said Daelyt.

"Does it mean that a mage is angry at the director or one of us?"

Daelyt laughed harshly. "No. It means that someone killed a mage, and the mage-guards don't like that at all."

Rahl shook his head. "But . . . if someone killed a mage . . . aren't they supposed to be registered or something?"

"There aren't any mages—not ones that are any good unless they're outlanders—except for the mage-guards. Killing a mage-guard will get you flamed on the spot, unless it's an accident, and then you'll spend the rest of your life—what little will be left—in the ironworks."

"Oh . . ."

"Exactly." Daelyt looked directly at Rahl. "How are you coming on the copies of the new schedule?"

"I have one done, and I'm starting the second."

At that moment, the front door opened, and Hassynat appeared, this time by himself. "Daelyt, what do you have that will handle five hundred stones in about three eightdays?"

"Five hundred stones' worth of what, Trader Hassynat?"

"Lead plates," replied Hassynat.

"Metals cost more, an additional two golds per hundredstone."

"That's banditry, even for you," complained Hassynat.

"Then why, with your score of vessels, are you looking for cargo space?" queried Daelyt with a laugh. "Might it be that you can carry more of a lighter cargo, items that weigh less?"

Hassynat looked to Rahl. "Is this the way you should treat one who would pay for cartage?"

"Daelyt has far more experience than do I, Trader Hassynat."

Hassynat laughed ruefully, although Rahl could tell it was largely for show. "You brigands stick together. Four golds a hundredstone? That's an additional ten golds."

"In addition to the cartage and valuation reserves," Daelyt replied.

"What vessel?"

"In two eightdays, we're expecting the *Legacy of the Black Holding* and then the *Legacy of Nylan.*"

"Those old tubs?"

"If you can wait almost five eightdays, you can have space on the *Founders.*"

"We'll take the *Nylan.* I'll be back tomorrow morning with a draft on the Exchange."

"The consignment forms will be waiting, ser."

Hassynat departed, not nearly so unhappy as his words might have indicated, Rahl realized.

"Captain Wyena won't be happy with that," Daelyt remarked. "Lead's a spavined mule to load and stow."

"I'll be gone for a bit." Shyret nodded to Daelyt as he hurried past and headed for the front door. He did not look at Rahl, who had paused from copying a revised port call listing for the Association ships.

"Yes, ser." Daelyt took out a consignment form. "You can make the copies for me, if you would, Rahl."

"I'd be happy to."

The longer Rahl was at the Association, the more worried he'd become. Not only were Shyret and Daelyt clearly hiding even more than their diversion of coins, but when renegade mages were involved in break-ins, far more was at stake than Rahl wanted to be involved with. But he didn't have that many alternatives, and the idea of being a mage-guard made more sense than anything else. That he might be right about that occupation being the best for him was even more disturbing. He really didn't know enough, but maybe he could visit the registry building on sevenday afternoon and talk to one of the mage-guards. He certainly didn't want to wait until he was forced to leave the Association . . . or even close to that long, the way matters had gone. By the end of the working eightday, he should know enough more to have a better idea about when to leave. At least, he hoped he would.

For the moment, though, all he could do was his job. He picked up the pen and resumed work on the schedule.

As on oneday and twoday, traders, factors, and more merchants than Rahl had seen before made their way into the Association, all wanting something. That meant Rahl was doing mostly copying, while Daelyt and Shyret, after he returned, sold and bargained, except for the time when Shyret sent Daelyt to the Exchange with the golds from the night before. Clearly, the director was having second thoughts about Rahl.

Yet what could Rahl do? Even if he sent a message—or even managed to persuade a captain to return him to Recluce, how would that help him personally? He had no real proof of what was happening. The ledgers reflected what Shyret said, and Rahl had no way to show that "spoilage" was not taking place. No one seemed to believe him anyway, and even when they did, all the magisters said was that it was his problem.

Outside, the sky grew slowly darker as the day progressed, and in midafternoon, after both clerks had eaten, Shyret departed again.

Not that long after, Guylmor and Sastrot—one of the other teamsters—made their way through the front door with a roll of something that was more than six cubits long.

"Got a carpet here for the director," Guylmor announced. "He said to put it here. Didn't say why."

"Just so it's at the side out of the way," Daelyt replied.

Rahl had to wonder why the carpet was in the office when it would have been just as easy for someone to pick it up from the warehouse.

Before long, Shyret returned. "The weather mages say that we'll have rain through the late afternoon and until tomorrow." He looked at Daelyt.

"We might get caught up on all the consignments, then, ser."

Another factor walked in. He'd been in before—a rope factor, as Rahl recalled, although he did not remember the man's name.

"Yes, ser?"

"When is the *Legacy of the Founders* due back?"

"We're looking at close to five eightdays, ser. The *Black Holding* and the *Nylan* will be here in about three."

"Thank you." With that, the man turned and left.

"He's got cordage on it," Daelyt said absently.

It was almost sunset before the last factor left, and the rain had begun to fall once more. Rahl was feeling more than a little hungry when Shyret approached the two clerks.

"It's late enough that we can close up. I need some quiet around here anyway. I have to reconcile some inventory before I can put down the right figures on the draft seasonal tariff report for the Imperial enumerators. Why don't both of you go eat? Lock the door. Just check back here after you eat and before you leave, Daelyt. I was hoping that you two could load that carpet in the wagon, and Chenaryl could follow me home with it, but I'll have to wait until it stops raining." The director snorted. "It never rains here, except on the days when you need it clear."

"Yes, ser." Daelyt inclined his head.

Rahl could sense a falsity about the director's words, but he couldn't figure out why Shyret would lie or why such an obvious statement about the inconvenience of the weather would ring false.

"You'd better go before the rain gets heavier," suggested Shyret.

"Yes, ser."

Daelyt quickly stacked his papers. Rahl didn't bother. He'd have more than enough time later. He certainly wasn't going out in the rain after dinner. Daelyt scurried out, leaving Rahl behind.

After Rahl locked the front door, getting wet while he fumbled with the large brass key, he dashed through the rain that had shifted from a drizzle to a steadier downpour. The gutters were almost full, the water in them moving quickly down the street toward the harbor.

The cantina was steamy, and Rahl found himself sweating as he sat down at the oily back table. He wiped rain and sweat from his face and looked at Daelyt. "Long day."

"There'll be more like that. Always are after the turn of fall."

"Be a moment or two!" called Seorya. "You could let us know you were coming."

"We would if we knew," Daelyt replied.

"The lead plates," Rahl began. "What was all that about?"

"That's simple. Lead is lead. It doesn't matter whether it comes from Hamor or Lydiar. The price is the same. Hassynat's probably got some fine cotton or linen scheduled for his ships, and doesn't have enough space for the lead. See . . . we tend to ship fuller on the legs out from Nylan, and they tend to ship fuller on the legs out from Hamor. Not always, but it's more likely to fall that way. Plus, the lead doesn't take the cubage, and the supercargo—or the master—or the crew—is likely to try and squeeze in more cargo. That can overload the ship. All around, they'd rather have us ship the lead." Daelyt grinned. "They also don't have to worry about spoilage. Lead doesn't spoil."

All that made sense, but . . .

"Here you go, you hardworking clerks!" Seorya set the two chipped crockery platters down, one in front of each man, followed by the two mug-like tankards that held the always-bitter beer.

For a moment, Rahl just looked at the fried flat bread wrapped around onions, pepper, and fish whose origins he preferred not to know, drizzled on top with too little cheese. There was one definite aspect of Seorya's cooking. It didn't matter what it was, because all Rahl could taste was the heat and the spices. Even the beer tasted like the spices after a mouthful or two of food. But, he reflected, there was enough so that he didn't go hungry.

"Frig!"

Rahl glanced up to see that somehow Daelyt had juggled his mug, and sloshed beer out before managing to catch the mug itself—as more beer spilled on his hands.

Daelyt looked at Rahl. "Can you see if Seorya or Eneld has a rag up there?"

Rahl got up and walked forward toward the steamy heat of the big iron stove.

Seorya had already seen what had happened and thrust a rag at Rahl, shaking her head. "It's a good thing you clerks aren't cooks."

"It's a good thing you cooks aren't clerks," Rahl shot back, grinning.

"That is true, because we'd all go hungry."

Daelyt was still trying to wipe and shake beer off his lower sleeve when Rahl returned with the not-too-clean rag. "Thank you." The older clerk used the clean section of the rag to wipe the beer off his hands and blot some off his sleeves.

Rahl sat down and worked to finish the mound of flat bread and spiced-fish-flavored onions and peppers. The beer seemed sweeter than usual, but that was welcome. Unlike most nights, Daelyt actually ate all of his meal, and Rahl wondered if Yasnela were with friends.

"We'd better get back," Daelyt said.

Rahl nodded and stood. He wasn't looking forward to slogging through the rain, even for the relatively short distance from Eneld's to the Association.

He yawned as he stepped out into the rain, which continued to fall as heavily as ever. Usually, right about sunset, there was a mage-guard around, but he didn't see any. He yawned again as he followed Daelyt across the street—far less traveled in the rain. He almost slipped stepping across the gutter to the sidewalk in front of the Association.

Daelyt obviously didn't like the rain, either, because he'd hurried ahead and unlocked the door.

As Rahl let the older clerk lock the door behind them, he headed for the desk to pick up the forms and papers he'd left. He looked around. Somehow, the office looked and felt darker, but the same lamps were lit as when they'd left.

"I need to check with the director. Why don't you put your things away? It's been a long day," Daelyt said before making his way back toward the study.

"I'll . . . do . . . that." Rahl yawned again. It *had* been a long day. His legs felt heavy, and he struggled onto the stool so he wouldn't have to stand while he stacked the forms and slipped them into the drawers.

He was beginning to feel sleepy. Far too sleepy. He put his head on his hands at the wide desk, but somehow, it slipped onto the wood. Then he tried to lift his hand, but it wouldn't move.

"He's almost out . . ."

"Get rid of the truncheon, and you can have what's in his wallet . . . lay him out on the old rug here, and we'll just roll him inside." There was a laugh. "Make him real comfortable."

Rahl struggled to move, to hear more, but a hot blackness rolled over him.

Luba

LVI

Despite the clouds overhead, the late-winter afternoon was almost as hot as fall or spring, and the hint of a breeze was acrid and carried the heat from the furnaces to the west.

"Move that shovel, Blacktop!"

The man knew his name was not Blacktop, but, for all the time he had been in Luba, he did not remember what it was. Until he remembered his name, he would answer to Blacktop. Then again, he had no idea how long he had been in Luba, only that he had been there at least for most of what the overseers called winter, hot as it seemed to him. For the moment, all he knew was that every single time he lifted the shovel, his arms and back ached, and every time that he took a deep breath, the air itself burned through his nostrils and all the way into his chest. He sweated all the time, and half the time, his beard itched from the salt that dried in it.

"Keep the chute full!"

He kept shoveling, evenly and just fast enough so that the overseer would not flick out his lash. He already had more than a few rents in the back of the sleeveless canvas working tunic, and scars on his back beneath those rents. He did not remember how he had gotten them.

"Stand back! 'Ware the wagon!"

Another wagon—pulled by heavily muscled sloggers—rolled to a stop in the unloading dock next to the chute that funneled the coal down into the coking furnace. The loading dock had been cut into the hillside, so that the wagon bed was level with the ground on which Blacktop stood. The top end of the coal chute was barely a span above the ground.

The wagon guide pulled a rope, and the side of the wagon dropped down. A portion of the hard coal rolled out of the wagon and onto the blackened and hard-packed ground some four cubits wide, where Blacktop and the five others stood between the wagon and the chute.

"Loaders! Back to your places! Get those shovels moving!" The overseer's whip cracked into the hot air.

Blacktop stepped closer to the side of the wagon and slipped the shovel under a pile of coal, then turned and lofted it in a low arc into the chute. So did the loaders on both sides, all working with the same motion—out of necessity.

Scoop, turn, and release . . . scoop, turn, and release . . .

Blacktop kept with the others until the wagon was empty. Then he lowered the shovel but did not otherwise move.

"Loaders back!"

He stepped back.

"Short rest, and I mean short."

Blacktop sat down on the concrete-and-stone support to the chute feeding the coking furnace below, a furnace whose stacks rose far above his head, even though the chute ran down the hillside for more than thirty cubits. He turned his head slightly, to let the slight movement of hot air help dry the sweat on his face.

Farther to the west, the furnaces of the ironworks rose up the hill, stairstep fashion, with the large iron pipes that fed the exhaust gases of one furnace into the belly of the next. On the west end of the valley were the mills. He'd been told they were mills, but he'd never been there. His job was simple. He had to shovel coal when he was told to, rest when it was permitted, eat when he could, and sleep the remainder of the time.

The great blast furnaces radiated heat and light into a sky that was gray by day and sullen red by night. Day and night molten iron poured from the furnaces into the sand molds, and when the molds were cool enough, the pigs were moved. At times, from a distance, he had seen wagons moving some pigs when still red-hot to the rolling mills and drop-forges to the west of furnaces. When his crew worked close to the furnaces, the combined clanging of the forges and the roar of the furnaces was deafening. Other wagonloads of pigs went elsewhere, but he had not seen where that might be.

Depending on where he was loading coal or shoveling broken slag into the disposal wagons, Blacktop could occasionally see the red-hot intensity of the furnaces and feel the heat. The reddish color that he only glimpsed reminded him of something . . . but he could not remember what it might be. It felt important, and nagged at him, in the few moments when he had time to think, but he could connect it with nothing before he had to go back to shoveling.

"Wagon away!"

The sloggers took up their traces, and the empty coal wagon creaked out of the unloading dock and back toward the black mountain of coal toward the east, even while another team of sloggers plodded forward, pulling the next wagon into the unloading area.

"Loaders! Stand by."

Blacktop stood and walked back to his position, second in the line of five.

LVII

The early morning was almost chill for Luba, and the warmth radiating up from the still-hot slag was welcome for most of the loaders working to shovel the chunks of waste into the disposal wagon, as was the heat radiating from the blast furnace above the slag pile. A crew of ten breakers stood well above the crew in which Blacktop worked. The breakers on the top of the slag pile carried sledges and bars to turn the solidified waste into chunks that could be carted away.

"Loaders! Stand and rest!" called the overseer in charge of the loaders. "Sloggers! Forward."

The disposal wagon pulled away, slowly at first.

Blacktop and the other loaders waited for the next disposal wagon, taking what rest they could before they once more had to shovel the broken chunks of slag into the wagon.

"Not taking this no more!" The tall man at one end of the slag breaking team abruptly straightened. He lifted the pointed iron bar and shifted it in his hand so that it was held like a javelin.

Without pausing, he hurled it directly at the overseer who stood above him and a good ten cubits to the south. The overseer jumped sideways, but his boots slid out from under him, and he fell and then rolled and skidded a good fifteen cubits down the side of the slag heap.

"Loaders!" snapped the overseer in charge of Blacktop's crew, "stand fast. Don't move."

Blacktop froze, only letting his eyes move to watch what was happening on the slag heap well above them.

The overseer picked himself up, almost resigned in his posture, but he did not attempt to walk or climb back up the slope. Instead, he walked side-ways, back south, and away from the breaker crew.

Five of the other breakers dropped their bars and sledges and also hur-ried after the overseer.

The man who had thrown the first bar scrambled southward and picked up another bar, and then a second.

"Stand fast, Grunt!" snapped the loader overseer. To back up his order, he cracked the lash just above the line of loaders, close enough that Blacktop could feel the brief breeze created by the lash.

In front of Blacktop, Grunt stiffened.

The unruly breaker began to trot after the overseer, throwing a second bar, and then the third. "Take that, you frigging bastard!" The breaker stopped.

Blacktop could not see why, but then, the overseer and the breakers who had followed him were out of his sight on the far end of the slag pile.

For several moments, nothing happened. Above and behind the slag pile, the massive blast furnace continued to roar. Warmth still seeped from the slag near the top of the pile. Two more breakers dropped their bars and followed the overseer.

The unruly breaker picked up another bar and held it, brandishing it, but not hurling it.

Blacktop waited, glad he was not shoveling the sharp-edged slag, and glad that he was not among the three remaining breakers, although he could not have explained why.

The wild breaker raised the iron bar, holding it before him.

A bolt of white flame arced from out of Blacktop's sight, but did not strike the man or the bar, instead spraying away from both, as if something unseen had acted as a shield.

"Frig you, white bastard!" called the wild breaker.

A second bolt of white flame arched out of the sky, and this time struck the iron bar. Flame sprayed off the iron and splattered into the breaker.

The man screamed and dropped the bar.

The third bolt enveloped the man, and flame flared everywhere. When it cleared, only ashes and dust swirled in the air, settling slowly.

Several moments passed before a figure in khaki trousers and shirt, with black boots and belt, appeared on the slag pile above the loaders. She pointed at the two breakers who stood at the end of the pile. "You two! You did not follow the overseer. You did nothing against the malefactor. Those who do not follow order or combat evil are evil."

One breaker fell to his knees. The other looked blankly at the woman.
Two bolts of white fire followed, leaving no trace of either breaker.

The uniformed woman turned and left, without another word.

"You saw the mage-guard," called the overseer. "That is what happens to anyone who fails in their duty. Anyone!" After a pause, he added, "Loaders, ready!"

Blacktop moved into position, waiting for the wagon side to drop so that he could begin to shovel slag into the disposal wagon.

Thoughts churned through his mind. Had he seen that before? He had known that something terrible would happen to the breaker who had tried to harm the overseer. He had known, but he could not remember ever having seen it happen. He had heard of mage-guards, but he had not seen one before. Or had he?

Why couldn't he remember?

LVIII

A mage-guard must never show uncertainty or be indecisive, but must act firmly and deliberately. Nor should a mage-guard delay acting when action is required, because a people equates inaction in the face of a crime or a disturbance with either indecisiveness, indifference, or ignorance, if not all three. Yet a mage-guard must also avoid the appearance of undue haste or careless swiftness, for those will create the impression of acting merely for the sake of conveying an impression, and that will reflect ill on the Emperor. . . .

A mage-guard must always wear his or her uniform in all public places and never conceal his or her identity, and that uniform must always show cleanliness and care.

A mage-guard must convey a mien of attentiveness and alertness and display equal concern for all law-abiding citizens, no matter what their position or station, as well as toward any outlanders, so long as they abide by the laws of Hamor. He or she should also never be cruel or vindictive, and never should a mage-guard display pleasure in meting out justice to malefactors. A mage-guard should not ever show discouragement or anger, no matter how heinous an offense against the Emperor and the laws might be.

Nor should a mage-guard ever use his or her position in a fashion that results in personal gain of any sort, or gain to any other person related to the mage-guard. No Hamorian mage of any persuasion may engage in any venture involving commerce in goods, in coins, or in any other instrument of commerce, either for payment or for any other consideration. Nor may any mage accept payment for services from any source, except from the Imperial Treasury, with the single and sole exception that healing practitioners may accept reasonable payment for healing services, and only for healing services.

Gifts to mage-guards are forbidden, except modest gifts by immediate family members . . .

> *Manual of the Mage-Guards*
> Cigoerne, Hamor
> 1551 A.F.

LIX

In the twilight, just inside the long cookshack, Blacktop stood in the chow line, shuffling forward behind the others. When he reached the spot just before the serving kettles, a white-haired man with a withered right arm and a wooden post for a leg below his right knee handed him a battered and shallow tin bowl.

"Take it, Blacktop."

"Thanks, Oneleg."

The old man grunted and handed another tin bowl to the loader behind Blacktop.

What the servers dolloped into Blacktop's bowl was the same at every meal. He thought it was, from what he could remember, a mixture of over-cooked quinoa, lumps of root vegetables, onions, peppers, a little olive oil, and meat shredded so much that it was impossible to tell from what it had come. Another server added a wedge of bread, and a third handed him a large tin cup filled with thin and bitter beer.

He left the servers and headed for the long wooden tables with the long wooden benches. He settled down beside the older loader called Brick. Blacktop ate quickly, using the bread to scoop out the stewlike mixture, but not ravenously. After each mouthful, he took a small swallow of the bitter beer. At some time—he could not remember when, not exactly—he had seen how the other loaders picked at men who gobbled their food, taking small morsels to annoy them. Small morsels were still food, he'd realized. It did not hurt that he was larger than most of the other loaders, but not enough larger that he stood out. His weather-tanned skin was more golden than brown, too, he had noticed, unlike the others, but his hair was blacker.

After he had finished, he turned to Brick. "What do they do with all the coke? Does it all go to make the steel?"

"You asked that before."

He probably had. "Sorry. I don't always remember."

"Might be for the best. You don't know what you've lost. Some of us do." Brick's voice thickened.

That was a thought. What had he lost? Would he ever find out? He didn't know what to say to that. "Tell me again about the coke."

"Frig if I know where it all goes, except to the blast furnaces. Only know that it takes a lot of coal to make it. Don't see it going elsewhere."

"And the steel goes everywhere?"

"All across Hamor."

Blacktop considered. Hamor had to be big, very big, with all the blast furnaces that filled the vast valley. That was another thing he should have known. "I wish I could remember."

"Even if you don't remember, Blacktop, you're smart. Specially for an Atlan. You do what you have to. Don't do more. Don't do less. See the sloggers?"

Too tired to respond energetically after a long day unloading coal, Blacktop gave the faintest nod.

"They're sloggers 'cause the wizard mage-guards burned their brains. You go against the overseers, and that's what happens. They can't talk, just grunt and pull the wagon traces till they can't pull no more."

"Why did the mage-guards do that? Did the overseers tell them to do that?"

"No. The mage-guards are above the overseers. Overseers just do what they're told, like us, except they don't get whipped. Coratyl said the high overseers have a special book, and so do the mage-guards, but the mage-guards' book is real different, real special."

"A book?" Blacktop asked. A special book? Hadn't he had a special book once? He thought he had, but there was so much he did not remember.

"You know, with letters on the pages? That's what they teach in school. Or didn't you go to school out there in the east?"

"I don't remember." He thought he must have gone to school, but he could not have said why. "I think so."

"Can you read and write? Like your name?"

Blacktop frowned. Then, slowly he used his forefinger to write the word *Blacktop* in the brownish gray dust that coated the table. The word was correct. That he knew, but it was not his name. Why couldn't he remember his true name?

"That looks like letters," Brick grudged.

Blacktop wrote the word *letters*. He thought there was another word for letters, and he found his finger tracing out another word. They both meant the same thing, but they were different words.

His head throbbed so much that he had to close his eyes, but he opened them quickly. Somehow, he was afraid that if he kept them closed for long, he would forget that he could read and write.

He traced another word. It was a name, but it was not his. It was a name he should have known, but he did not. Why couldn't he remember? His hands began to clench into fists.

"Careful now, Blacktop," cautioned Brick. "Last time you got all upset, they called in the mage-guards, and you were near-on as brainless as a slogger for almost an eightday. Weren't that me and Wylet kept telling you what to do, they mighta made you a slogger. A fella's head can't take that often."

Blacktop was angry. He didn't know why, but he wanted to kill someone, and Brick was telling him not to try. He had to trust Brick on that . . . because he couldn't remember. Had he killed someone before? Was that why he was here?

A heavy bell clanged.

"Clear the tables! Move out! Make it quick!"

Blacktop rose and turned toward the doors that led across the courtyard to the bunkhouse. Just before the door, he put the tin dish in one rack and the large cup in the other. Then he walked across the dusty packed earth. He was even more tired than usual.

Not that much later, in the hot darkness of the long bunk room, he lay on the thin straw pallet, looking at the underside of the tile roof. He could see the faint lines where the tiles had cracked and the sullen red gray of the night clouds seeped through. He *could* read and write. He had to remember that. He had to practice his letters, and what they meant, if only in the dust on the cookshack tables.

Could the writing tell him something? His name? Why he had become a loader in the ironworks?

In time, his eyes did close.

LX

The evening slop was worse than usual, and even Blacktop had to pause after scooping out the first half of it with his bread and swallowing each mouthful convulsively. He followed each with a small swallow of the bitter beer. He knew he'd want several swallows after eating to rinse away the rancid taste.

"Rather eat ground steel'n this shit," muttered Brick from where he sat beside Blacktop. "Or slag."

"Or coal," murmured someone else.

"Slag would cut your guts to pieces." Absently, Blacktop traced out the word *steel* in the dust of the tabletop, then the word *copper*. No matter how often the tables were wiped, there was always dust, either from the furnaces or the ovens or from something else. He frowned. There was something that linked the two. Pen nibs—they were copper-tipped, but how did he know that? He must have seen one. But what had he done that he would know that?

Abruptly, an image formed in his mind—one of a red-haired girl handing him a pouch that held pen nibs. He could not see them, but he knew that was what the pouch had held, and she had said, "Here they are." She had said more, but he could not remember what her words might have been.

"What's that?" asked the loader across the table.

"Nothing," replied Blacktop. "Just designs."

"They were words," said Brick from beside Blacktop. "I don't know 'em, but I know words when I see 'em." His voice rose slightly—just enough for two of the guard patrollers to move toward the table.

"He was just drawing in the dust," muttered the loader.

"How would you know, Flats?" demanded Brick.

Without another word, Flats rose and carried his bowl and cup to the next table, reseating himself with his back to Brick and Blacktop.

The two guards halted, then half turned, surveying the cookhouse for signs of other unrest. Both had their hands on the hilts of their falchionas as their eyes passed over each and every one of the loaders, breakers, and sloggers.

From under a lowered brow, Blacktop watched the two guards. He didn't want any trouble with the guards. He'd seen what happened when a loader went against the overseers or guards.

"They won't bother us none, so long as we're quiet," Brick said in a low voice. "Never have, anyways."

Blacktop finished the dinner slop without saying anything. The guards moved slowly until they were out of sight behind him. He wasn't about to look back because that would draw their attention.

Brick leaned closer to Blacktop. "They were words, weren't they?"

Blacktop nodded, just slightly.

"Can you write my name?"

Blacktop didn't want to, not at all, but without Brick's help he would have been a slogger. He leaned closer to the older loader, then wrote *Brick* in smaller letters in the small area of dust beside the older loader's tin cup.

"What are you doing there?" The words came from an overseer who strode toward the table, followed by the two guards Blacktop had lost sight of.

"Writing . . ." Blacktop admitted.

"You know your letters?"

"I seem to know a few, ser."

"Overseer, Blacktop."

"I seem to, overseer."

The overseer paused. "Don't do it anymore."

"Yes, overseer."

"You do it anymore, and you'll answer to more than me, Blacktop."

"Yes, overseer."

The mumbles that ran around the tables were so low that Blacktop could not make them out, but he had the feeling that most of the loaders were less than pleased at the attention he had brought to them. Just from a few words?

He finished the last sip of the beer, then rose, with a few quick words to Brick. "See you later." With his tin dish and cup in hand, he headed for the wash racks, where he left both. Then he turned and stepped out through the doorway and took the foot-packed walk to the loaders' bunkhouse. Overhead, the low gray clouds were tinged with a sullen red glow from the ovens and furnaces.

Later, as Blacktop lay on his straw pallet, looking up at the underside of the cracked roof tiles, he couldn't help but ask himself why the overseers were against his writing simple words in the table dust? It didn't make much sense, because he hadn't been writing anything, and whatever he'd written would soon be gone. Besides, Blacktop hadn't run across anyone else among the loaders and breakers who could read single words, let alone more.

What was it about words? But then, how did he know about them? It was as though his hands and fingers remembered more than his head, but he had to admit he was beginning to remember images. Still, why had he lost his memories, and why couldn't he remember more? And who had the redheaded girl been? Why had he remembered her when her face had looked so disinterested and as if she couldn't have cared less?

He looked at the tiles above, trying to find answers to those questions . . . and to others he could scarcely frame, questions lost in the fuzziness of a forgetfulness whose source he also could not remember. And beneath it all, he knew, was rage, a seething red force whose cause was also lost.

LXI

The next morning, as Blacktop filed out of the cookshack behind Brick, his eyes slit against a hot wind that swirled grit around the loaders, an overseer waited with two guards.

"You Blacktop?" asked the overseer.

"Yes, overseer." Blacktop blinked, trying to get the fine grit from his left eye.

"You're to come with me. The guard-captain has some questions for you."

Blacktop didn't want to accompany the overseer. Overseers usually meant trouble. He looked at the overseer and the guards behind him. He didn't see a mage-guard anywhere, but they were never far away. That he had learned. "Yes, overseer."

"Down the walkway there to the wagon. You go first."

The wagon that stood down the stone walk from the cookshack was one with two rows of seats behind the driver. Blacktop had seen such wagons occasionally, carrying guards, mage-guards, or others who were neither loaders, breakers, nor sloggers.

"Get in the second row, Blacktop. The one right behind the driver."

"Yes, overseer." Blacktop realized that each time he had to say those words, he could feel anger, yet he could not ever show such anger, not if he wanted to live. Or if he were ever to find out how he had come to the ironworks . . . and who had been responsible.

He climbed up onto the wagon.

The overseer and one guard took the seat behind him, while the other guard sat beside the driver, turned so that he was watching Blacktop. The driver flicked the leads of the two drays, and the wagon began to move, its iron tires crunching on the grit that covered the stone-paved lane.

Blacktop took in everything he could as the wagon continued southward down the gradually sloping way. The lane paralleled the blast furnaces, then continued across a stretch of flat ground. To both the right and left of the lane were structures with roofs but no walls. He had seen them from the loaders' enclosures and from the cookshack area, but had not been able to discern their function. Now he could see that they held iron. Some held stacks of heavy plate; others thinner plate, still others iron bars.

Beyond the warehouses to the west, he could make out a stone structure composed of multiple layers of arches. From the bridge, if it happened to be that, ran a smaller arched bridge to each of the blast furnaces. Farther to the south, the structure curved westward and ran toward the mountains. In fact, Blacktop realized, it ran right into the mountains. Unbidden, the word *aqueduct* came to mind. Of course, there had to be water for the furnaces.

Again . . . he wondered how he had known that, but that question could wait as he studied the area. He could also see that almost nothing grew in the valley, except sparse patches of grass and scattered scraggly bushes and twisted low evergreens. Just beyond the point where the storage warehouses ended, the lane began to climb a low rise toward a group of buildings set on a low mesa. As in the rest of the valley, little grew on the rock-strewn sides of the low mesa.

When the wagon reached the crest and the road leveled out, Blacktop could see that there were four buildings. He could also feel a cooler breeze out of the south, and he looked carefully past the structures. Directly south of the mesa was a gap in the low mountains that encircled the valley, and from that gap, he thought, the wind blew.

The stone walls of the buildings might once have been white marble, but all the stone was a brown-tinged gray. Even the narrow windows looked to be the same shade. The wagon creaked to a stop before the middle building. The archway had no columns before it, and only a single wide stone step to serve as an entry.

"Off, Blacktop."

Blacktop eased himself off the wagon, then stood and waited.

"Follow me." The overseer walked the fifteen cubits to the archway.

So did Blacktop, conscious that the two guards trailed him, ready to cut him down if he so much as stepped sideways. As he neared the building, he saw that the walls were old and pitted, as well as stained.

In front of him, the overseer opened the plain oak door and stepped into a square foyer. He turned right down a narrow corridor, walled in the same pale marble as the exterior of the building, but without the staining and pitting. The second door on the left was open, and the overseer entered.

A guard wearing a falchiona surveyed the overseer.

"Overseer Stolt reporting with the loader Blacktop, as ordered."

"Wait." The guard turned and opened the door to his left. He took a half step into the chamber, and said, "The overseer is here." After a moment, he stepped back. "The guard-captain will see you and the loader."

"Go ahead, Blacktop."

Blacktop walked through the door into a smallish chamber that held little besides a table desk, two chairs, a stool, and a set of file chests stacked against the wall on both sides of the narrow window before which the table desk was set.

The guard-captain was standing, waiting beside the table desk. She was a woman, with gray-and-white hair cut as short as any man's. Her shoulders were broad and muscular, and eyes watery gray and rimmed in red. Her face was so weathered that Blacktop couldn't tell what her age might be, save that it was beyond middling. Beside her was a mage-guard, a thin-faced man who looked to be nearly as old as she was. Neither smiled.

"You may wait outside, overseer." The guard-captain's voice was like rumbling gravel, slightly softened by sand. "Close the door."

"Yes, ser."

The guard-captain did not speak until the door closed.

"The overseer claims you were writing on the table, Blacktop."

"Yes, ser, but only in the dust. I didn't make any real marks on the table."

"That's good. We don't like destruction of any sort here in Luba. This is where all that Hamor builds begins." She laughed, softly, harshly. "That was not my real question. Can you write?"

"I think so, ser . . . it's been so long, and there is so much I don't remember."

"What did you do before you came here?"

"I don't remember, ser."

She glanced to the mage.

"He does not remember, Captain."

"Do you remember anything?"

"Just one or two things, ser. I remember a girl giving me a pouch, and I think it held pen nibs, and I remember being rolled into something hot and dark."

"Nothing else?"

"Just the words . . . and how to write them, ser."

The mage-guard nodded.

The guard-captain pointed to the stool at the side of the desk. "Sit down. There is paper. There is a pen. Write something."

Blacktop sat. Slowly, he took the pen. He had never seen it, yet it felt familiar. He looked down at the rough paper, and he realized he would have to be careful, or the point might snag . . . but . . . how did he know that? What could he write? He could feel the guard-captain and the mage-guard looking at him.

Slowly . . . he began.

The ironworks are in a valley in Luba. The blast furnaces roar night and day, and the coal goes into the ovens and comes out coke, and the coke goes into the furnaces . . .

"That's enough."

Blacktop cleaned the pen and laid it beside the inkwell. Both the guard-captain and the mage-guard had watched him do so.

The guard-captain lifted the paper, studied it, and handed it, without speaking, to the mage-guard, who in turn studied it.

"His hand is as good as an old-time scrivener's," offered the mage. "You don't see penmanship like that anymore."

Scrivener? Blacktop thought that word sounded familiar. Had he been a scrivener? But how would a scrivener come to be a loader in the ironworks?

"Except in the hills west of Atla, or in the mountains of Merowey." The guard-captain looked down at Blacktop. "Do you know numbers? How to write them?"

"Yes, ser . . . I think. I haven't written any, not even in the table dust."

"I'm going to give you numbers. I want you to write them down in a column, so that they can be added together." The mage-guard set the paper back in front of Blacktop.

"Yes, ser."

"Twenty-three . . . nine . . . seventeen . . . thirty-five . . ."

Blacktop wrote each number, lining them up from the rightmost column.

"Now . . . add them together and write down the sum."

Sum? Oh . . . that was the total, Blacktop recalled. He wrote *84* under the summation line.

"Might have been a clerk. That's a merchanting sum line."

"Your gain, Captain," suggested the mage-guard.

"Did anyone tell you why you were sent to Luba?" asked the guard-captain.

"I don't remember, ser."

"What do you remember?"

"Just being a loader, ser. Except I don't remember much of when I was first here, either."

"Would you like to do something else, with better food and a better place to sleep? It wouldn't be quite so hard, but you would have to write and do sums all day."

"Yes, ser." Blacktop didn't have to think about that long.

The guard-captain nodded. "Go out into the front room and wait."

"Yes, ser." Blacktop bowed slightly, then turned and opened the door, stepping out into the outer office.

"Get him a shower and clerk's garb. He can start at one of the plate-loading docks. Can't exactly do that much harm there if it doesn't work."

Just before he closed the guard-captain's chamber, Blacktop heard a few words of what the mage-guard said.

". . . wonder what merchant he offended . . ."

Why did they think he had offended a merchant? Because his writing and his ability to do sums suggested that he had been a merchant clerk?

What could he have possibly done? Even that thought tightened his guts, and he could feel the seething rage starting to rise before he pressed it back into the darkness within himself.

Within moments, the mage-guard emerged from the guard-captain's study and looked at the overseer and the two guards. "Thank you. You three can return to your duties. We'll take care of Blacktop."

After the three left, the mage-guard looked at Blacktop. "Let's go."

Another wagon carried him and the mage-guard down from the mesa, but the road they took was on the west side.

As they rode, the mage-guard began to talk. "Blacktop . . . your job is going to be very simple, but very important. We need to keep track of how much steel is produced. Each time a wagon is loaded, you need to write down the wagon number, where it is being sent, and how many sheets of each size of iron plate are in each wagon. You will need to write this down in a book called a ledger."

Ledger? He'd heard that before. It was a book where things were listed by name and number.

"Blacktop?"

"I'm sorry, ser. I was just remembering what a ledger was. I can do that."

For several moments, the mage-guard did not speak. Then he said quietly, "You may remember more in the eightdays ahead. Do not get angry. Before you say anything, think about everything that you do. Duty and performance can get you better positions in the ironworks. Sometimes, they can get you out of the ironworks. Violence and anger will only turn you into a slogger—if you aren't killed first."

"Yes, ser." Blacktop already understood about anger and violence.

At the same time, he wondered what else he would remember.

LXII

By midday, Blacktop had showered in cool water, changed into a tannish short-sleeved shirt and matching trousers, been assigned to a real bunk in a dormitory at one end of the mesa, and dispatched by a wagon to loading dock number three. The mage-guard accompanied him, still providing information.

"The loading dock is where the sheets of iron plate are lifted onto the short-haul wagons that take them to the river piers. From there they're barged up- or downriver. The head supervisor is Moryn. You call him and any other supervisor 'ser' or 'supervisor,' not that you wouldn't anyway."

"Yes, ser."

"All you have to do is pay attention and write down how much iron plate of what sizes leaves the loading dock."

That seemed simple enough to Blacktop, and he nodded as the wagon neared its immediate destination.

"You get two coppers an eightday for wages. It's not much, but you can buy things at the small chandlery next to the dining hall . . ."

Wages?

"You'll work from breakfast to dinner, but after today, you'll get an extra half loaf of bread at breakfast to take with you for a midday meal. A wagon picks up all the checkers and brings you back to the dormitory and dinner . . ."

Blacktop kept listening, trying to fix what the mage-guard said in his memory.

The loading dock was little more than a stone platform covered in heavy and battered planks. Behind it were stacks of iron plate. Each stack held a different size of iron plate, set three and four layers deep, with wooden wedges between each sheet. A swivel hoist powered by what looked to be a small steam engine was mounted north of the middle of the dock.

As the wagon came to a stop well short of the dock, Blacktop watched as the hoist operator turned the loading arm until it was positioned over a stack of plate. Then two men in beige shirts and trousers similar to those he now wore unfastened half the sling and slipped it under the iron.

Blacktop climbed out of the wagon, carefully, because he was now wearing stiff new leather sandals, and he wasn't used to them. He followed the mage-guard up a set of worn wooden steps on the northern side of the dock. There, the mage stopped, and so did Blacktop.

Shortly, a stocky man in a khaki shirt and trousers, a black-leather belt and scuffed black boots appeared from behind a stack of plate and walked toward them.

"That's Moryn," said the mage-guard quietly.

"What do you have here, Mage-guard Taryl?" asked the supervisor.

"You've been asking for a qualified checker for eightdays. The guard-captain found one."

The weathered supervisor studied Blacktop for several moments. "He looks like he's been a loader or a breaker. Now . . . how is that going to help?"

"He was a loader because he lost his memory, and the paperwork was somehow mislaid. The guard-captain and I have examined him. He writes well and does his sums adequately. His writing suggests he was at one time a scrivener."

"Tried to cheat his master, you think?"

Taryl shrugged. "Could be. Could be otherwise, too."

Moryn laughed. "Doesn't matter now. No one's going to make off with iron plate. We'll see how he works out." He turned. "What's your name?"

"Blacktop."

"That'll do." Moryn nodded to the mage-guard. "Thank you."

"We do try to help." There was a slight irony in the words, but Taryl said nothing more before vaulting back up into the wagon.

Moryn pointed to what looked like a tiny roofed building with walls waist high on three sides, and a high stool set behind a narrow counter. Another man dressed like the supervisor sat on the stool, shaded by the small roof. "See the kiosk over there. That's the checker's station."

Blacktop watched as the checker wrote something.

Moryn pulled out a sheet of paper and stepped back, smoothing it on the top sheet of plate in the pile nearest him. Then he motioned for Blacktop to look at it. "Here's the form you use. Each large block has a space where you write down the wagon number. Each wagon has a letter and a number painted on each side beneath the driver's bench. Each time the supervisor or wagonmaster calls out the size and thickness of the plate, and the number of plates loaded in a hoist, you write them down in the large space, and after the wagon pulls out, then you add up the total number of each size of plates, and put the totals in the smaller boxes here. Each box is for a different size or thickness of plate. It might be full span, half span, or quarter span in thickness, and it will be either full plate, half plate, quarter plate." Moryn rolled up the paper. "Do you have any questions?"

"Will they be loading anything besides iron plate, ser?"

"That doesn't happen often. Just write down what it is—iron bars, say, and total those separate from the plate."

"Yes, ser."

"Now . . . go stand next to supervisor Chylor and watch what he does for the next several wagons. Don't move away from the kiosk. If you get in the way of the hoist, there won't be enough of you left to worry about. Iron plate is *heavy*."

"Yes, ser."

As Blacktop walked carefully along the back edge of the loading dock toward the checker's kiosk, Moryn raised his voice. "Chylor! Blacktop's the new checker. He'll watch you until you finish this wagon."

"Got it, boss!" Chylor kept his eyes on the wagon and the hoist.

Blacktop stationed himself at the right side of the kiosk, just far enough back not to block the supervisor's view, but close enough that he could see the paper in front of Chylor, although he could not make out the words and numbers that clearly. Then he waited as the hoist rattled and the steam engine hissed, and the sling lowered its load.

"Two quarter plates, quarter span!" Moryn called out.

Chylor wrote and waited.

Blacktop watched.

After another sling delivery, Moryn announced, "Wagon away."

The six dray horses—not sloggers—strained for a moment before the wagon began to move. Chylor stood out from the kiosk, then walked to where Moryn stood. He did not look at Blacktop.

"Go ahead, Blacktop."

The former loader slipped into the kiosk and seated himself. Somehow, the stool and the counter felt familiar. Not the ones before him, but their arrangement. He studied the form on the counter, roughly half-filled out. Chylor's fractions for the thickness of the plate were sloppily written.

Blacktop found himself frowning. How did he know that? Why could he only remember so much, and no more?

The next wagon rolled up, and Chylor walked south of the kiosk, stopping just short of even with the driver, while Moryn moved back toward the kiosk.

Blacktop looked for the wagon number. It was faint, but right where Moryn had said it would be. He wrote down *D-21*, in the wagon number space, and waited, watching as the steam hoist rattled and swung a sheet of plate over the wagon.

"Forward about a cubit!"

More rattling and hissing followed the supervisor's directions.

"Easy down."

As the hoist lowered the plate, Chylor called out, "Full plate, one sheet, half span, first sling."

The wagon settled slightly under the weight of the plate. Then one of the hoist assistants unfastened the leather and cable sling, and the hoist operator lifted it, and the process began again.

"Full plate, one sheet, half span, second sling . . ."

After the loading was complete and the wagon rolled away, Moryn walked up to Blacktop. "Let's see."

"Yes, ser." Blacktop turned the sheet so that Moryn could see the entries.

The supervisor nodded. "Just keep doing it that way." He stepped back to where he had been watching and waited for the next wagon.

In the end, Moryn checked the entries for almost a half score of wagons before leaving the loading dock to Chylor's control.

For a moment, Blacktop hadn't seen why Moryn had waited so long, but then he realized that the head supervisor had wanted to see how Blacktop had entered all the different sizes and thicknesses of plate.

Blacktop settled himself on the stool and waited for the next wagon.

LXIII

As the mage-guard had told him, a wagon did trundle up to the plate-loading dock when Moryn stopped work at the loading dock somewhat before sunset. Both Chylor and Moryn got on as well, but they sat in the first three rows, reserved for guards and supervisors, and Blacktop sat alone in the seventh and last row.

From the plate-loading dock, the wagon continued along the dusty stone lane toward another loading area, one with stacks of steel bars. As the wagon slowed there, the wind picked up, swirling grit into Blacktop's eyes. He had to blink and blot them, and he realized that they didn't water or hurt as much as they had at the end of his day when he'd been a loader.

The single checker from the bar dock walked to the wagon, looked at Blacktop, then walked around to the far side, where he sat in the last row as far as he could from Blacktop. The supervisor squeezed in beside Chylor.

Once the wagon stopped outside the dormitory area where Blacktop had cleaned up earlier, he climbed down and followed the other checkers— he thought most were checkers—into the eating hall. There he found that they filed past a table with tin cups and tin platters, rather than shallow bowls. They also picked up forks and broad spoons before moving to a serving table.

Blacktop found himself served a heaping pile of spiced rice and a thick sauce that held root vegetables and discernible chunks of meat, as well as a half loaf of fresh bread. The beer actually foamed slightly and smelled better.

For a moment, Blacktop just stood, looking around the hall. The tables were old, but had been recently cleaned and polished, and, most surprisingly, since talking had been scarce among the loaders, the area was filled with the low murmur of voices. Scattered fragments of conversations flitted past him.

". . . problems with the big drop-forge . . . glad I'm not a mech . . ."

". . . don't ever want to piss off Dyeth . . . call a mage-guard and swear you struck him . . . they can't tell he's lying, either . . ."

". . . less than a season . . . be paid off . . . head home . . ."

Blacktop realized that two men at a nearby table were studying him.

". . . transfer from hard labor, more likely . . . look at the tan and the muscles . . . and that bushy beard."

He smiled and moved toward them.

"You're new here, aren't you?" asked the older balding man.

"I just started as a checker today," Blacktop admitted.

"You're welcome to sit down."

"Thank you." Blacktop settled onto the bench.

"I'm Zhulyn," offered the balding man, "and this is Faryn."

"Blacktop."

"Is that your real name?"

Blacktop took a sip of the beer before replying. He was thirsty. "No, I don't think so, but I can't remember my real name."

"But . . . you're a checker?" Faryn smiled broadly.

"I remember how to write and do sums. I just don't know how I got here."

Zhulyn and Faryn exchanged quick glances. "You must have really upset someone."

"Why do you say that?" Blacktop added quickly, "I know some things, but not others, and I'm trying to find out more."

"It's like this," said Faryn. "It's said that the only people who can take away memories are mages, and they can only do it if they use a special potion. If the Emperor's mages did it, you did something very wrong, and everyone would know why, and you'd still be doing hard labor. Because no one knows, that means someone broke the Codex, and to do that without getting caught means that they had to pay a great deal."

"Do you understand?" asked Zhulyn.

"Enough." The Codex was some sort of law, and whoever had taken his memories had broken it. He could feel his rage rising, but he suppressed it and forced a smile. "There's not too much I can do about what I can't remember."

Faryn nodded. "True enough. What's your station?"

"Plate-loading dock, number three."

"That's one of the places where they start new checkers."

"Where are you?"

"I work in shipping. We take all the checkers' sheets and put together reports for the Emperor's Minister of Trade." Faryn shrugged. "They think it's important. Who am I to argue?"

Blacktop hadn't heard of a minister before. He knew that. There was another word . . . *magister* . . . was that it? No, they were different. Magisters were from someplace other than Hamor. He turned to Zhulyn. "Where do you work?"

"I'm in receiving. I'm in charge of the coal section. We keep track of how much coal is mined and used in the coking furnaces."

Blacktop took a sip of the beer. He'd been right. It was better than what he'd gotten as a loader. He looked up. Several of the other checkers kept looking in his direction.

Faryn watched for a moment, then said quietly. "It's your beard. It's rather unruly."

Blacktop just looked at him.

"You can't have a razor here, but if you want to trim the beard now, you can borrow scissors from the guard station in the dormitory."

"Thank you." Blacktop began to eat, and before long the other two left him. No one joined him.

After he ate and left his platter, cup, and cutlery in the rinse tanks, Blacktop walked back outside and along the stone walk to the dormitory. Once inside the main door, and past the guard station, he stopped. There was a room to the left, one lit with high lamps affixed to the ochre-brick walls. There were five wooden benches, and against the outer wall, there was a single bookcase with books filling the six shelves.

Books . . .

He moved deliberately into the room and to the bookcase.

An older man with a trimmed gray beard who sat on one of the benches reading looked up. "They're for reading."

Blacktop smiled politely. "I know."

"You can read any one of them, but you can only take one to your bunk, and if you damage it, you'll have to work extra hours to replace it." The older checker looked back down at his book, pointedly ignoring Blacktop.

Blacktop stepped forward until he stood directly in front of the shelves. Some of the books had titles on their spines, but most did not. The older books had clearly been handbound, but there was a sameness about the newer ones that suggested . . . what? He just stood in front of the shelves for a time, realizing that he knew how to bind a book, how the signatures had to be sewn together, and how the backboards of the covers had to be just exactly so much smaller before the leather was stretched and sewed and glued.

He must have been a scrivener. He had to have been. How else would he know that? Except . . . how did he know that was what a scrivener knew? How did he know anything?

He closed his eyes for a moment.

When thoughts and questions stopped swirling through his mind, he picked out a book without a title on the spine and took it gently from the shelf, opening the cover. The title page read: *A World Geography and History.*

He opened the book and began to read, his eyes going down the page.

For age upon age, scholars taught that all true history began with Cyad and the ancient mages who carved a land of miracles out of the Accursed Forest of Naclos, and that Cyador lasted in prosperity and plenty until the black demons landed on the Roof of the World and sent forth the demon smith Nylan, who forged even greater weapons and toppled an empire in the course of an afternoon. This is, of course, a tale for children, if not nonsense. There were kingdoms east of the Westhorns long before Cyad rose, and many endured long after Cyad fell . . .

Blacktop kept reading. While the words made sense, he could feel that he should know more than what the words told him.

"You can read that, young checker?"

Blacktop lowered the book to look at the older man. "Yes. It talks about the stories that have been handed down as history . . . the first page does. I haven't read farther yet."

"Balderdash . . . if you ask me. Anyone who writes about the past is creating their own vision of what they think was. That's because they have to rely on the words of those who lived then, and no man tells his own story truthfully." He snorted and returned to reading his own book.

Blacktop took the history to the bench farthest from the other man, where he sat down and continued reading until the warning bells rang—the ones before the curfew bells. He reshelved the book quickly and started for his bunk room.

Abruptly, he turned and walked back to the guard station. The guard watched as he neared.

"Ser . . . I was told that I could ask for scissors to trim my beard."

"That you can. It might be a good idea. You won't look so much like a loader or breaker." The guard reached down and held up a pair. "Don't be long. The curfew bells will be ringing soon. The guard chief gets unhappy if you're not in your bunk room by then."

"Yes, ser."

"You can have the barber trim everything on sevenday afternoons or on eightday."

Blacktop hadn't even known about a barber. He also realized he had no idea what day it was. "Oh . . . thank you."

He hurried toward the bathing facilities at the end of the corridor.

The wall mirror in the shower room was old and wavery, but Blacktop managed to trim his long beard and enough of his hair so that he looked more presentable. Then he returned the scissors to the duty guard. He even got to his bunk before the bells chimed.

Later, in the darkness, he lay on the bunk mattress, his eyes open, ignoring the snoring coming from somewhere to his left.

In one day, everything had changed—and all because the guards had discovered he could write and do sums? Yet, somehow he had changed. He had learned more . . . or relearned some of what he had forgotten, and that had happened so gradually that he had not fully been aware of that change until just before the overseer had found him writing words in the table dust.

Now . . . he was in a far better place, and the guarding was so lax that he could easily have walked away. After a moment, he smiled wryly. And then what? The valley was desolate. There was nothing edible and no water, except in the guarded buildings in the valley, and everywhere else away from the ironworks, the dry rock and scrub bushes stretched for kays. The aqueduct that ran to the mountains must have been ten kays long. A guard on a horse could track anyone and run a prisoner down with little difficulty. And even if he did reach the mountains, what would he do? He had no real name, no real idea of what his skills might be, and no understanding of how he had come to Luba—or why.

LXIV

Cling . . . cling.

Blacktop groaned. He had not slept well, and his dreams had been disturbing. He'd killed a man. At least, he had in his dreams, and then people had begun to chase him. He could even remember some of the words from his dreams, from a shadowy figure who had attacked him with a truncheon. "We'll get you, we will. You're a white demon . . . the magisters will take care of you." Blacktop knew the word *magister.* It meant a kind of ruler, but why would the magisters be after him? There weren't any magisters in Hamor. Had he lived somewhere else?

And someone else had been saying words to him, warmer and sadder words, but the only phrase he recalled was something like "you won't be back . . . the past has no hold on you." Back where? And how could the past have had a hold on him, when he couldn't remember it?

Were those dreams memories? How could they be?

Despite the pounding in his skull, he knew he had to get up. The last thing he wanted was to go back to being a loader . . . or, even worse, a slogger . . . and that could happen if he didn't do his new job as a checker. He sat up on the edge of the bunk and swung his feet onto the worn reddish floor tiles. He could feel grit under his toes, grit that had not been there the night before. His clothes were on the rack at the foot of the bed, and the spare set was in the foot chest below it. He didn't feel like a shower, not with the cool breeze that blew through the bunk room, but it might help wake him.

After his shower, he pulled on his new garments and made his way back toward the eating area, where he filed into the line. Despite being among close to fifty checkers, not one looked in his direction or talked to him as he waited, then held out his tin plate for a large helping of an egg and quinoa hash. He also got a full loaf of bread along with his beer. It took him a moment to remember that half the bread—or all of it, he supposed—was his midday meal.

When he left the servers, he began to look for an empty space at one of the tables, carrying his platter, cup, and bread, easing his way between the checkers on the benches.

He saw Zhulyn, but the balding man did not meet his eyes.

Faryn did look up. "You look more civilized this morning."

Beside him, Zhulyn nodded, reluctantly, but did not speak.

"Thank you for the suggestion yesterday," Blacktop replied politely. Something about Faryn bothered him, but he couldn't have said what.

"I'm glad we could help." Faryn's smile was warm enough, but Blacktop felt it was false.

"Thank you." Blacktop moved on, slowly, listening.

"Why . . . encourage him . . . ?"

". . . a dangerous man once, young as he is . . . may be again . . ."

Him? A dangerous man? He almost shook his head, but sat down quickly when he saw an empty corner of one of the tables. The checker nearest him looked over, then looked away quickly.

What was it? The only thing that Blacktop could see about himself that looked different was that his skin was tanned darker and more bronzelike, as opposed to the light olive color of the other checkers—and he was taller and more muscular. But why would those things make a difference in the way the other checkers looked at him . . . or didn't want to talk to him?

He ate all the hash and drank all the beer, but decided to save the entire loaf of bread for later. After eating, he once more followed the lead of several checkers, and, before long, he stood outside the building with the others, waiting for the wagons and hoping he was in the right place.

Several more checkers hurried toward the group as Blacktop caught sight of three wagons coming toward the group. Which wagon was he supposed to take? Finally, he caught sight of Moryn and Chylor, who were heading toward the second wagon. He was one of the last aboard, seating himself next to the same gray-haired man who had been in the reading room the evening before.

"Good morning," Blacktop offered, as the wagon began to move.

"It is morning," replied the other, "and it is not that adverse. How did you find the *History*?"

"It's interesting," Blacktop admitted. "There's a lot I don't know."

"That's true for all of us, including those who write the histories. The only question is whether we realize it." The man looked away.

Blacktop did not say more.

Once the wagon stopped at the plate-loading dock, Blacktop hurried after Chylor toward the checker's kiosk. For a moment, when he saw the stacks of plate and heard a clanking around the steam engine, he wondered why nothing was guarded or locked. Then, he realized that there was no need for it. Without a wagon and a team and the steam hoist, how could anyone steal the iron plate? But why had he considered the need for locks?

"Blacktop!" called Moryn. "Before we start loading, we need to get the steam lift up and working. You'll help Hasyn. Shovel coal into the wheelbarrow and bring several loads over to the boiler on the lower level. The coal pile is over there."

Shoveling coal again? Maybe he was still part loader.

He went to the kiosk, where he stripped off the khaki shirt and set the bread under the counter. He wasn't going to shovel coal in a clean shirt. Then he headed off to find the shovel and wheelbarrow.

Both were beside the coal pile, and he quickly filled the wheelbarrow, then jammed the shovel into the coal and began to trundle his load in the direction of the steam hoist. As he neared the dock, he could see the boiler was on the lower level and Hasyn—the older man he'd been sitting beside on the wagon.

Hasyn was coaxing a fire from the banked coals remaining from the night before when Blacktop pushed the squeaky wheelbarrow up and stopped short of the open firebox door.

Hasyn looked up, then offered a wry smile. "Guess I'm stuck with you. I'm Hasyn."

"Blacktop."

"Can you lay down a shovelful of the coal just short of the reddish ones, spread out so they're not all clumped together."

Blacktop nodded. He eased the shovel into the coal and wiggled it so that there was a thinner layer of coal spread across the metal, then lifted it and eased the coal into place.

"Good. Styun never did figure that out."

"Another shovel?"

"Against the back."

Following Hasyn's instructions, Blacktop loaded the firebox under the boiler, emptying the wheelbarrow, then took the wheelbarrow back for another two loads of coal. One he added to the fire, the other he left, with the shovel.

"Obliged," said the steam mech. After a moment, he added, "There's a wash-water barrel over there. It's the one with the red slash. The blue one is for drinking."

"Thank you."

"Just don't take the histories too serious. The scriveners who wrote them never worked a loading dock or much of anything."

That was probably true enough, reflected Blacktop as he headed for the wash barrel to get the coal dust off his hands and arms. Then again, the mage-guard had said that he'd once been a scrivener.

For some reason, that thought created a tightness in his guts, and his fists had clenched without his even thinking about it. He forced himself to take a deep breath. Things were better than they had been. Getting angry wouldn't help. It wouldn't.

Except that he knew the anger and rage was still there, deep within.

LXV

For the next eightday, Blacktop continued his careful routine, following all instructions, and not intruding on anyone. The other checkers no longer stared at him—the shorter haircut by the barber on sevenday had doubtless helped with that—but none did more than address him civilly. While Hasyn, whom Blacktop often saw in the reading room, occasionally passed a few words with the younger man, mostly the steam mech remained pleasantly aloof.

On a sixday evening, with little else to do, Blacktop sat on one of the benches in the reading room, a heavy book in his hands. He glanced up at the sound of footsteps, then dropped his eyes to the text when he saw that the man entering the chamber was Hasyn.

"Still reading that balderdash?"

In fact, Blacktop had continued to read *A World Geography and History*. He knew that he would find something in it that would help him remember more of his past. He just didn't know how or what.

"It's interesting."

"Ought to read something that'll teach you."

"After I finish this, you can suggest something."

"By then, it'll be high summer."

"I don't think I'll be going anywhere, Hasyn."

The mech laughed, eased a book from its place on the shelves, then took the bench farthest from the one occupied by Blacktop.

The checker reread the paragraph he had begun earlier.

> . . . so-called founders of Recluce were anything but poor souls seeking a land for those oppressed by the hegemony of Fairhaven. Recluce was created by the machinations of the two most ambitious women in the history of Candar. The Tyrant of Sarronnyn colluded with the Marshal of Westwind in the consorting of the Tyrant's younger sister to the son of the Marshal. The purported "exile" of the couple to Recluce was in fact a well planned and well-financed effort designed to create another rival to Fairhaven and to reduce the ability of the High Wizard to circumscribe the depredations of both . . . The greatest irony of this effort was that their ploy resulted in the destruction of Westwind and the overshadowing of Sarronnyn by Recluce . . .

Blacktop paused, lowering the book slightly. He could not recall having read anything about Recluce, yet he did not think the words before him were right. Again . . . how could he *know*?

LXVI

Blacktop found his hands on cold iron—on a set of iron bars. He looked around. Someone was hurrying away from him, down the stone hallway outside the cell. How had he ended up in a cell? Was he still in Luba?

"So . . ." The voice was that of a guard who wore black, except for thin and bright blue piping on his tunic sleeves and cuffs. "How is our would-be mage tonight?"

Blacktop said nothing.

"Too bad Kacet can't help you now. No one can." The guard laughed. "Maybe the engineers can, but I wouldn't count on it. No, I wouldn't." Then he turned and walked away.

Blacktop's fingers tightened around the bars, as darkness—hot darkness—rose around him.

Abruptly, he was somewhere else, lying on his back, breathing rapidly. His body was damp with sweat, and heat radiated from him. An involuntary groan escaped him.

"Quiet!" hissed someone.

He closed his mouth. He was in the bunk room. He'd been dreaming, but the guard in the dream had called him a would-be mage, and said that someone couldn't help him. The name should have been familiar, but it hadn't been, and it had slipped away as he had awakened.

Had he once been a mage? Or had he tried to be one?

How could that have been?

He lay there for a long time. He'd had more dreams in the eightdays since he'd become a checker, but the one he'd just experienced had been the most vivid—and disturbing. He'd been in a cell. Had he really done something so terrible that he couldn't remember it? So terrible that his memories and past had been taken away?

He shivered, suddenly cold, although the late-spring night was anything but cool.

After a time, his eyes closed.

Then, something awakened him, and he got out of his bunk, except it was a pallet in a small cubicle, and his feet carried him through the dark toward the front of a building that felt familiar, yet he could not remember ever being there. When he reached the front door, his eyes fixed on the bar that held the door closed. Something whitish was seeping through the thin gap between the door and frame. As it thickened, it tugged, then shoved the bar out of its brackets so that one end clunked to the floor, and the door swung open, and a man stepped inside, falchiona extended.

The man turned and whipped up his blade, but Blacktop was faster, and his truncheon cracked the man's wrist and the bravo reeled back, out of sight, the falchiona clattering on the floor tiles.

Whhstt! A bolt of whiteness flew toward Blacktop, but it only splattered around him.

"We will have to handle you differently, dear boy," came the languid words from the chaos-wizard who stepped inside the front door.

The words chilled Blacktop, but he forced himself toward the white-shadowed figure.

The wizard lifted a falchiona of whitish bronze, flicking it toward the truncheon that Blacktop carried, but Blacktop managed a parry and evaded the blade enough so that the truncheon touched the wizard's forearm. Then Blacktop stepped inside and rammed the truncheon into the wizard's throat. The wizard shuddered, and light flared, and the wizard began to collapse in upon himself.

Blacktop jerked awake, more sweat streaming down his face.

Had it been just a dream . . . or had he killed a white wizard?

For a long time, he sat on the edge of the bunk, trying not to think or remember, hoping he could go back to sleep without dreaming.

In time, he did sleep, and if he dreamed, at least, he did not remember those dreams when he dragged himself up at the morning bells. A cool shower helped . . . a little, but he couldn't help but wonder if the reason he was in Luba was because he'd killed a mage. He didn't know if he had, but he wasn't about to ask anyone.

At breakfast, as he made his way to a table, he nodded to Hasyn, then to Zhulyn.

He'd no more than taken a sip of his beer when someone approached. "Blacktop . . . do you mind if I sit down?"

Blacktop had seen the checker, one of the few who looked close to his own age, looking at him closely, more than a few times.

"No . . . please do." He was getting more than a little tired of being ignored by the other checkers.

"I'm Masayd. I used to be a clerk in Swartheld. Did you work there? Hasyn said that you had a clerk's hand and that you wrote like a merchant-ing clerk."

Blacktop shrugged. "I don't know. I don't remember anything much before Luba. Someone told me I'd been given a potion so that I wouldn't remember." He paused. "What kind of clerk were you?"

"I was the junior clerk with Chalyndyr Brothers. They said I burned the ledgers to hide the coins I'd stolen." Masayd shook his head. "The whole three years I was there, I maybe managed to slip a silver out of the excess that wasn't covered. I never burned anything, but that lying Ventaryl swore

I did, and he was a mage-guard. That was after the other one vanished. Mage-guards were questioning everyone who wasn't bonded in gold. No outlanders, of course. They still need the trade from places like Nylan and Brysta and Valmurl." He looked at Blacktop speculatively. "You don't remember anything?"

Blacktop considered. "I had a dream . . . the other night. Maybe it was a memory, about a white wizard who followed a bravo into a building. I drove off the bravo, and the wizard said that he'd have to handle me differently."

Masayd stiffened. "Do you remember how the wizard spoke?"

Blacktop managed to offer an indifferent smile, eager as he was to hear what the former clerk might be able to tell him. "He spoke slowly, but it was lazy-like, and he called me 'dear boy.' That was in the dream anyway."

The clerk paled, and his jaw tightened. "That . . . that sounds like Asmyd. He was the one who disappeared. He always called all the clerks 'dear boy.' He was a slut sow's ass." After a moment, he asked, "Don't you remember anything more?"

"There was a flash of white, and then I woke up." Blacktop wasn't about to say that he'd killed the wizard, even in his dreams.

"They . . . they framed you, too, then." Masayd shook his head more violently. "They said I had something to do with his disappearing, but I didn't. I didn't. That lying bastard Ventaryl . . ." For a time, Masayd just looked down at the table.

Blacktop forced himself to eat slowly. Had Masayd been sent to Luba because of what Blacktop had done? Or had something more happened? There had to have been more . . . But what if there hadn't been? What if he had just killed the mage, and Masayd had been sent to Luba for it?

"Blacktop?"

"Yes?" He paused. "It might only have been a dream. I just don't remember more."

Masayd shivered and shook his head. "We've been framed. They wouldn't have blanked you if something hadn't been all wrong. I just wish you could remember more."

"So do I." That was more than true, yet Blacktop had to wonder if he really wanted to know all that he'd done.

Suddenly, Masayd stood. "Thank you. That helped. It really did."

"I wish I could remember more," Blacktop said.

"Maybe you will." With that and a faint smile, Masayd headed for the rinse racks.

Blacktop had to hurry to finish his breakfast and get out front to catch his wagon. Even though the sun was still a low glow behind the perpetual gray haze of the valley, he found he was beginning to sweat just standing and waiting. Once the wagon arrived, he sat beside Hasyn, although neither spoke on the trip to the loading dock.

He had just finished helping the steam mech load the boiler and returned to the checker's kiosk when another wagon—one of the smaller ones—rolled down the lane and came to a stop at the south end of the dock. The angular and thin-faced older chaos-mage—Taryl—hurried up the low steps and made his way toward Blacktop. Blacktop hadn't seen him since the first day that Taryl had brought him to the plate-loading dock.

Moryn moved forward, then just inclined his head and stepped back.

"I won't be that long," Taryl said in passing to the chief supervisor.

"Ser?" asked Blacktop.

"Blacktop . . . I've heard that you've been reading during your free time."

"Yes, ser."

"What have you read?"

"*A World Geography and History* . . . that's all."

"A good choice for a man who has no history or memory." Taryl paused. "Do you remember anything more?"

"I remember a building with a barred door, and I was on the inside. It was a building, not a dwelling, and it was dark."

"Hmmmm . . ." The mage-guard frowned. "Turn this way. Close your eyes."

Much as he did not wish to, Blacktop did. He felt *something*, the faintest tingling.

"Open them. Did you feel anything?"

"My head tingled . . . just a little."

Taryl nodded. "I'm not surprised."

Blacktop didn't like that, either.

"Do you recall ever wearing a copper bracelet on your wrist?"

"No, ser. I don't remember anything that I wore."

"If you remember that, or anything that you think is important, tell one of the guards that you need to have me see you. Do you understand? Don't wait."

"Yes, ser." Blacktop understood. He also understood he might be in even more trouble if he did remember who he had been and what he had done.

Moryn waited until the mage-guard and the wagon were well away from the loading dock before he approached Blacktop. "What was that all about?"

"I don't know, ser. He asked me if I had been reading, and if I remembered any more. I told him I'd had dreams, but I didn't know what they were. He said he'd check with me every so often."

Moryn frowned. "They want you to remember something. I hope for your sake that it's good."

So did Blacktop, but with the dreams he'd had of killing two men, and maybe more, he was less and less certain that he wanted to remember—or that it was to his advantage.

"Here comes the first wagon." Moryn turned. "Hasyn! Get that hoist ready!"

Blacktop laid out the forms and the pen and inkwell, then blotted his forehead. It was going to be a hot day, and full summer was still eightdays away.

LXVII

On fourday night, after dinner, as he did almost every night, Blacktop retired to the reading room. It was a space seldom frequented by any other than Hasyn and himself—at least not while he was there. At that moment, Blacktop had the small chamber to himself, and he extracted the *World Geography and History* from its place on the shelf and opened it to where he had left off reading the night before.

He had only read a few pages when the words seemed to leap off the page at him, as if they were tiny arrows aimed at his eyes.

> Recluce is ruled by a Council of Magisters, all of whom are black mages, and generally at least half are women, as a result of heritage forced on the isle by its founders, Creslin and Megaera . . .

Well over a century ago, after a series of naval engagements between Recluce and the Hegemony of Fairhaven in which the so-called black engineers unveiled a new class of steam-powered vessel that was extremely effective in decimating the Hegemony fleet, the "black engineers" created an engineering enclave and built the then-new city of Nylan at Southpoint on the southern tip of Recluce. To this day, a black wall divides the majority of Recluce from the enclave, even though virtually all trade now passes through Nylan. Nominally, however, the capital city remains Land's End at the northernmost point of Recluce, a matter of history and pride by the ruling magisters . . .

"The ruling magisters . . . the ruling magisters . . ." He mouthed the words, and they echoed through his thoughts, battering at him

Magister . . . magister . . . it was just a word, but it was more than a word, and he did not know why.

Still holding the book, he stood and began to pace . . . moving in circles, as if the walking might help him discover what he was so close to remembering. But . . . close as it seemed, he could not quite grasp whatever it might be.

Almost in desperation, he stopped pacing and opened the book again, trying to continue reading the book before him. His eyes dropped farther down the page.

Recluce is known for its practice of immediate exile of anyone who might be a chaos-mage or who attempts "improper" use of order-magery. While the black engineers allow a greater range of order-magery in the city of Nylan, exile from Recluce is immediate for any emerging white mages or wizards, and no one with such traits is even allowed to visit the isle . . .

Had he been exiled? Had they taken his memory as well? Exile . . .

An image appeared in his mind. He was standing in a chamber not that much larger than the reading room. At one end was a long black table, with four black chairs behind it. Four people in black sat in the chairs, two men and two women. The oldest—a gray-haired man—was speaking in a stern voice.

". . . you had no idea how you accomplished such destruction. You are in fact the perfect natural ordermage. Consequently, given our responsibilities, and particularly given the limited area of Nylan, we feel that there is little alternative to some form of exile."

Blacktop knew he had been in that room, and that the four had been speaking to him. They had exiled him. They had been in black, and they were magisters.

"Are you all right, Blacktop?" Hasyn stood in the archway of the reading room, a concerned expression on his face.

Blacktop? That wasn't his name. What was it?

Another image/memory appeared.

He sat at a corner table under a brass lamp suspended from the beamed ceiling by a large brass chain. Across from him were an older man and a beautiful woman. Her hair was light brown and curly, barely neck length, and her eyes were brown with gold flecks. He could not take his eyes off her.

The older man poured a clear liquid from the pitcher, half-filling each goblet. "Rahl, you must taste the leshak—it's a wine from greenberries and white grapes. Drink it in moderation. It's more powerful than it tastes."

He lifted the goblet, filled with a wine that had the slightest of green tinges, and took a small sip. The wine was smooth and cool . . .

Rahl . . . he was Rahl. He was the one who had been exiled.

Lights—whitish and reddish—flared across his eyes, and he staggered.

"Blacktop . . ."

Blacktop . . . No, he was Rahl. He was *Rahl*.

The entire reading room began to revolve around him, and he barely managed to put the book down on the nearest bench, before sinking onto it and holding his head in his hands.

More flashes of light flew across his eyes, and yet he knew that the lamplight in the room had not changed.

Rahl . . . he was Rahl, but how had he gotten to Luba? How had it happened?

Fragments of images swirled through his thoughts . . .

. . . listening to a mage-guard saying, "You don't have to wear the bracelet, not as an outlander, but you do have to have it with you if you leave Swartheld for any other part of Hamor," and taking the bracelet and putting it on his left wrist . . .

. . . dodging as a tall man in worn tans and a long knife darted in at him, then smashing the man's wrist with his truncheon and then his jaw, before pivoting barely in time to deflect the short staff of a second attacker, jamming the truncheon just below the center of the man's ribs—and watching the man die . . . and then seeing a mage-guard appear and throw two quick chaos-bolts to destroy both bodies . . .

. . . sitting at a long desk in the Merchanting Association and worrying about Shyret's dishonest maneuverings . . .

. . . standing at a doorway, looking a last time at Deybri before the door closed in his face . . .

. . . trying to walk back to the Merchanting Association, feeling sleepier, and sleepier, and then being rolled up in something—the carpet that Shyret had had waiting . . .

"Nooo!!!!"

"Blacktop! You'll have the guards on us!" Hasyn remonstrated. "Keep it to yourself."

Keep it to himself . . . to himself. Wasn't that what everyone wanted? Don't bother us with your problems and questions. Don't ask about things we don't want to hear. Don't complain when what we tell you doesn't make sense.

Even so, he closed his mouth, and found himself shivering in rage and anger, the tears streaming down his face.

He was in the ironworks in Luba, the ironworks of Hamor.

Slowly, he stood.

Hasyn looked at him, then stepped back. "Are you all right? You're not going to do anything stupid, now, are you?"

Rahl would have laughed, but he knew it would have become hysterical bitterness, a torrent he could not have stopped once he started. "No. I can't afford stupidity."

"You sound different." Hasyn continued to frown.

At that moment, Rahl realized something else. He couldn't sense what Hasyn felt. Nor could he sense what surrounded him. He could only see . . . and hear.

He had lost all his order-skills.

What had Shyret done to him?

He was a low-level clerk and checker in a prison ironworks in a land far from his birth, and he had been stripped of almost everything—his name, his memories, his order-abilities, what few coins he had possessed, and whatever future he might have had.

The utter unfairness of what had happened surged up within him. Every time he had needed help or assistance or wanted an explanation, someone had told him that they couldn't explain, or that it was his fault, or his problem, or that they were terribly sorry, but they really couldn't help him—and then all of them had turned their backs and left matters up to him, only to reproach him, or exile him, when they hadn't liked what he had done.

All of them except Deybri.

His whole body shuddered.

After a moment, he took a long and deep breath. He had to get control of himself. He had to. He looked up to see that Hasyn continued to back away from him. The older man kept glancing over his shoulder as he distanced himself from Rahl.

Rahl shook his head. "I'll be fine, Hasyn."

That didn't seem to reassure the steam mech, who turned and hurried out of sight down the corridor.

Rahl stood alone in the reading room. That seemed somehow apt.

Now . . . he had no choices, and no allegiances—except to those few who had honestly tried to help him. He could only do what he could, whatever that might be, in whatever fashion he could.

If he could do anything at all.

LXVIII

For much of the night, Rahl did not sleep. First, he tried to call up each one of the order-skills he recalled, but he had no use or even awareness of any of them, no matter what he tried. Then, exhausted, when he tried to close his eyes and summon sleep, one memory after another emerged, each jolting him back into wakefulness.

Beyond all the memories was a single question. If Shyret had been so worried that Rahl might reveal something, why hadn't he just killed Rahl? There had to have been a reason. Was murder too risky? Because he'd registered with the mage-guards, and if he turned up dead, someone would be unhappy? Except Shyret wasn't supposed to know that Rahl had order-skills, and he didn't know that Rahl had registered. Or did he? Or was it that if anyone from Nylan looked into his death, the investigation might reveal too much? Or that the magisters in Nylan might send an ordermage to inquire?

The latter was the most likely, and that irritated Rahl. His death might get someone to look into things, but his life and his questions wouldn't. He could feel the rage seething, and not that far beneath, but he blocked it away. Rage was not something he could afford. Not in Luba, and not if he wanted to get any sleep.

In the end, he dozed, fitfully, if that, trying to ignore yet another concern, that of how he could find a way out of Luba, a way that would get him out with both mind and body intact—even if he no longer could call on his order-skills.

He was awake with the first chime of the morning bells, a chime that splintered like miniature knives in his ears.

As he washed and dressed quickly, another thought re-occurred to him. Taryl had already discerned something because he had asked if Rahl had remembered wearing a bracelet on his wrist. And if Rahl didn't tell the mage-guard . . .

Once again, he was in an impossible position. He hadn't done anything really wrong, certainly not since ending up in Luba, but sooner or later Taryl would ask again, and if Rahl waited, that could do him no good at all. Rahl didn't want to tell Taryl, not in the slightest, but like it or not, he did remember the problems waiting had caused him with Puvort, and in Swartheld, and Taryl was likely to be even harder on him.

Apprehensive as he was, he made his way to the guard station.

"What do you want, Blacktop?" asked a guard that he did not know.

"The mage-guard Taryl, he said to leave a message with you, or whoever was on duty, if I remembered anything that he was asking me about."

"Yes?"

"I have," Rahl replied. "I'm just following his orders. That's why I'm telling you."

"I'll pass it on."

"Thank you, ser." Rahl inclined his head politely, and then made his way to the dining area. As he filed toward the servers, tin plate and cup in hand, several of the checkers looked in his direction, and then looked away even more quickly. By the time he had been served, no one would meet his eyes.

Why? Because Hasyn or someone had heard about how he'd acted in the reading room the night before? Or because word had spread that a

mage-guard would be seeking him out? Or because he appeared different—
even if he hadn't seemed so to himself when he had looked in the mirror
earlier that morning?

Rahl found a corner at one of the tables and ignored the way the checkers closest to him edged away. The egg and quinoa breakfast casserole
seemed far less edible than on previous mornings, but that might have been
because he'd had no basis for comparison from before he'd come to the
ironworks. Still, he ate it all, and drank every last drop of the beer, bitter as
it also tasted.

When he left the dining area, the guard by the door avoided looking at
him, and he stood by himself while he waited for the morning wagon to the
loading dock. He sat next to Hasyn in the last row of seats. Two of the hoist
sling-men sat in front of them.

"You all right?" murmured Hasyn.

"I had a hard night," Rahl admitted. "I'm better this morning."

"Guards say the mage-guards want to talk to you."

Rahl nodded.

"Best of fortune."

"Thank you."

Neither spoke for the rest of the ride to the plate-loading dock, where,
as usual, Rahl helped the steam mech with the coal and firebox before
washing the coal dust off his hands and arms and taking his place in the
checker's kiosk. Also, as usual, neither Moryn nor Chylor said anything to
Rahl, except to call out the hoist loads being set into the hauling wagons.

"Two half plates, ship cut, full span . . ."

"Three of the quarter plates, ship cut, full span . . ."

Rahl hadn't thought about it before, but the thicker ship-cut plates had
to be for warship hulls. The amount of iron being produced and shipped
dwarfed anything he'd seen or heard of on Recluce. Why were the Hamorians using so much iron? Because it could withstand chaos, and they used
more chaos?

Whatever the reason, he was careful to keep his tallies neat and his
sums correct, but, while the work was far easier than being a loader or a
slogger, he soon found it boring, and he had to concentrate on not letting his
mind wander.

In between wagons, when Chylor was not looking, he tried to order-
sense things, but he could not exercise any of the skills he had once possessed. Even after trying to recall what he could from *The Basis of Order*, he

had no success. That raised another question. Had Shyret discovered the book among his possessions as well? Or had Daelyt just taken his coins and disposed of his personal gear without really going through it?

The day dragged on, and Rahl dutifully entered plate types and quantities on the forms. By midafternoon, despite the shade provided by the roof of the kiosk, Rahl's shirt was splotched with sweat.

Although the sling-men were rigging another load, Rahl saw a two-horse team and a wagon approaching the loading dock. He watched as the wagon stopped. Taryl stepped down and walked toward the supervisor.

The mage-guard looked at Chylor. "I'll need some time with Blacktop."

"Ah . . . yes, ser. If we could finish this wagon . . . ?"

"I'll wait."

Taryl's patience impressed Rahl. The mage-guard seemed far less imperious than the magisters of Recluce—or even the Council Guards.

"Hoist on the way!"

Rahl checked the form and his pen.

"Three of the quarter plates, half span . . ."

Rahl made the entries for the remaining two loads, then waited.

"Wagon away!" called Chylor.

Rahl stepped out of the kiosk and moved toward the mage-guard.

Chylor took the seat in the kiosk. His look at Rahl was not particularly friendly.

Taryl motioned for Rahl to follow him, then turned and walked to a spot shaded by a stack of plate, where he stopped.

"You left word with the guards," said Taryl. "What do you remember?"

"Most everything . . . I think." Rahl smiled apologetically. "If there's something small I don't recall, how would I know I didn't remember it?"

Taryl just waited.

"My real name is Rahl. I was sent from Nylan to be a clerk at the Nylan Merchanting Association, and I'd been working there for most of the summer season until close to the beginning of fall. I was noticing some irregularities in the accounts, things being declared as damaged or spoiled in shipment, and some I was sure weren't. Someone tried to break into the Association one night, but I stopped them, and the bravo ran off. I never found out who it was. I was even thinking about leaving the Association and seeing if I could become a mage-guard, but then someone drugged me—it must have been Daelyt—and I can remember getting really sleepy and being unable to move, and someone rolling a carpet around me . . ." Rahl stopped.

"Why did you think you could become a mage-guard?" Taryl didn't sound particularly surprised.

"I didn't know if I could," Rahl admitted, "but the mage-guards where I registered said that anyone who had order- or chaos-talents could apply."

"Is there any way you can support what you told me?"

"I was a clerk at the Merchanting Association. Shyret and the others there might say that I was there. They might not. I always ate at Eneld's across the street. Seorya might remember me. I did register with the mage-guards in Swartheld, at the place off the main piers, but I don't know what happened to the registry bracelet." Rahl laughed bitterly. "It doesn't matter now, though. I don't have any order-abilities. At least, I can't find them or use them."

Taryl smiled. "You're lucky. When they use nemysa on someone without order, or chaos-abilities, that person almost never recovers his memory. With mages, a handful die, but any who live will eventually recover everything. It will be days, or eightdays, or longer. Generally, the more powerful the mage, the longer it takes."

"But . . . I wasn't that powerful."

"You're still young . . . it's Rahl, isn't it?"

"Rahl, that's right."

"Rahl . . . powerful mages start showing traces of ability young, but they keep getting stronger long after those with less ability—if they work at it properly."

Rahl was silent. Did he actually have a chance of regaining his abilities?

"We will have to send to see if they have any records remaining in Swartheld."

"With my luck, ser, those will have vanished as I did."

"That may be, but we will see."

"Ah, ser. What do I do now? Keep on as a checker at the loading dock?"

"That would not be wise for anyone, but particularly for you. The mage-guards can always use clerks, especially here in Luba, and being around mages might help you regain your abilities. Besides, that's where all mage-guards start in any case." Taryl paused. "You didn't say exactly, except about order-skills, but you were considered a black mage?"

"Of sorts. The magisters in Nylan said that I was a natural ordermage, and that I'd amount to little because, while I had skills, I was unable to learn others. I could either do things or not, but I never seemed able to learn what I couldn't do."

"There is a place for every level and type of mage in Hamor." Taryl's voice turned wry. "It may not be what one expected, but mages are not wasted or turned away here."

Rahl could hear the irony in the older man's voice, and couldn't help but feel sorry for him. Taryl had certainly not planned to be a mage in Luba.

The mage-guard turned and walked down the dock to the checker's kiosk and Chylor.

Rahl followed, hoping he hadn't upset Taryl.

"I'll be taking . . . him . . . with me," announced the mage-guard.

"Yes, ser. Ah . . . did he do something wrong?"

"No. Something wrong was done to him, we think."

To Rahl's eyes, the supervisor looked almost disappointed, but Rahl was more than glad to follow the mage-guard to the wagon.

LXIX

On fiveday evening, Rahl sat at the junior's table in the mage-guard's mess, with two others—Rhiobyn and Talanyr. He'd been issued two sets of khaki garments, similar to those worn by the mage-guards, except without any insignia, and a pair of heavy black boots that matched his new belt. His hair had been cut short, and the mages' barber had shaved him. He'd been given a kit with a razor as well, and was sharing an actual room with Talanyr, not a bunk room. He'd even been given a truncheon, although it was of oak, rather than lorken. It had been provided with the caution that weapons were not worn inside the station, but always outside.

While Rahl still could not order-sense whether mage-guards were order-mages or chaos-mages, he realized that all he had to do was look at their belts. Those who wore clips for a falchiona scabbard were chaos-mages, and those who wore the short retaining harness for a truncheon were ordermages.

Before him was a meal on a crockery platter—biastras, with pan-fried flat bread on the side. The beverage was not leshak, but a heavier ale. In the mage-guards' mess, in addition to the juniors' table, were two long tables for the mage-guards. One held seven women, and the other eleven men, although Rahl could hear comments back and forth between the tables.

He wrapped the bread around the biastra and took a modest bite. Spicy as the marinated meat was, it was not as hot as what he had tasted in Nylan. Either that, or he had gotten better used to the more highly seasoned Hamorian fare.

"How did you get here?" asked Rhiobyn, a youth who looked younger than Rahl and was more than a head shorter. "You sound like you come from Atla, except you speak better." His black eyes darted from Rahl to Talanyr.

"Good recovery, Rhiobyn," said Talanyr dryly.

The younger mage-clerk flushed under his olive skin.

"Someone drugged me with nemysa," Rahl said. "Mage-Guard Taryl discovered I could write when I started to get back some of my memories . . ." He continued with a brief explanation of what had happened after that.

"Taryl's a good sort," offered Talanyr quietly. "He's a lifer here, though."

"Why is that?" asked Rahl.

Even Rhiobyn leaned forward.

"I don't know exactly, but he did something to upset the Emperor's brother's mistress. That was when Halmyt was Emperor."

"Is Mythalt the Emperor now?"

"Where have you been?" asked Rhiobyn.

"I lost my memory, remember? He was the Emperor before that happened. I haven't heard any news in something like two seasons."

"He still is," Talanyr said. "He'll be Emperor for a long time. He's less than half a score older than I am."

"What's he like?"

Talanyr shrugged. "He's the Emperor. Who knows what an Emperor's like? I'd imagine he likes women and good food and being in charge. Who wouldn't?"

"Have there ever been mages who were Emperors?" Rahl ate another biastra, enjoying the taste of what he was thinking of as real food.

"The histories say that Sanacur the Great was, but that was a long time ago. Not recently, unless they've kept it hidden."

"How do you know all that?" Rhiobyn slurped his beer slightly. "I'm sorry."

"My father was the local scholar. He ran the school," replied Talanyr. "He insisted I know more than any of the other students."

"Where are you from?" Rahl asked.

"Jabuti—it's a little town in Afrit that's almost on the border with Merowey, in the western highlands."

"How did you get here?"

"How does anyone end up as a mage-trainee?" Talanyr laughed, softly. "I was ten, I think, when I decided to strengthen with order a basket I'd broken because I didn't want anyone to find out. I got away with it and a few other things for nearly five years, until a friend of my father visited us. He was an ordermage. Well, he wasn't that good a mage, and he'd been the historian of the mage-guards, but he could sense order and chaos. Since the Codex forbids isolated mages, except healers, before I knew it, I was in the juniors' school in Cigoerne, and, after four years, on my way here."

The Hamorian Codex forbid isolated mages? Magister Thorl had never mentioned that, Rahl realized.

"Who did you piss off?" asked Rhiobyn.

"Everyone, I think. The school head said that I concealed enormous arrogance behind a facade of politeness and humility." Talanyr finished his ale and picked up the pitcher in the center of the table, half-refilling the mug.

Rahl wondered if the school head had confused self-confidence and poise with arrogance, or if Talanyr had just been punished for being too able for someone from an out-of-the-way place. "How did you do in your studies?"

"Well enough. What about you?"

Rahl accepted that Talanyr didn't wish to talk about himself more. "I left school early. My father tutored me, and I read a lot. I was a clerk in Swartheld when a mage-guard . . ." Rahl shook his head. He'd only get in trouble by misleading them. "I'm from Recluce, and I upset a magister in the north. So they sent me to Nylan, and I didn't fit in there, either, because I couldn't learn order-skills the way the others could. That was why they sent me to Swartheld as a clerk."

Rhiobyn's mouth hung open.

"You can stop gaping, Rhiobyn," suggested Talanyr. "Hamor gets more than a few mage-guards from Recluce. Sometimes, Recluce even gets an ordermage or two from Hamor, no matter what they say."

Rhiobyn shut his mouth, if only for a moment. "But . . ."

"It takes time to recover from nemysa poisoning," Rahl replied, "and I need to learn more about the mage-guards." After a pause, he added, "The mage-guards could always use another clerk, Taryl said."

"That'd be the truth," said Talanyr. "We're more than an eightday behind on reports as it is."

"Do you write quickly?" asked Rhiobyn.

"Fairly quickly. I was a scrivener for a while."

"People still copy books by hand?"

"In most places except Nylan and Hamor, I expect," ventured Talanyr.

"But why? Printing is so much easier and less costly."

Rahl and Talanyr exchanged a quick glance before Rahl nodded to Talanyr.

"Printing presses don't work very well without order-magery, not the high-speed ones, because chaos breaks them down too quickly," Talanyr began, "and Nordla and Austra don't care that much for mages. Fairhaven has made it difficult for ordermages to remain in Candar anywhere east of the Westhorns."

"Austra and Nordla don't speak Hamorian," Rahl pointed out. "That means that the books would have to be translated first if they were printed here, and books are heavy. It would cost a lot to ship them."

"Who would want to do that when so few people would buy them?" continued Talanyr. "After all, Rhiobyn, how many books have you read lately?"

The slighter mage-clerk looked to Rahl. "How many have you read?"

"I was reading the *World Geography and History* . . ."

"That's good, but it's dated," said Talanyr.

"There weren't that many choices in the reading room for the checkers. I wasn't interested in reading about steam engines and hoists." Just how much had Talanyr read? Rahl wondered.

"Better than the reports you'll be copying tomorrow," predicted Rhiobyn.

LXX

On sixday morning, Rahl was seated at a long table in the rearmost room of the mage-guards' station in Luba, a small building tucked against the base of the eastern cliff of the mesa. The filing room had one skylight and no windows. The wooden surface was grained like oak, but different, and had an orangish shade to it, brought out more by an ancient oil finish.

Thelsyn, a gray-haired ordermage with a weathered if unwrinkled face, stood at his shoulder. "Young Rahl, it's simple enough. Each mage turns in daily reports of any incidents or occurrences. The task of clerks is to take the rough reports and turn them into final form. You make two copies, one for our files and one to be sent to headquarters in Cigoerne. Each season, the reports are bound before being dispatched. If you have any questions about a specific report, set that report aside and wait for the mage who wrote it to check in with you. They're supposed to do that twice an eightday. Most do." The last words were delivered sardonically.

"Yes, ser."

Thelsyn extended two sheets. "These are samples. Follow the example with regard to margins and letter size. You do know what margins are, I assume, since you are listed as once having been a scrivener?"

"Yes, sir. Is a standard hand acceptable?"

"Standard hand?"

Rahl took out the pen and wrote out the words "standard hand." "That's standard hand." He wrote another version of the words. "This is merchant hand."

Thelsyn looked at both examples, then laughed. "Whichever is faster and easier. They're both better than anything anyone else can do."

Rahl decided to use standard hand. He picked up the pen and took the top report off the pile to his right, then took a sheet of the smooth beige paper and set it before him.

"You must write well," said Talanyr from the far end of the table. Rhiobyn was serving as the duty messenger. "Thelsyn never says that."

"One advantage of my humble past," Rahl replied.

"More writing and less talking." Thelsyn stood in the doorway once more.

"Yes, ser." Rahl wondered how he'd managed to return from where he'd gone so quickly. He had seen the mage-guard leave.

"Remember that." Thelsyn turned.

Rahl returned his attention to the first report, from a mage-guard named Wenyna. Her writing was hurried but clear, once he realized that the hooked curlicue was an "e," and he was able to finish two copies of her daily report quickly.

The next one was a different matter. Rahl had to cross-check the scribbling against the roster of all the mage-guards even to make out the scrawled name—Shaelynt. He looked at the scrawled symbols on the sheet before him, struggling to make out the words, feeling as though he were working out some kind of puzzle. The first half page took him longer than two complete copies of Wenyna's report.

The report after that was better, if disturbing, because it dealt with a loader who had attacked one of the servers in the loaders' cookshack and thrown the old man into a kettle of boiling water. Why had the loader attacked the server? The servers were as much prisoners as the loaders and breakers.

After making that set of fair copies, he cleaned the pen. Then he got up and stretched and wiggled his fingers. He was little more than a glorified scrivener—except one without order skills.

Rahl could recall all too well that he had once thought he would be more than happy to have been a scrivener living in Land's End for the rest of his days. Now . . . if he didn't recover his order-skills, he'd be a clerk or a checker in Luba to the end of his life, and that was not what he wanted—even if he had no clear idea of what he did want.

Just after he'd reseated himself and started on the next set of reports, Thelsyn reappeared.

"Rahl, let's see what you've done."

"These here, ser."

Thelsyn picked up the completed copies and leafed through them. Then he nodded, turned, and departed.

After Thelsyn left the copying room, Rahl glanced to the other end.

"You must be good," observed Talanyr. "He always complains about mine and Rhiobyn's."

"He'll find something else I do to complain about."

"Such as talking too much," suggested Thelsyn.

This time, Rahl realized that the mage-guard had not really left the chamber, but used magery to create that impression. "Yes, ser."

When Thelsyn did leave, it did appear as though the mage-guard had actually walked out, but, to be safe, Rahl wrote out another set of reports and started on the next one before he said anything more.

"Does everyone just stay here in Luba all the time? The mage-guards and -clerks, I mean?"

"Oh, no," replied Talanyr. "This is lousy duty, but we're not confined the way the prisoners are. We get either sevenday or eightday off, usually eightday, and we can take the regular transport wagon to Guasyra. It makes a run after breakfast and leaves from the square there just about the time of evening bells. Or, if you're really adventurous, you can come back on the early-morning run."

"What's in Guasyra?"

"Good food . . . well, better food . . . women, if you're not too particular; young men, if your tastes run that way . . ."

Rahl winced.

"I thought not. You leave a girl behind?"

Deybri was anything but a girl, and Rahl hadn't so much left her behind as been forced to leave Nylan—and her. He'd kept having dreams about when he'd seen her the last time, and her words about the past having no hold on him. If it had no hold on him, why did he keep thinking about her?

"I wonder how much it would cost to send a letter to Nylan," he mused aloud.

"It's three coppers a sheet anywhere west of the Heldyn Mountains and four to the east," replied Talanyr, "and two silvers over that to any port in the world on a Hamorian vessel. I don't know about what it costs on other lands' vessels."

"More," said Rahl dryly. Still, he was now getting paid at the rate of five Hamorian coppers an eightday. If he were careful . . .

LXXI

As the sun shone over the eastern hills, Rahl and Talanyr sat in the third row of the long transport wagon while its iron tires rumbled over the stone road that rose gradually from the Luba Valley toward the southern pass. At Talanyr's urging, not that it had taken much, Rahl had agreed to accompany him to Guasyra on eightday. Rahl had certainly wanted to leave Luba and the ironworks, as much to know that he could as for any other reason, and it had been so long since anyone had wanted him to accompany them anywhere. On the other hand, he had but six coppers to his name. He tried not to think about that. At the very least, he could walk around the town and learn more about Hamor.

"The town's south of Luba, but isn't the Swarth River to the east?" asked Rahl.

"It is, but Guasyra sits on the north side of the Rynn. It's a small river that runs out of the mountains and into the Swarth, but, even without the cataracts east of it, it's not deep enough for the iron barges and the steam tugs. It's better that way. It's still a small town. Well . . . for around here. It's still three times the size of Jabuti."

"Is there a town where they load the iron?"

"That's Luba. It's just docks and loading, and it's almost as grimy as the ironworks. It's also ten kays farther away from the ironworks than Guasyra is, but it's a flat road almost the whole way, and that's easier on the drays that haul the steel. The Emperor Halmyt thought about building a canal east from the ironworks, but the high mages told him not to. He got so upset that he tried to have one of them killed, but whatever he had in mind didn't work, and his heart stopped."

Rahl glanced ahead. The road had begun to level out. Less than half a kay ahead, it entered a stone-walled cut between two hills of a dusky red sandstone. "And nothing happened to the mages?"

"One died, and two of them were sent to oversee the mage-guard station here. That's what they say, but when people talk about the Triad, you never know," Talanyr said. "One of the first things the Emperor Mythalt had to do was to find a new trio of high mages. That took a while."

"Do they come from the mage-guards?" Rahl blotted his forehead. Even the early sun was hot in summer, and the acrid odor of the ironworks still filled his nostrils. The ironworks never shut down, not even on eightday.

"They have to, and they have to have been a mage-guard for at least ten years."

"Does the time spent as a mage-clerk count?" asked Rahl.

"After you finish training—or for someone like you—once you're working in a mage-guard station."

The transport wagon rolled into the stone-walled cut in the hillside. The walls stretched upward almost fifty cubits, and the stone pavement was wide enough to accommodate two wagons side by side and ran from wall to wall, except for shallow gutters a cubit wide at the base of the walls. The sandstone blocks were all of the same size and precisely cut and finished, although weathered and worn in places. Rahl was glad for the comparative cool of the shaded defile.

"This looks old."

"Something like three centuries, Thelsyn said."

From one of the mage-guards in the wooden seat just before them came a murmured comment. "That's the sort of thing he'd know."

Talanyr grinned and shook his head.

Just after the wagon rumbled through the stone defile, Rahl could see a small valley spreading out to the south. Unlike the desolation of Luba, the greenery of grass and of trees was almost everywhere. The road began to descend, but not nearly so far as it had climbed out of the Luba valley.

"It's . . . different . . ." Rahl hadn't expected comparative lushness around Guasyra. He also realized that the air was clearer and smelled fresher.

"That's why it's good to come here when we can."

As they descended toward the town, the wagon passed through a stand of evergreens, and over a bridge that spanned a stone canal less than three cubits wide. On both sides of the road, below the canal were orchards. Dirt lanes led from the main road to steads among the orchards, but Rahl had no idea what the fruit trees were.

"Olives," supplied Talanyr.

At the northern edge of the town was a temple, one that, except for its smaller size, was identical to the one Rahl had seen near the park in Swartheld—a tall one-story structure with a gently peaked and tiled roof, with the dissimilar pair of spires on the end away from the road. The straight and narrow southern spire shone silvery in the morning sun, while the curled and twisted, and somehow feminine, northern spire shimmered a warmer bronze.

"What's that?" asked Rahl quietly.

Oh . . . that's a temple to Kaorda—the almighty god and goddess of both order and chaos . . ."

"God and goddess?" Rahl had trouble dealing with the idea of gods anyway, but the idea of one that was both order and chaos and male and female all simultaneously made it even harder. "How can he or she be both?"

"They don't have an image—that would be blasphemous—but the Kaordists say that his face is half of unworldly beauty and half of demented passion, and that the beautiful half is male and the passionate chaotic half is female."

"Oh . . ."

"I'm not sure I believe that, but it makes as much sense as the one-god believers."

Rahl nodded dubiously, his eyes taking in the outskirts of the town, which looked to be larger than Land's End. All the dwellings, outbuildings, as well as the shops, were constructed of the red sandstone blocks, and roofed with curved pinkish tiles

He saw women with children, and other women with laundry piled in baskets on their heads, and a youth pushing a handcart with a wooden cage filled with some sort of plumpish rodentlike animals. Two other young men were leading lambs.

"Eightday is market day—except for the Kaordists," said Talanyr.

The wagon slowed to a stop on the north side of a square, a good two hundred cubits on a side, each side flanked by the road. The square itself was raised a cubit above the surrounding sidewalk and contained by two courses of sandstone block and paved as well. In the middle of each side was a stone ramp leading up from the street to the square. As in the market square in Nylan, the space was filled with carts and tents and booths, and the sounds of haggling and selling easily reached Rahl, as did the odor of burning wood or charcoal. He scrambled off the wagon and walked around it to rejoin Talanyr. His fingers dropped to his belt to check the truncheon, but it was firmly in place.

He noticed that none of the other mage-guards headed for the market square. "Where . . ." He decided not to finish the question.

"Some of them have consorts or mistresses who live here. They can't live near the ironworks or in Luba."

That made sense to Rahl. If he'd had either, he wouldn't have wanted them to live near the ironworks.

"I thought we'd go through the market square first." Talanyr grinned boyishly. "We'll also avoid the women's quarter—at least until you're . . . more familiar . . . with the town. They certainly won't hurt a mage or a mage-clerk, but . . . it could be costly."

Rahl understood the unspoken message about the order-skills that had not returned—and might never. He followed Talanyr up the stone ramp to the market square.

"Who's your friend, Talanyr?" The mage-guard who walked toward them didn't look that much older than either of the two mage-clerks.

"Chovayt!" Talanyr turned. "I thought they were transferring you to Sylpa."

"Not until fall. That's when it rains all the time there." The broad-faced mage offered a hangdog smile.

"Oh . . . this is Rahl. He's new to Luba station."

"I'm pleased to meet you," Rahl offered.

Chovayt laughed. "Trust Talanyr to find someone else he can guide to the finer pleasures in life." He shook his head. "Just don't trust his taste in leshak and dovarn, or you'll have a headache for days." Abruptly, he turned. "There's trouble in the corner. Silverwork and gems."

Since Talanyr followed the mage-guard, Rahl ran to keep up with the other two. He didn't want to be left alone in a town where he'd never been before, especially when he had no order-senses.

Chovayt sprinted around a pile of baskets, and past a rack on which folded colored blankets were displayed, and down a space between stalls toward a cart painted a faded green. Talanyr was right behind him. A woman dragged her children out of his way, and several loaves of bread bounced on the paving stones. Seven handcarts were arranged to form an aisle, with four on the right and three on the left. The last cart on the right was painted a faded orange, and displayed what looked to be silver boxes and pins on an inclined board covered with black cloth.

An older gray-haired man sagged against the side of the cart, while a matronly woman stood in front of him and a girl perhaps eight or nine years old. She held up a wicker basket that she jabbed toward a bearded man who was scooping the silver items into a bag. "Thief! Mage-guards! Help!"

Another stockier man vaulted from behind the cart, brandishing a sabre. The other sellers were nowhere in sight, probably hiding behind their carts.

Chovayt had his falchiona out of his scabbard and Talanyr had a truncheon out as they engaged the thieves.

Belatedly, Rahl drew his truncheon, doubting that he could help much in the crowded quarters.

A third man, with a bag in his hand, darted from between two carts after Talanyr and Chovayt had passed those carts and began to sprint away from the mage-guard. Rahl stepped forward to block his escape.

In a single motion, the thief stuffed the bag into his shirt and came up with two long and sharp-edged daggers, one in each hand. Rahl dropped to one side, then came up and back with the truncheon. Hard as he struck, the man did not wince, but only paused, before jabbing the dagger toward Rahl, who jumped to one side, then slammed his truncheon down into the man's arm just above the wrist. That dagger clattered on the paving stones of the square.

The other knife slashed toward Rahl's unprotected side, but Rahl stepped inside, elbowing the knife arm away, and drove the truncheon straight up under the point of the attacker's jaw. This time, there was a crunching sound and a strangled scream. Still, the man staggered back, pulling away, trying to bring the dagger to bear on Rahl.

Rahl side-kicked the man's weight-bearing knee, then knocked the dagger out of his hand. The assailant collapsed into a shuddering heap. Rahl turned, keeping an eye on the downed thief, but trying to see what was happening with Talanyr.

One of the other attackers half sat, half sprawled against the side of a cart, his hands around his bloody forearm.

As Rahl watched, Chovayt's blade touched the shoulder of one of the other thieves, and chaos-fire charred the arm. The thief did not surrender, and a second chaos-fired slash charred his other shoulder, and he pitched forward.

Talanyr was fighting a taller bearded man who was clearly a better blade than the mage-clerk, but Talanyr held his own with the truncheon, despite retreating slowly. Rahl wondered where the fourth thief had come from. As Talanyr moved back, the bigger man grinned and darted forward.

Whsst! A small bolt of chaos-fire turned the bearded man's head into a charred mass, and he pitched forward onto the redstone pavement.

Rahl stood watching the thief he had stopped, not certain of what he was supposed to do next, and wondering why he had had so much trouble in dealing with the man.

Chovayt glanced around, then nodded toward Rahl. "Can you drag that sorry sow-carcass over here?"

"Go ahead, Rahl," said Talanyr. "If he makes a move, I'll smash whatever moves."

Rahl didn't want to get too close to the man he'd brought down. So he grabbed the foot of the uninjured leg and dragged the thief across the pavement one-handed, holding his truncheon ready in the other.

The fellow moaned. Rahl left him beside the wounded thief by the cart wheel, then stepped back.

"He's got a bag with stuff in it in his shirt."

A muscular woman appeared after his words, bent down and ripped open the shirt, pulling out the cloth bag. "My coins he took—and some scrip."

"That was a little messy," said Chovayt. "Mage-Captain Zillor isn't going to be happy. You two might as well move along."

"You're certain?" asked Talanyr.

Chovayt nodded. "He's on his way." He gestured at the two bodies and the two wounded thieves. "They aren't going anywhere."

Rahl couldn't sense anything, but Talanyr and Chovayt clearly could.

"This way," said Talanyr. "We'll walk down toward the local river docks until things cool off. We can go back later."

Rahl followed the other mage-clerk through the open spaces of the square and down the ramp on the south side. He could see how the vendors stepped back as they neared and passed, but he still could not sense what they felt. He was still trying to figure out what had happened. He'd struck the thief hard and solid, but he'd had trouble anticipating the other's moves, and his blows hadn't had the effect they usually did. Why? He almost shook his head. He'd been using order-skills before, and now he didn't have any. And . . . his previous truncheon had been lorken bound in black iron, which weighed more and conducted not only the force of his blows but the order behind them.

For a moment, he stopped, fighting the wave of rage that threatened to cascade over him, as well as the underlying sense of unfairness.

"Are you all right? You didn't get cut or anything?"

"No. I think I need a heavier truncheon, though." Rahl forced a smile. It wasn't Talanyr he was angry at, but Puvort and the magisters and rules of Recluce and Nylan.

"They might have some in the armory at the station."

"I'll look tomorrow." Rahl glanced back toward the market square.

"Chovayt is doing fine," Talanyr said.

"We weren't supposed to help him?" asked Rahl.

"No. We're always required to help another mage-guard, even if we're only clerks. But there's nothing to say we have to stay afterward. If we stayed, Zillor might have thought we'd distracted Chovayt. That's one of the tactics the thieves use. They've got a lookout who lets them know when the mage-guards are occupied and the farthest away from their target. If we hadn't been there, most of them would have escaped. This way, he can just say that we helped, and he has everything under control. It looks better for him. Besides, do you want to write up his reports, too?"

"You both used weapons," Rahl said.

"We had to. Chovayt couldn't use chaos-bolts in the market there at first, and I can't," said Talanyr. "Chovayt couldn't because the girl and her mother were standing too close to the two offenders. That's why he used the blade as a conduit for the chaos." He paused. "You're good with that truncheon."

"My father started me early. I had a lot of bruises for a while."

"It made things easier. Thank you."

Somehow, as Rahl crossed the street on the far side of the market square, walking beside Talanyr, he hadn't thought that there would be that many thieves in Hamor, not when the mage-guards patrolled everywhere.

"I'll show you around," Talanyr went on. "Later, we can go to the Nalyrra for a really good dinner."

"Talanyr," Rahl said. "I can't. I don't have any coins to speak of."

The other mage-clerk laughed. "I know. Tonight will be my treat, and it will be. You helped back there, and it's good to be with someone who can handle a truncheon and who's actually read a book. Rhiobyn thinks that you pick them for the color of the binding and how they look on a library wall." Talanyr laughed. "Besides, I don't have much to spend on anyway. You can treat me sometime when you've paid."

"I will." Rahl paused, then added, "Rhiobyn must come from coins."

"His family's coins have coins. They're merchanters in Atla. You wouldn't know it, because they hired tutors so that they wouldn't talk like Atlans."

"Like me?"

"You talk like an educated Atlan, and that's fine. Besides, I talk like an Afritan, and that's worse than an Atlan for most people."

Rahl just nodded. He had more than a little to learn about Hamor.

LXXII

Rahl had enjoyed Talanyr's tour of Guasyra, and the meal at the Nalyrra, but by the end of eightday, much of what he saw had become a blur, and he had been glad to climb on the wagon that night and ride back to Luba station. He could not remember his dreams, save that they were disturbing and left him feeling apprehensive when he woke.

As soon as he finished breakfast, he hurried to the armory.

The armorer was an older man, uniformed as was Rahl, except with the silver insignia of a falchiona crossed with a truncheon on his collar, rather than starbursts of the mage-guards. He stood behind a low counter and peered at Rahl. "You're the new one, aren't you?"

"Yes, ser."

"No 'sers,' young fellow. What do you need?"

"I was hoping you might have a heavier truncheon." Rahl held up the one he'd been issued. "This . . . well . . . I could do a better job with a heavier one."

"Heavier . . . hmmm . . . I might have something . . . just might . . ." The armorer turned and walked to the racks in the right-hand rear corner, murmuring to himself. "Now . . . where was that . . . saw it the other day . . ." After several moments, he turned and walked back to the counter. "This one here's been around ever since I've been here, but it's still solid as the day it was crafted." The armorer extended a dull black truncheon.

As he took it, for a moment, Rahl thought that it might be like the one he'd been given in Nylan, but he could see that the half guard was a touch thicker and the weapon was a trace longer. Still, there was an iron band below the half guard.

"It's black oak," added the armorer. "Only thing better than that is lorken, and I haven't seen any of that in years."

"Thank you." The older truncheon even felt better in his hand.

"Never let it be said that Vymor couldn't find the right weapon for you."

"Oh . . ." Rahl handed the truncheon he'd been issued to Vymor. "I only need one."

"We'll find a place for this one, we will. Best you be on with your duties."

With the effective dismissal, Rahl turned.

Once he got to the copying chamber, he set the truncheon aside and picked up the first report in the stack.

He'd finished both copies of that and was working on the second when Talanyr appeared.

"Thelsyn is going to start asking why I don't follow your example," Talanyr said as he took his place at the other end of the copying table.

"Because you already know what I need to learn."

"You know more than you think you do," countered Talanyr, "or Taryl wouldn't have made you a clerk."

"He just needed someone who could write quickly and accurately."

"That doesn't hurt . . ." Rahl broke off as Thelsyn stepped into the copying room.

"What doesn't hurt?"

"Writing quickly and accurately, ser."

"No, it doesn't, and I imagine that you both could do so with even greater results if your hands were as engaged as your tongues are."

"Yes, ser."

The mage-guard walked up to Rahl and inspected the first set of reports, then walked toward Talanyr.

"I just got here, ser."

"In mind, at least," Thelsyn said dryly, before turning and departing.

Rahl said nothing, but went back to copying and rewriting the almost illegible report of a mage named Sostrost. He had completed both copies of eight more reports by the time Taryl walked into the copying room in late midmorning, just before midday.

The thin-faced mage held an envelope in his hand as he stopped beside the copy table.

"Ser?"

"Rahl . . . we did get a report on you." Taryl offered a tight smile. "There was a Rahl who registered as an outland mage in Swartheld. You didn't register that you were from Recluce."

"I'm sorry." Rahl found his mouth open. "I thought . . . I mean when I said that I was working at the Nylan Merchanting Association, and I was an outlander, I thought that would have been clear."

Abruptly, Taryl laughed. "All of the mages or exiles from Recluce seem to think that there aren't any ordermages or chaos-mages anywhere but in Hamor, Fairhaven, or Recluce, and that most of the mages outside of Recluce are slaves of chaos." He shook his head. "Still . . . they didn't ask you?"

"No, ser. I said that I was an outlander working for the Association as a clerk and that my abilities were limited, but that I'd been told to register."

"Limited abilities?"

"I told you, ser . . . about what I could do. I can't do any of that now."

"And they didn't ask more?" persisted Taryl.

"No, ser."

"They should have asked, but not everyone follows the procedures as closely as they might have." Taryl's eyes lighted on the black truncheon. He raised his eyebrows. "You didn't like the issue truncheon?"

"Talanyr and I went to Guasyra yesterday. While we were there . . ." Rahl went on to explain what had happened. ". . . and the truncheon I'd been issued just didn't feel right. So I asked the armorer if he could find me one a little heavier. That isn't a problem, is it?"

"You took down a thief with two long daggers with just a truncheon?"

"Yes, ser."

Taryl looked over at Talanyr, who had been trying to remain unobserved. "You had something to do with this?"

"Mage-Guard Chovayt needed assistance, sir. There were four armed thieves there."

"I see." Taryl's voice conveyed a mixture of irony and skepticism.

"They were close to all the vendors, and there was no way to use chaos without hurting them, and there was a little girl."

"About the age of your sister?"

"Yes, ser." Talanyr's voice was subdued.

"Did Rahl face the man with daggers by himself?"

"Yes, ser."

Taryl turned to Rahl. "Exactly what did you do?"

"I knocked one dagger out of his hand. That took a while. Then I got inside his guard and broke his jaw and maybe his knee joint, ser. He did come after me with the daggers, and he had stolen coins from one of the vendors."

"Rahl . . . just how much arms training have you had?"

"My father started me with the truncheon when I was maybe eight, and we sparred a few times every eightday until I left. When the magisters were preparing me for exile, I worked with two of them every day for a season or so, but that was with more than the truncheon."

"Were they armsmasters or just trainees?"

"They were both armsmasters."

"Did they train you in dealing with blades and knives against your truncheon?"

"Yes, ser, and with a staff."

"Hmmm . . ." Taryl nodded slowly. "Once you know more about the mage-guards . . . well . . . we'll see. I'll be bringing a book to you later. I want you to read all of it, but I want you to read it carefully as well."

"Yes, ser."

"We'll also see about your sparring with Jyrolt when he comes through at the end of summer."

Rahl wasn't sure he liked that possibility, even though Taryl hadn't said exactly who Jyrolt was.

After Taryl had gone . . . Rahl thought about the registry. The mage-guard hadn't asked where he had been from, yet Taryl clearly thought that he should have.

Abruptly, Rahl smiled. He'd *sensed* that feeling from Taryl.

He also sensed another presence, if vaguely, one he did not see, and that had to be Thelsyn, checking up on them behind some sort of sight shield. Without hurrying, he picked up the next report and set to work, concealing a frown as he did. Why didn't Talanyr sense the mage-guard, or was the kind of shield Thelsyn was using designed to be more effective against someone trained in Hamor?

As he copied and rewrote the report before him, he tried to get a better sense of what order or chaos concentrations might be around, but as he tried to focus on that, his sense of where Thelsyn was, standing just outside the door, vanished totally.

Rahl tried to keep a pleasant expression on his face, despite the frustration he felt and the slight headache that had appeared with his efforts. With a slow and deep breath, he put his full attention into working on the report before him.

In midafternoon, Taryl reappeared, walking briskly into the copying room. He extended a thin volume bound in faded red leather. "It's my copy of the *Manual of the Mage-Guards*. I've ordered you a copy, but it's likely to be an eightday or so before it gets here. Most mage-clerks and beginning mage-guards get them before they're at a station."

"I'll take care of it, ser." Rahl took the volume.

"I'm sure you will. Besides taking care of it, read it carefully."

"Yes, ser."

"Once you get caught up on the reports, we'll start on evaluating your arms skills and work on training you in techniques and procedures. Part of those procedures, especially the reasons for them, are in the manual, and you'll be examined on them as well. As I said earlier, the next evaluation will be near the end of summer. If you're not ready, then the next one will be at the turn of winter."

"What am I supposed to know, ser?"

"Adequate skills in either blade or truncheon or both, techniques for handling trouble without using force, some basic skills in using order or chaos in support of your duties as a mage-guard, a complete understanding of the role and the duties of a mage-guard in Hamor . . . as well as the provisions of the Codex that you'll be enforcing."

"Is there a copy of that somewhere?"

"The Codex is rather lengthy. I'll get you a copy of the mage-guard summary. It's mostly common sense."

"Thank you, ser."

Taryl nodded brusquely, then turned and left.

Rahl looked after him. He still wondered why Taryl wanted Rahl as a mage-guard, so much so that Taryl had never actually asked Rahl if that was what Rahl wanted. Was that any different from the magisters of Recluce?

Somehow . . . Rahl thought it was, even if he couldn't say why.

He turned and looked at Talanyr. "Will you be evaluated at summer's end?"

"I'm supposed to be, according to Khaill."

"He's the station armsmaster?"

"As close to it as we have."

"Is it hard?"

Talanyr offered a wry smile. "It's not easy. Taryl said I wasn't ready in the spring."

"What happens if . . . you don't do well?"

"Oh . . . there's a place for everyone . . . but some of the places are worse than Luba. Some are better located, but the tasks are terrible. You might end up as a clerk in the Highpoint station."

Rahl had no idea what that might be.

"It's the mage-guard station that's on the highest point of the Great Highway . . . well . . . as much of it that's finished. It's so high that it snows until the turn of summer, and starts snowing again in early harvest. They don't send real clerks there, because it's hard duty, so mage-guards who have minimal skills are rotated in and out to handle the station chores, from copying to standing night watch duty. Up there, you just look for distress fires or trouble and stare out into the darkness . . ."

Rahl couldn't help but shudder. If he didn't recover his order-skills . . . would that be where he was headed? It was better than being a loader—or slogger—but it certainly wasn't what he wanted to spend the rest of his life doing.

LXXIII

For the next three days, Rahl, Talanyr, and Rhiobyn copied reports, slowly reducing the backlog piled on the copying table until, when Rahl arrived on fourday morning, there were only thirteen reports on the table—just those of the previous day.

In the evenings—those when he did not have desk duty keeping the logs and records for the duty mage-guard—he read both the manual and the short version of the Hamorian Codex. The abbreviated Codex, as Taryl had said, was mostly common sense. Mostly. There were several provisions that concerned him more than a little, particularly the one that restricted mages. He had read it several times, enough that he almost knew the words by heart.

> . . . no Hamorian mage of any persuasion may engage in any venture involving commerce in goods, in coins, or in any other instrument of commerce. . . .

Did the Hamorians really believe that mages could be that corrupt? Or was it just a way to assure that mages were all under the control of the Emperor? Or was it something else, as indicated in another section in the *Manual*, which gave commerce short shrift?

> . . . the principal duty of a mage-guard is to maintain order and contain chaos, not to protect commerce or to side with one individual against another or one group against another. All will cite order as their cause, but order is not a cause, nor is chaos, and one must be maintained and the other contained against all those who would misuse them . . .

Then there was the section dealing with the military.

> . . . any unregistered source or concentration of free chaos is forbidden within a quarter kay of any imperial military station,

port, or vessel. If such a source cannot be immediately removed, its immediate destruction is required and authorized . . .

While that made sense, given what free chaos could do around various explosives, the idea that immediate destruction was authorized and required left Rahl with a cold feeling.

But . . . there were reports to copy, and he could not change the Codex. He reached for the first report on the stack.

"Did you actually read the Codex?" asked Rhiobyn, from his place at the middle of the copying table.

"Of course he did," returned Talanyr humorously. "He didn't have it read to him by tutors as a child. Some of us actually had to learn to do our own reading. By ourselves."

"Sometimes, one wishes you had enjoyed a tutor, Talanyr. Then you wouldn't sound like one, and you'd recognize how annoying it is."

Rahl suppressed a smile and began to read the first report he had to copy.

He had finished four reports by early midmorning, when Thelsyn inspected what had been done. Shortly thereafter, Taryl stepped into the copying room. His eyes went from one clerk to the next. "Now that you clerks are generally caught up with the reports, we need to get on with your training. Talanyr, report to the duty desk for now. Rhiobyn, Mage-Guard Jaharyk will work with you. You know where to find him. Rahl . . . you come with me."

Rahl cleaned his pen and replaced it in the open-topped box, then capped the inkwell. He was the last to rise, if not by much.

Taryl did not speak until the other two mage-clerks had left. "We're going to see Khaill. He wants to test your weapons skills to see what sort of training you'll need. He has to report on the ability of all mage-guards each season, just as I do for their order-skills."

"You're the head order mage-guard here, ser?"

"Effectively. There aren't any titles here, except for Mage-Captain Wulmyrt. In the cities, most stations are headed by mage-captains, except for the largest, which have overcaptains. The districts are run by mage over-commanders, and they report to the Triad. I work with order-skills, and Jaharyk works with chaos-skills. We both know something about the other side, because some of the basics are similar and rooted in order. Now . . . go get your truncheon. I'll wait for you by the duty desk."

"Yes, ser."

After his difficulties in Guasyra on eightday, Rahl was not looking forward to sparring or having his weapons skills tested, but there was no help for it, and he hurried to the juniors' section of the west barracks wing of the mage-guard station. He returned quickly with the truncheon in place on his belt.

Taryl was beside the duty desk, talking to Talanyr, and Rahl stood back, listening.

". . . most of the time, nothing happens. The logs and duty book go into a dusty file. If there's trouble, and something goes wrong, though, the Mage-Guard Overcommander and the Triad demand all the records. If something's wrong, or missing, you'll end up at Highpoint station for the rest of your natural life, which will be far longer than you'd ever wish. Is that clear?"

Rahl didn't hear what Talanyr said in reply.

"Good." Taryl turned and motioned for Rahl to accompany him.

Rahl didn't dare say anything, and Taryl didn't volunteer anything, but Rahl did wonder what Talanyr had done to displease Taryl.

The exercise room was a long stone-walled room beyond the armory. The south side had three narrow windows, and there was a single small skylight. The floor was slightly roughened redstone, but a section of the northern end, perhaps ten cubits by fifteen, was covered in thick cloth mats.

A mage-guard was working there with two of the women guards on hand-to-hand tactics, but when he saw Taryl and Rahl, he said something to them and walked toward Taryl.

"Khaill, this is Rahl. I mentioned him to you."

"You did." Khaill resembled Magister Zastryl in bearing and in general size, but Khaill was older, with a worn and rugged countenance and fine limp brown hair. He was also stockier. He studied Rahl for several moments. "So . . . you're an exile, a merchanting clerk, a loader, and now a mage-clerk?"

"Yes, ser." Rahl met the mage-guard's glance evenly, without challenge, but without looking away.

"You prefer the truncheon, I hear."

"Yes, ser."

Khaill walked to the side of the exercise room and returned with a truncheon similar to the one that Rahl bore. "I would like you only to defend against my attacks."

With those words, he immediately jabbed his truncheon toward Rahl.

Rahl slid-parried and sidestepped, not wishing to give ground, then blocked the return strike, giving a half step, then moving forward to the left.

Khaill offered two quick thrusts in succession, and Rahl beat both aside, continuing to move, first to one side, then the other, not allowing the mage-guard to force him toward a wall.

After another series of engagements, Khaill was fractionally slower in recovering, and Rahl managed to step in and catch the other's half guard with enough force to jerk Khaill forward slightly. Rahl did not take the opportunity to strike, but beat Khaill's truncheon down almost to the floor, stepping on it for a moment, before dancing back, and then parrying the uppercutting strike

Khaill stepped up his attacks, but Rahl wove a defense effective enough that none of the mage-guard's blows came close to striking other than Rahl's truncheon.

After a time, Khaill stepped back. "That will do."

Rahl also moved back and blotted the dampness off his forehead.

"You have only recovered a small fraction of your order-skills, Taryl says. Is that correct?"

"Yes, ser."

The stocky arms-mage nodded. "Even so, your skills with the truncheon are more than adequate. Can you handle a falchiona?"

"I used to be able to . . . for a short time."

"Pick one out." Khaill gestured toward a rack set against the west wall. "Then put on one of the heavy jerseys."

Rahl studied the blunt-edged weapons in the rack, hefted one, then another. Although all of them felt somehow wrong, he finally selected the one that felt the most balanced in his hand. Was that wrongness because he was regaining some slight ability to sense order and chaos? The heavy jersey he struggled into had thin plates set in what looked to be shimmersilk and stitched over a padded woolen tunic. He was sweating even more heavily by the time he walked back to where Khaill waited, holding a falchiona similar to the one Rahl had selected.

"I don't want you to attack here, either. Just defend."

Khaill's weapon was clearly the blade, and Rahl felt far more awkward with the falchiona, but he managed to deflect most of the attacks, although Khaill did manage to strike the plates on his right shoulder twice. One would have been crippling in a real fight, although the other would only have been glancing.

The arms-mage stepped back. "Now, try to defend with the truncheon."

Rahl fared far better using the truncheon against the falchiona, although it was shorter than a blade, but that sparring only went on for a short time before Khaill once more stepped back.

"Interesting." Khaill nodded. "You can go, Rahl. I would like a few words with Taryl."

"Yes, ser." Rahl struggled out of the practice jersey/armor as quickly as he could and hurried from the exercise room.

Once outside the training chamber door, which he did not fully close, he slowed almost to a halt, listening and hoping to overhear what might be said.

". . . if he didn't have that hint of order all the way through," said Khaill in a quiet voice, "I'd have said he'd been trained as a bravo."

"In a way, he was . . . Recluce armsmasters, he said. He might do well in time, perhaps in a port city . . ."

". . . don't know where you find them, Taryl . . ."

". . . where I can . . . where I must . . . there are never enough."

Taryl's words would have chilled Rahl . . . except that the conversation suggested that Rahl might have a future away from Luba.

LXXIV

On fiveday, Taryl caught Rahl as he was leaving the mage-guards' mess at breakfast and drew him aside.

"Have you been studying the Codex and the *Manual*?"

"Yes, ser." Rahl had, particularly since he'd gotten his own copy and returned Taryl's, although he had noted which sections of the mage-guard's *Manual* had been the most perused.

"What is the one fundamental necessity for any land to survive?"

Rahl knew what he thought, but that wasn't what Taryl wanted, and he had to quickly think back on what was in the *Manual of the Mage-Guards*. "The need to maintain order, ser."

"What is the role of the Triad?"

"To assure that order is maintained and chaos is used only for just and lawful purposes, ser . . ."

"Why are all mages, except healers, forbidden to engage in commerce?"

Rahl remembered the prohibition, but he did not recall any reason being stated for it, other than the fact that mage-guards were not to take advantage of their position. "Because they could use their abilities and position to personal advantage?"

"They certainly could," Taryl replied dryly. "Why shouldn't they? Everyone else in the world does."

"Because they represent the Emperor," Rahl guessed. "If they represent him, they have to be impartial and above reproach, and if they get into commerce, they can't be either?"

Taryl nodded slowly. "Simple as that seems, a goodly proportion of mage-guard trainees have trouble with understanding it."

"But . . . ser . . . if those with order- or chaos-talents cannot be other than mage-guards or healers, but a number don't understand that . . . ?" Rahl wasn't quite sure how to finish the question.

"What happens to them? They're put in places where there's no temptation, like Luba, or the quarries, or Highpoint station, or the Afrit rubber plantations, or the mines." Taryl nodded. "That's enough for now, I'll be examining you at any time from here on. The questions will get harder."

"Yes, ser."

"Now . . . go get your truncheon. Talanyr and Khiobyn will do the copying today. You'll be accompanying Grawyl. He's one of the mage-guards who deals with loaders and breakers. You won't ever be a primary mage-guard here, because you don't handle chaos, but you need to see how they work. Grawyl knows that. Meet him at the duty desk."

"Yes, ser."

Rahl hurried back to his room, grabbed his truncheon, and made his way to the station wing of the building. Grawyl, whom he knew by sight, but not by name, was waiting. He was big—a good head taller than Rahl, broader in the shoulders, and his brilliant green eyes, black eyebrows, and short-cut black beard gave him a menacing impression.

"So you're the one Taryl reclaimed from the loaders. They didn't call you Rahl there, I'd wager."

"No, ser. Blacktop. That was before I got my memory back."

"Blacktop . . . Blacktop . . . oh, you were one of the quiet scary ones . . . ready to explode all the time, but you never did after the first time. Bushy black beard, wasn't it?"

"Yes." Rahl didn't remember exploding, only that there had been a time of heat and pain.

"I remembered you, and that means you shouldn't have made it." Grawyl laughed good-naturedly. "But then, one way or another, most of us here shouldn't have survived." He turned, expecting Rahl to follow him out to the wagons.

Rahl did, taking his place in the second seat beside Grawyl.

"Ready, ser?" asked the driver.

"Ready." Grawyl didn't look at Rahl while he continued. "We'll move from crew to crew. We check with the overseers. Some of them can spot trouble before it happens, and some don't know why something happened even afterward. Most of those don't last."

"What happens to them?"

"They get killed, or hurt—or they end up as workmen or something like it. There's always a need for someone."

As they sat in the mage-guard wagon that carried them northward through the already-hot morning air, Grawyl continued. "Only one rule here, really. Don't threaten. Just act. Threats mean nothing. But don't act unless you're sure of why you're acting."

Ahead of them, to the northwest, under the thin and hazy gray clouds, the air above the massive blackened furnaces shimmered and wavered from the heat radiated from the furnaces. Only the faintest hint of a breeze touched Rahl's face.

"Some mage-guards have a hard time remembering that the loaders and breakers, and even the sloggers," Grawyl went on, "are men. They do a job. If we hurt them, especially if we kill them, we've hurt someone, and we need a good reason. On top of that, there's one less to do the job. So, one of our jobs is not only to provide a stronger form of discipline than the overseers, but it's also to watch the overseers, to make sure that they don't abuse their power."

"In a way, you're protecting the workers, then."

"Who else do they have?" asked Grawyl.

For a moment, the only sounds were those of the creaking of the wagon and the rumbling crunching of the iron tires on the grit on the paving stones of the road.

"I try to avoid following a routine when I'm doing the inspections. That way, no one knows exactly when I'll be in any one spot. It's better that way. We'll be starting close to the middle of the coking furnaces. The overseer supervisor says that the loader crew on coking furnace three needs looking at."

The wagon began to climb the lower section of the road along the top of the short ridge to the east of the line of coking furnaces. Rahl glanced westward at the first furnace, a squat structure whose metal and once-yellow bricks had merged into a dark and dingy gray. A crew of loaders stood waiting by the dock as a team of sloggers pulled a coal wagon into place.

Farther westward, he could see the dark figures of breakers working on the slag outside the blast furnaces and more loaders at the base of the slag piles shoveling broken slag into wagons. The clinking of shovels barely rose over the distance-muted roaring cacophony of furnaces and mills.

When the wagon pulled off into a turnout short of the loading dock above the third coking furnace, Rahl followed Grawyl up the slope to a point just above the dock and coal wagon. From there, Rahl just looked at a loader crew—six bearded and sinewy men with shovels in ragged heavy trousers and armless canvas semitunics, their skin darkened and weathered by seasons of exposure to sun and heat. Their bodies and arms moved in rough unison as they scooped, turned, and shoveled the chunks of coal from the wagon into the chute that led down to the coking furnace. Even from fifteen cubits away, Rahl didn't recognize any of the loaders.

The second man in line paused, just slightly, but enough to throw off the rhythm of the loaders, and the third man growled under his breath. The overseer's lash flicked out—twice.

The second man didn't move, just took the lash, and struggled to fit his shoveling into the pattern of the others.

The third growled more loudly, muttering something to the second man.

Rahl thought he sensed something about the second man, but the feeling vanished even as he tried to identify it.

"Hold!" snapped Grawyl.

The overseer raised his whip but did not actually use it. "Stand and rest!"

Rahl could see the relief in the second man—that and a thin line of blood across his upper right arm. The third loader bore no obvious mark of the lash, but the stiffness of his body betrayed anger and rage.

Had that been what Grawyl had meant about him?

Grawyl stepped toward the line of loaders, and Rahl followed, but kept a half pace back of the mage-guard.

Once more, Rahl caught a flash of something like chaos, but not exactly, from the second loader in line. What was it? Then he almost shook his head. It was wound chaos of some sort, and it was strong, but his order-skills were still so unreliable that he hadn't been able to recognize it from farther away.

"Ser . . ." he said quietly, "the second loader is ill. I can't tell how, but he is."

"Thank you. I had that feeling from the way he moved." Grawyl turned toward the overseer. "Send the second man there to the sick barracks. He's not well enough to handle a shovel, and it's slowing the crew."

"Yes, ser." The overseer's tone was flat, not quite contemptuous.

Grawyl turned toward the man. "If you don't watch out more for your crews, I'll have you take his place as a loader."

The overseer blanched beneath his olive skin. "Yes, ser. I will, ser."

Grawyl said nothing, just stepped away and headed back toward the smaller wagon.

Rahl followed.

LXXV

It is always best when people do what they should because they choose to do so. Out of every score, one man or woman knows and understands his or her duty without being told or coerced. Out of the same score, one or two will not do their duty, except under the greatest duress. Of the remaining seventeen, some require but the slightest reminder to do their duty, and the rest require constant reminders of varying force and intensity.

Yet no ruler has ever had nor will ever have enough administrators and patrollers to stand over those nineteen day in and day out to assure that they obey the laws of the land, support their families or their parents, and wreak no wrongs upon others. How then does a ruler assure that all in his land functions as it should? While the forms of each are many, he has but two tools. One tool is praise and reward. The other is respect and fear.

Although a ruler must be both loved and feared, it is best that the ruler be loved directly. For that reason, all praise and rewards must be seen by his people as coming directly from him, while the methods that inspire respect and fear should be seen as coming from his faithful subordinates.

The requirement to inspire both respect and fear underlies all that a mage-guard is and all that a mage-guard does. For that reason, a mage-guard must always be courteous to all, but unyielding. A mage-guard should also always act so as to preclude any public disrespect of one citizen by another. He or she should be tolerant of all personal differences among the peoples of Hamor, but never allow such differences to result in physical violence between peoples. Nor should a mage-guard permit himself or herself any manifestation of intolerance of the Emperor and those who serve him. Where the Emperor is concerned, in person, deed, or reputation, a mage-guard must always act in a way that is both dignified and that brooks not the slightest hint of physical disrespect or civil disobedience, in matters large or small, for even the smallest signs of such disrespect, if not corrected, can lead to greater disrespect . . .

> *Manual of the Mage-Guards*
> Cigoerne, Hamor
> 1551 A.F.

LXXVI

In the darkness of the small room he shared, Rahl lay on his bunk, his eyes closed, thinking, as Talanyr snored softly. Almost an eightday had passed since Rahl had first sensed a hint of what Taryl felt, but his ability to sense other's feelings remained uncertain and weak, and those with any sort of shields were blocked to him. His practices with Khaill and some of the other mage-guards had sharpened his weapons skills, but he felt he had been forced to rely on physical cues where once he had sensed intent.

Why? Why had everything ended up as it had?

He knew he was fortunate that Taryl had sensed something—extremely fortunate, or he would have died young as a loader, probably killed by a mage-guard when he could no longer contain his anger and frustration. But why had he ended up in Luba? He'd hadn't done that much wrong— and so much less than most. He'd not understood what using order on Jienela had done, even if he had meant no harm, and from that one small mistake—and Puvort's nastiness—it seemed as though everything had followed, no matter what he had tried to do to avoid it. He hadn't had any choice in defending himself against her brothers, not the way they had been prompted by Puvort, and he had delayed no more than two days in deciding to seek mage training. One small mistake and two days delay, and his entire life had spiraled downward and out of his control . . . and the harder he had tried to find ways to stop it, it seemed, such as trying to understand how order linked to order, the worse matters had become, because all the mag-isters were continually pressing for him to gain greater understanding of order—if he didn't want to be exiled.

Another memory came back to him, of the night when he had enjoyed his first—and still the best—Hamorian dinner with Thorl and Deybri. She had deflected his attempt to enter her house with words about his need to know what he felt with his whole being. He could still see her standing there, her eyes warm and welcoming, yet sad, saying, "I can't make prom-ises for you."

Deybri . . . why did she continue to haunt him? There was no way he ever could return to Nylan, and it would be eightdays yet before he could accumulate enough coins even to send a single letter.

He closed his eyes even more tightly, not that it was necessary in the darkness. After a moment, he forced a long and slow deep breath, trying to relax, and yet to sense each item in the room separately.

When he had finished the exercise, he was less than satisfied. He could make out the beds easily, and the wardrobes, and the foot chests, but the smaller things were blurs, and once they had not been.

For all of his recent efforts, all that he had regained of his previous skills was the ability to feel the presence of strong order- or chaos-skills and the ability to sense what surrounded him without using his eyes. He could not even find the order-chaos links that he had twisted to explode the black wall, nor could he create even the weakest of order shields. He could not find the slightest bit of free order or concentrate it or move it.

And all of that . . . he had once done so easily, so effortlessly.

All that he had known was lost to him, and he was struggling just to master enough order to qualify as the lowest of mage-guards in one of the least desirable stations in Hamor.

He could feel the tears of rage and frustration seeping out of the corners of his closed eyes.

Why had it come to this? Why?

LXXVII

For Rahl, the next eightday was filled with more of what had gone before—copying reports, accompanying mage-guards on their rounds and duties, studying the Codex and his own copy of the *Manual* and answering Taryl's questions, and sparring with Khaill and, occasionally, other mage-guards. Upon occasion, Taryl would watch the sparring. More often he did not.

Late on sevenday afternoon, as Rahl left the exercise room after a series of sparring bouts with Khaill, Davyl, and Chynl, he found Taryl outside in the corridor, clearly waiting for him. The mage-guard carried a small satchel.

"Ser?"

"You're the best with a truncheon in Luba. Even Khaill admits it," Taryl said mildly. "You're better than most with a falchiona for a time."

"Thank you, ser, but . . . that is hard for me to accept." Rahl wiped the sweat from his forehead, wondering what Taryl wanted.

"Why is that so hard? You've obviously practiced for years."

"There must be others . . ."

Taryl laughed. "There are. Some of the blades at Cigoerne would cut you up if you used a falchiona against them, but you're close to holding your own with the truncheon against anyone." He paused. "You realize that you're using your order-senses in the sparring . . ."

"Not at first . . ." Rahl paused. "I mean, they're not there when I begin . . . and they're really still not there. I can't think about it at all, or they're gone."

"How are you coming in regaining your control of your order-senses otherwise?"

"I can sense order and chaos now and again, and sometimes I can find my way without seeing. It comes and goes."

The thin-faced mage nodded. "I'm not surprised. You've got order-energies wound in and around you so tightly that I'm surprised you can walk. Most mages would die for the amount of order that clusters around you."

"Then why can't I *use* them?" Rahl barely managed to keep from snapping.

"Let's take a walk . . . outside, where no one else is around." Taryl turned and headed toward the door at the end of the corridor.

For a moment, Rahl stood there. Was this going to be another meaningless and useless lecture, like so many he'd listened to over the past year? Would Taryl be just like the magisters after all? He hoped not as he hurried to follow the mage-guard.

Once on the flat ground south of the building, Taryl stopped. The sun was low in the western sky, just above the rugged mountains. He turned to face Rahl. "No . . . I'm not going to lecture you. You're the type for whom lectures are worse than useless. I have another sort of exercise I want you to work on."

Rahl nodded, grateful that Taryl would not lecture him but questioning silently exactly what the other had in mind.

Taryl withdrew two knives, still in their leather sheaths. "Catch." He tossed one, then the other, to Rahl.

"What am I supposed to do?"

"Turn with your back to the sun. Leave them sheathed, but juggle them. Toss one in the air, then flip the other into the hand that tossed the first, and keep doing that. I want you to do this *without* trying to sense or control the knives with your order-skills. Use only your eyes and your hands. Eyes and hands. Don't ask why. Don't question. Just do it." Taryl's voice was calm, but firm.

Rahl turned so that the sun beat gently on his back and took a knife in each hand, still in their sheaths. He tossed the first one up, then tried to flip the other to his free hand, where he caught it awkwardly.

"Keep them moving. Don't stop."

Rahl managed two more tosses before he dropped one of the knives into the dirt.

"Pick it up and keep going."

For the next several attempts, Rahl could only keep the knives in motion five or six times, but then he settled into a routine.

"Faster!" snapped Taryl.

Rahl dropped a knife.

"You need to pick up speed. Don't ask why. Just do it."

After a time, Rahl managed to keep the knives moving faster.

"Now . . . without stopping, turn and face the sun, but don't look at it. Concentrate on the knives."

Rahl managed the turn, if unsteadily, and kept the knives going.

"Concentrate on the knives. Close one eye, but keep looking with the other. Concentrate on the knives."

Rahl kept going, but it was hard because with one eye it was harder to judge distance, and he staggered several times.

"All right. Catch them and stop for a moment. Don't ask me any questions. Not a single one."

Rahl was just happy to stop. Even though there wasn't that much strength involved in the exercise, the air was warm, and he was sweating as much as he had while sparring. He blotted his forehead with the back of his left hand.

"Using order came easily and naturally to you, didn't it?" asked Taryl. "Before you lost your memory, that is."

"Yes, ser. For the things that I could do. For the others, I just couldn't. I did tell you that."

"The mountains look so dry from here, don't they?"

"Yes, ser." Rahl was puzzled by why Taryl was talking about the mountains, but he'd been ordered not to ask questions. He didn't.

"When you collect water from all the mountains, even from the dry ones like those west of Luba, you can fill an aqueduct. It's how you collect it that matters, and from how wide an area." Taryl cleared his throat. "Now . . . take the knives from their sheaths. Set one aside and toss the other from hand to hand until you're comfortable with the weight and balance. Just use your eyes and hands, nothing else."

"Yes, ser." Rahl tossed the single blade back and forth, watching as it crossed the space between his hands, the bare blade picking up an orangish red tinge from the sun low in the sky. A gust of wind whipped grit across his face.

"Keep tossing."

Even with one eye blurring from grit in it, Rahl managed to keep the blade moving.

"All right. Stop and pick up the other blade."

Rahl had the feeling he knew what was coming next, but he didn't ask.

"Now we'll start the first exercise all over again, with your back to the sun. You'll need to be more careful, and if you can't catch one by the hilt, let it drop. Just try not to drop them too often."

"Yes, ser."

Rahl was more than a little nervous. He'd never liked blades, and juggling two knives, even if they were only single-edged blades, didn't help much. He dropped one blade immediately.

"You didn't need to do that, Rahl." Taryl's comment was mild, almost resigned. "Start again."

Handling two naked blades forced Rahl to concentrate all his attention on the blades, and still he kept dropping them.

"Rahl . . ."

He forced even greater concentration on the blade juggling.

Abruptly, he could sense everything around him—the blades, the order-force around Taryl, and even the dull redness around the blades.

"Keep juggling . . ."

Rahl tried, but the distraction of regaining his order-senses overwhelmed him, and he ended up dropping both blades into the sandy dirt. His order-senses vanished. "Oh . . ."

"You had your full order-senses for a moment, didn't you?" asked Taryl.

"Yes, ser. But . . . how?" He realized he'd asked a question and stopped talking.

"Recluce doesn't have the answer to everything," Taryl said quietly. "Now . . . what did all that *feel* like?"

Feel like? Why did that matter? "Ah . . . I don't know."

Taryl sighed. "Too many mages think of order-senses as outside their bodies. For chaos-mages, in a way, that makes sense, because they need to maintain a separation from the body. Chaos can be extremely corrosive if it's not handled properly. For an ordermage, it's different. How you feel is important. Pick up the knives. You can rest for a moment, but then you're going to do this again, and when you get the feeling of your order-senses, don't try to use them or examine them. Just try to capture how they feel. Take in the feeling, just the feeling, nothing more."

Questions boiled up inside of Rahl, and he looked helplessly at Taryl.

"No questions now. When we're done, I may answer some. That depends on how well you follow my instructions." After several moments, the mage-guard nodded. "Pick up the knives."

Once more, Rahl was so distracted by the possibility that the exercise might help him regain his order-senses that he kept dropping the knives—once, twice, and then a third time.

"Rahl! Do you want to go back to being a checker?"

Rahl froze.

"You're not following my instructions. You're to concentrate on the knives and nothing else. Nothing! Do you understand me?"

"Yes, ser."

"Then do it."

Rahl took a deep breath, then put a knife in each hand and concentrated just on the knives. Toss . . . flip . . . toss . . . catch . . .

"Now . . . turn toward the sun. Don't drop the knives."

Rahl turned. Sweat was beginning to pour down his forehead.

Again . . . he had his order-senses.

"The knives . . . stay with the knives . . . stay with the knives . . ." Taryl's voice was somewhere between order and plea.

Rahl could barely see with the sun in his face, but he kept working with the knives . . . trying to follow Taryl's instructions . . . and somehow just trying to experience the feeling.

"Let the knives fall . . . follow them with your eyes, just your eyes . . ."

For several moments after the knives kicked up the dusty soil, Rahl could sense everything around him, but he made no attempt to use or explore that sense.

Another gust of wind hurled grit into his eyes, and they began to burn . . . and he lost his order-senses.

"Good." Taryl actually sounded satisfied, to Rahl's surprise.

"Ah . . ." Rahl stopped. Even asking if he could ask a question was a question.

"Yes. You can ask questions, but pick up the knives." Taryl extended an oily rag. "You need to wipe them off as well."

"Why . . . ?"

"Why does this exercise work? What I did was get your mind and body focused on something else, but something hard enough that your order-senses might surface if you weren't pushing them away by trying too hard to use them. That's why you do better sparring after a while, especially when you're working against someone good. What I had you do doesn't work for everyone. There are different ways of learning to handle order. From what I've heard, Recluce tries to get everyone to learn it by reading and thinking. There's a book. I imagine they gave you one—*The Basis of*

Order. Not everyone can learn that way. You're a natural ordermage. Some-day, you might even become a full ordermaster. That's if you'll listen to me and follow instructions." Taryl laughed ruefully. "You've been trying to *think* your way into regaining your abilities. That won't work for you. Not in my experience, anyway."

Rahl carefully wiped one blade clean and sheathed it, and then did the same for the second.

"Natural ordermages work better by feel, and you have to get the feel-ing for something. If you lock in the right feeling, it's almost effortless. Otherwise . . ." Taryl shook his head.

"What should I do now? After the exercises, that is?"

"Don't try to do anything with your order-sense. You may get flashes of it now, and you may not. If you do, just try to absorb the feeling. The more you can feel and identify that feeling, the sooner you'll recover order-handling ability." Taryl smiled. "You might want to get cleaned up before dinner."

As Rahl walked toward the small cramped shower room, he wanted to shake his head. A mage-guard in the ironworks of Hamor knew more about how to help him than all the magisters in Recluce. How could that be, when Recluce was the bastion of order?

LXXVIII

Over the next few days, little changed—except at odd times, Rahl would experience a return of his order-senses. The first few occasions were brief, but thereafter each time the feeling lasted a little longer—so long as Rahl did not attempt to *do* anything with what he felt. On eightday, he was the clerk-recorder for the duty mage-guard, and that kept him from joining Talanyr in going to Guasyra.

On threeday morning, he found himself once more assigned to follow a mage-guard. Dymat was not a chaos-mage, but an ordermage, one of the oldest mage-guards Rahl had seen, with silver hair and a long horselike face.

As they stood near the duty desk, Dymat studied Rahl, then shook his head.

"Ser?"

"I'll tell you later, young Rahl. Do you know what I do?"

"No, ser. Only that you're involved with the mills and forges."

"I'll explain on the ride to the rolling mill. We might as well get started. Besides, Klemyl is waiting."

Rahl only knew that Klemyl was one of the younger mage-guards at Luba station, slightly shorter than Rahl himself, with curly dark red hair and a high-pitched voice.

Dymat turned and walked quickly across the entry hall where the duty desk was located and out through the door to the wagon area. Three wagons remained, and Dymat hurried toward the second one. Klemyl was already in the forward bench right behind the driver. Dymat swung up into the second bench, and Rahl followed.

Klemyl smiled politely, nodded, then turned to face forward, addressing the driver. "We're all here. You can leave."

Rahl had the impression that, for all his politeness, Klemyl was less than pleased. Was that because of Rahl . . . or for some other reason? Rahl certainly hadn't had anything other than passing contact with Klemyl.

For several moments, as the wagon picked up speed under a gray summer sky, Dymat was silent. Despite the high clouds, the air was warm and would be stifling by midday. Rahl's nostrils burned slightly from the acridity in the air, and his eyes watered.

"What I do is simple, tedious, and vital to all of Hamor. In fact, this is true of what almost all the mage-guards do," began Dymat, his voice overly loud, at least to Rahl. "The production of iron plate, beams, and rods is most important for all of Hamor. The mills turn the pig iron into plate and other materials. They operate at high pressures and temperatures and contain many steam engines that provide power for the mills. If chaos should gain a foothold anywhere, production could be slowed or even halted for days, if not eightdays." Dymat smiled and looked at Rahl, as if expecting a response.

"I can understand that, ser."

"Speak up, Rahl."

"Yes, ser," Rahl replied, more loudly.

"You will see steam engines and steam tugs the like of which exist nowhere else. Do you know why?" Dymat looked intently at Rahl.

Rahl tried to think of a possible reason. If keeping out chaos was so important . . . "Ser, is that because—"

Dymat didn't seem to hear.

Rahl raised his voice. "Is that because those engines require the constant inspection of mage-guards to keep chaos away so that they will continue to work?"

"I see you can think. Not so quickly as one might wish," bellowed Dymat, "but one cannot have everything in Luba. No, one cannot."

Rahl merely nodded.

"We must keep chaos at bay all the time, and I will show you how." Dymat turned and looked ahead.

The wagon followed the road to the north, in the direction of the loading docks, but then took the fork that continued farther west. Before long, they passed south of the southernmost of the coking furnaces, and then south of the lowest of the blast furnaces built on the inclined slope that stretched to the north.

As Rahl studied the west side of the furnaces, he realized that the slope had to have been built—possibly by magery—because the slope was far too regular and the west side had been cut away, so that each furnace was exactly the same distance above the one below. He also noted that great stone causeways ran from the west side of the furnaces to the mills.

The driver turned northward, following another paved road toward what looked to be the southernmost mill. Then the wagon reached one of the stone causeways. It jolted once, then again, as its iron tires crossed something. Rahl looked down. The wagon had passed over a pair of iron-lined grooves in the stone, set almost three cubits apart.

The driver turned westward on the center of the causeway, and Rahl noted that another set of iron grooves bordered the north side of the stone pavement. Ahead was the mill, so large that it stretched at least four hundred cubits from north to south, and even farther westward. Shortly, the wagon halted some fifty cubits short of the east end of the mill. A huge arched portal gaped before them, an opening fifty some cubits across, Rahl judged.

"We get off here," announced Dymat, easing off the wagon.

Rahl joined him and walked beside the mage-guard toward the portal. He glanced back, but the wagon was on its way to take Klemyl to whatever his duty was. Rahl moistened his lips and took two hurried steps to catch up with Dymat.

From within the mill issued a thunderous rumbling, combined with dull and heavy impacts so powerful that the stone beneath Rahl's feet vibrated. Occasional shrieks, as if iron itself were being torn apart, punctuated the rumbling thunder.

Then, from the right side of the portal, an enormous flat wagon rolled forward, pushed by what could only have been the steam tug mentioned by Dymat. Both the wagon and the steam tug had iron wheels almost as tall as Rahl, and both were constructed entirely of iron. The steam tug had long drivers attached to its wheels. It took him a moment to realize that the massive wheels fitted in the iron-lined grooves. The steam tug measured a solid thirty cubits in length, and a plume of gray smoke issued from a squat stack near the front of the tug.

"Nothing like that anywhere else!" shouted Dymat. "Did I not tell you?"

"You did," Rahl called back, wondering how much pig iron or iron ingots the flatbed wagon could carry. He also couldn't help but wonder why there were no massive steam engines elsewhere in Hamor and nothing like the giant steam tugs. Then he nearly shook his head. How could there be? If such machines required constant attention by ordermages, if there were many at all, they would require all the mages in Hamor.

Dymat walked toward the open portal of the mill, and Rahl followed. They stopped some thirty cubits inside the portal. Under the high roof, supported by wide stone columns, the mill stretched almost a kay from where Rahl stood, and the noise from the welter of machinery battered at him. The air above the far end of the mill was so hazy that the details of the brick columns there were blurred.

Dymat gestured, then bent his head so that he was effectively shouting into Rahl's right ear. "The pigs come in hot, but not hot enough for milling. They go through what they call a regenerative furnace, then a hammer forge and a cogging mill. That's where they get cut and shaped into the slabs that go into the plate mill here. The slabs are about a hundred stones, and they get rolled by the big flywheel engines. The wheels are more than seven thousand stones, and they flatten the iron to whatever the thickness necessary. Most are quarter span, but for warship armament, they sometimes produce plate that's a full span in thickness. Just follow me." The mage-guard turned and began to walk down the open space on the left side of the towering furnace, from which waves of heat welled. The furnace looked more like a huge oblong box, but Dymat spent little time inspecting it, looking at it almost cursorily as he passed. At the end of the furnace was a set of massive rollers, each as large as Rahl's own body, set in an even more massive frame that extended from the slot in the back of the furnace to the next assembly, presumably the hammer forge, Rahl thought.

The hammer forge was even higher than the regenerative furnace. Through the structure of iron beams and supports, Rahl could make out what looked more like an enormous oblong that rose . . . slowly, and then came down with great force. With each impact on the red iron, iron sparks flew; the stone floor shook; and hot air gusted around him, air that was metallically acrid.

Dymat took a few steps, paused, studied, then took a few more, slowly making his way toward the western end of the giant forging apparatus. There he stopped well short of it and studied for a long time.

Rahl had no idea whether the ordermage found any chaos or not, because not only were his normal senses battered and numbed, but he had no feeling at all in the way of order-senses. But because Dymat did not seem disturbed, Rahl had the feeling that nothing was amiss.

At the west end, while Dymat continued to study the forge, Rahl watched as a section of reddish iron moved slowly over another set of the massive rollers toward the next assembly. Two men stood by a set of enormous levers. One looked briefly at the mage-guard, but his eyes went back to the slab emerging from the hammer forge and rollers that held and carried it forward.

The heat from the forge and the mill was far more intense than anything Rahl had felt as a loader.

Dymat paused and motioned for Rahl to join him.

Rahl nodded and stepped forward.

"Plate mill!" announced Dymat, gesturing toward the next assembly. "Slabs from the hammer forge come in here to the first set of pinions, then to the roughing rolls, and finally the smoothing rolls. Any chaos in the pinions or the rolls, and we'd have iron and steel exploding all over the mill. That's because they're turning, and there's already chaos being structure-trapped into the iron. You can see the chaos-red of the slabs. The iron can hold great chaos, even when heated to melting, but chaos in the mill . . . that's something else."

Again, Rahl followed as Dymat slowly inspected the plate mill. Once more, Rahl could sense nothing.

As he followed and watched the order mage-guard, Rahl was more than certain that, if there were any way he could avoid it, he wanted no part of being a mage-guard at the ironworks.

By the time Rahl had finished his day with Dymat and climbed aboard the wagon back to the mage-guard station, his eyes and lungs burned. His ears rang, and all he could smell was hot metal.

"Isn't it a grand place?" demanded Dymat.

Grand? That was one word for it, Rahl supposed. He nodded, then added, "Yes, ser."

There was just enough time before dinner for him to wash up and get the grime off his face and hands and out of the corners of his eyes. Even so, he was the last at the juniors' table in the station mess.

He could barely wait for the servers to place the pitcher of lager on the table, but he still allowed Talanyr and Rhiobyn to fill their mugs first. Then he filled his mug and immediately took a long swallow to ease his throat. After the fumes of the mill and having to shout to make himself heard to Dymat, his throat felt raw.

He immediately refilled the mug.

"Where did you go today?" asked Rhiobyn.

"The mill . . . with Dymat."

"Are you hoarse?" asked Talanyr with a grin, keeping his voice low.

Rahl nodded.

"It's not my favorite duty," Talanyr added.

Rhiobyn smiled broadly. "They won't even let us near the mills or the blast furnaces, except to light off a cold furnace. It's another benefit of being on the chaos side." He stopped as a server set a platter of burhka and noodles in the middle of the table and a basket of bread on the side.

"How can you even sense chaos in all that?" asked Rahl.

Talanyr shrugged. "I can't. It might be that being partly deaf helps." He frowned. "But Taryl can, and so can Dymetrost. It could just take higher-level order-skills."

Rahl nodded. That might be possible, and he was far from having any real control over whether his order-senses were present or not. Being able to sense chaos in the mills might be a true test of sorts, not that he was looking forward to anything along those lines. He filled his platter with the burhka and noodles, then took a small mouthful and a bite of bread.

"How is the arms training coming?" asked Talanyr.

Rahl swallowed before answering. "Much better. Khaill seems pleased, and I don't get many bruises anymore. I still sweat a lot. He makes you work hard."

Rhiobyn and Talanyr exchanged glances. Finally, Talanyr spoke. "If you're really good with weapons, you might get assigned to a city patrol station."

"From here?"

"It does happen, more than you think," Rhiobyn said. "That's for clerks and junior mage-guards. Most of the seniors will stay here."

"Is that because . . . ?" Rahl decided not to say more.

"It depends," replied Talanyr. "Some of the mage-guards actually want to stay here. Dymat likes his duties here. So does Dymetrost. Others prefer it to Highpoint or coastal duty in the north."

"If you could choose," asked Rahl, "where would you like to be stationed?"

"Someplace smaller near Atla. Really, I'd like Rymtukbo, but that's too close to Jabuti, and you never get stationed near your hometown. It's too hard to be fair if you know people. Sometimes, they'll move a mage-guard who's gotten too friendly, too. They do it more than once, and he's likely to end up here."

Rahl could see why the Triad would follow that policy, but was it necessary for all mage-guards?

He stifled a yawn and then took another mouthful of dinner. It had been a long and tiring day.

LXXIX

On fourday and fiveday, Rahl spent most of his time back in the copying room, because, whenever he was gone, the reports tended to pile up. At the end of each day, Taryl sent him off to spar with whoever was working out in the weapons exercise room, but more often than not, he ended up against Khaill or Taryl himself.

Right after midday on sixday, Taryl entered the copying room, carrying his satchel. "Finish up whatever reports you're working on and meet me in the training chamber."

"Yes, ser."

Taryl nodded and was gone.

"When he does that, I get worried," offered Talanyr from the other end of the table.

"You two have it easy," suggested Rhiobyn. "They don't throw chaos-bolts at you."

"Not yet," Talanyr replied, "but wait until an ordermage drops a shield around you, and you can't draw chaos from anywhere, and then he starts in on you with a staff or a truncheon reinforced with order."

Rhiobyn winced. "They don't do that in training."

Talanyr lifted his eyebrows. "They do what they think is necessary."

"As will I, if you don't get back to copying," added Thelsyn from the doorway. "You need to finish that report and get on your way, Rahl. You don't want to keep Taryl waiting."

"Yes, ser." Rahl dipped his pen in the inkwell. He finished Grawyl's report, both copies, and hurried off to the weapons-training area.

The door to the chamber was ajar, but when he stepped inside, he discovered that the space was dark, with the windows shuttered and covered in heavy dark cloth. Even the skylight had been blocked with something and shed no light on the training floor. A single tiny candle, surrounded by a frosted and heavily smoked glass mantle and set in the northwest corner of the chamber on the floor, was the sole source of illumination once Taryl shut the doors.

The thin-faced mage-guard held two heavily padded staffs. He extended one to Rahl.

Rahl took it and waited.

"We're going to spar and keep sparring for as long as necessary. You will not ask any questions, and you will follow directions."

"Yes, ser."

Taryl stepped back and took his staff in both hands. Rahl did the same.

In the dim light that was barely brighter than total darkness, at least to Rahl, Taryl's staff flickered toward Rahl's left shoulder, and Rahl parried, aware that Taryl was far better than Khaill or any other mage-guard he had faced. He concentrated on following both Taryl's body and the staff.

Even so, Taryl's staff immediately swept under Rahl's guard, and Rahl had to jump backward, his boots skidding on the stone pavement. He barely maintained his balance, and his next block was awkward and required a circling retreat.

Taryl moved forward, seemingly effortlessly, even as his staff cracked Rahl's wrist. "Concentrate. Do you think that you'll always be the best?"

Rahl forced his attention back to Taryl, trying to follow and anticipate the mage-guard's actions in the minimal amount of light afforded by the single shielded candle.

For the next series of passes, although Taryl did most of the attacking, Rahl thought he was holding his own, or as close to it as possible.

"Stop!" Taryl stepped back.

Rahl lowered his staff, warily.

"I'm going to put out the candle. You're to do the best you can. I'll tell you when I'm in position, and when to expect the first attack. I would suggest you concentrate on defense." Taryl turned and walked toward the corner and the lone candle.

Rahl swallowed. He was supposed to defend himself against one of the best he'd ever faced in total darkness—without any real control of the order-senses that had once allowed him to function in darkness?

Taryl bent over the shielded candle.

Then pitch-black darkness surrounded Rahl. He could barely hear Taryl's footsteps as the mage-guard approached.

"Ready?"

"Yes, ser." Rahl held his staff in a guard position.

Taryl's first blow was to the right end of the staff, forcing it almost to the floor.

Although Rahl neither sensed it nor saw it, he pivoted away, not fighting the pressure, but letting it swing him slightly, as he reversed the guard position with the left side of the staff, before stepping back—right into a blow across his left thigh.

He staggered, then hobbled back quickly, trying to keep his staff up and moving, attempting to weave a defense against an attacker he could neither see nor sense.

The padded end of Taryl's staff slammed into his chest, and, off-balance as he was, Rahl tumbled backward. His buttocks hit the stone floor hard, and he barely managed to hold on to the staff with his right hand.

"Get up," came Taryl's voice, calm, almost cold. "In a real fight, if you sat there and pitied yourself, you'd be dead."

In a real fight, thought Rahl, he wouldn't be blind and fighting a master mage. He scrambled to his feet and repositioned his staff.

No sooner did he have it up than Taryl's weapon clipped the back of his right calf.

"You don't always get to fight just one person," added Taryl, somewhere to Rahl's right. "You won't be able to keep your eyes on everyone."

Rahl turned . . . and took a blow to his left shoulder, and then one to his right. He retreated, but the blows kept coming, no matter how hard he tried to anticipate them.

"Stop thinking, and start feeling," came from Taryl, who followed the words with a slash to the staff itself, striking so hard that Rahl's fingers were momentarily numbed.

Rahl thrust wildly, and was rewarded with a return jab to his gut, just hard enough to double him up and send arrows of pain through his abdomen and chest.

It wasn't fair! Rahl struggled erect.

"No . . . it isn't fair," Taryl said out of the darkness, his staff lashing out and thudding into Rahl's thigh. "Life isn't fair. We don't get what we've worked hard to develop. Other people cheat and lie and prosper, and we do everything right and honestly and suffer. That's often the way it is."

Another staff blow—almost taunting—struck Rahl's left calf, and he danced leadenly to his right, trying to weave a defense against a mage he could not see.

"Superiors abuse their position and make us suffer." Taryl's padded staff thudded into Rahl's upper left arm. "It's not fair, but that's the way it is."

Rahl tried to keep his staff moving, but it was getting heavier and slower. In the darkness, the tears streamed down his face. This wasn't an exercise. It was sadistic torture.

"It's not fair when you can beat anyone in the light, and they make you spar in the dark."

Rahl threw out a parry, catching something. Then he stepped back to the left, only to run into another blow.

"We don't get to choose the way of the world. We have to deal with it as we find it. So . . . deal with it. You don't have the luxury of waiting for things to be perfect."

Rahl forced himself back into a defensive posture.

"Don't fight the darkness. Accept it."

Accept it. That was easy enough for Taryl to say. He had order-senses.

"Listen . . . if you ever want to be more than a checker or a clerk . . . listen. Listen to the darkness as well as the light."

Rahl tried, but, just as soon as he felt something, another blow struck from somewhere, no matter how he tried to defend himself.

"Feel . . . unless you want to die!" snapped Taryl.

The padded staff jabbed Rahl's chest.

Rahl backpedaled quickly, taking a deep breath and just trying to get a sense of the room, of the darkness.

There was a blur to his left, and he brought up the staff in a parry, actually avoiding being hit. He stumbled and took another blow, but grasped a brief image of Taryl and dodged the next thrust.

Slowly, Rahl began to sense where Taryl and his staff were, and even more slowly, he began to be able to block and to parry, to sidestep and to avoid some of the sudden attacks.

He still took blows, but they were far fewer, as his order-senses strengthened, and he was able to weaken the impact of many of those that did strike.

Still, his arms ached, and his legs burned. He was sweating heavily, and breathing loudly, and still Taryl pressed him, but . . . he could sense where the older mage was, and even the staff's position.

For all that, Taryl kept attacking, and Rahl was forced to defend . . . and defend.

At some point, he became one with his order-senses—but still Taryl pressed.

Then, abruptly, came the words. "That's enough."

Rahl could sense Taryl as the mage-guard moved to the south window and pulled away the black cloth covering and opened the shutters. Then he walked back to Rahl, who was as much leaning on the padded staff as holding it.

"Why did I do this?" asked the mage-guard, looking at the younger man.

Still sweating and breathing heavily, Rahl stared at Taryl. After a moment, he said, "Was it to prove my shortcomings?"

"In a way, but not in the way you think. Inside, you were still arrogant. You still are, but now there are some doubts. You have always had the feeling that you could overcome anyone, if the odds were anywhere close to even. Rahl . . . the odds are almost never close to even. Most times, the thieves and brigands—and the others you'll have to bring to justice—won't stand a chance against you. Some few times, it will be the other way. You have to understand, not just with your head, that there's always that slight chance that you might come out on the short end of the staff."

Rahl knew that. He did . . . didn't he? Except . . .

"Have you ever lost a fight anywhere except here?"

Rahl wanted to look down. "No. Not really."

"Would it have made any difference if you had been surrounded by three men with staffs or blades in that darkness, rather than me? Until the end, that is?"

Rahl had to think about that. "Until I could sense you . . . ah . . . probably not."

"Oh, you could have killed one or two, but not all three, and that's an instance where, if you're not totally successful, it doesn't matter. Ah, yes, I killed two, but the third killed me."

Rahl winced. He hadn't thought that, and yet . . .

"Good."

"I meant what I said about fairness. Life is not fair. Some people have ability; some do not. Some have wealth; most do not. Some are fortunate; some are not. Horrible things happen to good people, and fortune often smiles on the evil. That *is* the way of the world. A mage-guard's duty is no more and no less than to make the world less unfair by reducing the unfairness created by evil. But never think that you will make matters fair or just. You will not. You will only make them less unfair and less unjust." Taryl smiled ruefully. "Why else did I do this?"

"To force me . . . to become one—I think that's it—with my order-senses?"

"Exactly. You have still been thinking of yourself and your abilities as two separate and different things. For a natural ordermage, such as you, there can be no separation. This would have been easier if you hadn't been dosed with nemysa. It has a tendency to separate a mage from his abilities, in addition to suppressing memories." Taryl paused, then added, "Although it would have been hard for you in any case. The magisters in Nylan didn't do you any favors by insisting on all that book learning without also working on feelings."

Rahl stiffened. Was that why he'd been drawn to Deybri? Because she operated more on feelings?

"You remembered something important?"

"I was thinking about the only one whose words and acts made sense there, and she was the one who dealt more with feelings and acts."

Taryl laughed gently. "That's obvious."

"Ser?"

"You'll have to deal with that on your own, Rahl. Now, go get a shower.

You smell like a slogger. After that, you can go back to copying. You won't feel like much more than that for a few days. Oh . . . and I'll take the staff."

Silently, Rahl handed the staff to the mage-guard.

"And for the sake of both order and chaos, stop thinking about fairness in personal terms. With the skills you have, the world has been more than fair to you." Taryl nodded. "Go get cleaned up."

"Yes, ser." Rahl turned and began to walk slowly—and painfully—toward the showers. He had no doubts that the aches and pains would increase, but, he marveled as he closed his eyes for a moment, he could still sense everything around him, even the wound chaos of the rat dying of poison within the walls to his left.

LXXX

By eightday morning, when Rahl showered and dressed, his bruises had turned yellow and purple. All of them hurt to the touch, some more than others. Thankfully, most were concealed by his khaki uniform. Every movement still caused lingering pain or soreness . . . somewhere. Yet the dull aches and occasional sharp pains didn't matter so much, not now that he had his order-sensing back. He'd tried to create shields, but that skill evaded him—so far.

After a hurried breakfast, he stood outside the station building with Talanyr, waiting for the wagon. Rhiobyn was talking to Klemyl several cubits away.

". . . don't know what he did to upset Taryl . . . beaten within a span of his life . . . could hardly move yesterday morning . . ."

". . . Taryl . . . doesn't do anything without a reason . . ."

"Are you sure you can stand a wagon ride to Guasyra?" asked Talanyr. "You had trouble sitting still at copying yesterday."

"I can handle a wagon ride fine, and I'd like to get away from the station, even if it's a touch uncomfortable." Rahl adjusted his uniform visor cap, almost the same as that of a mage-guard, except there was no starburst above the black visor. With the heat of summer and the clear sky, he was grateful for the cap.

Under the early-morning light, Talanyr surveyed Rahl. "He really beat you up, didn't he?"

"He had to."

Talanyr nodded. "Sometimes, it's that way."

"I see Klemyl over there . . . and Rhiobyn."

"Rhiobyn fancies he can learn something from him, but Klemyl just wants to get to Guasyra to see his consort and his son."

"Doesn't Rhiobyn see that?"

"He was raised in Cigoerne, and that's where Rhiobyn wants to be." Talanyr laughed. "It's not impossible . . . but it's not likely."

The two turned as the long wagon rumbled up.

Rahl had to steel himself as he climbed aboard, and he let out a slow breath as he settled onto the hard seat in the fourth row.

"You're sure you'll be all right?" asked Talanyr.

"I'm fine." Rahl did have to sit with more weight on his left buttock. "Tell me about Jabuti, since I'll probably never get there."

"It's a little place smaller than Guasyra. There's only one market square, and it's not even on a paved highway. That doesn't matter much because it almost never rains or snows there. All the rain falls in the western forests below the highlands . . ."

Rahl sat back, if gingerly, and listened as the wagon began the long ride up the road to the pass, and then down to Guasyra.

Prompted by an occasional question, Talanyr was still talking when the wagon neared the twin-spired Kaordist temple, and the muted sounds of song wafted toward them on the still air.

"Their song sounds ordered," Rahl pointed out.

"They have disordered drums sometimes, I've heard."

Rahl was still half-listening to Talanyr and pondering why anyone would worship order and chaos—they just *were*—when the wagon came to a stop opposite the market square in the small town.

". . . anyway, despite what my father hoped, there wasn't much point in carrying the timber up over the passes, except for the little that people in Jabuti needed. It was so much cheaper to float it down the river and ship it to the coastal ports . . ."

"Always the golds," agreed Rahl as he eased off the wagon, concealing a wince. The odor of burning charcoal wafted past him, suggesting that the vendors were preparing their braziers for a day of cooking. He glanced

toward the raised platform of the square, where some sellers were still setting up awnings and tents.

"Let's head south, toward the river park," suggested Talanyr. "The vendors are running late. We can come back later. Are you game for trying a
place that serves Sylpan food? Not now, but this afternoon?"

"What's it like?" asked Rahl warily. Hamorian cooking seemed to be
prepared either as hot and spicy or hotter and spicier.

"Well . . . it's a bit bland. They say it's subtle. More fowl and rich sauces
and rice grasses."

Was any Hamorian cooking subtle? Rahl had his doubts. "I'd like to
try it."

"I thought you might." Talanyr grinned, turning westward along the
north side of the square.

Rahl could see Klemyl nodding to Rhiobyn, then hurrying northward
toward a narrow lane that angled to the northeast, leaving Rhiobyn by himself. The mage-clerk walked eastward, away from Talanyr and Rahl.

"Knives! Fine knives! The finest . . ."

"The best in spices, peppers to burn hotter than a stove . . ."

Rahl hurried his steps to catch Talanyr, and the two walked to the east
end of the square before turning south.

"The river park's on the far side of the center of town, but you'll have
a chance to see the merchant establishments on the way, such as they are,"
said Talanyr. "The square's on the north end of the main street, and the
park's just a few hundred cubits beyond the south end."

Rahl forbore to mention that he'd already seen the merchants' shops
once, if briefly.

Beyond the square, the first establishment was a tavern—The Iron
Bowl—but the maroon door was closed, as were the matching shutters.

"You don't ever want to go there," Talanyr said.

"Oh?"

"Costly, and not worth the coins."

Across the narrow paved street from the tavern was an apothecary, and
beside it an alchemist's. Both doors were open, and Rahl caught the faintest
hint of something that smelled like a combination of mint and brimstone.
The way the two shops were linked, and their identical narrow vertical windows, Rahl thought they might have the same proprietor—or have had the
same builder.

As they walked, Talanyr explained.

"... basketmaker's there ... use a river reed, and they'll actually hold water. That's what Klemyl claims, but it might be because his consort weaves some of them ..."

"... coppersmith ... honest work ... nothing special ..."

"... cooperage ... good workmanship, but he's got a problem because there's not much oak anywhere near here, and no spruce to speak of ..."

Before that long, the two stood at the north side of a green hedge. Rahl looked at it closely, realizing that the dusky green leaves concealed a myriad of thorns, all of which looked needle-sharp and were at least as long as his index finger.

"False olive hedge," explained Talanyr. "Some of the wealthier folk use them like walls around their grounds. The thorns can cause wound chaos if the cuts aren't cleaned quickly." He walked farther south along the hedge until he reached a set of brick pillars, clearly an entrance to the park beyond, an expanse of green, with brick walks and scattered broad-leaved acacias to provide shade to the tables set beneath them.

Following Talanyr into the park, seemingly empty, except for a con-sorted couple engaged in intimate conversation at one of the tables, Rahl glanced toward the river on the west side of the park. A low brick wall sep-arated the greenery from the water, except for the two piers that jutted out a good twenty cubits into the grayish water of the river. Two small girls stood on the nearer pier, and each held something, a sugared pearapple, perhaps.

As he continued to follow Talanyr along the brick walk, his eyes went back to the girls. A seagull swooped down toward them, and one threw up her hand to ward off the bird, but the other, startled, jumped back, then lost her balance and tumbled into the river.

Talanyr sprinted toward the pier. At the shoreward end, he yanked off his boots and belt, flinging his cap aside, and dashed to the end of the pier, where he plunged into the water.

Rahl rushed to the end of the pier, where he saw Talanyr swimming in circles around where the girl had been. Then Talanyr vanished beneath the water himself.

What could Rahl do? He wasn't that good a swimmer.

The other girl looked from Rahl to the river and back at Rahl.

"Go get her parents!" Rahl just hoped that Talanyr could rescue her before the parents arrived. "Tell them what happened."

Talanyr appeared above the water, then vanished again. After a moment, he reappeared, then dived beneath the slow-moving gray water again. When he finally emerged, he had the girl in one arm.

Rahl flattened himself on the timbers of the pier and took the girl from Talanyr. He opened her mouth and struck her back, trying to force water out.

Talanyr climbed out of the water. "Let me have her." He laid her on her stomach and turned her head to the side. Then he pressed her back. Water gushed, then oozed from her mouth. He repeated the motions several times, until no water issued forth.

"I've gotten the water out of her, but she's not breathing. She's not breathing . . ." Talanyr glanced up at Rahl. "Can't you do something?"

Rahl dropped to his knees beside the dark-haired girl, turning her over. She looked so pale and fragile. He could sense the combination of chaos and order that he knew was life, but it was faint and fading. What could he do? What would Deybri have done?

He had to feel . . . to sense. He gently grasped her wrists, then closed her eyes. He had to give her strength . . . if he could.

Feel—that was what both Deybri and Taryl had emphasized . . . if in their own and differing ways.

Rahl tried to re-create the feeling he'd had when he'd merged himself under Taryl's pummeling in the darkness. Slowly, everything seemed to darken around him, but he could sense a faint series of sparks, fading . . . fading. Gently, afraid to force anything, he *touched* one spark, and then another . . . and a third . . . and a fourth . . .

Somewhere in the process, darkness found him.

"Rahl! Wake up! You did it!"

Rahl found himself being shaken. "Oh . . . I'm awake." He looked around.

A wide-eyed and round-faced woman was wrapping a blanket around the girl, who, while still wet and pale, was clearly awake and breathing. A stocky man in a clay-stained apron stood beside the pair. Tears streamed down his face.

"Ser mage-guards . . . how can I thank you? I have so little, but my daughter, she is everything . . . everything . . ."

Rahl shook his head. "You don't have to give us anything." He grinned tiredly at Talanyr. "Except maybe a towel."

In the end, they followed the man—Kesyn the potter—and his consort, while Talanyr carried the girl, as protectively as though she had been his own daughter or younger sister. Then they sat on the shady side of a tiny court-yard, with Talanyr wearing an old blanket while his khakis baked in the sun.

"You are certain my Eysla will be well?"

"She will be well if she doesn't fall in the river again.," Talanyr replied. "Do you have a healer here?"

"Yes."

"If she has a fever, take Eysla to her. Sometimes, after people have been in the water, days later, they get chaos in the chest," said Talanyr. "There is none there now, but it could happen."

Kesyn nodded slowly. "You are the young mage-guards, is it not so?"

"We're mage-clerks," replied Talanyr, "and, if we do well, we will become mage-guards."

"You are from Atla?" Kesyn looked at Rahl.

"That is how I learned to speak," Rahl replied. "I'm an outlander."

Kesyn merely nodded and looked at Talanyr. "Afrit?"

"Alas, yes," replied Talanyr mock-mournfully. "Jabuti."

Kesyn nodded knowingly. "Wyala's cousin's consort's uncle came from there, many years ago. He said that it was almost as dry as Luba. He said it was so dry that he shriveled up, and the wind blew him here." A hearty laugh followed.

"Jabuti's not quite that bad, except in the late summer," replied Talanyr. "Astoy . . . that's another question . . ."

At some point, Rahl fell asleep in the canvas chair, only to wake with the sun well past midafternoon.

"You certainly slept the day away," said Talanyr, standing beside Rahl, wearing dry, but somewhat wrinkled khakis.

"Whatever I did tired me out more than I knew." Rahl sat up gingerly. Once again, he was stiff, if not quite so much as he might have been. He slowly rose from the chair.

At that moment, the potter reappeared.

"We should go, Kesyn," Talanyr said, adjusting his khakis.

"You do not have to go."

"My friend has recovered, and so have my clothes," replied Talanyr with a laugh.

"May order surround you and shield you, and may the strength of chaos defend you both." The potter stepped forward and threw his arms around Rahl. "I cannot thank you enough for my daughter, but you must know that I would have given anything that I possess to save her."

Rahl couldn't help but feel embarrassed. "We did what anyone should have done."

"Anyone did not save my daughter," announced Kesyn, stepping back. "You did." In turn, he embraced Talanyr. "Young mage-guards, you are what makes Hamor great, and may the Emperor reward you as I cannot."

Eysla stepped forward shyly from around her father's legs, then inclined her head. "Thank you."

Rahl smiled at the girl. "You are welcome, but please be careful around the river."

She smiled nervously, clinging to her father's trousers.

Rahl stepped back, not wishing to frighten her.

As Rahl and Talanyr walked back toward the market square, Rahl heard a clinking, and it was coming from him. He frowned, then put his hand in his single trouser pocket. He felt coins and drew them out. There were three silvers. How? He shook his head. Kesyn. It had to have been the potter, when he'd hugged Rahl before they'd left.

"Talanyr . . . Kesyn slipped these in my pocket."

"I know. I saw."

"I can't take them. I'll have to give them back." Rahl stopped.

Talanyr touched his shoulder. "You can't. You'll insult him, and what you did isn't against the Codex. You healed his daughter. She'd have died without you. Kesyn knows that. That's why you were the one who got the silvers."

"I couldn't have done anything without you. I can barely swim."

"Take the favor fate gave you, Rahl. Chaos knows you've had little enough favor lately. I was just glad we saved her."

The slight roughness in Talanyr's voice gave Rahl pause. Taryl had compared the girl who had been near the vendors and the thieves to Talanyr's sister. Rahl decided against probing something that painful. Instead, he looked at the silvers, then back in the direction of the potter's shop and dwelling. Kesyn was a proud man, but he shouldn't have given Rahl the silvers, but . . . if Rahl was too proud to take them . . . He smiled wryly and placed the silvers in his belt wallet. He did have a use for them.

"I'm glad you're not that stubborn," said Talanyr. "I'd heard that most mages from Recluce were insufferably stiff."

"Some are," Rahl conceded. His thoughts went to Puvort and Kadara, with their more orderly than thou attitudes, their insistence on there only being one way.

Suddenly, Rahl found his fists clenching and his entire body so tight that every sore muscle was even sorer. How could they be that smug? That certain?

Then, he stood alone, isolated, all his order-senses gone.

"Are you all right?"

Rahl stopped, slowly taking a deep breath, then another. He'd gotten so angry that the rage had almost taken him over—and he'd lost his order-senses. For a moment, he closed his eyes. What could he think of? Something warm, peaceful . . .

Deybri came to mind, and he concentrated mentally on creating her image in his mind, the waves in her brown hair, her smile, the gold-flecked brown eyes, the clear skin, and her warmth. He tried to picture her as he'd first seen her, in the mess at Nylan.

As his rage receded under that remembered warmth, he could feel his order-senses returning, if not completely.

"What was that all about?" asked Talanyr. "You just stopped and closed your eyes. Are you hurt?"

Rahl shook his head. "No . . . well, not . . ." He shook his head again. "It's hard to explain, except that . . . trying to regain what I once had isn't easy. Even keeping it isn't easy, either."

"I'm amazed at what you have done," Talanyr said quietly. "Not many escape the drudge jobs of the ironworks, and very few become mage-guards."

"I'm just a mage-clerk," Rahl pointed out.

"That's still a great accomplishment, and you will be a mage-guard. Taryl wouldn't spend so much effort on you if he didn't think so."

Rahl had his doubts, not about Taryl's efforts, but about whether anyone besides Taryl would see it that way.

"We need some dinner," Talanyr said. "Especially you."

"I could use something to eat."

They both laughed.

LXXXI

Rahl was up early on threeday, washed, shaved, and dressed well before breakfast. He looked over the letter he had taken two nights to compose and that he had finally written out in a final fair copy the night before. His eyes scanned the careful script that he had fitted on one small sheet.

My dear healer,

I am writing you for several reasons, the first of which is to tell you that the past does indeed have a hold upon me, one far stronger than even I would have believed possible, especially on that night when you uttered those words. Your image and memory have indeed redeemed me, though in ways you well might find ironic.

The second reason is to ask you to let others know that I have survived leaving the Merchant Association in Swartheld and, so far, the ironworks of Luba where I am now a clerk and working with order for further advancement in due course. What the future will bring exactly I cannot say, but I hope to convey such events in future letters, although they needs must be infrequent and brief.

Rahl had debated saying more about Shyret and what had happened, but, again, he had no proof. Without it, especially in a letter, there was no way he would convince anyone in Recluce what had really happened.

The third reason is to implore you, if you find it in your heart, to send word to my parents, Kian and Khorlya, scrivener and basketweaver in Land's End, some word that I am indeed well. I can only promise that when possible I will reimburse you for every copper or silver it may cost, and I would have done so myself, save that it has taken all that I have earned this season—and that is all that I have earned—to pay to send this one letter to you.

He'd debated many closings to the letter, but finally had written, "With all gratitude and affection." He hadn't wanted to be overly demonstrative, but neither had he wished to be matter-of-fact. He thought of Deybri every evening in the darkness. He did worry that he might just be thinking of her because he'd met no one else, and because, in such circumstances, absence did make the heart pine. Yet he thought it was more than that, but how could he know?

Finally, he folded the letter and slipped it into the standard envelope for Hamorian post. Then he made his way to the station's duty desk.

"Ser?" he said politely.

"Yes," replied Rymaen, the mage-guard holding the duty until after breakfast.

"I'd like to post this letter." Rahl extended the envelope.

"To Recluce? That's a far piece," observed Rymaen. "Let me see . . . that's three silvers and a copper for delivery in Nylan. Be four and two for Land's End."

Rahl handed over the coins.

"You must have saved every coin you could. She must be special."

Rahl laughed. "I did, and she is, but she's a healer, and she can get word to my family."

"You don't sound like an outlander, not at all."

"I've been here a while, but I learned from a scholar of Atla."

Rymaen nodded. "It'll go on the down-barge this afternoon."

"Thank you." Rahl turned and headed for the mess, where he was one of the first there. Since the breakfast foods were set out on large platters on a serving table, he helped himself, poured a mug of ale, and made his way to the juniors' table.

He'd only taken a bite or two when Rhiobyn dropped into the seat across from him, shaking his head. "How do you do it?"

"Do what?" Rahl had no idea what Rhiobyn meant.

"Sit down for report after report, copying each one without mistakes, without errors. After two or three reports, I want to blast something with chaos, or take a blade to it. And now, Thelsyn is telling me that, if I don't improve, I'll never be more than a clerk. I'm not a clerk, and that's not where my talents lie." Rhiobyn began to eat the battered egg toast, quickly and with precise rapid bites.

Rahl shrugged, and his shoulders twinged only slightly. "I was trained as a scrivener. That makes some of it easier. I also remember what it was like to be a loader. I'd much rather copy reports."

"Yes . . . I can see that when you've been lower-born and had to work drudge, copying would seem far easier, but don't you want more?" Rhiobyn didn't even look at Rahl as he took a swallow from his mug.

Rahl's immediate reaction to the other's unthinking condescension was anger, but he forced himself to take a sip of his ale before speaking.

"Don't you?" persisted Rhiobyn.

"Of course I do," Rahl said evenly. "But I need to be more careful than you. Being a lowborn outlander requires more patience, because

I have neither family nor wealth nor position upon which I can call."

"Oh . . . I hadn't thought of that. Not really." Rhiobyn frowned. "It must make matters terribly difficult."

"Not any more than for you," interjected Talanyr, settling into the chair beside Rahl and setting his platter and mug down. "It must be terribly difficult for you to evaluate matters in the longer run, since family, wealth, and position have so sheltered you from such considerations."

Rahl barely managed to keep from choking, even as he admired Talanyr's quick wit.

Rhiobyn looked startled. Then his face hardened. "You never did have much appreciation for the finer things in life, Talanyr."

"What are the finer things in life?" Rahl managed.

"They're . . ." Rhiobyn stopped and looked at Rahl. "Are you that naïve? Or are you trying to be witty like Talanyr?"

"I couldn't be witty in that fashion if I tried, not at your level," Rahl replied, ignoring the sense of hidden amusement from Talanyr. "I wanted to know what you thought the finer things in life might be."

"Exquisite music, such as performed by the Emperor's orchestra; fine wines, such as those of Phaleria; beautiful women, such as those of Cigoerne or Ilyra . . ."

"I thought as much." Talanyr nodded.

Rhiobyn took the last bite of his toast and ale and stood. "I hope you both have a day filled with what you seem to enjoy." He nodded and turned.

Rahl took another mouthful before speaking. "He really believes all that. Couldn't he sense what you were doing?"

"No. Most chaos types can't. Unless they have their chaos under total control, it keeps them from sensing what people feel. They can detect order and chaos, but not less obvious things. That's one place where order-skills are an advantage." Talanyr grinned. "You'll notice that ordermages have prettier girls and more devoted consorts."

At that moment, Taryl rose from the men's table and walked toward Rahl and Talanyr.

"I see you two have been agitating the young chaos-mage. Exactly what did you say to him?" Taryl's eyebrows rose in inquiry.

"He was asking me why I didn't seem interested in the finer things in life, ser," answered Rahl, "and I asked him what those might be."

Taryl smiled faintly. "How are your bruises?"

"Healing, ser. The soreness is mostly gone."

"Good. If you're going to bait your chaos colleagues, you'll need some more training. Meet me at the duty desk with your truncheon shortly. I haven't finished eating, but I won't be long."

"Yes, ser."

As Taryl turned away, Rahl wished he hadn't joined in the verbal sparring with Rhiobyn. Taryl hadn't seemed particularly upset, but . . . the last training session had been incredibly painful.

"He's not upset with you," Talanyr said quietly.

"He doesn't have to be for the results to be uncomfortable."

Talanyr chuckled. "True enough."

Rahl gulped down the last of his breakfast, then rose. "Have a good day copying."

"I almost wish I were doing whatever you'll be doing." Talanyr grinned. "Almost."

Rahl shook his head, then hurried toward his chamber. At least, he no longer had to worry about his meal dishes, as he had as a loader and checker. He reclaimed his truncheon and made his way back to the duty desk.

"Rahl . . ." said Rymaen. "Your letter's on the first wagon to the piers. It might even make the morning barge."

"Oh . . . thank you, ser."

"Just thought you'd like to know."

Rahl continued to wait by the duty desk, but when Taryl walked toward him, the mage-guard was accompanied by Khaill as well, and the arms trainer carried a practice falchiona, while Taryl carried a dark truncheon.

"Shall we go?" asked Taryl.

Rahl followed the two mage-guards out to the waiting wagon. Taryl sat with Rahl in the second seat, while Khaill sat in the seat behind the driver. No one spoke for a time after the wagon pulled away from the station building and headed toward the ironworks. The morning, like all the summer days in Luba, or so it seemed, was already hot and hazy, and light winds swirled grit from everywhere around those in the wagon. Rahl had to blot his eyes several times before they were off the lower section of the mesa road.

When they turned westward, past the coking furnaces, Rahl finally turned to Taryl. "Might I ask where we're going, ser?"

"To one of the mill buildings. It's a good area to practice certain things and learn about what can happen."

Inside, Rahl stiffened. He just hoped this session wouldn't be as painful as the last. Before he could ask more, the angular mage-guard had turned to look at the road ahead. Rahl could sense from Taryl's action and the coolness that surrounded him that he was to ask no more questions.

When the wagon stopped before the same mill in which Rahl had followed Dymat through his inspections, Khaill did not get off the wagon but turned to Taryl. "I'll wait outside until you need me."

Taryl nodded, then gestured for Rahl to follow him along the stone causeway into the mill.

As Rahl walked beside the mage-guard, he looked around, but did not see either of the massive steam tugs, but when he stepped inside the large open portal, he glimpsed the one on the south side of the mill, a good quarter kay away and moving slowly westward.

Taryl kept walking until he came to an open section of stone floor on the south side of the rollers that connected the hammer forge to the cogging mill. There he stopped and lifted his truncheon, nodding to Rahl. As far apart as they were, even shouting would have been lost in the sound-chaos of the mill.

Rahl raised his own truncheon, concentrating on Taryl with his eyes, rather than order-senses. With the struggle between order and chaos that surrounded him, and the thundering roar that melded the hammer forge, the cogging mill, and the plating mill, not to mention the hot chaos from the regenerative furnace, Rahl found it difficult to order-sense anything.

The mage-guard circled, then moved in, tapping the end of Rahl's weapon, then moving back and to his left. Rahl countered by edging to his right and moving forward, then trying a slight undercut.

Taryl parried and almost caught the edge of the iron band beneath the handguard's ridge, pulling Rahl forward.

Off-balance, Rahl jerked his truncheon free and danced back, momentarily disoriented by a reverberating *thud* from somewhere.

In a flash, Taryl struck Rahl's shoulder.

Rahl pivoted away, circling and trying to get a better feel for what Taryl was doing.

At first, Rahl was completely on the defensive, but slowly, ever so slowly, despite the distractions all around, and despite Taryl's skill, Rahl began to stop most of the mage-guard's attacks and even mount a few of his own.

Finally, Taryl stepped back, then motioned for Rahl to follow him out of the mill.

Rahl gratefully lowered his truncheon and, breathing heavily, walked after the mage-guard.

Even under the full morning summer sun, and without the slightest hint of a breeze, the unshaded causeway was far cooler than it had been in the mill.

Standing close to Rahl, Taryl said loudly, "You can rest for a few moments, but after that, you'll go against Khaill and the falchiona."

As far as Rahl was concerned, the respite was all too short, and he was all too soon standing back adjacent to the hammer forge and the cogging mill and looking at Khaill. From the side, Taryl watched intently, although Rahl had the feeling that the ordermage was watching Khaill more than Rahl.

Khaill moved slowly in toward Rahl, and Rahl half circled one way, and then back the other way.

Out of nowhere, the falchiona flashed toward Rahl, and Rahl could only block it, rather than parry or slip it, and the impact jarred his entire arm, even though he did manage to force the blade aside after the block.

From that moment on, Khaill pressed, and Rahl did his best to dodge, slide, slip, and deflect the longer and heavier weapon. Even though Khaill had managed to strike Rahl with the flatted blade several times, Rahl had managed to avoid a truly painful impact, and he was beginning to get a better sense of what the armsmaster was doing.

Suddenly, a chaos-probe jabbed at Rahl.

He deflected it—weakly—but he did manage to keep it from hitting him.

Khaill launched an attack with the blade, following it with another chaos-probe.

While Rahl managed to evade the blade, the jab of the probe threw him off-balance. Another probe followed, and Rahl managed to deflect it. Khaill was too strong for him to stop such an attack—but at least Rahl wasn't totally defenseless.

The attack of blade and probe continued . . . and continued.

Rahl's entire uniform was soaked, and his arm ached from evading and blocking an iron blade, and his body was sore in a few places from where the undefended or poorly defended chaos-jabs had struck.

Abruptly, Khaill stepped back, and Taryl moved forward, just enough to gesture for both to follow him out of the mill.

The wagon appeared, moving from a shaded overhang on the north side of the mill.

Rahl looked down at the truncheon, scarred, battered, and cut. If they kept him doing these kinds of exercises, he was going to need a new truncheon before long.

"You're getting better," Taryl said, "but you still get distracted when something unexpected happens."

Rahl bit back the retort he felt. Who didn't get distracted when something unexpected happened?

"We can't do this often, Rahl. Do you know why?"

Rahl hadn't even thought about something like that. He managed to keep his jaw from opening while he tried to find an answer. "I should, but I don't."

"Khaill is a chaos-mage."

Rahl wanted to shake his head. He should have thought of that. "Was that why you watched so closely, and why he only used just chaos-jabs and not bolts?"

"Partly. Also, we didn't want you burned if you failed to shield yourself adequately. As it is, by tomorrow those places where he got through will be twice as sore as the bruises you got from sparring in the dark. That's another reason."

Left unspoken, Rahl felt, was the point that training a so-called natural ordermage was far more work than other ordermages. Was that why Recluce had left him on his own? Or did they even know what he was?

LXXXII

After finishing the last of his breakfast, Rahl left the mess and began to walk toward the mage-guard duty areas . . . and the copying room, but he stopped beside the east-facing window because streaks of rain had created paths in the dust on the outside of the glass. He realized that he had seen no rain since early spring, not even the faintest of drizzles. The past eightdays since his sparring match in the mill had brought nothing new, just more copying, more rounds accompanying various mage-guards, more studying of the *Manual* and the abbreviated Codex, more questions from Taryl, and more and harder sparring with Khaill and others—although he had sparred only once more at the mill, and that had been with Taryl.

Outside, the rain was light, but it had dampened the dust and left traces of rivulets on the stone paving. Rahl studied the barren landscape to the east of the mage-guard complex for a moment. Although it had rained in Swartheld, he preferred to remember the last true rain he'd seen in Nylan, perhaps because it reminded him of Deybri, even though he really couldn't explain why he linked the rain to her.

Had he been too forward in his letter? Had she even received it? If she had, it would only have been in the past few days. He would like to have sent another, but he had only saved a little more than a silver from his less-than-modest pay since he had written her. He could but hope that she would find a way to let his parents know he was alive and well.

After a few more moments, he turned from the window and walked toward the copying room, nodding politely to the handful of mage-guards that he passed in the corridor.

Once at the copying table, Rahl settled into his chair at the front and picked up the report on the top. He couldn't help but smile, if wryly. Someone had switched the reports to be copied around. Those in his stack included the largely illegible and longer patrol reports, particularly those of Shaelynt and Sostrost. There was the faintest touch of chaos on Shaelynt's report, and that suggested that Rhiobyn had been at it again, probably late the afternoon before, when Rahl had been sparring with Khaill.

Rahl started in on Shaelynt's report and had struggled through deciphering the first few lines when Rhiobyn walked in, trying not to look in Rahl's direction.

"I see you didn't want to copy Shaelynt's report," Rahl said mildly.

"What do you mean?"

Rahl smiled pleasantly and continued to look directly at the other mage-clerk. "It's the oldest in the stack, and it has a touch of mage-chaos on it."

"I can't read what he writes. You can. I would have asked you . . ."

"I'd be happy to do it, but I do like to be asked."

"It might be nice," added Talanyr, who had followed Rhiobyn. "Even if Rahl is a trained scrivener, it might help your skills if you took on the harder copying once in a while."

"That just shows how backward Recluce is. Scriveners . . . what a waste. Why don't they print books?"

"They do in Nylan," replied Rahl, "and they have circular presses there."

"How do you know that?"

"They had me learn about one there. I helped operate it for a little while."

"A pressman . . . lowbred . . ." muttered Rhiobyn.

"Better lowbred and able than wellbred and condescending," suggested Talanyr.

"You have a comment for everything, Talanyr, and someday you'll choke on your words."

"That's possible," admitted Talanyr, as he settled into his chair at the copying table, "but at least I'll enjoy the taste of them."

Rhiobyn's only reply was a muffled snort.

Rahl returned his full attention to Shaelynt's report on having to remove an overseer for cruelty to a slogger team. The more he thought about it, the more seeming contradictions there were in Hamor. Men were used as laborers, even beasts of burden, and yet the mage-guards protected them. Hamor reveled in its fleets and commerce, but prohibited mages from taking any part in commerce. Good mage-guards—like Taryl—were stationed in places like Luba, and evil ones, like the one who had attacked him in the merchanting building, were stationed in Swartheld.

Would he ever make sense of it? Could he accept all the contradictions?

LXXXIII

After three days of intermittent drizzle, and a downpour on eightday, when Rahl decided he did not want to go to Guasyra, the weather cleared briefly on oneday, only to have the drizzling light rain reappear on twoday.

In late midmorning Rahl looked up from his copying to see Taryl standing in the doorway. Rhiobyn was sparring, and Rahl didn't know where Talanyr might be.

"Good morning, Rahl."

"Good morning, ser."

"What are the duties of the Mage-Guard Overcommander?"

"The overcommander is the direct supervisor of all mage-guard stations in Hamor, ser."

"That's a description, Rahl, but it doesn't tell me what he does."

Rahl tried to recall anything that might have been in the *Manual* or that Taryl or Khaill or any mage-guard had said. He didn't recall anything at all. "Ser . . . I imagine that he has to review the reports from the stations and decide whether those stations are well run. He must also have to report to the Triad, and make recommendations to them." Rahl looked directly at Taryl. "Ser, I've read the *Manual* and the Codex from cover to cover, and I cannot recall anything about the overcommander's duties."

Taryl laughed. "That's because there isn't anything written about it. What about the duties of the mage-captain here at Luba?"

"They're laid out in the duty book."

"Have you read it?"

"Yes, ser."

"Is there anything in the *Manual* about the duties of a mage-captain?"

"I only recall that mage-captains are responsible for the effective and loyal operation of their stations in the best interests of the Emperor and in accord with the standards set forth in the *Manual*."

"Why do you think that more specific requirements are not laid out in writing in the *Manual* or the Codex?"

Rahl had no idea. He couldn't even guess. "I couldn't say, ser. I don't know."

"Think about this. If a mage-captain is not honest and effective and loyal, of what use are detailed written procedures? Then think about this. Should Swartheld station be operated in exactly and precisely the same fashion as Luba station or Highpoint station or Cignoerne station or Atla station? Could you write a meaningful set of procedures that would cover all of them?"

"No, ser."

"That's why all procedures are set forth in the local duty books, and why the training and standards for mage-guards are as they are. We don't care so much from what background a mage-guard comes as we do about that guard's effectiveness, honestly, and loyalty. That's not to say we don't have our bad pearapples. That can't be avoided in any large group that has power, but we do our best to remove them when we find out." Taryl gestured. "Leave the copying. We need to work on something else."

"Yes, ser." Rahl rose, picking up his cap and following the mage-guard.

Outside, the rain had diminished to a light drizzle that seeped out of the low-hanging gray clouds. To the north, over the ironworks, the clouds held a reddish orange hue. Taryl walked to the waiting wagon and, after pulling a cloth from under the second seat and wiping it off, climbed up and sat down. He handed the rag to Rahl, who wiped off the other side before seating himself.

"Blast furnace number one," Taryl told the driver.

Blast furnace? Rahl didn't ask aloud. Taryl would tell him in his own good time.

Taryl waited until the wagon was headed away from the station before continuing. "A mage-guard, particularly one who is a natural ordermage, can never afford to be surprised or startled. He or she has to have an internal confidence, an assurance based on both experience and feelings. Your problems, I suspect, occurred because your confidence was greater than your experience, and because Recluce fears giving those such as you the necessary exposure to events and situations that will widen your experience."

Rahl hadn't thought of it in quite that way, but what Taryl said made far more sense than anything he'd heard in either Land's End or Nylan . . . with the exception of what little he had learned from Deybri, and he hadn't known enough to build on what she had said.

"Still . . . no matter what we do to prepare you, there will be the unexpected, but these and other exercises should give you an experience-based confidence that will allow you to face the unexpected. That is our hope, but you are the one who will have to make it work."

That sounded a little too much like the magisters of Nylan for Rahl, but he knew Taryl didn't mean it in the same way.

Before that long, the small wagon came to a halt on the southwest side of the southernmost of the blast furnaces. A misty steam surrounded the upper levels of the structure. Rahl followed Taryl along a stone walk toward the furnace, but he glanced westward along the causeway with the grooved iron rails that led to the mills. Halfway between was one of the steam tugs, moving slowly away from Rahl and toward the southern mill.

The misty rain continued to seep out of the clouds above, and heat and steam rose from the sand molds north of the walk, giving the hot air a damp and metallic odor. Taryl moved briskly to a portal at the base of the outer wall, then through it, as did Rahl.

Once inside, a wave of heat, like a wall of invisible flame, slammed into

Rahl, and he stopped well short of the circular brick wall that contained the crucible itself.

"See if you can raise a shield against the heat," suggested Taryl, who had already done that.

Rahl let himself feel everything around him before thinking about shields and trying to let them flow into place before him. The worst of the heat subsided, but he became even more aware of the raw chaos that lay beyond the crucible that held molten metal.

"Closer . . ." ordered Taryl. "Feel the power, but use your shields to keep it from you."

Rahl edged closer.

"Follow me." Taryl gestured, then walked to his left, toward the plug gate being opened by a pair of ironworkers.

Eventually, Rahl was standing almost directly beside the molten iron as it poured from the furnace along an inclined stone channel into the sand mold farther to the west. Even behind his shields, he was hot and sweating profusely.

Then, with a hiss and sputter, droplets of iron, like heavy chaos, splattered against his shields. For a moment, Rahl felt everything slipping, and he concentrated on holding the feeling of the shields, watching as the droplets struck his shields, then slid off onto the layer of sand over the stone floor.

After a time, Taryl motioned for him to step back.

Rahl did, following the mage-guard away from the lower levels of the furnace and then out through the narrow doorway. As he stepped out into the afternoon drizzle, mist and fog surrounded him.

"Your shields still absorb the heat-chaos," Taryl pointed out. "Let them go slowly."

The warm drizzle felt cool compared to the residual heat that had been held within his shields, and Rahl just let the pinpoints of rain bathe him for several moments.

"Each of those droplets of molten iron has as much force as a chaos-bolt," Taryl said. "More than the chaos thrown by most renegade or foreign mages."

"I didn't expect that," Rahl admitted.

"You weren't supposed to." Taryl offered a faint smile. "Now . . . tell me what you feel the difference is between the chaos in the furnace and the chaos when a mage throws a chaos-bolt."

Rahl considered before speaking. "The chaos in the furnace is . . . more chaotic. There's no sense of order about it at all. It's almost all power. But when a chaos-mage throws a bolt, it's different."

"How so?"

"It's like it has some chaotic order . . . but the order's not quite right."

Taryl nodded. "The chaos of the molten iron is what one might call honest chaos. A chaos-bolt contains a corruption of both chaos and order. That's one reason why it's so corrosive. It's also why an ordermage of equivalent strength can never be defeated by the power of a chaos-mage alone."

Rahl noted the careful phrasing Taryl used, but did not comment.

Taryl looked northward, where darker clouds were massing. "We need to get moving, unless you want to get soaked—or exhausted trying to hold an order shield against a downpour." He walked toward the waiting wagon.

With a smile, Rahl joined him.

LXXXIV

All mage-guard actions must be in accord with the Codex of Hamor and taken on behalf of the Emperor's best interests. Verbal or written ridicule or criticism of either a mage-guard or an administrator, or even of the Emperor, is not a violation of the Codex. Nor shall any book, pamphlet, or leaflet containing criticism be considered a violation of the Codex. Riot, civil disobedience, or physical violence in any form against the Emperor, his officers, any designated subordinate, or a mage-guard is a violation and should be halted instantly, by whatever means necessary. Likewise, incitement to civil disobedience, or physical violence in any form against the Emperor, his officers, any designated subordinate, or a mage-guard is a violation of the Codex and shall be punished as indicated . . .

In instances where compliance or violation of the Codex cannot be determined unequivocally, the possible malefactor shall be immediately taken into custody, and a superior mage-guard will review the situation and determine the outcome. In all cases, the outcome will be announced publicly. If a person is taken into custody in error, that person shall be released and given a writ that notes the custody was in error, and a public notice will be made. Likewise, if the person is guilty, the sentence will be pronounced and carried out publicly. No punishments or sentences will be administered privately or in secret, and the life of any mage-guard who does so will be forfeit, as will be the life of any superior who knowingly allows such to occur.

In instances of self-defense without witnesses, a full mage-guard inquiry will be undertaken. The results of the inquiry will be presented to the alleged attacker, or the attacker's next of kin, and a summary of the evidence and the findings of the inquiry shall be made public . . .

Manual of the Mage-Guards
Cigoerne, Hamor
1551 A.F.

LXXXV

Rahl spent the next eightday having his shields tested in various places, from the mills to the coking furnaces, and while having to spar with Taryl at the same time. By the following threeday, he had the sense that he'd actually recovered his ability with the shields, and he had far more understanding and control than he'd had in Nylan. After all that effort, he'd been happy just to copy reports on twoday.

He'd finished two more reports on threeday morning and was picking up the third when Taryl stepped into the copying room.

Taryl surveyed the three mage-clerks, then nodded at Rhiobyn. "If you'd accompany me, mage-clerk."

"Yes, ser." Rhiobyn rose with a bound, sounding far more cheerful than he had moments before.

Rahl paused in his copying, but waited until Taryl and Rhiobyn were well away from the copying room before he spoke. "What was that all about?"

"It's time for seasonal evaluations," Talanyr said slowly. "That's the only time Taryl ever calls anyone 'mage-clerk.' Jyrolt must be here."

"Rhiobyn seemed happy."

"That's because he's got an exaggerated view of his own skills."

"I wouldn't know," replied Rahl. "I've never seen him do anything."

For a moment, Talanyr looked surprised. "I hadn't realized it . . . I mean, I knew it, but it hadn't really struck me. You've never sparred against either of us. What mage-guards has Taryl had you work against?"

"Mostly Taryl and Khaill," Rahl admitted. "One or two others, sometimes."

"You never did say how you got those bruises, not in any detail."

"I was having trouble order-sensing things. So I had to go against Taryl with padded staffs in pitch-darkness until I could do it."

Talanyr's mouth opened. Then he shook his head. "You'll pass any arms evaluation."

"I thought . . . everyone . . ."

"No . . . you have to pass that level to get assigned to the city stations, but some mage-guards can never do that. That's why Rhiobyn won't make it. He gets confused in total darkness. He usually gets around it by using chaos to create light."

"Isn't that allowed?"

"Oh . . . it's allowed, but it takes more strength, and it makes you more vulnerable."

"As does talking when you should be copying," observed Thelsyn from the doorway. "Since it is possible that one or more of you might actually pass the evaluation, for the sake of either those who do not or the new mage-clerks who will be arriving in the next day or so, I would appreciate your making sure that there are no reports left uncopied."

"Yes, ser."

Rahl went back to work on the report before him, and Talanyr did the same.

Before all that long, Taryl returned and summoned Talanyr, leaving Rahl alone in the copying room. He forced himself to continue copying. He wasn't even certain if Taryl would have him examined. If not, would he spend more time as a clerk, or would he be sent some place like Highpoint?

He finished another report before Taryl returned and stepped into the copying room with Rhiobyn.

Rhiobyn looked shaken, but said nothing.

"Mage-clerk Rahl, if you would accompany me?" asked Taryl politely.

"Yes, ser." At least, he would be examined and evaluated, but what if he failed? He really had no idea what level of skill was expected, since he'd never seen what the other two could do—except for Talanyr's expertise with the truncheon in Guasyra—and the normally cocky Rhiobyn looked like he'd been coldcocked with a staff, if not worse.

Taryl walked quickly, leading Rahl toward the weapons-training area and in through the open door.

The only other figure in the chamber was a stocky and muscular man, slightly shorter than Rahl with broader shoulders and short brown hair. Like all mage-guards, he wore the khakis and black-leather boots and belt, with the sunburst insignia on his shirt collar. His eyes were a brownish green, and an aura of controlled chaos enshrouded him.

"Evaluator Jyrolt, this is mage-clerk Rahl," said Taryl evenly

"Ser." Rahl inclined his head politely, and when he straightened, Taryl was leaving the weapons exercise chamber.

"We'll begin with a few questions about what is expected of a mage-guard." Jyrolt's tenor voice was higher than Rahl would have expected from such a muscular figure.

Rahl waited.

Most of the questions were similar to those that Taryl had already asked Rahl, often several times in differing forms. A few were not.

"Mage-clerk, why are those mage-guards who embody order both uniquely qualified to serve the Emperor and fortunate to be able to do so?"

Rahl had to ponder for several moments before he had an answer, although he thought only half came from the *Manual.* "Because a peaceful land must be governed by order, and because it is difficult if not impossible for an ordermage to escape poverty and want without power, and it is difficult for an ordermage to obtain power without losing all or some of his skills."

"What about a chaos-mage?" asked Jyrolt dryly. "They could certainly hold power without losing their skills. They have for centuries in Fairhaven."

Rahl hadn't seen an answer to that question, or if he had, he hadn't remembered it. "A land must have order to remain peaceful. Too much chaos will not allow order. Does not Fairhaven spread its chaos-mages all across Candar?"

"Why does the Emperor allow his people to ridicule and criticize him, and why are mage-guards charged with enforcing that freedom?"

Rahl had read that section of the *Manual* and pondered it, but he'd never asked Taryl about it. He wished he had, because, again, he had to use his own interpretation . . . and hope. "Some people will always find fault. To punish them would only suggest that what they say is true, and more punishment would then be required, until all the mage-guards could do would be to punish those who spoke out, and before long there would be no order in Hamor."

"But would not too much criticism lead to unrest, mage-clerk?"

"It might, but if the unrest results in physical acts, then the mage-guard must stop it. That provides a balance. People can say what they feel, but they cannot act against the Emperor."

Jyrolt did not comment, and Rahl did not think that he had displeased the examiner, but with the other's shields, it was hard to tell.

The questions continued for a time longer, before Jyrolt declared, "Enough for the Codex and *Manual*. You must also be examined in weapons. With what are you most skilled?"

"Truncheon, and to a lesser degree, staff, ser. I can use a falchiona for a short period of time, but that gets most painful rather quickly."

Jyrolt nodded. "Then we will begin with the truncheon. Although you may have your own weapon, and may use it on duty, for purposes of evaluation, you will pick one from the case there." He gestured to a leather case set on the bench against the wall. "You are to choose first."

"Yes, ser." Rahl walked to the case, studying the truncheons. In the end, he picked up the longest and the heaviest, although it was of light oak, and he would have preferred dark oak or lorken.

Jyrolt picked one that was broader and slightly shorter, then moved to the center of the floor. "You are to wait until I attack the first time. Then you are to do your best."

"Yes, ser."

While Jyrolt was quick and skilled, after several passes Rahl realized that Taryl was better, and he began to see openings, although he could not quite take advantage of them at first, because he was uncertain whether they were merely feint-traps. But after another series, he slipped inside Jyrolt's guard, but pulled the thrust rather than striking with full force, and moved back.

Jyrolt immediately stepped back. "I doubt we need more examination with the truncheon. Pick a staff."

Matters with the staff were similar, except it took Rahl slightly longer.

The falchiona was another matter. Jyrolt was far better, and Rahl was hard-pressed, even retreating, just to avoid getting mauled, and he felt lucky to have taken only two or three blows, which Jyrolt had clearly pulled at the last moment. Just defending, by the end, even holding the falchiona was exceedingly painful.

Jyrolt again stopped. "Replace the falchiona in the case and return to the center of the floor."

Rahl did so, then stood there waiting.

"I want you to defend against my thrusts. Raise whatever shields you have."

"Yes, ser." Rahl took a moment, remembering to feel everything around him.

The first attack was a light chaos-jab—without any chaos-fire. From there, the jabs got more intense, and Rahl began to sweat even more heavily behind his shields.

Abruptly, a small chaos-bolt flew toward Rahl, but it burst against his shields, and he could sense the free chaos swirling around.

After a second bolt, somewhat stronger, flared away from Rahl, Jyrolt said loudly. "That will suffice." Then he turned to Taryl.

Rahl had not seen the other mage-guard enter, but that didn't surprise him. He'd been far too occupied in avoiding getting chaos-pummeled or -burned.

Jyrolt turned back to Rahl. "You may go. Mage-Guard Taryl will inform you."

Rahl inclined his head. "Yes, ser. Thank you." He wanted to blot his sweating forehead, but he did not, making his way from the training room.

Once outside, he did not close the door all the way but bent to examine his boot, trying to use his order-senses to catch what the two might say.

"Good weapons skills . . ."

". . . better than good, and you know it . . ."

"Shields . . . adequate . . . hard to tell . . . his experience is limited . . ."

". . . have had inexperienced mage-guards before . . . needs to be in Swartheld . . . we both know . . ."

"Enough of that now. Is this another of your future visions, Taryl?"

"I wish that it were not . . . dangerous for him, but more dangerous for us for him to remain here . . ."

"When then?"

There was a laugh. "Why not now? He could travel with you, and you could brief him." A pause followed. "Remember . . . he *is* a natural, and that means—"

"I know . . . I know. No lectures, just information and examples. More hands-on demonstrations . . . I suppose Mage-Captain Gheryk could assign him as an assistant to one of the patrol mages in those areas where they patrol in pairs. His arms skills are better than most . . ."

Rahl couldn't quite believe what he was hearing. Taryl was almost ordering his superior as to what to do. What exactly was Taryl?

He could sense someone coming. So he straightened and began to walk back toward the copying room, nodding politely as he passed Dymat. His thoughts were still swirling about the part of the conversation he'd overheard. Jyrolt was the examiner, but Taryl hadn't been all that deferential.

When he stepped into the copying room, both Talanyr and Rhiobyn stood and looked at him. Neither looked particularly pleased.

"What happened?" demanded Rhiobyn.

"I don't know."

"Didn't they test you?"

"Jyrolt tested my knowledge, my arms skills, and my shields, and then they dismissed me."

Rhiobyn nodded. "That's always how it is. We don't find out until later."

"What weapons . . . ?" asked Talanyr.

"Truncheon, staff, and falchiona. If he hadn't been kind, he would have turned me into chopped meat with the blade."

"You used a blade against Jyrolt?" demanded Rhiobyn. "How many times did he strike you?"

"Three, I think, but I was mostly circling, trying not to get chopped up."

The other two exchanged glances.

"How did you do with the truncheon?" asked Talanyr.

Rahl felt uneasy about answering that honestly. "I guess I did all right. I kept him from hitting me."

Talanyr's laugh was almost bitter. " 'All right,' he says. Taryl's the only one who's never been struck by Jyrolt."

Rahl wished he could have downplayed it, but he'd told the truth, if not all of it, and Talanyr would have known if he'd lied outright. "I just did what I could."

Rhiobyn just looked at Rahl, who could sense the other's bewilderment.

Rahl looked at the two reports that remained at his place at the copying table. "I suppose I'd better finish these." As he sat down, he glanced at Talanyr. "When will they tell us?" He paused. "What will they say?"

Talanyr shrugged, then settled into his chair. "They'll say whether we're ready to become mage-guards or not. If we are, Taryl will tell us whether we stay here as full mage-guards or where we'll be sent."

"If . . . if we're not ready . . . then what?"

"Taryl will say whether Jyrolt thinks we just need more preparation or whether we'll be mage-clerks for life."

Rahl winced at the thought of that.

Talanyr laughed, ruefully. "Sometimes that's not all bad. If they think your character is good, you can be sent to headquarters in Cignoerne or to one of the large city stations. They have a lot of reports to write and file in those places. Sometimes, clerks develop late into mage-guards."

Could that be what Taryl had been talking about with Jyrolt?

Rahl could only wait and wonder as he began to copy the next report.

He was finishing the second report when Taryl appeared. "Mage-Guard Rhiobyn . . . if you'd accompany me."

Rahl could sense the relief—and the nervousness—held within Rhiobyn, although he was smiling when he left with Taryl.

"Poor bastard." Talanyr shook his head.

"Why?"

"They'll send him to someplace like Ceostyr or Mludyn."

Rahl had no idea where either was.

"They're towns smaller than Jabuti or Guasyra, where you've got maybe two or three mage-guards, and none of the women he has his eye on in Cignoerne will ever consort him with that kind of assignment."

"You don't think he'll stay here?"

"He's too impatient. Haven't you noticed how patient and deliberate the mage-guards are here? They don't put up with trouble, but they don't lash out either."

Rahl had noticed that.

At that moment, Jyrolt himself appeared. "Mage-Guard Talanyr, if you'd accompany me."

Talanyr's grin and relief were more than palpable. Rahl grinned back at him. "Congratulations."

"Thank you."

Rahl got up and walked over to the reports that Talanyr hadn't finished and picked up the one on the top, carrying it back to his seat. He finished it and was wondering if he should start another when he sensed someone approaching—Taryl.

He looked up.

Taryl smiled. "Congratulations, Mage-Guard Rahl."

Rahl bolted to his feet. "Ser."

"Since we're alone here, I don't need to escort you off. Sit down."

Rahl sat, nervously, as Taryl pulled Talanyr's chair closer and seated himself.

"I shouldn't have to tell you, but you've posed a considerable problem for us."

"I had that feeling, ser, with my loss of order-skills . . ."

"That's not the problem I'm talking about. You have an aptitude with staff and truncheon that comes along maybe once in a generation. As an ordermage, you shouldn't even be able to hold a falchiona for more than a few moments, let alone use it. I know the pain of doing so is agonizing for you—any ordermage around can feel it—and I don't suggest you make a habit of picking up blades, but it's indicative of your ability. The problem is that you're a natural ordermage, and you have to learn things slowly, and by doing them. You can't rush things. We're not set up for handling mages like you, but you're already too far along to stay here."

Rahl still had no real idea of where Taryl was headed.

"Jyrolt and I have talked things over, and we're going to send you to Swartheld. This has several advantages and several disadvantages. You know some of the city, and you know commerce. But you're not a chaos-mage, and most mage-guards in the larger cities have to be. You'll be assigned to work with an experienced mage-guard there, but you're going to have to find a way to develop more order-skills on your own. We've worked on the ones you need to survive as a mage-guard, but if you want to do more than that, it's up to you."

Rahl considered Taryl's words without immediately replying. The thin-faced mage-guard had been more than fair, much more than fair. He'd effectively saved Rahl's life, and for that Rahl had no way of really thanking him, let alone repaying him. "I can't thank you enough, and I think you know that, ser."

Taryl smiled. "I do. The only way you can repay me is by continuing to learn and in time, perhaps, by saving someone else of such potential. Or keeping them from making near-fatal mistakes, but given the minds of the young, that is often impossible." The smile vanished. "One other thing. Hamor is generally a just land, but it is not a kind land. You will see injustice, and you will see good people broken and be unable to do anything. The hardest thing for you will be not to take the laws of the land into your own hands and use your powers to set things as you see they should be. *Do not do it.* That is the way to destroy yourself and all the good that the mage-guards stand for. The Codex is not perfect, but any alternative is worse. If you do not see that, please take my word for it until you do."

Although Taryl had not raised his voice, the concern and the conviction in his tone burned through Rahl.

"Yes, ser."

"You'll take one of the downriver barges to Swartheld, and you'll go with Jyrolt, tomorrow, because that's where he's headed next. That will give him a chance to brief you." Taryl stood and set the canvas bag he had carried on the table. "Here are your insignia for your cap and collars, as well as two more sets of uniforms and a cold-weather jacket. Oh, there's also a pouch with three silvers. Your pay as a beginning mage-guard is three silvers an eightday, and passing the evaluation entitles you to an eightday's pay." He smiled. "Now . . . put on the insignia and go find your friends. You're all free for the rest of the day, not that any of you would be worth much as copyists or mage-guards at the moment."

"Thank you, ser." Rahl still couldn't believe the pay. Three silvers an eightday plus lodging and two meals a day.

Taryl offered a last smile, then stepped back. "You earned it, and you'll keep earning it." Then he was gone.

Rahl had sensed a certain sadness in Taryl, as well as something else, but he couldn't very well chase Taryl and ask about it.

After taking his new and additional gear to his chamber and affixing the mage-guard sunburst insignia to his collars and visor cap, Rahl went looking for Talanyr and Rhiobyn. He found them in the small courtyard outside the mess.

Talanyr smiled as Rahl appeared. "I thought you'd make it."

"Well . . . I thought both of you would," Rahl replied. "You've both had much more training and experience."

"Where are you going? Or are you staying here?" asked Rhiobyn quickly, not quite looking at Rahl directly.

Rahl didn't want to answer that. "Taryl said I couldn't stay here." That was true, even if it had been said to Jyrolt. "What about you?"

"It could have been worse." Rhiobyn shook his head. "I'm being stationed in Heldya."

The town name was familiar, but Rahl couldn't place it mentally, and he glanced at Talanyr.

"It's on the east side of the Heldyn Mountains, about fifty kays north of the Great Highway. It's a lumber and herding center, and they say it's about three times the size of Guasyra."

Rahl looked at Rhiobyn. "It's not Cigoerne, but it sounds like a good-sized place compared to some of the stations you two have told me about."

Rhiobyn squared his shoulders and offered a smile. "They do have mage-clerks there. Taryl told me that."

Talanyr laughed. "You're fortunate. Clyanaka doesn't."

Rhiobyn glanced at Rahl, but Rahl had never heard of the name.

"I'm being assigned as a range guard on the northwestern high grasslands in Merowey. They wanted someone who could ride and knew plants and animals." Talanyr shook his head. "Taryl said that they've been asking for more help there for years, and I was a good fit."

Rahl could sense that Talanyr was pleased. "You really didn't want a city post, did you?"

"No. I'd hoped for a small town at least, but this is better. There is a town there, but most of the mage-guards patrol the grasslands against poachers and rustlers."

Rahl found both of them looking at him.

"They're sending me to Swartheld. They think that because I know something about commerce and trade . . . I guess. Taryl didn't say, except that I'd have to be paired with a very experienced mage-guard."

"That's tough duty," said Rhiobyn.

"I'd wager that's why Taryl worked on your weapons training so much," added Talanyr. "They get sailors and bravos from all over the world there."

"Is Clyanaka far from Jabuti?" asked Rahl, wanting to change the subject away from himself and Swartheld.

"Only some six hundred kays over roads that are barely that." Talanyr grinned. "But I'll be able to ride again, and not be so hemmed in. I miss the open skies . . ."

Rahl listened to Talanyr, realizing that he had been the first adult male friend Rahl had ever had . . . and that he would miss Talanyr's quiet steadiness in the days and seasons ahead. He doubted that he would miss much else about Luba station and the ironworks, except Taryl, who was far more than he seemed.

". . . and there aren't that many people around, except near the Clyan River . . ."

Even Rhiobyn listened as Talanyr went on.

LXXXVI

Although Rahl looked for Taryl on fourday morning to say good-bye, the older ordermage had already left the station, according to the mage-guard on duty. He still wished he'd been able to say a true good-bye to Taryl. He'd asked why Talanyr and Rhiobyn weren't taking the wagon, but Talanyr had pointed out that they were going upriver, rather than down, and that the next river steamer would not port at Luba until fiveday.

So Rahl found himself on the transport wagon to Luba port, seated beside Jyrolt, as they rode eastward. The older mage-guard dozed in the wagon, as if he were still exhausted from his evaluation efforts of the previous day. Rahl could not rest and contented himself with studying the highway and the barren flatlands that stretched toward a line of hills ahead.

The hills looked as though a massive layer of black basalt had formed and then been tipped on its side. The road itself ascended a long and gradual ramp to the lowest point in the hills. For a moment, Rahl wondered why the ramp was so long and gradual—until he realized that the iron wagons had to travel it to the river port.

Near the top of the road, Jyrolt stirred himself, stretched, and looked at Rahl. "You've been pleasantly quiet, Rahl, but I'd wager you have more than a few questions."

"Yes, ser." He paused. "Ser . . . what exactly is Mage-Guard Taryl's function at Luba station? Beyond training, that is? He is more than he seems, I feel."

Jyrolt raised two bushy eyebrows. "Why do you think that?"

"He sees more, but he says little."

"Ha! At least, you saw that, young Rahl." Jyrolt cleared his throat. "He was one of the Triad. Let us just say that he made an error. Only the great make errors of such magnitude. None thought it his fault, but he felt it was his responsibility, and he stepped down and came to Luba." Jyrolt paused. "There are rumors that a woman and a relative of the Emperor were involved. They are false. I will only say that the error involved judgment and magery, and none, save a few, will ever know the details, and none should. This is the last I will speak to you of it. Should any ask you, you should answer as I answered you."

"Yes, ser."

"Now . . . what other questions do you have? Preferably dealing with your assignment and duties."

"Taryl only told me that I had been assigned to Swartheld station and that I would be paired with an experienced mage-guard. I don't know enough beyond that to ask a good question, except for what my duties might be and what skills would be most useful."

"The most useful skills in Swartheld are skills with weapons, which you have, shields, and yours are adequate, the ability to sense when something is not as it should be, and a knowledge of commerce. Beyond petty thievery and violence, the majority of evildoing there lies in attempting to misuse trade for great personal gain . . . or worse, to obtain power over others. Your duties at first will be simple. You will patrol with another mage and keep order according to the *Manual* and Codex. I can't say where you'll patrol, because that's up to the city mage-captain and the station undercaptain." Jyrolt looked at Rahl, as if waiting for another question.

"What questions should I ask, ser?"

"Has Taryl been tutoring you on how to draw me out?" Jyrolt's tone was wry.

"No, ser."

"That sounds like something he'd come up with."

Rahl couldn't comment on that.

"Is it true that you were dosed with nemysa?" asked Jyrolt.

"I don't know that. I lost my memories for seasons, and Taryl told me that only nemysa could do that . . ." Rahl went on to explain all that had happened.

"Why do you think this Shyret wanted you to lose your memories?"

"He thought I knew something he didn't want known."

"Did you?"

"I had a good idea that he was claiming some goods were damaged, then selling them on the side and pocketing the coins. I would have been hard-pressed to come up with proof, and he was convinced that what he was doing did not go against the Codex. Without hard proof and as an exile—"

"You were exiled from Recluce?"

"Yes, ser. Because I was a natural ordermage. They claimed I couldn't be taught and was a danger to them for that reason."

Jyrolt fingered his chin. "This Shyret could not have known you were a mage, or he would not have used nemysa . . . unless he thought it would kill you well away from him. How long before you could remember?"

"I was not even aware of anything for more than a season, and it was another season almost before I remembered who I was."

Jyrolt nodded. "The dosage you were given might well have killed most mages, but there must have been something else. This merchant was right that the Codex does not concern itself with commercial manipulations, only with theft or fraud against those who buy their goods. There is a reason for that. Do you have any idea what it might be?"

Rahl did not. To him it seemed wrong that merchants could cheat each other.

"The Emperor cares only that honest goods are sold. To try to set the price, either directly or indirectly, always results in higher charges. To prohibit certain practices or to mandate that factors and traders only adhere to certain others only results in even more convoluted fashions of accounting and bookkeeping, and that makes gathering tariffs even more difficult. So the Emperor concerns himself with making sure that honest goods are sold and that the amount and value of the goods brought into Hamor, or produced here before sale, are accurate. What the merchants do to each other or their accounts is their business."

But if that were so, why had Shyret wanted Rahl removed or dead?

"I can see that you understand the problem. It is not a crime to remove someone's memories—rather it would be, except it can almost never be proved that it was caused by drugs rather than by an unfortunate accident—but it is a definite offense to murder someone. So why would a merchant partner do something that might result in murder over an accounting issue that is not an offense in Hamor?"

Rahl didn't have an answer for that, either, except that what he had seen signified far more than he had understood at the time—or even now.

"I would suggest that you say nothing about this matter. I can assure you that I will bring it to the attention of Mage-Captain Gheryk and Regional Mage-Commander Chaslyk. You are not to speak of it, except if asked, and only by those two officers, or by their superiors. This is for your protection as well. Do you understand?"

"Yes, ser."

"Now . . . let me tell you about how the mage-guards came to be . . ."

LXXXVII

By late afternoon on fourday, Rahl was standing midships on the main deck by the railing of the *Streamcrawler*—a squat steam tug that seemed mostly massive engine and boilers and little else. He had not expected there would be three long barges, linked by thick hawsers, all heavily loaded with iron plate and rods and beams, guided by a steam tug. Nor had he anticipated being on a river that stretched close to half a kay from bank to bank, yet one so deep that the water barely seemed to ripple except when disturbed by the passage of one craft or another, and not for long.

The black basalt hills overlooking the river port of Luba were behind them, at least thirty kays upstream, and had given way to a mixture of low, rolling hills to the east of the river and neat, irrigated fields to the west. On the broad Swarth River itself were all manner of craft, from the heavy barges to skiffs to small sailboats that were almost without keels and skittered across the dark waters in the light breezes. Only once in the entire afternoon had Rahl seen a river steamer, but it had been a handsome craft painted in crimson and green, with three full decks, and a handful of passengers dressed in finery on the uppermost deck, below the pilothouse, with scores of others on the main deck, some carrying what looked to be all that they possessed in large bundles.

As the sun dropped lower in the western sky, and the shadows crept across the water that was turning from dark blue to oily black, Rahl continued to watch the other craft on the river, as well as the hamlets they passed, as the tug and the barges glided downstream, with the muffled chuffing of the steam engine the loudest sound.

"The river's the heart of western Hamor," said Jyrolt from behind Rahl. "Have you ever seen its like?"

"No." Rahl had never really seen a true river. In the north of Recluce there were only streams. He'd heard that the Feyn was a goodly river, but he'd crossed it locked in a wagon and never seen it.

"You never will. It's the mightiest river in all the world, more than two thousand five hundred kays from its mountain headwaters to the harbor bay at Swartheld, and no real cataracts on it until you're well south of Cigo-erne. That makes travel between Cigoerne and Swartheld easy." Jyrolt laughed. "They say that all the trades and goods flow down the river, and the golds fly back up. There's a bit of truth in that."

As the mage-guard spoke, the captain called out, "Starboard for the bar!"

The tug eased away from the western shore. The heavy hawsers con-necting the tug to the barges creaked, and something groaned.

"Steady as she goes."

"Why is that?" Rahl finally asked the older mage-guard.

"Going upstream on the river takes good winds or a strong engine. It's much easier to send cargo down and sell it or ship it from Swartheld than to pay to ship upstream—unless it's something very light and valuable, like spices or dyes or perfumes or women's oils."

"With all those valuables, are mage-guards stationed on ships on the river? Aren't there brigands?"

"The river makes that difficult, but even if it did not, we would not put mage-guards on ships and boats. Who would decide which would benefit?" Jyrolt shook his head. "We have stations at all the major river ports, and we catch most of those few who have created chaos on the river, but those on the river have to provide their own guards."

Rahl couldn't help but frown.

"The mage-guards provide order, Rahl," Jyrolt went on. "You should know that our duty is not to protect commerce and coins, but to maintain order and contain chaos. The river is a channel of commerce. Except for those who serve the Emperor, almost no one who travels the river does so but for reasons of commerce, and commerce can and should take care of itself, so long as it does not create chaos or disrupt order. The same is true of people."

Rahl was having trouble with what Jyrolt was saying. How could one maintain order and contain chaos without protecting people? When he'd read that passage in the *Manual,* he'd wondered, but he'd assumed that maintaining order meant protecting people. Now, he wished he'd asked Taryl about it.

He *hated* to ask stupid questions, and he felt angry at himself for not understanding and even angry at Taryl for not explaining, but he had the feeling he'd best find out what Jyrolt and the *Manual* really meant.

"There's something I don't think I understand, ser, and I should."

Jyrolt just raised his bushy eyebrows.

"How can I be a mage-guard without trying to protect people who are innocent or who are likely to be hurt?"

The older mage-guard nodded slowly. "That is not a stupid question, simple as it might sound to some. You are at a disadvantage in some respects, because you were not lectured on this as most mage-clerks are, and your actions would indicate that you understood, and Taryl would have gone by your actions." Jyrolt's brow furrowed. "I'm not a lecturer or a philosopher, and I might not word this as carefully as they would, but . . . when anyone uses the word *protect*, they're talking about using force to stop an evil that is happening or will happen. The emphasis shifts from maintaining order and containing chaos to applying force to those who may or may not need it. Commerce is powerful enough by itself. When a trader talks about the need for protection, he or she is really asking for an advantage over others, backed by the force of the Emperor. This is also often true of individuals. That is why we do not talk about protection. The use of force against others is chaos. We oppose that, whether that force is chaos itself or order focused against someone. We seek to have anyone of any stature walk our streets without fear, and we seek to keep the laws that govern us simple and obvious. Why do you think mages are forbidden from commerce in Hamor? There are two reasons. The first is obvious. Many mages can sense what others feel, and some can use those skills to persuade through manipulation or force. That destroys any element of order in commerce. The second reason is that using such skills will eventually destroy the mage and all those close to him. Even Recluce and Fairhaven understand this, although they keep their mages from commerce in other fashions . . ."

Rahl thought he understood, but he had the feeling it was going to take some time for him to sort it out.

"As for those who suffer through no fault of their own . . . we do not turn them out. You have seen Luba. You have endured it. Did you see cruelty? Hard work, yes, but most of those there had brought chaos upon others, and we always look to sift out those who are otherwise. How else would you be a mage-guard?"

Rahl had to offer a faint smile at that . . . and yet . . .

Swartheld

LXXXVIII

On sevenday morning, Rahl sat beside Caersyn—the station duty mage—in the foyer that seemed half study, the same place where he had once gone to register, more than a year before. The mage-guard station was the same one Rahl remembered—right off the main piers of the harbor beyond the enumerators' building. What he had not noticed then were the two adjacent buildings almost tucked away farther shoreward toward the bluff and slightly to the south. One was the gaol, for holding offenders until they could be sent to the quarries or Luba, or until a case could be resolved, and the other served as quarters for unconsorted mage-guards. He had been given a small main-floor chamber, off the middle of the corridor, but it was his alone, for which he was grateful.

On the wagon, and on the barge downstream, Jyrolt had talked far more about the overall mission of the mage-guards, and about their history than about specifics of mage-guard duties. Rahl had found it interesting that the early emperors had been ordermages, not chaos-mages, and that one of them had actually created the mage-guards, but now he was listening carefully to Caersyn, because he needed to know more.

"Now . . . here's the duty book," said Caersyn, "and because I'm lazy, and you need to learn about Swartheld, you'll be doing the entries this morning. The captain likes them neat."

Rahl doubted that would be a problem.

"He'll be in shortly. He likes to spend some time with all the new mage-guards. Since nothing's happening yet, you might as well start reading the station manual." Caersyn pulled a leather-bound book from a shelf under the single drawer of the battered oak desk.

Rahl opened it to the first page.

He'd read four pages, when Caersyn whispered, "Here comes the captain."

Even before he reached Rahl, the dark-haired and blue-eyed Mage-Captain Gheryk radiated a cheerful strength.

Rahl stood. "Ser."

"You're our new addition, Mage-Guard Rahl?"

"Yes, ser."

"Good." Gheryk glanced at Caersyn. "I see you've already put him to work."

"Yes, ser. You and the undercaptain always start them here."

"I can tell I'm getting too predictable," replied the captain before turning his eyes back on Rahl. "I need to go over a few things with you. Why don't you come with me?" He grinned at Caersyn. "He'll be back before long."

"Yes, ser."

Gheryk led the way to a small windowless chamber less than twenty cubits away, where he settled behind a small desk and gestured for Rahl to take the straight-backed chair across the desk from him. The room was empty except for the desk and chairs, a small bookcase less than half-filled, and a wooden file chest.

"Welcome to Swartheld."

"Thank you, ser."

"You've been assigned to Swartheld port station. The other station is the city station, but it's on the south side. There's a naval station over by the piers, but the mage-guards there are in the navy. I'm in charge of both Swartheld stations, but the day-to-day operations are run by the undercaptains. Craelyt is the undercaptain here, and Demarya is the undercaptain of the city station. There's a map in the station manual that shows which sections of the city which station patrols, but you'll learn them all in time, because you'll be rotated over there at some point for familiarization. You won't meet Craelyt until tomorrow because he has today off, and I usually take eightdays off.

"Caersyn was right about putting you on the duty desk today, and having you read the manual. You'll also draw another set of uniforms and another pair of boots. Alternate the boots every day. They'll last longer, and so will your feet. There's one other thing. It's mentioned in the manuals, but I want to emphasize it. Mage-guards are never truly off duty, except when you're sleeping. You wear your uniform everywhere outside your quarters, except bathing or swimming, and you always wear a weapon outside the quarters. This is true in all towns and cities, even though it is mentioned only briefly in the *Manual of the Mage-Guards.* Part of the reason for this is that mage-guards are a group apart, and we are never to deceive others as to who and what we are. Another part of that is that there are never enough of us, and when we all wear our uniforms everywhere, we create the impression of a larger force." Gheryk leaned forward slightly. "Peaceful and orderly as it may seem, Swartheld is a dangerous city, Rahl, even for mage-guards. We do lose guards. Sometimes, we never find a trace of them."

Rahl nodded.

Gheryk's eyes sharpened. "That's a knowing look. What were you thinking?"

"I don't know if you know, ser. I was once a clerk here in Swartheld. I woke up one morning seasons later in Luba without any memories. It took another season before I recalled anything. I was agreeing with your observation that it's a dangerous city."

Abruptly, Gheryk laughed. "Oh . . . you're the one Taryl was inquiring about last spring. That's probably why Jyrolt left a note that he wanted to talk to me about you. You're the outlander who registered and had been a clerk with the Recluce trade outfit. You speak like an educated Atlan, and I didn't realize who you were."

"Yes, ser."

The mage-commander was the one to nod. "Seen that way, I'm beginning to understand why you were sent here. Mage-Examiner Jyrolt left your evaluation, but I haven't talked to him yet. Your weapons skills are impressive. He never exaggerates. I only wish you were on the chaos side. It's a little safer to be able to handle some of these bravos from a distance." He fingered his chin. "But . . . in crowded areas, one can't always use chaos. I think we'll have you on the piers to begin with . . . after you've spent an eightday on the duty desk as an assistant so that you'll get to know everyone, and they'll get to know you. You'll also have time to read the station manual and listen to the others about what is happening."

"Yes, ser." That all made sense to Rahl.

"Do you have any questions?"

"Just one, for now, ser. I'm sure I'll have more later." He paused, then asked, "Is there any way to send coins places safely, like to Recluce? I suppose I could get a draft from the Exchange, but . . ."

Gheryk raised his eyebrows slightly.

"I need to repay someone for a favor, for getting word to my parents that I was safe."

The captain's frown vanished. "You can send your Exchange draft with assurance through most bonded Hamorian factors. The assurance fee is a silver for the first five golds, and a silver for each ten above that, I'm told. That's only for a draft, though. You can't send actual coins, of course."

"Thank you, ser."

"Any other questions?"

"No, ser."

"That will be all . . . for now."

As Rahl headed back toward the duty desk, he came face-to-face with Jyrolt. "Ser."

Jyrolt looked at Rahl. "You've already met with Mage-Captain Gheryk?"

"Yes, ser. I didn't know exactly what to say. I just told him that I'd been a clerk and a registered outlander and lost my memories and woke up in Luba. He remembered Taryl's inquiry. I didn't want to say more after what you'd told me."

"Good. I'll explain the rest."

Rahl didn't sense any deception in Jyrolt, but he still worried as he rejoined Caersyn.

"The captain set you straight?"

"He was pretty direct." Rahl paused. "What are the undercaptains like?"

"Craelyt's our undercaptain," replied the duty mage-guard, "and he doesn't say much, except what needs to be said. Knows being a mage-guard, been one longer than even the captain. Likes to handle things quiet-like. Always pointing out that mage-guards aren't supposed to be seen, just supposed to keep things orderly."

Caersyn didn't seem inclined to say much more, and Rahl went back to reading the manual. He'd gotten through several more pages when Mage-Captain Gheryk appeared again.

"Anything I should know, Caersyn?"

"It's been quiet this morning, ser, but it's early. If there's trouble, it'll be tonight."

Gheryk laughed softly. "Sevenday nights." His eyes turned on Rahl. "Let's see your truncheon."

Rahl stood and handed it over. He'd oiled and polished it, but it showed the abuse it had taken at Luba.

"That's a sorry-looking truncheon you've got there. I thought that might be the case."

"It was the heaviest ironbound one they had at Luba, ser."

Gheryk glanced to the duty mage-guard. "Caersyn . . . would you check with the armory and see if we have any of those iron-banded black truncheons for Rahl? He'd take forever to get one because he'd have to explain, and then you'd have to go anyway. I'll wait here."

"Yes, ser."

Once Caersyn was well out of sight and earshot, Gheryk looked evenly at Rahl. Then he shook his head. "Jyrolt told me the rest of your story. I don't know whether I owe Taryl, or he owes me. Something is going on, and I don't like things like that. Until I learn more, you are not to tell anyone more than that you were a mage-clerk in Luba, and that you only have vague memories of Swartheld. That includes the undercaptains and duty supervisors. You are not to seek out anything of your past now, but if you discover more, and in time you may, you are to find a way to talk to me that is not obvious. Is that clear?"

"Yes, ser." Rahl could sense a certain anger deep within himself, and he immediately blocked it, although the effort limited his order-sensing, if not so much as letting it surface might have done.

"Good.

"Since you recall something of commerce, you will be assigned to work with Mage-Guard Myala. She is a solid chaos-mage, and I strongly urge you to listen to her. She's on leave until sixday, or I'd have you meet her now."

"Yes, ser."

"After your eightday assisting the duty mage-guard, you two will have daylight duty from eightday through sixday, with sevenday off. Later, you'll get the night shift . . ." Gheryk broke off as Caersyn returned, carrying two black-oak truncheons.

"This one's standard, and this one's heavier."

"I'd prefer the heavier," Rahl said.

"For you, that would be best," said the captain. "Later today, take the old truncheon and turn it in to the armorer and introduce yourself."

"Yes, ser."

Gheryk smiled. "I'm going to take a tour of pier two. There's a Jeranyi vessel there, iron-hulled and almost big enough to be a warship."

"Yes, ser."

After the captain had gone, Rahl said, "He's concerned about a Jeranyi ship?"

"Iron-hulled and big . . . sounds like a pirate coming in here as a trader. Not that we care about that so long as the crew behaves and they stay orderly, but pirate crews don't always do that."

"And sevenday nights? Why does that make a difference to the crews?"

Caersyn laughed. "It's not the crews. It's the locals. More of them are out on sevenday evenings, and they don't care much for outland sailors with lots of silvers. We shift more patrols to the eateries and taverns after dusk. So does the city station."

That also made sense to Rahl, although he wouldn't have thought of it.

"You a weaponsmaster with truncheon?" Caersyn asked, indicating a touch more than idle curiosity.

"Jyrolt said my skills were more than adequate."

The other laughed. "From him, that's praise. You get all those nicks in the old one working against blades?"

"Against Khaill and Jyrolt."

"With a truncheon? They're both armsmasters."

"Sometimes with a staff," Rahl admitted.

"Wondered why they'd send a new ordermage here. That explains it."

"The captain said I'd be working the piers, places where it's so crowded that sometimes chaos-bolts are hard to use."

"He say who you'll be working with?"

"Mage-Guard Myala."

Caersyn winced. "Better you than me. You make a mistake, and you'll know it."

That didn't surprise Rahl either. He looked down at the station manual. "I guess I'd better learn this."

"That you had."

The day was quiet until just past midday, and, after a while Rahl turned in his old truncheon. He'd only been back at the duty desk for a short time when an older mage-guard appeared.

"Caersyn, we've got something to be logged."

Rahl set aside the manual and reached for the duty book.

"Oh, Niasl, this is Rahl," Caersyn said. "Started today. What's up?"

"Good to meet you." Niasl offered a quick smile, then went on, "Hydlenese ship on pier two—the *Pyrdyan Pride* . . . has a chaos-mage on board. Man ran down the gangway, trying to leave. Mage flamed him. He's dead. The captain claimed he was a stowaway. He was too well dressed for that, but the mage never left the ship so we can't do much about him. We're keeping watch on the ship."

Caersyn looked to Rahl. "Enter that."

"Yes, ser." Rahl was already writing what the pier mage-guard had said, if adding a few words to make the report clearer.

"We'll add watch reports for the undercaptain and the captain," added Caersyn.

After Niasl had left, Rahl wrote up the two watch reports, under Caersyn's direction, and carried them to the two mage-guards' message boxes. When Gheryk returned, he read the report, but only nodded on his way past the duty desk, clearly preoccupied with something else.

Rahl wondered if it had to do with him and what Shyret represented, but he doubted it. While Shyret might well remain a problem for Rahl, Gheryk doubtless had far larger concerns than the shady trading of a Recluce factor.

At the end of the day shift, when another mage-guard appeared, Caersyn stood and stretched. "Ready to eat?"

Rahl was more than ready, since all he'd had since breakfast was the midday duty ration of bread and cheese, and he followed the older mage-guard.

As at Luba station, there were three tables in the mage-guard mess. One for men, one for women, and one for juniors, although Rahl noted that a female mage-clerk was seated at the lower end of the women's table. The junior table was empty.

Rahl took a seat at the lower end of the men's table.

"We're not real formal here," Caersyn said, "except for the places at the head. Those are in case the captain or undercaptain need to join us." He glanced around the table, where there were but five others. "It's a light night, because some of those without consorts go out on their own on sevenday." Caersyn raised his voice slightly "For those of you who haven't met Rahl, he got sent here after a stint as a mage-clerk at Luba station."

"Good training for here, they say," offered a graying and long-faced mage-guard. "I'm Hewart."

"Vosyn . . ."

The introductions went around the table as a mess attendant appeared and set several platters and pitchers down.

Caersyn served himself three chunks of the grilled fish and a heaping stack of hot rice cakes, and then covered them with fish sauce. "The mess meals here aren't bad, and you can't beat the price."

Rahl went easy on the spicy sauce, barely drizzling it on his fish and rice, but took a large chunk of the dark bread, the first fresh dark bread he could recall in a long time, perhaps since he'd left Recluce. As he ate, he listened.

". . . glad I'm not on tonight . . . Jeranyi bunch could be trouble . . ."

". . . worry about the Hydlenese . . . keep your shields up on that pier . . ."

"The portmaster should have put a Recluce ship beside 'em . . ."

". . . not one in port . . ."

"More's the pity."

"You hear about the new eatery opened down from Hakkyl's. Ventaryl says it's good."

Rahl recognized Hakkyl's, where he'd once had a good meal he probably shouldn't have splurged on, but the name Ventaryl also sounded familiar, but Rahl couldn't place it, even though he knew he'd heard it somewhere.

"He would . . . got nothing to spend his coins on but food."

Rahl continued to listen, and only answered politely on the few occasions when a question was directed at him.

When the meal ended, several of the guards, perhaps five or ten years older than Rahl, hurried out. Caersyn was talking with Hewart, and Rahl stood and turned. The woman mage-guard who was the last to rise from the other table looked familiar. Had she been one of those he'd encountered? He smiled faintly and looked away before she was aware of his scrutiny. He wasn't about to ask.

Instead, he headed for his small room. He might take a walk later, but at the moment, he just wanted to be alone, and to think. Behind his cheerfulness, Gheryk had been concerned about what he'd learned about Rahl from Jyrolt, and his concern had raised even more questions about what Shyret had really been doing. At the same time, what could Rahl do except learn his job and save coins?

At his new pay rate of three silvers an eightday, he could certainly send another letter to Deybri before long, but it would still be several eightdays before he had enough coins to pay for both the letter, the draft, and the assurance charge.

LXXXIX

Rahl hadn't slept all that well on sevenday night, although he'd been so tired that he'd had to stop reading the *Manual* because his eyes had stopped focusing on the words on the page. His thoughts kept going back to the points that Jyrolt had raised and Gheryk's concerns about them. Eventually, he did sleep, if fitfully.

There were even fewer mage-guards at breakfast, and Caersyn was not among them, although two of the three mage-clerks assigned to the station—Fhasyl and Zachyl—were already there at the juniors' table and eating heartily.

Vosyn called out cheerfully, "Morning, Rahl. You'll be standing desk duty with me today."

"Caersyn has eightday off?"

"This one, and he's headed to see his sister."

"More like her consort's younger sister. Hear she's really a beauty," said Hegyr, who nodded to Rahl. "They say some of the girls in Guasyra are beauties. You ever have any time to see them?"

Rahl offered a laugh. "See them? Yes. Do anything about it? Not exactly. Taryl kept us busy."

"They say he got on the Emperor's bad side. You hear anything about it?"

"I heard the talk, but I don't think it's true."

"Why not?" asked Hegyr, not challengingly, but with what seemed to be real curiosity.

"He's a strong mage," replied Rahl. "I've heard from senior mage-guards who should know that he's one of the strongest. If he'd gotten in trouble with the Emperor, then I think we'd either have had a new emperor or a dead ordermage."

Vosyn nodded, then gave a short laugh. "That's probably true, but your thoughtful answer takes all the pleasure out of all the rumors."

Rahl wasn't quite sure what he could answer. He just shrugged help-lessly.

Hegyr laughed raucously. So did the two mage-guards at the women's table.

"Maybe he'll keep you fellows from gossiping the way you're always accusing women of," added one.

"Watch out for Carlyse," advised Vosyn. "When she says she likes what you say, she's most dangerous."

"Watch out for Vosyn. He's worse," replied Carlyse dryly.

Rahl couldn't help smiling at the banter.

He finished his breakfast—overdone egg toast and dry mutton, with chunk of day-old bread and a healthy mug of ale—and then made his way to the duty desk. He hadn't been seated there long enough to more than check the duty log when Vosyn elbowed him.

"Undercaptain's coming," murmured the older mage-guard.

Rahl looked up, then stood as the undercaptain moved toward him. "Ser."

Craelyt was a slender man, and a good half head shorter than Rahl, but he carried himself with assurance, and muted chaos flowed around his shields. His brown eyes were alert and his face inquisitive as he studied Rahl, who could sense the chaos-probes against the light shields he'd come to maintain all the time. "You're Rahl?"

"Yes, ser."

"Order type, but highly skilled with weapons, is that right?"

"Jyrolt made the evaluation, ser. I just did my best."

"If he said so, none of us would dispute it. Just truncheon?"

"Truncheon and staff, ser." Rahl decided against mentioning his modest skills with a blade.

"Good." Craelyt smiled, an expression both warm and professional. "We're glad to get another good mage-guard." He glanced to Vosyn. "It's quiet today, and it will be till later. Tell him anything you think will help."

"Yes, ser."

With a nod to both mage-guards, the undercaptain moved away, almost silently, Rahl noted.

Craelyt had been quick and professional, and he'd offered a smile almost as warm as Gheryk's, but all his personal feelings were locked behind personal shields, and his were among the strongest Rahl had sensed in a long time.

"Good man, the undercaptain," offered Vosyn.

"How long has he been undercaptain here?"

"Six–seven years, I'd say. Gheryk was the undercaptain on the city side, and Craelyt was undercaptain here before the Triad made Gheryk the captain, and that was five years ago, just after I got here."

Rahl nodded.

"If you haven't already, write down in the duty log that I've taken the duty, and add that you're assisting under training."

Rahl had already written that Vosyn had taken the duty, but he added that he was assisting under training.

After that, for the entire day, there was only one report Rahl had to write up, and that was about a peddler unlicensed to solicit on the piers. He'd drawn a miniature crossbow—and been flamed down. The mage-guards had discovered he'd actually been a Jeranyi crew member. That explained how he'd even gotten past the outer pier guards.

Dinner on eightday was even quieter, and afterward, Rahl decided to take a walk on the piers to stretch his legs. He wasn't ready to wander around Swartheld—not yet.

When he left the quarters, it wasn't dark enough even to be considered twilight, despite the thickening clouds and the warm damp air rolling in from the northwest, both suggesting that more rain was on the way.

Pier one had only three vessels tied up, one without an ensign, but with the name SEADOG on a weathered plaque under and just aft of the bowsprit, and the others bearing the limp flags of Austra and Nordla. The *Seadog* was an ancient sea schooner without engines or paddles, and the other two were newer side-wheel steamers, with oak hulls, and both bore the signs of great care, with varnished railings and gleaming brasswork.

Rahl smiled as he made his way to the foot of the pier and past the portmaster's guard, who nodded and said, "Good evening, ser."

For a moment, Rahl was taken aback, almost looking around for a senior mage-guard before he realized that the pier guard was speaking to him. "Good evening."

Behind the guard was a raised stone stand with a vacant chair—the same one occupied by the first mage-guard Rahl had met in Swartheld, the one who had told him to register.

On the northern side of pier two, near the end, he could make out the bulk of a large iron-hulled vessel, probably the Jeranyi ship. He continued to walk toward it, although he did see another mage-guard ahead, walking in the same direction.

She paused short of the Jeranyi vessel, studying it, but turned as Rahl neared, waiting for him.

Rahl stopped short and nodded. "Good evening."

"You're not on duty." Her voice was firm, and almost as weathered as her face.

"No. I'm new." Rahl looked at her, sensing the chaos-energies behind her shields, realizing that she was only moderately strong in chaos-forces, certainly not able to overcome his shields, even though he was not sure they were yet what they had once been. "I just got here late on sixday."

"Oh . . . you're the one on desk duty. I'm Dalya." She smiled, then frowned. "I don't think we've met, but . . . you look familiar. Were you at Dibolti station?"

Rahl smiled in return, realizing where they had met. "No. I was an outlander. You were the one who told me to register when I first came to

Swartheld. One thing led to another, and I ended up a mage-clerk at Luba station, and I was sent here."

"Did you register?" There was a hint of laughter behind the hard voice.

"You scared me so much I went and registered right after I did what I was supposed to do."

A laugh followed his words. "Would that I had that effect on more."

Rahl glanced past Dalya at the Jeranyi ship. Even the steel plates of the *Wavecrest* felt as though they carried a low-level form of chaos.

She turned and followed his gaze. "You're an order type. What do you think?"

"Even the plates reek of chaos. I'm new, but I'd not want to encounter them at sea."

"There's not much we can do so long as they behave."

"One of the Hydlenese didn't yesterday."

"Saelyt told me that, but I didn't have any trouble with them or the Jeranyi."

"What do they carry on a vessel that large?"

"Whatever they want . . . Yesterday, they were unloading up when I came on duty. They had a couple score barrels of pickles. At least, you could smell the vinegar, and they had writing on the barrels that I thought said 'Feyn pickles.' "

Rahl hid a frown. Pickles so early in fall? Unless they were last year's pickles, but why would a Jeranyi ship be carrying Recluce pickles to Swartheld? Pickles weren't something that he'd seen on a manifest . . . but there was something about pickles that he should remember . . .

"What are you thinking?" asked Dalya.

"About pickles." He shook his head, hoping he could remember what he'd been thinking about. A raindrop struck the back of his neck, and he glanced up. The clouds overhead were definitely darker. "It won't be long before the rain gets heavier."

"I need to check pier three. Might as well get started before I get soaked."

Rahl nodded and walked back along the pier with her, passing a Sligan brig, then a battered Lydian side-wheeler with a bastard rigging he'd never seen before.

"Do you know who you'll be patrolling with yet?"

"Myala."

"Good woman, but don't ever try to mislead her about anything. She won't forget it."

"Thank you."

"I wouldn't have said much, but you did listen to me once."

Rahl laughed softly, the sound barely louder than the faint pattering of raindrops on the stone of the pier.

At the end of the pier, Rahl nodded slightly. "Good evening." He didn't really want to get drenched in the rain that was increasing in intensity with every moment.

"Good evening, Rahl."

As he hurried back toward his quarters, he just wished he could remember what it was about pickles. But he also had to take some time to relax and open himself up to sensing what lay around him.

XC

On threeday evening, after supper, Rahl left the mage-guards' mess and walked toward the pier-guard station. After five days of mostly sitting and writing, he was more than ready to leave the port area around the mage-guard station.

He'd already learned from the station manual that, during the working day, two mage-guards were stationed on the piers, one as a roving patrol, and the other with the two main pier guards at the entrance to the pier area. There were also guards armed with falchionas at the foot of each individual pier. After sunset, when the piers were cleared of vendors and wagons, only one mage-guard remained on a roving duty, and the two armed guards remained at the main guard post. There were no individual pier guards after sunset unless ordered for special reasons. The pier-duty mage-guard was supposed to remain close to the main guard post at night, except when conducting periodic inspections of the piers.

As he neared the main guard post, he could hear Dalya talking to the pier guards. ". . . still worry about the Jeranyi . . . good thing the Hydlenese left, but watch the crew on *Byneget Bay* if they come by . . ." As she caught sight of Rahl, she stopped. "You headed out?"

"Just for a walk. I need to refresh my memory about where things are."

Dalya nodded. "Understand there's a crowd at the Red Pier. If you go by there, I'd have the truncheon out."

"I appreciate that." Rahl smiled pleasantly.

Dalya turned back to the pier guards. ". . . probably not see much for a while yet . . . don't take your eyes off the Jeranyi . . ."

Rahl continued south until he reached the avenue that ran from the northeast to the southwest and several blocks farther to the southwest joined the boulevard that fronted on the Nylan Merchant Association building. He realized he was coming close to disobeying Captain Gheryk, but so long as he merely walked by the Merchant Association, he wasn't probing or seeking anything . . . and besides, it was on one of the main streets.

The fall evening was early enough that couples walked down the stone way in the center of the divided avenue under the false giant acacia trees, and carriages and a few riders traveled on both sides, although the traffic was far more sparse than in midday. Most glanced at Rahl—or his uniform—and nodded politely, but did not let their gaze linger on him long at all.

He did let his order-senses take in anything around him.

As he neared a bench on which a couple were entwined more closely than might have been decorous, he sensed someone behind the tree to their right, and he could sense a certain amount of greed—possibly a petty cut-purse. Rahl stepped past the couple, who barely seemed to note him and toward the tree, drawing his truncheon and wishing he had enough order control to become less visible.

A youth darted from the tree, then froze, looking at Rahl.

"Ah . . . ser . . . good evening, ser," the young man finally stammered.

"What you had in mind could get you in most serious trouble," Rahl said quietly. "Since you didn't do it . . . I won't take you in, but if I see you up to it again, it will go twice as hard." Even projecting his displeasure, he doubted his words would have that much effect. An offense hadn't actually been committed, and that meant he couldn't do that much except warn the boy.

Surprisingly, the youth paled, actually quivering, and stepped back. "Yes, ser. I won't even think of it. Please, ser."

"On your way."

"Yes, ser."

The young man practically ran from Rahl.

By now the couple had disentangled, and Rahl turned. "I wouldn't get so lost in each other in a place where cutpurses could make off with something." Then he nodded and continued on.

Behind him, he could sense relief.

"... if he told ... your consort ..."

"... not as though it's an offense ..."

Rahl shook his head slightly.

Before long, he crossed to the boulevard, but to the paved sidewalk on the north side. Ahead to his right, he could see Eneld's, where the lamps were still lit, but the lacemaker's windows were shuttered and dark. Across the boulevard to his left, he could see the Nylan Merchant Association. As he neared it, he slowed his steps, realizing that he still had his truncheon out.

A clerk Rahl did not recognize walked swiftly toward him and passed him, giving Rahl a quick and perfunctory nod. Rahl didn't sense any chaos or anything but faint worry and returned the nod.

Across the boulevard, the door to the Association building was locked, and the interior dark. The gates to the warehouse yard were also locked, but he could see at an angle a light in the upper-level window where Daelyt and his consort lived—or had lived, since Rahl had no idea even whether Daelyt was still working for Shyret.

Rahl shook his head.

Given the whiteness he'd sensed around the head clerk the year before, and Daelyt's consort's inability to walk far, he doubted that Daelyt had left the Association. Then, what would happen when Shyret was rotated to another port? Did the clerk remain? Follow the managing director? Find another position?

Rahl didn't know and wished that he did.

He turned his attention to the cantina immediately on his right, glancing in through the one window. Seorya was serving a couple—obviously consorted or related, or they wouldn't have been at the same table. She looked up as he passed, but he sensed no real interest or recognition, and that was for the best.

Rahl walked another two blocks, then crossed the boulevard and walked back on the south side. He did not change his pace as he passed the warehouse yard gates once more, although he did try to sense anything out of the ordinary. All he could feel was a sense of whiteness, not overpowering, but stronger than when he had been a clerk.

At least, he thought it was stronger, but, honestly, how would he know, with all the changes that had affected his order-abilities. He also sensed the presence of a pair of guards, not near the gates, but one near the doors to each of the two warehouses. The additional guard was a change. He did not sense anyone within the main building as he passed, but that did not surprise him greatly.

By the time he'd walked back to the avenue, the couple had vanished, and the walkway and the stone benches were all deserted. His boots echoed hollowly on the stone, the sound matched only by the clopping of the now-infrequent carriages.

He had to wonder about the greater chaos-mist around the warehouses—and the night guards—but there wasn't much that he could say or do. Not for now. He continued to make his way back to the mage-guard quarters.

XCI

Sixday morning began as any other morning had over the past eightday at the duty desk, except that Rahl was paired with Carlyse, the older red-haired chaos mage-guard who sparred verbally with most of the men.

Her first words to Rahl were delivered softly and with a smile. "You were a pretty boy before Luba, weren't you?"

Her words did not so much take him off guard as bring up the image of Deybri saying, "You're too much of a pretty boy."

When he didn't answer immediately, Carlyse laughed, not mockingly. "You've had to live with that, haven't you?"

Living with memories and thoughtless words was just a small unpleasantness in life. That Rahl knew, but he could still feel a torrent of rage that the words had stirred up. Had Puvort gone after him because he was good-looking? Had the magisters dismissed him because his looks had convinced them that he couldn't learn or think?

"That's the advantage of being a mage-guard, Rahl," Carlyse went on conversationally. "Your looks don't matter nearly so much. The uniform and what you accomplish do." She glanced at what he had already written. "Good hand, too. Mind if I ask how you ended up as a mage-guard?"

"I was a clerk, and I saw something someone didn't want me to, but I didn't think they knew I'd seen it. I was wrong, and I woke up working in Luba, without any memories at first. The overseers discovered I could write and handle numbers, and they made me a checker. Then Taryl found me and told me I'd been dosed with something. He made me a mage-clerk and started training me." Rahl shrugged.

"You were a mage, but you were a clerk?" Carlyse raised her finely drawn left eyebrow.

"I had limited abilities, and Recluce tossed me out because they said I wasn't trainable. I got a job as a clerk here. I did register, of course. But Taryl discovered that Recluce hadn't been training me right."

"He's good at that. He did something like that with Saelyt, and some others." Carlyse looked up as Captain Gheryk neared the desk. "Nothing happening, ser."

"That's always good." The captain paused. "Portmaster says we may be getting another Jeranyi ship. If you'd pass that along to the pier mages."

"Yes, ser."

Gheryk glanced at Rahl. "You finding your way around, Rahl?"

"Yes, ser."

"Good." With a warm smile and a nod, Gheryk turned and headed toward his study.

"Two Jeranyi ships here at the same time . . . that's always more work."

"Because the crews are disorderly?"

"Half of them act as if they don't care if they live or die, so long as they get what they want right now. We end up flaming or sending one or two to Luba or the quarries nearly every single time they port."

"Is that a lot worse than the ships from other lands?"

"They all have problems at times, but the Jeranyi make the others look like scared schoolchildren." Carlyse stood. "Just hold the desk. You know enough. I want to tell Suvynt about the Jeranyi while he's still at the pier gate. I won't be long."

While he sat alone at the duty desk, Rahl struggled to deal with the anger raised by Carlyse's question. Why did everyone have expectations based on what they thought they saw?

"Ser . . . ?"

Rahl looked up to see a youth, barely old enough to have the first hints of a beard, walking toward the duty desk. His accent was Hamorian, but not from a region Rahl recognized. "Yes? Can I help you?"

"I'm supposed to do something like get a bracelet that says . . . I don't know." The young man was trembling.

"Let's start at the beginning," Rahl said, extending his own order-senses and discovering the weak, but definite, hints of chaos, around the youth. "What's your name? Were you born in Hamor?"

"Kiehyt, ser. I was born . . . ah . . . in Cienta. That's near Heldya."

"Who told you to come here, and why?"

"I was working in the bakery, I mean, we came to Swartheld 'cause my uncle has a bakery, and the drought burned out the old place . . . ground wasn't that good anyway . . ."

Rahl listened politely.

". . . and Uncle Jeahat, he couldn't get the coals to light, and I just sort of looked at them, and they did, and he got scared and told me to come here and never come back there, and that if I didn't, he'd tell the mage-guards, and you'd send me to the quarries."

"No one is sending you to the quarries." Rahl hoped that was so, because the youth didn't look strong enough to lift a shovel, let alone massive stones. "We do need to . . . take care of some things, but you'll have to wait a few moments for another mage-guard to help."

Carlyse showed up within moments, looking from the youth to Rahl.

"Kiehyt. He's a chaos type," Rahl explained. "Not too strong yet, and he lit the oven coals in the bakery, and his uncle threatened him with the quarries and worse if he didn't come here. That much reads true."

Carlyse studied the youth, then nodded. "He'll have to go to school in Diancyr. He's older than most of them, but that's not a problem."

Kiehyt looked from Rahl to Carlyse and back to Rahl.

"You could be a type of mage," Rahl said, "but you need to go to a special school."

"I know my letters . . . I do. Don't put me in gaol."

"You need to learn more," Rahl said.

"No one's going to put you in gaol," added Carlyse.

"Come with me, Kiehyt." Carlyse's voice was gentle. Then she looked at Rahl. "I'll be with Saelyt beyond the undercaptain's office if anything comes up."

Rahl's anger had been submerged by his concerns for the very frightened Kiehyt, but once the youth left with Carlyse, even more questions burned through his thoughts. Why did people just throw out people who were different? Or those who didn't—or couldn't—obey every word slavishly?

Was there really that much difference between Puvort and the boy's uncle?

He didn't have answers to his questions, but he was far calmer when Carlyse returned, after completing arrangements for quartering the youth and having him sent south to Diancyr, a small town on the outskirts of Cigoerne where the mage-clerk school was located. After that, the rest of the morning and early afternoon went without incident. So far as he could tell, the duty mage-guard was basically a coordinator, backup, registry-receiver, and record-keeper combined, which explained to Rahl why the duty was rotated so that every mage-guard only stood duty—either day or night—only about once every two eightdays.

Rahl had noticed that he had not seen much of Undercaptain Craelyt, and it was a surprise when the undercaptain appeared at the duty desk in late afternoon with another mage-guard.

"Ser." Rahl stood.

"Rahl, I thought you ought to meet Myala, since she'll be the one you'll be partnered with for the next few eightdays." Craelyt offered a warm smile, stepping back and inclining his head to a wiry brunette with a sharpish nose and intense gray eyes. Chaos lurked behind moderate shields—chaos and controlled anger.

"I'm pleased to meet you," Rahl offered. "Captain Gheryk had high praise for you. He also told me to listen to you."

Myala nodded politely but not effusively. "I'll meet you at the duty desk right after early breakfast on eightday."

"I'll be there."

"It's good to meet you." She stepped back and glanced at Craelyt. "Thank you, Undercaptain. Now, if you'll excuse me."

"You're excused, not that I have to, since you're not on duty." Craelyt smiled warmly once again, waiting until Myala had departed before turning back to Rahl. "She's all to the point, Rahl, but a good mage-guard. She doesn't stay around here much when she's off duty, but that's understandable, since she has two daughters and a consort who like to see her."

Craelyt offered a parting nod and slipped away soundlessly.

Rahl sat and read the station manual again, then stood and stretched, then riffled through the duty log, reading some of the older entries.

"Rahl . . . you're getting jittery." Carlyse gestured. "Go inspect the piers. See if that other Jeranyi ship has come in yet. If it has, take a good look, and then tell Suvynt and come report to me."

"I can do that." He rose quickly.

"You don't have to be that enthusiastic." But she smiled.

Once outside the mage-guard station, Rahl stretched, then turned toward the piers. The afternoon was warm and muggy, as if the moisture dropped by the intermittent rains had never quite left.

Pier one was almost filled, if with smaller vessels, mainly from Austra and Nordla, and vendors and teamsters were everywhere, but matters were orderly. Rahl nodded to Hegyr, who was the roving pier mage, as they passed.

On pier two, there were fewer vessels, including the *Wavecrest* at the far end. Before Rahl reached the Jeranyi ship, he approached a wagon and team loaded with amphorae and barrels beside a comparatively large but four-masted and square-rigged Sarronnese ship. He could smell something pungent on the light breeze blowing off the harbor, something like vinegar.

"Friggin' careless sow's ass . . . idiot offspring of a gelded boar . . ." One of the teamsters was swearing and tossing heavy pieces of pottery into his wagon. He glanced up and broke off the stream of epithets. "Just upset, ser. Hoist crew dumped the amphora right on the stone . . . said it was our fault, left it for us to clean up."

"What was in it?"

"Some kind of special vinegar." The teamster's eyes were watering.

Rahl could feel the stinging in his own eyes as well. "That's unfortunate, but you're doing a good job cleaning it up." He nodded. That was one of the responsibilities of the teamsters. They could be fined—or worse—if they left garbage or refuse on the piers. So could a ship's captain.

The teamster nodded, then went back to work, mumbling in a lower voice. ". . . good job . . . frigging good job him . . ."

Rahl was slightly annoyed, but he couldn't blame the man. Besides, he was trying to think about where he'd smelled that before. Where had that been? He frowned.

Pickles! There had been barrels and barrels of Feyn River pickles in the warehouses at the Nylan Merchant Association, and they'd come off a Jeranyi vessel, and Chenaryl had been evasive about why a Jeranyi vessel had been carrying so many barrels of something with as little value as pickles. That had bothered him then, and it bothered him even more with what Jyrolt and Gheryk had said—and what Dalya had said the other night. But how could he find out if that had been true?

He was still thinking about barrels of pickles when he finished his tour of the piers and returned to the duty desk.

"Anything of interest?" asked Carlyse.

"Nothing besides a few broken amphorae of special vinegar. The teamster had them mostly cleaned up when I got there. There's still only the one Jeranyi ship at the piers."

"That's fine by me."

Gheryk came by several times, but only nodded, and Rahl was more than happy to leave the duty desk when Carlyse was relieved. He was quick to make his way to the mess. His stomach was growling in protest.

Through the first part of the meal, he kept thinking about vinegar and pickles, and finally decided to ask what had been fretting at him.

"Caersyn," Rahl began, "if we see something or remember it, or want to cross-check, is there any way to look at the manifests that are given to the tariff enumerators?"

For a moment, Caersyn's face had no expression. "What do you mean?"

"Well . . . the enumerators don't inspect every bale and barrel. What if we discover that a ship has been declaring, say, raw wool, but it's only raw wool on the outside of the bale, and finished cloth on the inside. It might be a good idea to see how many times that ship has been declaring low-value things . . ."

"Oh . . . I see what you mean. I don't know." He turned. "Do you, Woralyt?"

The heavier graying mage-guard nodded. "We've had to do that occasionally. Not in a while, though. We can go over to the enumerators and ask to review manifests . . . but you have to do it on your own time, not duty time, and you can take notes, but you have to leave the manifest there."

"I just wondered."

"That's how," replied Woralyt.

Caersyn nodded in agreement and took a long swallow from his mug.

Rahl decided he had to look at some of the manifests of a year ago . . . as soon as he could. He also needed to keep practicing Taryl's methods for expanding and improving his use of order-skills. He could sense that his shields were getting as close to what they had been, if not even stronger, and he was beginning to regain some of what he had lost, particularly in a deeper sensing of order and chaos; but he still only had the most general sense of weather and no sense at all of what lay beneath the surface of the ground. And he certainly couldn't bind anything together with order.

XCII

As with all mage-guards, Rahl had one day an eightday for his own use, and that was sevenday. After breakfast, he immediately headed to the building adjacent to the mage-guard station—the one that housed the tariff enumerators.

The staff enumerator behind the counter that he still remembered was pleasant enough.

"What can I do for you, ser?"

"I need to look at the cargo off-load declarations for all the Jeranyi vessels for last fall."

"You'll have to go through quite a few. We file them by day by ship name."

Rahl nodded. "That will be fine."

"Ah . . . I have to put your name and a reason on the form."

"I'm Rahl, and I think some factors may have been accepting mislabeled bulk goods." Rahl smiled politely. "Is that enough?"

"Yes, ser. If you'd come this way?"

Rahl followed the enumerator clerk down the corridor to a dimly lit chamber at the back of the building. File chests were stacked neatly in five rows, each row five chests high, and more than twenty long.

"The nearest chests here are the most recent. The ones more than five years old are sent to Cigoerne. Let's see . . . last fall should be about here." The clerk paused. "Let me or whoever's on the desk know when you leave."

"I will, thank you."

Even with his knowledge of manifests and declarations, it took Rahl most of the morning to find what he sought. Three Jeranyi ships had delivered Feyn River pickles to the Nylan Merchant Association in the fall of the previous year. One had been the *Wavecrest*, the other two had been the *Stormrider* and the *Dawnbreaker*. Each had delivered ten barrels. He wrote down the ships, quantities, dates, and consignees on a sheet of paper he'd taken earlier from the duty desk.

The number of barrels bothered Rahl. No one shipped that few barrels of something like pickles thousands of kays on an outland hull.

Then he returned to the desk. "Thank you."

"Did you find what you were looking for, ser?"

"I found the information. It may not be as helpful as I'd hoped, but thank you." Rahl made his way back to his quarters, where he tucked his notes into his copy of the *Manual,* before heading out for the afternoon.

High hazy clouds suggested that the afternoon would be hot and muggy, and he was sweating even by the time he nodded to the main pier mage, and well before he was walking down the shaded avenue toward the Nylan Merchant Association. The pickles had bothered him before, but he hadn't known why. He still didn't, although he felt he should.

There were far more people out on sevenday, and Rahl found it interesting to see and sense reactions. Most just ignored him or nodded politely. A handful, usually younger less-well-attired young men, tried to slip away before they thought he noticed them. Children often stared, and their mothers whispered to them.

It was almost midday when he reached Eneld's cantina, and, without really knowing why, he opened the door and stepped inside.

Seorya glanced at him and saw only the uniform. She looked back to the two women she was serving. One man at a corner table froze, radiating fear.

Rahl had to wonder what the fellow had done, but he just surveyed those in the cantina and then stepped back outside, catching one murmured comment.

". . . hate it when they do that . . ."

Rahl smiled wryly, then, as he had before, continued westward on the boulevard for several more blocks before crossing the street and heading back eastward on the southern side. He kept to a leisurely pace, but extended his order-senses as he neared the warehouse gates. This time they were open, but no wagons were in evidence, and Tyboran barely looked at Rahl. That was fine with Rahl. The two warehouses still radiated their diffuse white chaos, but Rahl couldn't identify any specific source from where he was outside the open gates. But then, he hadn't been able to do that when he'd been in the warehouses a year earlier.

Rahl glanced through the window of the Association building. Daelyt was sitting alone at the wide desk, talking to a trader or factor. Rahl nodded

He hadn't expected any change, but he was glad to know his feelings had been right. He didn't sense Shyret anywhere around, and he kept walking.

He was sweating even more heavily by the time he returned to the station, but he only paused to get some beer in the mess, before returning to the duty desk and a balding and black-eyed older mage-guard he did not know.

"I'm Rahl."

"Ashant."

"I've just been here an eightday, and I start on roving pier duty tomorrow. Is there a library here, or some books on cargoes and that sort of thing?"

"You mean what to look out for?" Ashant frowned, then nodded. "It's not a library, but there are a couple of bound folders on some of the tricks smugglers and shippers use."

Rahl wasn't certain that would help, but it certainly couldn't hurt. "Thank you. Ah . . . where are they?"

"Right in the small bookcase there." Ashant pointed to the wall beside the duty desk.

Rahl wanted to hang his head. Right within cubits of where he'd been sitting for almost an eightday. He could have been reading them for days. What a waste of time!

"They're pretty old, but they might be some help."

"I hope so." Rahl found a stool and began to read. The introduction was almost a primer on trade and declarations and manifests, things he'd learned in a few days in Nylan. The first section past that was more helpful, with a description of the tariff structure and rationale, the duties of the tariff enumerators and the support requirements laid upon mage-guards.

One sentence caught his attention. "The Emperor does not restrict or prohibit any goods or cargo, but the attempt to avoid tariffs by hiding or mislabeling is an offense against the Emperor . . ."

That meant that anyone could off-load anything, so long as they declared it accurately and paid the tariffs. Some tariffs were so high as to be almost prohibitive—luxury metals like gold and jewels in any quantities, or things like aqua regia, or aqua gloria, or cammabark, or explosives—but those made sense for various reasons. Tariffs almost everywhere were based on value in the case of precious metals and jewels, and explosives and corrosives could cause great damage if improperly handled or labeled. But vinegar wasn't that corrosive.

Rahl kept reading.

XCIII

On eightday morning, Rahl made sure that he was at the duty desk especially early. Even so, he'd only been standing there a few moments before Myala came in at a brisk walk.

"You're here. Good. Have you looked at the duty logs?"

"Yes. The Jeranyi ship—it's the *Wavecrest*—is still tied at pier two. The captain had said we should expect another one, but it hasn't arrived yet. There wasn't any trouble last night, and we have three offenders and one mage-clerk student waiting for upriver transport to Luba and Diancyr . . ."

"That's enough." Myala walked to the desk, ignoring Hewart, who was due to be relieved, and picked up the duty log. After scanning it a moment, she set it down. "Let's go."

Rahl followed her out of the building.

Without looking at him, Myala asked, "Do you know why they sent you here? Only a handful of the mage-guards here are order types. You're usually sent to the city station or Cigoerne or small towns."

"Taryl and Jyrolt were the ones who decided. They didn't tell me."

Myala's steps slowed for just a moment. "Taryl recommended you?"

"Yes."

"That's not good. When he recommends, he's usually trying to head off trouble, and it's never small trouble."

"That doesn't sound good." Especially since what Rahl had overheard confirmed what Myala was saying.

She headed for the main pier guard station where Hegyr had just finished relieving Niasl.

"It's all quiet, Myala. Only five or six vendors out there. No wagons. Niasl had to run off a pair of trollops earlier." Hegyr stood beside the pedestal that held the mage-guard chair. The umbrella was still folded.

Myala snorted. "You won't find any teamsters out on eightday, but trollops will try for their coins wherever and whenever they can find a willing sailor. It should stay quiet for a while, but if I see anything urgent, I'll send Rahl back. Otherwise, we'll check in after we patrol all the piers." With that, the compact mage-guard turned, taking quick and precise steps toward the base of pier one.

Rahl had to take three hurried steps to catch up with Myala, who, he was discovering, moved everywhere as if she were constantly in a rush.

Pier one was somewhat more than half-filled, with three ships—two schooners and a small coastal side-wheeler—on the north side, and an ancient Suthyan brig at the last set of bollards on the south. A vendor with a grill was already soliciting the crew.

"The best fowl in Swartheld . . . hot and juicy . . ."

Rahl had to admit that the grilled fowl did smell good, but Myala barely looked at the vendor or at the small boy who sat on a box beside the grill.

As Rahl accompanied Myala toward the base of pier two, she asked, "What do you know about the Jeranyi ship?"

"It's big and iron-hulled, and it's been here for an eightday now, and they haven't loaded or unloaded cargo in the last few days. There's an aura of chaos around it." Rahl paused, realizing something else. "Also, all the mage-guards have been talking about what a problem the Jeranyi crews are, but we haven't had any problems reported."

"Hmmmm . . ." That was all Myala said.

Before they reached the Jeranyi vessel, they passed a Brystan long-hauler, with side-wheels and the modified rigging that seemed to be common among Nordlan ships. The brightwork shone, and the crew was holystoning the deck.

Beyond the Brystan ship was an empty berth, and then the Jeranyi vessel. As he and Myala neared it, Rahl could see a pair of guards, attired more like ruffians than seamen, standing guard on the quarterdeck just beyond the top of the gangway leading up from the pier.

"Look at the guards," Myala said. "What do you see?"

Rahl looked again, with both sight and senses. The guards were armed with sabres that seemed similar, if not identical. Both were clean-shaven . . . "Oh . . ."

"What? Don't just say, 'Oh,'" said Myala tartly.

"They're dressed like ruffians, but everything else says they're more like guards or marines or soldiers."

"At least you can think, even if it takes some prompting."

Rahl could feel that hidden anger rising, and he wanted to use his truncheon on the waspish and condescending mage-guard, but he pushed the feeling away, finally managing to say, "I've only been a full mage-guard for two eightdays, Myala, and I'm certain I have much to learn."

Rahl could sense that she was taken aback at his words although she said nothing for several steps. Then she paused and continued to look at the ship.

So did Rahl, although he tried to use his order-senses as much as his eyes. The diffuse whiteness of chaos did not seem either stronger or weaker than when he had observed the ship before, and that suggested that it was either a part of the ship—or of cargo that had not been off-loaded.

"You're using order-sensing. What does it tell you?"

"There's something chaotic there, but I can't tell if it's the ship or cargo. It's not the crew, though."

"Could be explosives or powder. Sometimes they sense like chaos. That's what Hewart says."

"If they're really pirates, they'd have cannon . . ." Rahl studied the hull more closely. "It looks like the shinier sections below the railing they're smaller."

"Those are concealed cannon ports. You're probably sensing the powder in the magazines."

That was likely, but Rahl had his doubts that was all he sensed.

"I don't like it that they've been here an eightday. Ships don't make coins tied up for long periods in port, even pirate vessels. They could be waiting for a ship to leave, one with a profitable cargo, maybe the Brystan."

Rahl could tell that she wasn't convinced by her own words.

Abruptly, she turned. "Nothing will happen this early. We might as well finish the first tour, and then we'll leave a watch report with the duty desk."

Again, Rahl had to hurry for several steps to catch up with her. After even such a short time, Myala was wearing on him. He wondered how her consort stood it, but maybe he needed the time when she was on duty to recover from her presence.

XCIV

Oneday was far different from eightday. Even by midmorning, the piers were crowded with wagons and vendors, unlike the comparative handful of sellers on eightday. There was actually a cool breeze, and the sky was bright and clear. While Rahl was grateful for the cooler and drier weather, he worried about the Jeranyi vessel still hulking at the end of pier two, with yet another set of clean-shaven guards. The diffuse white chaos that enfolded the ship seemed unchanged.

"Still the same," noted Myala. "They're waiting for something. That something won't be good."

Rahl didn't think so, either, but what could he say, especially as a very junior mage-guard who'd been warned away from looking into his own past too closely?

As they moved away from the far end and toward the base of pier two, Rahl caught sight of the captain walking toward them, on the far side of the small tent of a vendor who was grilling kebobs of ground and spiced meat. Gheryk continued to stroll casually toward the two mage-guards before stopping and smiling broadly.

"Myala . . . keep on your patrol. I need a word with Rahl, and then I'll send him back to you."

"Yes, ser."

Rahl could sense her puzzlement, but he was more worried about the deeper feeling of irritation and concern that Gheryk was trying to conceal behind his shields.

"The tariff enumerator wanted to know if something was happening." Gheryk looked at Rahl with a faint smile. "I thought I told you just to watch things for a while, until you knew more."

"Yes, ser. I haven't pried around the Nylan Merchant Association, ser. But . . . the other day, when I was on the piers—Carlyse sent me out, ser—there was a teamster cleaning up some broken amphorae, and they had vinegar in them. The smell reminded me of something I'd forgotten."

"Go ahead." The captain's voice was neutral.

"Just before everything happened last year, I'd noticed that the Merchant Association had received some barrels of Feyn River pickles. I remembered that because of the smell of vinegar that was spilled on the pier on sixday. I couldn't help thinking about it, because the Association never shipped pickles, and I'd asked Chenaryl—he was the warehouseman. He said they'd come off a Jeranyi ship. I never had a chance to do anything, but I wanted to find out if he was telling the truth."

"Was he?"

"Yes, ser," Rahl admitted. "Three Jeranyi ships sent the warehouse pickles. That was what I found out from the enumerators' manifests. Ten barrels each."

"What does that mean to you?"

"I don't know, ser. Except with the valuations, no one could make coins on pickles."

"So the head of the Association was part of a Jeranyi smuggling operation. Not all that smart of him. He's taking all the risks, and that leaves them in the clear. No wonder you ended up in Luba."

"Yes, ser." Rahl wanted to say that he knew there was more, but he couldn't even guess what that might be.

"We'll watch for that, and I'll ask the enumerators to let me know if any Jeranyi ships off-load pickles or anything in small quantities." Gheryk smiled almost paternally. "You've got a good head for this sort of thing, but you need more experience. You've told me, and that's fine . . . but don't do any more snooping. Just watch the ships and the piers and tell me. You understand?"

"Yes, ser."

"Good. Now . . . get back on your patrol with Myala, and if she asks, and she will, tell her I was giving you another standard talk about not seeing smugglers tied to every bollard."

"Yes, ser." Rahl nodded politely. He could sense that the captain, while mollified to some extent, was still worried and irritated.

Myala was watching as another Hydlenese ship was maneuvering into the south inshore berth on pier three when Rahl caught up with her.

"What was that all about?"

"The captain was giving me a talk about not seeing smugglers tying up at every bollard. He also said to listen to you and not to say much until I know more." That was mostly true, and Rahl had the feeling that, for all of her other strengths, Myala was not that good at reading feelings.

"Good advice." She laughed, a harsh bark, and gestured toward the sleek modified schooner. "See that rig? They can put on enough sail to run down anything—or outrun most anything. It's probably one of those pirate-smugglers that the captain told you not to look too hard for. We can't do anything unless they break the Codex, but the crews are usually more trouble."

She started toward the end of the pier, skirting past a vendor, when Rahl sensed pain and fear. He turned, sensing a man wrenching something from a girl behind the tent.

He sprinted toward the base of the pier, at an angle, pulling his truncheon out. The two teamsters beside a wagon jumped out of his way, as did several others.

"Thief! Thief!"

"That way!"

The man dashed toward the side of the pier, then saw Rahl. For an instant, his face froze, until he saw the truncheon, and out came two long knives. He rushed Rahl in a headlong attack.

Rahl barely had to move, stepping to his left, and striking hard enough to snap the bone above the wrist on the arm nearest him. The pain froze the man for an instant, and that was enough for Rahl to use the truncheon a second time. The second knife clanked on the stone.

Even so, the man staggered and tried to lurch away.

Rahl clipped him on the skull, pulling the blow slightly, but with enough force that the combination of order and impact was enough to leave the thief sprawled on the stone.

Rahl rolled him over and pried the purse from his limp fingers, then stood.

At that point, Myala arrived.

She looked at the two teamsters. "You two! Carry him to the gaol. Rahl, here, will show you the way. Rahl, you can write up the report there. Then go to the pier gate and wait with Hegyr, and I'll pick you up there. It won't hurt to have two mages there. If there's anyone else, you might be able to sense it."

Rahl nodded, then handed her the purse. "He took this from a girl in the tent by the vendor we were passing."

"I'll get it back to her."

Rahl turned to the teamsters and gestured. They lifted the limp figure and followed him. As he led them across the base of the pier, he realized that no one on the pier had said anything, and that all the locals had scattered out of his way. That suggested that the mage-guards weren't that averse to using chaos-flame with bystanders nearby.

Once they reached the gaol, Rahl held the door for the teamsters, who lowered the thief onto the tiles and departed the building as quickly as they could.

The duty gaoler looked at the limp figure laid on the floor of the entry to the gaol, and the crooked arm, then at Rahl, who still held his truncheon. "Another idiot. Lucky he ran into you, rather than one of the chaos types." After a pause, he added, "You need to fill out the report."

"You'll have to help me. I can write it, but I don't know the form. This is my first eightday."

The gaoler shook his head and took a sheet from the small file case on the table. "You have to learn, but the older ones always do this. Most of the spaces tell you what to fill in . . ."

After Rahl finished writing out the gaol report, including the details on the theft and his own actions, he signed the form, and two more guards carted the still-unconscious thief through an archway and to a cell. Then Rahl left the gaol and made his way back toward the pier station, where Hegyr was monitoring wagons and pedestrians.

As he neared the pier mage-guard, Rahl observed the undercaptain talking to Hegyr. Before Rahl could do more than smile, Craelyt turned and left Hegyr, drawing Rahl well away from the street. "Young Rahl, it's good to see you out here on the piers. Where have you been? I don't see Myala."

"I just took a thief to the gaol, ser."

"Still alive?"

"I saw him first and took him down with a truncheon." Rahl smiled wryly. "I did break one arm and knocked him out."

"That's what you're supposed to do. You filled out the report?"

"Yes, ser."

"I understand you were over at the tariff enumerators' on sevenday."

"Yes, ser."

"I had another question for you. Isn't it rather ambitious to think you can detect smuggling after just a week at the duty desk?"

"I wasn't trying to detect smuggling, ser, but I wanted to see what sorts of cargoes the Jeranyi were declaring. Everyone has been saying how dangerous they are, and . . . I just thought . . ." Rahl offered a hopeless shrug. "Anyway, ser, the captain already set me straight, ser."

Craelyt laughed, a soft sound that was somehow warm, yet without humor. "Just remember, Rahl, we do see more than what might appear, even with outland trading houses."

"Yes, ser."

Craelyt clapped Rahl on the back. "Good work with the thief. Just keep to the piers, and you'll do fine." The undercaptain smiled again, then walked briskly away, in the direction of the mage-guard station.

As he stood there for a moment, Rahl felt the slightest chill, warm as the fall sunlight was. There was something about the undercaptain . . . more than the shields that hid everything personal about him. But what could Rahl do?

He shook his head and walked to join Hegyr.

"What did the undercaptain want, if I might ask?" murmured the other mage-guard from where he sat on the raised chair, his eyes on the wagon approaching the piers.

"He wanted to know what I was doing away from Myala. I took a thief to the gaol. So he decided to encourage me to keep paying attention to what I learned on the piers."

"Sounds like the undercaptain. Always wants us to stick to the job at hand. 'You've got enough to do handling your own duties. Don't try to do anyone else's.' "

Rahl had to work to keep from laughing at Hegyr's imitation of the undercaptain's false-hearty tone.

XCV

Rahl woke before dawn on twoday. For a time, he just lay on the narrow bed, enjoying the comfort of the thickest and most comfortable mattress he'd ever had, but his thoughts began to drift to the uneasy feelings he had about the Jeranyi and Shyret. Even though he'd promised he wouldn't attempt to snoop around the Nylan Merchant Association, he couldn't help but feel how much easier something like that might be if no one could see him. He knew that was possible for both ordermages and chaos-mages, and he recalled vaguely something about light being made to flow around things. Had it been something someone had said, or had it been in the *Basis of Order*? For a moment, he wished he still had his copy. Then he recalled what Taryl had said about his need to "feel" rather than think when he learned a new skill.

But how could he feel light passing around him?

He sat up and put his bare feet on the floor. The smooth stone tiles felt cool, especially in the warm confines of his chamber. While he had left the small window open, there had been no breeze the night before.

Could he think of . . . no, *feel* light as if it were a breeze? The only source was the window, just like the breeze—when there was one.

Rahl closed his eyes, trying to feel the light rather than see it.

Something happened, and he opened his eyes. He was in total darkness. How . . . what? Had he gone blind?

Just as suddenly the light reappeared.

What had occurred? Why hadn't he been able to see?

He knew he had to feel to use his order-skills, but he still had to understand what had happened. He'd been feeling the gossamer-like flow of light—and he had sensed the flow, but when he had opened his eyes, he hadn't been able to see. Why couldn't he see? He could see now.

He took a low and slow deep breath and tried to relax, again closing his eyes. This time, when he felt something he couldn't quite describe happening, he did not open his eyes, but just tried to experience the feeling. As though he were in darkness, he could in fact order-sense what was around him. Still holding on to that feeling, he opened his eyes into darkness, yet he could sense everything around him.

After several moments more, he released the sense of diverting light, and his vision returned.

It wasn't his eyes, but why couldn't he see when he had the light flow around him? It was like he was in his own private cave. Suddenly, he felt stupid. In a cave, or in a windowless room at night, there was no light to see by. If he flowed the light around himself, his eyes had no light to see with, either.

Getting the same feeling was far harder with his eyes open. After a time, he did manage it, but he had to stop the exercise because he was feeling light-headed. At that point, he washed and shaved and dressed and headed for the mess.

Only Hegyr, Vosyn, and Carlyse were seated when he walked in and sat down across from Vosyn and Hegyr.

"Good morning."

"It is morning," conceded Vosyn. "Whether it's good remains to be seen."

"Any morning that you're healthy and alive is a good morning," replied Hegyr.

"So you say." Vosyn took a bite of egg toast, chewing it slowly, before saying, "We've had worse egg toast. I don't remember when, though."

Rahl started in on his platter the moment the server set it before him, and the egg toast didn't seem all that tough to him. He hadn't realized just how hungry he was until he'd finished off two stacks of egg toast, four tough strips of ham, and a greenish sour fruit that was too squishy for his liking—not to mention more than a mug of ale.

Carlyse glanced over from the women's table to Rahl. "Bringing down that thief yesterday must have taken all your strength."

"It just happened. He was stupid." Except, Rahl realized, the thief had been hidden behind the canvas of the vendor's tent and probably hadn't even seen the two mage-guards and doubtless thought he was unseen.

". . . Myala was pissed, you know," Carlyse bantered. "She really likes to flame thieves. Hear you smashed his arm. Wager you never thought that mangling a thief's arm was going easy on him."

"Real easy," added Hegyr.

Rahl had his doubts, recalling his days as a loader in Luba.

"Hear about south Merowey?" asked Vosyn. "No one's saying much, but the administrator's declared independence."

"Independence from what?" asked Carlyse. "The world?"

"I'm serious. So is he. You know he's Prince Golyat, and he's the older brother of the Emperor. They say that he's getting help from Fairhaven. Under the table, of course. That's why there aren't many warships at their berths across the harbor."

Rahl managed not to frown. The *older* brother wasn't the Emperor? Yet he was an administrator who served the Emperor.

"That won't last long," opined Hegyr.

"You'd better hope not," countered Vosyn. "The last revolt, the Emperor drafted a good fifty mage-guards to help the army."

"That was more than a century ago."

Rahl ate and listened.

"As good as their chatter is, Rahl, you'd better get moving," suggested Carlyse, "unless you want to give Myala good cause for writing you up for being late. She goes by the manual and then some."

That was the last thing Rahl wanted, and he left the mess quickly. He was at the duty desk just behind the waspy mage-guard.

"Let's go," was all Myala said.

Rahl checked his truncheon, adjusted his visor cap, and followed her.

Myala's and Rahl's first sweep of the piers confirmed that the Jeranyi vessel, with its guards, was still tied at pier two.

By midmorning, when Myala and Rahl were making another tour of pier three, Rahl could see another iron-hulled vessel doubling up at the end berth and the gangway coming down onto the pier. "There's that other Jeranyi ship."

"We'll take a closer look." Myala's voice was almost an order.

Rahl found himself bridling at her tone, but he said nothing, just matched his pace to hers as they walked toward the just-docked ship.

Once they neared the Jeranyi vessel's stem, Rahl began to count the crew. Those he saw numbered more than twice what he'd known on the *Diev*, and he had the feeling that there were far more crew members belowdecks than he saw topside.

"Too large a crew for a merchanter," Rahl observed quietly.

"Obviously." Myala's tone was dryly condescending.

Rahl could make out the same concealed gun ports as on the other Jeranyi vessel, and roughly the same level of concealed chaos as he'd noted there as well; but, after Myala's last comment, he kept his observations to himself. He also didn't see any signs of the deck crew preparing to off-load cargo, and that was normally one of the first things a merchanter did once she was secured to the pier.

On the way back down the pier, on the far side, Rahl smiled pleasantly at an attractive brunette girl, clearly using her obvious charms to help her father sell an array of brightly colored shirts and tunics. Then, as they passed the cart and half tent that shielded the father and daughter from the sun, Rahl waited until Myala looked in the other direction. Then he concentrated on feeling the light flow around him, although he kept walking a pace behind her and to her left.

He could sense her turning, then looking. "Rahl?"

He waited only until she turned her head in the other direction before releasing his hold on the light flow. "I'm right here. I had to adjust my boot."

Her eyes narrowed. "Adjust your boot, both my left elbows. You were ogling that vendor girl."

Rahl shrugged as expansively as he could. "What can I say?"

"Not on duty."

"I won't."

"You just did." Myala snorted.

"I won't do it again . . . at least for a while." He offered a grin.

"Don't be so obvious."

That confirmed for Rahl that Myala, and possibly many of the chaos-type mage-guards, had limited order-senses. Certainly, Khaill and Jyrolt—and Craelyt and the captain—possessed a fuller range of senses, but then, since the mage-guards co-opted all the mages in Hamor, one way or another, it made sense that many, especially the patrol mages, were not so talented.

While the day had already been long and was far from over, he'd learned more than a few things, but he was far more worried about what he hadn't learned—such as the connection between the Jeranyi ships and Shyret and the Nylan Merchant Association. He tried to tell himself that it wasn't his duty.

That didn't seem to help much. He still worried.

XCVI

Twoday evening, in deserted areas around the quarters, Rahl worked more on using the light flow and on sensing his way around when using it. He had to give up early because it was exhausting, even though he didn't feel worn-out at the time. He just felt drained and light-headed afterward. He had to drag himself back to his quarters, pausing to banter some to Vosyn in the corridor, before escaping to his chamber and his bed, where he soon collapsed into a deep sleep. That lasted until sometime before dawn, when a series of nightmares tormented him.

When he awoke he was sweating, but he remembered little of the dreams, save a short fragment where he and Deybri were on separate ships passing in the afternoon, and all he could do was watch while she was carried farther away. Something about that bothered him even more than the idea of separation, but he couldn't put a finger on it.

He cleaned up, shaved, dressed, and hurried through breakfast to get to the duty desk before Myala. As he waited, he had to wonder why Taryl had been so insistent on his being stationed in Swartheld. Even to him, it was clear that the chaos-mages had a clear advantage over him in dealing with problems. Rahl's sole edge was that he seemed to be able to sense some trouble earlier than they could.

Myala said little once she arrived, just nodded and headed out, clearly expecting him to follow her. Once again, Rahl had to take several quick steps to catch up with her.

By the time Rahl and Myala had reached the end of pier two on their first patrol, a third Jeranyi ship was tied up at the seaward end, almost directly opposite the first Jeranyi ship. Like the other two, the new arrival was overcrewed, guarded, and not preparing to off-load cargo immediately.

"Have to admit that I can't ever remember seeing three of those big Jeranyi ships in port at the same time." Myala turned. "Best that you go and report that to the duty desk, and the captain and undercaptain if they're in the station. Otherwise, leave a watch report, but make sure that the duty mage gets it to them. Then I'll meet you at the main pier guards' station."

"I'll take care of it." Before Myala could add some caustic remark or observation, Rahl was on his way.

He didn't have to look far for the undercaptain because Craelyt was actually at the duty desk when Rahl hurried inside the station building.

"Ser!"

"What sort of trouble are you about to report, Rahl?"

"We now have three of the large Jeranyi vessels, two on pier two and one on pier three. All have concealed gun ports, and all are carrying excessively large crews, and those crew members look more like soldiers or marines than merchant crew. Also, there doesn't seem to be any cargo coming aboard or being off-loaded, even for the one that's been at pier two for over an eightday."

"Have we had any crew trouble from them?" Craelyt glanced to Nyhart, the duty mage-guard.

"No, ser. None at all."

Rahl forbore to point out that alone was unusual.

Craelyt shook his head regretfully, "You know they're trouble, and so do I, but we really can't do anything so long as they behave themselves, just because they *might* do something against the Codex."

"Yes, ser."

"It's important you watch closely, though," Craelyt added. "If they're going to try anything, now would be the time, with the revolt brewing in

Merowey. More than a few of the Emperor's warships have been dispatched to keep arms and ammunition from being shipped to the rebels. If they can pull off something here, there aren't enough warships to chase them." He looked to Rahl. "Just keep a careful watch on them."

"Yes, ser." Rahl inclined his head politely, then stepped back, turned, and left the building. With the undercaptain's shields firmly in place, Rahl hadn't been able to sense anything except what Craelyt wanted to reveal— and that had been mild concern. Rahl was more than mildly concerned, even if he couldn't have explained why, but he hoped that he'd been able to hold most of those feelings behind his own shields. He also couldn't see why Craelyt was just mildly concerned when the Jeranyi might be taking advantage of a revolt—especially one started by the Emperor's brother. That whole situation seemed strange to him. Wasn't the older brother the one who inherited power? Why was it different in Hamor?

The late-morning sun beat down through a cloudless green-blue sky, and the fall day was beginning to feel more like summer by the time Rahl reached the station where the pier guard and Hegyr were monitoring the traffic entering and leaving the piers. Rahl blotted his forehead and adjusted his visor cap.

"What's happening?" asked Hegyr from the high and shaded seat, even as he kept his eyes and senses on the wagons and pedestrians moving toward the piers.

"There's another Jeranyi ship on pier two. Just reported it to the under-captain. That makes three."

"It's not as though we need more trouble. Poor Niasl."

"He's on the night watch?" asked Rahl.

"He is." Hegyr broke off. "You there! Stop that wagon! Now!"

Rahl moved forward, his hand on his truncheon.

"Your rear axle's cracking," added Hegyr, "and we're not about to have broken-down wagons on the piers. Go up to the turnabout and get back here. You try to make the pier, and you won't have a wagon."

The teamster nodded. "Yes, ser."

Beneath the man's impassive exterior, Rahl could sense anger, probably because the fault wasn't his but belonged to the trader who owned the wagon.

At that moment, Myala arrived. "Did you find them?"

"I reported to the undercaptain and told the duty mage-guard. The undercaptain said to keep a close watch on them."

"We'll take a look at pier three first, this time."

Behind Myala's back, Hegyr gave the smallest of headshakes and then a sympathetic broad grin. The wide piers were crowded; but as always, everyone stepped back when either of the two mage-guards moved toward them.

At the foot of pier three, Myala turned to Rahl. "You go up the south side, and I'll take the north. When you get to the end, we'll meet, and you tell me what you've observed." Then she left Rahl standing there.

He wanted to shake his head at her abruptness. Instead, he took his time, moving along the edge of the pier, trying to sense chaos or trouble. He was halfway out on the wide pier when he saw ahead of him a wagon bearing the familiar emblem of the Nylan Merchant Association, drawn up short and waiting for another wagon to move into position alongside a Spidlarian clipper. Rahl walked over to the teamster seated on the wagon. "I haven't seen Guylmor recently."

"He hasn't been around for almost a year."

"Why not?"

The teamster shrugged. "He was killed in a loading accident at the warehouse. That's what they told me."

Rahl could sense both the truth of the man's statements—and his unease. "Sorry to hear that. Where are you picking up cargo?"

"The *Duumbreaker* way at the end. If that boat's ass up there will ever get out of the way, beggin' your pardon, ser."

"Do you know what it is?"

"Never really know, not until it's off-loaded. They give me the declaration, and I give it to Chenaryl. That's his problem. Usually, from the Jeranyi, it's something in barrels." The teamster shrugged.

"Good fortune!" Rahl nodded and moved on.

As he walked away from the teamster and past the clipper toward the Jeranyi vessel, Rahl had a definite feeling that he was being watched, perhaps even by a mage. Guylmor's "accident" also disturbed him more than a little, though, because it had occurred not that long after he'd been drugged with nemysa, and there were too many coincidences for his liking. There was also almost no hard proof of anything, and both the captain and under-captain weren't that different from the magisters in being unwilling to take Rahl's unsupported word about matters.

XCVII

On fourday, Rahl woke with a feeling of apprehension, yet outside his window, the sky was clear, the air refreshingly dry and cool. At breakfast, Carlyse was even more ebullient than ever.

"Rahl . . . when are they going to give you your own duties?" She laughed, loudly. "It's got to be soon, because Myala just glared when I asked how you were doing, and if she couldn't find anything to complain about, then there wasn't much."

"She was just in a hurry to leave," Rahl countered. "She's in a hurry all the time."

"Can't be all the time," interjected Hewart. "She's got two daughters."

Both Dalya and Carlyse shook their heads.

Caersyn howled with laughter. "If anyone could hurry that, she could."

Zachyl, alone at the juniors' table, looked up wide-eyed.

Rahl still had the feeling it would be some time before the captain or the undercaptain would let him do much in the way of true mage-guard duties without supervision, and he still rushed through his breakfast.

Once he was on the piers with Myala that morning, her matter-of-fact attitude and marginal instruction and information seemed to confirm that feeling. Her only truly informative comment did not come until close to midday on pier one, when she gestured toward a heavyset man wearing a loose and cheap cloak of thin material.

"Cutpurse or thief, if he gets the chance. Thin fellow under the cloak. He may drop the cloak on someone, and like as not, he'll jump into the water and dodge out to one of the fishing boats. Not a real fishing boat, but it's hard to tell."

"Then he's going after a lot of coin."

"Exactly. Not worth the trouble otherwise."

"Do we . . ."

Myala laughed, softly but harshly, because the man turned and walked back off the pier. "He won't be back today. He knows we'd recognize him. He might come here for days before he acts. Good thieves aren't hasty."

Rahl hadn't thought of using the harbor water as a way to escape chaos-bolts, but it certainly made sense.

After that, the rest of the morning was quiet, although Rahl could still detect the miasma of white chaos every time he and Myala passed any one of the three Jeranyi ships. All three maintained their armed guards at the top of the gangways, and there was no sign of any cargo loading or unloading.

Slightly after midday, for the first time since he'd been a mage-guard in Hamor, he saw a wagon platform with slaves being sold—two lithe women and three youths, and all were dark-haired. According to the Codex, slavery was not allowed, but permanent indenture was. Rahl didn't see any difference in that, except that children of those permanently indentured could not be indentured for the debts of their parents—or by their parents.

He glanced to Myala. The older mage-guard said nothing, although Rahl could detect greater tenseness in her as they passed the wagon.

"... look at those bodies ... strong and agile ... look close now!"

Rahl couldn't help the flashback to Fahla and her brother, nor the rush of anger at Puvort and the magisters. To enslave or indenture children because they had not turned in their father? That still struck him as wrong, no matter what the magisters said.

"Some of them have no memories," Myala said quietly.

"Why?" asked Rahl in a low voice.

"The harlots who drug men and steal from them are heavily dosed with nemysa and indentured. They say that's because they wouldn't last in the quarries."

"And the children?"

"They're cutpurses and thieves. It's kinder than working them to death."

Rahl had his doubts, and he couldn't help but wonder how much choice any of them had had. He almost laughed bitterly when he considered how little choice he'd really had. Those in power, and those who drafted rules like the Codex, seemed to think there were more choices in life than there were. What choices did an urchin child have? Being indentured to who knew what kind of owner? Begging? Stealing? Or starving to death?

Thankfully, for the next several rounds of the piers, Rahl didn't see any other indenture wagons.

Slightly after midafternoon, as they left pier one and headed for the base of pier two, Rahl caught sight of two empty Nylan Merchant Association wagons just ahead of them moving through the crowds to pier two. Since there weren't any Recluce ships tied up, he suspected that they would be unloading from one or both of the Jeranyi ships.

Fhasyl, the juniormost mage-clerk, was hurrying through the crowd, looking this way and that—until he caught sight of Myala and Rahl and trotted up to them.

"Sers!" The young man stopped short and inclined his head. "Mage-Guard Rahl, the undercaptain has requested that you join him and the armsmaster in the exercise area." He turned to Myala. "He should be back by late afternoon, ser. That's what the undercaptain said."

"Patrolling might be easier," Myala said dryly. "Only come back if you can still walk."

"I'll manage." What he might manage was another question. He turned to Fhasyl. "Lead on." Part of that was because he'd only seen the arms exercise room once, and he'd had the feeling it wasn't used that much. Fhasyl was likely to get him there more directly than he might on his own. Even so, he kept his eyes and senses alert, and that was difficult because he didn't like the idea of the Merchant Association's wagons heading toward the Jeranyi ships.

"Ser," inquired Fhasyl, "is it true that you were once a laborer in Luba?"

"Yes. I spent a year there."

"But . . . ser . . . ?"

"I was an outland clerk here before that, and I had some small magely abilities. I was registered, but didn't think I'd ever be a mage-guard. Then I lost my memories and ended up in Luba."

"Did you really break a thief's arm?"

"Yes. He had a pair of long knives."

"And you did it with a truncheon?"

"I'm not exactly a chaos-mage, Fhasyl."

"Oh . . ." The mage-clerk led Rahl past the quarters building and to a side door on the north side of the gaol. "Here, ser."

"Thank you."

Fhasyl vanished even before Rahl had the door open.

Inside waited the undercaptain and another mage-guard.

Craelyt smiled politely and nodded to the wiry man in the black of an armsmaster. "Ah . . . Rahl . . . I showed Boltyk your arms evaluation, and we thought it might be best to see how it compares with our standards. Then, there's always the possibility that you might have something to teach us."

Rahl pushed away his irritation at being pulled off the pier and smiled politely, inclining his head to both. "Sers, I will be most happy to help in any way possible."

"I'd thought a series of sparring matches might be most illustrative," suggested the undercaptain.

"Since your weapon is the truncheon, perhaps we could begin there," added Boltyk.

Unlike Craelyt, the armsmaster's shields were less than complete, and Rahl could sense the combination of doubt and contempt as Boltyk moved to the center of the exercise space and raised a golden oak truncheon slightly longer and thinner than Rahl's black weapon.

Rahl laid his visor cap aside on the bench against the wall and slipped his truncheon from its holder before moving out opposite the armsmaster.

"Begin," said Craelyt quietly.

On the possibility that Boltyk was letting the contempt show in order to make Rahl angry and careless, Rahl simply wove a defensive screen for the first several passes, getting the feel for the other's moves and rhythm.

Craelyt did not depart but watched closely.

Rahl saw several openings, but let them pass, taking his time and measuring the other, realizing that Boltyk was not nearly so good as Taryl or even Khaill with the truncheon.

Then Boltyk lunged, and Rahl anticipated both the half feint, and the counter, and slashed the truncheon out of Boltyk's hand. Then he stepped back.

Rahl could sense the astonishment, but Boltyk merely reclaimed the weapon. "If you would . . . another round."

Rahl nodded. "As you wish, ser."

The second time around, the armsmaster was more cautious, but, again Rahl disarmed the other and just tapped his shoulder blade and darted back before Boltyk could react.

The armsmaster stepped back and turned to Craelyt. "The report on his skills with a truncheon is more than accurate. At least, with truncheon against truncheon."

"Let us see about staffs," said the undercaptain.

Boltyk produced two staffs, padded, if lightly. Rahl took the one that was slightly shorter because he liked the feel and balance better. He set his truncheon on the bench beside his cap.

After two rounds, the results were similar.

"I'd like you to defend against a practice blade, next," said Craelyt.

"In that case, ser, might I use a practice truncheon?"

"Take mine," suggested Boltyk.

In the two rounds with the truncheon against the blunted practice falchiona, Rahl managed to keep the other's blade from ever hitting him and disarmed Boltyk both times.

Rahl had to keep his emotions under shield and to avoid smiling in satisfaction as he inclined his head to the armsmaster. "Ser . . . if you require more . . ."

"I think you've answered any doubts the armsmaster might have had about your abilities, Rahl." Craelyt smiled warmly.

Rahl caught the sense of consternation and dismay from Boltyk. The doubts, if there had ever been any, had not been those of the armsmaster, or at least, not primarily or exclusively his.

"If you have no further use for me here, sers, the piers are crowded today, and there are three Jeranyi vessels out there . . ."

"Oh . . . of course, you should return to duty," said Craelyt.

"Thank you, ser." Rahl retrieved his visor cap and truncheon and stepped outside, leaving the door just barely ajar. There was a slight breeze, one that felt more than welcome after the closeness of the exercise room. He paused, extending his order-senses, to see if either man would reveal anything.

". . . better than any bravo on the streets with his weapons. No one here can touch him, except maybe Gheryk."

". . . still worry about his standing up to chaos," replied Craelyt.

". . . something that goes with being a mage-guard . . ."

". . . later, then . . ."

Rahl quickly moved away from the gaol building and walked swiftly ·toward where the pier mage-guard would be stationed. He glanced to the west. There, the sun was barely above the hills behind the far side of the harbor, and the handful of warships at the naval piers were already in shadow.

As he hurried along the side of the crowded road, peddlers and even teamsters moved or slowed to let him pass, but his progress was still slower than he would have liked. Ahead of him he could see a Nylan Merchant Association wagon moving past Caersyn rather than Hegyr. He looked farther south and thought he saw the other wagon. While he did not want to sprint after it, he moved even faster. From what he could tell the wagon held only barrels—pickle barrels; but they didn't quite feel like pickle barrels, although he could smell the faint odor of vinegar long before he reached the pier-guard station.

There, he found Caersyn. "I didn't know you had pier duty."

"I don't, not usually. Hegyr got so sick this morning that the undercaptain asked me to fill in." Caersyn's eyes remained fixed on the next wagon that was headed past him toward the piers.

"Have you seen any Nylan Merchant Association wagons?"

"There was one a bit ago. There may have been more, but I don't pay much attention to whose wagon it is, just what's on it."

Rahl could sense the evasions behind the other's words.

Whhsttt! A chaos-bolt flew from somewhere.

Rahl strengthened his shields, but, even so, was rocked back, and barely managed to avoid crashing into the stone pier that held the mage-guard's chair.

Whhstt! Whsstt! Whsst!

For a moment, it seemed as though chaos-bolts were everywhere, and most of them seemed aimed at Rahl, although his shields held. Screams and yells added to the confusion, and the handfuls of people on foot near them scattered. The teamster who had just driven his wagon past Rahl and Caersyn struggled to keep control of his team.

The chaos-bolt attack ended as suddenly as it had begun, but by the time Rahl gathered himself together, he could detect no sign of free chaos . . . or of a chaos-mage. Either that, or the mage had such tight shields that he or she was effectively invisible to Rahl's order-senses.

Caersyn held on to the chair in which he had had been seated. He leaned to one side, looking dazed. Rahl glanced past the stone post that anchored one of the iron gates to the piers, not that Rahl had ever seen it closed, and along the wall beyond it. He thought he sensed something, but he was looking for the duty pier guards, either, and that was unusual.

The faintest scraping sound alerted Rahl, and he turned to see six men in worn blue moving toward him from behind a donkey cart. Two had sabres, rather than falchionas, and one carried something like a billhook, while the other three had cudgels. Rahl glanced toward Caersyn, but the mage-guard lay sprawled in his seat, moving slightly. Rahl couldn't very well leave, although that would have been the sensible thing to do had he been there alone.

Rahl had the truncheon out and immediately charged the man with the billhook before the man could lift the heavy weapon. Rahl got well inside both blade and hook. The truncheon went into the man's throat, and Rahl's knee into his groin. The billhook clattered on the stone.

Then Rahl dodged the wild swing of a cudgel and struck across the fellow's forearm, reinforcing the blow with order.

He danced back, away from a wiry bravo with a sabre. Unlike the others, the man was at least a passable blade, and Rahl had to deal with him while trying to avoid the others as they closed on him.

The other blade darted toward Rahl.

Whssst! Whsst! Two chaos-bolts slammed into the second blade, and he went down.

A weaker chaos-bolt burned the shoulder of a cudgel-wielder.

The remaining blade danced to one side, as if to keep Rahl between him and whatever chaos-mage was coming to Rahl's assistance. He moved again, and Rahl struck. The sabre went flying, but before Rahl could move to disable him, another chaos-bolt, one of the weaker ones, caught him full in the face, and he pitched forward onto the stone pavement.

Rahl turned.

Myala stood less than fifteen cubits away.

The man who had carried the billhook was dead. So were the two blades. The others had run off.

Myala looked at Rahl. "For an ordermage, you're not bad."

"I'm very thankful you arrived." Rahl looked up the mage-guard chair, where Caersyn sat, still looking slightly dazed. "Are you all right?"

"I will be . . ." Caersyn shook his head. "That first chaos attack . . . it took a lot out of me. I could barely get those last two off."

"Chaos attack?" asked Myala.

"I thought I'd wait for you here," Rahl said. "We've always done that before. Just after I got here, someone fired chaos-bolts at us. Then, right after that, those six came in."

"Against two mage-guards?"

"Caersyn was knocked out for a bit," Rahl explained. "They must have sent most of the chaos against him. I don't know where the pier guards went."

"One had gone to relieve himself, and the other started running when the chaos started to fly," Caersyn said. "I saw that."

"We'll take the pier," Myala said, looking at Caersyn. "You're in no shape to finish your duty. You go find the undercaptain or the captain and tell him what happened. Have the guards send out another pier guard."

"Probably best that way," Caersyn admitted. "You're sure?"

"What else can we do?" asked Myala. "It's getting toward sunset, and the piers are clearing anyway."

Only after Caersyn was well away, and Rahl had dragged the three bodies and their weapons over to the gate pillar and laid them out, did Myala speak. "Weak-assed excuse for a chaos-mage. And letting a guard go off . . . that's inexcusable. Why was he on duty? Do you know?"

"He said he was filling in. Hegyr was too sick to stand duty. That's what he said."

"I don't like it. The weakest chaos-mage in the station with an order-mage."

Rahl had his own doubts, but he said, "They might not have known I was going to be here. They started the attack with chaos-bolts."

"Hmmm . . . that's true." Myala gestured to the teamster moving southward and away from the piers. "Hurry it up. Time to clear the piers!"

The driver flicked the long leads, and the wagon, laden with bales of wool, began to move a trace more quickly. Behind him were two vendors, pushing carts.

"What about the Jeranyi crews?" asked Rahl.

"Some have been going ashore, but they've been going like most crews . . . that's in groups of two or three, or sometimes all alone." She gestured toward the three bodies. "They don't look like Jeranyi. The others didn't, either."

"So what were they after?" asked Rahl.

"I don't have any idea. That's why I sent Caersyn to get the undercaptain."

Just before the sun finished dropping behind the distant hills, three pier guards appeared with a cart. Two began to load the bodies onto the cart. The other took station by the gate.

Suvynt had accompanied them. "I'm here to relieve you. The undercaptain asked if you would meet him at the duty desk to brief him on what happened."

"We can do that." Myala's words were clipped.

Rahl could sense her displeasure.

Neither spoke until they were a good fifty cubits from Suvynt.

"Would have been easier if he'd just come out and seen it," was all that Myala said.

Rahl couldn't help but feel that somehow the attack had been aimed at him, but how could he say that? He had not one shred of proof, only his feelings that it was all linked to the pickle barrels, the Jeranyi, and Shyret and the Nylan Merchant Association warehouses. The problem was that he couldn't figure out any possible reason why the Jeranyi would want him dead. How did any of them even know who he was? And why would the Jeranyi even care?

Almost as soon as they stepped into the mage-guard building and neared the duty desk, Craelyt appeared, as if he had been waiting for them.

"I'm sorry that I couldn't come out to see what happened, but the captain left word that I was to meet him here for something urgent." Craelyt's shields were even tighter than usual, and not a trace of any emotion escaped, but his voice was warm. "I heard that you both had a difficult time at the pier-guard station."

"You could say that, ser," replied Myala.

"Caersyn said that there was an attack on the pier-guard mage post," Craelyt said. "I'd like to hear your account of what happened?" His eyes were fixed on Rahl.

"After I finished sparring here, ser, I returned to the pier-guard mage post to meet up with Mage-Guard Myala . . ." Rahl related what had happened from the chaos-bolt attacks onward. He did not mention the Nylan Merchant Association wagons or the pickle barrels. ". . . and then Myala sent Caersyn to find you. He didn't seem in any condition to finish his duty."

"He'll have to have several days off," Craelyt agreed. "Were you able to discover anything about the chaos-mage who attacked? Did you see who it might have been?"

"No, ser. There was almost no warning at all," replied Rahl. "Then, as soon as Caersyn was staggered, the bravos and ruffians appeared."

"Did they say anything?"

"No, ser. Not a word."

"Did you notice anyone entering or leaving the piers while you were engaged?" Craelyt turned to Myala. "Did you?"

"I was close enough to see that no one did. The vendors and teamsters ran and stayed away until it was over."

"Does either of you have any idea what this was all about . . . or what they might have had in mind?"

Rahl had an inkling of what might be involved, but nothing solid enough to be considered an idea, and he wasn't about to tell Craelyt. Telling the undercaptain didn't feel right, and Rahl in fact didn't actually *know*. "I don't know, ser. I thought it might have something to do with the Jeranyi ships, but Mage-Guard Myala has been watching them, and there's nothing strange going on there."

"Is that right?"

"I wouldn't say quite that, Undercaptain," replied Myala, "but we haven't seen anything so far."

"Why do you think they might be a problem?"

"Because, ser, we've never seen three of their pirate vessels in port for this long at any time since I've been a mage-guard," replied Myala. "That suggests trouble."

Craelyt kept questioning them until he had asked the same questions in different forms at least three or four times. Then he smiled and looked at Myala. "I'm sure your report, and that of Mage-Guard Caersyn, will cover everything. You both have had a long duty. Go and get some rest."

"Yes, ser."

Rahl followed Myala out of the station, but she did not even look back as she kept walking away, presumably to her home and quarters. Rahl could detect a mixture of both anger and apprehension.

He watched her for a moment, then looked toward the quarters building and the mess. Finally, he turned toward it. He *was* hungry.

XCVIII

All through dinner, as he ate mechanically, Rahl kept thinking about the attack and all the pickle barrels on the Nylan Merchant Association wagons. It would have been better if the last bravo hadn't been flamed, because they might have been able to find out who had been behind the attack. He frowned. That blast had come from Caersyn, but Caersyn wasn't at the table, and neither was Hegyr.

"You're looking worried," offered Vosyn.

"More than that," added Hewart.

"How often do attacks on mage-guards happen?" asked Rahl.

"Not that often, but they do happen," replied Vosyn.

"Usually at night," said Niasl. "I've had two in maybe ten years. Always with a renegade mage, like what happened to you. They know they have to distract or disable the duty mage-guard. It's usually so that they can raid one of the ships while most of the crew is ashore."

Rahl nodded. What had happened to him just didn't feel like that. "How is Hegyr? Caersyn said he was pretty sick."

"He's better," interjected Dalya from the women's table. "He was hotter than burning cammabark this morning."

Cammabark! Vinegar! Rahl almost froze in his seat. Why hadn't he remembered sooner? Was that what was in the pickle barrels? Another thought struck him—he shouldn't have been able to smell the vinegar in pickle barrels because they should have been sealed more tightly. So the pickle barrels had been opened recently. But why would Shyret be in league with the Jeranyi?

Rahl forced himself to finish his meal before excusing himself and heading in the direction of his room, but he didn't enter it, but slipped out the side door and made his way through the dampish evening toward the main mage-guard station building.

Nyhart looked up from the duty desk. "Evening, Rahl. You're not doing some evening duty, are you?"

"No. I was just thinking about something. Have you seen the captain?"

"No. He was supposed to meet with the undercaptain, but he never did. That's what the undercaptain said. No one's seen Captain Gheryk since midafternoon. He might be meeting the regional commander about the rebellion in the south. Do you want to leave a report for him? Or see the undercaptain? He's around somewhere. He might be out on the piers."

"I'll see what I can do. Thank you." Rahl smiled and made his way from the building. He didn't want to talk to Craelyt, and he didn't like the fact that the captain was nowhere to be found. Yet what could he do?

He couldn't just report his suspicions, not after the captain had pointedly told him not to investigate anything to do with his past, and yet he didn't feel that he could just let things happen, not the way he felt.

Finally, he turned toward Swartheld itself and walked southward through the darkness beside the road from the piers. When he neared the pier-guard station, he raised the light shield, keeping well away from Suvynt. The night mage-guard turned and studied the area along the wall from the pier gate, but when Suvynt turned away, Rahl climbed up the low wall, still holding his light shield. That wasn't hard, since the wall had been designed far more to keep wagons out of the pier area than to stop single individuals from leaving.

Once on the other side, Rahl moved a good hundred cubits away from the piers before dropping the shield. Once he reached the section of the avenue where it divided into two sections, he crossed the pavement and took the walkway that ran down the middle, moving at a fast clip, truncheon in hand. Overhead, the leaves of the giant false acacias rustled in the slight evening breeze that brought a faint scent of cooking from somewhere.

He passed a couple on one bench, and neither more than looked at him. Two young men nodded politely as they passed him, and Rahl only sensed mild apprehension. Then, as he neared another bench closer to the boulevard, someone sprinted away across the far side of the avenue. Rahl did not follow him.

When he neared the Nylan Merchant Association, he could tell that Eneld's cantina was still open, as much as from the boisterous voices as from the mixed odors of melted cheeses and fried meats.

> . . . *sailors are a fearsome lot but never fear,*
> *A sailor's gone so much he's never here . . .*

Laughter greeted the last line of the song.

Rahl shook his head. Even from across the boulevard, he could feel the diffuse white chaos, far stronger than the last time he had passed by, but he walked farther to the west before crossing the street, using a passing carriage as partial cover, and then headed back eastward.

From a good fifty cubits away, Rahl could see that the warehouse gates to the Merchant Association were shut. He could also sense two guards, and possibly three, stationed in the courtyard near the gates. While the warehouse doors were also closed, Rahl felt that there were more than a few people inside.

Before reaching the ironwork gates, Rahl raised his light shield, and then began to climb the brick wall, carefully, and as quietly as possible. Just before the top, his left trouser leg caught on a projection or a rough brick, and he almost lost his balance and nearly tumbled backward. Breathing heavily, he hung on and lowered his leg, eventually working it free and creeping upward. At the top, he peered over, but did not see or sense anyone nearby.

Climbing down was almost as difficult, because he did not wish to land hard enough to alert the guards. He finally stood in the shadowed corner between the warehouse and the outer wall, dropping the light shield and using his order-senses to survey the courtyard.

Two guards watched the gates, and three men were harnessing a team before the stables under a single lantern. Across the courtyard, the door to the Association building was open. As Rahl watched, two other men each carried two large buckets inside, then returned almost immediately with their buckets clearly lighter, only to fill them from the barrel set just outside the door. From what Rahl could discern, both men were Jeranyi.

He had to hurry, and he had no time to return to the mage-guard station. Girding his light shield around him, he moved quickly along the front of the first warehouse until he came to the door. He paused for a moment. There had been no light from the quarters above, and he didn't sense any life there, and there should have been. Yasnela never left the quarters in the evening in the middle of an eightday, and Daelyt never left her. Rahl's lips tightened.

The warehouse door was latched from the inside, but he could smell vinegar, an odor so powerful that it forced its way out through the narrow crack between the sliding doors. Rahl took another step, and his boot skidded off a rope that ran between the doors on the stone. He staggered but caught his balance.

His truncheon was too wide, but his small belt knife might be thin enough to reach the latch through the crack and lever it up. He eased the knife from his belt and slipped it between the timbered edges of the two doors. The tip just barely reached the metal latch bar, but skittered off the metal.

Could he somehow lengthen the end of the blade with order?

Rahl concentrated on that, but either the order-extension wasn't long enough or strong enough because the blade tip still skittered off the iron. Then he placed the blade tip against the latch lever or plate, concentrating on linking the two with order, and slowly sliding the blade upward.

The latch unlocked with a muffled *clunk*.

Rahl froze for a moment, certain that someone must have heard, so loud had the sound appeared to him. But the men harnessing the wagon teams didn't even look up. After a moment, Rahl slowly eased the doors apart, just wide enough for him to slip into the dark warehouse. He managed to avoid the rope as well. Quiet as he tried to be, his soft footsteps echoed slightly.

Even with his night vision, it was difficult to make out much in the dark space before him, but he used both vision and order-senses to survey the warehouse quickly. He did so a second time because all the racks were empty, and except for a row of barrels near the door, there were no signs of any goods anywhere. Not any goods . . . not a single barrel, bale, or crate. Not even a single amphora.

Why was it totally empty?

When he turned his attention away from the storage area, he realized there was a figure lying on the stone floor beside the barrels. Rahl stepped closer. The dead man was Chenaryl, and his body lay sprawled on his back. His throat had been cut. Rahl glanced upward. How many had the Jeranyi killed beside Chenaryl, Daelyt, and Yasnela? He paused only for a moment. He didn't have time to dwell on that, nor did he want to. Not now.

Nine barrels beyond the body stood on their ends, the heads removed. The tenth smelled of vinegar and a long rope led away from it, the one that ran to the doors. Rahl inspected the nine quickly. All were marked as containing Feyn River pickles, but the staves inside were dry. One held a scrap of cloth caught between the edges of two staves.

He nodded. The barrels had held Jeranyi, but why had they wanted such concealment? The tenth held cammabark—the rope was a long fuse. He didn't have the answers as to why the warehouse was empty or why Jeranyi wanted to fire the Merchant Association compound, and he wouldn't find them in an empty warehouse.

Rahl slipped out through the narrow opening in the doors and, once more under the concealment of his light shield, made his way toward the rear warehouse. He slowed and flattened himself against the rough stone wall in the alcove between the two warehouses as he sensed Jeranyi carrying wooden buckets with covered tops through the open doors of the second warehouse to the two wagons waiting in front of the stables where the teams were being hitched.

"Move it!" hissed someone. "Think we got all night?"

"You took your time with that woman upstairs . . ."

Rahl pushed away the sickening feeling.

"Keep the buckets away from the lanterns!" snapped another voice in a sibilant order.

At that, Rahl remembered what he'd been told about cammabark—that it was even more unstable than black powder and no longer used in most places, especially in munitions and explosives, because the slightest spark could set it off. For all that, he edged forward, concerned about quiet, and around the front corner and toward the warehouse doors.

As Rahl eased toward the doors, he listened, struggling to understand the thick Jeranyi accent of a language that seemed half Low Temple and half Hamorian.

"Zebal . . . your group hits the warehouses to the southeast. Make sure the first one goes up with double the bark. That'll get everyone moving that way. Then get as many others as you can. You know how to get back to the ships. After places start going up in flames, no one's going to question sailors hurrying back to get their ships clear of the harbor."

Rahl just stood there for a moment, less than ten cubits from the open warehouse doors. Once the Jeranyi left the Merchant Association warehouse, no one could act in time—except him, and there were almost a score of Jeranyi in a courtyard lit by a single lantern.

At that moment, Taryl's caution flashed into his mind—don't use your abilities to break the laws trying to set things right. But . . . if he didn't . . .

"That's it!" came a voice from within the warehouse. "Last bucket's coming out, except for what we're leaving."

Rahl moved forward, using his senses to determine how many Jeranyi remained in the warehouse. There were two.

Holding the light shield in place, he slipped inside, letting the sailor with the bucket pass him. Then he moved toward the heavyset figure who had affixed the fuse to the last barrel.

Rahl slammed the truncheon across the other's temple, using both order and force. The sailor hit the stone like a heavy flour sack, and Rahl expanded the light shield to cover them both. The sailor with the bucket glanced back, trying to see into the dimness, then turned and continued out the door.

Rahl hurried after him, catching the man five paces outside the warehouse. Holding his light shield tight around himself, he struck again with the heavy truncheon and cloaked them both with the shield.

The heavy wooden bucket clunked on the stone. The sound of the sailor's fall was more like a scraping muffled thud.

"Where's Boreat? He was just here."

"Check the warehouse. Make it quick."

Rahl jammed the truncheon into its holder and ran toward the lantern hanging on the outside bracket. When he lifted it, the outcry was immediate.

"Who doused the lantern?"

"Arms out!"

Rahl forced himself to walk back to the bucket, still sitting on the stone. Then he pulled out the lantern's reservoir plug and carried both lantern and bucket to the nearest wagon. Between hauling the bucket even that short distance one-handed, avoiding the sailors who could not see him, and holding the light shield, he was beginning to feel light-headed. He set the bucket on the tailgate, then began to pour the lamp oil into the bucket, leaving a trail to the side of the tailgate where he puddled more. Then he wicked up the lamp and smashed the mantle against the side of the wagon. Flames licked up.

Rahl sprinted the twenty cubits to the stone wall at the rear of the courtyard, hurling himself over the rear wall, coming down so hard on the alleyway pavement that arrows of pain shot from his boots up through his legs. He dropped the light shield at the impact.

Two figures in gray looked at him, and one raised a crooked staff, then saw the mage-guard uniform and backed away.

Another Jeranyi tumbled over the wall and started to run.

Rahl threw up full shields and dropped to the base of the wall.

CRUMMP'I'I'I!

Even within his shields, Rahl found himself being shaken. Stones and assorted other debris slammed against him, rattling him back and forth even more.

When the ground stopped trembling and objects stopped pelting him, Rahl staggered up, still holding his main shields, but not his light shield, because he could sense the inferno behind the remnants of the stone wall. He wanted to hurry away from the blazing heat, but had to make deliberate haste, given the scattering of stones and chunks of flaming roofing and wagons and other less attractive items.

At the end of the alley, he turned northward, moving at almost a run. Another explosion echoed through the night. Rahl thought that was most likely one of the warehouses . . . or the other wagon. A third explosion followed, and then a fourth, the last most likely the main Merchant Association building. Most of Swartheld was built of stone and tile. Rahl just hoped that would restrict the spread of fire, but the low clouds just east of him and overhead were beginning to turn a faint ruddy red.

Rahl forced himself to walk, quickly, but to walk.

A long whistle, with three short blasts, sounded. Bells began to clang. Because of the heat and falling flaming debris, Rahl had to go farther north to get on the avenue back to the harbor. He could only hope that those in Eneld's cantina had survived and that not too many others were hurt, but what else could he have done?

As he neared the pier-guard station, Rahl could sense Suvynt's agitation.

Rahl looked back once more. To the southwest, a low flickering of orange marked where the Nylan Merchant Association had been. Then he frowned. Why would Suvynt be so agitated?

Rahl used the light shield and the wall to get past the duty mage-guard, glad that most of the chaos-mages weren't nearly so good with order-sensing.

Once he was near the mage-guard station, Rahl released the light shield and sat down on a shadowed bench near the tariff enumerators' building. He just had to rest for a moment . . . and think.

No one would know what he had done—not until the captain returned and questioned him, and then he'd be in more than a little trouble. But what else could he have done? Better that the Nylan Merchant Association went up in flames than a half score or more of other trading houses.

The other question was what else could he do? What should he do?

He shook his head, then stood and walked toward the mage-guard station. He just hoped that the captain had returned.

The duty area in the mage-guard station held only the duty mage-guard, who looked up as Rahl entered.

"Has the captain returned yet, Nyhart?"

"No. No one's seen him. Even the undercaptain was looking for him. Suvynt sent word that there's a huge fire somewhere in the merchant area. Have you seen it?"

"You can see the flames from the piers," Rahl admitted.

"The captain might be at the city station," suggested Nyhart.

Behind Rahl, the main door opened. Both mage-guards turned as Undercaptain Craelyt strode into the building.

"Nyhart . . . see who's available to strengthen the watches on the pier-guard station and have them report to me there," ordered Craelyt. "You can leave the desk for a while. Get one of the mage-clerks to act as a messenger."

"Yes, ser."

"Rahl, you come with me."

"Yes, ser."

Craelyt turned and headed out, clearly expecting Rahl to catch up with him.

Rahl had almost to run for several steps before he drew abreast of the swiftly walking undercaptain.

Craelyt was taking the shorter—and darker—way to the pier-guard station, the one on the south side of the mage-guard building, where there were no lights and little beside refuse bins, pavement and the stone wall that separated the harbor and mage-guard buildings from the warehouses and other commercial establishments farther to the south.

"So . . . where have you been this evening, Rahl? You left the mess before I could find you." Craelyt voice was almost jovial, but Rahl could sense the buildup of chaos around the undercaptain.

What could Rahl do? He still didn't know where the captain was, or how exactly the Jeranyi and Shyret had been connected. "Where is the captain, ser?"

"He seems not to be around. It could be that he's at the other station with all the trouble they're having. That's not your concern. Your concern ought to be following orders, and it's clear that you haven't been."

Although Craelyt had not said anything incriminating, there was no one with him, and that alone suggested to Rahl that all was not as it should be.

"Ser? Exactly how have I not been following orders? I've been exactly where I've been ordered to be. I've been tested for my arms skills, and I've stood duties under instruction."

Craelyt stopped and turned, facing Rahl. "You were told not to snoop around the Nylan Merchant Association. You kept doing that. You were told to report to the captain. You didn't. Those failures alone are enough to send you to Highpoint, if not worse."

"There wasn't anything to report, ser." *Not until today,* Rahl added to himself. "I never even entered the Nylan Merchant Association building, and I've never seen or talked to anyone who I worked with or talked to." All that was certainly true.

"You know, Rahl, you're one of those types I dislike. You follow the letter of the rules and ignore their spirit. That's as much insubordination as outright disobedience."

Rahl tried again. "It's not against the Codex or the *Manual,* ser, to walk the streets of Swartheld and to try to recall the memories someone stole from you."

Craelyt smiled, coolly. "Always blaming someone else, aren't you. *They* stole your memories. Why can't you admit that you forgot? *They* wouldn't explain things so that you could understand, but you never made any real effort. *They* insisted that you take responsibility for your actions, and you just accused *them* of failing to understand. I know your type, always blaming others. It's too bad you never could really control your abilities, Rahl. You'd never be more than a half mage, if that. You know, the magisters on Recluce were right to exile you. You're the kind that always wants someone else to explain. You've never really worked that hard. Taryl was wrong. He always is."

Rahl could feel the rage surging through him. Just who was Craelyt to make such statements? He certainly hadn't been a loader in Luba.

"The mage-guards don't need whiners like you."

Whhhstt!

The force of the fire-bolt threw Rahl backward, almost into the wall. He staggered, both at the force of the chaos-bolt, and at the suddenness.

Whhsst!

Rahl's shields barely held back the second blow. Why was he having such trouble? Craelyt's chaos-bolts weren't that strong. He dodged to one side, behind a stone refuse bin.

"Coward. You always were."

For a moment, Rahl's rage surged. Then he swallowed. Anger! That had been what Craelyt was doing. Taunting Rahl enough to get him angry without Rahl's totally realizing it so as to weaken him. The chill of that realization drained away all fury, and Rahl concentrated on feeling everything around him, letting himself take in the order that was everywhere.

Whhsstt!

Chaos splashed around Rahl, but with his shields gaining strength every moment, he stepped out from behind the stone and walked toward the undercaptain.

For the first time, Rahl caught a sense of uncertainty as he approached the other man, but Craelyt barely hesitated as he drew the shimmering falchiona. Rahl quickly pulled out his truncheon.

"Exercise rooms are for boasting. Let's see how you are when it counts, whiner." The undercaptain's blade flashed toward Rahl.

Rahl slid the heavy blade away, twisting the truncheon just slightly so that the falchiona's edge would not bite into the dark oak and catch, then used an upward stroke to knock the undercaptain's blade away.

Whsstt!

The chaos sleeted away from Rahl's shields, and Rahl moved forward, again deflecting the falchiona, this time downward.

Craelyt went into a crouch for an instant in order to keep control of his weapon.

Rahl slammed the truncheon down on top of the heavy blade, then stepped on it. Without hesitation, he let order flow into the truncheon as he slammed the truncheon into the side of Craelyt's face. The order flow staggered the undercaptain just enough that he hesitated, if fractionally, as he dropped the falchiona and lunged toward Rahl with a long dagger.

Rahl swung to the side and brought the truncheon down on Craelyt's forearm.

With the snap of bone, the undercaptain paled, but he mustered enough chaos to fling more at Rahl, enough to stop Rahl for an instant. Craelyt swayed on his feet, and Rahl struck—this time across the undercaptain's temple. Even before the older mage-guard's body toppled toward the stone pavement, it began to disintegrate.

Rahl's mouth dropped open. Had the undercaptain been that imbued with chaos?

After the moment or so it took Rahl to compose himself, he looked down where Craelyt had fallen; but there was little enough left of the undercaptain but his falchiona and a few other metal items. Rahl left them, backing away, and hurrying to the pier-guard station.

Now . . . what could he do? The captain was missing, the undercaptain dead at his own hand, and Rahl had no idea whom to trust among the senior mages—or who was even around of the few he thought he *might* be able to trust.

As Rahl hurried toward the pier gates, Suvynt turned and took several quick steps toward the junior mage-guard. "Rahl! What's happening?"

"There's a big fire in Swartheld. The undercaptain ordered Nyhart to gather up the available mage-guards and send them out here. He wanted to put more patrols on the piers and to back you up. I came ahead, but he was supposed to be right behind me." Rahl glanced back over his shoulder.

"He'll be here, then."

Rahl looked toward Swartheld. From what he could tell, the fire didn't seem to be spreading. He sincerely hoped not.

After a time, he looked to Suvynt. "Did the undercaptain send anyone out before me to patrol the piers?"

"No."

"I'd better start that. Tell the undercaptain that's where I am."

"Are you sure?"

"That's what he said he wanted done. There should be more mage-guards coming, but I'm not a chaos-mage, and there should be at least one of you here."

"True enough." Suvynt nodded.

"I'm going to check pier two, where the Jeranyi ships are. If anyone had anything to do with that fire, they might have." Rahl turned and walked swiftly toward the base of pier two, not waiting for any response from Suvynt.

One of the Jeranyi vessels was already moving away from the pier, her concealed gun ports uncovered. The other had two guards at the foot of the gangway, and another pair on the quarterdeck. The vessel still reeked of whitish chaos.

As he neared the ship, but far enough back so he could not be seen clearly, he once more raised the light shield and used his order-senses to make his way toward the guards, angling in from the side. Then he used the truncheon to tap one on the calf.

"What . . ." The guard jumped.

"I didn't see anything," answered the other sailor. "Stop being so jumpy . . ."

". . . feels like someone's here . . ."

". . . imagining things . . ."

Rahl slipped behind the two and eased his way up the gangway, moving slowly so that his weight did not flex the gangway. Just short of the opening where a section of the railing was swung back, he slipped onto the railing and moved aft along the narrow flattop for close to five cubits before setting his boots on the deck.

". . . wish they'd get back . . ." came from one of the quarterdeck guards.

". . . you can see one fire . . ."

". . . thought there should be more . . ."

A long hiss of steam issued from the stack above the superstructure and aft of Rahl, confirming his suspicions that, despite the quiet appearance, the ship was ready to steam at any moment.

He moved silently across the deck toward an open hatchway, then, sensing no one in the darkness inside, entered. He tried to sense the chaos of powder or cammabark, but within the iron of the vessel, his order-senses were more limited. Another passageway intersected the one he had taken, and it headed aft. Rahl followed it to a ladder leading down. At the base of the ladder, the sense of chaos was stronger . . . and someone was headed his way.

Holding the light shield tightly around himself, Rahl flattened himself against the bulkhead. The crewman turned his head from side to side, paused, but then continued forward past Rahl, so close that Rahl could feel the faint breeze of his passing. At the next passageway, Rahl turned outboard. After less than ten cubits he stepped through a hatch into a gun bay.

Directly to his right was a heavy cannon. Set inboard and to the left of the cannon was a metal powder locker. Since he could sense no one nearby at the moment, Rahl released his light shield and looked around the gun bays, lit by a single safety lantern set within a metal bracket on the inboard bulkhead. Aft of him was another cannon, also with a locker. There was another cannon forward, but all the lockers were secured with heavy padlocks.

What could he do?

He could hear the massive steam engines beginning to turn over. The Jeranyi captain wasn't about to wait much longer, and then crewmen would appear to man the guns.

He glanced to the lantern, then walked over to it. He couldn't duplicate what he'd done at the warehouses, but there just might be another way. He didn't try to think about it—thinking wasn't the way for him to handle order. He just slid the retaining clips out, and lifted the lantern, carrying it and setting it down directly beside the powder locker. There, he turned up the wick, adjusting it for the most heat possible.

He studied the heavy lock, then attempted to use order to manipulate the tumblers inside.

Sweat was pouring down his face before he could open the lock and lift the locker lid, propping it open with the attached lever.

He repeated the process with the nearest two other lockers before returning to the first locker and the lantern, where he used his belt knife to help rip and cut a strip of cloth from his undershirt. He sheathed the knife and then pulled the filler plug from the lantern, then threaded the strip of cloth into the reservoir until he held just one end. Next he pulled the cloth from the reservoir and twisted it into a makeshift wick.

He lifted the lantern and held it over the powder bags in the locker, tilting it so that lamp oil fell on the bags, puddling slightly in one spot. He set the lamp on the powder bag next to the oil that was already sinking into the cloth. Then he ran his makeshift wick from the puddle to the reservoir and then up to the top of the lamp mantle, poking it just inside the mantle. Quickly, he wicked up the lamp and turned. While the passageway through the hatch was empty, he decided on caution and raised his light shield, even as he began to move at almost a run.

At the base of the ladder topside, he slammed into a crewman. As the sailor staggered back, Rahl scrambled up the ladder and along the upper passageway, and then out onto the main deck.

"Lines away! All hands to battle stations! All hands to battle stations!"

Behind him, Rahl could sense that his impromptu fuse was burning too fast. The gangway had been lifted, and even if he could jump to the pier, the pier was so wide he wouldn't be able to reach the far side in time, and he'd be fully exposed to the blast or fire . . . or both. Yet the ship was so close to the pier that he might well get crushed between the hull and the solid stone wharf wall.

He tried to hurry aft, unseen, trying to follow one sailor, and then another.

"There's a mage-guard on board . . . on the main deck aft!"

A whitish powder exploded, and Rahl kept hurrying along the railing, although he could sense that he was covered with something. He dropped the light shield and discovered he was covered with a luminescent powder, like glowing flour.

"There!"

"Get him!"

Rahl flung himself over the railing, scraping against the hull as he fell. He could barely swim, but he didn't have much choice. The water was chill, despite the warmth of the air, and his entire body spasmed as he plunged under the surface.

A muffled explosion pressed the water around him, and momentary knives stabbed into his ears. Then both subsided, and he struggled to reach the surface.

Flame was everywhere, and he ducked back under the water, trying to struggle away from the ship. He kept paddling until he reached the smooth stone wall of the pier, which he could barely grasp, and pulled himself up just enough to get another breath before using his fingers to push himself under the water toward the base of the pier.

Another quick breath, and he ducked underwater and tried to keep moving toward the shore. He was so light-headed, but he couldn't give up, not yet. *Pull and breathe, and duck, and pull and breathe and duck . . . pull and breathe . . .*

The water was so deep he couldn't feel or sense bottom, and he had to keep half-swimming, half-pulling himself toward the base of the pier.

Finally, he was well clear of the flaming hulk that had been a ship, but there was no way he was going to be able to make his way much farther, especially since another vessel was tied up before him, with frantic activity on its deck. Stars pinwheeled across his vision, points of intolerable light and pain.

"There's someone in the water!"

"It's Rahl! I knew he was down here . . ."

"How did he . . . ?"

"The blast must have thrown him into the water."

". . . have to get him out . . ."

". . . not that far from the ladder . . ."

Rahl strained, trying to find the ladder, and finally seeing the niches carved into the stone, and the iron railing beside them. Slowly, so slowly, he tugged himself to it.

His fingers were raw, and he could hardly grasp the rough iron of the ancient railing. Somehow he managed to get his boots onto one niche, then another . . .

Hands pulled him up the last steps, and hot darkness swept over him.

XCIX

You don't look back . . . look back . . . The past has no hold on you." The words echoed through the hot darkness, only to be replaced by other phrases, one after another. "He doesn't seem inclined to listen . . . not inclined to listen . . . has to learn everything the hard way . . . everything the hard way . . . it's up to you . . . life doesn't provide private tutors . . . use your skills without thinking . . . you lack adequate forethought . . . just keep to the piers . . . do your own job . . . always blaming others . . . whiner . . ."

The words vanished, only to be replaced by the image of a brown-haired woman in healer green, looking sadly at him even as her image dwindled into the distance and vanished.

Deybri . . . vanishing once more . . .

Rahl coughed, then shuddered.

His face felt as though it were on fire and still burned. Slowly, he opened his eyes. He was in an unfamiliar chamber, and it was light outside the single narrow window. How long had he been struggling through the darkness? What had happened?

"You're awake. Good." The voice belonged to Hewart, who stepped closer to the bed on which Rahl lay.

"Where . . . ?" Rahl croaked.

"In the infirmary. You're lucky to be alive. Very fortunate," Hewart said, looking down at him. "Suvynt said that you'd gone to check on the Jeranyi vessel, or we wouldn't have been looking for you."

"Captain . . . undercaptain?" Rahl croaked.

"No one can find the captain. We think that he might have been killed by the blast on the Jeranyi ship. Someone killed the undercaptain. At least, it looks that way. All we could find was his blade and boots, and insignia and parts of his cap and uniform. It looks like a Jeranyi plot. You were just lucky."

"Who takes over . . . in charge?"

"The regional commander is running things, but Jyrolt and someone from Luba are coming as well. The Jeranyi were up to more than what anyone knows happened, so far, anyway, but no one's quite sure what happened. They think it might be tied into the rebellion in Merowey."

"Rebellion . . ." Rahl tried to remember. He had known something about that, about the Emperor's brother being behind it. How could that be tied to the Jeranyi? He didn't know, and it was still hard to think, and his face burned, and his breathing was labored.

"You don't have much order left in you, Rahl, but you should be all right before long." Hewart lifted a mug of something. "Heavy beer. It'll help a lot."

Rahl had to swallow slowly, and his throat was more than a little sore, but he got all the beer down.

"Good." Hewart smiled. "Now you need to rest."

Questions swirled around in Rahl's head, but before he could ask any more, the hot darkness rose and swallowed him once again.

C

The heat and fever continued, and Rahl drifted in and out of it for several days. The words and phrases echoing through his head became fewer, but the dreams more vivid—if scenes from his past were truly dreams, particularly those involving Puvort and Kadara. The dream-scenes were seldom pleasant. Even the dreams of Deybri included the time she had chastised him for trying to shield himself against nonexistent chaos in learning how to handle the falchiona.

In time, he did wake from the fever, on oneday morning, according to Hewart, who had hovered over him and clearly had some ability as a healer.

"Have I just lain here the whole time?"

"Hardly . . . you've eaten and washed and talked, but you weren't really here," replied Hewart. "You had as much of an order-loss fever as a real one, and there was some wound chaos in your throat and lungs. That was probably from being so close to the Jeranyi ship that caught fire and exploded. You talked some."

"Ah . . ." Did he really want to know what he'd said? "What did I say?"

"Most of it didn't make too much sense, especially at first when you mostly muttered and whispered, but you did keep saying that you tried to find the captain and tell him, and something about the Jeranyi getting caught in the fire of the Nylan Merchant place, but that made sense, because that was where the big fire happened." Hewart looked embarrassed. "Did you have a girl named Deybri? You kept saying her name."

"She's a healer, but she was never my girl. I wish she were," Rahl admitted.

"Rahl . . . what happened on the pier? Do you remember?"

How much should he say? Rahl took another swallow of the beer in the mug on the table beside the bed before answering. "I thought one of the concealed guns on the pier side of the ship exploded, and then there were more explosions. I felt like the whole ship would explode and there was nowhere to go. So I jumped into the harbor." All that was true, if hardly complete.

"That was smart. It probably saved your life. Did you see the captain?"

Rahl shook his head. "I was looking for him, but I never saw him."

Hewart looked to the infirmary door. "There are some important mage-guards here who need to talk to you. They've been waiting."

Rahl could feel a chill go all the way through him. "Who?"

"The regional commander, Jyrolt, and a mage-guard from Luba named Taryl. I never heard of him, but both the others defer to him, and I never saw a regional commander ever defer to anyone except the Emperor, the over-commander, or the Triad."

"I heard that he was once part of the Triad." Rahl just hoped Taryl would understand and could help. Otherwise, he was likely headed for Highpoint or Luba, if not worse.

"Oh . . ." Hewart looked to the infirmary door as it opened. "I think they're here." He moved away from Rahl's bed.

Taryl was the first one into the room, and he merely looked at Hewart, who immediately stepped back, then departed after Jyrolt and a third mage-guard entered.

"Rahl," began Taryl, "you know Jyrolt, and this is Regional Mage-Commander Chaslyk."

"Ser . . ." Rahl inclined his head to the tall and muscular figure, whose black eyes, olive skin, and angular face created a physically commanding presence. Even so, Taryl dominated the room.

"I have this feeling," said Taryl, a slight smile upon his face as he looked at Rahl, "that you know far more than you've said about the situation here in Swartheld."

Rahl noted that Jyrolt felt more than a little nervous. Chaslyk, despite shields at least as tight as Craelyt's had been, was both concerned and angry.

"Before we begin, however," Taryl added, "I'd like you to tell me hon-estly what you think each of us is feeling."

Rahl didn't want to, but Taryl had saved his life, and he owed the older mage-guard. After a brief hesitation, he said, "Yes, ser. You're somewhat amused. Mage-Examiner Jyrolt is nervous and worried, and Regional Mage-Commander Chaslyk, behind his shields, is angry and most concerned."

Chaslyk's concern grew more intense.

"Do you know why I asked that question?" Taryl was still smiling.

"I don't *know*, ser, but I would guess it might have something to do with Undercaptain Craelyt."

"What happened to him?" Chaslyk's voice was cold. "Did you have anything to do with his death?"

"Commander." The coolness in Taryl's one-word address froze the senior officer. "I think we need to hear what happened from the beginning. Then you can address specific questions to the mage-guard. If you would, Rahl . . ."

"Yes, ser." Rahl cleared his throat. "It began even before I was drugged and sent to Luba. That was when I smelled the vinegar in the Nylan Merchant Association warehouse and saw the barrels of Feyn River pickles . . ."

"Pickles?" murmured Chaslyk.

Rahl paused, and Taryl looked at Chaslyk. Chaslyk, seething beneath his shields, closed his mouth.

"There was no reason to ship pickles . . ." Rahl went on to explain how he'd ended up in Luba, been discovered and trained, returned as a junior mage-guard to Swartheld, and then how he'd been reminded of the pickles and discovered the link between the pickles and the Jeranyi, and what had happened afterward. The only thing he omitted was his killing of Asmyd, the mage-guard who had tried to kill him back when he'd been a clerk. ". . . and when the ship was about to explode, I jumped in the harbor."

"Why didn't you tell anyone?" asked Chaslyk.

"I did, ser. I told Captain Gheryk that I thought there was a tie between the Jeranyi and Shyret as soon as I figured that out; but I didn't know what it was except that they were shipping barrels marked as pickles, and that didn't make sense. I probably should have recalled earlier that cammabark was always shipped damp in vinegar, but I just didn't. He told me that was something serious and not to snoop around more, and that he'd take care of it. I didn't snoop any more, but when I saw the three Jeranyi ships and all those pickle barrels headed for the Merchant Association warehouse, I realized that there might be a terrible problem, and I went looking for the captain. I never found him, and the undercaptain wasn't there, either, or I would have reported what I discovered to him. But when I couldn't find either one, after what had happened with the attack on the pier-guard station and the strange way Caersyn acted, I didn't know who I could go to."

"Do you know why the undercaptain attacked you?" asked Taryl.

"No, ser. I knew he was angry that I had discovered what was happening with the Jeranyi, and he was quite clear in telling me that my investigating was insubordination. He also didn't want me to tell anyone else."

"You actually heard the Jeranyi giving orders to attack other merchanting warehouses?" demanded Chaslyk.

"Yes, ser."

"It appears that all of the workers at the Merchant Association were killed. We did find the remains of the director and a clerk."

All of them? Rahl had suspected that, but it was another thing to hear it.

"Why do you think that this Shyret was cooperating?"

"Because the warehouse was empty of all goods, ser. I would guess—it's only a guess—that he sold or moved them and was going to claim everything burned. I'd been drugged, and one of the drivers was killed in an accident. I don't think it was an accident. Also, one of the clerks before me had just disappeared. When I learned all of this, and remembered that Shyret was going to be moved to another post this year, it made more sense." Rahl paused. "Oh, there was one other thing. When I was a checker in Luba, another checker who'd been a merchant clerk said he'd been framed. His name was Masayd, and he claimed that a mage-guard supervisor named Ventaryl destroyed certain records and did things for certain factors when the undercaptain told him to, but he didn't say which undercaptain."

That brought Chaslyk up with a start.

"I didn't tell anyone that," Rahl added, "because I didn't know who the undercaptain might be, but Masayd thought he was telling the truth."

Jyrolt nodded. After a moment, so did Chaslyk.

"Why didn't you trust the undercaptain?"

Rahl shrugged, almost helplessly. "Ser . . . I wish I could tell you. He kept his shields so tightly all the time . . . oh, and the other things were that he really emphasized that I should keep away from the Merchant Association—but the captain told me not to tell the undercaptain anything, and I didn't. And when the undercaptain pulled me off the pier while the Jeranyi were loading the pickle barrels—"

"The captain told you not to tell the undercaptain?"

"Yes, ser. He said to tell no one but him anything, and to approach him only in a way that was not obvious."

Taryl looked to the regional commander.

Rahl could tell that Chaslyk's anger had almost vanished, but his concerns were far greater.

"Pickles . . ." There was an actual note of humor in the commander's voice. "Total disaster averted because a mage-guard smelled pickles." He shook his head. "Years from now, it will make a great story. Right now . . . I'd appreciate it if you'd keep it to those of us here."

"Yes, ser." Rahl couldn't hide his puzzlement. There was obviously far more going on than he knew.

Chaslyk straightened. "Jyrolt and I have a few more items to take care of, including taking to certain mage-guards. I believe you can handle what else Rahl needs to know, Taryl. If you would excuse us . . ."

Taryl smiled. "I can do that." Taryl smiled at Jyrolt. "My congratulations and condolences, Captain."

Captain? Jyrolt was being made captain of the mage-guard stations in Swartheld? Or somewhere else?

Taryl did not speak until the infirmary door closed once again. "There is more, of course. It appears Shyret was killed earlier, but his body was badly burned. We have found no records, even at his dwelling, but his house and the barn upon his grounds are filled with goods, and there were more than a thousand golds in a hidden strongbox there. We have seized the golds and goods as reparations for the damage created by the Jeranyi and Shyret. Furthermore, all Jeranyi vessels have been banned from all ports in Hamor." Taryl snorted. "That will do little good because they will simply sell their stolen goods elsewhere, or transfer them to other vessels for consignment sales here, but at times even the Emperor must make great and meaningless gestures."

"What was the purpose . . . ?"

"Of the attack? If they had succeeded in destroying all the warehouses, they would have reduced trade to a fraction of its volume for some time. A good amount of the Emperor's revenues come from the tariffs. That would have made it more difficult to fund the efforts against the rebellion in Merowey, and the Emperor would have been required to send at least some warships on patrols and efforts against Jeranyi pirates, and perhaps waste time and effort blockading and bombarding the port of Jera. Any success would have been slight at best, but not doing so would have signified weakness and indifference, and those are even more costly. Using warships against the Jeranyi would have resulted in fewer ships to patrol the approaches to Sastak and the smaller ports in the southwest and would have made it easier and less costly for the rebels to obtain supplies. It also would have raised the prices that the Jeranyi could charge for what they sold. At least for a time." Taryl paused.

"Ah . . . ser . . ." Rahl wasn't quite sure how to ask what was to become of him, and he was even less certain he wanted to know.

"You're worried about what might happen to you?" The former Triad mage nodded. "That's understandable for a junior mage-guard who created one of the largest fires in years in Swartheld, even to prevent a worse conflagration, not to mention killing a superior and disobeying direct orders."

Rahl tried not to swallow. "I remembered your words, ser . . . the ones about not taking matters into my own hands, but . . . if I didn't . . ."

"It happens that way, but I'm glad you did think about it first." Then, surprisingly, Taryl grinned. "You still need some reminders that you have much to learn. It has been decided that your talents are not being used to their fullest here in Swartheld. Also, there will be speculation about how you survived the explosion and who killed Craelyt, not to mention the captain's disappearance."

"That had to be Craelyt," Rahl interjected.

"Without a doubt, but . . . how could anyone really prove it?" continued Taryl. "Then, too, it would be difficult for any captain, even Jyrolt, to concentrate fully on what he must do to rebuild the port station when he knows that one of his junior mage-guards is as . . . capable as you are, as well as inexperienced in understanding all that the mage-guards are and must be."

Was he being sent to Highpoint or worse? Or merely some small village in the middle of nowhere? That might be a relief.

"Several of the mage-guards here were at the least inadvertent accomplices of the undercaptain. Caersyn, Suvynt, and Saelyt have already been sent to new postings. Caersyn is on his way to Highpoint. Now . . . Jyrolt and Chaslyk will have to interrogate Ventaryl as well, if he's still around."

Rahl shook his head. "Accomplices?" He'd suspected Craelyt of something, but what had he been doing?

"Oh, you wouldn't have known that. Craelyt was an occasional guest of Shyret's. The director's house staff confirmed it. We'll never know everything, but Craelyt was passed over for captain when Gheryk was appointed. We did find a set of instructions for dealing with a large fire in Swartheld in Craelyt's desk."

"So he could show skill in handling it and become captain after Gheryk perished in the fires?"

"That's most likely, but we won't ever know. Not for certain."

Taryl still hadn't said what Rahl would be doing or where he would be posted next. Or even exactly why Taryl was in Swartheld.

"Now . . . about you. You definitely need more training, but you won't get what you need here in Swartheld, even if you could stay, and the same would be true of other cities, especially Atla or Cignoerne or even Sylpa. You also are an ordermage from Recluce, and that makes you especially useful for your next posting. The Emperor and the Triad have decided that I will act as their emissary to Recluce and that you will assist me in explaining to the magisters exactly what happened in Swartheld. This is necessary to assure that Recluce does not use its black ships against our shipping or traders and will accomplish several other ends, which we can discuss at length on the voyage."

"The magisters at Land's End will not even—"

"We are emissaries not to the magisters at Land's End but to those at Nylan. They already are the true powers of the isle." Taryl offered a friendly smile. "Now, we need to get you some new uniforms, including full-dress. We leave on threeday on a fast naval frigate. You also look like you could use a decent meal."

"Yes, ser."

For a moment, Rahl just sat upright in the infirmary bed.

He was heading back to Nylan—aboard a Hamorian warship—as the aide to an emissary from the Emperor. Back to Nylan . . .

"Get yourself cleaned up and dressed, and we'll find somewhere decent to eat," Taryl said, breaking into Rahl's reverie.

Rahl smiled and swung his feet over the side of the bed and onto the cool tiles of the floor. He was still light-headed, but that would pass.

What wouldn't pass was the thought that he would have to face the magisters again . . . and Deybri, especially Deybri.

Sometimes, he did look back.

CI

In the late afternoon of twoday, under clouds that promised, but had not delivered rain, Rahl stood on the avenue in Swartheld, looking at the burned-out walls of the Nylan Merchant Association and the heaps of masonry, ashes, and rubble within them that had been warehouses, stables, and the main building.

Behind him, Eneld's cantina was open, if with broken and battered shutters, and stacks of rubble in the side alleyway waiting to be carted away. The odor of Seorya's heavy cooking mixed with that of ashes and death.

He stood there silently, in his mage-guard uniform. In less than a day, he would be boarding a warship on a mission back to Nylan. His eyes went to the still-smoking rubble that had been the first warehouse—with the rooms above that had housed Daelyt and Yasnela. Both were dead, although Rahl had no way of knowing exactly how they had died, only that they had. For what it was worth, he wished that Yasnela had not been alone; but he knew that she had been, trapped by her crippled leg when the Jeranyi pirates had emerged from their concealment.

In his own way, Daelyt had been trapped as surely as Rahl himself had been constrained, all because Daelyt had loved Yasnela. With what Rahl had been paid, he certainly could not have maintained a consort, and especially not one who was crippled. Even had Daelyt made three or four times what Rahl had—and that was doubtful—Daelyt could not have supported and quartered a consort in Swartheld. So, because he had loved his consort, Daelyt had helped Shyret in his scheme to divert golds from the Association, not knowing or understanding where that would lead. What would Rahl have done if he had been faced with a similar situation—and his consort had been Deybri? Would he have been able to walk away? Especially if he were not a mage?

Chenaryl, too, was dead. He had been more guilty, in a way, because he'd pocketed golds from the "spoiled" goods. Tyboran the warehouse guard and Guylmor—the first driver—had been killed just because they had been inconvenient to either Shyret or the Jeranyi. Shyret had wanted more golds than his ability could honestly provide. So had Chenaryl. Daelyt had wanted to have the love of a beautiful—if crippled—woman. The innocent had died as well—Captain Gheryk, Yasnela, and the merchant clerk before Rahl.

Yet, reflected Rahl, regardless of their relative guilt, they'd all been slaughtered by the Jeranyi or their agents. For what? So that the pirates could amass more golds after they had burned the merchant quarter of Swartheld to the ground? And so that an undeserving undercaptain could become a captain?

But the causes went deeper than that. The Jeranyi had acted because the revolt in Merowey offered them an opportunity. Craelyt had acted because he believed himself better than he was, and because the mage-guards had not seen his corruption of spirit—or not wanted to. Even the Nylan Merchant

Association was far from free from blame. They had taken Rahl, either because he was inexpensive help or because they were beholden to the magisters, and the directors of the Association had never truly looked at what was happening in Swartheld. With what he had known after two eightdays, Rahl had discovered something was wrong—and he had had no experience at all. Surely, an experienced trader could have discovered the problems. So why hadn't anyone? Or had they not wanted to look too deeply?

None of them had wanted to see what they had found unpleasant. Was he any different? He hadn't wanted to deal with Jienela . . . or with the strain he had surely placed on his parents. Or with . . . he could name more than that.

His eyes went back to the tumbled rubble that had been the Merchant Association building.

As he stood there, another question came to mind, an old question, one that he had asked himself more than once. Why exactly had he been exiled? It had not been just because he had avoided real responsibility. Or that he had been self-centered. Or even because he was a natural ordermage.

After all he had been through, he could see that, at least in the case of the magisters of Nylan, his exile had not been a personal thing for the magisters—except maybe for Kadara. They'd honestly worried about what he might do. But why? Hamor allowed both kinds of mages, and the land didn't seem any poorer. If anything, more folk were better off. And Fairhaven

He moistened his lips.

Perhaps that was part of the answer to both questions.

In Recluce, and especially in Nylan, commerce and trade had to serve order. So did the view that the magisters of Nylan had of order and what sort of magery was accepted. The Nylan Merchant Association had to follow those unspoken yet ironclad rules. Nothing could be allowed that conflicted. In Nylan, the rules were frozen in the words of *The Basis of Order*; in Land's End, nothing that suggested any change was allowed. Beyond that, did that many really care? Deybri did . . . and some others, like Khalyt the engineer, or Thorl, but most wanted life to go on peacefully and without unpleasantness, and if a director of the Merchant Association pocketed a few hundred more golds, so long as it wasn't obvious, no one cared, or cared that much.

They only cared if their view of order happened to be challenged, as Rahl had done, if totally inadvertently.

Yet, was Hamor any different? It, too, had its rules. In Hamor, magery was governed by rules, as it was in Recluce, but almost all forms of magery were allowed. In reality, the rules and practices of magery served commerce and trade, something Rahl had not understood because everyone insisted vigorously that the mage-guards did not protect commerce.

Yet, in practice, as Rahl realized, looking at the ruins before him, the greatest protection of commerce was the maintenance of order and the separation of magery and commerce. If mage-guards were required actually to serve commerce, in time they would come to control it. *That* was why mages could not be engaged in commerce in Hamor. In that way, at least, Hamor was more honest.

When Rahl thought of it in that fashion, the difference between Hamor and Recluce was both profound and so obvious, yet nowhere had he actually read or heard those differences spelled out that clearly. And those differences told him that there never would be a place for him in Recluce, a realization doubly ironic as he prepared to return there on a mission he had not asked for or sought.

He smiled, sadly and wryly, as he turned from the ruins, the ruins of his own past, in a way, and began to walk back toward the harbor. He glanced up at the sky, but the clouds had thickened, and he didn't expect sunlight, not for a time; but the sun would shine, in time, not on a scrivener or a clerk, but on a mage-guard of Hamor.

And he would see Deybri . . . but would it be in an entirely new light?

HAMOR

Dolari

Northpoint

Swartheld · Luba

Guasyra
Cigoerne

Heldya · Highpoin

Quarries

SWARTH RIVER

Westyr

CLYAN RIVER

Jabuti

Kysha

Clyanaka

Alsenyi

MEROWEY

Dawhut

AWHUT RIVER

Elmari

Saslak

Nubyat

SOUTHERN
OCEAN